THE ERRANTRY
OF BANTAM FLYN

AUTUMN'S FALL SAGA

Jonathan French

OPEN ROAD
INTEGRATED MEDIA
NEW YORK

To my Dad, who taught me twelve laws of modern chivalry
and a knightly oath which begins:
"On my honor, I will do my best to do my duty . . ."

ISBN: 978-1-5040-9518-1

This edition published in 2024 by Open Road Integrated Media, Inc.
180 Maiden Lane
New York, NY 10038
www.openroadmedia.com

Woe to the dwarrow,
Of the two others,
Our dead rest not,
A man there shall be,
In earth, in stone,
Mortal and shunned,
Nor under waves.
Friend to folk Fae,
Neither flame, nor rot,
Though weak he seems,
Our cold flesh touches,
Ever on his shoulder,
Nor worm, nor crow,
Winged and deathless,
Dine within our tombs.
A watcher will sit.

We are food for one,
A great champion,
Wind's ancient mother,
To complete the three,
Called to her gullet,
Guided by lust,
We march on blackened feet.
For glories new.
All are risen,
Though strong of limb,
All go forward,
A mile-tamer gone,
In death enslaved,
Deep in the horns,
A feast of corpses.
All foes to the ground.

Till the end of days,
These hunters bound,
She will glut upon us,
Together in purpose,
So that she may live,
Shall seek with blind eyes,
Last upon the earth.
The eater of corpses.
To see her slain,
Upon frosty bough,
A blade must be wrought,
And rime-ridden root,
Three must be gathered
And there decided,
And the eater sought.
The fate of our race.

Her bane to be forged,
Follow you this skein,
Tempered and cooled,
To seek such an end,
Eight times in the hearts
To set these links fast,
Of beloved issue.
And make you this chain.
One you must find,
Heavy is the burden,
Among her lost children,
Long will be the search,
To wield this doom,
Many paths unwoven,
And see mother slain.
Many lives undone.

—The Rune Caster's Augury

PROLOGUE

Four of the men huddled together in a tight circle, cradling their bowls.

"There's horse-meat in here," Stig heard one of them whisper. Even in his carefully hushed tones, the delight in the man's voice was obvious. A childish, pathetic joy. Stig, standing well apart with his own bowl, scowled in the darkness. Their guards had not wanted to risk a fire. The thin broth was cold. Cold like the wind that tore through Stig's old tunic, cold like the snow that covered his feet to the ankles. Give a thrall a bowl of stewed horse-meat and he plays the groveling wretch. All around, the sounds of slurping filled the frozen night as the men supped greedily. Stig continued to stare at the shadowy form of the man who spoke.

Debasing them all with his sniveling gratitude, he made them lower than slaves. Stig wanted to kill him.

It would not be difficult. Stig could throttle the fool even with his frost-numbed fingers. The other thralls would only watch and the warriors would merely laugh, maybe place bets. Murder had landed Stig in bondage, he saw no reason not to repeat the offense now. No reason save he would spill his own stew.

Stig slurped at the broth, glancing around the night-shrouded depression where the warriors had ordered them to halt.

The moon infused the snow with a blue, frigid light, the men growing from it as shapeless, black stalks. Around the cold stew pot, the half-dozen remaining warriors stood watch, their hot breath emerging from their beards in steamy torrents. Stig and the other thralls outnumbered them at least five to one, but the guards leaned lazily on their spears, unconcerned with the possibility of escape or revolt. Fear kept the thralls obedient. Fear of night on the tundra, fear of the berserkers who had split away from their group not an hour ago, fear of Crow Shoulders.

Stig risked a glance at the man.

He sat astride his horse at the top edge of the depression, his cape of feathers twitching in the wind as if quivering with the remembrance of flight. Stig stared up at the dread form, glad the warlord's own gaze was turned away, across the hoary fields where his sons had gone. For what purpose Crow Shoulders had sent the berserkers out, Stig did not know, but he guessed it was bloody business. They had taken the majority of the warriors with them, nearly three-score men. Such a force could produce a good many fresh corpses come the dawn, if the bundle of tools near the stew pot held any importance.

They were wrapped tightly in a large hide and dragged on a sled by several of the hardier thralls, the wooden hafts peeking out from the end of the covering. Shovels and picks, no doubt. Crow Shoulders must expect to put a pile of enemies in the ground on this raid. Why else bring thirty-odd thralls on a forced march through the night and feed them horse meat? Some blistering labor was ahead, for certain. That was fine by Stig. He could dig a grave as well as any man, and the work would keep him warm.

The pot was not yet empty and some of the thralls were brazen enough to approach the guards for more broth. They ladled it out freely, so Stig quickly took a place in line for a second serving.

Why not? The warriors were sure as shit not going to eat this swill, and an empty pot was less weight to carry back. Only one man separated Stig from the stew pot when a bellow came down from the ridge. Crow Shoulders waved an arm, then turned his horse and rode out of sight over the lip of the depression.

The warriors slammed the lid down over the pot and started growling at the thralls to get moving. Stig swallowed a curse and tossed his bowl into the snow. To add to his luck, he found himself picked to help haul the sled and soon he was straining up the icy incline, leather straps cutting into his swollen hands as he pulled the heavy load of tools. The going was easier once they left the depression.

A white expanse of harsh tundra lay before them under the moon. Stig's feeble shoes crunched through the crust as he struggled across the plain, huffing in time with the man pulling next to him. He kept his eyes downcast, watching his stinging feet.

Sweat began to form on his flesh, mating with the cold air and causing him to shiver. No one offered to spell him, just as he had not offered aid to the miserable curs forced to pull the damn sled earlier in the night. He stumbled hard, knees, wrists and chin scrubbed raw by the hard-packed snow.

"Fuck," Stig hissed.

The thrall beside him groaned as their progress was arrested, but was too winded himself to voice much complaint. As Stig struggled back to his feet, his eyes fell upon something large and black on the horizon. It rose above the plain, at this distance nothing but a dense shadow, blotting out the stars. Stig continued trudging forward, his eyes now fixed on the dark mass ahead, each step chiseling at the distance until details began to form.

It was a hill, alone on the plain and oddly devoid of snow.

Even from a distance Stig could tell it was no natural child of the landscape. The slope was too regular, the summit too flat. Atop the hill stood a great tree, its branches reaching high and wide. Between the boughs, the stars seemed to flicker, winking in and out of existence, an illusion caused by the leaves still crowning the tree despite the unforgiving grip of Winter that had reigned in Middangeard for thousands of years.

They were still a goodly distance from the hill when the bodies began appearing. They were scattered across the plain, limp and unmoving save for where the wind plucked idly at their cloaks.

Stig was glad to see they were all Crow Shoulders' men. He would not need to break his back chipping holes in the frozen earth for their graves. They would get a pyre as befit a warrior and the flames could do the work. Each looked to have been felled by arrows, the shafts now sprouting from their corpses where shield and mail failed to protect flesh. Stig wondered how many men Crow Shoulders had lost to this charge and he counted at least a score before he lost track, the slain growing more numerous as they crossed the final distance.

Mutters and murmuring rose from the thralls as the hill and its tree drew near. As a group, their steps slowed and the guards began barking at them to keep moving, punctuating their words with blows from their spear shafts. Thralls they may be, broken by debt or misdeed, but none among them were from foreign shores.

They were men of Middangeard all and taught from boyhood to avoid such hills with their single, deathless tree.

The glow of torches bathed the snow at the base of the mound, illuminating the mounted bulk of Crow Shoulders and his surviving warriors. Stig reckoned that near thirty still drew breath, but it was the berserkers he counted carefully. They stood apart from the others, receiving praise and horns of drink from their father. All twelve had survived, Stig noted sourly, allowing the common warriors to shield them during the charge. Their thickly muscled bodies were limned in steam and clothed in the skins of bear and wolf, the hides of the predators unable to contain the savagery of the men beneath. Not slaked with mere blood, they breathed heavily and drank deeply, the mead splashing down their shaggy cheeks to mix with the gore at their feet.

Short, stocky corpses lay all about the base of the hill and upon its slopes. The large, well-used weapons of the berserkers had butchered them well, severing every head, but Stig still knew the slain defenders for what they were.

Svartálfar.

Dwarrow.

Guardians of the Warden Trees.

One of the warriors was entertaining his comrades, holding his torch towards the hacked form of a dwarf and watching as the flame dwindled the closer it came to the corpse. The torch guttered and nearly died within an inch of the dead flesh, but the warrior snatched it away at the last moment and the flame sprang back to life. The spectacle drew laughter from the men nearby and several spat on the fallen, headless dwarfs.

Stig was shoved roughly from behind and he turned to find one of the guards glowering at him.

"Get these passed out!" the man ordered, waving an aggravated arm at the sled.

The other thralls were being bullied towards the sled as Stig bent to untie the ropes. His numb fingers were clumsy, but he soon had the rough, cold cords loose, shoving the hide aside. The tools clattered as they rolled free of the bundle, wood clunking against wood, metal scraping against metal. Stig bent and snatched one up, handing it to the closest man. Then another and another. They were not spades, nor picks. Axes. They were all axes.

Dread settled between Stig's shoulder blades, quickly capering down his spine, quivering through his ribs and squeezing his bowels. Soon, all the thralls had axes, every last man, but though their hands gripped weapons, their faces held nothing but fear.

Stig looked down at the sled, at the single remaining axe.

His hands yet remained empty. How many times had he yearned for the means to fight back, to spill the blood of those who held him in thrall, to liberate himself?

Now, the very tool that would offer that chance lay within his reach and he had as much desire to seize it as he would a glowing coal.

"Get them up the hill."

It was Crow Shoulders who spoke, his voice calm and cruel.

The warriors pushed at the thralls with their spears, but not one step was taken. The men stood rooted, their jaws slack beneath wide eyes fixated on the tree above. The warriors showered them with cuffs and curses, shoving the thralls forward with such force that many fell to the snow, but none took one step willingly towards the hill. One thrall, an old, skinny greybeard, looked sternly at Crow Shoulders and tossed his axe down into the snow.

The warlord's horse stamped and shuffled a bit, but the man astride did not move. Rough, wet laughter spilled out of the berserkers and they strode forward, pushing through the crowd of thralls, heedless of the axes. The twelve of them surrounded the greybeard, still laughing. Stig caught one last look at the old thrall's face, the glimmer of brave defiance frightened off by the man's own wails. The fists of the berserkers rose and fell, then, a moment later, their feet. Stig heard bones snapping over the high-pitched screams. One of the berserkers bent down and the screams increased to something no longer human. The smells of blood and shit settled heavily in the cold air. One of the thralls next to Stig vomited, the stew he had so recently consumed spewed violently onto the snow.

When the berserkers stepped back, the old thrall lay upon the ground, his chilblained legs broken at sickening angles, the pale tubes of his entrails lolling out of the red ruin of his belly. The greybeard was no longer screaming, but he was still breathing. The berserkers had tied a rope about his neck and one of them went running up the hill, dragging the dying man behind him. When he reached the summit, the berserker tossed the rope over one of the tree's stout branches and hauled the thrall into the air. His legs shattered, the man could not kick. He could only hang and strangle, his guts dangling in coils.

"Up the hill," Crow Shoulders commanded.

Stig snatched up the last axe with a quavering hand and followed his fellow thralls slowly up the hillside. The thought of fighting back came to his mind, no doubt came to all their minds, but someone would need to be first. It was not Stig. Nor any of the others.

The Warden Tree loomed even larger once they reached the summit. A dozen grown men, arms outstretched, hands joined, could not have encircled the trunk. Stig could hear the choking sounds of the hanged thrall coming from above, but he did not look up. From below, Crow Shoulders' voice drifted up on the blustering wind.

"Bring it down."

Stig licked his chapped lips, flexed his blistered fingers around the axe haft. All around, the thralls milled uncertainly around the tree. All twelve berserkers were on the hilltop now, bolstered by as many warriors.

"Fell it! Bring it down!"

Stig craned his neck upwards. The branches seemed to bend down towards him, creaking with menace, the leaves hissing.

A cornered animal issuing a warning.

A thrall fled. Bolting away from the tree with a desperate squeal, the man dropped his axe and dashed for the edge of the hill.

He made it less than ten steps before two spears struck him in the back, their flight almost lazy. The thrall stumbled a few more paces then pitched forward on his face, his last breath rattling in his pierced lungs.

There was nothing for it. Stig swallowed hard and swung.

The axe bit deep into the wood and the sting of the impact shot through Stig's cold fingers. Dull thuds began to fill his ears as other thralls set upon the tree. Stig swung again, sending a chunk tumbling from the tree and a pain up his arms. The tree was shaking with the force of the repeated blows. Stig could feel the chopping pulse through his feet, his heart. But there was another sound, lower, yet usurping the chorus of the falling axes. A groaning, coming from the stricken wood.

Stig had felled many a tree. He knew the aches, the cramps, and the soreness that came from such labor. The pain that lingered in his limbs after each swing was different, deeper, unnatural. He had worked a notch out of the trunk the size of a man's head and continued to send his blade into the ever-widening wound, but with each bite of the axe, his own pain grew. His muscles did not burn with exertion, they froze, began to harden. Sweat did not rise on his flesh, no, each swing leached the heat from his body.

Cries and moans floated up around him as the other thralls suffered. They chopped and hacked, their movements growing sluggish. Next to Stig, a man fell, pitching forward as he swung. His axe sank into the wood, but there it remained, the man having slumped down onto the roots, his face pressed into the bark. Stig looked down to see the man retch a thick gob of inky fluid, pushed with a grey tongue between blue lips. The fallen thrall inhaled deeply, then moved no more, his eyes staring sightlessly, weeping black. A whine of fear escaping his throat, Stig threw himself behind his axe, chopping with desperation. All around him, men began to die. He could feel his joints swelling, trying to burst, his breath crackling in his chest. A pitiless cold gripped his heart, compressed his crystal-filled lungs, but still he swung, trying to kill the tree before it killed him. Only a few axes could be heard now, popping irregularly into the trunk, but Stig worked at the wood, sending chips flying. The head of his axe squeaked as he pulled it free, only to slam it home once more, deepening the cut as he choked on the turbid muck of his insides.

At last, a mournful creaking signaled the tree's impending fall. Stig took one final, furious swing and the wooden wound yawned wider as the trunk tumbled over. The thick branches snapped with deafening finality as the tree struck the ground, infesting the air with swarming snow.

Stig found himself lying on a pile of bodies. He coughed, spitting bile into a dead face, and began to crawl over stiff arms and legs, away from the splintered, accusing stump of the fallen sentinel.

There was no sign of the berserkers or the warriors. Nothing moved on the hilltop, nothing except the falling snow and Stig.

Grasping with blue-black fingers, he dragged himself along, every breath an ordeal. He could feel something leaking out of his eyes, his ears, leaking only to freeze upon his flesh. His heart had slowed to a flutter, he could feel it dwindling in his chest, barely pulsing against the frozen earth, which began to tremble.

Beneath him the trembling became a tremor, the snow dancing over itself as the hill shook from its core. Stig crawled for the edge and tumbled down the slope in a cascade of snow and soil as the ground eroded beneath him. He rolled to a stop at the base of the rotting hill, watching numbly as the slope began to fall in on itself. Swiftly, horribly the hill decayed and a great, gaping hole opened in the remains. From within the dark cavity, a sound grew, beginning as a vibration, then growing into the low, undulating rhythms of song.

Figures appeared, slowly lurching out of the hole. They were thick of limb and short, the dirt of the grave settled in hair and beards black as pitch. The moonlight caught in their colorless eyes and was sucked in by flesh paler than the snow. Mouths open, they sang their dirge, crawling forth from the ruined hill, too many to count.

Stig struggled to stand, turning away to flee on feet crippled with frostbite. He stumbled into something, the sudden hindrance spilling him back to the ground. He rolled onto his back and found a familiar, bloodless face staring down at him. It was the thrall who had fled, the points of two spears protruding from his chest. The dead man reached for him, but Stig knocked its hand away, scrambling to his clumsy feet once more.

He ran, ran as best he could across the tundra. The song of the exhumed dwarfs chased after him, the unending tones enveloping the night. Stig stumbled and careened across the white expanse, seeing the arrow-ridden bodies of Crow Shoulders' warriors, the men who died charging the hill. They began to twitch, to move, heeding the song. Stig felt his breath failing, but still he ran on legs no longer flowing with blood. He was dying. The tree had killed him and there was nothing to be done now. Nothing save run and hope that when he soon fell, he was far from that dread song and did not rise again.

ONE

The cattle were diseased.

Ingelbert knew little about livestock, but the poor health of the beasts showed with every plodding step as they passed through the main gate of the Roost. He risked a glance at the Old Goose.

The aged knight was not pleased. He glared sourly as the clansmen entered the castle yard, their shoulders loaded with goods and despondence. Ingelbert looked away, finding the featherless, slick-scarred flesh of the Old Goose's head difficult to behold for long. Coburn were a fearsome sight even when not so viciously deformed.

The clansmen had already begun dropping their burdens, putting them down with no care for order or organization. Making a proper count would be difficult, but Ingelbert said nothing.

He never did.

The half-dozen cows were easy enough to note, but Ingelbert did not dare open the heavy ledger he held close to his chest. He waited between the Old Goose and Worm Chewer, feeling every bit the weakling human beside the intimidating knights. Behind them, a trio of squires stood vigilant, spears smartly in hand. Ingelbert felt the first runnel of sweat liberate itself from his skin and run unpleasantly down his back. He busied himself ensuring that none of the clansmen had neglected to wear visible iron. Thankfully, he found bracelets made of old horseshoes on every wrist. The collar of blunted nails around Ingelbert's own neck was already beginning to chafe and he resisted an ever-present urge to tug it away from his throat.

Dawn was an hour old, a bright promise for another suffocating day. Ingelbert shuffled his grip on the ledger, not wanting his dampening palms to further curl the pages. The coburn surrounding him did not sweat, but Ingelbert's nose gave evidence to what his eyes could not prove. For all their proud bearing, in the midst of an unseasonably hot Albain spring, the rooster-men stank.

Worm Chewer gave a grunt and spat out a sticky gob of something that had entered his beak still wriggling. Ingelbert was unable to suppress a shudder. He turned his attention back to the yard, where three of the clansmen had detached from the pitiful caravan. Áedán mac Gabráin led from the center. The exertion of the uphill approach to the castle had reddened his face to match his beard. The men flanking him were younger but of similar coloring, and bore the stocky build inherent to the Dal Riata.

"You can begin your count," mac Gabráin said before he stopped walking. "Me and the lads will be gettin' on."

"The cows are stricken," the Old Goose replied, never taking his gaze from the animals.

Mac Gabráin drew to a halt before them, taking a moment to rub at the callouses on his hands before answering. Ingelbert noted a bitter amusement in the chieftain's face.

"They'll serve well enough for the tannery."

1

It was true. The coburn ate little red meat, but their need for leather was constant. Still, it was a waste. Ingelbert and the other human residents of the castle would miss the beef.

"To it, straw-head." Mac Gabráin tossed his words at Ingelbert and a thumb at the goods behind him. "I'd be home before the heat's much higher."

Ingelbert looked to the Old Goose, drawing several impatient expulsions of breath from mac Gabráin and his men. The scarred knight nodded.

"Proceed, Master Crane."

Relieved, Ingelbert opened the ledger, freeing the charcoal stick from between the pages and moistening the tip with his tongue. He was of a height with the coburn, who over-topped the clansmen by a full head, but for all his stature he could not match any in this company with brawn. As he took his first steps, he was keenly aware of his gawky frame and weedy limbs punctuated by knobby knees and elbows. Living in the midst of such fearsome creatures as the coburn was a constant reminder of his feeble physique.

"Wait."

Ingelbert was pulled back roughly, a strong, feathered hand closing around his thin arm with a jerk. He stumbled, dropping the ledger to the dust of the yard. Still fighting for balance, he found himself in Worm Chewer's grasp.

"Who is that?" Worm Chewer demanded, his free hand pointing across the yard.

Ingelbert followed the coburn's outstretched arm to where the remaining clansmen sat scattered among the haphazard piles of goods. Worm Chewer's gesture singled out one man in particular.

"Who is that?" the knight repeated, his head turning with the words to look upon Áedán mac Gabráin.

The chieftain turned to view the man in question, giving him the most cursory glance before returning to face them.

"My wife's sister's boy," mac Gabráin's voice betrayed his irritation. "Domnal."

The Old Goose took a step forward.

"We've not seen him before."

"Nor would you," mac Gabráin returned. "He's not been here before!"

The Old Goose did not match the clan chief's raised tones.

"Bring him forward."

Mac Gabráin rubbed at his beard and took a few frustrated paces. For a moment, Ingelbert thought he meant to defy the Old Goose, but then, with a resigned slump of his shoulders, mac Gabráin waved his arm at the man.

"Domnal! Come here, lad."

Domnal advanced without hesitance, only a hint of sore feet slowing his steps. He came and stood next to his chieftain. He was freckled and hairlipped, but clearly not a simpleton. Homely and clever. Ingelbert knew such a face well. He considered them to be of similar age, past the middle twenties at least, but the muscles and careworn lines granted by a life of hard work could have fooled Ingelbert's estimation. The Dal Riata often appeared older than they were.

"Have a look," Áedán mac Gabráin said, hooking a finger up under the bracelet on Domnal's wrist. "He wears what you require!"

Ingelbert went to tug at the ugly torque about his own neck and found himself still in Worm Chewer's grip. Feeling his movement, the knight released him.

The Old Goose looked the newcomer over. To Domnal's credit, he met the coburn's eye.

"Bring the anvil," the Old Goose commanded. The squires behind him went swiftly into the keep as Áedán mac Gabráin muttered a string of curses.

"You trust not my own kin?"

"Pardons," the Old Goose replied with little courtesy. "We must be sure."

"Then test him on the one you wear," mac Gabráin demanded, pointing at the Old Goose's neck.

The collars were an uncomfortable nuisance, but one from which even the Knights Sergeant were not exempt. The Old Goose ignored the suggestion and merely watched as the Dal Riata chieftain grew more incensed. Ingelbert felt the tension mounting and hoped this was not the day that saw the long alliance between the Valiant Spur and the clansmen crumble.

The squires were not long in returning. Ingelbert heard creaking wheels and the babbling voice of the prisoner long before they were dragged into sight. The anvil was affixed to a sturdy cart of oak and pulled into the yard by two of the squires. The third hauled the stumbling goblin along by a length of steel chain connected to manacles that bound the creature at wrist and ankle. His short, bandy legs could not meet the coburn's long, sure strides and he fell several times as they crossed the yard. The goblin's scalp was raw and freshly bleeding, what remained of the normally grey-toned flesh now an angry red. Scraping his head along the wall of his cell again, Ingelbert surmised. All in loyalty to a uniform the fanatic was no longer allowed to wear.

The squires brought both anvil and captive to where Ingelbert and the others stood. Domnal tried to remain resolved in the presence of his chieftain, but Ingelbert saw confusion and fear rippling at the corners of the man's face at the appearance of the Red Cap, who kept up a steady stream of vile insults at everyone surrounding him, spitting at them when words failed. His curses turned into wordless squeals of protest when the three squires began forcing him towards the anvil. The goblin was half their height and could not have matched one of them in strength even were he not under-fed and bound, but desperation powered his struggles. The squires were grunting with effort and issuing curses of their own by the time they forced the goblin to his knees before the piceous weight of the anvil.

"Iron," the Old Goose intoned, the word directed at Domnal.

At this, one of the squires seized the goblin's left arm, locking the elbow straight. Another grabbed the goblin's wrist and began pushing his hand towards the anvil's base. The goblin strained so firmly against this effort that Ingelbert feared he would break his own arm. His eyes bulged, his teeth ground together, but inch by unstoppable inch his hand moved toward the metal. At the last second, the goblin tore free, wrenching his arm away. The sudden movement unbalanced the coburn and they stumbled, their weight pushing the goblin forward. His face slammed into the anvil.

The sound of sizzling flesh was quickly drowned out by the goblin's screams. Ingelbert's tightly closed eyelids were powerless against the distinct smell of septic skin burning.

"Iron," the Old Goose repeated. "Virulent to all Fae."

Ingelbert opened his eyes to find the goblin being dragged away. He was still conscious, though half his face was a bubbling ruin. The curses and threats still dribbled weakly from his half-fused lips.

"Yet nothing but a common metal to the mortal races of coburn," the Old Goose continued, "and man."

The knight gestured for Domnal to approach the anvil.

"And *this* man," Áedán mac Gabráin yelled as he stepped between Domnal and the anvil, "has iron about his fucking wrist! He is no Fae skinchanger, he—"

"If he is not gruagach then he has nothing to fear!" The Old Goose's voice rose for the first time.

"The ornaments can be cheated," Worm Chewer stepped in, his tone blunt. "Made from pewter, lead. Or enchanted, given time. The anvil lays all doubt to rest. Lay hand upon it, boy, and let's have done."

Domnal looked to Áedán mac Gabráin for guidance. The chieftain cast a fiery look at both knights before giving him a nod.

The young clansmen took a hesitant step towards the cart. Next to him, Ingelbert felt Worm Chewer tense slightly. The Old Goose's stance changed subtly, the butt of his spear no longer resting on the ground. Ingelbert took a deep breath, hoping no one heard it shudder. Domnal's next steps were swifter, his arm raised. He paused, his hand hovering inches above the pitted surface of the anvil. Ingelbert saw the apple of the man's throat rise and descend heavily. He lowered his hand onto the metal. The only noise was Ingelbert letting the wind out of his lungs.

Domnal stepped away quickly, rejoining his chieftain.

"We are through here," mac Gabráin muttered, waving his men to follow as he turned to go.

"All of you," the Old Goose stopped them.

The clansmen turned as one, the anger of their chief reflected on every face. There was a long moment of terrible stillness. Neither side moved nor spoke. It was mac Gabráin who finally broke the silence. He no longer shouted. His voiced had dropped to a low growl.

"Damn you. We are not like this one," the chieftain flicked his chin towards Ingelbert. "We are not your servants to be ordered about."

"My duty is to safeguard this castle, mac Gabráin," the Old Goose replied. "Not your injured pride."

The clan chieftain's eyes widened, the whites burning amidst his ruddy face.

"You would speak to me of pride? The swell-chested cocks of the Valiant Spur?!" Áedán mac Gabráin thrust a finger at the Old Goose. "Do not think I do not know where this danger comes from, coburn. This castle that you safeguard is the womb that birthed this evil!"

"It matters not," the Old Goose said, keeping control of his own voice. "The gruagach are a threat to your people, as well."

"Because of you!" mac Gabráin gave the coburn a final jab of his finger, then used it to tap his own chest. "You came to me. Yours were dying behind these walls, and I offered aid. Not one in my clan was taken before that."

"You do not know that," Worm Chewer threw in. "The gruagach do not reveal themselves needlessly. It is impossible to know when they infiltrated the Roost or your clan before we began to be vigilant."

"Vigilant," the clansman scoffed, pulling the twisted horseshoe from his wrist and casting it disdainfully upon the ground. "Trinkets and charms and anvils. How have they helped? How many have the gruagach murdered in spite of all your precautions?"

"Twenty-seven."

Ingelbert found every face in the yard turned to him. He had not meant to say it aloud.

"In, in total," Ingelbert stammered, unable to stop himself under the harsh scrutiny of the clansmen and the grim stares of the knights. "Eight from the castle servants. The former chief steward, the smith's, um, the smith's daughter. Two . . . two from the kitchen staff, one scullery boy. The kennel, that is, the kennel master, the tanner's apprentice and the, um, the chronicler. Not me, the one before, the chronicler before me.

"The clansmen have lost nineteen, but two of them were not, not Dal Riata but from neighboring, uh, neighboring clans. Both were men, shepherds who were more than likely killed some distance away in their own lands and their forms worn by the gruagach to come here. Áedán mac Gabráin's folk, that is, your folk, make up the remaining seventeen. Six men, two of which . . . were elderly, seven women all fairly young, though one was a widow. And four, um . . . four children. Three girls and, and one boy."

Ingelbert was sweating freely now, the sun bearing down on him less intensely than the eyes of Áedán mac Gabráin.

"And how many coburn have the gruagach slain, straw-head?"

Ingelbert had not expected the question, but he knew the answer. He responded immediately, knowing hesitation would not soften the number.

"None. That is . . . no, none."

"None," mac Gabráin repeated, giving both the Knights Sergeant bitter looks.

"Our order knows your people have suffered greatly," the Old Goose said, breaking the awkward silence. "No knight or squire has yet been slain, but though our own have not yet bled, do not mistake, Grand Master Lackcomb values the friendship of the Dal Riata and grieves for your losses. Do not allow the gruagach to divide us now."

Áedán mac Gabráin did not respond, but after a moment he strode purposefully over to the anvil and placed his hand firmly upon it, gesturing for his men to do the same. They obeyed without hesitation and none of them suffered ill at the iron's touch.

Satisfied, the Old Goose bowed his head to the chieftain. The clansmen made their way across the yard and out the gate without another word.

"That may be the last we see of Dal Riata goods," Worm Chewer said, pushing another wad of night-crawlers into his beak.

The Old Goose nodded gravely. "I will report to the Grand Master. Áedán mac Gabráin is not an ally Lackcomb would want lost." He turned to Ingelbert. "Begin your count, Master Crane. And be sure to have the squires touch iron to the cows before you approach."

Ingelbert did not risk a verbal answer. He simply nodded and stuck the tip of his charcoal to his tongue. Worm Chewer stayed in the yard while Ingelbert began his inventory of the dry goods. He worked quickly and efficiently, comfortable in his task and eager to be out of the yard before the sun was much higher.

The squires touched an iron horseshoe to each of the cows and found nothing sinister about them save their health. The beasts were herded out of the yard, destined for the pens near the tannery and the knacker's mallet.

When all was accounted for, Ingelbert walked back to where Worm Chewer waited and shut the ledger, his charcoal tucked securely between the pages. The Knight Sergeant spat in the dust and, with a grunt, led Ingelbert out of the yard in the direction of the Middle Bailey. Ingelbert knew the way, of course, but it did not matter. He never went anywhere without escort.

The Roost was a vast stronghold of halls, towers, barbicans and keeps, all stoutly perched atop an imposing escarpment. Such a castle should have been a hive of activity, but Ingelbert and Worm Chewer encountered no one between the yard and the Bailey. The gruagach had murdered eight of the castle's denizens. Fear had claimed the rest. Now the daily functions of the castle limped along with barely a quarter of the manpower needed to maintain the needs of the Order. Productivity was further retarded by the need for every human servant to be constantly guarded by at least one-armed squire. As annalist, Ingelbert merited the protection of a member of the Knights Sergeant. The last man to hold his position was discovered to be an impostor and slain. The body of the actual chronicler was never found.

Ingelbert had come to the Roost to record the deeds of the knights, preserve their history and maintain the castle library.

However, the servants' mass desertion forced him to perform more than his titular duties. He spent the rest of the morning in the chandlery, dipping wicks. Worm Chewer sat on a barrel, performing the ghastly habit that gave him his name. Some of the other Knights Sergeant often helped Ingelbert in his daily tasks, especially Yewly the Salted, who was an old sailor and loathed to be idle. Not so with Worm Chewer. After several hours, Ingelbert gathered up a bundle of finished candles for his own use and left the chandlery.

A lazy spring rain had begun to fall, the drops slow and swollen. It did nothing to cool the day. When Ingelbert and Worm Chewer entered the Campaign Hall, the air was heavy and close, the stone walls slick with moisture. Ingelbert's chambers were located beneath the hall, in a large storeroom converted for his use.

He took a heavy iron key from his belt and unlocked the thick oaken door that was the only entrance. Worm Chewer stepped in first to ensure the room was indeed empty before stepping back into the corridor. Ingelbert entered and closed the door, locking it once more with the key and throwing the large bolt. He undid the clasp of the squint and slid the small iron door aside. Worm Chewer peered at him through the bars.

"Will you be wanting supper brought?" the knight asked with little interest.

"No, um, no, no need," Ingelbert told him.

The coburn nodded, spit and turned away. Ingelbert heard his spurs clicking on the stones as he left.

Closing the squint, Ingelbert took a deep breath and immediately removed the collar of nails. Another day done. No one would bother him further, at least until the morning. It was scarcely past midday, but the knights had taken to leaving Ingelbert to his tasks as chronicler without a guard, so long as he kept the door locked and barred. Feeling some of the tension flee his body, he turned and faced his haven.

After the shape-changers' attempt to set fire to the library, the Grand Master ordered the more important contents moved.

The storeroom was quite spacious, but after transporting the multitude of scrolls, tomes, ledgers and maps, along with all the tables and shelves necessary to house them, the room shrank considerably. Now it was something of a warren, choked with stacks of dusty parchment, piles of musty books and colonies of furled charts. Ingelbert hated the Roost, but here, here in this room, he gained a sense of safety. It was foolish, he knew, for one was never truly safe from the duplicitous terror that stalked the castle.

But here, he was safe from the fallacies of verbal interaction. He might very well have caused the long-established alliance between the Knights of the Valiant Spur and the Dal Riata to crumble today, all because he spoke and, as always, spoke poorly. He envied the servants who had fled. He shared their fear, but his fear did not grant him the courage to run. Here, at least, in his storeroom among the books where there was no need for speech, here he could do some good.

Ingelbert deposited his collar and the fresh candles on a desk already buried and sat down in his chair. There were messages from the Knights Errant to record, come from all across the Tin Isles. Most had taken months to arrive, the news old and largely unconfirmed, but Ingelbert carefully scrutinized each one, cataloging the information in a system of his own invention. Now he could immerse himself in comparing the newest missives with older reports, tracking the individual knights' movements, mark his maps and cross-reference their words with their fellows' to glean a clearer picture of the current state of the Isles.

News from surrounding Albain was regular, provided more by the human clans than the Knights Errant, few of whom quested so close to the Roost. Middangeard warriors continued to plague the Isles, but Blood Yolk reported engaging several of their ships off Albain's eastern coast, while Pitch Feather repelled a raiding party in the lowlands. To the south, in Ingelbert's homeland of Sasana, there was little of note, though Sir Barn Lochlan had sent disturbing word of an entire village massacred and the corpses of the slain eaten. The knight could not say what had done the slaughter, only that it appeared the work of several large creatures.

Little trickled in from Kymbru, but that was unsurprising as the knight they called Poorly Well was nigh illiterate. Nothing from Outborders either, but that was expected. The Dread Cockerel never sent word.

The source of the most anticipated news, however, came from across the water to the west, where lay Airlann, the Source Isle. Many of the knights were occupied there, lending aid in the aftermath of a Red Cap uprising. Though Torcan Swinehelm and the majority of his army were slain at the ruins of Castle Gaunt, the goblin general had left a large contingent to hold Black Pool, a city he had taken with support from Middangeard reavers. Reports from Black Pool were regular. Two of the Knights Errant, Bronze Wattle and Sir Girart the Wake, had pledged their swords to the city's liberation.

A core of resistance had formed among the populace not long after the walls fell, bolstered by sellswords paid by the deep coffers of Black Pool's enigmatic leader, the Lord of the Pile.

Ingelbert had varying reports about this goblin potentate. Originally, he was said to have been executed by Torcan Swinehelm, but now Bronze Wattle wrote of his return, rallying the people of the city to push the Red Caps out. Whatever the truth, the resistance had gained much ground. Fully half the city had now been reclaimed, harkening back to a period in Black Pool's long history when the city was divided among warring factions.

The coburn penchant for colorful sobriquets notwithstanding, they did a great deal of good in the world, and though Ingelbert had served the Order only a short time, he had quickly come to respect the mission of the Knights Errant. He knew only their names, for they returned to the Roost once every two years, and Ingelbert had arrived at the castle in the middle of the latest errantry. He delved into their messages, hoped for their success and yearned for fresh reports, but he had only seen one in the flesh, Sir Pikard the Lucky, the aging knight who had recruited him. Soon, he would meet the rest.

The two years were nearing an end.

There were no windows in the storeroom, but Ingelbert had grown accustomed to reckoning time in his paper-strewn den.

The sun would be down, the watch posted and the castle filling with shadows. The pall of fear that draped the fortress during the day would now solidify into calcareous dread. A companion by day encountered alone in a corridor at night was to be feared. An alteration in the action or mannerism of a friend was something to be distrusted. The company of others was to be shunned since anyone could be a monster wearing familiar flesh. Alone, no one could harm you. Alone, no one could help you.

Ingelbert stayed immersed in his work until the bitter watches. At last, when his heavy lids could no longer stay perched above his dust-reddened eyes, he retired to the small alcove that contained his bed. The night did little to abate the heat. Ingelbert slept fitfully and fought a losing battle with his damp bed linens.

Resigned to restlessness, Ingelbert rose and returned to his desk.

He needed to occupy the final hours before dawn in order to keep the trepidation that dwelt ever in his mind at bay. He reached into the chaos of his work and plucked a heavy volume from the nest of parchment.

It was a prodigious work, bound in green leather darkened to near black with the oil of countless palms, the pages curled and stained with the curiosity of ages. Ingelbert had discovered the book in the library after the fire, when he and half a dozen squires were tasked with moving the annals to a safer location. It had no title that Ingelbert could discern and was written in a runic script that he knew to be the archaic language from which the tongue of Middangeard was descended. Many sleepless nights had been whiled away staring at its pages, the tedious translation of which had yielded little more than mundane lists. Yet Ingelbert returned to the task more nights than not, finding the numbing exercise a balm to his regularly troubled thoughts. He spoke the tongue of Middangeard, but the words contained within this discarded book were only distantly related. He found the translation of each individual word not unlike untangling a ridiculously overwrought knot. So long as he continued to worry at it, eventually it would unravel. The banality of the discovered words never seemed to dampen his satisfaction.

He had just dug the word for honey from among the runes when he heard the noise in the corridor.

Ingelbert tensed.

It was not yet dawn, he was certain. His appointed escort never arrived before the sun. He sat frozen at his desk, listening, waiting for the sound to have been an invention of his ears, but it continued. Steps on the flagstones and coming closer. Ingelbert groped around his piles for the dagger he knew to be present, though rarely seen. He tried to make a silent search, but when the weapon remained hidden, panic infused his movements and soon paper and books were thrown noisily to the floor. The footsteps were just outside the door when his hand at last fell upon the weapon's sheath underneath a stack of maps. The sudden, forceful knock caused him to jump, knocking the dagger off the desk to fall between it and an overburdened bookshelf.

Ingelbert did not move. He stared at the door, unwilling to take his eyes off of it to look for the fallen dagger. The knock came again, louder.

"Master Crane," an unfamiliar voice issued through the door.

Ingelbert remained where he was. What could he do?

Continue to stand here shaking like a frightened child and hoping whoever was without would go away? He could wait for one of the Knights Sergeant to arrive and—

"Master Crane," the voice punched through, punctuated by a strong fist on the door.

Wiping the sweat from his forehead, Ingelbert approached the door and with a shaking hand unclasped the squint. He slid it aside and found two coburn in the hall. The younger one stood bearing a torch behind the older, who regarded Ingelbert through the opening with a placid expression. Both wore iron collars about their necks.

"Ingelbert Crane?" the older coburn asked.

"Yes?" Ingelbert managed.

"Pardons for waking you," the coburn said. "But as is custom, we would have our names recorded in the castle book."

"Names?"

"Sir Corc and Squire Flyn."

"*Bantam* Flyn," the younger of the pair added, laughter in his voice.

A hint of annoyance played across the older coburn's brow before he returned his attention to Ingelbert.

"We have returned."

TWO

Dawn was minutes away when Flyn rolled the barrel directly down the center of the squires' barracks. The heavy tub thundered across the floor, the mail shirt within slapping sharply with each rotation. Curses, shouts of alarm and groggy protests flew at Flyn from both sides as the squires shot up in their bunks.

When Flyn reached the end of the barracks he hopped over the barrel and turned to face the long, low room. Two dozen rudely-roused faces glared at him. Flyn gave them a hearty wave.

"Top o' the morning, my young struts!"

With a laugh, Flyn bent back to the barrel and started pushing it down the aisle between the beds once more. This time, the complaints were followed by several flung objects, mostly surcoats and skullcaps, but one pewter mug sailed past, missing widely thanks to sleep-addled aim. The haphazard missiles did nothing to curb Flyn's progress or his laughter. The squires regained enough of their wits to add words to the rough din of complaints.

"Who the blazes?!"

"Jackanapes!"

"Get out!"

"Pardons, boys!" Flyn replied without remorse. "Have to get this armor clean. Make the Order proud and all that!"

A large, clawed foot stamped down over the barrel, causing Flyn to come to an abrupt stop. He looked down at the long talons between his hands. They flexed, leaving deep scratches in the wood as they gripped the curve of the barrel. A foot that size could belong to only one coburn.

"Hello Gulver," Flyn said without looking up.

The barracks had gone quiet.

Flyn straightened and found his eyes level with a breastplate.

"Had the late watch, then?" Flyn said, looking up the rest of the way to meet Gulver's face.

Of all the coburn in the castle, Gulver was by the far the biggest. None in the ranks of the squires or the Knights Sergeant came close. Among the Knights Errant, only the Mad Capon rivaled Gulver in size, but where the knight was notoriously fat, Gulver was a walking mass of muscle. When last Flyn saw him, he was lying senseless in the mud of the tourney field, the result of a quarterstaff strike to the head. A strike Flyn had delivered.

"See lads," Flyn said, clapping Gulver companionably on the shoulder and turning to address the entire room. "The leech was worried, but I told him . . . Gulver has not any brains to scatter."

Flyn was rewarded with a few chuckles.

"Well, go on then," Flyn said to Gulver, keeping his hand on his shoulder as he stepped around the barrel. "Give it a good kick and help a fellow out."

Gulver did as suggested. The barrel bounced mightily across the floor before careening into one of the bunk posts, causing the occupant to swear loudly as the impact rocked his bed.

After the crash, the only sound in the barracks was the steady hiss of sand escaping the burst slats of the barrel.

"You should not be here, Flyn," Gulver rumbled, shrugging away from Flyn's touch. "You should be in the Campaign Hall, waiting for the others to return from their errantry."

Flyn found himself surprised at the lack of anger in Gulver's voice. Even as the big coburn walked away from him, there was a noted absence of aggression in his movements. Coburn males were known for their posturing, especially within the ranks of the squires, where everyone was on the lookout to prove their prowess. Destroying the barrel had not been a challenge, then.

Gulver had simply called his bluff.

"I am not spurred yet," Flyn replied, keeping his tone light.

"I am afraid you must still count me among your company. Just another bantam!"

"No," said a squire Flyn did not know. He stepped into the aisle, glaring with flinty eyes. "You are *the* bantam. Bantam Flyn! Count yourself so great, you title yourself with the name the Knights Sergeant use to demean us. The first of us. The best of us."

Flyn knew when he was being mocked. And this stranger had all the physical clues of challenge that Gulver lacked. This was inevitable, though Flyn was surprised at the source.

"What is your name?" he asked.

"Drincoin," the squire answered, placing far too much pride in the response.

"Drincoin," Flyn repeated, affecting a hushed reverence.

"You have squired, what? A year?"

"Eight months," the youth replied without hesitation, confident even in his lack of experience.

Flyn was no longer surprised. This is where he should have expected the challenge. From himself. A fresh squire, too sure, too foolish to be of much use to anyone save his own overinflated sense of prowess. But there the similarities ended. This Drincoin was not Flyn. The way he stood, the placement of his hands, the weight of his body shifted too far to his left shoulder, his beak lifted too high. This fight would be over quickly. The trick would not be to win it, the trick would be to teach these others watching, so that he was not challenged again.

"Well, Drincoin," Flyn said. "You seem eager to show me what you have learned in so lengthy a tutelage."

"Eager to show an overstuffed braggart where his jests are not welcome," Drincoin said striding forward.

Gulver extended his monstrous arm, blocking the squire's path.

"You lot have watches to post," Gulver said to the entire barracks. "And drills to work. Do not keep the Knights Sergeant waiting. To it, now."

The big squire had barely raised his voice and Flyn was impressed to see the squires scramble with alacrity at his words. All save Drincoin, who continued to stare over Gulver's arm at Flyn.

Gulver leaned down until his beak was very close to the brash squire's face.

"To it."

Drincoin blinked, gave Gulver a respectful nod and withdrew.

"My gratitude," Flyn said once the squires had filtered out of the barracks.

"I did you no favor, Bantam Flyn," Gulver said, wearily setting about the chore of removing his armor. "The Order needs every able body. I did not need you killing some young strut. Even if he is a green fool."

"I would not have harmed him overmuch," Flyn replied.

He took a step forward and began helping Gulver with his pauldron straps. The brute tensed for half moment, then gave a grunt of appreciation, slumping heavily onto the nearest bunk. Flyn worked quickly and soon had Gulver free of his harness. He hung the various components on hooks along the barracks wall and then sat on the bunk opposite the huge squire. The two regarded each other for a long time and Flyn could not help but recall all the times they done just this after hard days of training. He smiled.

"How fares your skull?"

Gulver blew out a frustrated laugh.

"Fortunately thick. Curse you for the lightning-quick ponce you are, Flyn! I was a fortnight in the infirmary for that blow!"

"Even trees fall to lightning," Flyn returned. "Whereas you are still standing, you feathered mountain."

Gulver chuckled, working the stiffness of the armor from his neck and shoulders. "You returned with Constant Corc?"

"I did," Flyn nodded. "And do not call him such."

Gulver gave a conciliatory nod. "Any of the others?"

"We are the first," Flyn replied. "Not been here but two hours."

"And you are only now subjecting us to your damn pranks?"

"It took me that long to find a barrel."

They both laughed heartily at that, drawing a few grumbles from the other squires returned from the night's watch now trying to sleep.

"I met the new chronicler," Flyn said in more hushed tones.

"Inkstain?" Gulver snorted. "A wonder he still lives. Never met a human so useless and craven that the gruagach don't bother to murder him."

There was a long silence.

"How long, Gulver?" Flyn ventured at last. "How long have the skin-changers been in the castle?"

Gulver's brow furrowed as he calculated. "You been gone, what, a full year and half another? Likely, they were here even before you left. Leastways that is what the Knights Sergeant think, what little they tell us. Things are grave. There are whispers that the squires up for errantry will be denied. With the dangers now lurking within the Roost, we are too few and too valuable as a garrison to let any go."

Flyn absorbed the big squire's words. Like Gulver, Flyn was two years away from being knighted, but unlike Gulver he had special dispensation. If these rumors were true, there was a chance he would not be granted knighthood as promised, but stuck back in the castle to man the walls and guard the servants against skin-changers. Flyn fought a rising anger.

"You meet with the Grand Master today?" Gulver asked, bringing Flyn out of his darkening thoughts.

"Yes," Flyn said, realization dawning.

So. All eyes were on him. The Order could not dub him a knight and then decline to bestow the same honor to the squires who had served dutifully for the required six years. If the whispers Gulver spoke of bore any weight and the squires were to be nothing more than a standing army, he could not hope to escape such a fate.

"How many with the required years have petitioned for knighthood?"

"Seven," Gulver said. "But only four have a chance of being given spurs. The others . . ." Gulver waved a massive hand, dismissing the remaining candidates and Flyn with one gesture.

"Now get you gone. I need sleep."

Flyn stood, slapping Gulver on the knee. The squire lay his bulk down on the rough straw of the bunk. Flyn retrieved his hauberk from the ruins of the barrel, purposefully shaking the sand off on Gulver's feet. His little goad was wasted. The brute was already snoring.

Flyn returned to the Campaign Hall, where a room had been prepared for him and Sir Corc. Several of the other doors along the corridor were now closed, evidence that a few of the Knights Errant had also made it back to the castle. Flyn wondered who rested behind those doors. It was always the most debated question among the squires. Who would return every two-year and who would not. The knights had not been away quite so long this time, having been recalled to the Roost a year and a half ago for a funeral and an accompanying tourney. A tourney which had changed the course of Flyn's life.

Not bothering to close the door to the chamber, Flyn sat upon a low stool and began inspecting his mail shirt. It could have used a few more passes in the barrel. Frowning, he snatched up an oiled cloth and gave the links an aggressive scrub.

"It is time."

Flyn did not look up immediately. He gave the mail a final once-over, squinting hard. Still unsatisfied, he raised his head.

Sir Corc stood in the doorway.

Well into his middle years, the knight remained thick of arm and deep of chest. His feathers retained most of their chestnut color, only here and there paled with grey. His armor showed dents, the crimson of his surcoat faded, but both were kept clean. Well-worn, hard-used, but donned with pride, their imperfections a testament to the many years and countless miles spent in honorable service. Flyn did not know how he did it. He had never seen Corc take oil to his breastplate, nor a whetstone to his sword. Those chores he saved for the darkest watches; the nights he spent awake while others slept, the lonely mornings when he rose before the sun.

Every night, every morn.

"I will be just another moment," Flyn told him. "Last bit of tarnish here."

Sir Corc's stare shifted briefly to the mail draped over Flyn's knee. He nodded once before turning away, his broad shoulders filling the narrow corridor as he left.

"Sir Corc the Constant," Flyn said to himself, pausing in his futile scrubbing. Once he would have said it with disappointment, even disdain, muttering it away from the knight's hearing as a private slight. He was still careful to say it out of earshot, but there was no disrespect in his voice. It had become something of an oath to Flyn, a reminder. Sir Corc hated his title, given him by his sworn brothers years before Flyn's time. If they thought themselves clever, if they sought to make sport, they were fools. Just as Flyn had been a fool. He often wondered whether the name was something the knight was saddled with during his days as a squire; days filled with ceaseless drills and the belittling tutelage of the Knights Sergeant. Flyn could not imagine the Old Goose screaming at a young Corc, calling him "bantam" and slapping him with the blade of a practice sword. But surely it must have happened, for Sir Corc learned his lessons well.

Flyn had fought him twice and been soundly defeated. Flyn, who was the best of the squires. Flyn, who had bested the famed Bronze Wattle and stood against the Forge Born. Flyn, who once sought to win glory and titles far surpassing any who had come before him. Flyn, who would now have an audience with the Grand Master looking like a begrimed sellsword.

He bent back to his armor, pressing the rag deeply into the rings, but patches of stubborn rust remained. He had tried to clean the shirt before they took ship, rolling it in a barrel of sand across what flat ground existed on their little island. Across and back again, for hours. He even stooped to recruiting Pocket to his cause, resting on a rock as the little gurg pushed determinedly at the heavy barrel. For all their efforts, the mail continued to look dingy and they shared a good laugh at their failing.

Flyn stopped suddenly, the memory of Pocket freezing him in place. He should not even be thinking of the boy. Not here. Sir Corc had made sure he understood, badgering him the entire voyage that they were not to utter the child's name, not even to each other. Flyn had not needed to be told. To the few in the castle who might remember him, Pocket had to remain what he was the day he left. A changeling orphan who ran away from his duties in the scullery, never to be seen again. At least, not alive.

Banishing all thought of the boy and all hopes of shining mail, Flyn quickly donned his armor and weapons. He found Sir Corc waiting for him in the Campaign Hall proper. They strode out into the Middle Bailey, Sir Corc leading slightly, ascending the nearest steps to the battlements and using the wall walks to cross over to the middle gatehouse, or as the squires affectionately called it, the Midden Gate.

"Because it is the shittiest place to stand watch!" Flyn recited with a laugh, reaching forward to bump Sir Corc's shoulder with his fist. The old knight had to know the joke, it was near as ancient as the Roost, but he gave no notice to Flyn or his jibe. Flyn was unperturbed. It was Corc's way.

The guards checked that Flyn and Corc were wearing the required collars of iron nails and also had them place hand upon the blunted blade of an old tourney sword for added measure.

Once through the gatehouse, they descended into the Inner Bailey and Sir Corc led them to Mulrooster's Tower. They were again checked by guards before being admitted into the tower, but once inside they went unchallenged up the stairs to the Grand Master's chambers. Sir Corc entered without knocking, a familiarity which said a great deal about the knight, and about his relationship with the sole occupant of the room they now entered.

Grand Master Lackcomb turned away from the window as they stepped inside, fixing them with his good eye. The other was milked over, colorless and dead. Nearing his seventies, Lackcomb still possessed a powerful frame, radiating the vigor of a much younger coburn. Indeed, Flyn found it difficult to believe that the Grand Master was a full twenty years Sir Corc's senior. Scars from dozens of battle wounds lay nestled in Lackcomb's feathers, but his most famous injury was self-inflicted. An ugly, puckered strip of tissue ran across the top of the old war bird's head, all that remained of the comb he had sliced off with his own hand. That, at least, was the legend. To Flyn's knowledge, Lackcomb had never uttered a word to refute it.

Sir Corc went to one knee before the Grand Master. Flyn realized he should follow, a lurching heartbeat later.

"Rise," Lackcomb commanded with a hint of impatience.

Flyn need not have worried about the delay in his decorum, for once they were back on their feet the Grand Master forgot all about him, directing his gaze and his questions only at Sir Corc.

"Any of the others?" Lackcomb asked.

"Pyle Strummer, Poorly Well and Wex the Ganger have arrived," Sir Corc answered. "I saw Blood Yolk when we put in at Grianaig. He should not be but a day or two behind."

"Needs to pay his crew of wreckers and pirates," Lackcomb surmised. "So. Five returned. Out of three dozen."

"It is early yet," Sir Corc said. "The two-year mark is still a week hence."

"We will not get a full count," Lackcomb's response was too quick, almost angry. Flyn risked a glance at Corc. The knight's face was unchanged, and he said nothing, as was his way.

Lackcomb went back to the window. "Bronze Wattle is dead."

"What?" Flyn could not stop himself from asking.

Lackcomb plucked a piece of stained parchment from his desk, only to toss it immediately back down with a flick of his wrist.

"I have had word from Black Pool. The Red Caps attempted to retake Sweynside. Bronze Wattle led a force to stop them at the Goat's Tongue Bridge. He succeeded, but the goblins have taken to poisoning their arrows. Sir Girart confirms it. He is dead."

Flyn's beak was agape. He could not fathom it. Bronze Wattle was considered by many to be the best knight of the Order.

He was respected by his fellow Knights Errant and revered by the squires. His fall was a grave turn.

"You fought him, bantam."

It took Flyn a moment to realize Lackcomb's words were directed at him.

"You fought him," Lackcomb said again, ignoring Flyn's lack of attention. He came around the desk and approached, drawing closer with every word. "In the tourney field. You fought him and emerged the victor. You beat him, but I wonder . . . can you replace him?"

The Grand Master was now directly in front of him, leaning in close. Flyn met his penetrating stare with a solid one of his own.

"No one can replace Bronze Wattle, my lord," he answered with surety. "But I know Black Pool and have experience against the Red Caps. If my lord deems it fitting, I will go to the city and take up Bronze Wattle's struggle."

Lackcomb considered this, his milky eye seeming to search Flyn's face for a hint of weakness. Flyn knew it would find none.

At last, the Grand Master turned back to Sir Corc.

"Is he ready?"

Flyn was suddenly grateful Lackcomb no longer stared at him, for that milky eye would have detected any doubt that played across his face. He was unsure how Corc would answer. There had been no great love between them in the beginning. A mutual lack of respect at best, outright hostility at the worst, especially on Flyn's part. He kept his face forward, fighting an urge to look over at Sir Corc, knowing to do so would be both pitiful and pointless. The knight's face was ever unreadable. Even now he considered the question before him, every moment he remained silent furthering Flyn's fate back to the squires.

"He is," Sir Corc said at last. Flyn allowed himself a small smile.

"And what of you?" the Grand Master pressed the knight.

"Are you ready to give up your own errantry and at last join the ranks of the Knights Sergeant?"

Flyn did look over at Sir Corc now. This was new. Corc had never spoken of such an offer, but Corc never spoke of much to anyone. The knight's response to this question, however, came quickly.

"As before, my lord," Sir Corc said. "I must decline."

"These refusals are wearing thin, Sir," Lackcomb said.

Corc said nothing.

"This castle is under siege from within," the Grand Master told them. "We are not an order of farmers or shepherds. We are warriors. And dependent upon the surrounding human clans to sustain us. Human clans who now grow to distrust us. The numbers of young struts who enter the Roost with visions of knighthood wanes each year. We are losing our servants within the walls, we are losing our knights without. I have need of trustworthy knights here, Sir Corc."

"With respect, my lord," Sir Corc replied, "the needs of the Tin Isles are also great. I can still be of most use in the world."

Flyn saw the Grand Master's face darken at these words.

Anger began to creep into his brow, into the edge of his voice.

"You did a great service to Airlann with the slaying of Torcan Swinehelm," Lackcomb said. "But after, you left the Source Isle and, despite recruiting the best leech this Order has ever had, what has occupied your quests since?"

"I have been chart—"

"Charting the Knucklebones!" Lackcomb cut him off. "Aye, I know. You sent word. And how, tell me, does the distinct mapping of countless miserable spits of rock in the ocean help the causes of the Valiant Spur?"

Sir Corc remained stalwart under the Grand Master's disapproval. The charting of the northern islands was a lie, one which the knight had not told lightly. The opinions of his brother knights had never mattered to Sir Corc, Flyn knew, but such thinly veiled vexation from the leader of the Order could not have been easy to endure. Still, the knight bore the weight with the same implacable resolve that shaped him.

"It would be prudent to know exactly what lies just off our northern shores," Sir Corc responded. "It may seem an inglorious task, my lord, but that does not lessen its importance."

"And what of this gruagach incursion?" Lackcomb demanded, his patience frayed. "Of what importance do you place that? I have need of swords here, Sir Corc. Swords, and minds keen enough to wield them. The Knights Sergeant need new blood to help shape the squires."

"I am ill-suited as an instructor, my lord," Sir Corc said.

"You shaped this one!" Lackcomb returned, thrusting a finger at Flyn.

"No, my lord," the knight disagreed. "He shaped himself."

"Damn you, Corc, your place is here!" Lackcomb pronounced, slamming a fist down upon his desk.

"My lord," Sir Corc said evenly. "By tradition, each knight sworn and spurred may quest where he will, without interference. You have no power to keep me here."

The Grand Master's eyes widened at this defiance. Flyn saw his feathers begin to bristle and glanced to the corner of the room where Lackcomb's renowned pole axe, the Coming Dawn, rested.

By rights, all were allowed to challenge the reigning Grand Master for governance of the Order. Lackcomb had thrown down his predecessor, just as every Grand Master before him had for centuries. Flyn tried to imagine a contest between these two veterans. The outcome of such a battle was far from certain.

Fortunately, the Grand Master cooled, his gaze and his voice adopting an icy bitterness.

"True," he said. "I have no power over you. But I do have the power to grant or deny petitions to knighthood."

Flyn felt his blood go cold.

"If I grant this one the honor," Lackcomb continued, nodding at Flyn, but keeping his eyes fixed on Sir Corc, "then I must consider the other seven eligible squires. That is a tenth of the castle garrison lost to errantry. That is a cost I can ill afford, Sir Corc. Not without recompense. So, I ask you again. Will you join the Knights Sergeant? For that is the price of the bantam's spurs."

There was a long silence.

"Flyn," Sir Corc said at last. "Please await me without. I would speak with the Grand Master alone."

Flyn gave the knight a respectful nod, leaving the room without the slightest sign of obedience to Lackcomb. Not wanting to pace about in the confines of the tower, Flyn made his way down to the Bailey and out into the hot day. Maybe the sun's heat would eclipse the rage boiling up in his blood.

Damn Lackcomb and his deals!

Flyn himself had struck a bargain with the Grand Master when he left with Sir Corc. He was to accompany the knight to Airlann and upon his return he was to be awarded his spurs. Now, it appeared, that promise was as empty as the Roost. Sir Corc would be a fool to agree to any terms set by Lackcomb. And Flyn knew the knight was no fool, just as he knew Corc could not join the Knights Sergeant. His mission was far more important than the falsehood he fed the Grand Master.

Pocket must be protected, his identity kept safe, the very fact that he still lived kept secret! That was Sir Corc's charge. Even coming here, leaving the little island in the Knucklebones where they had lived hidden for over a year, had been difficult for the knight. Turning Pocket's safekeeping over to others, even trusted allies, tested Corc's sense of duty. Would he possibly reveal his true purpose to the Grand Master? That, in Flyn's estimation, was the only way Lackcomb might see reason. Is that why Corc had sent him away?

Flyn's steps led to the Great Hall. He satisfied the guards that he was no skin-changer and entered the cavernous, echoing structure that housed the grandeur of the Order. During feasts, the Great Hall was filled to bursting with revelers. Now it loomed quiet and abandoned. It was difficult to imagine a feast held in the Roost now. The castle was a changed place.

Flyn strode slowly towards one of the immense tapestries that lined the walls. Each of the huge and ancient works depicted a momentous scene from the Valiant Spur's long history. Flyn craned his neck up to the shadowed recesses of the ceiling where the hulking tapestries began their dizzying descent. He shook his head in amazement. Pocket used to clean these dust-laden fossils. Flyn could not imagine a more tedious, thankless and needlessly dangerous task.

A memory crept up on him, something Pocket had told him, disregarded at the time and quickly forgotten. Flyn cast about the Hall until he spied the tapestry depicting the Battle of the Unsounded Horn. Here the weavers had attempted to capture the first time the Knights of the Valiant Spur went to war, winning a great victory against one of the Goblin Kings. Flyn's knowledge of such history was spotty at best. The battle was some eight hundred years in the past, he thought, and waged against one of the Sweyns.

The Second? Third? He could not recall.

Pocket had known. The boy's memory for Order lore was impressive. Flyn now dug into his own memory, trying to recall what the lad had told him.

"To the left of Mulrooster," Flyn whispered aloud, trying to conjure Pocket's own words. "Two! Two to the left . . . sundering the Red Cap banner."

Flyn found the figure. A coburn, charging with the rest into the goblin ranks. He wielded a large, two-handed sword, cleaving the standard of the goblins along with its bearer. Flyn shrugged the harness which held his own blade off his shoulder. It was the only way to draw a sword of such length. He pulled the wide blade free from its scabbard, the steel flawless, rippling and beautiful.

Coalspur.

The sword was named for its previous owner, a former Grand Master. Flyn had come into possession of the sword after the tourney held in honor of the fallen and well-respected knight.

Pocket seemed to think the weapon was depicted in the tapestry, but during his time at the castle had never gotten close enough to the actual sword to know for certain. But after living on the tiny island with Flyn, the boy had become quite familiar with the blade.

Flyn held Coalspur up before him, between his eyes and the tapestry. The weavers had been skilled, imbuing the embroidery with remarkable detail. The size of the sword was accurate. The shape of the cross-guard and pommel exact. It could be the same sword, insomuch as a sword rendered in cloth could compare to an actual weapon. His momentary curiosity sated, Flyn was about to turn away when something in the tapestry caught his eye. Upon the grip of the sword, between the hands of the wielder, was a mark, a symbol of some kind. Flyn looked at the grip of Coalspur, wrapped in old, stained leather. Drawing his dagger, Flyn split the leather and unwrapped the grip. There, inscribed on the handle, was the same mark. It was a simple symbol, but like the rest of the sword, expertly wrought. Flyn inspected it for a long time without gaining further insight into its meaning.

At a loss, he sheathed his dagger and slung the harness across his back once more. Propping the greatsword up on his shoulder, he turned to leave the hall and stopped short. A dozen paces away, silently watching him, stood the Dread Cockerel. Even in the ill-lit vastness of the Great Hall, the knight was an imposing figure, tall and predatory. The Dread Cockerel's armor was the same soot gray as his feathers. Flyn noted he still bore mud stains from the road, his longsword at his hip.

"Just arrived?" Flyn ventured in his friendliest tone.

The Dread Cockerel said nothing.

There was a grudge here. This was the knight that Flyn was supposed to fight at the tourney to determine the champion and the rightful winner of Coalspur. But the Dread Cockerel had killed Sir Tillory the Calm, a latecomer to the contest, and disgraced himself. The sword had gone to Flyn. Judging by the way the Dread Cockerel now stared, it was obvious he still coveted the weapon.

Flyn laughed.

He had avoided a fight with Gulver. And been robbed of one with Drincoin. If this, the most debased and villainous of the Knights Errant, wished to cross blades, then Flyn was happy to oblige. He saw the Dread Cockerel's hand drift slowly to the grip of his own sword.

"Sir Wyncott!"

The voice resonated across the Great Hall. The Dread Cockerel's head swung slowly towards the doors of the Great Hall and Flyn followed suit. Sir Corc walked purposefully towards them, his hand resting on the pommel of his sword.

"Sir Wyncott," Corc repeated as he drew near, stopping mere paces from the Dread Cockerel, whom he addressed. "Unless you have dealings with my squire, I would like a word with him."

The Dread Cockerel stared down at the older knight for a moment, then turned his attention back to Flyn. His eyes flicked from Flyn to the sword in his hands and back again. He then strode out of the Hall without a word. Flyn watched him go, waiting for the thud of the closing doors before taking a deep breath and facing Sir Corc.

"Well?" he asked. "Am I to be knighted?"

The knight's normally stolid face told him all he needed to know. Flyn gave a resigned nod to the floor and another thump on Sir Corc's shoulder as he passed, a sign of no ill will. Flyn needed a strong drink, unfriendly company and blunt advice. He knew where to find all three.

"Where are you bound?" Sir Corc called after him.

"To the infirmary," Flyn tossed the words over his shoulder, "to find Master Loamtoes."

THREE

"Curse all constipated shepherds," Deglan muttered through gritted teeth, leaning heavily into his muddler. Twisting his already sore wrist, he worked determinedly at the flax seeds, grinding them into powder. "Not a proper ailment among the whole lot. Red-haired, ruddy-faced, sheep-shaggers! Nothing ever wrong with them but boils and backed-up bowels."

"Still talking to yourself, you mouldy old mushroom?"

Deglan looked up from his work to find Bantam Flyn leaning into the infirmary. The young coburn was armed and armored, a cocky smile playing across his face. A smile Deglan was pleased to see wither when Flyn noticed Banyon Deaf Crower was also in the room.

"I was just telling the Knight Sergeant, here," Deglan said casually, "about the inherent hardiness of the Dal Riata."

"Sir," Flyn greeted Deaf Crower respectfully, but Deglan noted he did not straighten his relaxed posture. A tiny defiance, but obvious. The squire was angry.

"Successful journeys, Squire Flyn?" the Knight Sergeant asked.

"In purpose, if not in promise," the squire answered with a laugh, taking a few swaggering strides into the infirmary.

Deglan saw Deaf Crower frown at this elusive answer.

"Sir Banyon," Deglan said to the Knight Sergeant. "Clearly, young Flyn needs something to do. Why don't we let him take over your duties here for the day. I think I can find plenty of unpleasant tasks to occupy him."

"Aye," Deaf Crower agreed. "This one was always troublesome when idle." The Knight Sergeant gave Flyn a warning glower as he passed.

"Thank you, Sir," Deglan said.

"Staunch," Deaf Crower replied, giving Deglan a quick nod before leaving the infirmary. The Knights of the Valiant Spur had their own ways and customs, but they had taken quickly to using Deglan's rank from his days in the gnomish army. It was a small victory, but one which gave Deglan a small twinge of pride.

"Your bodyguard?" Flyn mocked after the Knight Sergeant was gone.

"Make yourself useful," Deglan said, tossing the muddler at the young cock's smirking face. Flyn caught it deftly.

"I came for a drink," he protested.

"Then bloody well earn it," Deglan told him.

The young coburn removed the harness that held his ludicrous sword and began unenthusiastically grinding the flax, the task quickly chasing some of the rancor from his body.

It was well over a year since Deglan had last seen the young strut and he was suddenly struck with his vibrant appearance. Most coburn possessed impressive colors in their tail feathers, but Flyn was truly unique. The rich golden brown feathers which covered his head and shoulders gave way to blazes of deep blue on his arms, while his legs were a lustrous green. Even the ubiquitous comb and wattle were a deeper red. The observation surprised Deglan. He had never given the appearance of individual coburn much notice during his long life. His tenure at the Roost was clearly affecting him.

"How are you still alive?" Deglan jabbed, digging through his shelves until he found the right ceramic jug. He pulled the stopper and sniffed, just to be sure. The whiskey the Dal Riata distilled was rough stuff, but it served well enough.

"Even I find difficulty getting myself killed charting islands," Flyn replied, throwing a bitter chuckle into the last two words.

Deglan poured two cups and handed one over. Flyn put the muddler down and drained the cup in one toss, extending his arm for a refill. Deglan handed him the jug instead.

"Wise healer," Flyn said with a wink, taking the jug and upending it for a long pull.

While the squire was drinking, Deglan saw Sir Corc step through the door. They locked eyes for a moment, all the greeting needed between two old soldiers. Flyn noticed the knight now, too.

Sir Corc took a few slow steps over and held his hand out for the jug. Flyn had the decency to look mildly ashamed and after a moment's reluctance, relinquished the whiskey. Sir Corc regarded the jug for a moment, then raised it and took a measured pull.

Deglan could not help a bark of laughter at Flyn's shocked expression.

"I am sorry, Flyn," Sir Corc said, his voice unaffected by the liquor.

"No pardons needed, Sir," Flyn replied, taking the muddler up once more. "I have found a new calling. Leech's apprentice."

"Who would have you?" Deglan asked, getting a laugh from Flyn and managing the barest grin from Sir Corc.

"True," the squire said, returning to the grinding. "I could simply challenge Lackcomb and become Grand Master."

Deglan felt a momentary flutter in his gut as he saw the idea take root on Flyn's face.

"Do not even think about it, you puffed-up popinjay!" he warned. "We are plagued with enough dangerous creatures in this castle pretending to be something they are not, without you having delusions of leadership!"

Flyn shook his head. "Even if I could best the old bird, there would be no end to the challengers. The Dread Cockerel first among them, I'd wager." Flyn seemed to remember something, then looked quickly to Sir Corc. "What was it you called him? Sir Wyncott?"

"Every one of us comes here with a name, Flyn," the knight replied, "before we are draped in pride and titles."

"I have a name," Flyn said, thumping the muddler ineffectually into the bowl. "I have a title. And I have pride. Seems I shall have no knighthood to accompany them."

"Not until the gruagach are driven from the Roost," the knight agreed.

"Should they not have moved on by now?" Flyn asked, looking up at Deglan as he did. Sir Corc also looked to him.

Deglan bit back a string of retorts. They thought he failed.

They needed to be told the right of it, but not here.

"I have some medicines to deliver to the clansmen," Deglan told them. "Fancy a walk in the hot sun?"

Soon, the three of them passed through the main gate and began the slow, sloping descent from the escarpment which the castle surmounted. The highlands of Albain spread out below them, the grey-green of the rocky landscape adorned with smears of purple heather and yellow wildflowers. It was a rolling country, beautiful in its ruggedness. Not too distant, the placid waters of Loch Halket rested heavily in the embrace of the rocky hills, the human village of Glengabráin near its banks. The mid-morning sun blazed across the surface of the water and warmed the wind, which flowed in rhythmic pulses across Deglan's face. He had not seen a Spring since last he left Airlann, well over a thousand years ago. It was a welcome change from his home-land, the Source Isle of Magic, where Autumn now held perpetual dominion.

The steepness of the grade was tough on Deglan's short legs, but he voiced no complaint, waving Flyn off when the squire offered to carry the heavy satchel laden with remedies for the Dal Riata. Deglan could accomplish what he set out to do and of that these two needed to be reminded. Despite the growing distance from the walls, they did not speak for a long while.

Deglan had not saved Pocket's life. Whatever dread Magic he inherited from his human half had done that. But the malice and power of the Goblin Kings' iron crown had left the changeling hanging on the brink. His Fae blood was poisoned, his flesh scorched, his organs failing. Deglan had mended all that, saving the boy from a life of permanent decrepitude. He lived, but the Red Caps and the gruagach, both of whom sought the gurg for their own ends, needed to go on believing him dead. A body needed to be taken to the Roost and burnt in the tradition of the Order. For that, Deglan volunteered. Pocket was thriving, there was no more need for a healer on the little island where they hid. Besides, the task at hand would require deeds that would test the honor of a knight. Deglan had left the Knucklebones with nothing but his herb satchel and a letter from Sir Corc. By the time he reached the Roost, he had a corpse to pass for Pocket.

"I upheld my end," Deglan said at last, keeping his voice low and his attention fixed on the downhill path. "Your damn ruse did not work."

"It was a fool's hope that it would," Sir Corc said. "The blame is not yours, Master Loamtoes."

Deglan whirled around. The coburn were more than twice his height, but he fixed them with his most baleful stare, thrusting a warning finger up at their faces.

"Do not coddle me! I put on your little mummery, and placed myself in the service of your precious order on top of that. I have seen more wars than every coburn in the history of the Valiant Spur combined. So get your teat out of my mouth!"

"Pardons," Sir Corc said humbly.

"And like the young cock said," Deglan hooked a thumb at Flyn, "no apologies from you, either." Deglan waited a moment to be sure his words had sunk in. Satisfied, he lowered his hand.

"How fares the boy?"

"Well," Sir Corc replied. "Moragh keeps great care of him."

"Who guards him while you are here?" Deglan asked. By necessity of secrecy he and the coburn had shared no correspondence since he left the island.

"Curdle Milkthumb arrived a day before we departed," Sir Corc said.

"Good," Deglan approved. "I was worried you were going to say the other one."

"Muckle remains in Toad Holm," the knight assured him.

Deglan was relieved. Of the two hobgoblin sorcerers, Curdle was the more unlikely candidate for a guardian, but Deglan would rather have the seer watching over Pocket than the corpulent Jester. Muckle Gutbuster was not to be trusted, though Deglan refrained from voicing it to Sir Corc, who had a longstanding alliance with the fat scoundrel.

"What news from my cesspit city?" Deglan asked, turning back to the path and beckoning the coburn to continue their trek with a wave of his hand.

It was Flyn that answered, taking a few hurried steps to draw even with Deglan. "Curdle says they have weeded out some of the corruption. But there remain Red Cap sympathizers within the Wisemoot and among the people."

Deglan gave a growl of disgust, spitting off the side of the path to rid himself of the sour taste that filled his mouth. He hated goblins, always had, but now he hated the gnomes even more. His own damn people! They were distantly related of course, gnomes and goblins, but it was a fact that should fill any decent gnome with shame.

"They need to supplant that lack-wit, King Hob!" Deglan declared, more to himself than the coburn. He was convinced the king was behind the treachery that had taken root in Toad Holm. It was Hob's fool decree that the goblins be allowed back into the city, in order to reintegrate them into gnomish society. Infection was supposed to be purged, not invited to be a bloody neighbor. That was the reason Deglan had renounced his city so long ago, vowing never to return. He broke that vow, only to find his worst fears come to life. After helping stop the Red Cap resurgence under Torcan Swinehelm, Deglan had been all too happy to resume his self-imposed exile, this time leaving Airlann behind entirely.

"And what of the Seelie Court?" he inquired. "Did Curdle manage to contact the elves?"

Deglan scowled as Bantam Flyn dodged the question, looking back at Corc for aid.

"No," the older coburn answered.

"Buggery and spit," Deglan swore. "Then Jerrod's crown remains at Castle Gaunt."

Corc nodded. "As does the last Forge Born."

Deglan grunted. "Coltrane is a capable guardian, but that damn crown needs to be destroyed and Irial Ulvyeh is likely the only one left with the craft to do it!"

"The Elf King remains unfound," Corc told him.

Bitter bile rose in Deglan's throat. Blasted elves and their elusive ways! If the Seelie Court had only made itself known, the Red Caps may never have regained power, but Irial and his kin had been silent for centuries. Their absence had forced Deglan to seek aid in Toad Holm and, when that failed, to try and stop Torcan Swinehelm's uprising with nothing but a handful of allies. They had succeeded, but it nearly cost them all.

"We never should have left the crown," Deglan groused.

"There was no other choice," Corc replied.

The truth of the knight's words made Deglan's whiskers itch and he ran an aggravated hand down his chops. None of Kederic Winetongue's surviving men dared go back into the citadel after witnessing the terrible frenzy of the Unwound, no matter that they were once again inert. As Fae, the hobgoblin sorcerers Curdle and Muckle, could not have handled the iron crown and lived.

Neither could Deglan, plus he was bound to the same task as Sir Corc and Flyn: Pocket's safety, and the boy needed to be as far away from the heirloom as possible. That left only the piskie Rosheen's companion, the man Padric, and he had not the power to keep the crown safe. Indeed, the remaining Red Caps holed up in Black Pool still believed him to be the Gaunt Prince's heir. Likely, they would be seeking him and it would not help the lad's safety to have possession of the Goblin Kings' artifact. So, it had been left at Castle Gaunt, under the guardianship of Coltrane. Deglan was thankful the Forge Born never needed to sleep.

They walked the rest of the way in silence, coming down off the escarpment and onto the relatively flat herd trails of the Dal Riata. Deglan had made this journey many times over the last year and every time he found himself wishing for a sturdy riding toad beneath him. Another vow made, but this one he kept. Never again, not after Bulge-Eye.

So, with a sweaty back and cramping legs he led the coburn into Glengabráin, chief village of the Dal Riata. He was welcomed warmly, though he noticed the coburn received several dubious stares. Sir Corc weathered the looks with his usual stoicism, but Deglan kept an eye on Bantam Flyn. The squire was eager for a fight, though he tried to hide it. Relations between the Valiant Spur and the Dal Riata were strained enough without Flyn spilling blood over a few mistrusting glares.

Deglan made his deliveries quickly, relating instructions when necessary and administering examinations when needed. His assessment to Banyon Deaf Crower was more than simple grousing; the Dal Riata truly were a hale breed. Humans had always seemed a bit uncouth from Deglan's perspective, but compared to the mortals of Airlann, the clansmen of Albain were downright barbarous. They dwelt in rude, one-room huts with only the most rudimentary stonework. In the exceptional heat of Spring most of the children scurried about naked, but Deglan had seen them go barefoot even in the colder seasons. Their crops, and therefore, their diet were limited, yet they thrived, seeing themselves though famine and illness with a resilience Deglan had quickly come to respect. Despite their doughty self-reliance, the Dal Riata still benefited from his presence. A Fae healer was welcomed even in the most superstitious human settlements. Deglan's herbcraft had saved more than a few lives since he took up residence in the Roost, his services required more often among the clansmen than with the coburn. Like the knights, the Dal Riata were fighters. Less trained, less well armed, but no less brave, and they shared a common threat.

The plague of the gruagach.

The poisoned livestock and blighted crops were hard enough, but the fear, the ever-present fear of a loved one being taken, used as a mask for a murderer, that took the greatest toll.

Deglan could see in the eyes of the men, aye and the women as well, the helpless frustration of having an enemy they could not fight. The same look Deglan had seen in countless humans when their children fell ill, he saw now in every adult member of the clan.

Powerless, desperate, willing to sacrifice anything for the lives of their offspring.

The gruagach *were* a sickness: entering unseen, a silent assailant, the infected ignorant of the danger until the symptoms arose and by then it was too late. Ugly death followed swiftly. The clansmen could not combat the skin-changers with any more success than they could disease. But Deglan could. It took a careful patience to wage war against invisible foes. Fevers. Malignancies.

Gangrenous wounds. All had to be allowed to run their course and faced in a mad game of careful timing. Treated too soon they would return, too late they would kill. Deglan had stared down illness and injury unblinking for thousands of years, he would be damned if a bunch of shape-changing assassins would make him flinch now.

His rounds complete and his satchel now empty, Deglan led the coburn away from the village, following the bank of Loch Halket. He strolled for a ways, until the village was lost from sight.

Looking out over the water, he spied a few Dal Riata fishermen, drifting in their currachs, well out of earshot.

"These people have suffered much," Deglan said, not taking his eyes off the boats.

"And only we three know the reason," Bantam Flyn said.

Deglan looked up, but the young coburn's words were directed at Sir Corc. "Unless you revealed all to the Grand Master?"

"No," was the knight's only reply. Deglan could tell by Flyn's expression he already knew as much.

"Pocket's secret must be kept," Deglan said. "But we cannot continue to allow the gruagach free reign."

"The Roost is nigh inaccessible now," Flyn declared.

"Guards posted. The clansmen kept at a distance. Iron about every neck." A thought crossed the squire's face. "Except yours. Deglan, how do they ensure you have not been replaced?"

"Iron affects me as it does all Fae," Deglan said, rolling up his sleeve to reveal a bandage across his inner forearm. He peeled back the linen, showing them the strip of burned flesh underneath.

"I submit to voluntary exposure every fortnight."

"Earth and Stone," Flyn swore softly, causing Deglan to smile. It was a gnomish oath.

"Besides," he said, covering the burn once more, "a gruagach can assume your form, but that is all. It will not possess your knowledge or your memories. That is why they must be careful who they replace. Any of those shape-changing bastards would have to know a master herbalist's skills if they wanted to kill me and have none be the wiser."

"You burn, they burn," Flyn said carefully. "Forgive me, Deglan, but that proves nothing. You could still be one of them."

"No," Sir Corc said sharply. "A gruagach will revert to its true form when exposed to iron."

"Actually," Deglan told them, "the lad has a point. All the precautions in the castle and they are still succeeding, still killing. I do not think they are changing." The coburn stared at him quizzically. Deglan motioned to the collar of nails around Flyn's throat. "Remove that hideous thing and toss it here."

Flyn hesitated, looking to Sir Corc for guidance.

"No need for permission," Deglan grumbled. "Toss it here."

Slowly, Flyn removed the collar, stalling a moment longer before tossing it down.

Deglan caught the collar in his bare hand, keeping his eyes fixed on Flyn. The first thing he felt was an unpleasant itching in his palm, then his throat became hot and scratchy. He felt a flush course through his body and his eyes began to water freely.

Focusing, Deglan grit his teeth against the bile that rose in his mouth. Molten fluid filled his ears and a roaring that forced his eyes shut. Breathing became difficult as his airway constricted. The contents of his guts soured, threatening to spill stinging down his legs. The itching in his palm was quickly turning into a burn as the first muscle spasms wracked his spine. With a hiss, Deglan let go, dropping the metal onto the wet rocks at his feet.

Staggering over to the loch's edge, Deglan bent and dug his fingers into the cool, yielding mud. He felt the rocky grit in his hands and opened himself to it, asking the Earth to mend him. The roaring fled his ears and air passed unhindered into his lungs. He spat the foul contents of his mouth into the water and rose, returning to stand before the coburn. They looked down at him, the squire with concern and amazement, the knight with a puzzled frown. Deglan held up the hand he used to grip the iron, palm forward, fingers splayed. There was no mark upon his flesh.

"I am eight thousand years old," Deglan said, his voice raw.

"Or near enough as to make little difference. And I held that iron for what, half a minute? Fae can withstand the touch of iron for brief periods. The older we are, the greater our will becomes to resist it. The shape-changing gifts of the gruagach have always given them more resilience to iron's effects. It is said their lord, Festus Lambkiller, has completely overcome the aversion."

"You think the lord of the gruagach is in the Roost?" Flyn asked.

"I think," Deglan replied, "we are being preyed upon by some very old and very cunning skin-changers. They have not yet moved in force against the Order, it is not the gruagach way and it profits them nothing. They have been waiting."

"Waiting for me," Sir Corc said grimly. "The gruagach who tried to take Pocket in Black Pool knew me by name."

Deglan nodded his agreement. "Now that you are returned, it is only a matter of time before they move against you."

"Then we need to strike first," Flyn declared.

"To do that, we would have to know the identities of every skin-changer in the castle," Sir Corc said.

"Exactly," Deglan said, giving both coburn a pointed look.

Flyn was the first to understand. Realization slowly dawned on the strut's face and he produced a smile. "You know who they are."

"Do not go slapping me on the back yet," Deglan scolded the young squire. "With skin-changers nothing is certain."

"If you have a plan, Master Loamtoes, we would hear it," Sir Corc said.

"Iron may be the Fae's only weakness," Deglan told them, "but in our strengths we are also vulnerable. The gruagach may look like anyone they wish, but there is one mortal trait they cannot emulate. They do not succumb to illness. They are never sick."

"Clever gnome," Sir Corc said approvingly.

"Well, I have not been idle for a damn year!" Deglan told him. "I have kept account of every person I have treated for any malady since my arrival, also noting those who remained healthy. There are certain herbs which will cause a human to become quite ill, but are harmless to Fae-folk. These I have slipped into the food and drink of those I suspected to be gruagach. Sometimes I was wrong, but slowly I cobbled it together. Whether through nature or my own meddling, four of the castle servants have remained free of all ailments."

"The servants," Sir Corc repeated. "Not our brothers in the Order?"

"No," Deglan admitted. "You coburn may be mortal, but you are not as susceptible as humans to illness and poison. Your blood is thicker and you are damn hard to kill, traits I am hopeful have kept the gruagach from trying to replace any of you."

"Hopeful," Flyn said. "But we cannot be certain."

"We cannot," Deglan agreed. "Which is why I have not gone to the Grandmaster with my findings."

"Lackcomb is no gruagach," Sir Corc said and Deglan heard a tinge of annoyance in the knight's voice.

"Perhaps not," Deglan conceded. "But who would he first confide any information I provided him?"

"The Knights Sergeant," Flyn answered readily.

Deglan looked back at Corc. "Can you vouch for all of them, Sir? Because if even one of them is a gruagach, all could quickly go to ruin."

Sir Corc said nothing, his silence voicing his assent.

"I needed to wait for your arrival," Deglan continued, "for allies that I could trust, before confronting those I suspect. The four servants for certain, but it is possible there are more. If I know the gruagach, they will only take open action with all their numbers. If we face the four, we will draw out the rest. But anything we do, we do alone. It is your decision, Corc."

The knight removed himself a few paces and thought for a long moment. Deglan watched him stare at the stony shore, recognizing the look of an old warrior weighing his options and not liking any of them. At last, he walked back to them.

"Tell us, Master Loamtoes. Who are the four?"

Deglan took a deep breath. "The tanner's apprentice, Aonghas, and the mason's boy, Earc. Both gruagach. That lass in the laundry who cannot speak, she is one too. Muirne is her name. And the chronicler, Ingelbert Crane."

FOUR

Flyn gave the ropes a final, cautionary pull. They were tight against the strain of so much weight, creaking slightly as he strummed the tension with his fingertips. He was not much of a craftsman and had been forced to work quickly. The Knights Errant were arriving with more regularity and soon the castle would be filled with armed coburn. The gruagach would need to make a move soon. Feeling confident his knots would hold, Flyn plucked his torch out of a decaying sconce and descended the tower stairs, stopping at every landing to look up and inspect his work.

This drum tower was one of the oldest in the castle, all but forgotten and rarely visited. The rotting stairs hugged the curve of the wall, leaving the center of the tower a wide, yawning shaft.

There were six landings along the creaking spiral, one near the top leading to the battlements, another several turns down that held a door to a connecting gallery. The remaining landings housed doorways, now sealed with masonry, which once led out into the Upper Bailey and long-abandoned corridors within the curtain wall.

The foundations of the tower went deep and the base level was home to a final passage that wound around in the dark, leading eventually to the Under Hall for those who knew the way.

The Roost was an ancient citadel, built atop the indomitable crag in the earliest days of the Order, when the elves still guided the coburn in the ways of honor, combat and service.

The original keep was long enveloped as the stronghold grew over the centuries, reflecting the might of the Valiant Spur in its prime.

This drum tower, no doubt, was once a key point in the elder defenses, now choked out of use by the bloated maze of fortifications it helped spawn. Flyn was surprised the servants had not used it to store grain.

Reaching the end of the stairs, he hopped down to the rough floor of the base level, craning his neck upwards to view his work from the very bottom. His efforts were lost to distance and shadow. Perfect.

The torch was near its end, but the fat lamps he had left burning at the bottom still had life. Flyn dropped the guttering shaft and took up his water skin, taking a long drink. He was not much for honest labor, though setting a trap for your enemies was neither honest nor honorable. It was not how knights fought and the plan had troubled Sir Corc, but Deglan had put him to ease with his usual eloquence.

"Skin-changing bastards are the fathers of trickery. I say we shag 'em with their own prick. And smile all the while!"

Flyn laughed aloud at the memory.

The cranky old gnome had been right about the castle servants. The lads apprenticed to the tanner and the mason were never far from Sir Corc, though he made it easy on them. Every castle servant was required to have a coburn escort, so Corc had arranged to be Deglan's permanent guard and the two spent as much time holed up in the infirmary as possible, making it simpler for the gruagach to watch them. For his own part, Flyn had volunteered to ensure the safety of the mute laundress, enjoying the irony for a few hours before giving her the slip, as planned. It was fortunate he had established a habit of shirking his duties years ago, lest the Knights Sergeant and his fellow squires wonder about his absence. Still, it had not been easy gathering the needed materials and hauling them into the tower unseen, but he used the forgotten passages of the castle to his advantage.

Flyn was more worried about being discovered by the Knights Sergeant than the gruagach. The skin-changers he could fight, but not the discipline of one of the senior knights. He would not be much of an ally to Corc and Deglan if he was relegated to scraping gong out of the garderobe shafts as punishment for leaving the laundress unguarded. And he could expect no more special dispensation as tourney champion, either. While the Grand Master had not made any official pronouncements, Flyn was destined for two more years squiring at least. His only hope to avoid that fate lay in the success of their plan.

It was not only for himself that he plotted with such pains, however.

Flyn looked to the base of the stairs. There, under the musty timbers of the first landing, was a small curtain and behind that curtain, a home. A former home. Flyn took one of the fat lamps and approached the stairs, keenly aware he had wanted to do this since entering the tower, but avoided it until his work was done.

He had to crawl on his knees and free hand, struggling to maneuver between the support beams, in order to reach the curtain. Careful to keep the flame of his lamp away from the cloth, he pushed the hanging aside. The light fell upon a tight space created by the tower wall and the scaffolding of the stairs. Within, a small bronze brazier sat, long cold. The rats had made merry with the straw-stuffed feed sack that once served as a bed. Nailed to a stair beam across from the bed hung a tattered map of Airlann.

Flyn had hoped it would be difficult to imagine Pocket here, sitting alone beneath the stairs. The image, however, was easily, painfully conjured. The boy had oft spoke of this place, a haunted longing creeping into his voice and face. Flyn had not known of this tower outside a vague perception of its location, much less Pocket's lonely nook within. He had once asked Moragh about the place. The former mistress of the Roost's kitchens had smiled sadly, the expression affecting only half of her palsied face. She gave him clear directions, starting from the kitchens, of course. It was mere curiosity then, but when the time came to choose the site for their ambush, Flyn had insisted it be here. There was a pinch of poetry to it. If the gruagach wanted Pocket, they could come here, to the place he once dwelt alone and often afraid. The place he was forced to hide because he was shunned and feared by the castle's human servants on account of his changeling blood.

They had given Pocket a new home, he and Sir Corc, Moragh and Napper. The thought of the skinny, old cat made Flyn smile, realizing now that Pocket had rarely sat beneath these stairs alone. The pair remained inseparable, the ratter at Pocket's heels or in his arms everywhere he went. Fishing had become the boy's principal interest, though there were few other choices on the island. Flyn fashioned several wooden swords and often invited the boy to learn swordplay. It was half lark and half drill, but Flyn got the distinct impression that the little gurg, once so enamored of knighthood and all its trappings, was merely humoring him. It was a more solemn Pocket that emerged from the sickbed, with nary a hint of the sorcery he had wielded in the moments he wore Jerrod's cursed iron crown. He had calmed the Unwound in those moments, commanded them back to the torpid slumber that kept them from covering Airlann in blood. He had restored Flyn's life in those moments, his and Corc's along with several others. In those moments, the child was the most calamitous being to walk the Tin Isles in a thousand years. That was difficult to imagine, given the boy's gentle nature and tragic beginnings.

He was a changeling, an unwanted get, hated by his human kin, but loved still by his mother, in whose veins the blood of the Goblin Kings survived. Beladore, descendant of Jerrod the Second and his son, the Gaunt Prince, duped like so many mortal women, into the arms of a gruagach wearing her husband's face. A husband who then tried to slay her misshapen child and would have, if not for a wandering warrior, a Knight Errant of the Valiant Spur. Sir Corc the Constant. The knight had continued to watch over Pocket in the years that followed, mostly from a distance, but the gruagach closed in, intent on obeying Festus Lambkiller's command that all gurgs be returned to him. Corc took Pocket away from the Roost, to better protect him, ignorant that the boy's human blood was a direct link to the Goblin Kings of old.

Half Fae. Half warlock. Sought by two immortal races bent on using him to subjugate the Source Isle. Such a person was too dangerous to live and so, Pocket had died at Castle Gaunt. A few knew the truth, that he still lived, but fewer still were aware of the deeper truth. He was no longer a danger to anyone. The Magic of the Goblin Kings no longer coursed through him, but also gone were his Fae gifts. Pocket had not been able to change his form since recovering from the ruination of the iron crown. Not the slightest change. Flyn was certain, for he watched the poor gurg try and try again. He was nothing now but a young boy, forced to live out the rest of his mortal life in exile because of who he once was, what he could have become. Flyn knew the Red Caps and the gruagach would never stop hunting Pocket, just as he knew that he and Corc, Moragh and Deglan, Curdle and Muckle, would remain steadfast in their guardianship.

It had been difficult to leave the island, especially for Sir Corc. Flyn had grown restless during their sojourn and secretly yearned to be away, back to the Roost to receive his spurs and on to greater challenges. But when it came time to depart, Flyn found he was reluctant. Pocket occupied his normal fishing spot on the rocky shores, the wind and the spray playing in his hair. Napper lay close by, contorting his body to match the rare patch of irregular sunlight that managed to peek through the bleak clouds.

"Never known a cat to be so comfortable near the ocean," Flyn said as he approached.

"He knows fish are soon to follow," Pocket replied, reaching back to scratch the cat's upturned belly. Napper soaked up the attention as he basked in the sun, his eyes blissfully shut. Flyn came up and stood beside them, unable to sit comfortably on the rocks while wearing his sword harness. He looked out over the choppy, slate-grey waters that he would soon cross to return to Albain.

"Weather could turn against us," Flyn said, knowing it was a falsehood. "We may not sail today."

"I think you will," Pocket stated, scrutinizing the sky.

"Curdle arrived in the night. Sir Corc will want to be gone soon."

"Only so he can return sooner," Flyn told him.

"Without you."

It was a statement of fact. Pocket placed no blame or guilt in the words. Flyn squatted down beside him.

"I will come back when I can," he said.

Pocket looked over at him and smiled. "You were meant to be a knight, Flyn."

The boy never failed to surprise him. It was permission.

Permission to seek glory unfettered by any attachment.

"I will come back," Flyn insisted. "Who else will listen to all the tales of my many great deeds?"

"Not Sir Corc," Pocket giggled.

"No," Flyn agreed with a laugh. "Not Sir Corc. Moragh, mayhaps?"

"She will pretend to," Pocket retorted, his laughter growing.

"Oh, you wound sir. You wound," Flyn said, placing a hand over his chest. He reached back and quickly, but gently, plucked Napper off the ground. "Surely, you will lend ear to my heroic exploits, Old Orange One?" The cat adopted the wide eyes and flailing limbs of unwanted handling, quickly wiggling free to hop back down onto the ground before turning to give Flyn an earnest look of wounded dignity.

"Or perhaps not," Flyn said with feigned defeat. "Looks like you will be the sole recipient of my boastful tales, Pocket my lad! Be honored!"

"Where will you quest?" Pocket asked, a hint of the old eagerness coming back to his face. "Once you get your spurs. Will you go back to Airlann?"

Flyn knew the answer to that readily. He had for years, but it was not a quest Pocket would want to hear. Or Sir Corc. Neither of them would find it worthy. He would not smother Pocket's rekindled ember of enthusiasm with talk of deposing tyrants.

"I think," Flyn said with an embellished sign, "I shall find a lonely bridge over calm waters and let none cross unless they best me in honorable combat or give me a single white rose." Flyn leaned close to Pocket, fixing him with a droll stare before whispering, "Of course, I shan't tell them about the rose."

That was the last laugh they had shared. Flyn had ruffled Pocket's hair and then embraced him. Unlike Napper, Pocket did not struggle to free himself.

The fat lamp was sputtering when Flyn shook himself out of his revelry. He began to back out of the nook when the dwindling light fell upon something in the remains of the mattress.

Flyn reached in and plucked the small object out of the squalid straw. It was a horse, skillfully whittled out of wood. A toy. Flyn placed it carefully in his belt pouch. He would give it to Corc so that the knight could return it to Pocket. As an afterthought, he took the map of Airlann as well. It would give him a good excuse at his next destination.

Dusk was old when Flyn emerged from the Under Hall. He was not to meet Corc and Deglan for several hours yet, and he still had one more task to perform. Of all the humans Deglan suspected of being a skin-changer, only the chronicler, Ingelbert Crane, had yet to act in a way which confirmed the gnome's suspicion. The man stayed closeted away in his makeshift library most of the day and on the rare occasions he did emerge, he took no interest in anything other than candle-making and the tallying of supplies.

Deglan said that Crane had never been ill, despite his gawky frame.

The gnome had also managed to dose the man's food with herbs which should have induced a severe, though fleeting, sickness with no apparent result. Still, thin as Crane was, it was possible he was not eating what was brought to his chamber.

They needed to be sure, and Flyn had taken it upon himself to discover if the chronicler was indeed a skin-changer. The gruagach did not possess the knowledge of their victims, and Flyn had just the test for the supposed annalist of the Order's history, one which would help prove his true nature.

Quickly crossing the Middle Bailey, he made for the Campaign Hall and the storeroom beneath. The door to the squint opened much more quickly than the last time Flyn had knocked.

"Yes?" The uncertain voice matched the look in the eyes that stared through the bars.

"Master Crane," Flyn said, casually hooking a finger under his collar of nails and giving it a superfluous shake. "It is Bantam Flyn. I have something here for you and a few questions if you can spare the time?"

"Oh," came the reply. "Um. Yes. Yes, certainly. A moment."

The door to the squint closed and Flyn heard a bolt thrown back and a key turn the lock. Ingelbert Crane opened the door to admit him, then quickly secured it with the bolt once more, though he did not bother with the key. Once inside, Flyn turned to face the man, causing the tip of the sword on his back to knock over a stack of books resting on the floor. Ingelbert gave a choked cry of alarm and Flyn watched as he darted forward, eyes wide with distress. He moved awkwardly yet nimbly, managing to right the stack quickly without upsetting any of the other precarious piles.

As a coburn, Flyn was unclear on the physical attributes that humans found appealing, but he was fair certain this gangly scribbler possessed none of them. His face was long, punctuated by a hooked and protruding nose, beneath which rested thin lips and a knobby chin. The whole unfortunate visage was surrounded by a thick mass of hair the color and texture of wheat chaff. He was young and tall, but slump-shouldered and sunken-chested, his arms barely discernible beneath the sleeves of his voluminous tunic. Flyn noted strength in his hands, however, the fingers long, the knuckles pronounced. They were also covered in black smudges, especially under the nails and on the heels.

"Inkstain?" Flyn said aloud.

Ingelbert straightened, though his eyes kept darting back to the pile of books he had fussed over. "Yes? Um. Yes. I'm sorry. What?"

"Inkstain," Flyn repeated. "I was curious if you were aware that was the name the squires have given you."

"Oh," Ingelbert gave an overexaggerated nod. "Aware. Yes, I was aware. That they call me that. Inkstain, yes."

"Good," Flyn said cheerily. "Because I was likely to slip and call you that instead of Master Crane. Did not want to offend."

"No! No no. Offend? No," the chronicler said, though it was obvious he did not much care for the name. "It is, ah, it is an appellation far superior to straw-head, as, uh, as the Dal Riata have taken to calling me."

"Titles find you in the Order," Flyn told him. "Best to embrace them, believe me."

"Right," Inkstain agreed with a nod, his attention still on the pile of books.

"Here," Flyn held the rolled map out. "I thought you would want this."

"Oh, yes," the chronicler said, taking the map. "I have been anxiously awaiting this!"

Flyn found himself confused. "You have?"

"Oh yes," Inkstain said, sidling past to get to his beleaguered desk. "Your map of the Knucklebones, yes? The charting done on errantry by, um, Sir Corc the Constant?"

This chronicler was well-informed.

"No," Flyn clarified. "Those are not yet complete. Likely years before they will be. No, this is just an old map of the Source Isle I found."

"I see," Inkstain said, sliding into his chair and unfurling the map with no dampening of enthusiasm. "And where, um, where did you find it?"

Flyn had the dodge ready. "I should not say. I was ducking guard duty. You understand. But this was all that was around, be assured."

He waited while the man inspected the map with care, his substantial nose pressed close to the faded illuminations. After several tedious minutes, it dawned on Flyn that the chronicler had forgotten he was in the room.

"Well?"

Inkstain jumped slightly, looking up sheepishly.

"Um," the chronicler cleared his throat. "Right. Yes. It is old. I will have to examine it, that is, examine it alongside other maps I have of Airlann to, ah, get a firm estimation of the age. Um, thank you. Yes. Thank you for bringing this to me."

"A trifle," Flyn waved him off. "And I will give you something more. A word of advice. Sir Corc and his title? Best not to use it around him."

"Right," Ingelbert replied, nodding more thoughtfully than Flyn felt warranted. "He does not, ah, he does not embrace the Constant as you have Bantam, and I, Inkhead Strawstain?"

It took Flyn a second to realize the man had just jested. He laughed approvingly, drawing a shy, but proud smile from the chronicler. If this endearingly awkward man truly was a gruagach, then Flyn was a one-legged goblin.

"No," he said still chuckling. "Sir Corc does not approve of titles for anyone. I must remember to ask him the Mad Capon's true name."

"Is he?" Inkstain asked. "Is he, ah, as fat as they say?"

"Fatter," Flyn replied, shaking his head. "But fast and fierce for all his suet."

"Remarkable," Inkstain marveled. "It will be most interesting to see the names made manifest. Put faces to all the reports."

"You come from Sasana," Flyn stated, noting Crane's accent.

"Oh, um, yes. Gipeswic," the man replied, his face momentarily reflective. "So do you. That is, come from Sasana. Not Gipeswic. Arrived and pledged to serve on the same day as Squire Gulver. Though no community of origin was listed for either of you, if I recall."

"You have a good memory," Flyn said, shrugging out of his shoulder harness. "I was hoping your memory might contain something about this."

Flyn held Coalspur out to the chronicler, still sheathed.

Inkstain stood slowly, his mouth going slightly slack. He looked the sword over with widening eyes and glanced up with uncertainty. Flyn nodded and held the sword out an inch farther.

The man's black-smeared hands took the weapon firmly, the blade resting horizontally across his palms.

"The sword of Grand Master Coalspur," Inkstain began.

"Dwarf-forged. It was carried by him until his death by fever and, in honor of his final wishes, offered as prize in a tourney to honor his memory. A tourney won by Squire Flyn. Um, that is, you. A tourney won by you."

The man had the right of it. Still, that was recent history.

"Is there anything prior to that?" Flyn pressed. "Anything from the annals mentioning such a sword being wielded earlier, perchance at the Battle of the Unsounded Horn?"

"The Unsounded Horn?" the chronicler pondered. "That was before the annals were kept. We have, uh, songs written much later in commemoration, but nothing contemporary, nothing from the day. The Order was in its infancy, still governed mostly by elven war masters. All of the original knights—The Five Score—were, ah, illiterate. All recruited from feral coburn communities. Even Mulrooster, the first Grand Master, was little more than, uh, than a barbarian."

"What about this here?" Flyn asked, directing Inkstain's attention to the glyph he discovered beneath the grip wrapping.

Inkstain inspected it for a long time before answering.

"I, um, I cannot say offhand. I have seen similar runes, certainly, but it is not, um, it is not something I can immediately decipher. A mark of the maker, perhaps?"

"I met a dwarf who claimed to be the maker," Flyn told him. "In Black Pool. His name was Fafnir. One of Corc's many contacts. He said he forged it for Grand Master Coalspur, but a near-identical sword bearing this same mark appears on a tapestry of the Battle of the Unsounded Horn in the Great Hall."

"Ah," the chronicler sounded, still peering at the rune on the grip. "Well, that might solve it. The tapestries were made centuries after the events they depict. It is possible the artisans used knights and weapons of the current day as the basis for their images." Crane squinted as his thoughts grew deeper. "However . . . if the dwarf you met in Black Pool told the truth, this sword is no more than fifty years old and the tapestry was commissioned at least two hundred years ago. It is interesting. I will, um, do some research and see if I can find an answer."

"My thanks," Flyn said as Ingelbert offered the sword back gingerly. This man was no danger. He could confidently tell Deglan he had been mistaken. "I will take no more of your time, Master Crane."

Inkstain gave a tight-lipped smile and a bobbing nod. He gathered the key off his desk and headed for the door, but stopped short, remembering something.

"Oh! Squire Flyn. Could you maybe help me with, um, my own little mystery. That is, if it's not too much trouble?"

"Learn to sing," Flyn said with a small laugh. "The women will swoon in droves."

"Women?" the chronicler was puzzled for a moment. "Oh! No, um, no. Singing, right. Swoon. Um. No, Sir Corc the Con—" he caught himself. "That is, Sir Corc."

"Sir Corc is the mystery?" Flyn asked.

"Well in a way, in a way, yes," Inkstain said, slinking back to his desk to rummage through the stacks until he produced an aged ledger. "I was hoping you could, well, because you have traveled so much with him, that you could answer something for me?"

Flyn found himself intrigued. Sir Corc was not, in truth, a knight that was often the subject of much interest. Ingelbert seemed to be looking through the ledger, his fingers flipping deftly while his eyes scanned the pages. After a moment, he held up a finger, but kept his eyes focused on the book.

"Sir Corc has served the Order as Knight Errant for thirty-one years," the chronicler stated. "His very first errantry, he requisitioned from the quarter-master one mule, one broadsword, one dirk, two daggers, one mace, one shield, one hauberk, one breastplate with pauldrons, one surcoat, one cloak, two tunics, two blankets, one iron pot, one pound smoked herring, three pounds beans, five pounds oats . . ."

Flyn's mind wandered as the chronicler continued to list the provisions. Where was the mystery here? Was the man mad?

". . . and one sack of onions. This list does not change for thirty years. Every errantry, the same supplies without deviation."

Ingelbert looked up from the ledger with a look of amazement, even respect. Flyn decided he was mad.

"Sir Corc the Constant," he shrugged, heading for the door.

"Yes," Inkstain's voice agreed. "Constant. Unchanging. Until Coalspur's funeral, when suddenly the list of supplies changes. The provisions more than double—"

"Because I went with him."

"—in addition, a pot of honey—"

"I have a weakness for sweets," Flyn laughed, unbolting the door.

"—and one page's tunic, newly made in the colors of the Valiant Spur."

Flyn froze and slowly turned to face the chronicler.

"In his earlier days," Inkstain continued, his face a mask of fascination, "Sir Corc often did not return for the two-year, preferring to remain on errantry and only send written reports. He begins coming with regularity about ten years ago, after bringing a foundling to the Roost that was entered into the castle book only as Changeling Infant, later amended with the name Pocket."

Flyn tensed. His gaze fell to Inkstain's neck. He wore no iron collar. Flyn cursed himself for a fool. How had he missed it?

"The boy is later reported to have run away after being suspected of poisoning the castle's former steward, a man named Bannoch. He died the same day you and Sir Corc left for Airlann."

Flyn quickly surveyed the room. Coalspur would be useless in such tight confines. Besides, the sword was steel. He would need iron. His eyes found a dagger on the desk.

"The boy's body was later returned to the castle by the current leech, Master Loamtoes, who also bore a letter from Sir Corc vouching for him and relating a report of a Red Cap uprising put down at the ruins of Castle Gaunt. Now Sir Corc, after questing unfailingly in Airlann for three decades, has begun inexplicably charting the Knucklebones."

Flyn took a careful step forward. Ingelbert's stammer was gone, his words certain. The mask was slipping.

"So, the mystery I have been trying to solve is this gurg child, Pocket. Flyn, wh—"

Flyn darted forward, knocking piles of parchment aside to snatch the dagger from the desk. He grabbed Inkstain around the throat with his free hand, lifting him out of the chair to slam him into the shelves behind. The chronicler's eyes bulged with fear and he tried to scream, but Flyn squeezed down on his throat, choking off the sound.

"You will never find him, skin-changer!" Flyn hissed, pressing the blade of the dagger against Inkstain's sallow face, just beneath the eye. An eye that was weeping. Flyn waited a long span, keeping the iron pressed to the flesh. Deglan said the strongest gruagach could endure its touch, but there was no strength in the man he held pinned to the wall. Only tears and choked sobs.

At last, Flyn let Ingelbert down gently. The man's knees gave out as soon as his feet touched the floor, spilling him into his precious papers.

"Master Crane," Flyn said feebly, stooping to help him rise.

"Forgive me."

The chronicler recoiled, a wordless protest forced between his coughs and gasps. Flyn tossed the dagger back on the table, disgusted with himself, and took a few steps away to give the man room to breathe. It was some time before Ingelbert regained his composure, clutching the chair to help himself stand. He rubbed at his throat with a stained hand.

"It, um," the man said at last, his voice thick. "It was just curiosity. Sir Corc clearly, um, clearly loved the gurg. I just, I just wanted to know why he died."

"Dangerous questions, Master Crane," Flyn replied, grateful the man kept his face turned away. He was too ashamed to look him in the eye.

"Less dangerous than, than the answers, it would seem," Inkstain returned. "The boy is not dead. That is why, that is the reason the gruagach are here." They were not questions. This man's mind worked quickly, and accurately.

Flyn could think of nothing to say. He bent and began gathering the strewn papers.

"Leave them!" Inkstain snapped.

Flyn let the papers drift back to the floor. He turned to the door and was stopped by a sudden knocking.

"Master Crane, are you within?"

Opening the door, Flyn found Worm Chewer in the corridor. The Knight Sergeant frowned, looking over Flyn's shoulder to the disheveled room.

"What goes on here?" Worm Chewer demanded. "Master Crane, are you well?"

"I am, I am fine, Sir," Inkstain replied.

"I can explain," Flyn began.

"You can explain as we walk," Worm Chewer cut in. "It was you I come to find. The Grand Master wants a word."

"The Grand Master?" Flyn asked. "Why would he—"

And then he noticed it. The smell. Rather, the lack of smell on Worm Chewer's breath.

"The taste of worms not to your fancy, gruagach?" Flyn asked with a smile.

Worm Chewer lunged.

FIVE

Ingelbert tried desperately to dodge the struggling coburn as they plowed through his storeroom. He was not quick enough.

Bantam Flyn, reeling from the speed of Worm Chewer's charge, bowled into him, knocking his feet from the floor and the wind from his lungs. Blinded by roiling nausea and a storm of falling parchment, Ingelbert pressed himself against the base of the bookshelf. His shins and knees were struck painfully as something battered into him. He drew up into a ball and threw up his arms, but his warding limbs continued to be pummeled. Through watery eyes, Ingelbert saw the coburn grappling above him. His own chair, toppled during the combat, was caught between him and the combatants, bludgeoning him as the coburn fought. A grunt of pain and frustration escaping between his teeth, Ingelbert seized a chair leg in each hand and shoved. The chair struck the coburn in the legs, upsetting their balance. They toppled, still grappling, onto the floor less than an arm's length from him.

Bantam Flyn was pinned beneath Worm Chewer, the knight's hands around the squire's neck. Ingelbert issued a wordless noise of dismay. This was madness! First, he is threatened by the rash young squire who believed him a gruagach and now Flyn levels the same accusation at one of the Knights Sergeant! Let Worm Chewer beat him bloody. Such a harsh lesson would serve him well.

An acrid smell filled Ingelbert's nostrils, the same awful reek given off by the goblin's flesh when it burned against the anvil.

He watched, terror and understanding rising, as Worm Chewer's hands began to sizzle, smoke appearing beneath his fingers where they gripped Flyn's iron collar. A trilling noise came from Worm Chewer's throat, shrill and rhythmic. It was not a cry of pain, Ingelbert realized. It was laughter.

Flyn strained against Worm Chewer's grasp, fighting to break the hold, but the knight continued to throttle him, continued to laugh, his beak opening wider. As the laughter reached a peak, Worm Chewer's beak split, peeling back over his head, swallowing the feathers that now began to recede about his neck. The pink, fleshy interior of the coburn's mouth began to swell, growing upward out of the maw formed by the ever-widening rictus. Three slits appeared in the damp, puffy tissue, two blinking open to reveal black, merciless eyes, the third widening into a mouth filled with yellow, horse-like teeth.

Ingelbert kicked away from the revolting sight, crawling backwards until he hit another bookshelf. He gained some distance, but could not turn away from the gruesome transformation. The gruagach's newly formed head stretched, as bones hardened beneath the malleable flesh, lengthening into a leering visage. The face moved inexorably towards Flyn's, slavering.

"The gurg," the gruagach's wet voice demanded. "Tell me."

"I'm prettier than you," Flyn rasped.

The gruagach raised Flyn's head off the floor, then slammed it back down against the flagstones.

"Tell me."

The smoke was now pouring from the skin-changer's hands, but he showed no sign of slackening his grip. Ingelbert looked frantically around the debris for his own collar. Once safely in his study, he had removed the irritating choker, placing it on his desk, the contents of which were now strewn about the room. Ignored by the gruagach, Ingelbert scrambled to his feet and rummaged desperately for the iron chain.

He found his dagger first.

Snatching it up, Ingelbert looked back to the gruagach. It paid him no mind, repeating the simple command to Flyn, bashing his skull into the floor when he would not answer.

"Tell me."

Flyn said nothing, a defiant grin lodged across his beak.

Ingelbert gripped the dagger firmly, blade held down. He fought the churning in his gut, raised the weapon above his head and charged. The gruagach's arm whipped out, almost too fast to see. Light exploded across Ingelbert's vision as he was back-handed across the face, sending him reeling against the edge of the open door. His shoulder smashed into the heavy wood, delivering a final blow to his balance. He felt the cold of the floor against his face before the pain from the gruagach's strike. Blood filled his mouth, the metallic taste oddly invigorating. He placed his hands flat against the floor, dimly aware neither of them held the dagger, and pushed himself to his feet.

Ingelbert found himself facing the open doorway, the empty corridor beyond beckoning him to flee. If he ran, he could get help, but not in time. Flyn would die. If he stayed, they would both die. Ingelbert was no warrior. There was nothing he could do against the speed and strength of a Fae assassin. The gruagach had swatted him down, an insect crushed and forgotten. He was insignificant. A maker of candles, a scribe, hiding among his books with black smudges on his hands, saddled with an ignominious name by the proud warriors he served.

Inkstain.

Ingelbert turned away from the portal and stumbled to a cabinet. Flinging open the door with a shaking hand, he removed a sizable ceramic jar from among its dozen identical fellows. He made it himself. The ink. He doubted that any in the Order knew that, or cared. He was the chronicler, and often wrote, but the stains mostly came from the process of making the ink. His own recipe. Dried hawthorn. Water. Boiled wine. Those were little more than thickeners. The main ingredients were oak galls, for their acid.

And iron salts.

The gruagach was screaming at Flyn now, the squire barely putting up a struggle, all but limp in the skin-changer's clutches.

"TELL ME!"

Ingelbert did not bother with the stopper. He strode up behind the gruagach and smashed the jar into its open mouth, using the force of the blow to pull its head back. A howl erupted from the skin-changer as the thick, black fluid flowed into its mouth. It spat and sputtered, spraying ink and spittle into the air.

Ingelbert ground the remnants of the jar into its mouth, feeling his hand sliced by teeth and pottery shards. The gruagach reached up to tear at its own throat as the liquid burned down its gullet.

Flyn was free.

Ingelbert pulled back hard on the gruagach, giving the squire room to plant his feet in its midsection and kick, launching the skin-changer away. Ingelbert clung to its back, the force of the coburn's kick sending them careening into the door, slamming it shut. Even wounded, the gruagach's power was monstrous and Ingelbert felt his hold slipping as the creature pulled them forward.

He heard the sound of iron scraping on stone as Flyn snatched up the fallen dagger and leapt to his feet. Ingelbert and the gruagach were hammered back into the door once more as Flyn thrust the blade home. Ingelbert held fast to the screaming skin-changer, his shoulders, back and skull thumping painfully into the iron-studded wood as the squire stabbed again and again.

After an eternity, the screaming stopped and the creature went limp.

Ingelbert shoved it away to fall in a heap and let his own legs relax, sliding down the door until he sat on the ground. Dull pain burrowed into his entire body, except in his lacerated hand where it declared itself sharply. Bantam Flyn seemed to be well recovered already, though his feathers still stood out from his body with residual aggression. The coburn looked down at the body of the gruagach, but seemed to stare past it, deep in thought.

"We thought they would come for Corc," he half whispered, then shook himself out of his momentary brood and quickly gathered up his fallen greatsword. "On your feet, Master Crane!"

Ingelbert found it difficult to blink. He stared numbly at the ruin of his make-shift library. It should have irked him, seeing it in such disarray, but he was too exhausted to fuel any emotion.

"We must move," Flyn urged, striding over and lifting Ingelbert to his feet. The strength of the coburn seemed undiminished after the gruagach attack. Ingelbert felt a sudden flush of anger at the physical contact. This strutting ruffian had laid hands upon him enough this night! He shoved the coburn back, surprising them both. Words failed him, as they often did, so he simply glared at the squire, hoping the look would warn against any future attempts to touch him.

"Pardons, Master Crane," Flyn said. "But time is short. You must gather up any of these records about the boy Pocket and come with me."

"Gather, gather up?" Ingelbert felt a laugh creep into his voice. "Look at this! I will not be able to find anything rightly for days. Weeks! It will take time."

"We do not have time," the coburn replied. "We must get to Sir Corc with all haste."

"We must get to the Knights Sergeant, you mean," Ingelbert corrected him. "Inform them of what has happened here."

"Use your eyes, Master Crane," Flyn gestured at the still form of the gruagach. "A moment ago *that* was one of the Knights Sergeant. We would be fools to trust in any of them. Now, I beg you, any information you have on the gurg orphan must not fall into gruagach hands."

"Impossible," Ingelbert said throwing his arms up with defeat.

"Then we will have to burn it all."

Ingelbert's blood went cold. He met the coburn's insistent stare, fearing and hating the certainty he saw entrenched there. But he did not look away when he spoke.

"These, these are the annals of the Valiant Spur," he told the squire, failing to keep the incredulous tone from his voice.

"The collected history of the Order beginning with Mulrooster and the Five Score, leading down for sixteen centuries to this very day. You, who have inherited that mantle of honor, would, would, you would burn it?"

"Find the records, Master Crane," was the squire's cryptic answer.

Ingelbert did not know why the gruagach wanted this boy Pocket, nor why it was so important to keep him from them. He had stumbled onto something with his damnable curiosity, something Flyn did not want known. That the squire believed strongly in his cause, Ingelbert had no doubts. Flyn's needless assault on him proved his devotion to protecting the gurg. If burning the annals was the course Flyn chose to ensure the secret, Ingelbert would be unable to stop him.

He set to work, ferreting through the scattered documents.

There was not much here, in truth, that pertained to Sir Corc or the boy, but laying hands on it became the challenge. He found the ledger containing Sir Corc's supply record without difficulty, then used it to secure the loose documents as he unearthed them.

Bantam Flyn had moved to the door and opened it enough that he might peer down the corridor, dagger in hand, watchful for anyone approaching.

Ingelbert hoped someone would come, the Old Goose perhaps, someone who could stand up to this hot-headed bravo and deter him from this unfathomable path. They remained undisturbed, however, and soon Ingelbert had all he was likely to find. He doubted it was everything, but for the safety of the library, he would not divulge such to Bantam Flyn. Plucking a large sling bag from its peg on the wall, Ingelbert shoved the recovered records inside then looped the strap over his head and onto his shoulder, finding the weight greater than anticipated.

Flyn turned from his vigil at the door and gave Ingelbert a confirming nod, then checked the corridor once more before stepping out, motioning him to follow. The squire led them quickly down the passage and up the stairs to the main floor of the Campaign Hall. The place was still and quiet. None were about.

They discovered why when they stepped outside.

An unmistakable glow could be seen pulsing over the Steward's Gate, a flush of orange invading the night sky.

Somewhere, beyond the wall in the Lower Bailey, the castle was afire.

"The tannery," Ingelbert surmised.

"Damn," Bantam Flyn hissed, his hand running quickly across his comb as he wrestled with some thought. "Come!"

To Ingelbert's surprise the squire turned away from the glow and led them at a run up the slope towards the Midden Gate and the Upper Bailey. Four squires were usually posted here at all times. They found only two, lying in the undignified sprawl of death. Flyn paused at the corpses only long enough to relieve one of its iron falchion, then pressed on at speed. Ingelbert kept pace, the strap from his heavy satchel pressing painfully into his collarbone. The squire made straight for the nearest stairs to the battlements, ascending them two at a time. Grateful for his long legs, Ingelbert stayed on the squire's heels, following him along the wall walk towards a neglected corner of the stronghold. Here an ancient drum tower stood, devouring the battlements in the bloat of its old, curved body.

Flyn approached the closed door to the tower, pausing to listen before carefully pushing it open a hand's breadth. Ingelbert waited while the coburn listened again. Flyn then turned, flipping the dagger in his hand deftly to catch it by the blade and extended the grip to him. Ingelbert took the weapon, uncertain of what Flyn expected him to do, but before he could give voice to any questions, the squire put a finger up to his own beak, signaling silence. Ingelbert swallowed hard as the squire crept through the tower door, the curved blade of his newly acquired falchion leading.

They carried no torch or lamp and Ingelbert caught a brief glimpse of a wooden landing before moon and stars were banished as Flyn closed the tower door behind them, leaving Ingelbert in a darkness deeper than night. He felt the squire advance past him, but feared to move lest he step off the landing and into the hungry abyss of the tower shaft. Ingelbert knew the vision of the coburn far exceeded that of humans, even in the dark, but it seemed the squire was ignorant of such a fact.

He was about to issue a hiss at his would-be guide, when he detected a slight variation in the sea of darkness. Just at the edge of his slowly adjusting eyesight, Ingelbert made out a hint of contrast.

It grew clearer with each passing moment and Ingelbert was able to deduce the outline of the platform on which he stood against the slightly brighter interior of the tower shaft. A line of shadow became rope, suspending a large, irregular shape over the drop. The scant light seemed to come from below, and Ingelbert cautiously slid his feet along the square of blackness that was the landing until he came to the edge. Far below, a lone lamp burned, revealing five figures, one faced by the remaining four. Ghosts of voices echoed up along the round walls, rendered unintelligible by distance.

Motion at the corner of Ingelbert's trammeled sight made him look over to see Flyn's silhouette crouched at the landing's far end, near the stairs that descended the tower in a long spiral along the wall. The coburn's head appeared to be cocked, as if listening to the conversation below. After a moment, Flyn gathered something from the floor of the landing and approached.

"Stay here," he hissed. "Deglan may not be in position. If I give the signal, cut the rope tethering the net. You will need this."

Flyn's shadow gave a quick motion and Ingelbert felt the leather of the harness and the balanced weight of Coalspur placed into his hand.

"Flyn!" Ingelbert whispered, feeling a sense of panic rising to match his confusion. "I cannot—"

"You can," Flyn insisted.

"No, listen!" Ingelbert felt his hushed tone slipping. "I cannot, cannot see!"

Ingelbert felt the dagger snatched from his hand and shoved into his belt, then something smooth and wooden put in its place.

"A torch," Flyn explained. "You will find flint in a pouch on my harness. Light the torch when the fighting starts."

"More fighting," Ingelbert said dispassionately.

"Oh yes," Flyn chuckled softly in the darkness. "This will not be won with words."

The squire turned away, but a thought made Ingelbert reach out and grab his surcoat, stopping him.

"What, um, what is the signal?"

"Inkstain. Cut. The. Rope," Flyn replied softly. "Except I will be yelling."

"Buggery and shit."

Deglan uttered the curse under his breath as the four servants emerged from the tunnel into the base of the tower. The words had come unbidden and, quiet as they were, Deglan worried he might have been heard. Skin-changers had keen senses.

He peered between the support beams of the tower stair, under the landing where he had concealed himself. They skulked in wearing their false identities, their movements so fluid, so predatory, Deglan wondered how they ever passed for human. He need not have concerned himself with discovery. They had eyes only for Sir Corc.

The knight stood a few paces from the base of the stairs.

Though his back was turned, the composure with which he awaited the gruagach was obvious in his stance. Deglan had never seen a worm on a hook behave with such serenity. Of course, no worm was ever so well armed. The broadsword and stout mace hanging close to hand on the knight's belts were both iron, replacing the similar weapons of steel he normally carried. To say nothing of the honed steel caps strapped over the coburn's natural spurs, prominently visible from Deglan's low vantage point. Plate covered Corc's torso and mail his legs, sure protection against fishhooks.

Deglan hoped they would be enough against these shape-changing killers. He would feel more confident if Corc had more support than one gnome herbalist hiding in a changeling's former hovel.

Flyn had been here, Deglan was certain. The steel hand axe was in place under the stairs, next to the thick rope tethered to one of the beams as planned, but no sign of the young strut. He and Corc had arrived earlier than arranged, for the fire had forced their hand. The gruagach were making their move and the time for planning was ended. Deglan clutched the axe, waiting, hoping he would know when to strike.

The gruagach spread out in front of Sir Corc, not yet brazen enough to attempt to surround him, but Deglan could see in their movements the attempt would not be long in coming.

Aonghas, the tanner's apprentice and Earc, son of the master mason he had expected. A tragedy. Each lad was no more than fifteen. He had been less sure about the mute laundress, Muirne, but here she was, none of the wide-eyed meekness present now in her face. The fourth wore the guise of a Dal Riata clansman Deglan did not recognize. It no longer mattered. Likely there were many and more that slipped his notice, damn them.

"You intrude here," Sir Corc's voice resonated off the tower walls.

"Do you mourn, coburn?" Muirne mocked the knight and mocked the memory of the girl who in life never spoke a word.

"Do we interrupt your false respects? Paid to a boy not dead."

"You intrude upon this castle," Sir Corc replied evenly.

"Leave here, do not return and you will be spared, though you deserve death."

"Death is ours to deliver," Earc proclaimed, his freckled face turning sinister. "We dispense it at our desire. It is not within your power to bring us to our end, mortal duckling."

"Enough," the knight commanded sharply. "Show your true selves. I'll not parley while you wear the faces of the innocents you murdered."

The gruagach laughed at this.

"You think to set terms, knight?" Muirne asked, amused at the notion. "Your fellows flutter about while your glorious dovecote burns. The young cock you have taken for a minion is dead. We have come for you, Sir Corc the Constant. For ten years you have defied us. Ten years which must have seemed so long a resistance to you. So tiring, such unyielding vigilance. To us, the time was but a moment, no longer than it takes to yawn."

Deglan tightened his grip on the axe as the gruagach began to close around Sir Corc. The knight did not take so much as half a step backward, calmly drawing mace and sword.

"The boy you seek is dead," Sir Corc said. "If you think to find him through me, you will find that course futile."

"We know he lives," Earc's voice dripped. "We need you not to find him. We need you dead for when we do. Lord Lambkiller commands."

Laughter filled the tower. The sound made Deglan smile.

Bantam Flyn plummeted from above, slashing as he fell.

His blade caught Earc where neck met shoulder, cleaving him to the belly. The ugly wound hissed as Flyn landed behind the twitching gruagach, its human features changing violently as the creature died. Sir Corc wasted no time, stepping forward with a sweep of his mace, catching Aonghas in the hip and sending him sprawling. In the same motion, the knight tossed his broadsword to Flyn, who caught it and engaged the remaining two gruagach, a sword whirling in each hand, driving them back. Muirne and the clansman moved with preternatural speed, splitting off from each other and retreating to the far wall. Flyn did not pursue, but kept his attention on his adversaries as he stepped back to join Sir Corc who kept watch on Aonghas, now recovered from the mace blow.

Knight and squire stood back to back, one slain foe at their feet.

Deglan could see their time on the island had not been wasted.

They fought well together.

The three gruagach watched the coburn intently, eyes blazing with calculated malice. They began to change, soft flesh giving way to scales and black fur, fingers stretching into vicious claws. Tusks emerged from faces now devoid of humanity, shoes burst to reveal cloven hooves. The gruagach gave Sir Corc what he demanded.

They showed their true selves.

Deglan checked the angle of his swing and waited for the signal to cut the rope.

Ingelbert lit the torch as soon as he heard Flyn's mad laughter. He had only caught glimpses of the squire making his way stealthily down the stairs, often losing him in the uncertain light.

The daring coburn had been half a turn above the final landing when he leapt, at least a dozen yards above the ground, a feat which would have pulped the bones of a man. Bantam Flyn landed unharmed, cutting down one of the figures below. It was difficult to discern what was transpiring from such a height, but the transformation of the gruagach was plain. Flyn, and what Ingelbert guessed to be Sir Corc the Constant, were standing against three creatures of the same ilk slain in the records room. If the prowess of that gruagach were any indication, a victory for the coburn was far from certain.

Flyn had instructed Ingelbert to cut a rope at his signal. In the light of the torch, Ingelbert could now inspect his surroundings and the trap he was supposed to help spring. What Flyn had called a net turned out to be at least two dozen rusty mail hauberks haphazardly fashioned together to create a ponderous web of iron.

A crude framework of wood held the thing splayed wide. At the junction of the planks an iron ring had been fastened and tethered to a rope, suspending the entire construction over the tower shaft.

The rope appeared to run down the wall behind the stair scaffold, no doubt to its final tether point.

Ingelbert was impressed. He would have thought the use of a pulley to be beyond the ken of one like Bantam Flyn. The squire had even thought to give him Coalspur, the reach and weight of the greatsword being necessary to sever the sturdy rope. If the net fell true, the gruagach would be crushed and, even if they survived, held fast by the weight and the iron. Of course, so would anyone else unlucky enough to be beneath when it fell.

Placing the torch in a wall sconce, Ingelbert glanced over the landing. The coburn still battled the gruagach, staying close together near the center of the tower floor. Trying to lure their enemies in, Ingelbert surmised. He hoped the coburn were sure in their ability to get clear if the signal came to cut the rope.

Unless . . .

Ingelbert's hair stood up with the revelation. It was a failsafe. A last, desperate measure to ensure the gruagach did not prevail. The coburn were not staying close to the center to lure the gruagach in, they stayed so that should they fall, their defeat would place the gruagach in position to be destroyed. Ingelbert knew Flyn's dedication to his cause was strong, now he knew just how strong.

The door to the tower was flung open. Startled, Ingelbert turned to find a short, soot-covered figure lurching onto the landing. The torchlight fell upon a face half covered in oozing blisters and blackened flesh. It was the goblin captive, the one the Order kept to test on the anvil. Bulbous, crazed eyes fixed on Ingelbert. A halberd, the shaft broken in half, dangled from the goblin's hand, the head spike scraping across the landing boards.

"Smoke," the Red Cap gibbered, advancing. "Smoke! And Fire!" The goblin charged, shrieking and swinging the halberd wildly. Ingelbert stumbled away, trying to bring Coalspur up to ward the blows. The halberd blade crushed into his forearm, snapping bones. The agony forced a scream from Ingelbert's lungs and he dropped the greatsword. The goblin pulled the halberd back, preparing to ram the spike into Ingelbert's bowels. He stumbled away from the coming thrust and his guts jumped to his throat.

His foot struck nothing but empty air.

He fell, terror screaming in his skull. Twisting, Ingelbert caught the dangling net with his good hand, but his sudden weight caused the wooden framework to snap. He fell again as half the mail tore free, swinging him further away from the landing. His hand had caught in a jagged hole in one of the hauberks and the rusted links bit into his flesh. He kicked desperately over the dizzying void, his motion tearing more of the net free from its moorings. Sweat and blood slicked his fingers and they began to slip. He cried out in helpless anguish, trying to bury the metal deeper into his flesh so it would hold him. There was nothing else to do. Ingelbert looked up to see the grinning face of the goblin staring down at him, waiting lustfully for him to fall.

SIX

Flyn took his eyes off the gruagach for half a moment.

Hearing a stricken cry from above, he shot a glance upward.

Someone dangled from the net.

"Inkstain," he cursed.

Deglan's voice burst from underneath the stairs behind him, bellowing a warning. Flyn barely got his blades up in time to parry the skin-changer's claws. The gruagach were fast, too damn fast, and one had wasted no time exploiting Flyn's momentary distraction. Claws swept and raked, squealing against iron as Flyn interposed his swords. Sir Corc made no move to aid him, ensuring the other two gruagach did not rush in and overwhelm them.

Turning the scything attacks aside with the broadsword, Flyn whipped the falchion low at the creature's legs. The gruagach sprang away, as Flyn had anticipated, the blow a feint for the thrust of the broadsword which followed. He went for the throat, the kill, but the gruagach ducked its head, knocking his blade away with a crooked tusk. Flyn pressed the attack, but could not find an opening, succeeding only in driving the gruagach back.

"This dance grows tiresome," he said, stepping back to Sir Corc's side.

"Who is above?" the knight asked, nodding upwards without taking his eyes from the gruagach.

"Crane," Flyn replied. "The *human* chronicler."

"He will fall." It was not a question.

"And bring a lot more than the weight of one skinny man with him," Flyn said.

Corc took a moment, considering.

"Go," he ordered.

"That will leave you three to one," Flyn pointed out.

"I will deal with them," the knight said.

"I do not doubt," Flyn went on, "but such a deed is worthy of song. The notoriety, Sir, you would never survive."

Flyn rushed the middle gruagach. It braced to meet him, its arms held low and wide. They no longer ended in claws, having reformed into sinewy tentacles, flexing and curling with anticipation. That was unexpected. Movement at the edge of his vision told him the other two were converging. Flyn smiled. He brought the falchion up in a great arc over his head and around for a powerful disemboweling slash at the creature in front of him. It hopped backwards, avoiding the cut. Flyn released his hold on the grip, sending the curved blade spinning at the gruagach coming in from the left. The creature could not check its charge. The falchion wind-milled, thumping through the air before slamming into the gruagach, the blade biting deep. The gruagach was knocked off its feet, landing hard on the stones and sliding to a halt, the sword still embedded in its chest. Flyn dove to the side, over swiping tentacles, and rolled to his feet next to the fallen gruagach. It yet lived, struggling to stand, smoking black blood pumping out from around the falchion's blade. The gruagach from the right was almost upon him and Flyn waited a final heartbeat before turning to bolt for the stairs.

"Stay there, you old mushroom!" he yelled as he passed over the first landing, knowing Deglan was below. "I shall return in a trice!"

Heavy thuds resounded on the stairs behind him. One of the gruagach had given chase. He had hoped for both. A tentacle whipped up between the stairs ahead of him, coiling around the boards. So, the other was not chasing, it was climbing to head him off. A high-pitched squeal issued from below and, just as quickly as the tentacle appeared, it was gone. Corc must have wanted a word.

Flyn ignored the sounds of pursuit behind him and pounded up the stairs, looking up the tower shaft on the run.

Ingelbert still hung from the net, but the man was flagging. Even had he the strength of a fomori, it would not save him. The rig holding the mail was coming apart, shaken to pieces by the chronicler's panicked movements. Someone else was up there as well, leaning over from the top landing, but making no move to help Inkstain. Flyn climbed as swiftly as he could, but he still had several turns to complete before reaching the top.

He was not going to make it.

Deglan waited for Flyn and the gruagach to pass over before crawling out from beneath the stairs. He did not care what the young strut said, he was not about to cower under there any longer. Something had gone amiss. Keeping the axe in hand, Deglan emerged to see Flyn across the tower, flying up the stairs, already half a turn up, the gruagach not half a dozen strides removed. The other tentacled monstrosity had climbed under the stairs, hauling itself up by a one of its loathsome appendages to intercept Flyn. Sir Corc had already covered the distance, swinging his mace around to land a crushing blow to the creature's fur-covered knee. The tentacle uncoiled from the support beam, the gruagach squealing as it came tumbling to the ground. The knight raised his mace for the killing stroke when the beast swept a tentacle into his legs. Sir Corc fell onto his back, the mace flying from his hand.

Cursing, Deglan moved to help him. Something grasped tightly at his ankle and his leg was jerked out from under him. He hit the floor, wrists and elbows bashing painfully. His chin scraped across the rough stones as he was dragged backwards. Flipping over he found a tentacle wrapped firmly around his leg and the gruagach Flyn had felled with the thrown falchion pulling him in. The beast had traded its tusks for a mouth full of fangs, its jaw unhinging, ready to receive him. Deglan still had the axe and he hacked at the heavily muscled coils. The blade chopped deep, but the creature held fast, undeterred by steel. He kicked hard at the mouth with his free leg, the fangs snapping at his foot. Hot, viscous blood splattered Deglan's face and the tentacle went loose, twitching and writhing against his liberated leg.

Sir Corc pulled his mace out of the ruin of the gruagach's skull and helped Deglan to his feet.

"Took your damn time," Deglan grumbled, glancing over to the broken remains of the other gruagach beneath the stairs.

"Should have known you would not need my help."

The knight did not respond. His gaze was fixed skyward.

Deglan looked up just as a horrible, hopeless scream pierced the tower. Ingelbert Crane fell, his limbs flailing helplessly. A second later, the heavy iron net broke free and plummeted after him.

Deglan and Corc began to shuffle back, out of the path of the crushing trap and the poor, doomed youth. Above, Deglan spied Flyn on the stairs. He was two turns below the top landing and no longer running. The gruagach was almost upon him, but the squire ignored the danger, his eyes fixed on Crane, tracking his plunge. The squire dropped the sword in his hand, bouncing slightly on his feet.

"No, you daft cock, no," Deglan muttered.

Flyn jumped.

The gruagach launched itself after him. Arms outstretched, Flyn sped towards Crane, seeming to hang in the abyss for a single, terrible heartbeat. Behind them, the gruagach reached out with a clawed hand. The iron net slammed into it from above, denying its pursuit, missing the coburn by a finger's breadth. Deglan winced when Flyn collided with Crane midair, his forward momentum altering the man's dive into a rapid, diagonal descent. Flyn held onto Crane as they fell together, twisting his body to direct their flight towards the narrow stairs. If he overshot, they would crash into the tower wall above. If they fell short, the inevitable floor would be their end.

The mass of mail, and the ensnared gruagach struck the ground. Deglan threw his arms up against the dust and debris, his ears ringing with the concussive impact. He coughed, grit filling his mouth. A strong, feathered hand clapped him on the back and he followed Sir Corc as the knight ran for the base of the stairs.

They found Crane half a turn up, bloody and motionless.

Flyn lay underneath him. He had taken the brunt of the fall.

"Do not move them!" Deglan called to Sir Corc, while he scrambled to catch up. He stepped carefully around the knight and inspected Crane. The man was unconscious, but breathing. His pulse was weak and he had at least one broken arm, though Deglan's battlefield days saw the work of an axe blade, not the fall.

His spine was intact, so Deglan motioned for Sir Corc to move him.

The knight lifted the chronicler carefully, laying him back down just up the stairs before returning to stand over Deglan's shoulder as he examined Bantam Flyn.

The squire's eyes were closed and he was not breathing.

Deglan slapped him.

"Enough of your foolery!" he admonished the young strut.

Flyn began to chuckle, cracking an eye open.

"Next time, remind me," the squire groaned. "Despite the feathers, I cannot fly."

Flyn's legs were trembling by the time he reached the top landing. A return climb up had not been a welcome prospect, but Coalspur had not fallen with Inkstain. He found the greatsword easily enough, though no sign of the short figure he had spied callously watching the chronicler's plight. Bending down, he retrieved Coalspur from the planking and with an exhausted sigh, began the long descent back to the ground floor.

By the time he arrived, Corc had dragged the gruagach corpses against the wall and piled them up, heaving the iron net atop them. They had laid Inkstain out, using what was left of Pocket's old bedding to cushion him. The chronicler's face was pale, drawn up in pain even in unconsciousness. Deglan knelt beside the man.

"Will he live?" Flyn asked, approaching on unsteady legs.

"If he wakes," Deglan said, scowling. "We need to get him to my infirmary."

Flyn took a deep breath, placing the sheathed point of Coalspur on the ground, he leaned heavily on the cross-guard.

"We need to get him away from the castle."

Deglan looked up, his scowl deepening.

"He knows," Flyn explained, his words addressed to Sir Corc. "He knows Pocket is alive."

The knight walked a few paces closer, regarding him steadily. He said nothing, waiting.

"We were wrong about him," Flyn told him. "He is no gruagach. But he is clever and asked questions. About you, the boy."

"Does he know where?" the knight asked, betraying no emotion.

"Not from my words," Flyn replied. "But he will reason it out, mark me. It is too dangerous for him to stay. Too dangerous for Pocket."

"Let me get him stable," Deglan said. "A day or two, then you can take him back with you."

"We may not have a day or two," Flyn said. "Four gruagach lay here, but a fifth Crane and I slew. Corc, it was Worm Chewer."

The knight absorbed this, nodding grimly.

"And something attacked Crane above," Flyn continued. "I cannot be sure, but it looked to be a goblin."

"Buggery and toad shit," Deglan spat. "They let it loose."

Flyn looked to Sir Corc for clarification, but the knight stared down at the gnome, equally puzzled.

"They caught one," Deglan told them. "A bloody, bandy-legged Red Cap! Killed some of the Dal Riata stock and murdered one of the cowherd's sons about half a year ago. Had it chained up since. They use it to proof iron."

"Torture," Sir Corc said, a growl of displeasure in his voice.

"No less than that gray-skinned bastard deserved," Deglan declared. "But I wager the gruagach set him free. Fire-loving fuck is running about, setting the Roost ablaze!"

"A distraction," Sir Corc said. "One that does not thin the gruagach numbers."

"They came after us," Deglan said and then pointed at Flyn.

"And him. Five dead. Likely all there is."

"We cannot know for certain," Flyn said. "There may be more. Or will be given time. They killed at least three of us tonight, a formidable knight included. Crane must be taken away."

Sir Corc considered his words, looking down at the still form of the chronicler.

"I will take him," the knight said.

"No," Flyn returned forcefully, then dropped his voice, leaning close to the knight. "With Worm Chewer gone, the Grand Master will press you even harder to join the Knights Sergeant. You cannot accept that honor for the same reason you cannot shoulder this burden. Pocket needs you."

"I can take the man to the island," Corc replied, his voice barely a whisper. "He will be safe there."

"And a prisoner," Flyn said, his voice equally hushed. "We cannot save his life and steal his freedom. Enough innocence has been bound to that place."

Sir Corc fixed him with a hard stare, troubled at his words.

"I will take him," Flyn affirmed, losing the whisper to add weight to his words. "I know from whence he came. I will see him home."

"No," Sir Corc shook his head. "This is not for you to do."

"I can, Sir," Flyn assured him.

"Listen to me," Corc insisted, but Flyn waved him off.

"My mind is made."

"You fail to—"

"I will not fail, this I—"

"DAMMIT, BANTAM!" Sir Corc grabbed him roughly by the shoulders, shaking him. His outburst traveled up through the tower, finally dying out in the shadows above. The old knight took a deep breath.

"Heed me," he said, his voice calm once more. "You fail to see. You are still a squire. If you do this, it will be desertion. A dishonorable act. Leave now and your knighthood will be forfeit. Flyn, you will never be able to return."

Flyn smiled, holding his mentor's gaze, and waited for him to understand. It did not take long. Corc's face softened, his grip on Flyn's shoulders relaxed. Flyn had known the consequences before he spoke and now Sir Corc was aware.

"I was never meant for knighthood, Corc. Too brash. Too proud. Disdainful of rules. This is better."

Sir Corc struck him. It was an openhanded blow, little more than a cuff, but the force sent Flyn to his knees, as it was meant to.

Flyn looked up at the knight, perplexed. It was the buffet, a ceremonial blow of humility delivered to remind the recipient of his oath. The knight's oath. Flyn had seen it performed before, the culmination of the dubbing ceremony.

"Know you the words?" Sir Corc asked, drawing his sword.

Flyn knew them well. Long had he yearned to speak them aloud.

"In service shall I wander,
my life a shield for the meek.
All injustice shall I conquer,
no wealth or mate ever mine.
My honor undimmed, my vigil never ending,
Until peace blesses all lands, or the sun sets its last."

Sir Corc nodded, extending his sword.

"I, Sir Corc, Knight Errant of the Valiant Spur, do on this field of battle, dub you knight."

Flyn bowed his head, clinging to Coalspur and feeling the taps on his shoulders.

"Rise now, Sir Flyn and take your place among us."

Flyn stood and as he did so, Sir Corc knelt, unbuckling the steel caps from his own spurs.

"In the first days of our Order," the knight said, "Mulrooster led the Five Score. One hundred knights, the first knights, trained by the elves. Those worthy warriors were given the first spurs, forged with elven-craft long vanished from the world. Forever sharp, they could not be sundered. Over the centuries many of the elven spurs were lost when the knights who wore them fell in forgotten lands. A few have survived and been passed down from one knight to the next over many generations."

Sir Corc buckled the spurs on Flyn's feet and rose.

"Receive them now."

Flyn tried to keep the wonder out of his face. He knew of the elf spurs, every squire knew of them. Bronze Wattle's spurs were said to be one of the last pair extant. That Sir Corc possessed such a legendary heirloom was never spoken. Flyn should not have been surprised.

"You need not gift me these, Sir," he said.

Sir Corc held up his hand. "They must be passed on."

Flyn looked down at Deglan, the gnome's sardonic grimace unable to keep the smile from his face.

"Well," the herbalist said, "if we are going, let's be off."

"We?" Flyn asked.

"Yes, we. I will be going with you."

"No," Flyn said, looking to Corc for support. "Loamtoes, you are too important to the Order. You are needed here."

Deglan's face crinkled and he jabbed a finger at the prostrate Inkstain.

"Do you know how to set bones? Reduce a fever? Feed a man in a torpor? If you take him out on the road without me, it won't bloody matter what secrets he knows! He will die. Besides, bugger living in a place where I must burn myself just to prove I'm me!" Flyn looked to Corc again, unwilling to fight the cantankerous old stoat.

"Very well," Sir Corc agreed.

"I will need some things from the infirmary if he is to have a chance," Deglan said, rising to his feet.

"There is a sally port through the Under Hall," Corc said, nodding towards the lower passage. "It is not far from here. Master Loamtoes, you and I will take Master Crane out. Tell Sir Flyn what you need and he will see it done."

Sir Corc then turned to Flyn.

"We will meet where we last took leave."

Flyn nodded. He remembered the place. A small copse of scrubby trees at the base of the mount where he had first met Pocket. After Deglan made Flyn memorize his necessities, Sir Corc lifted Inkstain off the ground, eliciting some fussing from the gnome and they disappeared down the dark passage.

Flyn slung his greatsword, then climbed the stairs once more, his legs working with renewed vigor. He retraced the route he and Inkstain had used to gain the tower. From the battlements, he could see no evidence of more fires, but kept an eye out for sign of the escaped Red Cap as he made his way down to the Middle Bailey. He kept to the shadows, knowing he could trust no face he encountered and, even were they proven friend, he wished to avoid questions. Inkstain's sudden disappearance would be easily accepted. Once the gruagach body was discovered in the records room, the missing chronicler would be blamed on the skinchangers or cowardice. Either way, he would not be long sought.

Flyn himself would be branded a rogue and a deserter.

Many, especially among the squires, already thought him a knave, and this act an inevitable end. Let them think what they will, he never cared overmuch for the opinions of others. There was only one in the Order whose esteem he valued, whose spurs he now wore.

He feared for the future of the Order. Long had the glory of the Valiant Spur been in decline, but never in its history was it so beset. Flyn hoped they had snuffed out the gruagach threat this night, but it was a tenuous victory at best and one dearly paid. It would be many long years before the shadow of fear was purged from the Roost, years measured by the lifespans of the Dal Riata, who would tell stories of the cursed castle long after those who witnessed these dark days were in their graves.

Flyn reached the infirmary unchallenged and quickly set to work gathering the required supplies. He took all he could carry, slinging a heavy rucksack over his shoulder. He paused before leaving, going over the gnome's list in his mind one last time.

Certain he had forgotten nothing, he turned to leave.

Gulver blocked his path.

"Hold," the huge squire said. He bore a halberd in his hand, but its haft rested on the ground.

"Unless you are a skin-changer, step aside," Flyn told him.

"I cannot let you leave, Bantam Flyn."

"Supplies for the leech," Flyn explained, hefting the rucksack. "Let me pass."

He took a step forward, but Gulver did not budge.

"I know you," the brute said. "You forget. I know the look of you when you flee."

"Gulver," Flyn said, walking over slowly and placing a hand upon his shoulder. "I must go."

"No," Gulver brushed his hand away. "It is a mistake you make. You will throw it all away. For your pride! Lackcomb refuses your knighthood, so to spit in his face you will forever shame yourself."

Flyn lowered his eyes to the floor. It was better for Gulver to think this than know the truth. Still, it was painful. He stepped forward, shouldering past. Gulver shoved him back.

"You will not go! Not to where I know you are bound."

"You know nothing," Flyn told him, anger edging his voice.

"I do," Gulver replied. "I know that look. The same one you wore the day we left. You mean to return. Tell me I read you wrong. Tell your brother he is wrong."

Flyn looked into Gulver's face. The brute was right, he did know him. He would not lie. It would serve no purpose. Flyn pushed through the doorway and this time, his brother let him pass.

"He will kill you," Gulver's voice followed him down the corridor. "If you return home, Gallus will kill you."

SEVEN

Black thoughts.

They always came, unbidden, when a life balanced on Deglan's skills as a healer. After thousands of years honing his craft, doubt rarely entered his mind, but the grim consequence of failure, the death of those under his care, he never kept at bay. Immortality had awarded him vast knowledge, and a vast number of dead to tally those he failed. Fae-folk never succumbed to age and only the most insidious diseases conjured by sorcery could lay them low, but violence could take an immortal's life, especially if inflicted with damnable iron. Deglan had watched many a Fae shudder to stillness beneath his hands, but they were only an acorn in the immense forest of mortals he had watched die.

Fragile and ephemeral from the newly born to the venerable, humans had perished before Deglan's eyes despite his best efforts in numbers now impossible to reckon. Often he had been perfect; catching the malady early, having the exact medicines close to hand, administering them with precision, adapting to fluctuating symptoms seamlessly, doing everything correctly. And still they died. These simple, short-lived beings, almost witless in their immaturity, would pass away, spitting in the eye of great wisdom learned across hundreds of their fleeting generations.

It used to enrage Deglan to be so denied, his careful attentions rejected by a thing so young, so ignorant. What right did a mortal child have not to survive when pitted against his powers?

But die they did. All of them. Deglan would save a babe from fever only to return, seemingly a day later, to watch that same babe, now a bent-backed old woman, shivering with some ague that refused to be cured, forcing a final breath before the next sunrise.

At his most bitter, he yearned for the days of the Rebellion.

War was a calamity, a waste of life, but at least the wounds, the disease, the starvation, all stemmed from a single identifiable source.

You could hate the enemy and vent your fury in the task of trying to bury more of his friends than your own. You would stitch, cauterize and amputate. It was bloody business filled with screams, and yes, dying, but during those long years in the gnomish army, riding proud as a Staunch of the Wart Shanks, Deglan never buried a child. Battle claimed its share of innocents, he knew, but he was spared such despair, locked away in a soldier's life, his service promised to those who swung the sword, not those who suffered in the path of the swath.

It was selfish and shameful, but, by Earth and Stone, it was easier! There was something justifiable in a warrior's death, a fate accepted if not deserved. Deglan hated the war and like all the other crotch-rotten bastards he rode with, spoke a fine lie about wishing it would end, but once it did, had no place in a world of relative peace. Bugger him, there were many times he missed the war and bugger him twice if he would have voiced it aloud. He was not alone.

Faabar had missed it, too. The noble fomori lacked the subtlety to hide it, however, and Deglan often chided him mercilessly for his wistful thoughts of past glory. They had both settled in Hog's Wallow, living pitifully within the shadow of Bwenyth Tor, the site of their last battle. The Wallow began as little more than an outpost for supplies destined for the fortress. The gnomes quickly abandoned their above-ground settlements after the Restoration of the Seelie Court and Bwenyth Tor, like so many of the great Fae strongholds, was abandoned to ruin. Soon, humans came there to live, to raise their families, grow their crops, tend their animals and die too quickly. Faabar became their champion, his mere presence enough to ensure they lived unmolested. Deglan earned the name Faery Doctor, much to his displeasure and they both faded into the tedious, miserable cycle of mortal tranquility.

Then, after nearly nine hundred years of decaying pride, Faabar was injured in a ploughing mishap, crippled by a spooked ox. Deglan had done what he could to mend his friend, but for all his art it was not herbs or potions or salves that made the fomori whole again.

It was the return of war.

The phantom threat of an Unwound rose in the countryside surrounding Hog's Wallow and, for the span of a firefly's glow, Faabar's sense of duty, of purpose, was renewed. They went on patrol together, unbeknownst to either, for the last time. They found no Unwound, but discovered the return of Torcan Swinehelm and the liberation of the last Flame Binder. Faabar died fighting them.

Deglan had wept for him, helped to bury him, but even in grief he knew it was a worthy end for a warrior, far better than a pathetic death caused by a vacuous beast of burden. Deglan returned to the familiar habits of war and left the life of a Faery Doctor behind, discarded in the ash of Hog's Wallow. There were goblins to fight and he was a Staunch once more. Curse him, he had been relieved. No more human frailty, no more sheep blights, no more children to save. Or so he thought. In the end, he had saved another, a girl, though not from illness. Saved, and for her continued well-being, given up.

Deglan shook his head, keeping the memory from nesting in his head.

Black thoughts. And not one of which would help save Ingelbert Crane.

The chronicler lay upon the turf. He was still unconscious and his breathing had become labored. His forearm was swollen, the skin turning an ugly purple, obvious even in the torchlight.

There was a gash as well, caused no doubt by a heavy blade swung by that gap-toothed Red Cap, but Deglan was less concerned with the wound than he was the shattered bones beneath. If he did not tend to them soon, the man faced losing the arm entire and Deglan did not think he would survive the cutting. He also worried about injuries to Crane's organs. His slight build would have done little to help him endure the force of the fall he suffered. But for Flyn, he would be dead already.

"Where is that preening wastrel?" Deglan demanded. He needed his herbs and instruments. There was little he could do for Crane in a benighted cluster of trees. Sir Corc did not answer, but continued to work, constructing a litter for Crane. If Deglan did not get his supplies soon, it would end up becoming the chronicler's bier.

The sounds of someone approaching caused Deglan to look up from his wounded charge. Sir Corc straightened, his hand hovering over his sword hilt.

"You need but call and I appear," Bantam Flyn announced, striding out of the darkness and into the little clearing.

He came swiftly to where Deglan knelt, swinging a rucksack off his shoulder and handing it down. Deglan emptied the contents quickly, but carefully. The young strut had done well. A hasty inventory revealed nothing forgotten. Selecting a certain bottle, Deglan peered at it in the flickering torchlight, verifying its contents.

"Liss-more and yarrow," he muttered to himself, breaking the wax seal and pulling the cork. Titling Crane's head back, he slowly poured the potion past the man's slack lips. That done, he went to work setting and splinting the fractured arm. Much more was required, but he needed fire, boiling water, better light and time.

None of which they appeared to have.

Corc had finished the litter and Deglan waved his permission to move Crane as he got to his feet, gathering up his supplies and repacking them. Thankfully, Flyn had remembered his satchel and Deglan filled it with the vital components, placing the surplus back in the rucksack. This he placed on the litter between Crane's feet alongside the chronicler's own bag. The damn thing had still been around Crane's body when they reached the copse.

Deglan had removed it during his examination, paying it no mind at the time. Now he saw it was stuffed with books and scrolls.

"Do we need this extra weight?" he asked, thumping the bag with his foot.

"It all comes," Flyn answered.

"Comes where, exactly?" Deglan pressed.

"Gipeswic," Flyn said. "On the eastern shore of Sasana."

Deglan's knowledge of the lands to the south was limited.

"And how long will that take?"

"A month overland," Sir Corc said, frowning down at the litter and its occupant. "Mayhaps longer. You could go east from here to the coast of Albain. A fortnight would bring you to Caer Caled where ships may be found to bring you south."

"Ships," Flyn agreed, "and Middangeard raiders."

Sir Corc only nodded once, clearly aware of the risk.

"East would also mean crossing over the Mounds," Flyn went on.

"Or through," Corc added. "There are passes."

Deglan knew enough about the landscape of Albain to recall that the mountain range crossed nearly the width of the region. It would be unavoidable if they made for the opposite shore.

The port of Grianaig on the western banks was nearer the Roost, but that would leave them facing a long voyage either around the top of Albain through the Knucklebones or an even longer one down the length of the western shore through the Airlann Channel between the Source Isle and the unforgiving land of Kymbru.

Those were dangerous seas, filled with storms, bloodthirsty kelpies and kraken that could drag a boat down to its doom. Even if they made it through the channel alive they would still need to round the southern end of Sasana and circle back north to reach the eastern shore.

Deglan did not much care for sea travel, preferring his feet pressed solidly to Earth, but at present, the route was not his primary concern.

"We need to get this gawky scribbler out of these damn trees and somewhere I can work. Let's begin there."

Sir Corc nodded his agreement and handed his torch to Deglan, then stooped to pick up the head of the litter. Bantam Flyn took up the other end. The knight led them out of the copse and down the last stretch of hill from the escarpment, reaching the relatively flat ground below the castle.

In the distance, Deglan could see the glow from the hut fires in Glengabráin and the moonlight reflecting off the loch behind. If only he could take Crane down to the village and see to his injuries there, but it was too dangerous. Any gruagach hiding among the Dal Riata would be on the watch for them. One or even two would not likely cause a threat. Skin-changers rarely moved openly against their quarry without numbers in their favor.

For all Deglan knew there were half a dozen of the slippery bastards hiding among the clansmen, there was just no sure way of knowing.

Not unless they asked.

"Bugger me for a blind fool," he chastised himself, then raised his voice at the coburn walking ahead. "Make for the pasture land."

"Why?" Flyn tossed the word back at him.

"Where else would you look for a cow?" Deglan barked.

"Deglan," Flyn said slowly. "I am sorry to tell you this, but planting yourself in manure will not make you taller."

"Shut up and walk, you!"

They skirted the borders of the village, Deglan extinguishing the torch before they entered the fields. Despite their differences, gnomes and coburn saw equally well in the dark, the moon providing adequate light to guide them. The Dal Riata kept a night-watch over their livestock and it took some doing to avoid the eyes of the drovers. Deglan took the lead, moving low and quiet towards the edge of the pasture.

It was impossible for the cowherds to keep an eye on every beast during the night and there were always strays. So long as the majority of the herd was kept safe from predators and thieves, the few that wandered were rounded up the next morning. It did not take Deglan long to spot an animal separated from the rest in the warm night, unseen by the clansmen. He motioned for the coburn to set their burden down and wait. Leaving then, he crept into the pasture.

The cow shied away from him as he approached, but did not retreat. Deglan was not overly fond of the brainless brutes, but he had need of this one. Reaching into his satchel, he produced a bundle of dried speedwell. Deglan valued the plant for its aid in curing congestion, but it was a rare find due to the livestock and their tendency to eat all they could sniff out. He held the fragrant plant out towards the cow. It caught the scent, its wet nostrils flaring, and plodded forward in single-minded pursuit.

Deglan led it back to where the coburn waited and shot Flyn a warning look against any remarks as he passed. He made for the edge of a small wood bordering the pasture where the Dal Riata swine foraged. The cow was in tow and the coburn came along behind, bearing Crane between them. Deglan stopped at the tree-line, casting a long glance back the way they had come to make sure they had not been spotted.

"Needed to visit your sweetheart before we left?"

"I know over a hundred plants that can kill you, Bantam Flyn!" Deglan growled. "Now put that litter down, both of you. I will need help."

The coburn approached, Corc with silent patience and the young strut with bemused uncertainty.

"Flyn," Deglan said, handing over the bundle of speedwell.

"Feed this to the four-legged lout. Slowly! And get a good hold around its neck. Sir Corc, help keep hold of her."

When he was sure the coburn had a firm hold, Deglan took a bronze lancet out of his satchel, gently feeling along the beast's neck. He found a good vein, ensuring it was not the artery and quickly pierced the flesh with his lancet. The cow gave a groan of protest and lurched, trying to pull away, but the strength of the coburn held her fast. Deglan stuck his free hand under the flow of blood, cupping his palm to allow the fluid to pool, hot to the touch.

He approached the edge of the wood, his dripping hand raised.

"Deglan what—?" Flyn began, but a hiss from Sir Corc silenced him.

Deglan waited, watching the trees.

The cattle of the Dal Riata were prized. Hearty and strong, they produced sweet milk, supple leather and tender meat. When Deglan had arrived at the Roost, he tended to the clansmen as often as needed, but was never summoned to treat the stock. He should have suspected then, but he had other concerns on his mind.

The gruagach were in the castle and among the Dal Riata. Murder, fear, distrust, all of these the gruagach spread. And disease.

However, only in the last month had the cattle become afflicted.

Curse him for a blind old gnome, he should have seen the clue.

Fae are protectors.

From the beginning, that was their purpose. Magic had made them, gifted them with immortality and entrusted the greatest among them with the guardianship of the Elements. Above them all were placed the elves, destined to be the stewards of Magic and the guiding hand for all Fae. Upon mortal man's arrival to Airlann, it was the elves who decreed that all Fae-folk should help elevate them from savagery and further distance them from the caves they had so recently left behind. Even the least of the Fae found purpose then. The piskie, the clurichaun, the fenodyree, once mere servants of the Seelie Court, established themselves as tutors to the humans, using their gifts to aid and protect aspects of mortal life.

For years uncountable it was so, until man betrayed the trust of the elves, using Magic learned at their knee to supplant them and attain dominion over the Source Isle. These human oathbreakers became the Goblin Kings and though they were few in number, the atrocities committed during their reign sullied all mankind. Some Fae, like the gruagach, refused to forgive and turned their powers to man's destruction. Many, however, kept to the old ways.

The blood covering his hand had cooled, becoming sticky between his fingers.

She appeared at the edge of the woods, walking between the trees, silent and graceful. Her tall, lean form was clothed in a simple dress of rough wool, darkly dyed. Even in the moonlight, her unbound hair shone, the deep red of fallen leaves.

The bright eyes and pointed ears suggested elf-kind, but her skin was grey and beneath her dress Deglan knew her feet would be hooves.

After the Restoration, the baobhan sith had sided with the gruagach, refusing the Seelie Court's command that humans be left in peace. All but a few. Those who honored the peace were driven from Airlann by their vengeful kin, forced to find homes in other lands where they could continue to live in harmony with humans.

Here in Albain, they were called glaistig and their province was bestowing blessings to livestock. Of course, such a boon did not come without price. The glaistig were blood-drinkers.

"Why do you summon me, Earth warden?" the glaistig demanded, fixing Deglan with a penetrating stare. "And why do you dare lay hands on animals under my protection?"

Deglan refused to be intimidated. "Are they? Because it looks as if you have failed in your duties. These beasts are ill."

"Some natural culling is needed for the good of the herd," the glaistig answered, defiance lifting her chin.

"Toad shit!" Deglan scoffed. "The gruagach have driven you away. Why do you protect them?"

He watched anger flare in the glaistig's face, anger mated with fear.

"I protect myself, gnome!"

Deglan chose to soften his approach. "Why did you not come to me? Surely you must have seen me, another Fae aiding the people here."

"You aid the coburn," the glaistig accused. "It is their interests you serve."

"My lady," Sir Corc said, taking a step forward. "The Knights of the Valiant Spur wish for the prosperity of the Dal Riata. Long has it been so."

"You held them off," Deglan jumped in, not wanting to give the glaistig time to dispute the knight's statement. Sir Corc had not been here over the past year and seen the extent of the rift the gruagach had driven between the Order and the clansmen. "The cattle only recently took sick. What has changed?"

The glaistig did not readily answer. Her eyes left Deglan, looking beyond him into the night, towards the village.

"The gruagach left me be," she replied, her gaze returning.

"When they first arrived. They told me they had dealings with the coburn, but the Dal Riata would not be touched. They lied. They began murdering the humans . . . their children, using them to gain access to the castle. I stood against them, but more arrived. Too many now to fight."

"How many?" Deglan asked, fearing the answer. "How many now live as clansmen?"

The glaistig looked from him to Sir Corc and back again.

"Thirty," she told them at last. "More are coming."

"Buggery and spit," Deglan exhaled.

It was more than even he feared. The five they killed tonight were meaningless. They could not take Crane into Glengabráin. More than that, the gruagach had

Pocket's scent, they were not giving up the hunt now. If the glaistig was right, they would soon have the strength to challenge the Roost.

"My lady," Sir Corc said again. "Do you know the faces these gruagach now wear?"

The glaistig eyed him for a moment, then nodded.

Sir Corc went to one knee before her. "You need not trust my Order, you need only trust me. If you help me unmask these gruagach, I swear I will do all within my power to see that they do no more harm to the Dal Riata. Come with me to the castle and I will marshal the Valiant Spur to this cause. What say you?"

The glaistig fixed the knight with her bright eyes, evaluating him. "Agreed."

"Then it shall be done," Sir Corc promised, rising. "My friends must journey far from here. Can you procure an ox and wain to aid them? You have my oath, the family will be well compensated for its loss."

"Wait here," the glaistig said and slipped back into the woods without a sound.

Deglan turned to Sir Corc, dropping his voice. "Is this wise? Removing yourself from the Roost may be the best way to deter an attack now."

"I agree," Bantam Flyn said from behind them.

Deglan looked to the young knight and saw that he still stood next to the cow, arm firmly around its neck. He let loose a snort of laughter.

"Who is in love now?"

Flyn glanced down at the cow, then chuckled himself, releasing his hold. The animal took several quick, skipping steps away, then continued its retreat back towards the pasture at a more leisurely pace.

"Corc, I agree," Flyn repeated, coming to stand with them.

"Best we all get far from here."

"I cannot continue to ignore this threat," Sir Corc told them. "If it means open war, so be it. Too long have these killers been allowed to skulk about unchallenged."

"You can kill rats in a barn as you find them," Deglan offered, "but you will never know how many hide underneath the straw." While Corc considered this, Deglan went to check on Crane.

The liss-more was taking effect. The man's breathing was more even, his face less pained, but Deglan was far from satisfied.

He had bought a little time, maybe eased some of the internal bleeding, but the chronicler's survival was not certain. He hoped the glaistig did return with a wain. An ox was slow, but Deglan did not fancy trying to haul the man about on a makeshift litter over the highlands. He remained kneeling next to Crane, glancing up to find the knight still deep in thought. Flyn stood close by, scanning the darkness. Eventually, Sir Corc came to stand over Deglan, motioning the younger knight over.

"The Roost is not yet overrun," he said. "There is still strength enough within the Order to fight. The Knights Errant are returned, we may never have a better chance."

"And what of Flyn's words?" Deglan asked. "About where you are most needed?"

This gave the knight further pause. He was clearly torn between oaths. The first, the same Flyn had sworn not an hour ago, but for Corc it was decades old and long adhered. The other was newer, more personal and once melded seamlessly with the demands of knighthood. No longer. The old bird was at a crossroads. Deglan knew such a plight well, but he suspected the knight had chosen his path.

"I intend to return where I am needed," he said slowly.

"After." Deglan saw Flyn tense, his head darting over to look hard at the older knight.

"But," he barely whispered, "Pocket?"

Corc put a reassuring hand on Flyn's shoulder.

"The gruagach wish me dead and in that they may succeed, but my life is all they will get from me. In victory or in defeat, Pocket will be safe. A more formidable guardian than me watches over him and will continue to protect him once I am gone. He is not where he is by chance."

This should not have surprised Deglan. Sir Corc the Crafty, he should be named, though the knight would appreciate it no more than any other title. He was a great warrior, but along with skill at arms he possessed foresight, patience and a good head for strategy. Deglan had lived on that little island for several months and never saw any sign of the protection to which Corc now alluded, but he did not doubt it was there. It would be no damn good if it were obvious. He wondered if even Pocket was aware of its existence. Deglan was impressed. If Corc had been alive during the Rebellion, he would have been a great asset. In that war or any other.

A creaking sound drifted towards them out of the dark. It did not come from the wood, but from the stretch of field between them and the village. They all turned and saw the slow progress of an ox outlined in the moonlight. The glaistig walked beside, the beast following her without the use of lead or switch. Tethered to the shaggy animal was a two-wheeled haywain, its deep bed empty.

"I have cured this one of the skin-changer's malady," the glaistig said, stroking the ox's wide head. "He will go as directed without the need for much prodding. Treat him well."

"You have my word," Deglan told her.

Flyn and Corc loaded Crane, litter and all, into the bed of the wain.

"There are few settlements between here and Caer Caled," Sir Corc told the younger knight. "Once you leave the lands of the Dal Riata, be wary. The Mounds are inhabited by none but the Painted Men. They are unpredictable."

Bantam Flyn accepted the advice with a nod.

"Here," he said, shrugging out of his harness and holding his greatsword towards Sir Corc. "Trade swords with me. Coalspur should serve the causes of the Valiant Spur."

"It will be," Sir Corc said, pushing the weapon gently back.

"I wish you success in errantry, Sir Flyn."

"Luck in battle, Sir Corc," Flyn replied. He lingered a moment, then jumped up onto the driver's bench of the wain and took up the reins. Deglan crawled up into the bed next to Crane and hunkered down. Sir Corc walked around to the back of the wain.

"Fare thee well, Master Loamtoes," he said.

"Until our next meeting, good knight," Deglan replied.

Flyn gave a click at the ox and the wain began to trundle forward, jostling Deglan a little until he settled into the rhythm. He watched behind as the figures of the glaistig and the coburn grew steadily distant. Before they were lost from sight, Deglan raised a hand in parting and he saw Sir Corc return the salute.

"Do not worry, Bantam Flyn," Deglan tossed his words towards the front of the wain without turning. "Corc will not be brought down by some sorry rabble of skin-changers."

There was silence for a long time, then Flyn's voiced drifted over the creak of the wheels.

"How can you be sure, Staunch?"

Deglan smiled to himself in the dark.

"A soldier's intuition."

EIGHT

The hare perked up its ears, body going stiff with sudden alarm. Flyn rose, arm cocked back. His target bolted, long legs propelling it in unpredictable directions across the scrub and over the stones. Flyn threw the rock anyway, missing the retreating hare by miles. He laughed into the wind and slumped down to sit on the quivering grass.

"Bantam Flyn," he said, shaking his head with amusement and watching his would-be prey disappear among the hills. "You are no hunter."

He always fancied himself skilled with a throw. Many a restless night had he spent in the squires' barracks flinging knives into makeshift targets, drawing jeers or cheers from his fellows with each successful toss. Of course, grain sacks hung from the ceiling did not hear, see and smell you coming, then take to heel in panicked, dodging hops that made mockery of the surest aim. A rock was a poor missile, but Flyn knew he would have fared no better with the finest bow. He was outmatched.

"The contest is yours my long-eared friend."

Standing, Flyn gave the now-hidden hare a salute and turned to make his way back across the rolling terrain. Four days out from the Roost and they were still in the foothills of the Mounds, the ground alongside the track they followed rising steadily upon either side with every ponderous mile. The highlands of Albain were an inconsistent marriage of grass-clad glens, rocky tumbles and boulder-choked gullies. Stands of trees huddled sporadically in the hilly expanse, which Deglan had informed him were alder, birch and rowan.

Flyn enjoyed goading the old gnome, pretending not to listen during his tutelary rants, but in truth the herbalist's knowledge had served their bellies well. He constantly pointed out edible plants as they traveled and while Flyn could not recall every one of them over the last several days, he had become adept at spotting gorse, often handing the reins over to Deglan while he jumped down from the wain to gather the yellow blooms. Crow-berries were more scarce, but Flyn made a point to keep his eye out for them, more for the challenge than the sustenance. Due to the daily spring rains and numerous highland streams, water was plentiful and they were far from starving, but Flyn could feel the meager meals taking their toll.

It was the height of spring and game was afoot, but their need to stay on the move made trapping impossible. Flyn spent the early morning scouting ahead and hunting when the opportunity presented, but thus far his efforts had brought nothing to the cook fire. There were deer and wild goats that ranged the foothills and often Flyn saw them in the distance, but without bow or spear it would be a waste to pursue them. Still, his morning forays gave him something to do while Deglan tended to Inkstain and the ox, both better fed than their caretakers.

Returning to camp, he found Deglan carefully pouring watered-down honey into the chronicler's mouth. Flyn had wondered why the herbalist had wanted him to gather a pot of the stuff from his infirmary. He discovered the reason their first morning out. The sticky mixture was the man's only means of nourishment so long as he remained senseless. Deglan had thought of everything.

Flyn had stood guard the better part of that first day, while Deglan worked, grinding herbs and mixing potions. He made a plaster from wood anemone and other ingredients Flyn could not name, using it to cover Inkstain's broken arm. At one point, the gnome's face grew grim and he quickly drew a small, sharp blade.

With a practiced, steady hand he made a small incision in Inkstain's side so that he could insert a hollow, bronze tube. There had come a hiss of rushing air and Inkstain took a deep, shuddering breath in his sleep. After that, Flyn had refrained from watching, finding his stomach stayed calmer if the mysteries of healing remained mysteries.

Three days later, the chronicler had not regained consciousness. Deglan told Flyn he had done all he could; it was up to Crane now. They had settled into a routine, their days spent traveling, foraging and seeing to Inkstain's comfort.

"Sneaking some of that honey while I am away?" Flyn asked Deglan as he approached.

"Herbs are good for healing," Deglan replied casually, not taking his attention from feeding Crane. "They are also good for seasoning roast chicken."

Flyn laughed. They were not fresh taunts. He knew Deglan would never do anything to endanger the health of one under his care, no matter how hungry he was himself. It was all part of the routine. Flyn untethered the ox from a nearby tree and began yoking him to the wain.

He used to think about what life would be like as a Knight Errant. For years an image would form in his mind, unchanging.

He, Sir Flyn the Jocular or Flyn Quickblade or the Laughing Cock, striding alone down a forested path in unknown lands, sword and armor his only possessions, seeking his next adventure. Bloody foolish notion. Daydreams do not provide for the necessities of the road; the beans that need boiling, the latrine that needs digging, the pack animal that needs tending. Such things did not fit well in tales and tapestries, where a hero needs nothing but shining steel and an honorable cause.

The disillusion was not fresh for Flyn. Sir Corc had taught him much, not least of which was a good mule was just as important to a knight as a sharp sword. Flyn found himself wishing Backbone were with them, but Corc's doughty beast was enjoying a life of ease on the island with Pocket, who would not be parted from him.

"You will have to do," Flyn told the ox, tousling the shaggy hair between its horns. He had refrained from naming the animal, knowing that they would have to give him up once they took ship at Caer Caled, where they would likely trade him for passage. Of course, they would have to reach the port first.

At the end of the sixth day the track led them close to a small loch resting at the feet of the Mounds. The peaks rose all around, dominating the sky, conquering the horizon. Just beyond the loch gaped the mouth of a corrie, admitting the track they traveled into a shadowy pass between the mountains. They camped near the banks, using the entirety of the next day to rest the ox and attempt some fishing. Deglan gave over some of the gut string he used for sutures and Flyn fashioned a hook out of one of the herbalist's heavy needles. It was tedious business, but by dusk Flyn had caught a sizable charr. Deglan collected some herbs from the surrounds to season the catch and they shared it over their nightly fire. It grew quite cool after the sun fled, despite the warmth of the season, and they lay Inkstain near the flames as they ate.

"Do you think he will wake?" Flyn asked, knowing Deglan was sick of the question.

"He better," the herbalist replied, sucking on a fish bone.

"This is a long damn way to travel simply for a funeral."

Flyn let it rest for another night. The cranky stoat liked to appear callous, but since their journey began Flyn had seen him checking on the chronicler through the long nights, hardly sleeping himself. He wondered what the gnome would do once Inkstain no longer needed him. Whether the man lived or died would soon be decided, but either outcome saw the end of Deglan's concern.

Would he return to the Roost? He left eagerly enough, with no care for what the Order would think of his sudden desertion. It was a question Flyn did not voice. He knew the only answer he would receive was a bitter tongue-lashing. Besides, the old mushroom was most content when miserable.

The next morning they entered the mountain pass.

As slow as the wain had traveled on the track, this was worse. Flyn spent as much time clearing boulders from their way as he did on the driver's bench. The ox was strong and labored tirelessly against the steadily increasing slopes, but by midday Flyn had abandoned riding in the wain entirely, both to lighten the load and to help push the wheels over the worst of the boulders.

At last they came to a saddle gap and Flyn marveled at how high they had climbed. The pass through the range went on ahead, but to either side the slopes gave way to a splendid view of the surrounding countryside. To the north, a vast loch spread out in a deep valley and the view south awarded dense forest. Such landmarks could be used to help determine their location, but without a map it was pointless guesswork.

They did not linger long in the saddle, for the wind tore savagely through the gap and the day still held hours of light. The pass became more level after the saddle as it ran the length of a wooded ridge and Flyn was able to ride in the wain once more. The trees gave way to thick scrub after a mile or two and soon the pass became flanked by irregular cliff face.

It was not long before Flyn spotted the first of the watchers, though they made no attempt to hide themselves.

Perched on the cliffs above, they were little more than silhouettes. They seemed taller than the Dal Riata, though no less muscled. Even from a distance their lack of clothing was obvious, but some did appear to be wearing helms. He saw spears in their hands along with axes and the occasional sword. One stood with a pair of dogs and two had falcons perched on their wrists. None moved, but simply stayed fixed to their vantages until the wain passed from sight. Flyn said nothing at first, but after the tenth sighting he tossed a warning over his shoulder into the bed.

"Deglan."

"I see them," the gnome's voice uttered from behind.

"Painted Men," Flyn declared casting a reassuring look at Coalspur resting on the bench next to him.

"The Pritani, aye," Deglan agreed. "Have not laid eyes on one in a long, long time. Was hoping they had gone and gotten themselves extinct."

"Old friends?"

"Old enemies."

Flyn kept the wain going at a steady pace, watching the path ahead, but threw continual glances upward, keeping a running count of the sentries. He was up to twenty when the wain passed away from the cliffs and entered a wooded bowl, blocking the sun and the view above. The trees pressed close to the trail, some of the boughs hanging so low Flyn had to duck his head to pass beneath.

"Fancy an ambush?" he asked no one in particular.

Flyn had his greatsword and one dagger, plus his spurs. His armor lay stored in the wain, the mail too encumbering for all the pushing and scrambling required over the course of the day.

Deglan had retained the steel hand axe from the tower, but that was all the arms they possessed. The Painted Men would not even need to catch them off guard if they chose to attack.

They traveled through the bowl, sharing no words. There was nothing for it, they had to keep moving. Time passed, slowed by tension, and with the trees hiding the sun, Flyn lost all sense of how long they had been in the bowl. The ground began to gradually shift uphill and the trees thinned. Passing from beneath the shadows of the branches, the wain emerged once more into the sun. A broad, towering cliff face hugged the track to their left, while a bank of loose stones dropped away to the right, ending in a sparse mountainside wood far below.

Flyn looked up for signs of the Painted Men, but the cliff was too high, too sheer, to house any but an eagle. He craned around and looked down into the bed. Deglan met his gaze, a sour twist to his mouth, the axe in his hand.

"Are we to be allowed to pass?" Flyn asked lightly.

Deglan did not answer, but scanned the cliffs above before turning his attention back to Crane.

They passed the remainder of the day unchallenged and unwatched. The sun began to set before they found a good place to make their camp and they were forced to prepare for an uncomfortable night on the track. The cliff face still dominated the left of the trail, but the drop to the right had leveled off somewhat, becoming a mass of crags. Flyn released the ox from the yoke, tethering it to a boulder. There was little fodder for the animal and they all went hungry. They built no fire and Deglan stayed in the bed of the wain with Inkstain. Flyn donned his mail and stood watch, keeping his dagger unsheathed and in hand. Coalspur he left in its scabbard, propped against the tail of the wain, never out of arm's reach.

The stars were veiled by clouds, and most of the moon eclipsed by the surrounding cliffs, but Flyn would have no trouble seeing any attackers. It was difficult for him to comprehend a human's night blindness. Anything giving off heat, he could see.

The ox, Deglan, Inkstain, all were visible to him as shifting phantoms of red and orange, almost as if they were made from dull flame. Unless they were colder than the surrounding air, he would see the Painted Men coming, likely before they saw him. Flyn hoped they knew as much about coburn and were discouraged from taking action.

"What sort of foes are these Pritani?" Flyn asked, knowing Deglan did not sleep.

"Not one to say," Deglan replied quietly. "Never fought them myself."

"You said they were old enemies."

"To the Fae," Deglan said. "Fought a war with them in the Age of Spring, long before I was born."

Flyn chuckled. "Hard to imagine you were ever born."

He expected a biting retort, but none came. There was silence for a long time. When Deglan spoke again, there was something in his voice Flyn had never heard before. Patience.

"We were all young once," the gnome said. "Me. The world itself. Earth and Stone! Even the elves were once freshly woken. We always talk about the humans as a younger race. In truth, they are just as old as the Fae. But life is so short for them, they seem to be forever starting over, learning and relearning what they have already been taught. They are constantly . . . new."

Flyn listened intently, but kept a watchful eye. He noticed Deglan did not refer to the coburn in such terms even though they were as mortal as man. Still, he did not dare interrupt.

"But slow as their progress is," Deglan went on, "humans do eventually change. All except the Pritani. You can look at them and see man as he was ten thousand years ago. They were one of the first tribes to come to Airlann. Savage and naked, they struck the shores of the Source Isle in their crude boats, raiding and killing. The Seelie Court was all powerful in those times, but war and violence were a rarity, something that was discussed as a curiosity, not practiced or prepared for. The Age of Spring was a time of art and music and prosperity. Not bloodshed. The elves could have turned their Magic on the Pritani, but they did not. You do not seek vengeance on a spirited horse that escapes its pen and causes destruction. Man was something to be domesticated, not punished.

"What they failed to see was the Pritani's unwillingness to be tamed. All attempts at peace failed. The elves wished to share their knowledge and elevate these men out of barbarity, but the Pritani were scornful of such aid. They discovered the Fae weakness to iron and learned the mystery of its forging, casting aside their bronze weapons. They made ink from iron, tattooing their flesh so that their entire bodies were wards against immortals. That is how they earned the name Painted Men. They came in droves to Airlann, bringing ugly death to the Isle. The peaceful Fae, for all their power, could not combat such insatiable hunger for blood."

"How did they emerge victorious?" Flyn asked.

"The fomori," Deglan said, a slight hitch entering his voice with the words. "They were a mortal race then, living among the shore cliffs. Battle suited them well and they quickly learned the craft of war. They repelled fresh invaders from making landfall, then marched inland, crushing the Pritani as they found them. The Painted Men were pushed off the island and the few that survived settled here in Albain, never again able to manifest the might to threaten the Fae.

"The fomori continued to guard Airlann's shores. The Fae had all but neglected the big, bestial race to that point, but the fomori were now their salvation and could no longer be ignored. The elves gifted them with immortality and they continued to serve the Seelie Court."

Flyn let the tale settle in his mind. He had never heard it before, but he was never one for history.

"Deglan," he said, as something occurred to him. "The coburn also helped the Seelie Court win a war. We were not granted immortality."

He heard the gnome grunt. Clearly, the thought had never crossed his mind.

"Different war. Different time," Deglan ventured. "The power of the elves was severely diminished after the Rebellion. The Goblin Kings ushered in the Age of Autumn when they supplanted Irial Elf-King and it long held sway before we retook the throne. Irial's daughter died fighting the Gaunt Prince, and the king succumbed to grief. The Restoration is generously named, Bantam Flyn. We never did regain what was lost. The Seelie Court has remained silent for centuries, the Fae have all but withdrawn from the world and man backslides into barbarity. Another few hundred years and we may witness all mankind once again resembling the Pritani."

"Well, you will witness it," Flyn pointed out.

"Perhaps," Deglan grumbled. "Not sure I want to."

"If it helps," Flyn said, reaching for his sword, "we may not survive the night."

A wash of red bodies was approaching. He counted about a dozen, appearing, disappearing and reappearing as they picked their way through the crags off the track.

"Buggery and shit," Deglan hissed. Gnomes saw well in the dark, their eyes enhancing what light was available. Likely he saw the movement in the rocks, but to Flyn the warm flesh of the humans shone. He motioned for Deglan to duck down, fearing the Painted Men would begin hurling spears. They were certainly close enough.

Flyn's mind raced. He was confident he could approach his enemies unseen, but remaining silent would be near impossible.

His steel spurs would sound on the rocks and even if he removed them, the clink of his mail might give him away. Armor was not something Flyn was willing to relinquish.

He spied one radiating form on the far left, well away from his companions. If Flyn could reach him unnoticed and dispatch him painfully, noisily, it might frighten the rest and send them running. It was not an honorable way to kill, but these Pritani courted such an end by sneaking up in the dark. It might work, but if the others were not spooked and rushed the wain, Deglan would be left exposed.

The romance of the lone Knight Errant dissolved, as Flyn wished he stood beside Sir Corc. Muckle Gutbuster would not be unwelcome either. Still, he was unafraid. He had fought against greater numbers many times. His fellow squires at the tourney, the Red Caps and the Unwound at Castle Gaunt, all had outnumbered him. These skulking savages would not succeed where greater foes failed. Nor would he play their cowardly, sneaking game. Let them come! He would best them and a dozen more.

But they did not come.

For hours Flyn watched them. They moved rarely, only shifting slightly as they too waited through the long night. Flyn lowered his sword and leaned upon the cross-guard, but he did not relinquish his vigil.

The Pritani moved off just before dawn, scrambling back across the crags and vanishing before the first light touched the rocks. Flyn was stiff and weary. He turned to Deglan, finding the gnome looking at him with red-rimmed eyes. Flyn made a halfhearted gesture at the still form of Inkstain.

"Scribbler will sleep through anything."

Deglan gave him a token grin, then winced as he stood up.

Flyn heard his joints pop.

They worked quickly to get the ox yoked and set off once more. Flyn kept his mail on as he drove, keeping an eye out for any threat. He was grateful when the cliff face finally receded and they once again ran the back of a ridge. The sky opened up on either side, a clear blue adorned with bright sun and pure clouds. Within hours, they descended into a lush valley. Grass and wildflowers covered the flat expanse for a goodly distance and Flyn let the ox come to a halt.

"We will rest here for a spell," he told Deglan as he hopped down from the bench. "Let this noble beast graze awhile."

A queer, ululating cry went up through the valley. Flyn snatched Coalspur from the driver's bench as figures began leaping up from the dense foliage at the edges of the valley.

"All sides!" he heard Deglan yell from the bed of the wain.

Flyn tore his greatsword from its sheath, discarding the harness as he ran around to the back of the wain. The gnome was right, the Pritani were rushing in from every direction, too many to count. Flyn put his back to the tail of the wain and braced himself.

He heard the ox give a wail of distress and the wain lurched forward as it tried to flee. There was nowhere to go. The Pritani closed in, surrounding them, staying half a spear's throw removed.

In the light of day, Flyn got his first true look at the Painted Men. What he thought were helms from a distance turned out to be hair, grown long, formed into wild shapes with lard and dyed with woad. Some wore hide breeches, but many were naked, the hair above their genitals styled and colored the same as that on their heads. They were long of limb and thick with muscle, screaming their war-cries through beards of yellow, green and blue.

Spears, axes and swords were brandished over their heads, each bladed in iron. The color of their skin was near impossible to tell as every man was covered in intricate tattoos, the swirling lines and bestial pictures detailed in black, blue and copper.

Flyn held Coalspur before him, gripped firmly in both hands. He kept his stance wide, ready to spring to either side to meet the direction of the inevitable charge. He allowed himself a smile.

This was a battle well suited. The valley offered the space needed to bring Coalspur to bear. The long reach and sharp steel would lay these unarmored brutes low, while Flyn's own mail would help protect him from their crude iron. He could unleash his full speed and strength, tear through their ranks with blade and spur, leaving dozens dead. It would be a glorious, bloody, pitched battle. The Pritani would be cut down by the score, learning what a coburn was capable of at the cost of their lives.

And still he would fall.

There were near a hundred Painted Men in Flyn's field of vision alone. Three times as many likely encircled the wain, more than he could hope to defeat. If he could close the distance he would make them pay, but if they stayed well removed and began raining spears upon him, the battle would be done.

Quiet settled over the valley. The Pritani had ceased their screaming. They lowered their weapons, readying them for the charge. Flyn watched as those before him hunched slightly, the muscles beneath their tattooed flesh coiling. The calm before the kill.

"Creule-hun!"

The strange words came from behind Flyn. He turned to see Deglan standing in the wain, his axe ready and a puzzled expression across his face. Inkstain stood behind the gnome on unsteady legs. He swayed alarmingly, his head flopping around on his neck as he tried to look up. Flyn shot a glance back at the Pritani and found all eyes focused on the reeling chronicler.

"Creule-hun!" Inkstain cried again, his unused voice hoarse and wavering. He waved his good, quivering hand at the Painted Men as he spoke, more strange words issuing haltingly from his pale lips. Flyn saw doubt creep into the faces of the men surrounding them and they began to take several paces backward.

Inkstain continued to call out to them in the strange tongue, his hand shooing feebly in front of him. The circle broke and the Pritani shuffled away, keeping their wide eyes fixed on the chronicler as they moved away.

Soon they were gone, leaving nothing in the valley but the wind.

"Flyn!" Deglan cried out. Inkstain was collapsing, the gnome struggling to keep him from falling.

Flyn leapt into the wain and took the man's weight, lowering him back down to the bed. Inkstain's face was wan, sweat shining on his skin. His eyes were again closed, but Flyn could see them rolling around beneath the fluttering lids. Deglan went to work, rummaging in his satchel while Flyn peeked over the sides of the wain.

The Painted Men were truly gone.

"By the Hallowed, Staunch," Flyn exclaimed. "What did he say?"

Deglan shot a frown up at him. "How would I know?"

"Well," Flyn shrugged, "you are *really* old."

A sound came from Inkstain's lips, barely discernible at first.

The chronicler's eyes remained closed, but his voice grew stronger.

"Creule-hun," he forced out. "Difficult . . . to translate. Jumping. Jumping . . . sickness."

"Jumping sickness?" Deglan said, his face scrunching.

"Plague? You told them you had a plague?"

Inkstain nodded weakly. Flyn smiled.

"He speaks Pritani," he said happily.

"Not, not Pritani," the chronicler said weakly. "Qrutani. They were, were Qrutani. Different dialect."

"Bugger a toad," Deglan whispered, his jaw slack.

Flyn laughed, giving Inkstain's leg a squeeze and Deglan's shoulder a slap as he clambered up onto the driver's bench. He gave the reins a gentle snap and the ox trudged forward. Flyn could hear Deglan working behind him, instructing Inkstain to swallow a few concoctions. After a mile, he could hold his tongue no longer.

"Six thousand year old doctor," he called back. "And you never thought to tell a bunch of barbarians he had the plague?"

Deglan's stream of curses lasted the next several miles.

NINE

Ingelbert's head still ached. It felt as if a leaden weight was pressed between his brain and his skull, grinding one to pulp and the other to dust. His eyes had trouble opening more than a squint for days, a pressure forcing them closed, causing a sickening roar in his ears. Often he would wake to the feeling of a great weight on his chest, compressing his breathing, but upon inspection found nothing. Nothing that could be seen. The problems lay beneath the skin, in his lungs and ribs. Master Loamtoes told him his hurts would take time to properly heal, but Ingelbert wondered if he would ever truly recover.

He had never been strong, envying other young men their comfort with physical labor. And yet he found it difficult at times to understand their inability to remember exact details or reason out quandaries he deemed simple. He knew from experience that not all burly men were dullards, but even the cleverest he had known seemed to struggle with mental challenges he found all too obvious. It did not take him long to perceive that it was no deficiency on their part, but a useful abnormality in him. He learned quickly, retained everything and could recall in an instant, traits that had served him well, making his lack of somatic prowess less a drawback. His present injuries, however, made him realize how capable, if not formidable, he had truly been. Walking under his own power, once so simple as to be inconsiderable, was now a feat Master Loamtoes used to measure his rehabilitation.

Ingelbert rose from his bed, unable to keep the wince from his face, but he managed to bite back the whimper. He tried to keep from waking Master Loamtoes whenever he needed to move about in the midst of the night, but the gnome always sensed his stirring and sat up in his own bed, ready should he be needed.

Ingelbert gave the herbalist a conciliatory wave of his plastered arm, keeping his blanket clutched closed under his neck with his good hand as he shuffled over to the table holding the basin and ewer.

The room of the fishwife's hut was mean, but Deglan had seen it was furnished with the needed comforts. Ingelbert filled a cup from the ewer and drained it in several long swallows. The water was warm and a touch brackish, flowing sluggishly down his throat, but Ingelbert had a thirst of late. Master Loamtoes dosed him with a surfeit of teas which eased his aches, but the craving for drink never abated.

He did not return to bed, finding the pressure in his chest more bearable while standing. The swollen wood of the door caught upon the stone lintel as he dragged it open. He was too weak to force it, but he managed enough of an opening to fit his slim frame through. Outside, the wind from the sea met his throbbing skull, increasing the pain for a moment before it was eclipsed by a light-headed numbness marginally less unpleasant.

Night near the port was a dreary presentation of sounds and smells, with little to see beneath a seaside moon. The air carried a fetid mixture of turf-smoke, rotten fish, salt and sour bodies. Everything was wet and unwashed.

Gipeswic.

Ingelbert witnessed little of the journey here. He had floated in and out of consciousness, initially due to his injuries and later because of Deglan's medicines. There were vague pieces of moments, little more than sensory echoes, that he could summon.

The rough jolting of the wain, the heat of countless campfires making him sweat, rough voices haggling with Bantam Flyn and the long, queasy passage on board a groaning ship. That memory was the most vivid, though beclouded with nausea and an impotent dread of a destination unknown. His last complete recollection was the scarred goblin and the horrifying fall. He had been at the Roost in Albain and now he was in Sasana, hundreds of miles away. It was a queer thing to have come so far with nothing but disjointed fragments to fill the gap in time. It was almost too ludicrous to fathom. And yet he found himself in Gipeswic, one of the largest port settlements on the eastern shore of Sasana, having had no choice in the matter.

Once they arrived, he remembered Master Loamtoes asking him where his kin resided, but Ingelbert had said nothing. His ability to speak was well returned, it was simply that there was no answer he could give. So he remained silent, allowing his infirmities to excuse him from any further questions.

Bantam Flyn had seen them lodged in the hut and stayed barely a day. From his sickbed, Ingelbert was dimly aware of the coburn leaving, exchanging a few words with Deglan outside the door. He heard something about Flyn's intention to journey upriver, but chose not to waste his limited ardor to discern further details. Near a week had passed and the coburn had not returned, though Ingelbert could read in Deglan's demeanor he was not expected. Wherever Flyn had gone, Ingelbert was well quit of him.

Him, the Valiant Spur, the Roost and all its denizens. It had not been his wish to abandon his posting, but since the choice had been made for him, he felt no small amount of relief. No more iron collars and armed escorts, no more constant fear and doubt.

Still, he would have preferred not to have ended up *here*.

The hut where they stayed was one of several that belonged to a widow who survived not just her husband, but her children as well, inheriting their property as each was eventually claimed by the sea. No doubt her usual tenants were drunken stevedores or dockside whores, looking to pass a night or two in relative comfort, but the hard-earned coin of such itinerant locals could not compare to the advantages of having a Fae healer take up lodging to ease the myriad aches and afflictions of her aging body. Deglan went daily to her own hut nearby to see to her complaints, always returning with a deluge of his own. The week spent in residence made them both ready for Ingelbert to be fit enough to take their leave. He knew the gnome had been making fruitless inquiries throughout Gipeswic concerning him.

Ingelbert shivered slightly in the damp dark, though the air was fairly warm. Somewhere in the jumble of fisherman's huts and sailors' flops, a baby began to wail in the night. Ingelbert smiled, knowing it was not a genuine response. He did not know what else to do. His injuries prevented him from fleeing down the greasy cobbles. It was an unexpected feeling, but that unseen infant, crying in the dark, seemed to Ingelbert to have the worst fate he could imagine. To be helpless in this sprawling sea-side settlement, new to life and its hardships, unable to alter a single facet of its existence, all direful thoughts. How fortunate that babes are denied memory, for without such designed ignorance, Ingelbert did not think a person born would reach maturity free of the grip of madness.

Abruptly, the crying stopped, but there was nothing sinister in the silence. Ingelbert did not know in which of the low, sodden dwellings the baby lay, but somewhere it was soothed. A tired mother, waking in the late watches to care for a child dependent and trusting of her surrounding compassion, a trust which she had not broken. Might she even be smiling? It was difficult to imagine anything but bitterness in this harsh place, but somehow Ingelbert sensed the tenderness in the sudden absence of that distinct, needful sound. The breadth of varied human experience in a shared environment, separated only by a paltry amount of years, was fascinating.

Ingelbert heard the door scrape open behind him. He could smell the tea before Deglan handed it up to him. He took a cautious sip from the steaming cup, allowing the fragrant vapor and infused liquid to work on his head. Ingelbert looked down to see Deglan standing beside him, staring out with a frown across the muddy lane where rats plied the refuse piles behind a sagging storehouse.

"Place is a bloody spawning pool for disease," the healer grumbled, his lips crinkled with disgust.

Ingelbert blew on the contents of his cup and hummed his agreement.

"A week more," Deglan continued. "Maybe two and you should be hale enough to travel. Go where you will. That," the gnome cocked an eye at Ingelbert's plaster-encased arm. "That will take a while longer."

"If you, um," Ingelbert said. "If you give me proper instructions. I am sure I can, I can remove it myself."

Deglan nodded slowly, returning his scrutiny to the shadowy lane. "You are a smart lad, Ingelbert Crane. That was clear at the Roost."

Ingelbert wondered about the truth of the gnome's statement. They had served the same Order for over a year and this was as many words as they had ever shared. Ingelbert had never needed the herbalist's care and Deglan never needed anything from anyone.

"Smart lad," Deglan repeated almost to himself, then he looked up at Ingelbert with a calculating look. "Too smart to come from this stinking harbor. You know your letters, history and I cannot figure how many damn tongues. Even the sharpest fish-counting clerk in Gipeswic does not possess a quarter of your brain. And I know! I have talked to all of them. No one here knows you, Master Crane."

"No," Ingelbert said. "No, they would not."

He heard the gnome issue a snort. "Confounded Flyn."

Ingelbert let that go unanswered for a long time. He did not consider himself a spiteful man, but he found it satisfactory at times to allow the sentiments of the more visceral to speak for him.

The impetuous coburn had, in an alarmingly brief acquaintance, drastically affected his life. Living in the Roost had been a treacherous path since the first day Ingelbert stepped through the gate. He knew Flyn was not to blame for the danger, but prior to the arresting rascal's involvement, it was a danger he had learned to manage. Now, he was purposeless and that caused a certain amount of resentment. He was content to ride in the wake of Deglan's ill-humor for a moment.

Still, it was unjust to allow the gnome to continue to work tirelessly on his behalf without answers. Ingelbert realized the herbalist must have come on this unexpected journey to save him and for that he was grateful. Bantam Flyn had only brought them here because of Ingelbert's own words. If he was misguided, then Ingelbert could only blame himself.

"Do you, do you know what a Gautland cabbage is, Master Loamtoes?"

The gnome looked up at him with an impatient grimace.

"Raiders from Middangeard often, often plunder these shores," Ingelbert went on. "Gipeswic has, has fallen prey to them many times. They have even held it a time, that is, a time or two. But a Sasanan warlord always takes it back . . . eventually. Mostly, the fjordmen come, pillage and, and leave. They take. They take riches, they take lives, those they do not kill they take as thralls. The, the Gautland cabbage is the only crop they sow. It is what the locals call the children born after a raid."

Ingelbert did not look down at the gnome to see what impact, if any, his words had. Deglan was obviously well seasoned in the ways of the world, it was likely he knew the tragic details of a Middangeard raid or was at least wise enough to glean them.

Ingelbert did not want to see pity on his face, nor could he bear to see apathy. It was simpler, safer just to look out in the dingy streets while he related his own besmirched beginnings.

"I was born here. I do not, do not know if my mother saw herself as, as fortunate or deeply cursed. The dead could be mourned, the taken missed or, or even forgotten, but those like her had a living reminder of the . . . the stain of Middangeard. She was alive and, and free, but was forced to care for a, a, a raper's get. Forgive me such base words, Master Loamtoes, but I cannot waste eloquence on such ugly deeds."

He paused. Spoken words were never his strongest ally and here he was referring to his own eloquence. It was needless pride.

Deglan was a trained and learned being. Ingelbert was attempting to justify his unseemly origins to this skilled healer with displays of intellect. His quick mind would not allow him to conceal even his own vanities.

Enough, then. Let the truth speak unmasked by feigned rhetoric.

"I can still, I can still see her . . . her face, though I was no more than three when she died. Certainly, I would have followed ere long, if not for the kindness of a great man. He had come through Gipeswic many times and I was not the first Gautland cabbage he harvested. His name was Parlan Sloane and he took me to his, to his sanctuary, the Orphanage of the Dried Tear."

Ingelbert tossed any fear of judgment aside and looked down at Deglan. The gnome's face was grim, but there was confusion also, still forming along his sun-browned face. Ingelbert surmised it was his last words that caused the perplexity.

"You, you know of the Dried Tear?" he asked.

"I know it," Deglan affirmed. "It was founded by the Fae, but I thought it destroyed."

"Ah yes, it was, yes," Ingelbert said. "And rebuilt a century ago. It is an ancient place and there I was, um, educated. Through kindness and learning the lost can find themselves. Those were, those were Parlan's words. Twelve years I stayed, learning all I could, but those who find refuge at the Dried Tear may only do so until adulthood.

"At fifteen, I left and found a place as, as a bee-keeper's apprentice not a dozen leagues from the orphanage. Nearly ten years later, I saw Parlan Sloane again. He traveled through the hamlet where I lived, returning from another long search for lost children. A coburn journeyed with him, a Knight Errant of the Valiant Spur called Sir Pikard the Lucky. They told me news of the Tin Isles, of the Red Cap uprising in Airlann and Sir Pikard expressed the Order's need for able minds. Of course, nothing was said of the gruagach incursion.

"I, I had no intention of going, but before departing Parlan Sloane drew me aside. He repeated his old words to me. 'Through kindness and learning the lost can find themselves.' But then he said, 'I have shown you kindness and you have learned more than any under my tutelage, but you will never find yourself so long as you continue to hide.' There was . . . there was disappointment on his face. The next day, I began my journey to the Roost."

Ingelbert felt a sudden anger well up and he tossed the remainder of the tea out of the cup to splatter on the wet cobbles.

It was a useless and petulant act, done before he could stop himself.

He felt weak, sick and pained, his ample memory unable to conjure a time when he did not feel so.

"You blame Flyn," Deglan said. It was not a question.

Ingelbert felt his throat constrict, an uncontrollable quivering taking hold of his chin. He often wished he possessed the ability to forget.

"He accosted me," Ingelbert managed. "Threatened to, to, to burn the annals. Took me to that tower. Put me in the path of that, of that burned goblin. Brought me here. Here!" He kept the tears from coming, another foolish feat of pointless pride. A burning question came to the surface, one he had convinced himself held no import. "Where has he gone?"

"Inland," Deglan answered, waving a hand vaguely. "To hunt a wyvern, he said."

Ingelbert's perception was not dulled by his self-pity. "You do not believe him."

The gnome brushed at his muttonchops with his knuckles and shook his head, lips down-turned with consideration. "He seeks to lead the life of a Knight Errant, though the Valiant Spur will never recognize him as one of their own. Not now."

"You think I should be grateful to him?"

"He did save you from that fall," Deglan said, looking up at him with an appraising frown. "But to your mind, he put you in the position that led to it. You may be right. Damned if I can answer that, but here is what I do know. He did not abandon his knighthood for you."

"The boy," Ingelbert said. "Pocket."

Deglan nodded firmly. "Flyn. Corc. Buggery and shit, even me! We are willing to give our lives to protect him. You too now know he is alive. But it is not ours to decide if you should surrender your life for this cause. That is your choice to make. Flyn understood that. He took you away, so that if you survived, you could make that sacrifice or not. Many would have let you die, Master Crane. It would surely have been simpler."

"Who is he?" Ingelbert asked. "Pocket. Who is he?"

The gnome seemed to wrestle with the question for a moment, his eyes leaving Ingelbert's to search the surrounding darkness. Eventually, he looked back.

"The Dried Tear," Deglan said. "You know your history. When was it destroyed?"

"One hundred and twenty-two years ago," Ingelbert answered immediately.

"By whom?"

"Festus Lambkiller. Lord of the gruagach."

"You say it has been rebuilt," Deglan said. "Tell me, were any gurgs among the orphans while you resided there?"

Ingelbert shook his head, certain Deglan already knew the answer.

"When Lambkiller burned the Dried Tear to the ground," the gnome said pointedly, "he caused the deaths of dozens of orphans, humans and gurgs alike. For centuries his people have slunk about, duping humans into their arms and creating these poor, stunted half-breeds. Gurgs have been around since man and Fae first made contact and up until recently, the gruagach seemed as content to abandon them as humans. But within the last ten years, Lambkiller, who once killed gurgs without a thought, is bent on finding every last one and returning them to the gruagach fold."

"They are important to him," Ingelbert surmised. "Or one of them is."

Deglan pointed a finger up at him. "One of them is."

"You think it is Pocket he seeks."

"We damn well know it is!" Deglan barked at him in a whisper, then he took a deep breath and the sudden frustration left his face. "He is just like you, Master Crane. An orphan who will never know who his father was, only that he was an evil fuck who cruelly used a woman. You inherited your height and flaxen head from your Middangeard father. Pocket received the limited abilities of a changeling from his. But unlike other gurgs, his human half gave him gifts as well. His mother was a descendant of the Goblin Kings, possibly the last of Jerrod's bloodline. That is what Lambkiller wants! That is why Pocket is hunted! And that is why we can never allow the gruagach to find him!"

Ingelbert absorbed all the gnome said. It was truly fascinating and explained much of what he had not already reasoned out. He still had a few minor questions, but refrained from asking them, knowing the herbalist was in no mood for further inquiry. Deglan turned to go back into the hut, taking the empty cup from Ingelbert's hand. At the door he paused.

"One more thing," the gnome said. "You can carry anger towards Bantam Flyn, or me, or whoever you like. We made the choice to save you and spirited you away. Now you know why. What you do from here is your choice. The Roost was a dangerous place and you are to be commended for serving there. But make no mistake, Ingelbert Crane, just because it held more threat than tending bees, you were still hiding."

After Deglan went back inside, Ingelbert remained without for a long while, contemplating the healer's words and his own mind. He was relieved to be away from the Roost and he was angry for being removed as well. Was there sense in the retention of such disparate passions? He wondered if an answer held any importance.

He was away, whatever the cause or justification, and in need of new purpose. Entering the service of the Valiant Spur was a means of dispelling Parlan Sloane's disapproval of his sequestered existence. Now Master Loamtoes, who held equal wisdom, deemed he had accomplished little to that end. Ingelbert knew well his shortcomings, but he was not arrogant enough to dismiss the gnome's assessment without consideration. Such contemplation would have to wait, however, for his body grew tired, requiring the tedious business of slumber.

Deglan was away from the hut when Ingelbert woke the next morning. His appetite was returning and he broke his fast on black bread with butter and weak ale. There was salt pork and herring on the board as well, but Ingelbert left them untouched.

While he ate, his eyes fell upon the satchel he had taken from the library. It had lain nearly forgotten in the corner of the hut while he recuperated. Stuffed within were all the documents that Flyn had made him hastily gather from the records.

Opening the flap, Ingelbert was surprised to find them intact, certain Flyn would have condemned them to the fire by now.

He was even more surprised to find the great, green leather-bound tome within the satchel. It was the volume of lists he had been translating and had nothing to do with Pocket or Sir Corc.

Ingelbert did not remember putting it in the satchel. Seeing the thick book sent a stirring through him, rejuvenating him more than any of Deglan's teas.

He got dressed as quickly as he was able in breeches, boots, tunic and jerkin, then slung the satchel over his shoulder. It was quite heavy and his ribs ached at the weight. He briefly considered removing all but the green tome, then thought better of it. Deglan had said it was his choice to help protect Pocket or not. Ingelbert was uncertain how he could do that, but leaving these records lying about was not wise. And they still belonged to the annals of the Valiant Spur. He may no longer serve as chronicler to the Order, but the documents were still his charge and he would not abandon them. Deglan had acquired a stout walking stick for Ingelbert in preparation for his returned perambulation. It stood propped next to the door and Ingelbert took it up in his good hand before heading out.

Gipeswic by day was a teeming hive of wet labor. The town was built on the estuary of the River Orr and centered on the docks. Construction and expansion of the quay was constant, with embankments and revetments raised to accommodate the need for sufficient moorings. Ramparts had also been built around the quay to deter Middangeard raids, but Ingelbert doubted Gipeswic had suffered its last sacking. He made his way along a slick lane parallel to the waterfront, which was alive with haggling merchants, scurrying urchins and mud-covered laborers working on the ever-expanding earthworks. Stevedores loaded and unloaded the numerous moored ships, while sailors prepared their vessels for port or a return to sea.

Ingelbert avoided the press of bodies, not trusting his weakened state to stand up against such a jostling. He skirted the docks for quite a ways before putting his back to them, striking more to the north. His childhood memory of the town gave him few solid recollections, but he knew where to find the river. When he was young, the crossing was merely a ford, but in the years since his departure, Gipeswic had constructed a solid bridge of stone, linking the banks of the Orr and allowing passage just upriver from the estuary. He made his way through the cattle market and then was forced to go around a boisterous rabble of drunken knaves betting on the dog fights.

His shoulders ached and his ribs were sore by the time he reached the outskirts of the northern edge of Gipeswic. Here the land began to rise, spreading away from the town in verdant downs to the horizon. This was the land used by the townspeople to bury their dead. Somewhere among the grass-covered barrows his mother lay in the earth. Ingelbert let the wind cool the sweat on his skin and surveyed the seemingly endless green humps, knowing not even his limpid view of past days could steer him to her resting place. Planting his walking stick firmly ahead, he set off across the downs. He had no destination in mind, merely seeking any quiet, secluded place he could rest with his book. The sky held few clouds and the sun covered the fields. Ingelbert grew hot from exertion and an irksome itching began to grow under the plaster encasing his right arm.

It occurred to him that Deglan would not know where he had gone and it may very well appear that he had fled entirely. It was not something Ingelbert had considered before leaving, the sudden impulse to escape the confines of the hut allowing little forethought. He did not know what the herbalist planned to do once his services were no longer needed. It may be he intended to return to the Roost or his homeland in Airlann. Deglan would certainly not remain in Gipeswic, and without him Ingelbert would have no lodging. He very much doubted the fish-wife had much use for a scribe or a beekeeper. Nothing for it, Ingelbert put such thoughts out of his mind.

By mid-morning, he found a tiny copse that afforded good shade and a sweeping view of a shallow dale containing an expanse of flat heath. Ingelbert slung the satchel off and eased himself down among the roots of an old oak, resting his back against the broad trunk. Wishing he had remembered to bring a skin of water and maybe one of the fresh pears Deglan kept in the hut, Ingelbert looked out across the field, feeling the quivering in his legs begin to subside.

After a time he opened the satchel and removed the green tome, his plastered arm making the task more difficult than expected. He opened it to a random page, marveling at the columns of strange runic script, so like the languages of Middangeard and yet indiscernible at first inspection. Thankfully, his own sheaf of parchment containing the translations of the two dozen or so words he had coaxed from the runes still lay nestled in the book. Oddly, the tome appeared to be nothing but a continuous list. There were no full passages or even sentences. It was a prodigious catalogue without any system of organization that Ingelbert could perceive. Initially, he had tried to translate the words in order, hoping to find some basic alphabetic structure, but after the first ten words he found nothing connecting the register.

Leech.

Coal.

Beans.

Tar.

Fletching.

And on and on. Every deciphered word as random as it was innocuous. The task was made even more difficult by the apparent lack of a set character meaning. The order of the runes was complex and yet subtle, the translation of one word giving little insight into linguistic rules that might govern the entire symbol structure. He had to wrestle every meaning one by one, pulling on every strand of language he knew until a definition began to form.

The long hours he spent on one rune often made the script appear to swim on the page, his eyes watering from concentration. But then, as wax in a mold, the word would set and always Ingelbert felt an absolute certainty in the accuracy of his translation, as if the meaning should have been obvious from the start.

Eventually, he abandoned all attempts at order and made a game of opening the book to any page and working on the first entry that struck his fancy. He would never complete the project, even with a lifetime of effort, not unless he could uncover some reliable key. Still, it was a distraction and a puzzle, one which he never grew weary of trying to solve. There was a solace he found within the pages of the mysterious book and a calm triumph whenever he dug out new understanding from the runes.

He had no quill, nor ink and therefore no method to record anything he translated, but that did not concern him overmuch. In his weakened condition, Ingelbert doubted he would manage to make any progress. Nevertheless, he peered at the open pages, propping the weighty volume up with his thighs. He did better than he anticipated, chiseling the word for boar out of the archaic mess just before the sun reached its apex.

The horsemen entered the field while he was trying to decide whether to head back to Gipeswic or attempt another word.

There were three of them, all on fine steeds and bearing falcons on their wrists. They reined up less than a furlong from where Ingelbert sat, but took no notice of him. They did not dismount, but appeared to be waiting, talking among themselves while occasionally tossing looks back from the direction they came. Soon, a group of six men on foot caught up with the riders, coming into the field at a hurried pace despite the bundles they each carried.

The majority of the baggage looked to be wicker cages. The riders at last dismounted as three of the servants took hold of their horses. The remaining men stayed by the stacked cages, each reaching inside one to remove what proved to be rabbits.

Laughter drifted across the heath as the falconers jested with one another, one removing the hood from his bird. He gave a signal and one of the servants released his rabbit, the animal quickly darting across the open field. With an almost lazy motion of his arm, the first man released his falcon and the bird launched itself into the air, pursuing the fleeing rabbit with rapid and single-minded purpose. The falcon swooped low, its talons lowering and opening, before snatching at the ground. It pulled up and away, revealing the struggling rabbit caught in its talons.

Ingelbert returned his attention to his book.

Hunting held no interest for him. The men were clearly of wealthy, landowning stock, likely the sons of huscarls of some thegn that kept a manor nearby. Many powerful men dubbed themselves kings in Sasana, each wishing to expand his already vast holdings, but in truth no individual could claim rule over the land entire. This close to Gipeswic, it was Eorl Wehha who laid claim to a crown and his thegns were pledged to defend the town, but had they ridden to aid the port with any measure of swiftness during the last raid, Ingelbert would never have been born. The power of the gentry was never much use as far as he was concerned and it was an aspect of life he had not missed during his time in Albain.

A cry of anger pulled Ingelbert back to the men in the field.

The third falconer had missed his rabbit and was cursing as his fellows shared a chuckle at his expense. The bird was returning, its flight slow and silent as it made a wide turn. It was then Ingelbert noticed it was not a falcon at all, but the largest owl he had ever seen. Even from a distance Ingelbert estimated the wingspan nearly matched his own height. The owl returned dutifully to its fuming master, landing on his outstretched arm. Ingelbert had seen many a hunter use falcons, peregrine, goshawks, but never an owl.

He watched four more rounds and the two falcons only missed once between them, whereas the owl failed to catch a single rabbit, much to the increasing fury of his handler.

"Releasing too soon," Ingelbert muttered to himself, seeing the problem.

Looking back down at his book, Ingelbert plucked his notes from between the pages so he could record the translation of boar, then remembered he had nothing to write with. Trusting to his memory he placed his notes over the proper page and went to close the book when his eyes fell upon one of his earliest translations.

Owl.

He looked over the word for a moment, then glanced back out to where the falconers stood.

"Huukayat," Ingelbert said with a small smile as he looked at the owl on the man's wrist.

The massive wings unfolded and the hunter gave a shout as the bird took off. It settled into a low glide, silently speeding over the grass. It took Ingelbert a moment to realize it was heading directly for him. He barely gained his feet, spilling the great tome to ground. The owl swooped in under the canopy of the oak and Ingelbert's view was dominated by its unfurled wings, orange eyes and large talons. He threw up his arm to defend himself, feeling the air against his flesh, a momentary buffet of wings against his shoulders and then nothing but a gentle weight pushing down on his arm.

Opening his eyes carefully, Ingelbert found the owl perched on his injured arm, its powerful claws gripping the plaster cast. It looked down at him with a look of indifference, preened briefly under its wing then swung its head around to look at its master and his servants approaching the copse at a run. Ingelbert waited nervously, adjusting his stance to better accommodate the weight of the owl, which was lighter than he expected given its intimidating size. Two of the servants reached the copse first, slowing down when they saw Ingelbert. Seeing the owl was not lost, their faces relaxed.

"It's here, my lord!" one of them called to the hunter, who was several strides behind. He stamped into the copse, the look of annoyance on his fleshy face only deepening when his eyes fell on Ingelbert.

"Give him over," the hunter demanded, holding out his arm.

Not certain what to do, Ingelbert extended the owl towards the man and made a slight tossing motion to no effect. The hunter waved impatiently at his servants and one of them stepped up to Ingelbert, taking the owl from him with a practiced hand.

"It is, uh, it is beautiful," Ingelbert said, not addressing anyone in particular. "A rodzlagen eagle-owl, if I am, um, not mistaken. Native to Middangeard."

"Damn useless is what it is," the hunter griped. He was at least a head shorter than Ingelbert and younger, though his chestnut colored hair was already thinning above his sweating forehead.

The other two hunters now approached the copse on horseback. They had their servants in tow, falcons on their wrists and smiles on their faces. They were of similar coloring to the hunter on foot, though both older and comelier. One had a well-groomed beard, the other was clean-shaven and wore a circlet of gold upon his brow.

"Did your owl find a new master, Edric?" the bearded horsemen asked with a hearty laugh.

The one named Edric did not answer though he continued to glower at Ingelbert. The man wearing the circlet guided his horse skillfully into the trees, reining up before Ingelbert and nodding down at him.

"Our thanks for retrieving the bird," he said.

"No, no trouble," Ingelbert replied, then motioned to his cast. "I think he was attracted to the, um, to the white."

"What do you know of it, churl?" Edric nearly spat at him.

"Peace cousin," the rider said. "You should be more gracious."

The bearded rider laughed at that. "Edric, gracious? As likely as that owl catching a rabbit!"

"Damn you, Raedwald!" Edric cried shrilly, but his cursing only fueled the other's laughter.

Ingelbert's legs were beginning to feel shaky, so he bent to retrieve his walking stick.

"Forgive my kin," the rider before him said. "My brother Raedwald lives to make sport of our cousin. As men, they are still boys. My name is Wuffa, how may I address you?"

"Oh, um, Ingel—Ingelbert Crane, my lord."

"Well, Ingelbert Crane. Our thanks again."

The hunters and their servants began to leave the copse. As Edric waited on his horse to be brought, Ingelbert approached him.

"My, my lord," he ventured.

The man turned and regarded him with a sneer.

"I, um, I think the owl would strike true," Ingelbert went on undeterred, "if you would wait, that is, wait longer to release him."

Wuffa and Raedwald had turned in their saddles, looks of interest on their faces. Edric gave him a withering look.

"What?"

"Well, um, owls do not see well up close. They track more with hearing than, ahh, than sight when prey is near. I think, I think if you wait for the rabbit to be further distant, give your owl more time to see it, he will not miss."

Edric regarded Ingelbert through squinted eyes for a moment, then glanced passed him and motioned for his servant to bring the owl over. Ingelbert stepped back as the hunter took the bird on his wrist, regarding it with interest.

"Tell me," the man said, not taking his eyes off the owl.

"What good is a bird of prey who cannot see what is right in front of it?"

With that, Edric snatched a dagger from his belt and punched the blade into the owl's torso. The bird gave a piteous cry, its wings flapping spasmodically. It went grotesquely limp, falling off Edric's wrist to land in the dirt where it twitched, bleeding.

Ingelbert stood stunned and sickened, unable to move. He looked into Edric's small eyes and the man smiled at him, then mounted his horse.

"Curse you for a black bastard, Edric," Raedwald said with disgust and spurred his horse out of the copse.

Ingelbert leaned heavily on his walking stick to keep from falling down next to the dying bird, watching as Edric, still smiling, rode away. Ingelbert bent and gathered the owl up awkwardly in his arms. Its eyes were closed, its beak opening to take tiny breaths. He could feel its heartbeat slowing beneath his hands. Wuffa remained in the copse, staring down from his horse grimly.

"My lord," Ingelbert pleaded. "If, if you would help me get him back to, to Gipeswic. I have a friend, a, a Fae healer. He could save him."

"I am afraid no horse will be swift enough, nor Fae magic strong enough to save the poor creature now. Look."

Ingelbert looked down. The owl was still, it breathed no more.

He stood for a long time clutching the bird, only vaguely aware of the departure of Wuffa and his men. Was there no end to the evil deeds he would witness? Was there no end to his inability to stop them? Damn Edric!

And damn Flyn. And Deglan. Damn Parlan Sloane as well.

This is why Ingelbert chose to hide. This is why he yearned for distance from the world. If he could do nothing to prevent the iniquity of men, of skin-changers, of rapers, then he could be sure to take himself far away from their reach. He refused to feel shame for who he was, let others judge as they will.

Ingelbert laid the owl beneath the oak, knowing the bugs would soon be upon it, but he lacked the strength and the tools to dig a grave.

"Huukayat," he said in parting, placing a hand on the gorgeous feathers.

He gathered his book and stuffed it back into the satchel.

Shouldering the bag, he turned and began the long walk back to the town of his unwanted birth.

TEN

"A bear on a boat," Flyn said, shaking his head and laughing as he tossed Pali a chunk of uncooked goat. "It still remains a marvel."

From the tiller, Milosh smiled at him, the gentle river wind playing through the man's dark, curly hair. That hair contained a little more silver and that smile a bit more gold, but otherwise the years had done little to change him. Milosh's clear, deep voice eased effortlessly into song, his smile broadening.

"A bear on a boat,
saw a coburn tall and asked, Oh! What could it be?
Never have I seen a rooster of size
Enough to rival me!
Fear not nor care, was said to the bear,
Your balls are bigger still!
What good be they, the bear did say,
When a cock goes where it will?"

Milosh held the final note for an impressive spell, his strong voice filling the river from bank to bank. When he finished, the man looked back to Flyn, his eyes dancing in his swarthy face.

"Not your best," Flyn critiqued with good humor, tossing his own voice so that it reached the stern.

Milosh shrugged theatrically, leaning on the tiller as he piloted the boat with an expertise his casual posture could not conceal. "Age begins to dull my wits."

Flyn heard Tsura issue a small breath of exasperation. He looked down at where she squatted amidships, tending both the small sail and the cooking pot. She did not believe her father's proclamations of decline any more than Flyn did. For that matter, Milosh did not believe them either. Most of what the man said was jest and he remained as canny as ever.

A grumble from Pali reminded Flyn he still had one piece of meat in his hand. He tossed it to the bear, then left him to eat at his usual spot at the bow. Pali was neither chained nor caged, a testament to the wondrous abilities of Milosh Ursari.

"I learned a few bawdy lays from a hobgoblin Jester," Flyn called to Milosh as he made his way amidships. "I shall have to teach them to you."

"I eagerly await this education!" Milosh answered.

Tsura shot Flyn a reproachful look, but like her father's claims of dotage, there was little weight in her disapproval. Milosh may have changed little in a few years, but his daughter was fully transformed. Tsura had been a slip of a girl when Flyn last saw her, but now she was a woman grown. She possessed the bright eyes of her father and the olive-hued skin of the Tsigani people. Her thick, black tresses were unbound, falling down her back and past her slim waist. In the prime of her youth, Flyn did not doubt she would be a woman that human males found desirable. He wondered what Inkstain would think. Of course, the chronicler had no hope of winning her, for the Tsigani were notoriously clannish and Milosh would never relinquish his daughter to an outsider.

The Tsigani were not native to Sasana or anywhere in the Tin Isles. As Flyn understood it, their ancestors came from lands far to the southeast of Outborders. Some far-traveling Middangearders had raided their homelands in the distant past and taken several of their women as thralls. The fjordsmen were not shy about fathering children on their slaves and Tsigani blood reached Sasana when the raiders established footholds in places like Gipeswic, Rattlesdan and Norwyk. But the Tsigani do not forget and a group of their best warriors pursued their captive kin. It took many years, but they eventually freed all of those with Tsigani heritage from thralldom. Not wanting polluted blood to mix further with their people, the warriors and the former thralls remained in Sasana, slowly breeding the taint of Middangeard out over the generations. This was the legend as Milosh told it and Flyn suspected at least a small portion of it was actually true.

Whatever their roots, the Tsigani were now a tight-knit race of vagabonds. They wandered the rivers of Sasana in their ramshackle vessels, plying a myriad of traditional family trades among the human settlements. The work of their silversmiths was much prized and the gifts of their singers renowned. A gift which Milosh displayed with gusto.

"Bury my body in the loam, burn to the ground my hearth and home,
Unearth my riches and scatter my flocks, but leave my wine alone!"

Flyn knelt beside Tsura and took over management of the sail. She did not utter a word of thanks or breathe relief for the help. This was not a lack of gratitude, but merely the way the Tsigani mind worked. They were a wayward people, passing from one place to the next, each stop containing faces that came and went in cycle. To Tsura, Flyn's six-year absence was the same as if he had been gone only a day. They settled into the old rhythms seamlessly, holding no resentment for a time apart, nor fawning over a reunion.

Upon leaving Gipeswic, Flyn had avoided the trade roads and stuck to walking along the riverbank, first following the Orr and then the Stour. He spotted the first Tsigani boat at dusk on the first day out and called to them.

"Please pass the word! The coburn called Flyn travels westward along these banks and seeks Milosh Ursari!"

After that it was simply a matter of time. Flyn continued his journey on foot, never losing sight of the water. Two days passed and then, early this very morning, a gaudy boat with a bear in the bow rounded a bend in the river. Flyn had given a merry shout, waving his arm at Milosh, Tsura and Pali. The Tsigani may not be overly sentimental, but Flyn did not hesitate to show his joy upon seeing them again.

After all, these were the people who taught him how to laugh. They spent the afternoon sailing upriver and listening to Milosh sing, quickly lulling Flyn into a strange nostalgia. It all felt so comfortable, so familiar. Only Tsura's maturity revealed the passage of time. That and the steel spurs on Flyn's feet, the greatsword close to hand and the martial training that had become ingrained in his body.

"No husband?" Flyn asked Tsura after a time.

The girl did not blush or dip her chin demurely. She met his eyes squarely.

"Only a Rudari man has approached Father. He refused."

Flyn nodded.

The Rudari were a tribe of miners and the only Tsigani that did not wander. They were prosperous, but viewed as somewhat inferior, only slightly better than an outsider. Tsura cocked her head ever so slightly towards the stern, listening more than turning.

Milosh continued to sing at the tiller.

"He awaits the Atsinganoi," Tsura said. She did not whisper, which would have been a sign of disrespect, but had ensured her father did not hear before speaking so plainly.

Flyn was not surprised. "He told you that?"

"Of course not," Tsura said with a wry smile. "But I know his mind."

"Is that what you want, Cricket?" Flyn asked, knowing she would not lie to him.

"Cricket," she repeated with genuine affection. "You know, I do more now than just hop about the boat singing. Should I still call you—"

Flyn burst out laughing, cutting her off. "No!" he waved a pleading hand at her. "I beg you, do not."

Tsura smiled at his embarrassment and for a moment the little girl who hopped around the boat returned.

"My wants do not matter," she said, her smile fading. "We are the last Ursari in Sasana and Milosh has only me. If our art is to continue, marrying one of the witch-men is the only course. Father thinks not of me in this, nor does he think of himself. The Rudari would give him wealth for my hand, but he refuses. Even the Aurari, the goldsmiths, I think he would turn away. He thinks only of the Ursari. An Atsinganoi man holds the strongest chance of fathering a child with our gifts."

Flyn knew Tsura was right. He also knew that such a match would condemn her to a life of hardship.

The Atsinganoi had Magic in their veins and were shunned by most humans. They often posed as traveling entertainers, fortune-tellers or hedge healers, using their arcane talents to earn coin and kind, but many saw through the ruse. Even humans trusting of the Fae were intolerant of Magic-wielders in their own race. Flyn suspected such condemnation stemmed from the tyrannical legacy of the Goblin Kings, though not one of those mad warlocks had been of Tsigani stock. The men who became the Goblin Kings had learned their craft from the elves before betraying them, but no such tutelage was the root of Tsigani power.

They brought it with them from their homeland and never spoke openly of its source to an outsider. Not all were born with gifts and when they manifested they were as varied as the tribes themselves.

The Atsinganoi were the most potent, occupying a queer position in Tsigani culture as revered outcasts.

Flyn did not want that for Tsura, but he said nothing, for it would offend Milosh. Tsura too would not react well to judgmental words from him, such was the fidelity she held for father and tribe.

It was not Flyn's place to gainsay. For all his camaraderie with the Tsigani, he was and would forever be, an outsider.

Milosh steered the boat to the bank just before sunset and Flyn jumped into the shallows with the mooring rope in hand.

Once the vessel was secured he unlatched the bow ramp so Pali could shuffle his furry bulk to shore. Flyn gave the massive bear a companionable slap on the rump as he passed. Tsura handed down the supplies needed for their nightly camp, then allowed Flyn to carry her to shore. She could have used Pali's ramp to avoid the water, but this was an old game.

"You used to be lighter," Flyn teased.

"You used to be stronger," she shot back, reaching beneath his beak to pull gently on his wattle as she had always done.

He let her down with calculated roughness, then went back to the boat for Coalspur and his armor. Milosh had gone ashore and was busy collecting firewood. Pali shambled around not far from the man, never leaving his side unless directed. Flyn watched the pair from the deck.

The Ursari relationship with their bears went beyond mere training. It was a mystical connection, one that was commonly overlooked by the peasants that Milosh and Pali entertained. Were it not, the Ursari would suffer the same mistrust as the Atsinganoi.

Thankfully, a man singing and a bear dancing was a jovial spectacle that humans could accept, ignorant of what Flyn had seen many times. Pali understood complex verbal commands, whether Milosh spoke in the tongue of the Tin Isles or the Tsigani ancestral language. It was as if the words were unnecessary and the bear was actually responding to Milosh's will directly. Yes, Pali would stand on his hind legs or sit when told to do so, but he would also refrain from eating if bidden, defying all instinct. Tonight, Milosh would have the bear patrol the borders of the camp to keep them safe while they slept. Pali would fight, kill and even die at Milosh's word, protecting the man and his daughter to his final breath. This was what the Ursari truly were and what Milosh sought to preserve.

That night they shared Tsura's savory fish stew by the fire, Pali receiving several of the catch to eat raw. They sang traditional Tsigani songs and Flyn taught Milosh the raunchy ballads passed to him by Muckle. The moon rose above the river and Pali went lumbering off into the shadows, huffing all the way. Flyn kept his weapons close to hand, but knew there would be no need for them.

This was what he had experienced for countless nights in his life before the Roost. He would need no fire to keep warm and expected to sleep deeply as he only could in this company.

Milosh stared at him over the fire, a calm grin cracking beneath his black mustachios.

"So," he said, nodding at Coalspur leaning on the log next to Flyn. "A dream fulfilled."

Flyn considered this. "Almost."

"There is more to being a knight?" Milosh had a way of asking questions that both mocked and displayed deep concern.

"For me there is less," Flyn replied. "And more."

"You once loved song, not riddles," Milosh said, wagging a finger at him.

Flyn looked from Milosh to Tsura. They waited, their gazes neither impatient nor imploring. The same eyes.

Flyn considered telling them everything. His time as a squire, the tourney, his travels in Airlann, the siege of Black Pool, battling the Unwound at Castle Gaunt. Once he would have enjoyed boasting of these exploits, but now he simply wanted to unburden himself of them. He could relate everything that had happened to him in the intervening years, even explaining his unsanctioned knighthood and Pocket's importance. Flyn trusted Milosh and Tsura completely, knowing any secrets he shared would never be betrayed. He wanted them to understand him, what time had made him, but it was nothing but a self-serving wish. Such knowledge would only endanger them.

"You are right!" Flyn proclaimed, jumping to his feet. "No more riddles. I am a Knight Errant of the Valiant Spur. Sir Bantam Flyn, at your service!"

He performed an ostentatious bow, drawing laughter from his audience.

Milosh's gold teeth shone in the firelight as he smiled mischievously. "Bantam? As in . . . small?"

Flyn knew where this would lead. "It is a champion's title," he said quickly. "Bestowed to honor my singular achievement of early knighthood."

"Did I not also give you such a name?"

Tsura shoved Milosh's arm lightly. "Father. Stop."

Milosh beamed at them both, took a deep breath as if he were going to say something and then clapped his mouth shut.

Flyn gave him another bow, this one of relieved gratitude, then sat back down.

"What of your brother?" Tsura asked. "Did he attain the same dream?"

"Gulver still trains," Flyn said with a show of pride. "He will one day be a member of the Knights Sergeant, I have no doubt. Perhaps Grand Master. Such paths as I will never walk."

"You underestimate yourself," Milosh admonished, retrieving a wine jug sitting nearby and holding it forward.

Flyn reached around the flames and took it. "That is not something I am often accused of."

He took a mouthful from the jug, fond memories flooding his mind as the wine touched his tongue. Position within the Order was forever lost. Sir Corc had dubbed him knight, but he lacked the power to erase his desertion. Flyn could live the life of a Knight Errant and even claim allegiance to the Order, but he could never return to the Roost, nor elevate his position. Unless . . .

Unless he challenged and defeated the reigning Grand Master. That remained the traditional right of all coburn. Grand Master Lackcomb himself had won leadership without ever having been a knight, or even a squire for that matter. He famously came striding into the Great Hall as an unknown youth and bested Grand Master Coalspur, winning both the leadership of the Order and the respect of his predecessor. A similar act would be Flyn's only road back to the fold, but he had never been driven by a lust for leadership. No, he was now what he aspired to be and that was enough.

"Let others bear the burden of governance," Flyn said, handing the wine jug to Tsura. He winked at her. "Me? I was made to wander."

Milosh laughed heartily at this. "Then you have returned to the proper bosom!"

Tsura took a swallow of wine. "You mean to travel with us then?"

"Is this allowed?" Milosh asked with feigned shock before Flyn could answer. "Can a knight stoop to travel with we Tsigani on his, how do you say, errantry?"

Flyn chuckled, knowing the man had purposefully misspoke.

"Nothing would give me greater joy," he answered. "But first I must ask a boon."

"You need but name it," Milosh said with a wide smile.

"Take me back," Flyn told him, "to where you found us."

Milosh's smile plummeted from his face. He looked at Flyn unblinking for a long moment, then took a deep breath, rubbing his hand over his mustachios.

"You wish this?" he asked at last.

Flyn nodded.

Milosh regarded him grimly for a moment. "A boat may sail upriver, but the waters that bore it downstream have long since moved on."

"Wise words," Flyn said. "But you know me for a fool, Milosh."

Milosh smiled sadly, then stood. "Very well. I shall take you there." Flyn met his eyes. "My thanks."

The man dipped his chin, then bent down and kissed Tsura.

"Fair night, my Cricket."

Milosh headed for the bright Tsigani tent that would shelter twice their number. As he passed, he thumped Flyn on the shoulder with the heel of his fist without pausing.

"And fair night to you too, Little Pecker."

Tsura threw a hand over her mouth, her eyes squinting with mirth.

"Lovely," Flyn said with a chuckle. "Too much to hope he would abandon that."

Tsura removed her hand, revealing her smile and shook her head at him. "Never."

"I still say Gulver had it worse," Flyn insisted.

Tsura broke out in fresh laughter. "Big Pecker!"

Flyn added his merriment to hers. "Yes! Much, much worse. By the Hallowed, my brother is an enormous bastard. I am far from small for a coburn!"

"If you say," Tsura said, placating him.

"Alas," Flyn breathed. "Well if nothing is to change, let us keep to all traditions."

He extended his arm to the side, beckoning Tsura with his hand. She gave a girlish giggle then bounded over to nestle under his arm. Flyn relaxed his shoulders against the log, legs stretched out before him and hugged the girl close, remembering when she were small enough to curl up in his lap, encircled in both arms. As a child she was fascinated by his feathers and used to run her finger along the edges. That habit returned as they sat together staring into the campfire.

"Did you ever accomplish them?" Tsura asked after a time.

"All those daring deeds you told me you would do?"

"No," Flyn admitted. "I am afraid I have slain no kraken nor dragons. The Slip Noose Gang is still at large and I have never even seen a giant." He paused a moment for effect. "Oh. I *did* best one of the greatest knights of the Valiant Spur in single combat, scale the walls of Castle Gaunt, fought at least a dozen Unwound and played a small part in saving the Source Isle from war, enslavement and death from the Red Caps. Otherwise . . . no, I have done nothing daring of any significance."

Tsura gave a sleepy breath of amusement, clearly believing he jested.

"When Father saw you standing on the bank, he said, 'What took him so long?'"

Flyn chuckled at that.

"He is proud of you, Flyn," Tsura told him, looking up from his chest to catch his eye.

"I ask too much of him," he replied.

Tsura's face pinched into an expression of soft assurance.

"That is not possible."

Flyn accepted this with a nod, then returned his gaze to the fire, stroking Tsura's hair until she fell asleep. He remained awake a long time, knowing he did ask too much. So much was already owed this family.

It was Milosh who agreed to tell Gulver and Flyn where to find the Roost. They were lost youths then, with no knowledge of the world. The Ursari tribe, such that it was, had taken them in, given them a place. They were anxious to become knights, but barely knew north from south, much less the distance to Albain and the location of the legendary fortress of the Valiant Spur.

Milosh promised to tell them, but only when he deemed them ready and not before. That was the bargain, to live with him, his wife and their toddling girl-child, learn to be more than they were and when the time was right, he would set them on the path they desired. Eight years passed before Milosh made good on his promise. Those years bore sweet and bitter fruit. Flyn and Gulver learned much from the Tsigani. They shared their labor, their laughter, their music. They also shared their pain. Milosh's wife died giving birth to a son. The Atsinganoi mid-wife did all she could, but the child followed his mother to the grave within a day.

Milosh bore his grief with pride, but for many nights after the loss, Pali could be heard moaning mournfully in the darkness. Tsura had been no more than six and it was Flyn who held her close while she wept, beginning this nightly ritual of comfort in his embrace. The Tsigani do not speak of the dead, believing the words of the living snatch their departed loved ones away from paradise, so Tsura's mother's name was never uttered again.

Flyn spent two more glorious days on the river with the Ursari and then, on the morning of the third day, Milosh steered the boat to shore. It was an unlikely spot on the bank with no discernible place to make a good landing. Thick reeds hung out over the water from a muddy embankment. Flyn turned to give Milosh a questioning look and then he saw the man's face.

"Here?" Flyn asked.

Milosh's silence was an answer.

Flyn looked back to the shore. He knew Milosh would remember, but seeing the spot he was amazed. There was nothing to distinguish it from the shoreline for a league in either direction.

It was an inconspicuous stretch of river that Flyn would have sailed past without a thought. And yet, he knew in his bones it was the exact location he sought. His complete faith in Milosh's knowledge of the river told him so and something else, something deeper, almost a pain that crept into his chest and soured his guts when he looked at the reed-choked bank. He never would have found this place on his own, but having been led here, his body screamed to be away.

He had dragged Gulver as far as he could, his brother's blood mapping their slow, cruel progress. Fatigue had long overtaken him, but Flyn had continued to pull, hauling on the limp bulk until he was reduced to sliding backwards on his rump.

Reaching the river defeated him. His body was spent and his brain exhausted, neither offering any way to attempt a crossing. Flyn did not know how long they lay in the reeds, surviving on river water and worms. Gulver rarely woke and his periods of lucidity grew shorter and shorter. They were filthy and starving, their world shrank to mud, blood and the gurgle of the river.

And then, around a bend came a boat. With a bear in the bow.

"How long do you need?"

Flyn came out of his haunted memory to find Milosh standing beside him.

"A few days," he replied. "No more."

Flyn made ready, donning his mail and strapping the elven-made spurs to his feet. Straightening, he found Tsura standing before him, Coalspur held in her hands. Flyn found the sight oddly disturbing. He had never seen Tsura touch a weapon and it appeared the greatsword held her, even as it lay sheathed in her grip.

Reaching out, he took it from her quickly.

"My thanks," he said, slinging the harness across his back.

"We will continue on," Milosh told him. "But I will sail back through here in five days' time."

Flyn nodded, extending his hand and they clasped arms firmly, Milosh giving him an affectionate slap on the face. Next, he embraced Tsura, the girl stiffening a little at the feel of his armor.

"Safe travels, Cricket," he said when he released her.

"Safe travels," she replied. "Sir Bantam Flyn." Then she reached up under his beak and shook his wattle, making them both laugh.

Flyn glanced to where Pali sat in the bow, gazing at the three of them impassively.

"Take care of them, you hairy lummox," he called to the bear.

Pali snorted at him, then turned his attention upriver.

Flyn stepped up onto the side rail and jumped to shore, his talons sinking into the mud as he landed. He turned to face the boat once more. Milosh held Tsura to his side.

"If I am not here in five days," Flyn told them. "Forget my name. I do not want to be pulled out of paradise."

Father and daughter raised their hands in acknowledgment and parting. Flyn raised his own hand, then turned away and began to trek through the reeds.

Nearly fifteen years separated him from the last time he had come this way, desperate and fearful. He was unsure of the exact path, so he simply struck out directly away from the river, traversing the marshy land slowly. Soon, the reeds and mud gave way to overgrown fields and sparse woods. The sun was concealed behind a mantle of clouds which relieved themselves by midday, sending heavy, warm drops to accompany Flyn as he marched across the scrub land. The shower passed swiftly and the clouds were burned away, leaving the afternoon air clammy.

Flyn found nothing in the landscape familiar. It was possible he would explore the country for days and never find his way. This *was* a fool's errand. Time and happier memories had dispelled any hopes of retracing those agonizing steps he had taken while dragging a dying brother. It was for the best. Too long had he held onto the burning notion that this was where his errantry must begin. He could make his way swiftly back to the river, cutting across country to get ahead of Milosh's boat. There was no need to wait five days, he could be back among the Ursari by nightfall and begin his life anew. All Knights Errant chose how and where they lent aid. If Blood Yolk could sail with a rabble of pirates and pay them to hunt Middangeard raiders at sea, then surely Flyn could find a place on the rivers. The Tsigani were an abundant source of information. He could live with Milosh and Tsura and Pali, wander Sasana and go where his sword was needed. By the Hallowed it would be a good life!

Laughing to the world, he set off at a run, holding the sword harness tight against his body, vaulting rocks and logs. He must have sped a league before slowing, the landscape becoming too wooded to allow such headlong flight. Making his way quickly through the trees, Flyn emerged onto an expanse of field adorned with hedgerows and he went sprinting once more over open ground, knowing the river would soon appear before him.

And then he saw it.

It was nothing really. A break in the hedge, one among dozens, and beyond, a measure of sun-dappled field edged with forest. He stopped short, halted in his tracks by the sight. Just as Milosh had recognized a seemingly insignificant stretch of riverbank, so now did Flyn see a clear and memorable path. He nearly screamed aloud, fury igniting inside of him. He could have run right past, he *should* run right past. Flyn took a deep breath and looked back across the fields, in the direction he knew the river lay not an hour's run distant. Making a choice, he turned and walked slowly through the break in the hedge and across the field. Within minutes he reached the edge of the forest and without pausing, strode into the trees.

The smell was the first reminder. A rank, leaden stench born from a mating of life and death. Cooked meat, rotting food, wet feathers, smoke from dung fires, piss, shit and blood. Not the blood of the battlefield, the blood of birth. All these fetid odors settled into his nostrils, growing more pronounced as he walked deeper into the wood. He fought the urge to draw his sword, knowing that the comforting weight of steel in hand could quickly bring death charging to claim him. Ahead, in a dark clearing of long-felled trees stood a miserable cluster of crude buildings.

Each was made of a pit dug an arm's length deep in the soil, then covered by a rough framework of branches smeared with manure. Most of these pitiful structures were roughly rectangular, but the largest was round, situated near the center of the clearing, standing a broody sentry over the half-dozen smaller huts. Black smoke rose from a hole in the conical roof, a foreboding testament to its continued occupancy. Flyn had hoped to find it in ruin.

He approached the nearest of the sunken huts, grimly aware it had been expanded since his youth. A small, muddy slope at one end led down to the door of the hut, covered only by a filthy hide. Ducking, Flyn pulled the curtain aside and leaned into the murky hut. Nine coburn females lay within on beds of squalid straw. They turned to stare at him, squinting at the sudden light.

Most were greatly pregnant, their feathered bellies swollen. Two, however, had recently delivered. A sinewy, pulsing cord ran from between their legs to translucent, blood-filled sacks laying in the damp straw. Beneath the thick, gently writhing membrane, Flyn could detect the curled forms of the infant coburn within. In another moon's turn, they would emerge, tearing free of the egg sack and entering the harsh world of the clutch.

Flyn only recognized one of the females. She had been brought to the clutch the year before he and Gulver fled, a young, new prize. Fifteen years of endless childbearing had worn her down into a pitiable wretch and she looked at Flyn vacantly, turning away quickly when comprehension dawned. Not comprehension of who he was, but the realization of who he was not.

Disgust rising within him, Flyn let the hide fall back over the door and turned away from the birthing hut. No one moved about the clearing, likely driven to shelter by the earlier rain. Flyn could hear the distinct grunts and squeals of swine foraging nearby, unseen in the thick of the trees. He stepped up out of the pit and made for the central hut. Despite its size and circular shape, this building was no different from the others and Flyn was met with another hide door. He paused before entering, slinging Coalspur's harness off his shoulder before pushing past the curtain.

Smoke filled the gloom despite the hole in the roof. A pig, spit over the central fire, was being turned by a young female not yet of breeding age. Another female of similar age scraped at a sheep's hide stretched over a tanning frame. A dozen more occupied themselves with various chores in the dingy living space.

None of them wore more than a filthy woolen shift. Several had children clinging to their legs. Flyn's heart fell when he noticed two were male. They peered at him from behind their mother's legs, both years away from adolescence. All eyes were now upon him, but quickly looked away. The confused and frightened stares turned to the rear of the cavernous room where a creaking platform stood.

Upon it, sitting on a hideous chair made of animal bones was the only other adult male coburn in the hut.

Gallus.

He glowered down at Flyn for a moment, then stood, taking up the massive club that rested against his knee. His grimy feathers were the color of rancid milk, encrusted with dirt and soot.

About his waist hung a loincloth of uncured leather secured with a girdle of bronze discs. A coburn's comb and wattle grow with age and, it was said, with the amount of blood he sheds. Gallus's comb had long been torn away, the victim of countless battles. His wattle, however, hung to his belly, a ropey mass of red, blubbery flesh, adorned with swells of purple and blue. Age had done nothing to diminish him, his shoulders still broad and powerful. He was a scarred, knotted, hardened tree, grown stronger with the passing of long years and fed at the roots with the blood of foes.

"You one a mine?" Gallus asked, his voice a harsh, wet grinding.

"Yes," Flyn told him. "Yes, father. I am."

ELEVEN

Smoke drifted up out of the whale's blowhole. A bedraggled cluster of fishermen ambled into its gaping maw without an upward glance at the row of countless teeth in the beast's upper jaw high above. Deglan watched with a scowl as the men disappeared down the shadowy gullet, still talking wearily among themselves. He stood before the cavernous mouth wondering what possessed mortal man to construct something so damn hideous. Deglan hated whales when they were made of flesh and blubber, but this calamity of wood deserved its own disdain.

"By Earth and Stone. This should be put to the torch."

The Guild Hall of the Anglers was the largest building in Gipeswic and home to the wealthy ruling body of the town. From end to end the hall was fashioned in the likeness of a whale, or as close as the craftsmen could come to it with timber and planking.

Giant, cumbersome, sinister and revolting. Deglan reckoned they had captured the essence. The only way in or out of the place was through the mouth and it was said the upper jaw could close, sealing off the structure at nightfall. Deglan intended to be well away by then.

"Alright," he said, turning to face Ingelbert. "Shall we go into the belly of the beast? Get this done."

The gawky lad raised his long nose out of the ponderous volume he carried, but only long enough to stammer his reply.

"Um. Yes. Please, go on. I will, I will await you here."

"Oh no!" Deglan strode over and took the chronicler by his bony elbow. "I will not have you slipping off again, Master Crane. Besides, I may need a translator in here."

He began pulling the man towards the whale's mouth.

"Master Loamtoes," Ingelbert protested. "You speak the same tongue as these men."

Deglan did not ease his pace. "You would be surprised how often a shared language seems not to help when I talk to people."

They passed between jaws that a dozen horses could walk through abreast and entered the expansive antechamber of the hall.

The Guild Masters did not waste money on fanciful ornamentation or even much light, no doubt wanting the entrant to feel fully that they had been swallowed alive. Only a few fat lamps burned dimly on the support beams. The ceiling above was supported by an endless march of massive crucks, the timber framing conveniently akin to the bones of a great fish. Deglan found himself impressed.

The dramatic facade aside, the interior was ingeniously done and must have required considerable time and skill to construct.

Ahead, a group of heavily armed men stood before a wooden partition that was only half the height of the hall. The flickering glow of firelight and the sound of voices drifted up from over the top of the partition. The armed men stopped Deglan and Ingelbert when they approached. There were ten of them, all bearing spears in hand, swords at the waist and clad in dingy mail.

Mercenaries by the look of them. Several racks and tables stood in the corner where the partition met the sloping side walls. Upon them various clubs, daggers and hatchets were haphazardly tossed.

A bearded goat, tied to one of the table legs, stared at Deglan with a disinterested expression, its jaw chewing ceaselessly.

"Weapons?" one of the men asked through a yawn.

"Yes," Deglan affirmed. "You have a lot of them." He took a step toward the iron-studded door at the center of the partition.

"No," the man said, waking up enough to stoop and quickly place a hand on Deglan's chest, halting him. "Yer to hand over all weapons."

Deglan looked down at the mercenary's grubby paw with a sneer, then met his lazy gaze.

"We cannot bloody well unscrew our heads now can we?" he barked.

The mercenary smiled at this. "Think yer clever, do you?"

"The lad is," Deglan replied, hooking a thumb over his shoulder at Ingelbert. "Damn genius. Not me. My head is just at an inconvenient height for most men. Be careful if I decide to lean forward right fast."

This drew several dim-witted chuckles from the other men.

The man blocking Deglan's way smiled even broader, then slapped him companionably on the chest before removing his hand.

"Right then," he said, still grinning. "In you go."

Deglan returned the grin. He knew how to deal with men like these. Mercenaries fought for money, but they preferred to get the money without the fighting. Such a life created a contrary creature, constantly bored and looking for a fight, yet wanting nothing more than to avoid one. Provide some momentary distraction, some spark of entertainment and they became swiftly agreeable. These thugs would still be talking about the feisty old gnome over their drink and dice a week from now.

The door was unbolted and opened, revealing a large chamber beyond. Deglan stepped through, Ingelbert at his heels, and the door swung shut behind them. They found themselves at the top tier of a circular gallery containing rows of benches. A shallow stair lay directly before them, leading down to the floor of the large chamber. One man stood down there, facing away from Deglan and responding to questions being posed to him by a group of imperious-looking men sitting on a looming dais. At least two hundred people sat scattered among the benches watching the proceedings with various degrees of interest, but the gallery was far from full.

"Name?"

Startled, Deglan looked to his right to see a sour-faced man staring down at him expectantly over the top of a lectern.

"Where did you come from, you creeping vulture?" Deglan demanded.

"Um," Ingelbert broke in hurriedly. "This is, um, Master Deglan Loamtoes, herbalist and healer."

The sour-faced scribe gave Deglan a withering look, before directing his attention to Ingelbert.

"Business before the hallmote?"

"Bugger if I know," Deglan declared before Ingelbert could stammer an answer. "You bloody summoned me here!"

The droning from the floor of the chamber lulled for a moment at Deglan's outburst, but quickly resumed when the interruption did not continue.

"My business," Deglan said through a deep breath, "is to discover why you summoned me, so I can quickly depart your bloody big fish. Good enough?"

The scribe wrinkled his nose and scratched something into a ledger before making a show of speaking only to Ingelbert. "Sit anywhere. Quietly. Until his name is called."

Deglan found a spot on the benches in the upper row, knowing Ingelbert's legs were not quite up to stairs. The chronicler sat beside him, instantly returning his attention to his tome. That book had become an obsession ever since the man returned from his sudden and unannounced jaunt into the burial lands. A jaunt which set his recovery back at least a week. Deglan had not been pleased when Ingelbert returned to the fishwife's hut in a cotter's cart. The man who owned the cart said he found the lad a half mile from the city walls in a swoon, but was at least able to get a residence out of him before he collapsed entirely. The exertion had rendered Ingelbert bed-ridden for another two days.

Deglan did not fault Ingelbert for wanting to move about.

The confinement of infirmity often made people a bit anxious, but not informing him first was a foolishness Deglan did not expect from such a clever man. And something had happened to him while he was away. Ingelbert was even more diffident than usual, engrossed in the translation of that particular book. It was an obsession, one fueled by an inner fury. Ingelbert hid it well, but Deglan saw it nonetheless. He did not pry. It was his duty to heal the man's body, not to lance whatever was festering in his mind.

Down on the floor of the court, the same poor fool was still being questioned. The six men seated upon the dais all swam in an air of self-importance. Richly dressed and fat, each was a product of too much rich food and too little honest work.

"We are in the belly of the whale," Deglan whispered, nudging Ingelbert with his elbow and pointing to the corpulent guild masters. "And the big girl is pregnant."

Ingelbert merely hummed in response, not even glancing up from his work. Defeated, Deglan turned back to the doings of the court with a scowl, resigned to a lengthy span of boredom. This hallmote reminded him too much of the Wise Moot in Toad Holm.

A lot of swollen bastards passing judgment as easily and frequently as they passed wind, with the same repellent result. They alleviated their own concerns to the discomfort of everyone else.

Deglan had half a mind to get up and leave. He had broken no laws that he was aware of, unless tending to the sick was a crime in Gipeswic. If they wanted him out of town, well and good. He had no great love of the ocean and would happily put his back to it within the coming days. If Ingelbert had not overtaxed himself, they could have been long quit of this salt-smelling heap of driftwood. Bantam Flyn was not coming back to Gipeswic, the young strut had said so himself. He and Deglan had agreed to meet on the isle where Pocket was hidden in two years' time. Until then, Deglan would do as he pleased.

The fat men on the dais made some pronouncement on the poor sod below and he left the floor wringing his hands, head bowed, likely fined deeper into unyielding poverty.

"Bugger this," Deglan muttered as he stood, turning towards the way out. Let them seek him out. He was not about to sit through any more of this tedious tyranny.

"The Guild Masters call to presence, Hafr the Ever-Boastful!"

The already somber room grew even more still. Further along the back row of benches, someone stood. Ingelbert was one of the tallest men Deglan had ever known, but the individual making his way towards the nearest stairs was no man and at least half again the height of the chronicler. This Hafr was the first giant Deglan had seen in Gipeswic, and judging by the nervous expressions on the judges' faces, he was well-known here.

His hair and beard were the color of old bones, both plaited into a single braid, one dangling from the nape of his neck, the other from his chin. Ringlets of silver and gold adorned his thick, knotted arms and about his neck was an intricate torque from which hung polished stones. His only clothing was a kilt of various animal hides and a sizable drinking horn swung from his belt. A heavy thumping sounded whenever he stepped with his left foot and Deglan noticed the telltale stride of an amputee. Several more mercenaries appeared in the upper gallery and around the dais as Hafr made his way down the stairs.

Deglan returned to his seat. This hallmote might prove to be very entertaining after all.

When the giant reached the floor, he moved assuredly despite the hitch in his step. From the mid-calf down his leg was replaced by a metal-banded wooden peg, the end shod with a studded, steel cap. The guild masters leaned into one another, conspiring behind their hands as the giant waited, reaching under his kilt to scratch at his fruits. At last, the judges came to some agreement and each settled back into his seat as one of them spoke.

"Hafr," he began, his voice pinched and high. "You have been—"

"You leave out many titles," the giant interrupted carelessly, his voice a rumbling mumble.

The guild master's mouth hung open for a moment, then he rallied. "This council will not suffer—"

"Hafr is more than Ever-Boastful," the giant proclaimed. "I would hear them all."

"We will not humor such—"

"If you will not, Hafr will speak his own glory."

The giant turned his back on the affronted faces of the guild masters and looked up into the gallery. Spreading his massive arms wide, he raised them above his head.

"Before you stands Hafr!" he boomed, slowly circling as he spoke. "Champion of Utgard! At my name the legs of men run with piss and women become wet with desire! I am named Ring-Breaker and Troll-Killer! The Wyrm Wrangler! Slayer of thousands and kneeler to none! The storulvir name me brother and the Summit King names me friend! Behold Hafr the Ever-Boastful and know my words hold truth. Doubt them and my hands shall deal death!" Even Ingelbert looked up during this brash display. Deglan caught the chronicler's eyes and rolled his own.

"Giants," he scoffed. "I know a couple of plants that will turn the Ever-Boastful down there into the Never Ever Not Shitting."

Ingelbert wrinkled his mouth at the sight of the huge braggart. The rest of the assembly was no more impressed than the chronicler, but Hafr seemed satisfied, lowering his arms before turning back to face the guild masters.

"You were not to return to Gipeswic," the appointed speaker accused the giant hurriedly. "The fighting pits have been closed. There is no longer a place for you here."

"Hafr seeks no more glory in your pits," the giant replied, waving a massive hand dismissively. "Bears and dogs and small, weak men. These are not worthy foes. Hafr is only passing through."

"Then take ship with all haste," the guild master commanded, finding enough courage to lean forward slightly when he spoke. "Your ban includes the lands of Eorl Wehha as well. There is nowhere for you to go but back across the water."

The giant found the last statement amusing. Perhaps it was the way the man pointed ostentatiously, as if commanding a child to leave the kitchens.

"Hafr will soon sail back to Middangeard," Hafr said with a dangerous chuckle.

"See that you do," the speaker replied airily. "And make no trouble while you are here or it will go hard for you."

The giant considered this for a moment. "I make trouble and what? Hafr finds himself again standing here before the fat men? Then he demands trial by combat, maybe."

This last was not a question. Deglan watched the moist faces of the guild masters blanch. The brute had them there. Unless they had another giant or a fomori on hand for their judicial champion, these merchants had little hope of enforcing any threats made against one such as Hafr. Their coffers may be large enough to convince their mercenaries to face him, but that was not the sort of entertainment mercenaries found agreeable. They would take the money and flee, like as not. Best just to hope Hafr spoke the truth and was simply passing through. Hope, and stay out of his way.

The guild masters came to the same conclusion. The speaker dismissed the giant with a tentative wave of his hand. Hafr snorted loudly, clearing his throat and turned to the stairs, the thudding of his false leg signaling his ascent. No one moved or spoke until the giant was gone from the chamber.

"The Guild Masters call to presence, Master Deglan Loamtoes!"

"Well," Deglan whispered to Ingelbert as he stood. "I am a quarter of that giant bastard's size. See if I can manage to frighten these louts half as much."

As he made his way down the stairs to the court floor, Deglan could feel the eyes of the assembly following him. Prior to Hafr's boisterous interlude, half the men in the gallery had been dozing, but now everyone was attentive. Deglan was more annoyed than afraid, but still, if he had done something to earn the guild masters' ire, he doubted a demand of trial by combat would prove effective for him. He walked to the center of the floor and looked up at the judges on their dais, his neck craned back uncomfortably.

"We thank you most sincerely for joining us today, Master Loamtoes," the speaker oozed at him, looking around at his colleagues, who all gave fawning signs of agreement.

So. They wanted something from him. This changed everything.

"No gratitude necessary," Deglan replied agreeably before going to take a seat in the front row of the gallery. He was not about to stand before this council of rotundity and tie his spine in knots if they were going to lick his boots. A few murmurs rose from the assembly behind him at this lack of respect, but the guild masters' faces remained masks of amity.

"It has come to our attention that you are a healer of considerable skill," the speaker said, all smiles.

"You have gout," Deglan replied, mirroring his expression.

The speaker's smile drooped, but only slightly. "Sorry?"

"Gout," Deglan repeated with exuberance. "So do you, you and you." Deglan indicated three more of the guild master's with a casual wave of his finger. "Likely the rest of you will get it ere long. Sumptuous feasting, excessive quaffing of fine spirits. That will do it. No real cure for you four, but I can provide some relief. A regular extract of naked lady will help your swelling go down."

The men looked flummoxed, staring at him slack-jawed.

"Do not get too flushed," Deglan told them. "Naked lady is a flower. The meadow saffron. The bulbs contain what you need, so you have to wait until they are in bloom. 'Course that is not until autumn. You have a long summer ahead, I am sorry to say. Unless you send a boat to Airlann. Always Autumn there. Naked lady aplenty! Not a trouble for men like you, boats to spare and all. In the meantime, I suggest bland food, less wine and some form of physical activity that does not involve a woman doing all the work. Oh, and cherries. If you have them."

Deglan stood, giving the transfixed guild masters a quick, sharp nod before making for the stairs.

"Master Loamtoes," one of the judges stammered. "A moment further, if you please."

Deglan turned on his heel, but did not move from the stairs.

"Clearly," the speaker said with a self-effacing breath of laughter, "we have been well informed as to your skill. Many a report has reached our ears from the docks, attesting to your ability to cure various ailments. The local barbers and leeches have sat idle since you arrived here."

At last, the damn point of this summons.

"Worry not," Deglan told the judges. "I am leaving within the week. Your boys will have their trade back soon enough. They can go back to bleeding people and pulling teeth."

"No," another of the guild masters piped up. This man appeared to be the youngest of the six and the only one whose heart was not likely to give out in the next five years. "You misunderstand, Master Loamtoes. Gipeswic must thrive. There is no place here for charlatans and hedge surgeons. Not when a Fae physician is a valued citizen."

Deglan fixed them all with his most shrewd glare, looking for the deception.

Seeing his dubiousness, the original speaker jumped back in.

"We are willing to construct a residence and infirmary to your exact instruction. We shall run all other claimants to medicine out of town if you so desire. We will provide you with any servants you require and if you wish to take apprentices, we will make certain you receive only the best and brightest of Gipeswic's sons as pupils. And. We will pay you a yearly sum of eight hundred sceattas."

This caused a stir in the gallery as men expelled their breath and began murmuring to their neighbors.

"Money," Deglan confirmed.

He had witnessed mankind invent and forget the concept several times during his life. Minted coins were only the latest of man's attempt to attach value to a paltry thing for the sole purpose of hoarding it. In Deglan's youth, the Fae knew nothing of physical wealth. Immortality drove the pursuit of perfection, not comfort.

The elves taught that each individual possessed an inherent love, what humans might call talent. Once this love was discovered it was to be honed for the benefit of all. Elven farmers nurtured their crops and fed their community, asking nothing in return. Surely, the harpist who delved daily into his art to provide music to ease his fellows deserved to eat from the bounty they provided, breaking bread at a table lovingly crafted by the carpenter who sat beside him. Not until the Usurpation did the Fae learn the inevitable imbalance of trade. Dispossessed and hunted, surviving hidden in the wilds while everywhere the Red Caps marched and slaughtered, the elves were forced to abandon their harmonious generosity.

They took to the human ways of barter and payment. And where the elves trod, the rest of the Fae followed. Mankind was not to blame, they had not the gift of eternal life nor the aid of Magic.

This was how they survived, knowing no other way.

"Of course," the guild master continued, "any money earned from the rest of the population would be yours to keep."

Deglan wrinkled his brow. "Rest of the population?"

"Yes," the fat merchant said, his smile broad. "The sum we would pay naturally covers the members of the Guild of Anglers and their families. We have no interest in what fees you charge the rest of the townspeople, provided our needs remain paramount, of course."

So, if one of these bloated bastards is passing a stone and one of the dockside whores is about to give birth, then luck be with the whore because Deglan surely would not be.

"I see," Deglan said. And he did. "Remember what I said about the cherries."

He turned and began making his way up the stairs.

"Master Loamtoes!" one of the whale's pups called after him. "You have not given us an answer!"

"Yes I have!" Deglan responded without slowing his climb.

Ingelbert must have managed to keep his nose out of his book during the encounter, for he met Deglan near the door at the top of the stairs. Once outside the chamber, Deglan passed the mercenaries without a word, then thought of something and turned to face them.

"Eight hundred sceattas a year?" he asked the sellswords.

"What's that worth?"

The lusty gleam in the eyes of the men was all the answer he needed.

"Earth and Stone!" he swore, making his way quick as he could towards the blaze of light outside the whale's mouth. "I should take the damn offer just to poison those sacks of suet."

When at last they escaped the jaws of the guild hall, Deglan paced a moment, fuming. Ingelbert stood by, watching him with patient concern. The bustle of the street surged around them, people moving slump-shouldered about their daily business.

Charcoal burners and dung collectors pushed handcarts, wearing the soil of their professions on their faces next to hard-set jaws.

Swineherds and muleskinners led their charges through the congested lanes, the animals adding to the noise and reek that assaulted the senses. Rat catchers, scullery maids, oyster shuckers and fruit vendors, all of these and a myriad of other toiling vocations plied the streets, scraping a living out of the filth. And none belonged to the Guild of Anglers.

These were the people the whales would see excluded from his care. Or at the least, pushed aside in favor of their own health.

What did it matter? Even without the Anglers' selfish stipulations, Deglan could not handle the well-being of a town this size. Already, he awoke to a line outside the fishwife's hut, one that barely diminished come nightfall. The guild masters were not fools.

Deglan would need the offered servants and apprentices if he were to stay in Gipeswic, but when would the time present to train them? They wanted their own brats taught at his knee, but if Deglan were to take an apprentice it would damn well be a fellow gnome. He had always intended to do it one day, pass on what Ruhle Nettle had taught him countless years ago. Maybe now was the time to send word to Toad Holm and inquire about a likely candidate.

The direction of his thoughts halted his pacing.

"Buggery and spit! Why am I considering this?"

"Are you?" Ingelbert asked.

Deglan shot a look up at the chronicler's long face. "No."

"So, um, then back to the Roost? Or Airlann?"

"Yes."

"Which?"

Deglan opened his mouth to answer and nothing came out.

He did not know.

Across the muck of the street stood one of Gipeswic's many wine sinks. These truculent establishments were hastily erected all over town whenever an influx of sailors made port and were in need of cheap, foul drink. This particular one was little more than a pavilion made of sailcloth, sheltering the drunken patrons from the worst of wind and rain, but doing nothing to keep their tuneless caterwauling or the sour stench of their cups from spilling into the street.

The giant, Hafr, emerged from under the filthy tent, drinking horn in one hand and a tether in the other. Deglan was puzzled to see this tether attached to a goat, the very goat from inside the guild hall. The giant took a few guzzling swallows from his horn, then began leading the goat down the muddy lane.

"What do you think?" Deglan pointed the odd sight out to Ingelbert. "That a pet or his evening meal?"

And then Deglan saw it, his blood running cold. Slung across the giant's back was an imposing sword, no doubt collected from the mercenaries on his way out of the guild hall. Deglan knew that sword. Even sheathed and from a distance, he knew it. There could not be two like it in the world.

"Ay!" Deglan called after the giant and then hurried after him. "Ay, you!"

He left Ingelbert behind, but the chronicler's long legs quickly caught up to him.

"Deglan?" the man inquired nervously. "What are you doing?"

Deglan did not bother to answer. The street was crowded and the press of people made progress difficult. Everyone was taller than him and he pushed against a teeming barrier of legs and backsides. Hafr was taller still and was easily visible over the throng.

The giant's limping gait slowed him, but the townsfolk did not impede his movement, readily parting to get out of his path.

Deglan elbowed his way forward until he reached the small trail of abandoned street left in the giant's wake.

"Stop, you towering fuck!"

Deglan felt Ingelbert place a hand on his shoulder, trying to pull him back and stop him from yelling at the same time.

"Deglan," the chronicler pleaded. "Enough. What is wrong?" Shaking roughly out of the man's grasp, Deglan approached the giant. Hafr had stopped and was now turning slowly, looking to see who had cast insults at his back. Deglan had to look up a long way to meet the giant's eyes. He was not afraid. Hafr was no taller than Coltrane, the Forge Born who was made of living iron. No taller than Faabar, who Deglan had stood beside and counted as a friend, as a brother for nearly two thousand years.

Faabar, whose sword the giant now carried on his back. A sword Deglan had last seen resting on the fomori's scorched chest before placing the final stone on his cairn.

"Where did you get that blade?" Deglan demanded.

Hafr scowled down at him, then took a long pull from his horn. The immediate passersby had stopped, gathering around to gawk. Deglan ignored them.

"Answer me, you daft bastard."

Hafr spit. A stream of warm, pungent wine spattered down on Deglan's face. He coughed and sputtered, hearing the booming laughter of the giant and the accompanying mirth of the crowd which followed. Deglan wiped the dark liquid out of his eyes with his sleeve, finding Ingelbert kneeling by his side and Hafr again walking away. He took a step after him, but Ingelbert grabbed his arm.

"Master Loamtoes," the man said, confusion spread across his face. "He, he could kill you! Whatever, this is about. Let it go."

"No," Deglan growled, snatching his arm away.

He caught up to Hafr again and darted around to get directly in his path. The giant stopped, looking down at him with renewed amusement.

"You want to share another drink, maybe," Hafr sneered, raising the horn to his lips.

"I want to know how you came by that sword."

"You are too small for such a weapon, I am thinking," the giant replied.

"And I thought you too mighty to be a grave robber," Deglan returned.

Hafr's grin vanished. "Hafr Ring-Breaker despoils not the dead. I claim only what is won from those I slay."

"You did not slay the wielder of that sword," Deglan said through clenched teeth.

The giant shook his head impatiently. "Nay. It was a gift, not plunder. It was given to Hafr by—"

Deglan cut him off. "I know damn well who gave it to you! Take me to him."

There was a moment's pause before the giant answered.

"He is not here, maybe."

"He *is* here. You said a gift. Not paid for or bartered for. A gift. And a dwarf's gifts are not bestowed freely. You owe him something. He is here."

Hafr's face betrayed the truth. "Maybe he would like not to see you."

"Oh he won't," Deglan affirmed. "But if I kill him, you will no longer owe him a debt."

The giant guffawed at this, then took a thoughtful swig from his horn before answering. "You? Slay he? This, Hafr would see. I go to him now. If you follow, you follow."

Without another word the giant started off again, tugging at the tether until his goat fell into step beside him. Deglan found Ingelbert a few paces removed.

"Go back to the hut," Deglan told him. "I will return directly."

The chronicler shook his head. "I, um, I think I will go along."

"You may regret that."

"Or you will if I, ah, if I do not."

Deglan had no argument for that.

They followed Hafr into the craftsman's district, passing stalls and shop-fronts occupied by cordwainers, wheelwrights, poleturners and billiers before reaching the hot, smoke-laden, clangorous alley that housed the smiths. Here, the buildings were made of stone and roofed in tile to reduce the risk of fire. A chorus of ringing hammers and roaring furnaces besieged Deglan's ears, the air in his nostrils dry and burnt. Within the forges, they passed sweating blacksmiths bent to task over their anvils with hammer and tongs while apprentice boys pumped the bellows, fetched water and shoveled coal.

Hafr limped to the end of the alley where a courtyard containing a well was formed by several of the larger workshops.

The grandest had a vaulted roof supported by stout beams and open to the yard along the entire face. Hafr eased himself down upon a low wall and gestured towards the place with a grin. Deglan looked up at Ingelbert and nodded, before the two of them entered the stifling heat of the great smithy.

No fewer than three forges were housed within and could have been tended by a dozen soot-stained bodies, but the workshop was occupied by only a solitary figure. Deglan's rancor rose at the sight of the stocky, solid frame of the dwarf, his broad back turned as he smote the anvil.

"Fafnir," Deglan spat the name.

The hammer fell again and then the dwarf turned to face them. He had changed since Deglan last laid eyes on him. The rust color of his hair had dulled somewhat and his beard had grown longer. His upper lip was still shaved, but the flesh of his face had lost its ruddy complexion, replaced with a sickly pallor. Still, he remained the same steel-peddling meddler he had always been.

Fafnir's keen eyes took Deglan and Ingelbert in with a glance, squinting with interest.

"The sour gnome herbalist," he said, nodding at Deglan to mark his recognition. "Hog's Wallow. You are a long way from Airlann."

"As are you, dwarf," Deglan snarled. "I see the distance from the Source Isle is already taking a toll."

Fafnir ignored this. "How can I be of service?"

"Faabar." It was all the answer Deglan could give, nearly choking with rage. He took a few steps further into the forge, picking up a smithing hammer lying on a nearby bench.

The dwarf nodded slowly. "You think I dishonored him."

"YOU DEFILED HIS GRAVE!"

Deglan could feel his entire body shaking as his voice reverberated against the rafters. "Faabar was my friend. I buried him with my own hands. And you? You dug him up to take back a damn sword. His sword!"

"I retrieved the blade," Fafnir admitted. "And covered the bones of the fomori once more."

Deglan had known it to be true, but upon hearing it from the dwarf's own lips, his fury boiled over. With a cry of anguish he threw the hammer at Fafnir, but he was clumsy with grief and tears blurred his vision. The flung tool spun past the dwarf, slamming into a rack of shields and sending them crashing to the ground.

Deglan howled in frustration and made to charge Fafnir, but Ingelbert restrained him.

"Does your avarice know no end?!" Deglan screamed as he struggled in the chronicler's grasp. "How dare you?!"

Deglan wanted to kill him, even if it meant using his bare hands. The dwarf was taller and far brawnier, but it would not save him. This was the creature who had come to Hog's Wallow, tempting Faabar with promises of steel. When Fafnir returned a year later with the weapon, Faabar was injured and Deglan had ensured the dwarf came nowhere near his friend. But then death and fear had come to their village, forcing Faabar from the sickbed.

He received the sword and, along with Deglan, the piskie Rosheen and a coal-haired mortal youth, set out to end the threat to Hog's Wallow. It was a decision that would end his life. Faabar had died standing against the goblin Flame Binder and his Red Cap zealots, sacrificing all to protect the community he loved. It was the beginning of a long and anguishing ordeal for Deglan, one which put Pocket in his path and continued to steer the course of his life.

Fafnir had not even flinched when the hammer was thrown.

He stared placidly, waiting.

"How did you even know where he was buried?" Deglan demanded.

"No weapon I have forged can hide from me," the dwarf told him.

Deglan surged forward again, but Ingelbert held him fast.

"And you could not let it remain where it was?"

"The price for the sword had not yet been paid."

"He traded dearly for it!"

"No!" Fafnir's voice raised for the first time. "There was yet a debt outstanding."

"What?" Deglan scoffed. "To endure your presence on the road and guard your fucking goods?"

"He agreed to travel with me, yes."

"Liar!"

"Think on it, gnome!" the dwarf barked. "After a thousand years living among sheep and peasants, what did your friend possess of value? What could he have given me for so fine a sword? No, his desire was to leave Hog's Wallow, no longer to stand a useless guardian to a rabble of herdsmen. He yearned for greater purpose and I offered him a place. The sword was payment, herbalist. Payment for service the fomori did not render. Believe what you will, but a sword is not what your friend wanted. It was freedom from a life devoid of glory."

Deglan had ceased struggling. Could it be true? Had Faabar truly meant to abandon Hog's Wallow? If so, he had kept the fact hidden for over a year while he waited on the sword to be fashioned and delivered. Would he ever have told Deglan, or simply slunk away in the night, shameful and silent? They had fought together, bled together, saved each other many times during the Rebellion. At the siege of Bwyneth Tor, when the provisions ran out and they were forced to eat the gnomish mounts, it was Faabar who slaughtered Deglan's toad when he could not bring himself to do it. Why had he not told him? They were as kin.

Deglan froze, paralyzed with realization. The answer was clear.

Faabar, who knew him so well, was unwilling to suffer the censure he had witnessed Deglan dole out for centuries. Deglan would have judged him, harshly and freely, maybe even hated him. Even now, with his friend in the ground, he struggled with a rising bitterness.

Deglan was too old not to know the truth when he saw it.

His anger waned, replaced by a cold disgust for himself. He cocked an eye over his shoulder at Ingelbert.

"Alright now, lad," he said. "You can let me go."

Ingelbert removed his hands and Deglan took a deep breath, then looked up to meet Fafnir's implacable stare. Anger flared in Deglan once more, but he turned away from the despicable steel-monger before it could overtake him. Putting a guiding hand on Ingelbert's elbow, Deglan began to leave the forge.

He stopped before he stepped outside, one question still remaining.

"How long?" he asked without turning. "How long was Faabar to serve you?"

The answer came quickly. "Fifty years."

Deglan winced, unable to stop himself from facing the dwarf.

"So now that giant whoreson serves in Faabar's stead?"

"As you say," Fafnir nodded. "My wares still require protection and I have not another year to waste forging a new blade."

"I warned Faabar against dealings with you," Deglan said.

"Bargains with dwarfs never end well."

"And yet," Fafnir replied, "his bargain with me was not his end. Fate chose differently. He went off in search of an Unwound instead, and if I recall, it was you who set him on that path. A path from which he never returned."

The spit in Deglan's mouth soured. "Let us go, Master Crane."

Outside, Hafr still waited, smiling as he watched his goat feed from a pile of refuse. Feeling weary to the bone, Deglan walked over and stood before the giant.

"You have many titles Hafr the Ever-Boastful," Deglan told him. "But one thing you will never be is Faabar of the Brindlebacks."

With that, he made his way out of the courtyard and along the narrow alley until the clamor of the craftsman's district was well behind. When he reached the high street, he turned away from the direction of the docks and the fishwife's hut. He walked briskly, distancing himself from Ingelbert.

"What are you, um, what are you going to do?" the chronicler asked.

"Tomorrow? I have no idea," Deglan replied without slowing. "Today, I am going to get very drunk."

Ingelbert watched the herbalist go. He had no wish to pursue him. In truth, he had wanted free of the irascible gnome's company all day so he could devote time to the translation of the green book without distraction. Ingelbert could be obsessive, single-minded. It was a facet of his nature he accepted long ago.

Once he set his acumen to a task, it was difficult to steer elsewhere.

This might have been crippling were it not for another aspect of his cognition. He remembered everything.

Turning, Ingelbert headed back down the smith's alley. He found the giant now within the large smithy, standing in the center where the roof was highest. The dwarf was busy righting the rack that Deglan had upset with the flung hammer, picking up the scattered shields.

"Um," Ingelbert ventured. "Excuse me."

Hafr looked around, glancing down and smiling.

"Behold," the giant snorted, getting Fafnir's attention. "The gnome sends the weakling back. Challenge you to a duel, maybe."

The dwarf peered at Ingelbert for a moment. "How can I be of service?"

"The sword," Ingelbert said.

A low growl bubbled in the giant's throat. "The sword is Hafr's now. It will be claimed by another only when I am slain. Come, puny one! Test Hafr's words."

Ingelbert looked up at the glowering brute, then shook his head, ignoring him. "No," he said, looking back to Fafnir. "Not that sword. Another, ah, another sword."

The dwarf's eyes narrowed slightly. "Hafr. Leave us."

Casting Ingelbert one final, threatening look, the giant curled his lip and shrugged, thumping out of the workshop, his goat following.

"Giants are uncouth," the dwarf said apologetically. "But as guards, they have few equals."

"Save fomori," Ingelbert pointed out.

Fafnir touched the side of his nose. "Just so. Fomori are near as strong and more even-tempered. Of course, they are Airlann-born. We immortal children of Middangeard are a lesser stock. Prone to chaos and wickedness, as the Fae are quick to remind us."

Ingelbert knew his history. "Well, um, your people were slow to come to Airlann's aid, during the, ah, the Pig Iron Rebellion."

"And only then for a price," Fafnir said darkly, stooping to pick up a fallen shield. He held it in his thick, powerful hands for a moment, studying its shape. Then he shook his head with a sad chuckle and hung it on the rack. "I am afraid the grudges the Fae hold against we dwarrow go far deeper than their Rebellion. No, the roots of that enmity run to the eldest days."

"When your people were still ruled by the huldu," Ingelbert said.

Fafnir's gaze snapped up, a curious smile growing above his beard. "What is your name?"

"Ingel—um, Ingelbert Crane."

"Ingelbert the Learned," Fafnir said approvingly. "You know the dworgmál word for elves. Tell me, do you know any more of my people's tongue?"

"Yes," Ingelbert said softly. "All, all of it."

"Very good," the dwarf nodded, looking Ingelbert up and down. "Though I would not say the elves ruled us."

"That is the legend," Ingelbert replied.

"Legend to you mortals," Fafnir said, still smiling. "History to us. Let us just say the dwarrow and the huldu were once . . . allied, when we both dwelt in Middangeard. But those bonds were severed and the elves left our homeland, settling in Airlann. It was long, long ago and our kindred atrophied with the passing of many thousands of years. To this day, the huldu and their Fae subjects look upon the races of Middangeard with contempt. Magic's cast-offs." Ingelbert had a vague notion of what the smith spoke. It was an archaic myth, with no written record that Ingelbert had ever encountered. It was little more than an oral tradition, one of many almost nonsensical stories concerning the creation of life. That Magic made the world was accepted, molding it from the Elements to create a celestial guardian against some unfathomably ancient emptiness. Airlann, the Source Isle, was said to contain the slumbering essence of Magic, near spent from its long struggle with chaos. The elves were Airlann's stewards, Magic's chosen people, and they were also given dominion over the Elementals, the Fae races charged with protecting Earth, Fire, Water and Wind, the foundations of creation. This, every orphan at the Dried Tear was taught.

But there was another tale, an older tale not oft told, of Magic's original keepers. The immortals of Middangeard. The dwarfs, giants, elves and an unnamed race inscrutably referred to as demons. They were each entrusted with an Element, but greed and lust for power drove them to conspire against one another. In some tellings there was a great war, in others a grievous betrayal.

Whatever the events, the Elementals of Middangeard failed, their powers stripped and their land left a frozen waste. All except the elves, who were favored by Magic and given Airlann, to begin anew.

Ingelbert had never given the story much thought. He loved history and the discovery of knowledge, but the origins of the molding of the world were unrecorded, unreachable, lost to a time beyond mortal reckoning. As far as he knew, even the oldest Fae had not lived during those events. After so long, certainty was impossible, leaving only belief. Ingelbert was uncomfortable with belief, trusting only to what he could possess with proof.

"And mistake not," Fafnir continued. "We may have come late to Airlann's aid, but we had our own concerns. Irial Elf-King lost his throne to the human sorcerers and their goblin worshipers, but was too proud to seek the help of the dwarrow for many years. At last, when things were most dire, the Fae stooped to treat with us. A bargain was struck, and yes, we demanded remuneration, but we paid dearly as well. Vindwor Secret Keeper, our high king, was laid low at the Battle of Nine Crowns, defeated by that wretched warlock the Gaunt Prince."

This Ingelbert knew to be true. The Battle of Nine Crowns was the last bloody chapter in the history of the Rebellion. The Forge Born had been defeated, Jerrod the Second was dead and all that remained of the Goblin King's forces was an army of Red Caps led by his son. Though small in number, every goblin in the ranks was a fanatical veteran and loyal to the death, but the Gaunt Prince did not commit them. He commanded his generals to scatter and go into hiding, choosing to meet the armies of the Fae alone. And there, on a rain-soaked field, the last scion of the Goblin Kings challenged the leaders of the Rebellion to combat.

Wishing to see no more of their subjects slain, the lords of the Fae accepted. One human prince against eight of the most powerful beings to draw breath. But the Gaunt Prince was no ordinary man and by the time he fell only Goban Blackmud, king of the gnomes, remained alive.

Nine monarchs. Eight deaths. The Battle of Nine Crowns.

"Your herbalist companion hates my kind," Fafnir uttered, "but his liege-lord survived that day. Since the fall of Vindwor, we dwarfs have had no other high king to unify us, only scattered, insular lords guarding their hoards and holds."

"I think," Ingelbert said slowly, "Deglan's ire is born from your mistreatment of his, um, of his friend."

Fafnir looked at him with regret. "I cannot return the sword to the fomori's grave, Ingelbert Crane. I cannot."

"Again, Master Fafnir," Ingelbert replied, "I am not here about that particular sword. It is of Coalspur that I wish to speak."

The dwarf's brow furrowed with confusion.

"That is," Ingelbert clarified, "the sword forged for Grand Master Coalspur of the Valiant Spur. The blade now bears his name in honor and is carried by a coburn named Bantam Flyn."

Fafnir nodded with recollection. "I know him."

"Yes. Um, he said you met in Black Pool and that you claimed, claimed to be the maker of the sword."

"I am."

"Wonderful," Ingelbert said. "I am, um, that is, I was formerly the chronicler of the Valiant Spur, and squire Flyn, now Sir Flyn, came to me in regard to the weapon. He had questions, ah, questions which I could not answer."

Fafnir's face began to show mild impatience. "Yes?"

"Well, Flyn believed that you told him the sword was a gift for Grand Master Coalspur, who died only a few years ago, but he, that is, Flyn, Flyn saw what he believed to be the same blade depicted on an old tapestry celebrating the Battle of the Unsounded Horn. That, ah, particular battle took place many centuries ago. Even if the sword were merely used as a model, the tapestry predates Coalspur's captaincy of the Order by several hundred years. This is most puzzling, Master Fafnir."

The smith stared at him for a moment, his expression blackening. Then he laughed, heartily and loud.

"You are a most interesting man, Ingelbert Crane! You are no longer in service to the coburn, yet you pursue answers like a wolf who has caught the scent of blood." The dwarf chuckled for a moment longer, then gathered his breath. "Like you, the coburn are a mortal race. It is difficult for mortals, especially young ones, to conceive how we immortals view the past. I have lived a long time fashioning weapons and do not recall now which of the knights I forged the sword for. I know every inch of the blade, Ingelbert Crane, but the coburn who first received it is just another shadowed face in the throngs of those I have outlived. It seemed more . . . courteous to deceive Flyn then explain a lapse in memory. The coburn are a proud race, I did not wish to offend the young squire needlessly."

"I see," Ingelbert said. And he did. By his own admission, the dwarf found it easier to lie. "Well, I will not, um, trouble you further."

Fafnir offered his hand. "Master Crane."

Ingelbert took it, clasping the dwarf's thick forearm, feeling the corded muscles, hard as metal. He tried to break the grip, but Fafnir held him fast, looking at him intensely. Ingelbert had seen that expression before, in his own face. Parlan Sloane had secretly done a charcoal sketch of him one day at the orphanage. Ingelbert had been reading.

Just as he began to be alarmed under the dwarf's scrutiny, Fafnir released him.

"Fare you well, Ingelbert the Learned. I hope our paths cross again."

Ingelbert merely nodded and hurried out of the workshop.

He spent the rest of the day on a quiet stretch of shore a fair distance from the docks, digging words out of the green book.

There was a crowd of sick and injured milling about outside the fishwife's hut when Ingelbert returned at dusk. Deglan was not within, however, and Ingelbert was forced to tell the infirm hopefuls they would have to come back on the morrow. Once alone, he ate a light meal and toyed with the notion of seeking Deglan out. A drunken gnome should be simple to find, even in a place as big as Gipeswic. He dismissed the idea, however, knowing the cranky healer would not respond well to being sought out.

Unable to stop himself, Ingelbert recorded the information about Coalspur in what was left of the annals he still possessed.

Fafnir had withheld something, of that Ingelbert was certain, but he had taken the inquiry as far as he was willing. What did it matter? He was no longer the chronicler, not truly. He was like Deglan, adrift, clinging to the wreckage of another life.

Rain began to patter on the roof of the hut and Ingelbert retreated to his bed. The plaster around his injured arm itched terribly. When Deglan returned, he would make a point to ask when the dreadful thing could be removed. He fell asleep listening to the rain, the runes of the green book still dancing across his closed eyes.

He had latched the door before retiring and awoke in the dead of night to a rapping on the swollen wood. It was light, irregular and it took Ingelbert's drowsy senses a moment to differentiate the knocking from the patter of the rain.

Disentangling himself from his bedding, he shuffled across the room, surprised Deglan was not yet cursing at him. Ingelbert removed the latch and opened the door.

Ingelbert's breathe seized in his chest as something fast barreled out of the darkness, striking him at shoulder height. His face was slapped wetly and he flung his arms up for protection, but the attack ceased as quickly as it began. Leaving the door open in case he needed to flee, he turned into the hut, arms still raised.

There, perched atop one of his bedposts, orange eyes fixed on him, was an immense owl. Not just an owl, a rodzlagen eagle-owl. The owl. Ingelbert's brain was spinning as he stared, slack-jawed and panting. The coloring, the size, the markings on the feathers, all identical. He was certain. Only how could it be? He had watched the bird die!

Slowly, cautiously he approached, hands raised. The owl watched him come, unconcerned. By inches, Ingelbert reached for the owl and it allowed him to stroke its wet feathers. Carefully, he hooked his knuckle underneath the downy feathers of the owl's breast and lifted them up, finding the evidence. A thin, grey scar adorned the flesh beneath, exactly where Edric's dagger had sunk to the hilt. Breathless, Ingelbert looked into the owl's face. It regarded him for a moment, then blinked before turning once more to face the door.

The same bird, back from the dead. Ingelbert was certain, he just did not know what to believe.

TWELVE

Flyn slept with the pigs.

The old sow had grunted in protest when he crawled into the grub hut, but did not rouse herself in anger nor move even an inch to make space for him. Wedging himself between the sow's ample bulk and the side wall of the hut, he huddled just inside the dripping opening, hugging Coalspur to his chest. He had been content to sleep out in the warmth of the spring night, but the rain forced him to seek shelter. Gallus would not suffer another male in his hall, so that left Flyn with no other choice. It was not the first night he had spent in the company of his father's swine.

He often used the grub hut as a haven during his youth.

Gulver, even at a young age, was soon too big to squeeze into the low, cramped enclosure, so Flyn never had to compete for this particular hiding place. Many a bitter, winter night had been endured nestled among the stinking warmth of the pigs, though he had been smaller then and now found the sanctuary far less comfortable.

Unlike the sunken huts inhabited by Gallus and his mates, the pigs' shelter was built at ground level, a long rectangle of stacked stones with a low roof of crude thatching. The pigs entered the hut at the end of one of the long sides, the first to enter turning to make its way to the opposite end of the enclosure, which was just wide enough for a full-grown pig to lie down. The others followed, snuggling side by side until the last, always the big sow, had just enough room to lay with her head facing the opening.

Seven sleeping pigs and Flyn, all squeezed in a row. He was suddenly reminded of the village in Airlann Deglan often spoke of and once called home.

"Who resides in Hog's Wallow now?" he muttered to himself.

His feet stuck out into the rain, as did the last third of Coalspur's sheathed blade. Within minutes of hunching down, Flyn's back began cramping, protesting the tight conditions and the weight of his mail. It was for his armor's sake that he crawled into the grub hut, the steel rings already suffering from the effects of his errantry. The tarnish would soon turn to rust without proper time spent with oil and rag, time Flyn would need to spend out of his armor, which he could not risk. So, there was nothing for it but to stay out of the wet as best he could. Fortunately, Flyn had no such worry with his sword.

When he first received Coalspur, he spent countless hours tending the weapon with oil and whetstone. It was not until after the battle at Castle Gaunt that he discovered his efforts were needless. Despite cleaving into the hard iron skin of many Unwound, the blade suffered neither notch nor nick and had not dulled in the slightest. During his time on the island, the salty spray had done nothing to affect the metal's luster. Dwarf-forged steel was much prized, but Coalspur's undiminished edge and resistance to degradation was unlike anything Flyn knew to be possible. He reckoned it unique until Sir Corc gifted him with the spurs of elf-make, now strapped to his soaked talons and resting in the mud.

Mail. Sword. Spurs. He was well girded against the attack that was soon to come.

It was a marvel Gallus had not assaulted him the moment Flyn stepped into his miserable hall. For his part, Flyn gave no provocation. He had kept his head low, never meeting his father's eyes for more than a few moments. Surely the old bird suspected a challenge. It was not Flyn's intention to offer one. He simply made his presence known, which Gallus accepted with an indolent curiosity. Once the question of Flyn's parentage had been answered, Gallus returned to his seat and signaled one of the females to bring food. It was rough fare; hard bread and a pottage made with peas, onion and pig fat. Flyn ate standing, while Gallus peered down at him, evaluating the threat. No further words were spoken and Flyn was careful to keep his eyes on his meal, knowing that even a lingering glance at one of the females would insight violence. To waste food was a sign of disrespect and weakness, so Flyn mopped the bowl clean with his bread before choking it down. The taste was painfully familiar. When he was finished, he placed the bowl on the ground and bowed his head to Gallus before turning and leaving the hall. The dozen strides to the curtain covering the door were the longest Flyn could remember taking, his ears straining for sounds of a charge at his back.

It was all a dance. Displays of obedience and domination, each participant ever searching for signs of doubt, over-confidence, cowardice. All a dance, and one in which Flyn had come here to participate, at least until he could change the tune to suit his own steps. He smiled to himself in the darkness. Only a Tsigani would think of this as a dance. Gallus knew nothing of music or grace or shared joy. Likely he now lay in his hut, at his ease with several of the youngest females in his bed, without a care for the sudden return of one of his wayward sons or the danger such an appearance could pose.

It was the coburn way.

No ruling male, no matter how strong, could keep his clutch forever. Some were claimed by disease or mishap, others killed by their own mates. Most though, most were simply deposed by a younger male, either an outsider in search of females or a son ready to replace his sire. And, at least once, an alliance of sons who thought themselves ready.

Flyn stared out into the downpour, at the ugly, old trees and the depressed clump of huts. In the rain they appeared as sodden lumps, boils upon the flesh of the forest. He had hoped to find his birthplace abandoned or, at the very least, under the reign of a new master, but in his heart he knew such a hope was a useless dream. Gallus would not have succumbed to illness or age. Gallus would not have been slain by some wandering strut lusting for a clutch to claim. Gallus's mates would never dare conspire to murder him. He was indomitable. An untamed, savage tyrant living in the heart of the wilds, his very presence keeping the settlement of mankind at bay.

During his youth, Flyn had seen his father defend his mastery from rivals on four separate occasions. Every challenger had been brutally defeated. Only one had survived. Gallus knew he would one day fall, but the thought plagued not upon his mind. No, within that decrepit hall rested a creature unafraid, while out here in the damp, reeking shadows, squatted a knight, the rain melting him back to childhood.

Flyn was awakened by the big sow pushing her snout into his shoulder and squealing with aggravation. She almost knocked him off his cramped and tingling legs when he stumbled out of the grub hut to allow her to pass. Grunting, the sow headed for the woods to forage, her six piglets following close at her heels.

The rain had ceased, the first shards of rising sunlight intruding into the forest from the east. Flyn attempted to stretch the soreness from his neck and shoulders, but only succeeded in increasing his desire to remove his hauberk and be free of its weight. He walked to the border of the clearing so that his blood could chase the stinging from his legs. He was careful to keep the door of the hall in sight, so that he would be visible when Gallus emerged.

Movement caught his eye and he looked across the clearing to see one of the younger females disappear into the birthing hut, likely bringing food to the mates lying in their confinement. Once Flyn saw her, he began to notice the others. The whole clutch was stirring with activity. Females fetching water, tending the toft, scraping hides. They were all about, over a dozen at the least with an equal number likely hidden from view within the hall. Counting the mothers Flyn had seen in the birthing hut, Gallus must possess over thirty females, more than he had before Flyn fled. Gallus had been conquering. How far must he have ranged to find clutches he had not already despoiled? How many other tyrants must he have slain to gather this many females? Flyn estimated half their number were active mates, the rest daughters, old and new. Known as beldams, these females were spared Gallus's desires, but were destined for a life of never-ending labor and servitude.

Despite the drudgery, the females of Flyn's memory were a garrulous lot, their chatter as endless as their chores. Now, they moved and worked so silently, Flyn had hardly known they were present. Heads were bowed, steps were cautious, communication limited to gestures. They only grew this cautious when a rival male was near, sensing the inevitable conflict, doing nothing that might hasten its arrival. Of the children, he saw no sign, their mothers having hidden them away in hopes of protecting them. Flyn yearned to tell them he had not come to spill blood, that he was a knight of the Valiant Spur. He wondered how many would know what that meant. It mattered little. To speak to any of the females, even the beldams, would only bring about what he sought to avoid.

Besides, these were Gallus's brood. Nothing would ease their fear of him. As he watched the females move about, Flyn felt a stirring in his loins. It crept up on him, sudden and disturbing, quickly rising from an unwanted twinge into a prepossessing ache. Lust for flesh, lust for blood. These females need no longer suffer the dominion of an aging, filthy brute, not when Flyn could throw Gallus broken upon the earth and claim all he once possessed. Flyn would protect the females, see them free, see them safe. He could take them away from here, he could take them to more civilized lands. He could take them.

Perhaps only one, the youngest and most comely, the most willing. He was young and charming, his feathers resplendent.

Surely the females would welcome his touch, desire his caresses.

They would compete for his affections, fulfilling his every whim in order to become his favorite. His father's blood would still be hot upon his hands when he took the first to bed and expelled the balance of his passion in the release of willing flesh.

The curtain to the hall was thrust aside and Gallus ducked through the opening, a brace of spears clutched in one hand. Flyn saw him through a swimming haze of crimson, the sound of his own blood drumming through his skull.

No wealth or mate ever mine.

A cold weight settled into his gut and he looked to the ground, breathing deeply.

My honor undimmed.

The words of his knightly oath struggled to the front of his brain and he fought to hold them fast against the furious tide of red anger flooding his veins. Looking up, he saw Gallus approaching.

Flyn kept very still, willing the teeming appetites to leave his body before his father sensed them.

The spears rode Gallus's fist carelessly, the butts almost dragging on the ground. It was a ruse. Flyn could see the readiness in his father's stride, the possibility of quick action loaded into every muscle in the old bird's body. It was infused in Gallus's motion just as it was in Flyn's stillness. Damn! He had been so careful, but now there was nothing to be done. In another few steps, Gallus would know Flyn's desire, however unbidden. He would smell it.

Coalspur was propped on his shoulder, still sheathed. Sir Corc had once told him that a greatsword was a weapon best used on the open battlefield or for the slaying of monstrous beasts.

Unless in experienced hands, such a ponderous blade could prove a hindrance in a duel, a lesson Sir Corc had beaten into him when Flyn once drew the blade on the knight in anger. Luckily, he had learned a great deal since that defeat and now counted his hands well experienced.

Gallus stopped before him. Now that he was down from the platform in his hall, Flyn was reminded where Gulver received his immense size. Despite the passing years, Flyn still had to look up slightly to look his father in the eye. His age was impossible to determine. He looked to be somewhere between Sir Corc and Grand Master Lackcomb, but could have been older than both, or younger for all Flyn knew. Gallus was molded in the headwaters of barbarism, the weariness of existence fueling a bottomless well of spiteful vigor.

Flyn nearly struck out when his father's free hand raised.

Pinching the edge of Flyn's mail sleeve with his fingers, Gallus emitted a derisive laugh from the back of his throat. He looked at the armor with disdain, then cast the same look into Flyn's face before removing his hand. He turned and walked several paces into the brush, keeping his spears in hand as he squatted. After a moment the stink of Gallus's emptying bowels filled the air.

Flyn silently cursed himself. A few scant hours in the company of females and he was nearly overcome by the territorial instincts that plagued his race. The Valiant Spur's vow of chastity was not an idle one. Without it, there could be no brotherhood and the Order would have torn itself apart centuries ago. It was mere luck that his father had not sensed his heat.

Finished, the old bird rose and walked out of the bushes.

"Your mother? Which one?"

The sudden, blunt question took Flyn off guard. There was no care in the inquiry, just a selfish need for information.

"Eadlin," Flyn managed to answer.

Gallus nodded with immediate recall. He knew all his property.

"Dead."

Flyn fought to keep the rage from his voice. "I know. I was here. Claennis took me in, after. She was mother to Gulver."

Gallus's expression darkened with uncertain anger. "The big'un?" Flyn nodded. Gallus tossed a bitter breath of laughter in his face, the anger at the memory of the challenge replaced by the one of his triumph.

"Dead?"

"No," Flyn replied, risking a mote of joy.

"You were t'other," Gallus said. It was not a question. The look Gallus gave him caused Flyn to shift his weight subtly, but the attack did not come. The baleful look in his father's eyes faded as quickly as it had come.

"Claennis was a good hen," Gallus pronounced as if that ended the matter.

Flyn did not need to be told. She had kept him and Gulver alive and unharmed for longer than their father would normally have suffered, using his favor of her to extend his forbearance. But even Claennis' influence did not last forever. Gallus went raiding, bringing fresh mates upon his return and Claennis found herself replaced by a younger female. After that, each passing day saw Flyn and Gulver's existence grow more treacherous.

"When did she die?" Flyn asked.

"Winter," Gallus replied, pulling at his long, heavy wattle.

"The one after you pair run off."

There was no sadness in the response. It was merely a statement of fact. The only thing Gallus had buried more than enemies was mates.

"Come," he commanded, heading off into the woods without a backward glance.

Flyn fell into step behind, shocked that Gallus would expose his back. Was it a trap? A test? No. Gallus's coarse brain understood the notions of honor, even if he did not adhere to them.

Flyn was not the first knight his father had encountered and he expected no skulduggery.

They walked away from the brood huts and into the expanse of the forest. After a few minutes, they passed one final hut, smaller and well away from the others. Flyn had no memory of this lone dwelling. Gallus passed it by without consideration. Flyn began to hear a sharp, rhythmic sound cracking through the trees, soon joined by the unmistakable grunting of pigs. Gallus led him towards the sounds and eventually they came to a large oak.

Beneath its branches, Flyn's former bed fellows rooted around for acorns. These were being knocked to the ground by a lone coburn brandishing a thin, long-handled club. Flyn's heart sank. There was another adult male in the clutch after all, if male he could be called.

He was barely out of adolescence, shorter than Gallus by a head, his comb and wattle pale and underdeveloped. His shorter stature made it difficult for him to reach the acorn-laden upper branches, but he wielded his felling club purpose-fully, hopping up to strike the nuts from the tree. Flyn could see one of his feet was deformed, the talons curled inward on withered toes, making his task all the harder. The youth's body was fleshy and would likely have already fallen to fat if better fed. Capons were prone to heaviness.

Gallus called wordlessly, but in the midst of his labor, the lad did not hear. With a snarl of frustration, Gallus strode over and snatched the club from the plump coburn's hand. Startled and off-balance, the capon fell hard to the ground.

"Up!" Gallus ordered, throwing the club down at the youth.

It struck against his warding arms and Flyn saw him wince as the wood bashed against his bones. The capon scrambled to his feet, his face the numb mask of one long accustomed to such abuse. His eyes, however, grew wide when they caught sight of Flyn. Within that stare Flyn saw a fate avoided.

Gallus's sons had three choices when they came of age.

Challenge him. Flee. Or stay and be castrated. This poor young strut did not seem the fighting sort and, with his clubbed foot, must have seen little hope in flight. So, he stayed and surrendered to mutilation, becoming a slave to Gallus's will, a tormented servant who posed no threat of rivalry for mastery over the clutch. This was why the coburn race was so formidable. The weak did not breed. Gallus, displeased at the capon's distraction, redirected his attention with a backhand across the beak. The youth stumbled again at the force of the blow, expelling a small whimper of pain, but managed to keep his footing.

"See to the traps," Gallus instructed and the capon hobbled away into the woods.

Flyn found his fingers aching from gripping his sword so tight. He had suffered similar treatment at his father's hands and worse, but the life of a capon must have been the cruelest sort. In the pecking order of the clutch, a castrated male was beneath even the beldams. In a hard winter, he would be the first to starve.

Gulver and Flyn, faced with this fate, made a different choice and it nearly cost them their lives.

"That one's not mine," Gallus waved a spear contemptibly at the departing capon. "It's mother was already swollen when I claimed her."

Flyn swallowed his rage and said nothing.

The rest of the morning was spent trekking circuitously through the forest, checking Gallus's many traps. Only one proved fruitful, the capon whistling back to signal them towards the game.

The ensnared fox hissed and growled with vicious desperation right up until Gallus plunged a spear into its body. Freeing the limp animal from the trap, the capon draped it over a shoulder, the blood staining his russet-colored feathers.

By midday they came to a sizable woodland stream and followed its banks until they reached the edge of a rocky rise. Here, the water cascaded over the boulders, forming a deep pool below before the stream continued on its course through the somber trees.

Without pause, Gallus began climbing down the moss-covered rocks towards the pool, one hand still clutching his spears. The way was slick with slime, but the old bird made the descent with ease, his movements sure and practiced. Flyn slung Coalspur's harness over his head and situated the sword across his back, inwardly cursing the drenching his mail was sure to receive during the climb.

The capon had turned away from the ridge and was making his way down the sloping woods, skirting the outcropping to avoid the scramble down the rocks. Such a path was longer, but obviously easier and less hazardous with the youth's clubbed foot. Gallus had nearly reached the bottom, but Flyn stepped back from the rise and caught up with the capon.

"What is your name?" he asked.

The young coburn looked over at him quickly, taken off guard by his sudden presence, then cast another furtive glance back towards the ridge. Gallus was out of sight, hidden from view by the wooded slope.

"Wynchell," the capon answered, his voice soft and high.

"I am Sir Bantam Flyn," Flyn said, the words sounding strange as he spoke. His instinct was to be less formal, to eschew all knightly titles and laugh and clap the lad merrily on the back. He refrained from any joviality, however. This poor strut did not need any more hands laid upon him, nor be pandered to with forced friendship. "Have you heard of the Knights of the Valiant Spur, Wynchell?"

Regardless of good intention, Wynchell, it seemed, was not receptive to friendship, forced or otherwise. He did not answer and said nothing further as they made their way down the wooded hill, keeping his eyes on the placement of his unsure steps.

They reached flat ground at last and Wynchell led them assuredly to the pool. Gallus was hauling an eel trap from the water when they approached, turning to stare at them with a mocking leer.

"You take the cripple's way?" he asked Flyn. "Too craven to climb?"

Flyn refused to be baited. He pointed up at the waterfall and then tapped his mail-clad chest. "Rusted be the knight who courts a wet embrace."

Gallus's brow wrinkled at this, trying to determine if he was being insulted. He took several paces forward, then tossed the eel trap roughly at Wynchell without taking his eyes off Flyn.

"A true coburn," Gallus growled, "fights in his feathers."

Flyn had a dozen clever retorts for that, but he kept them to himself. He would not bait any more than he would be baited.

He shrugged out of his sword harness, attempting to make the motion appear casual, but Gallus's eyes narrowed. Let him be suspicious, Flyn would have Coalspur close to hand. He propped the sword up against the rock face, then sat down on a boulder. He knew Gallus wanted to keep him in sight, but he would be damned if he was going to help the old tyrant hunt or fish.

Wynchell dared no such rebellion and was already pulling the catch from the traps. The eels wriggled in his hand, sinewy and slow, before he tossed them upon the ground where they lay to gasp in the open air. Gallus speared one deftly, lifting it up to pluck it off the blade. It was still writhing when he bit into the soft flesh at its belly, tearing a pulpy pale chunk free with his beak. Wynchell shot a quick, hungry glance at Gallus while he ate, which Flyn did not fail to notice. He and Gulver had cast that same look many times, envying their father's food far more than his mates.

Sometimes the old bird would share, but they went hungry more often than not, relying on what little Claennis was able to sneak them. This day, Gallus was not in a charitable mood and made no offer to share.

"You should give the lad some," Flyn said.

Gallus laughed at this. "It's fat enough."

"He is hungry, Gallus," Flyn pressed. "He works tirelessly."

"Too many hens to feed," Gallus muttered as he continued to tear into the eel.

"Aye," Flyn agreed. "Too many."

Gallus's head jerked up from his meal, the feathers at his neck bristling. He fixed Flyn with a dangerous stare.

"You think to take a few?"

"Knights take no mates," Flyn said pointedly. "You know this."

Bits of eel flew from Gallus's beak as he guffawed.

"Castrates in metal shirts! Look you," he kicked some mud in Wynchell's direction to get his attention. "Another cockless coward! Oaths and honor is all that is 'twixt his legs. Would not know what to do with a pullet even if he could get her to lie with him. Ran from me so I couldn't cut him, then went and did it himself so he could join a gaggle of other capons."

"The Valiant Spur has trained the greatest coburn warriors in history," Flyn said with his own laugh. He could play this game.

And win.

Gallus spat. "Weaklings and loons, the lot of you! Unable to take a clutch.

Greatest coburn? Bah! We who hold mates are the strongest there is. Yours is an order of lesser sons."

"And yet," Flyn returned without rancor. "Only the mightiest may lead us. One who must receive all challenges and defeat all rivals to retain mastery."

"Then I am your master," Gallus declared. "For I have done no less."

"You are surrounded by females," Flyn replied airily.

"Waiting for you to grow weak with age or take ill, so they can bash your head with a rock. The Grand Master of the Valiant Spur is ever in the company of armed males who by rights may contest his leadership at any moment. I ask you, which is the greater warrior?"

Gallus let the remains of the eel fall to the ground. He took a single step toward Flyn, his wattle darkening angrily.

"Me," he hissed. "I have fought one of you knights. And he pissed hisself when he died, same as all I have killed."

Flyn shrugged dismissively. "He was not Grand Master Lackcomb."

"And what of you?" Gallus's voice was wet with fury. "Why have you not challenged this great warrior? Do you fear him?"

Flyn met his father's gaze without blinking. "As you say, I am a lesser son. I am no Gallus."

His father seethed, chewing on these words.

Flyn resisted a smile. The witless brute had made it too easy.

Gallus's knowledge of the world was limited and Flyn doubted he would even attempt the journey to Albain. Certainly he had traveled far to depose other rivals, but never as far as the Roost.

For all his displays of vitality, Gallus was no longer young and would be risking all over a matter of pride. He was driven by base desires, not a need for glory. Even if by some madness he found his way north, Lackcomb would stand victorious and if not, Gallus would not long hold command. The knights would never suffer such a barbarian to lead them. It was all a jape, but a worthy deed nonetheless. A seed had been planted in Gallus's dim mind. Flyn had made him doubt his own prowess and mocked him in a single stroke. All in all, a grand bit of knavery.

They returned to the clutch by dusk, Wynchell depositing the prizes of the hunt in the hall before retreating to his exiled hut.

Flyn was again invited to sup with his father. He ate standing as before, but this time was offered a jar of beer, thick with dregs. He asked for another jar before taking his leave, which his father granted. As he neared the door, Gallus's voice made him pause.

"Tomorrow. You leave."

"Tomorrow," Flyn agreed with a dip of the head. "I leave."

He stood outside the hall for a long while, leaning on his sword and watching the door as the moon rose higher in the night sky. Neither Gallus nor any of his mates appeared during his vigil and, once he thought it safe, Flyn made his way into the woods.

A light burned behind the curtain of Wynchell's sunken hut and shadows moved about inside. Flyn purposefully made plenty of noise as he approached and the signs of motion within the hut ceased.

"Wynchell," Flyn called softy. "It is Bantam Flyn."

After a moment, the curtain drew back and the cautious face of the capon leaned out. Flyn held up the jar of beer and sloshed the contents gently.

"I would purchase a place of repose," he said with a smile. "The pigs tire of my company."

After a brief consideration, Wynchell pulled the curtain further aside and gestured for Flyn to enter.

Within, a single pallet of straw and odd hides lay beside a smoking fire pit. Nothing cooked over the flames, the only evidence of a meal were a few broken acorn shells lying scattered on the ring stones. Wynchell remained standing by the door, eyes lowered. Flyn handed the beer out to him.

"No need to share," he said. "Every drop is for you."

Wynchell hesitated for just a moment, then took the jar from him, tipping it to his beak for a healthy swallow. The pullets' brew was foul to the taste, but filling as a loaf of bread. The lad was not likely to begrudge the intoxicating effects either, a rare escape for such a beleaguered brain. Flyn leaned Coalspur up against the wall of the hut, then began removing his hauberk. He let out a deep sigh of relief after shedding the weight of the mail. He deposited it on the ground then sat down heavily, stretching his legs out before him.

"My thanks," Flyn said with genuine relief. "I could not have stood another day encased in metal."

Wynchell sat down across from him, the beer already dispelling some of his timidity. The lad finished the jar quickly, but they sat silently for a long time, the flames of the fire pit waving between them.

"Are you going to kill him?" Wynchell asked at last, staring into the empty jar.

"No," Flyn told him, unable to mask the regret in his answer. "It is forbidden for a member of my order to slay a mated coburn, unless it is to defend ourselves."

"Then why have you come?" the capon demanded.

Flyn laughed deeply then and saw the confusion in the lad's face turn to anger.

"Take no offense," Flyn said, still chuckling. "It is myself that I mock. It is a worthy question, Wynchell, for a truth it is. And I fear I have no answer that will satisfy you." Flyn looked wearily at the ceiling of the hut, allowing his mirth to subside. "Once, not long ago I would have killed him . . . sought vengeance. We Knights Errant are tasked with walking the world, lending aid and strength of arms against evil. Gallus was the greatest evil I knew to exist and I dreamed of returning so that I could take his life, all oaths be damned. Now, though far removed from the ideals of the Valiant Spur, I must keep them close to heart.

"Still, I needed to see it again. This cursed place. I did not know what I would find here after so many years, but even having escaped, I needed to see it in order to be free. To be free of him."

The capon regarded him grimly and Flyn gave a remorseful shrug.

"As I said, the answer would not satisfy you."

Wynchell shook his head slowly. "I would never have returned. Not here."

"Perhaps," Flyn allowed. "Perhaps you are not as foolish as I. But imagine what you would do with strength, with training at arms. If you *knew* you could defeat him. Would the contempt of this place be enough to keep the lust for his blood at bay? Or would your hard-earned prowess lure you back with promises of retribution?"

"I will never have the chance to know," Wynchell replied bitterly.

Flyn leaned away from the wall towards him. "You are wrong. Join the Valiant Spur and one day, such a test will be before you." That took the lad by surprise. His beak hung open and a glimmer of hope appeared in his plump face, but it faded quicker than the sparks rising from the fire.

"I am a cripple," Wynchell said. "And I know Gallus lies. You are not capons. I would trade the scorn of one for the contempt of many? No."

"We are not all capons," Flyn conceded. "But one of the most famed and feared of the Knights Errant is and none within the Order dare mock him. You are a cripple and that will draw jests from your fellow squires, but if you can endure Gallus's hatred, it will seem as nothing. The Knights Sergeant will make a fighter of you, Wynchell. And the squires will become as brothers. It is a far better life than the one you now know."

"How did you know of them?" the capon asked. "Trapped here, I have heard stories as you must have, but how did you know it were true?"

Flyn smiled sadly, the lad's question dredging the muck of his memory.

"The same as you have come to know," he said. "A knight came to the clutch. By the Hallowed, he was impressive! His armor made him appear monstrous, invincible and he bore weapons unlike anything I had ever seen. A sword at his hip, broad shield upon his arm and a pole hammer, the type I later learned to be called a crow's beak. And his spurs! They were the most wondrous. My clutch-brother, Gulver, and I were young, younger than you. We could not take our eyes off of him. Even the females stared openly at him.

"Gallus was away on a raid and the knight came every day into the clutch. He ignored the mates and beldams, but gave Gulver and I food to share with them. At night, he would take his leave and camp well removed, but for near a week he would spend the days telling me and Gulver about the Valiant Spur. The knights were ever in need of new struts, he told us, and that there was a place for us in this magnificent hall called the Roost. I could not fathom a castle then." Flyn smiled and looked up at Wynchell. "But the food would be plentiful, the knight told us. That was enough for me. Gulver was less certain, he had his eyes on the clutch even then, but I told the knight I would go with him. I dreamed of what it would be like, seeing myself clad in armor before a great feast, wearing spurs and eating my fill. That was my vision of knighthood.

"And then Gallus returned. The knight tried to speak with him about recruiting me, but he may as well have entreated a wild boar. Gallus attacked and suddenly the knight did not appear so invincible. Shield. Sword. Mail. None of it saved him. It was not the first time I had seen my father kill. A wandering rival and an elder son had already been slain before my eyes, but this was the worst. He fought with such disdain, such rage."

It was not something Flyn had thought of in a long time, but once conjured, the memory was difficult to dispel. He could still hear the sounds of the knight's bones breaking beneath his armor, the pleas for mercy. But the word yield meant nothing to his father. Flyn suddenly wished the beer jar was not drained.

"After it was over," he continued quietly, "Gallus made Gulver and I bury the body. Armor, weapons and all. I tried to sneak the spurs away, but Gallus saw and beat me bloody. For years, I conspired to dig up the knight's arms and fight Gallus. I marked a tree near the grave with a carving of two spurs so I could find it again. I never did find the courage to do it, however, and I am glad of it, knowing now it would have been a grievous disrespect to the knight."

Flyn shook his head and snorted at himself. "Sir Haward the Lambent. I looked up his name while I was a squire, years later. He remains listed in the Order's records as 'lost to an unknown end.' Gulver and I never revealed we knew his true fate."

Wynchell accepted his tale with a nod, though it was clear the lad had not understood all he heard. The clutch was a quagmire of ignorance and were it not for his time with the Tsigani, Flyn would have undoubtedly remained illiterate and unlearned. He still struggled with the ways of letters, though Sir Corc had bolstered his practice during their sojourn on the island. Pocket was his fellow pupil and they nurtured a friendly competition over who could compose better verse. The gurg was far more skilled, but Flyn retained the edge in terms of wit and prurience. One of his pieces managed to make even Corc smile. Such companionable memories seemed to intrude in the murky squalor of the sunken hut and Flyn banished them quickly before they became sullied by the bleak touch of his revisited past.

"How did you become a knight then?" Wynchell pressed, the possibility taking hold.

"It was years later," Flyn said. "My clutch-brother wanted to challenge Gallus. Gulver had always been big and had grown larger than our father. The choice was upon us. Fight. Flee. Or stay to be cut. We thought Gulver had a chance of defeating Gallus, so we struck a bargain. He would present challenge and if things went ill, I was to come to his aid."

Flyn took a deep breath, expelling it in a rush.

"Things went ill. Gulver fared well at the first, but he was poorly fed, outmatched. It was time for me to join the battle. I saw it, but I could not move. All the blood, all the broken bodies my father had made of breathing enemies . . . my courage fled. No. It was never there. Claennis intervened at the last, throwing herself over the ruined body of her son as Gallus prepared for the killing stroke. She pleaded with him and I found myself finally moving forward. Gallus had not yet decided on mercy, but I began dragging Gulver away, expecting us both to die at any moment. I did not stop until we reached the river. We were taken in by humans and Gulver eventually recovered from his wounds, but it was many years before he forgave me."

Wynchell glowered at the jar in his hand. "Gallus will never let me go."

"You are not of his blood," Flyn said, knowing his words would be harsh, but necessary. "You chose castration to combat. He does not value you, Wynchell. There are enough females here to do his bidding, enough mouths to feed that hold some measure of worth to him. You, he will part with."

The capon accepted this with dour resolve. "What if you are wrong?"

"Then I will fight him," Flyn answered firmly. "Either way, you and I leave for the river tomorrow. My human friends will come soon and give us passage. I must remain on errantry, but you shall journey north to Albain. When you arrive at the Roost, speak with Gulver and tell him from whence you come. You will find an ally in him and soon, a brother. Me you can count as one from this moment."

Flyn smiled and extended his hand across the fire. Wynchell, after the briefest consideration, took it and they clasped arms firmly.

In the morning, Flyn donned his mail and strapped the elf spurs to his feet. He took up Coalspur and stepped up out of the sunken hut, finding Wynchell and the pale light of dawn awaiting him. The capon had no possessions, wearing only his hide clout and an eager, if nervous expression. Flyn gave him a reassuring thump on the shoulder, then headed for the hall.

The females were already at work in the clutch, but paused in their chores as Flyn and Wynchell passed. Flyn caught the eye of the closest and stopped long enough to give her a wink and a bow.

She turned away quickly, returning to her work. With a smile to Wynchell, Flyn pulled the curtain back and entered the smoky hall.

They found Gallus atop his platform, not yet risen from his bed of furs. Hearing them approach, he untangled himself from the drowsy arms of three mates and peered down at them through the dim, not bothering to stand.

"Get gone," he said, his voice thick and wet. "You will find no food to break fast here."

"I take my leave," Flyn told him. "And Wynchell travels with me."

"He stays," Gallus said dismissively and settled back down on his pallet.

"No."

Flyn had not raised his voice, uttering the denial calmly and evenly. He may as well have sounded a war horn. Gallus shot up from his mattress, throwing his mates off him as he gained his feet.

He snatched up his heavy club and leapt off the platform, landing nimbly in the dust. He gave Flyn a warning look, his wattle swelling.

The females scrambled down from the platform and scuttled out the door, hugging the walls as they passed.

"He is to become a knight," Flyn stated. "He will earn his spurs and serve the Tin Isles. He will be a warrior, Gallus."

The old bird's baleful glare flicked to Wynchell. "See to the pigs."

Flyn said nothing. He did not even glance at the capon. If the lad gave in now, there was no hope of him bettering his life.

Wynchell did not move.

"The pigs!" Gallus roared, taking a step forward and thrusting with his club. The blow caught Wynchell in the gut and he fell to his knees, the breath rushing out of him in an agonized grunt. The capon coughed painfully, but slowly rose on wobbling legs. He stood and, though he kept his eyes downcast, did not budge. Gallus made a sound of disgust in his throat, then raised the club with both hands and swung.

Flyn stepped in, catching the downward swing in his hands.

The gnarled wood bashed into his palms, but he held firm. Gallus's feathers bristled, his neck and shoulders seeming to double in size.

His eyes blazed at Flyn, his beak opening with a menacing hiss.

"Let him go, father," Flyn said, nearly whispering. "Give him his freedom. Or give me what I want. A reason to kill you. I told you I was not the equal of my Grand Master. That is true. I am greater. This is no lesser son that stands before you. I am Sir Bantam Flyn, knight of the Valiant Spur and I have bested far worthier foes than you. I will take this lad from your miserable clutch or, by the Hallowed you louse-ridden savage, I will separate your head from your shoulders!"

Gallus's eyes continued to burn, but the pressure on the club lessened. Flyn released his hold, pushing the weapon away as he did and forcing his father to take a step back. Gallus breathed heavily, his talons scratching slightly at the dirt, but he made no further move. Flyn took one step back and placed his arm around Wynchell, then guided him towards the door. He turned his back on his father without fear of attack.

Outside, the females stood motionless by their tasks, watching the hut, waiting to see who would emerge.

"Are there any farewells you wish to make?" Flyn asked Wynchell.

"My mam died a few summers back," the capon replied with no small sadness.

Flyn squeezed his shoulder warmly. "Then let us be rid of this place."

They made their way across the clearing, passing a pair of females kneeling in the toft garden. For once, they did not look away and Flyn looked into their faces. Wide, bright eyes met his.

Confusion. Wonder. Desperation.

Flyn stopped.

He stood transfixed, the two females holding him fast without touching him. He should take them as well. Just these two.

He did not know if they were mates or beldams, but it was unimportant. They needed him, they desired to be taken away.

They desired. No, he could not take just two. All, all must go! What could he do with thirty pullets? He could give them the clutch. Let them rule themselves. But then they would be vulnerable. Another strut could come along and there would be no one to protect them.

No one to claim them. He would stay. Stay and serve them. Let them serve him.

He turned back towards the hall.

"Bantam Flyn?" he heard a voice, distant, nearly drowned in the throbbing furnace of his skull. "Sir? What are you doing? We must go!"

He saw red. A swimming crimson, the bodies of the females shining figures of hot white. They would be his. Shrugging out of the harness he ripped Coalspur free, tossing scabbard and belt aside. Why deny what he had come for? Why hide behind oaths and honor, vows taken to an order that no longer wanted him? He would take his vengeance and claim his prize. This tyrant would no longer roam the lands, drawing breath and breeding misery. He would die this day.

"GALLUS!"

His cry ripped through the trees, the echo lost in the pulsing of his raging heart.

The curtain of the hut was torn down and his father rushed forth. A round shield of rough bronze was strapped to his arm, the hand underneath clutching his spears and in his other hand he bore the weighty club. Flyn laughed at the sight. Bronze and wood! The uncouth barbarian and his crude weapons against the finest steel.

Flyn felt his feathers lift away from his flesh and he sunk his talons into the loam, his sword held before him in both hands.

Gallus charged and Flyn rushed to meet him, raising Coalspur above his head. He would end this with a single stroke.

The distance was eaten away and Flyn swung, bringing his sword down in a strike that would split Gallus from shoulder to belly. His blade struck nothing but soft earth as Gallus spun away, bringing his club around to slam into Flyn's exposed back. It caught him high at the shoulders, pummeling him through his mail and sending him stumbling forward. He whipped around to face Gallus once more, slashing out with the length of his blade, a warding blow to keep his enemy from pressing forward.

So. He was fast. Unarmored, he would need to be.

Flyn laughed.

Gallus's club was nearly as long as Coalspur, but he wielded it easily in one hand, keeping it low and to the side. Flyn lunged, feinting a thrust at his father's shield before whipping his blade around for a slash that would tear through the bronze. Gallus ducked the attack, hammering the edge of his shield into Flyn's thigh. He felt the blow even through his mail. Gallus was inside his guard, but Flyn released his right hand from the grip of his sword and punched downward, catching Gallus in the face, then slammed Coalspur's pommel into his shoulder. Gallus shrugged off the blows and continued his bull rush. Flyn did not resist, but rolled with the momentum, falling to his back and kicking his feet into Gallus's belly, sending him sprawling to the dirt.

Flyn scrambled to his feet, his back suddenly exposed. He turned quickly, but just as he faced his father, something slammed into his ribs, knocking the wind from his lungs. Looking down, he found a spear piercing his left side. Ignoring the pain, he looked up in time to see the second spear flying towards him. Swinging Coalspur, he batted the flung weapon aside, shattering the wooden haft. Gallus had dropped his club to hurl the spears and now retrieved it from the ground. Flyn used the moment to pull the first missile from his side.

His mail had taken some of the brunt, but not enough to prevent the head from sinking half its length into his body. Blood flowed freely through the torn links of his armor. Gallus also bore wounds. Two patches of feathers around his mid-section were slick with blood, the result of the elven spurs. His injuries, however, did not slow him. He charged again, his shield leading. Flyn swung a sweeping cut at his legs, but Gallus was already in the air, leaping the blade and hurtling towards him, swinging his club down with all the force of his descent. Flyn parried the blow, shearing a foot of length off the club, but as Gallus landed, he once again slammed the rim of his shield into Flyn's leg, this time just under the edge of his mail. Blinding pain was quickly replaced by a terrible numbness and Flyn felt his leg buckle. His fall brought him eye to eye with Gallus.

His father smiled.

Flyn flung an elbow into the hateful sneer, sending the brute reeling. Gallus rolled away, but stopped just outside of Coalspur's reach, regaining his feet. He began circling Flyn. The old bird was cunning, stepping to the side of Flyn's injured leg, knowing he could not match the speed for long and thus expose his flank. Flyn did not wait for the opening to appear.

He charged forward, but did not attack, allowing an opening in his guard. Gallus took the bait and swung his club viciously. Flyn caught the blow on his blade, the force of Gallus's stroke sinking the steel into the wood. With a downward twist of his sword, Flyn tore the club from Gallus's grip, then head-butted him in the face, sending him stumbling back. Pressing his attack, Flyn dragged Coalspur into the air above his head, then brought it down in a fast arc. Gallus swung his shield up into the stroke, interrupting the swing before Flyn could put his full weight behind it, but the dwarf-forged steel sundered the bronze. A grunt issued from Gallus as steel bit bone and bright blood spurted, running in rivulets off the barbarian's elbow. The impact drove him to a knee and Flyn planted a foot in his chest and kicked him onto his back.

He stabbed down with the greatsword, but Gallus cast the remains of the shield in his face, upsetting the finishing blow. The blade sunk deep into the ground as Gallus rolled away, kicking at Flyn's legs as he did and catching him with a spur. Gallus had no knightly caps of steel, but his natural talons were sharp enough to tear flesh, drawing blood.

Flyn pulled Coalspur from the mud, but Gallus barreled into him as he turned, knocking him off his feet and sending the sword flying from his hand. A fist punched into his face twice before the ground rose up and bashed into the back of his skull.

Dazed and disoriented, blazes of sickening light splashed across his vision as Gallus struck him again and again. He could not breathe, a hand pinning him to the earth by the throat. Blinded and scrabbling, Flyn tried to break his father's throttling grip, but it was no use. Gallus's strength was unconquerable.

Desperate for air, Flyn kicked his legs free from beneath his father and slammed his spurs into him with all the force he could muster. He heard Gallus growl in pain and the grip around his throat slackened. He kicked with the spurs again, but Gallus did not release him. Again he drove the spurs deep. With a bestial scream, Gallus wrapped his other hand around Flyn's throat and began lifting him off the ground. Flyn dug in with his spurs, grinding them deeper into his father's back, but still the brute raised him higher. Gallus was standing now, holding Flyn before him by the neck. Flyn looked into his blood-crazed eyes, leaving one spur embedded to support his own weight, kicking again and again with the other. Gallus opened his beak wide in a terrible howl of fury, then thrust his face forward at Flyn's, biting into his wattle. There was a wet sound and excruciating pain as the soft flesh was torn away from under Flyn's beak. He felt Gallus fling him aside and he hit the ground heavily, sliding in the muck.

His vision cleared and he saw Gallus stumbling for his club.

Hot blood pumped down Flyn's neck, but he paid no heed, casting about until his eyes fell on his sword, lying on the ground a dozen paces away. He crawled towards it, snatching at the grip and rolling to his back. Gallus advanced towards him, his steps unsteady, the club dangling in his hand. Flyn managed to rise, the weight of his armor trying to drag him back to the earth. Coalspur was an unwieldy weight in his hands, the blade swaying drunkenly in front of him. He needed to end this. Now.

There was not strength enough in him for another great swing. He would need to get in close, plant the blade in Gallus's middle for a draw cut. Disembowel the bastard. Flyn widened his grip on the sword, placing his left hand down at the pommel, inverting his right hand so that the heel butted up against the cross-guard. It was something Corc had taught him, calling it the oar-grip.

Gallus was nearly upon him and Flyn planted his feet, crouching low. The club came up. Flyn sprang, ducking his head into his shoulder, allowing Gallus's blow to fall. He nearly lost his feet as the club slammed into his left arm, but he barreled through the impact and the agony, pushing the edge of the blade into his father with his full weight. He heard Gallus grunt in pain and Flyn stepped out to the side, dragging the sword along with him. A scraping filled his ears, metal on metal. Flyn looked to the ground, and saw his father's guts. One pale, glistening loop trailed among the remnants of Gallus's severed girdle of bronze discs.

Amazingly, Gallus kept his feet, his face still, his eyes drunken. He took one solid step forward before his legs gave out, but even as he struck his knees, the old tyrant continued to stare up at Flyn with stubborn wrath.

"Farewell, father," Flyn said, raising Coalspur over his head for the ending stroke.

Something struck him hard upon the shoulder before he brought the sword down. A fist-sized stone tumbled to the ground at his feet. Another came arcing at his face, causing Flyn to duck gracelessly. Looking about, he saw the females closing in on him from every direction, flinging rocks.

"Enough!" Flyn demanded from behind his warding arms.

"I only seek to help you!"

The stones continued to pelt him, many blunted by his mail, but others striking painfully into his fingers and head, his feet and elbows. The closer the pullets came, the better their aim and Flyn was now awash in a battering storm. He cursed and cried out in protest, trying to cease the assault while searching desperately for a way to win free of his encircling attackers. A rock cracked horribly into the back of his skull and Flyn screeched with rage and pain, whirling around with his sword drawn back. If he could not reason with these misguided harridans, he would cut them down!

The pullets did not recoil from his blade. They held their ground, well within Coalspur's deadly reach, and continued to cast rocks, stooping to fetch clods of mud when the stones were exhausted.

Flyn paused, lowering his sword. He could not do it, would not. He could not fathom the females' defense of their oppressor, but he would not slay them for it, peril to himself or no.

"Peace!" he cried at the pullets. "I will go! On my word! I will go!" The hail of debris began to slacken. Flyn turned to make good on his promise and was lifted off his feet when the club smashed up under his beak. He felt a crack and blood filled his mouth, choking him. He must have risen, for he was on his feet when Gallus hit him again, the wood crushing his ribs. Somehow, the tyrant had regained his feet, holding his escaping entrails with one hand while he swung the club with the other. Coalspur remained in Flyn's own hand, but he could not bring the sword up in time. He heard the dull rush of wind as the club swung again, slapping sharply into his mail, feeling bones snap beneath. Gallus disappeared. There was only the beating of the club, coming from everywhere at once, swatting him about in a maelstrom of pain.

He was on the ground.

Gallus loomed above him, visible through only one eye, the other swollen shut. The savage was gutted and yet lived.

Flyn laughed through his shattered beak. There was nothing else he could do.

Sounds. Soft and sharp and regular.

Flyn's eye opened and found Wynchell. Half of Wynchell.

The capon struck downward at something unseen. Dirt flew. He was waist deep in a hole, digging. The plump lad took a breath, straightening his back and saw Flyn looking at him. Spade in hand, he stepped out of the unfinished grave.

Flyn's grave.

Wynchell stood over him, his face a melted candle of fear, fury and despair. Flyn tried to speak, tried to raise an arm towards the youth, but could accomplish neither. Wynchell swallowed hard, then raised the spade, poising the cutting edge over Flyn's neck.

The tool trembled above him and Flyn, waiting for the descent, spat blood.

With a powerless moan, Wynchell dropped the spade and bent down, grabbing at Flyn's shoulders and tugging. Feebly, Flyn buried his heels in the dirt, trying to stop the lad from pulling him into the hole. He only slid a few inches and then he felt his mail being tugged off his body. Flyn choked on a hundred screams as the capon fumbled to get him out of the armor, but at last the task was done. Wynchell tossed the hauberk into the hole, while Flyn lay panting and whimpering.

"You must go," the youth's face appeared above him. He was weeping. "Can you move? You must go!"

Flyn felt something being wrested from his grip. Coalspur.

He clutched down hard on the grip, growling and shaking his head.

"You will go quicker without it," Wynchell protested.

Flyn shook his head again and rolled onto his side, the pain in his ribs nearly ridding him of consciousness. His belt lay within reach, discarded after Wynchell stripped him of his armor. Flyn grabbed for it, looping it around Coalspur's crossguard. Thrusting his other arm out before him, he sunk his fingers into the loam and pulled, dragging himself along.

"The pullets tend to Gallus's wounds. You must be gone soon." Wynchell helped him rise, but the lad was not strong enough to support him. Flyn managed only a score of steps before collapsing once more. After a few moments fighting to breathe, the capon helped him again, and again he stumbled along weakly before falling. Flyn did not know how long this occurred, but it was near dark when the lad finally gave up.

"I must get back," Wynchell muttered and without another word he was gone.

Flyn lay in the grass, in the wind, for a long time.

He crawled through the long night, his injuries often forcing him into a swoon. His progress was torturous and he had no concept of time or distance. He still bled, leaving a trail behind him. Gallus would have no trouble finding him if he pursued. Flyn needed to cover ground, put space between him and his father. He crawled.

He fled.

Dawn came and Flyn emerged from a stupor born of exhaustion. His harness was gone and he dragged Coalspur along behind him, unsheathed, tethered to one foot with his belt. The sun grew high and Flyn had long left the shelter of the forest. He crawled through the scrub land, the heat pressing down on him from above. It had not rained and his tongue became a dry lump, his throat a dusty, empty well.

It was a row of hedges that defeated him. Thick with bramble, they grew across his path as far as he could see in either direction. He tried to crawl through, but the bracken was too dense.

Flyn tore at the hedge, snapping the thorny limbs with raw hands.

It was no use. Snarling, Flyn gave up the fight, lying limp in the underbrush.

Bested by a bush. Killed by his father. This was the death he deserved. A fool's death, sought and found.

Bantam Flyn. Deserter. Lost to an unknown end. A far better entry in the annals than the truth.

Flyn rolled to his back. He wondered how long Coalspur would lie with his bones until being discovered. Wincing, he reached down and untied the sword from his foot, using the belt to pull it to his chest. He unwrapped the belt from the cross-guard and was about to fling it away when his good eye fell upon his pouch. Fumbling, he undid the clasp and reached inside, finding a single object. He drew it out and held it before him against the harsh blaze of the sun.

It was the small wooden horse he had taken from under the stairs of the tower. Pocket's horse.

He had meant to give it to Sir Corc to take back to the boy, but had forgotten during the flight from the Roost. Held between his fingers, Flyn used the little horse to eclipse the sun. He opened his split beak, muttering the words through the pain.

"Very well, my little king. Very well."

Flyn carefully returned the horse to his pouch, then affixed Coalspur to his foot once more. Rolling back to his stomach, he chose a direction and began crawling along the hedgerow, looking for an opening. Hours later, he found one.

The sun was setting when he heard the river. He crawled on and at last he saw the water. Flyn tumbled down the muddy embankment and splashed onto the bank. He pulled his sword loose and struggled to his knees. With the last of his strength, he thrust the blade into the mud and collapsed. Coalspur was over five feet of bright steel. Flyn hoped it was enough to catch an eye, even in the dark. He shivered as the darkness spread, his body wracked with fever, but he failed to crawl up the embankment and out of the wet. Trembling and spent, he slept in the mud, waking in fits from tormented dreams.

It was full night when he awoke, the moon glinting off the current. Something was approaching, treading boldly through the shadows. Flyn lay helpless, unable to move. Against the starlight a tall shape appeared, coming from the scrub land. It stood upon the embankment, facing him, looking down at him. Agilely, it jumped down onto the bank, landing solidly in the muck. Flyn saw talons approaching and the shadows of long tail feathers.

Gallus.

Come to finish him.

The figure loomed over him, its arm raising. Flyn thought he saw a glint of mail.

"Corc?" Flyn's voice was barely a rasp.

The figure did not respond, but continued to outstretch its arm, slowly. Towards Coalspur.

A bellowing roar sounded through the night as something thundered heavily along the shoreline, throwing water in massive torrents as it charged. The figure whirled to face the lumbering mass of shadow and Flyn heard a sword quickly drawn. Mud and water splattered Flyn as the two shapes met, the deep roar continuing to burst over the sounds of struggle. Then all went quiet, save for a low growl that came nearer. Four large feet squelched in the mud around Flyn and the moon fled, the huffing creature standing over him, straddling him.

Splashing signaled the rapid steps of others approaching, bringing voices.

"Father! They are here! Pali's hurt!"

The steps came closer and the moonlight returned as the bulk stepped from over top of him.

"I have him, Tsura. Check Flyn."

The girl knelt in the mud next to him. He felt his head being lifted.

"He is alive. Father, it is grave."

"Help me get him to the boat." Milosh's voice was calm.

"We will get him to the Atsinganoi."

"N-no," Flyn managed, his own voice sounding distant.

"Gnome. Gipeswic."

And then he let the blackness claim him.

THIRTEEN

Ingelbert squinted hard, pinching at the corners of his throbbing eyes. The moon was socked in by fog and the fat in his lamp was nearly spent. He could barely see the scrawls on the page, his mind wandering while his eyes remained fixed on the same word, the last he had translated for some hours.

Rain.

It was the first time a word had been repeated in the green book. At first, Ingelbert thought he had inadvertently doubled back, reworking what he had already unraveled, but then he began to find the word on other pages. Every page.

Try as he might, he could coax nothing more from the symbols. He flipped the heavy volume closed with a frustrated expulsion of breath, the thud of the pages drawing several glances from the remaining patrons in the wine sink. Ingelbert ducked his head back towards his table and fidgeted idly with the spoon stuck in the now-cold bowl of uneaten soup. The wine jug was also untouched, but its contents were not for him. Indeed, the only thing the rough establishment offered Ingelbert of any value was a place to work in the late watches.

He sat outside the sagging pavilion, preferring the open air when the nights were dry. The wind still played at the pages, but it was a smaller annoyance than the boisterous singing of the crowds within the tent proper. Knowing the surly proprietor was unlikely to refill the fat lamp, Ingelbert stood, taking up the green book and supporting it in the crook of his arm. He stared at the wine jug resting on the knife-scarred surface of the table and considered leaving it behind. The swimming stares of the drunks at the surrounding tables were also affixed to the jug, dumbly hoping it would remain when Ingelbert left. It would cause a scuffle if he abandoned it. He knew from experience. Loosing another tired breath, Ingelbert hooked a finger in the loop of the jug and swung it off the table. He could hear the low grunts of pathetic regret issue from the drunks as he walked away.

Trudging wearily down the rough lane, Ingelbert glanced upward, scanning the eaves of the warehouses on either side. It was several minutes before he finally caught sight of Gasten, flying silently from one roof to the other, keeping just ahead of Ingelbert's progress. Had the owl not moved, Ingelbert would never have seen him. Each time he landed, Gasten became lost in the darkness, blending into the shadowy thatching and sooty tiles.

There was always a brief flash, when the owl's eyes caught the diffuse moonlight as he turned to stare down at Ingelbert, and then even that evidence of his presence vanished. For all the owl's quiescence, Ingelbert was always certain he remained nearby. That was why he named him Gasten, a Middangearder word for restless spirit. A ghost.

But the bird was corporeal enough. Ingelbert had touched him, felt his feathers and even managed to get the owl to perch on his arm. He appeared to breathe, his magnificent breast rising and falling, but Ingelbert had yet to see him eat, try as he might to tempt him with vermin bartered from one of Gipeswic's rat catchers. Still, Gasten may have hunted on his own in the daylight hours when he stayed away. The rodzlagen eagle-owl typically sought their prey at dusk, Ingelbert recalled from his reading, but he had not been able to witness Gasten's activity during that time, for he only showed himself at night. He knew the owl was once dead, whether it remained so was unanswered. Be it renewed life or awakened death that now animated him was a mystery, but such was a minor detail to Ingelbert. He was more fixated on the cause.

There were many wondrous things in the world, the Fae not the least of which. Ingelbert had returned to the place where he encountered the vile Edric and the other hunters, to the copse where Gasten died. He had hoped to find evidence of a Fae dwelling in the area. A woodwose possibly, perhaps even an elf, some being capable of returning the owl to life. He spent a day wandering, even entreating aloud for any Fae to reveal itself, but it proved a fruitless search. It was a practical investigation, almost desperate, but without access to a proper library, Ingelbert knew of no other way to seek answers. He wanted to ask Deglan about it, but the gnome was in no fit state to humor any questions.

Ingelbert continued along the streets. He was not alone despite the late hour. He made a point of ignoring the beggars and hoped he was ignored in kind by the clavigers, Gipeswic's permanent watchmen. Brawny and generally ill-tempered, the clavigers kept the peace night and day, prone to settling disturbances with the stout maces they carried, especially after the sun went down.

Ingelbert kept his eyes directed at the cobbles, resisting the urge to glance skyward for Gasten. Soon, the cobbles ceased, giving way to the sticky mud of the unpaved tracks that dominated most of the town. Ingelbert made for the north wall. The gates would be shut until morning, but there remained a means of exiting the town, one that he had become well-acquainted with during the past week.

Gipeswic's north wall contained two gates. The first, called the Foot Gate, opened to the barrowlands and was the principle entrance for all traffic from the road. Further west along the wall stood the larger River Gate, a complex construction built astride the River Orr. When opened, it allowed vessels traveling along the waterway to enter the town and proceed down to the bay. No foot traffic was ever allowed into Gipeswic at night, but the guards at the River Gate had the power to admit boats at their discretion, an arrangement made with the wealthy guild masters to ensure no hindrance to the fruitful trade route from the river. On either side of the River Gate, a pair of sally ports were set into the wall, allowing the gate wardens access to the banks of the Orr should they need to inspect a boat before allowing it into town. The guards at the River Gate were not opposed to allowing people to exit the walls through the sally ports, for a price of course.

As Ingelbert approached the River Gate he could hear the raised voices of the guards. Two of them stood on the fortified bridge above the gate, leaning over the parapet and shouting, waving their arms at whoever was requesting entrance on the far side of the wall. Their cargo must not have been important.

Ingelbert approached the sally port on the west side of the gate.

The guard posted there slouched lazily against the wall, his pike leaning next to him.

"Looking to go out?" the man yawned.

"As long as it is, um, as long as it is safe."

The guard pushed himself off the wall and began fumbling with a ring of heavy keys on his belt.

"Aye, it's safe," he said, cocking an eye up at the commotion above. "Just some river rats trying to get in. Bloody gypsy swindler and his whore." He turned and began unlocking the sally port, first the heavy grate, then the thick iron door beyond.

Ingelbert followed the guard into a low, narrow tunnel running the thickness of the wall and leading to another set of doors These the guard also unlocked, long practice allowing him to complete the task in the dark. The argument from the gate intruded into the tunnel as the final door was opened, admitting the scant moonlight. Ingelbert pressed a few coins into the guard's waiting palm. He would not be able to do this much longer, not unless Deglan began treating the townsfolk again.

Ingelbert stepped out of the tunnel and heard the door slam shut behind him. He looked briefly to his right and saw a ramshackle boat anchored on the near bank. A short man of middling years stood in the bow, craning his neck up towards the guards on the bridge. He wore the gaudy clothes of an entertainer and his long dark hair was curly, framing his bearded face.

"Please, you must understand!" the man pleaded. "We must come in now!"

"We warned you to be gone, Tsigani!"

Ingelbert turned away from the river, inwardly cursing the men on the gate. The river wanderers were ever maligned in Sasana.

"I tell you, I must see the gnome herbalist!"

Ingelbert paused, but only for the briefest of moments.

Everyone was looking for Deglan. Even if this poor man managed to gain admittance to Gipeswic, he would only join the ranks of the dozens of sick and injured desperately seeking the gnome's aid.

None of them would succeed.

No matter, the guards would remain the gypsy's biggest obstacle. "Get gone!"

"Send word to him, at least," the man pressed. "Tell him that Sir Flyn is gravely injured and requires his help!"

Ingelbert spun around and ran back to the bank.

"What did you say?" he asked as he drew near the boat, still on the run. The man had not noticed his approach and was startled, snapping his head around in alarm. In the same moment, a throaty groan issued from the bow of the boat and what Ingelbert had taken for a pile of fishing nets and old furs shifted heavily, sprouting a wide head that also turned to look at him. Ingelbert skidded to a sudden halt at the sight and slipped on the wet grass along the bank, dropping his book and the wine jug as he fell unceremoniously onto his backside.

The guards on the parapet must also have overlooked the animal. Shouts of alarm mingled with curses and threats as Ingelbert saw several bows drawn back, aimed down at the boat.

The gypsy man threw up his arms.

"Wait! No! I beg you, he is not a danger! He too is injured, he is no threat to you!"

All the shouting was agitating the beast, a bear, Ingelbert now saw as his brain caught up with his eyes. It stood, huffing and complaining, causing the boat to rock and the men on the gate to draw their bowstrings further back.

"Bloody witch-man!" one of the guards swore. "Trying to smuggle that monster within the walls!"

The gypsy was desperately trying to calm the men on the wall and the bear at the same time, his eyes and beseeching hands darting between them.

"This is not true," he said. "The bear is hurt, as is the knight who is below decks. I swear! Come see for yourselves and know I speak the truth!"

The guards let out a derisive laugh. "Think we are to fall for that?" Ingelbert scrambled to his feet, leaving his belongings and waved up at the guards. "I will look!"

His words caused four bows to swing in his direction and he hopped back involuntarily. "Dammit, hold!" Deglan was wearing off on him. Ingelbert was not normally one for swearing.

When the arrows did not immediately loose, he swallowed hard and recovered what dignity he could muster. "I, um, I will look. If you would just, ah, if you would just lower your bows, I will go aboard."

There was a pause as the guards considered this.

"Go on then," one of them said at last, easing his string slightly and directing his fellows to do the same, but they returned their aim to the bear which was now circling slowly on the deck, ridding itself of the coverings which had kept it concealed.

Ingelbert approached the side of the boat slowly. "What, what is your name?" he asked the short man quietly.

"Milosh Ursari," the man answered calmly, still stealing glances up at the parapet.

"My name is Ingelbert Crane and I, I have a question for you, Milosh Ursari,"

Ingelbert said. "If I attempt, that is, if I come aboard, what exactly will be the actions of your, um, of your bear?"

Milosh's face grew still. "He will not harm you." The words were an oath.

"Very well." Ingelbert extended his arm and stretched his leg out over the water, placing a foot on the rail of the boat as Milosh grabbed his hand and helped haul him onto the vessel.

Ingelbert took one more quick glance at the bear, now no more than a stride removed. It had appeared large from the shore, now it was positively huge.

"Pali, down," Milosh instructed the bear and the great beast eased itself back onto the deck with a low moan.

Ingelbert returned his attention to the gypsy. "You say you have Bantam Flyn aboard?"

Milosh's face rippled briefly with shock and then relief.

"You know him?"

"I do."

"Then come."

Milosh led him to the stern of the vessel where a small stair led down below decks. The man pushed back a curtain at the base of the stair and stepped aside to allow Ingelbert to pass. He had to duck in the low hold, his height a hindrance. Within was a cramped cabin. It looked as if the gypsies typically slept in hammocks, which swung empty from the low roof. Flyn lay on the floor, a woman kneeling beside him, tending him.

She looked over her shoulder as Ingelbert entered. Her skin was tanned by the sun and her near-black, unruly hair fell down her back, tied into a quick tail. She was more somberly dressed than Milosh, but had the same coloring in her hair and eyes, though far younger. Concern was lacquered across her face, and a little fear, just at the edges, but her entire visage emanated a strong resolve.

Truly, she was beautiful.

"Tsura," Milosh said. "This man knows Flyn."

"We need the gnome," the woman said to no one in particular.

"I, um, I am acquainted with, ah, with Master Loamtoes as well."

"Inkstain." The weak, quavering voice caused all eyes to look down. Ingelbert had been so taken aback by the woman he had not so much as glanced at Flyn. He did so now and his stomach lurched. The young coburn's face was nearly unrecognizable. One eye was swollen completely shut, encased in discolored, puffy flesh. The other was barely open and fluttering rapidly, leaking fluid. The top half of Flyn's beak was misaligned, a wide crack running up from the bottom edge and cutting across beneath his nostrils. Below, what remained of his wattle was a shredded mess, oozing blood and pus. One of his legs was bent at an unnatural angle, the feathers beginning to molt off the inflamed flesh.

"Inkstain," Flyn repeated, his voice surfacing through wet and ragged breaths.

Ingelbert stood frozen, his mind unable to reconcile the sight beneath him. Bantam Flyn, once so proud, so intimidating, so full of life. This was the coburn who had made him laugh, made him trust, then turned in an instant and lifted him into the air, thrusting a knife in his face. Ingelbert had feared him then, a fear which had never truly diminished. Until now. There was nothing to fear here. The imposing young warrior now lay broken on the floor in the dark hold of a creaking boat. Dying.

Ingelbert leaned down past the woman and gripped Flyn's hand. "Hold fast, Sir." He felt the slightest squeeze in response. He straightened and looked at Milosh.

"Take your boat back upriver," he told him. "Just far enough so that you are out of sight of the gate."

"You cannot get us into Gipeswic?" It was the woman, Tsura, who asked.

Ingelbert met her piercing eyes. "Um, no, I am afraid, afraid not. It would take more money than I have and even then . . ." *You are Tsigani.* But he left it unsaid, just as he left unsaid that it would be pointless to enter the town. Deglan was not there. "Wait. Wait a little longer."

He tried to give Tsura a reassuring look, but was unsure of his success. He turned and quickly made his way up out of the hold.

Milosh followed close behind.

Ingelbert waved up at the guards. "It is as he says. But the knight is dead. They will be on their way."

He turned to find Milosh giving him a quizzical look.

"Trust me," Ingelbert whispered. He could not risk that one of the guards might actually take pity and allow the boat to pass. It would only cause more delay and time was not Flyn's ally.

"You will return?" the gypsy asked.

"I will return," Ingelbert promised and jumped back to shore. He gathered up his fallen book, but the wine jug had cracked when he fell. It was just as well. Ingelbert turned from the river and hurried off, keeping the town wall to his left. He ran as fast as he was able, looking up once to see Gasten keeping pace in the sky above him, his broad wingspan silhouetted against the night sky.

Ingelbert counted the towers along the wall as he sped past. At the fifth he put Gipeswic to his back and ran across the expanse of cleared ground, dodging the stumps of trees felled long ago to build the town, its walls, houses, warehouses and docks. At this pace Ingelbert would be lucky not to trip on a sinister rock or root and break his neck, but he did not slow. Flyn had once risked himself to save Ingelbert's life. He could do no different.

Soon, a small wood appeared on the horizon, a dark stand of trees watching over the glow of several distant fires. Ingelbert's legs doubled their efforts and his feet pounded forward. His lungs were burning, his head was unpleasantly light and he felt sick to his stomach, all the signs of sudden, unaccustomed physical strain. His injuries from the fall were mostly healed, save his plastered arm, but the exertion was taxing him, bringing dormant pains back to bloom. Still, he did not slow until he reached the wood. Gasten flew straight into the canopy without rustling a single leaf and was lost from sight in the branches.

The smell of wood-smoke and unwashed bodies was thick beneath the trees. Low, crude structures were scattered about, hovels of mud, rough-cut timber and rotting, untanned hides.

Figures huddled around the half-dozen pitiful cookfires, many dressed head to toes in stained rags, faces covered with deep hoods, heads swaddled in filthy bandages.

Deglan had left the fish wife's hut to escape the ever-increasing number of towns-folk seeking his healing arts. But even in a town of Gipeswic's size, there were few places he could hide for long before word of his new lodging spread. He could not disappear, so he took up residence in a place where he was certain to remain undisturbed, seeking solace where the good townspeople would never dare come. The leper camp.

There were some two dozen exiles in the camp and most barely glanced up as Ingelbert came into the ring of light, breathing heavily. They were used to his nightly visits now. He wasted no time, striding between the fires with purpose. He was too well-read to fear the disease, knowing it was rarely catching so long as one was careful. Deglan, being Fae, was entirely immune and the stricken inhabitants of the camp had accepted his presence readily.

He could not cure their affliction, but had provided considerable relief and promised to halt the progress of their disfigurement. It was a simple matter for the herbalist. The malady was obvious and required no real work for such a skilled healer as Deglan. He did not even need to remain sober.

Ingelbert made straight for one particular hovel and thrust the hanging aside. The lepers had graced Deglan with the best dwelling in the camp, big enough for Ingelbert to stand in, so long as he bent nearly double. The gnome lay on a straw pallet, facing the wall. He jerked when Ingelbert entered, casting a bleary-eyed look over his shoulder.

"Just leave the jug," Deglan mumbled, then turned back to the wall.

"There is no wine," Ingelbert told him. "And there is no time. You must come with me now. Flyn—"

But Deglan had only heard the first statement. He rolled over with a scowl. "No wine? Dammit boy, what good are you? You have only—"

Ingelbert knelt forward, getting right in the gnome's sour face. "Enough! You must rouse yourself from this besotted disgrace. Bantam Flyn is injured! He needs our help, Deglan! Your help!"

Confusion wrinkled the herbalist's face. His breath reeked of stale wine. "Flyn? He is here?"

Ingelbert nodded. "He is dying."

Deglan stared at him with a lost expression for a moment, then his puzzlement melted into a frown. He rolled to a crouch and reached out so Ingelbert could help him stand. He cast about the hovel and began stumbling around the tight space, gathering up his satchel and various jars strewn about the room. Upon inspection, several turned out to be empty wine jugs, which the gnome let fall back to the ground. Most of the oddments he stuffed into his bag, but one particular item he kept in his hand. Ingelbert was no herbalist, but he recognized the green, leafy plant. Boggard's posy.

He was alarmed when Deglan began quickly tearing the leaves free and stuffing them into his mouth.

"Stop!" he exclaimed, reaching over to snatch the remainder out of Deglan's hand. "It's poisonous!"

"To you," Deglan snarled through a mouthful of leaves and batted his hand away. "I am not so drunk that I need my judgment questioned." He continued to chew and shoved a few more of the leaves into his mouth before waving impatiently. "Now lead on."

Ingelbert led them out of the camp swiftly. Deglan said nothing to the lepers, though his departure caused a stir in the poor wretches. Some of them stood, limping along behind until the edge of the wood. There they stopped following. Ingelbert glanced back at the shrouded, forlorn forms. Near a score stood together, watching him and Deglan leave. Near a score, and yet each of them seemed so very alone.

"What happened?" Deglan demanded, his words thick with chewing.

Ingelbert directed his attention forward. "I, uh, I do not know. Flyn is with some Tsigani, on a, on a boat on the river."

"Is he conscious?"

"Barely."

"Tell me what you saw."

Ingelbert related the injuries as best he could as they walked, but was forced to stop when Deglan became violently sick, his sudden retching driving him to his knees. The gnome vomited a dark, thick gob of undigested plant, followed by a rush of sticky fluid. After, he remained on his knees, coughing and breathing laboriously. Deglan took a moment to collect himself, spat once then rose and waved Ingelbert onward.

"Any bleeding wounds?" Deglan pressed.

"Not that I could see," Ingelbert told him. "Internally, perhaps. Um, I mean, definitely."

He heard the gnome curse in the darkness, then suddenly Deglan grabbed his wrist jerking him to a halt.

"Easy! You almost walked directly into that damn hole."

Ingelbert peered ahead and in the poor moonlight could just make out a difference in the depth of shadows before him.

"Best you follow my lead," Deglan said. "It's a wonder you found your way with those human eyes."

Ingelbert stood perplexed for a moment. His vision did seem to suddenly be worse, though he had no trouble getting to the camp. He never did, and he never brought a torch or lamp. Curious.

Before setting off behind Deglan, Ingelbert looked up into the dark veil of the sky with his now trammeled sight. Gasten was nowhere to be seen.

***

Deglan's head was splitting. The boggard's posy had done its work, but it would be another few hours before he was fully recovered. He inwardly cursed himself for a drunken fool as he scrambled along the river bank.

"Where is this damn boat?" he asked Ingelbert.

"Should be just ahead," the man replied. "Just out of sight of the walls."

And then, after a bend in the river, Deglan saw it. An ugly vessel, more akin to a small barge than a boat, though it did possess a single mast and a long bow. Lamps were lit on board.

"Buggery and shit," Deglan intoned slowly, separating each word. "There's a fucking bear."

"Right." Ingelbert sounded a touch sheepish. "Forgot to, um, warn you about that."

"Damn thing is hurt," Deglan grumbled. "Can see that from here. That what injured Flyn?"

Ingelbert's response was uncertain. "I do not believe so." A man stood on deck alongside the bear, speaking to it in soothing tones. Ingelbert hailed the man as they approached.

"Milosh!"

A ramp had been lowered from the boat to the shore and the chronicler traversed it in two easy strides, undeterred by the shaggy beast. Deglan was less eager to be so close and remained on shore.

"Ah!" the one named Milosh proclaimed. "Ingelbert, you have returned as you said. Deepest thanks. The men you sent have already come and taken Flyn into town. You have the gratitude of the Ursari."

Ingelbert's mouth hung open. "Men? Um, I do not . . . wait, no—"

"What men?" Deglan growled.

Milosh looked down at him, his face falling, then looked back to Ingelbert. "Four men, they came with a mule and a litter. The dwarf that led them said—"

Deglan's skin flushed. "Dwarf?" Forgetting the bear, he stamped up the ramp and looked up at the gypsy. "Reddish beard? Shaven lip?"

Milosh nodded swiftly.

"Fafnir," Ingelbert said.

"He said you sent him," Milosh told the chronicler. "You and Master Loamtoes—"

"I am Master Loamtoes!" Deglan fumed. "And we did not send anyone."

"Then why would he come?" Milosh asked. "I do not understand."

Deglan glared up at Ingelbert and they shared a long look, but the chronicler was equally perplexed.

"What by Earth and Stone would that steel-peddling bastard want with Flyn?" Deglan muttered, mostly to himself.

"He forged Flyn's sword," Ingelbert offered.

"Another debt?" Deglan snorted, rubbing a frustrated hand along his mutton-chops. "What? Recollect the weapon and leave the strut to die?"

"Is my daughter in danger?" Milosh asked, his voice taking on a new, almost panicked edge, while next to him the bear began to growl low in its throat.

Ingelbert's head shot up. "Tsura?"

The gypsy man nodded, his eyes widening. "She went with them. She would not be parted from Flyn. I let her go! I told her I would come in the morning when the gate opened."

Ingelbert was struggling to give the man an answer, some reassurance, but he only stammered, groping for words.

"Milosh," Deglan said firmly, infusing his voice with as much calm as he could muster. "I do not believe your daughter will be harmed. Fafnir . . . may be trying to help."

It might be true. He may have hated the dwarf, but there was no evidence to suggest his actions were malevolent. When Deglan and a band of other desperate fools had camped at the King's Stables, preparing to launch an assault on Castle Gaunt, the piskie Rosheen had told him it was Fafnir who helped lead the people of Hog's Wallow away from the Red Cap raid that destroyed their village. He had also prevented her from entering the fort of Kederic Winetongue and delivered her to Sir Corc in Black Pool, a deed which may have saved her life. Rosheen had borne no love for the dwarf, but by her own admission he was capable of worthy, if not altogether selfless, deeds.

"How, how could he have known Flyn was here?" Ingelbert asked. The lad was shaken. He hid it well, but it was not like him to forget even the smallest detail.

"Same way he found Faabar's grave," Deglan reminded him.

"Fafnir said no blade he forged could hide from him. Likely smelled Flyn coming or however dwarfs do it. He was prepared, that is damn certain."

"I must get beyond the walls," Milosh declared. "Find my daughter."

"Ingelbert will do that," Deglan told him.

"She is my only child. I must—"

"You must stay here," Deglan cut him off, trying to ignore the threatening sounds rumbling out of the bear. He cast a thumb at the animal. "I don't fancy trying to heal that damn thing without you present." He did not wait for the man to raise further protest, turning quickly to face Ingelbert. "Get back into town. Find Flyn.

Dawn is only a few hours away. Keep him from being moved further and send the girl back here so I know where you are. Understood?"

Ingelbert nodded firmly. He was clever, not asking what he should do if he could not find Flyn and the Tsigani girl. Such a question would not do Milosh any good. Ingelbert hurried back down the ramp and was soon lost from sight around the bend.

"Do you have any medicines on board?" Deglan asked Milosh. "Herbs? Unguents?"

The gypsy nodded and went below decks, returning swiftly with several bundles. Deglan looked them over. There was some vervain and eyebright, both dried.

Deglan had no way of knowing if they were harvested at the height of their potency, but it was better than nothing. His own supplies were severely limited.

"I am going to look at the bear's wound," Deglan told Milosh pointedly. "I trust you can keep him calm?"

Milosh nodded confidently. The gypsy went and knelt by the bear's head, whispering to him in the Tsigani tongue and stroking his wide head, caressing his ears. Deglan approached slowly, his gaze shifting involuntarily to the claws curving out from the animal's massive front paws.

"What is his name?" Deglan asked, trying to keep his voice from shaking.

"Pali."

Deglan took another cautious step. He was now within the beast's reach.

"Listen here, Pali," he said. "I know I look small and delicious, but mark me, any great, smelly brute that tries to eat Deglan Loamtoes will choke on him. As our mutual friend Flyn likes to say, I am a moldy old mushroom and you can bet your shaggy hide I'm the poisoned kind."

The bear looked up at him with unconcerned eyes, breath rushing out of his big, wet nose. Deglan got close and circled the animal, examining it only with his eyes. There were a few small cuts around Pali's head and neck, but those appeared to be knitting fine on their own. However, there was a long, deep gash that ran along the shoulder and across the upper back.

"I am going to touch him now," Deglan told Milosh and waited for the man to nod an assertion. Even with the bear lying flat on its belly, Deglan had to stretch up on his toes to properly inspect the wound. Pali gave a grunt and shifted slightly when his fingers probed the split flesh. Deglan froze, hoping this was not the last patient he ever treated. Thankfully, Milosh was well in control and Pali quickly settled.

"This is a sword wound," Deglan said. "Can you tell me what happened?"

"Little," Milosh replied, his voice still low and soothing. "It was night when we found Flyn, darker than this one. Pali got to him first and drove off the other coburn."

Deglan's brow furrowed. "Other coburn?"

"Truly," Milosh replied. "It was too dark to see much else, but it was a coburn that threatened Flyn."

"Another coburn with a sword," Deglan mused darkly.

"Might have been one of his brother knights looking to help him."

"No," Milosh said firmly. "Pali would not have attacked unless Flyn was in danger."

Deglan stepped away from the bear. "I will need to prepare some herbs, but I think he will mend."

Milosh looked greatly relieved. "I thank you."

Taking his bowl and muddler out of his satchel, Deglan sat on a coil of rope. "You raised him," he said to Milosh. "Flyn."

The man nodded. "He and his brother Gulver. Though only partially. They were adolescents when they came to us."

Deglan let his surprise show. He was not aware Flyn had a brother. Deglan knew Gulver from his time at the Roost, a bloody big bastard without any of Flyn's careless charm.

"They were always very different," Milosh said, picking up on Deglan's astonishment. "Flyn was like a river during a strong rain. Fast flowing, accepting all that life dropped upon him and using it to fuel his course. Gulver was more a lake, large and quiet, stagnant on the surface, but beneath, great depth." The gypsy laughed softly, his face suffused with memory, and then worry crept in. "And Tsura. She is simply the sun. She is warmth and light, yet blinding and distant, too great for me to ever understand."

"She will return, Milosh," Deglan told him. "Fear not."

"Do you have children, Master Loamtoes?"

Yes. He almost said it, but caught himself.

"No," he said. "No, I have no children."

Damn the wine. Blink had been on his mind often of late.

He had crawled into a bottle to drown out the pain of Faabar's lack of trust in him, but only succeeded in swimming through a choppy sea of tormented memories. Spirits summoned ghosts, funny thing that. He regretted giving her up, but only because he was alive. Had they all been killed at Castle Gaunt, he never would have doubted his choice. Of all the possibilities this was not the harshest. What if he had chosen to keep Blink close and the battle had gone ill? He could bear the pain of her absence, but he could never have lived with her loss. She was safer with Madigan. That was what he told himself then and that was what he had to keep telling himself now.

The thought of the Sure Finder brought another thought to Deglan's mind and he took it up quickly, relieved to turn away from useless regrets.

"I knew a man once," Deglan told Milosh, "with an uncanny connection to a pair of hounds." He remembered the words Curdle had used, repeating them aloud. "Three minds that function as one. Is that the way of it for you and the bear?"

Milosh wore a thin, almost sad grin. "It is one of the rare gifts of my people. But for me it is less about the mind and more a sharing of spirit."

Deglan kept his focus on crushing the herbs. "That young man, Ingelbert Crane, has an animal connected with him."

"The owl."

Deglan peered up at the gypsy. "You know?"

Milosh dipped his chin. "I sensed it."

Deglan found he was not at all surprised. He was beginning to like this crafty old bugger. "He thinks I have been too drunk to notice. But a week soused is not enough to make me blind. Tell me Milosh, this owl that is following him, it is not the same as the man and his hounds, not the same as you and Pali, is it?"

Milosh was quick to answer. Quick to confirm his fears.

"No. No, it is something different."

***

Ingelbert's mind raced, surging along even faster than his feet. He was not skilled at stalking men, but in the hunt for answers, he was more than adept. He headed swiftly for the River Gate, though he did not believe Fafnir had come from there. The dwarf undoubtedly had the coin to bribe the guards, but the sally ports would be too small to admit the mule and the litter Milosh spoke of.

Likely, he used the Foot Gate or was already outside the walls when night fell. Either way, Ingelbert was certain the dwarf would be found back in Gipeswic.

In the hallmote, the giant Hafr had told the guild masters he would soon be sailing back to Middangeard. He was in service to Fafnir. Gipeswic was the only port for many leagues.

If Middangeard was the dwarf's destination, then leaving the town was fruitless. But what of the giant? Milosh had made no mention of him. His false leg. It slowed him, so the dwarf had not brought him along. Fafnir was in a hurry. Why? Even if he sensed the sword, could he possibly have known its bearer was injured. He had brought a litter and a mule to pull it, which pointed to either foreknowledge of the coburn's injuries or a premeditated plan to incapacitate him. Four men. Milosh said he brought four men. Did Fafnir believe that was enough to subdue one such as Flyn? Surely not. Ingelbert had little contact with the dwarf, but he did not strike him as a fool. They must have had a different purpose. In Gipeswic, the most numerous and readily available men for hire were sailors.

So, part of a ship's crew and a necessity for haste. Fafnir meant to sail tonight!

Reaching the River Gate, Ingelbert hailed the guards. The same man who escorted him out opened the sally port, a suspicious look on his stubbly face.

"That gypsy boat gone?" he asked, blocking the tunnel with his body.

"Just up river," Ingelbert told him. "They will be returning when the gate opens in the morning."

The guard sneered sourly at that and for a moment, Ingelbert feared he would not allow him to pass. Then the man held out his hand and flicked his fingers impatiently. Ingelbert paid him and the guard stepped aside. Once through the tunnel, Ingelbert waited a moment as the guard locked the inner doors.

"Four men and a mule did not come this way tonight, by chance?" he asked, trying to make the question sound unimportant.

"Possibly with a dwarf?"

The man looked at him curiously for a moment, then spit and shook his head. Ingelbert nodded and went on his way, waiting until he was around the corner of a building before breaking into a run once more.

As he thought, Fafnir had not used the River Gate. Milosh's boat had been moored to the west bank, the ramp still down from when Flyn was offloaded. Fafnir would not have been able to ford the river with a mule pulling a litter, which meant he was on the wrong side of the water to use the Foot Gate. That left only the Bog Gate, located far along the wall, near the south side of town.

Ingelbert may very well have entered Gipeswic first, giving him time to get to the docks ahead of Fafnir.

He flew through the grimy lanes. In the lonely hours just prior to dawn, the streets were nearly deserted, inhabited only by the lowest of beggars, the most wretched harlots. The desperate.

Ingelbert ignored the pleas for coin and the promises of pleasure as he headed for the waterfront. What if Deglan was correct and the dwarf was truly offering aid? Then why lie to Milosh? All of Gipeswic knew that Deglan now squatted with the lepers. If Fafnir had wanted to bring Flyn to him, surely their paths would have crossed between the camp and the boat. It was all wrong.

Ingelbert took the most familiar path, not wanting to risk losing his way. As he passed the fishwife's hut, he noticed a lone goat tied to the rain barrel out front. His physical pace at last outran his mind. Too late did he remember where he last saw that exact goat.

Hafr stepped out of the alley, not ten paces ahead.

Ingelbert halted, noting there was room on either side of the giant to run past, but nothing outside his reach. His sword was still sheathed across his back, but that did nothing to diminish the menace that seemed to fill the air around his massive form. The giant smiled, toying with the long braid dangling from his thick chin.

"At last you come. Hafr was growing restless waiting."

Ingelbert refused to be intimidated. "Where is Flyn?"

"Come," the giant beckoned him with a huge hand. "Hafr will take you to him."

Ingelbert needed to go. It was why Deglan sent him. Find Flyn. Find Tsura. Ensure they were safe. He knew the giant was involved from the start. Nothing here was a surprise. He should follow him. It was the logical choice. But it was all wrong. Too many unknowns.

"Why, why have you taken him?" Ingelbert demanded, hearing his courage faltering.

Hafr found the question amusing. "You think you have a choice, maybe. This would not be correct."

Ingelbert heard movement. He turned to find a pair of clavigers had stepped into the street behind him, brandishing their heavy maces. Another stood in the alley to Ingelbert's right. They were here to keep him from running, to take away the one advantage he had over the hobbled giant. There was nowhere to go.

"Help me," Ingelbert pleaded with the one in the alley, knowing it was useless. "They have taken, taken a friend of mine and and, and a woman. They have them at the docks, I, I think. Please." The claviger stared back at him remorselessly.

"Feeble words," Hafr chuckled, "are not as heavy as dwarf gold, I am thinking. Now. We go."

Ingelbert cast about, to left, right, ahead and behind. He was surrounded. Three men and a giant, all armed, all stronger than him, each looking at him with amusement. They did not bother to move, taking no step towards him, confident in his weakness. Why did Deglan send him? He was not the man for this. Fighting was for men thick of muscle, thick of head. Like the two louts behind him. He stared at them, their witless faces, leather jerkins and iron helms making them nearly indistinguishable. These were the sort to wage battle, to bellow and sweat, swinging heavy weapons and spilling blood. They were molded of sinew and violence. Meat meant to consume other meat and be devoured in kind. Ingelbert was not a threat, not a foe. These types of men were meant to kill each other and become food for burrowing creatures that dwelt in the mud.

The claviger on the left began to tremble, a mere shiver quickly growing into a spasm. His limbs twitched erratically, stiff joints responding to the jerking compulsion of resistant muscles.

Sweat poured from the man's flesh, his face a blank mask of helpless confusion. Air escaped from him in a constricted squeal, causing the man next to look over in alarm. The twitching claviger's arm jerked upward, his mace slamming into the face of his comrade with a wet squelch. Blood and pulpy bits of teeth spattered the street. The struck man fell, his head wobbling unnaturally atop a grotesquely pliant neck.

Ingelbert recoiled from the dead man and his convulsing killer. He heard the claviger in the alley swear and turned to find him standing transfixed with horror. He had dropped his mace and now held his hands out before his goggling eyes. Beneath his skin, small mounds pulsated, thousands of them, rising and falling, pushing at the flesh. His hands, his face, his neck, al were beginning to ripple as something, some *things*, writhed beneath his skin, crawling to the surface. The man screamed as the mounds tore open, each birthing a glistening worm. Blood oozed from thousands of holes as the worms came forth, turning the wailing man's body into a disintegrating mass of wriggling, living tendrils.

The first man had collapsed, his limbs seizing so violently that Ingelbert could hear his bones snapping. His hand still clutched his mace in a death grip, the weapon swinging on the end of his uncontrollable arm, battering his own body, his own face.

Ingelbert's knees gave out, spilling him to the ground. The men died around him, their tortured screams joined by the one rising from his own throat. He gagged, his hollow stomach forcing its way upward. He rocked forward, choking, and smelled the contents of his bowels in his breeches, stinging against the back of his legs. Through eyes cloudy with feverish tears, he saw the giant limping towards him, the greatsword now in his hands, muttering in a guttural language Ingelbert could not comprehend. Coming to kill him.

A weight pressed into Ingelbert's left shoulder, followed by piercing pain. He cried out, finding Gasten perched upon him, the owl's talons gripping powerfully into his flesh. He felt them puncture deep, could feel the agonizing pressure on his collarbone as the owl squeezed. Gasten flapped his wings, pulling upward.

Ingelbert was forced to stand, lest the meat and bone of his shoulder be torn free.

Hafr had paused at the sight of the owl, his face full of grim disgust. It was all Ingelbert could do to keep his feet. He swayed, his entire body brimming with nauseating pain, anchored by the relentless stabbing of Gasten's talons. He was no longer capable of running. Hafr took another step towards him, watching him intently. And another. A few more strides and Ingelbert would be within the reach of that terrible sword. Gasten dug into his shoulder, causing him to wince and whimper, tears smoldering on his cheeks. Curse the owl and curse Hafr's loathsome hide! He would stand here, unable to flee, unable to fight and be cut down.

A wave of uncertainty spread across Hafr's face. He grimaced slightly, his stride faltering. Removing one hand from the grip of his sword, Hafr reached up under his arm, feeling tenderly at his side. A weeping boil stood up on the giant's flesh. Another appeared on his thigh, bubbling up black and angry. Then another near his throat. And another. Hafr growled as the affliction spread, his jaw muscles clenching against the pain. He took another step forward.

Ingelbert's skull flooded with a wave of excruciating dizziness and he fell to one knee. Gasten's wings battered into his head, his face, the claws crunching into him, but he no longer had even the strength to scream. Hafr came on, raising the sword over his head.

"Fated or not," the giant growled, his face covered in seeping sores, "you die now, wizard."

The blade came down in a rush of air and Ingelbert watched its terrible descent. Numbly, he reached up to catch the blade, horrified at his own actions but unable to stop himself, he did not want to die.

There was no pain, no blood. The heavy sword should have split his hand down the length of his arm, a cord of wood under a woodsman's axe. It would not have taken a giant's strength to accomplish that. There was a dense, metallic ring as the edge struck his palm, the massive blade stopping just above his head. The giant snarled and tore the sword back. Ingelbert slumped back onto his rump, his mind swimming in terror while his body succumbed to hopeless exhaustion. He watched as Hafr raised the blade once more. Ingelbert did not know how he stopped the first blow, but he was certain he could not do it again.

"Enough!"

Hafr, sword still poised to strike, turned.

Fafnir stood alone in the dark street behind the giant. He approached slowly, his eyes never leaving Ingelbert. Even under the shadows of the hood he wore, it was clear he was smiling.

"A man there shall be," the dwarf said, his voice lowered with hushed reverence. "Though weak he seems, ever on his shoulder, winged and deathless, a watcher will sit."

FOURTEEN

Deglan clutched the railing of the *Wyvern's Jest*, trying to keep his eyes fixed on the sky and away from the all-encompassing surface of the water. Before setting sail, he had choked down a bitter concoction he brewed to prevent seasickness, but the potion served only to keep him miserably hovering at the edge of vomiting.

Closing his eyes only made the qualmish motion worse, and he refused to go below decks. He felt trapped enough on the ship under an open sky. The damned thing had seemed huge docked in the harbor at Gipeswic, but now, floating on an endless expanse of choppy sea, it was a tiny, insignificant toy. Behind him, Deglan could hear the forty-man crew laboring on the deck, going about the inconceivable business of sailing. Shouts and curses were punctuated by the snap of sailcloth and the abrasive whistle of rope.

Deglan stayed well out of the way. He hated boats and knew nothing about the mysteries of keeping one on course. So long as it continued swiftly and kept him out of the maw of some great, toothy fish, he was content to suffer the journey and hope for its quick conclusion.

"A thousand dripping poxes on you, Fafnir," Deglan muttered at the distant horizon, willing the dwarf's ship to appear ahead, but there remained only that queasy blur where the clouds met the ocean. Hakeswaith sidled up next to him. Deglan did not bother to look over, weary of the man's presence after near two days at sea. Besides, the odious whaler had a face best avoided, all pockmarked flesh, tanned and stretched over a cadaverous, bald skull. His jaw had been broken at some point earlier in life, leaving half his mouth set in a permanent snarl, displaying teeth brindled with rot.

"Talking to yourself's a sign a madness, stunty," Hakeswaith rasped, the hint of a laugh in his voice. He thought himself clever, using the insulting name, but he was not a big man himself, barely a head taller than Deglan. Still, his wiry limbs were knotted with cruel sinew. Small men were often dangerous, especially the ones who were beaten by those of larger stature until they learned to beat back. It was no wonder that Hakeswaith earned his coin by slaughtering whales.

"Aye," Deglan agreed, taking a step away. He could smell Hakeswaith over the sea. "The mad gnome's likely to slit the throat of a sleeping man. Good to remember, that."

He felt the man tense. Hakeswaith could not differentiate jape from threat, the prickly bastard. That was the other thing about short men, they saw slights every-where. The whaler leaned down close, pressing his hideous face next to Deglan's ear and the vicious iron blade of his harpoon under his nose.

"You listen here, stunty," the whaler threatened, his voice shaking. "Try any of your Fae evil on me and I'll bugger you with this."

Deglan winced, more at the man's breath than the harpoon.

He said nothing further, keeping his gaze fixed on the waves.

Hakeswaith stayed close for a moment longer, seething, then slowly removed the harpoon and backed off a step once he believed Deglan properly cowed. Let the buffoon think him afraid, so long as he soon went away, as far away as he ever got on this abhorrent hulk. Every man on board was a wrecker, equal parts sailor and fighter, but Hakeswaith was the one tasked with keeping an eye on Deglan. He was a malodorous, quick-tempered and conniving shadow, always lurking about with a suspicious eye. The ship, the crew, all were being funded by the Guild of Anglers, but Hakeswaith was their creature.

"To protect you, Master Loamtoes," the corpulent merchants had said fawningly. "To personally see you come to no harm on your expedition and are returned safely to Gipeswic."

Deglan had no doubt they wished his safe return. He was now an investment. He had a ship, a crew of fighting men and a bodyguard. All were presented as gifts of good faith, of course, but the truth was plain, and none so happy about it as the guild masters.

And why not? Deglan owed them now. Was owned by them now.

The ship was his prison, the crew were his guards and Hakeswaith, his warden. All part of the bargain.

He had been left with no choice.

Milosh's daughter, the girl Tsura, had returned to her father's boat just after dawn. The gypsy man was making preparations to sail into town, bear and all. Deglan had decided to stay on board, just in case Milosh ran into any resistance at the River Gate. Tsura came rushing along the bank just as they set off, breathless but otherwise unharmed.

"They have taken him, father," she exclaimed as soon as she was on board. "They have taken Flyn!"

"Where?" Deglan demanded, drawing a confused look from the girl.

"Tsura," Milosh explained, "this is Master Loamtoes."

Tsura accepted this with a quick nod and answered Deglan's question, but it was Milosh she addressed. "The dwarf and his men. I did not realize anything was wrong until we reached the harbor and they began loading Flyn onto a longship. By then it was too late! I tried to follow Flyn on board, but the men restrained me."

"Did they hurt you?" Milosh asked.

The girl shook her head impatiently. "Father, we must find him. Free him!"

"The dwarf," Deglan urged. "Did he say anything? Do anything?"

"He left," Tsura replied. "As soon as Flyn was on the ship, he left. Alone. It was not long before he returned. There was a giant with him, carrying the thin man who said he would help us."

Deglan's mouth soured. "Crane?"

"Yes."

"You said the giant was carrying him? Was he injured?"

"Possibly," Tsura said. "He looked poorly, but I could not see if he was even awake. They all boarded the longship. Two men stayed on the pier and kept me until the ship was out of sight, then they let me go."

Milosh reached out and embraced his daughter then, more for his own sake than hers. The girl was tired and angry, but the only fear on her face was clearly for Flyn. Deglan had just learned the cocky knight had a brother and now here was a sister, worried but resolute.

"Any indication of where the ship was bound?" Deglan asked her.

Tsura's response pained her. "No. All ships must first sail out of the inlet. Even during the day it would be difficult to see a ship's heading by the time they reach the ocean."

"Likely back to Middangeard," Deglan muttered to himself.

"But I would have to be sure." He took a quick look over the gypsy boat. "Milosh? Is this thing seaworthy?"

"Only within sight of the shore," the gypsy said.

"It would not matter if we could go into open water," Tsura put in. "We would never catch them. That longship has a larger sail, plus thirty oars and the men to pull them."

"Damn," Deglan swore. "What by Earth and Stone is happening?" He took a moment to gather his thoughts, finally looking up at Milosh. "I need to get to the harbor, can you take me in?"

"Of course," the gypsy replied and immediately began getting his boat underway. Tsura sprang to help her father.

The gate guards did try to harass the Tsigani, but one look from Deglan and a warning that they interfered with the Guild of Anglers was enough to see them quickly through the River Gate and down to the harbor. Deglan had invoked the name of the guild out of anger, but the ruse quickly formed into a plan. However, he had one other deal to strike before he went and sold himself to the fish merchants.

The sun had just fully cleared the edge of the ocean when Deglan hurried off Milosh's boat, now docked in the busy harbor.

Instructing the Tsigani to stay put, he took his satchel with him and made for the end of a long, empty pier thrusting out into the bay.

When he reached the edge he stared down at the briny water distastefully. Drawing a lancet from his satchel he pierced the meaty flesh on the heel of his hand and clenched his fist, allowing his blood to drop into the water lapping at the posts below. Then he sat down on the pier and waited.

Soon, his call was answered.

During his long life, Deglan had purposefully limited his contact with the Water Fae, finding them unsettling. Especially the suire. Naturally, it was one of those creepy bastards who emerged, rising up out of the dark water in the shadow of the pier. He was man-shaped from the waist up, possessing the arms, hands and torso of a human, albeit one slabbed with muscle, but there the similarity ended. His skin was a pale grey, slick and glossy, his eyes pits of lifeless black. Thick, matted locks, the color of kelp, fell heavily across his wide shoulders and hung from his face in a wild beard. Beneath the water, his lower half would be a long, powerful fish tail covered in scales and edged with sharp fins. Deglan shuddered.

"What is it you want Earth-blooded?" the suire asked, his voice deep and resonant, but the tones were queer, following no familiar patterns of inflection that helped to indicate his mood.

Deglan could not tell whether he was being addressed with courtesy or aggression.

"I seek the aid of the undine," Deglan answered, trying to keep his own voice neutral. "My name is Deglan Loamtoes. With whom do I speak?"

"My name, sung above the waves, would be meaningless to your ears," the suire said. "We are far from the shores of the Source Isle, but I serve the keepers of the Shaping Element and was the nearest to your plea. Present it to me, a messenger of the undine."

So, it seemed Deglan's fellow Elementals were too important to converse with a lone gnome spilling his blood in the Water. He would much rather have dealt directly with the undine, who at least had proper legs and spoke with some damn clarity. Still, there was nothing to do now but proceed.

"I need to know the course of a ship recently departed from this shore. It contains a pair of mortals who have proven themselves friend to the Fae. A coburn and a man. They have been taken captive by two children of Middangeard, a dwarf and a giant. I mean to follow."

The suire smiled at this, showing a mouthful of pointed teeth. "You mean to swim? Be careful gnome, lest the waters dissolve you into nothing but silt."

Deglan snorted appreciatively. Dark, mocking humor he understood, strange voice or no. "I will procure a ship," he told the suire. "But I ask for a guide."

The suire seemed to think for a moment, his black eyes covered briefly by pale membranes when he blinked. "Procure your craft," it told him at last. "I will return to you before you set sail with word of the ship you seek."

Deglan bowed his head. "You have my deepest thanks."

The suire said nothing further, diving back swiftly beneath the water, his tail fin breaking the surface before he was lost from sight.

By noon, Deglan was in bed with the guild masters and a ship was being outfitted for his use. Fafnir would have less than a day's lead.

On the pier, minutes before departing, Tsura had insisted on going with him. Milosh forbade it, but the girl invoked some Tsigani taboo of family and honor that Deglan did not understand, causing her father to relent. She marched up and made her intentions known. Deglan, looking beyond her, caught sight of her father's despair and quickly squashed the girl's designs.

"You will stay where you are!" he snapped. He threw an outstretched arm at the ship and the rough-looking crew behind him. "No sense having a lass on board stirring up these lusty brigands. I have enough to worry about without having to save you from a gang of rapers every night. If we come back from this at all, you'll have some fish-reeking wrecker's bastard in your belly. There will be no bear on this boat to protect you, girl. And I do not intend to save Flyn's life only to have him cut my head off when he discovers I brought you into danger. You are not welcome on my ship. Now get back to your father!"

The hateful look in Tsura's eyes could have knocked down the walls of the Roost, but Deglan did not waver. Eventually, she did as he bid. His words were harsh, but he had no need for the gypsy girl to love him. What he needed was her fear to eclipse her love for Flyn and that was no small feat.

The suire returned as promised and informed Deglan that Fafnir's longship did indeed sail directly for Middangeard, bearing northeast at speed.

Now, nearly two days later, they were still in pursuit, not once having caught sight of their quarry.

"The men don't fancy this race across open water," Hakeswaith said bitterly, looking to use his perceived intimidation of Deglan to his advantage. "Should have made eastward, hugged the shores of the Leek Men, then headed northward 'round the Horn of Cimbria."

Deglan cursed inwardly. It was not the first time he had heard this complaint. "Those we chase have no fear of being out of sight of land," he said. "So neither will we."

"S'fuckin' unwise," Hakeswaith spat. "That dwarf of yours employs fjordmen sea dogs. Middangearders have strange ways. They's can navigate a true course with nought but seein' a whale's spray and a flight of gulls. Tisn't natural. Foolish to follow, stunty."

"Thankfully," Deglan pointed out airily, "your masters disagreed when they gave me the means to follow whoever I damn well please."

Hakeswaith's reply held a sneer. "They didn't *give* you nothing, stunty."

Deglan ignored that, though he knew the man was right.

The ship had a captain, of course, a man whose name Deglan forgot the instant he learned it. He had command of the men and the management of the vessel, but her course was entirely Deglan's to direct. Hakeswaith, the captain and the entire crew could hate him and more than likely did, but they yearned for the coin of the guild masters and feared their displeasure. For now, the acquiring of the first and the avoidance of the second hinged on Deglan getting what he desired. And what he desired was the return of his comrades. He cared not one bit for the crew's feelings about their voyage. Let them worry. The Middangearders may have uncanny prowess on the water, but Deglan was not without his own advantages.

As if bidden by his thoughts, a trio of suire appeared alongside the ship, their tails and rippling backs cresting out of the water as they kept pace. Deglan could hear the men behind him cursing in disgust and alarm at the sudden presence of the suire. It did not matter how many times they arrived to give report, the sailors reacted with scorn. Hakeswaith breathed an oath and snapped his harpoon up, readying to throw.

"Stay your hand!" Deglan barked, looking over at the man for the first time. "Unless you want this whole ship drug to the bottom by a damned kraken, you witless barnacle."

The whaler gave him a look dripping with disdain, but lowered his arm. Deglan would have to tread carefully. Hakeswaith was just the sort to let a thirst for petty vengeance overcome any desire for coin or fear of reprisal from the guild masters. He would deal with that when it came, for now he had no use for the man and returned his attention to the suire.

One of them had caught hold of the ship's hull and began climbing, hauling himself up with ease, using nothing but his bulging arms and the long nails at the ends of his strong fingers.

Deglan thought it was the same individual he spoke with at the Gipeswic pier, but he was far from certain. With the exception of the genders, he found it difficult to tell one suire from another.

Likely they thought the same of gnomes.

The suire reached the railing of the ship and pulled himself up, resting his arms on the rail, allowing his tail to hang out over the water. His black eyes locked on Hakeswaith and he displayed his pointed teeth.

"Get you gone, slayer of whales!"

Hakeswaith returned the stare with one of equal loathing before skulking off.

Deglan bowed his head to the suire. "What news?"

"The other ship continues along its course," the suire told him. "The men on board row tirelessly, never ceasing. And they have the wind. You are not gaining."

"Buggery and shit," Deglan swore under his breath, not wanting the men to know. "How long before they reach land?"

"Difficult to determine, since we do not know where they mean to make port. Soon they will reach the Jutland Sea between Middangeard and Cimbria. Once there, there are many places they might go."

Deglan clenched his teeth in frustration. He knew from maps that Cimbria was a sizable peninsula, thrusting out from the north of Outborders, almost stabbing into Middangeard and separated from that land only by the Jutland Sea. He did not believe Cimbria was Fafnir's destination. Likely he would sail around the Horn and land somewhere in Middangeard, but Deglan had no proof of that theory beyond his gut. In truth, it did not matter where Fafnir landed. Once off ship, Flyn and Crane would be lost. Deglan had no friends in Middangeard, no allies to call upon. The Fae held no sway in those frozen lands. No, he must catch the dwarf on the open water while he still had time.

Deglan ran a hand down his whiskers, making up his mind.

"I need the sylphs."

"You cannot call the Wind Elementals without Earth beneath your feet, gnome," the suire intoned.

"But the undine can," Deglan told him. "Here upon the ocean, they can entreat the sylphs. I beg you, go to your masters. Tell them of my plight and ask that they converse, Water to Wind."

"On behalf of Earth," the suire mused. "I will try. But I remind you, even if my masters will do this thing, there is no certainty the sylphs will listen. The tamers of Wind are fickle."

"As you say," Deglan agreed. "But I must try."

The suire only blinked once, then let go of the railing, pushing itself away from the ship. It turned adroitly as it fell, twisting to enter the water arms first and disappeared beneath the waves with barely a splash. Again. Deglan could do nothing but wait. The suire spoke true, the sylphs were a fickle lot. But these days, in absence of the Seelie Court, the same could be said of all the Elemental Guardians. Even Deglan's own people, once so redoubtable, had fallen into corrupted idleness. Irial Ulvyeh's long, slow withdrawal from the world had not benefited his subjects. The Elf King had an influence over the Fae that could not be matched.

Though in the elder days, Deglan remembered rarely agreeing with the direction he chose to wield that influence. But king or no, Irial, like any father, was unalterably affected by the death of his daughter. Aillila's destruction at the hands of the Gaunt Prince robbed the Fae of a true victory at the end of the Rebellion and made mockery of the Restoration. Irial was returned to the throne, but his line and his heart were sundered into fragments of hopelessness. The Elementals soon began to govern themselves without his guidance. The old alliances were now tenuous, at best.

Deglan had one of the crew inform the captain to hold his course and fly every sail. He hoped it would not be a wasted effort.

The sylphs were just as likely to rob them of the Wind as bestow its power. Hours passed and the day grew old. The *Wyvern's Jest* continued along at much the same speed she had managed since the voyage began. Deglan remained at the foredeck as the sky bathed the clouds in lurid shades of orange and purple, vainly enticing the retreating sun to remain aloft. The stars had not yet showed themselves when Hakeswaith returned to the rail.

"Captain says we are putting in once we reach Skagen," he jeered. "Dwarf ship or not."

Deglan grimaced. Skagen was a notorious refuge for seamen that clung to the very tip of Cimbria's Horn. Deglan had never been there, but even in distant Airlann tales were told of the place.

"No," he said gruffly. "Unless the longship has docked there, we will sail past."

"Captain says no," Hakeswaith insisted sullenly. "He says that you can talk to your filthy fish friends there if you like. Depending on what lies they tell you, he'll decide whether we's to press on or make for home."

"If this tub returns to Gipeswic without my friends the deal is forfeit," Deglan said through clenched teeth.

The whaler shook his head gleefully, his bent jaw twisting further into a hideous smile. "Nah! I don't see that. Captain says your deal with the guild masters was just for the *Jest* and the men to crew her. Run down the longship, *if* it were possible." Hakeswaith shifted his harpoon to the crook of his arm and clasped his hands together, shaking them and bending at the knee in a mummery of begging. He pitched his voice high. "Please, please grant me a ship, for I must finds me friends and I promise to become your stunty pet doctor once I'm back!" Hakeswaith straightened, laughing at his own mocking display. He pointed a scabby finger at Deglan, his voice returning to normal. "Guild masters couldn't guarantee you'd find yer mates and neither could you. Not a deal they woulda made. No, just the means to search is all you got. And the Captain has hisself a deal too, stunty! Ensure that you come back, and I reckon *that* deal's more important to the Anglers when all's done. So, we'll get our money for a job well done, while you'll have to stand before the big merchants and whine that we done you wrong. Even if they side with you, let you go out again, your dwarf's ship will be good and gone and your friends made thralls to some fjordman jarl or the like. No matter what, you'll be back in Gipeswic soon enough, lancing the boils on the guild masters' fat asses and dragging their ugly brats out of the cunnys of their fat wives!"

Hakeswaith rewarded himself with a good chortle after his little speech.

"You belong to the Anglers too, Hakeswaith," Deglan said, fixing the man with a knowing smile.

"Aye. I do."

"The bargain has me treating all guild members," Deglan informed the man, turning to face him. "Not just the masters. For the next fifty years. Were I you, I would make damn sure you never fall ill or suffer injury during that time, which I might add, will be the rest of your miserable life. Because I promise you, you stinking, broke-mouth son of a dockside whore, you will not recover from anything which brings you under my care."

Hakeswaith's chuckling ceased and he suddenly became very still. He regarded Deglan with a blank stare, his stretched lips quivering around his blackened teeth. When next he spoke, his voice was just above a whisper.

"So you mean to kill me then, eh stunty?"

"It is no worse than your designs for me."

"Well then," the whaler hissed, moving his harpoon back into his hand. "Nothing could be clearer. When two bastards hanker for the other's blood, the only course is for one to strike first."

"Your masters want me for a pet," Deglan pointed out.

"Your words. Kill me and you will get nothing."

"Some things are worth more than coin."

Deglan flicked an eye across the main deck, careful not to move. The sailors went about their business, unable to hear the deadly turn in the conversation over the roar of the *Jest* plowing through the waves. Toad shit! Too late Deglan realized he should have spent more time winning a few friends. Hakeswaith was about to make his move, curse his pride! Deglan swallowed hard and hoped he could hold the whaler off long enough for someone to take notice. Surely some of the crew wanted their payment and would step in.

Laughter tickled through the air. It was light, a giggle as from a girl, but somehow it presided over the cacophony of the ship. Deglan thought maybe he had imagined it, but he saw Hakeswaith wearing a confused expression, his face upturned, eyes searching the rigging. More laughter followed, deeper, yet still full of frivolity, joining with the girlish giggle. The main sail snapped to fullness, straining against the ropes. The crew cast about, every man searching for the source of the laughter. More voices joined in, male and female, all young, lusty and unrestrained. Squeals of delight and playful, wordless taunts mixed with the exhalations of amusement. The sail began to ripple, but not from a slackening of the wind. Deglan saw it stretch and run, as if someone swiped their fingers along it at speed from behind the cloth. He looked closer as the laughter intensified and could see other shapes, familiar shapes, begin to press against the sail. Impressions of faces, hands, well-formed limbs and shapely bodies.

The *Wyvern's Jest* began to crash through the sea as it picked up speed, the keel rising and falling, slamming into the water, sending sprays of foam over the rails to drench the deck. The crew scrambled about, trying to wrest the vessel back under control while keeping their eyes fixed to the main sail where the sylphs frolicked with abandon. Moans of pleasure filled Deglan's ears, pierced with the occasional shriek of delight. The sail had transformed into an ever-shifting menagerie of nubile forms, fluidly intertwined.

As the sylphs cavorted, the ship continued to gain speed, pitching so violently that the sailors had trouble keeping their feet.

Deglan watched as they spilled onto the deck, their mouths open, emitting screams and curses unheard over the gaiety of the Wind's children. Next to him, Hakeswaith slipped, the harpoon tumbling from his hand as he collided with the rail before taking a hard tumble to the deck. Amazingly, Deglan kept his own legs beneath him. Then he felt it, a gentle pressure of hands, made of the very air, holding him upright, steadying him against the harsh jolting of the ship.

Hakeswaith scrambled away, joining the line of sailors hastening below decks. Deglan was left alone, standing in the prow of the speeding ship. Sheets of water exploded on either side of him each time the keel hammered down. His vision became an alternating vista of endless stars and surging ocean, accompanied by a chorus of reckless merriment. He was terrified. He began to laugh.

The night sped by in a dreadful, glorious mirage. The sylphs were gone with the rising sun, departing with a final, satisfied sigh.

Ahead, the blood bright orb blazed, showing Deglan the ship now faced due east. Distant shores lay to the south off the *Jest's* starboard side, but both land and sun held no importance for Deglan. He had eyes only for the longship, now visible just ahead.

The crew was making its way back onto the deck, every man shaken from the night's events. Seeing the captain emerge, Deglan called him over and pointed at the longship, close enough to see the sweep of her oars.

"Can you catch her?" Deglan demanded.

The captain squinted at the other vessel and the terror of the night fell from his weathered face. "Aye," he growled. "We can catch her!"

The *Wyvern's Jest* was a larger, bulkier craft, but the captain knew his trade, using his broader sails to deprive the longship of wind. After an hour's dance, they were no closer to their prey, for the men in the longship bent their backs to the oars, keeping the vessel ahead. The Jest had no oars and soon they settled into a stagnant chase, neither ship gaining or losing distance.

Finally, by midday, inch by painstaking inch they drew nearer the low, sleek length of the longship. Deglan looked down from his vantage on the deck. He could easily make out the giant, Hafr, standing tall in the stern. His sword was drawn and he beckoned the *Jest* to come onward with the blade, bellowing a challenge. There was no sign of Fafnir, nor of Flyn or Crane.

Deglan's heart sank. Had he been duped? Had the dwarf changed ships? Surely the suire would have noticed. And then he saw it. A small canvas was erected near the prow, no doubt to shelter the prone forms of the chronicler and the coburn.

The captain appeared at Deglan's side, his face grim.

"We only outnumber them by ten men," the man said.

"And with that giant on their side, the odds are still greatly against us if we try to board. I do not know how much longer we can keep up with them. Should the wind fail, they will again pull ahead and we may not catch them a second time. They are within bow shot. I say we give them a few volleys."

"My friends are on board that ship," Deglan said, scowling up at the captain. "A stray arrow and all this is could be for nothing."

"It will thin out their oarsmen," the captain urged.

"Decrease their speed. They may give up the chase."

Deglan glared back at the longboat, hating his options. Just then, from beneath the canvas, Fafnir emerged, walking down the aisle of the ship between the oar benches. He was hunched as he moved, clasping his cloak tight about his neck. He stopped in the center of the longship and turned to face the *Jest*, pushing his hood away from his head. Across the watery expanse separating the ships, he and Deglan locked eyes.

"Give the order," Deglan told the captain. "But tell your men to keep their aim clear of the prow."

The captain nodded and hurried across the deck barking commands. In quick order, half the wreckers had bows in hand, gathering on the port side of the fore-deck and along the rail. At the captain's word they drew their strings back, angling their bows high and let loose. The shafts sped away, arcing high over the water.

Deglan watched their descent, as did Fafnir, but the arrows fell short. The wreckers adjusted quickly and let loose another volley.

Again the shafts flew and Deglan held his breath, knowing that this time they had the distance. Fafnir watched them come, a shower of broadheads about to rain on he and his men. And then the shafts began breaking mid-flight, or flew suddenly off the mark. They snapped or spun away, flung aside by some unseen force. Not one found their target.

Deglan let out his breath in a curse. The wreckers issued oaths of their own and began setting fresh arrows to their strings.

They sent another volley at the longship, but Deglan did not watch their flight. This time he kept his eyes on the dwarf.

Fafnir stood and waited, stooped, unmoving. At the last moment, as the arrows fell near, his head moved slightly, subtly, as if counting the coming missiles. As his eyes touched each one, they splintered or were cast aside to fall harmlessly into the water. The archers around Deglan stood dumbfounded, each looking slack-jawed to his mates for answers. Only the captain spoke, ordering the men to lower their bows.

On the longship, Fafnir raised a hand and his men ceased rowing. The *Jest* quickly drew even and Deglan looked down into the vessel, noting the smirking face of the giant before settling his gaze on Fafnir. The dwarf looked haggard, sallow. His hair and beard were thin and wispy, blowing in the sea wind. The rust color had dulled, darkened to nearly black. However, despite his changed appearance, Fafnir's voice remained strong, calling up to the deck.

"Master Loamtoes! You are unexpected. We thought perhaps you were pirates."

"You would not have fled pirates with as much vigor, dwarf!" Deglan shouted back.

"I have no reason to flee from you, Master Loamtoes. It is not a foe behind that demands haste, but the destination before me, for I have no more time."

Deglan choked on a building rage. "No more riddles! Explain yourself!"

"Not here," the dwarf said placidly. "Follow me to Skagen and we may talk."

"No! I will not allow you to slither away again. Where are my companions?"

"We are here, Staunch," a familiar voice called out.

Deglan's head whipped over to the prow of the longship.

There, standing just outside the makeshift tent, were Flyn and Ingelbert. Deglan's breath caught in his throat. They were alive!

The owl was perched on Crane's shoulder and Flyn was even armed, his sheathed greatsword cradled to his chest. Neither were as Tsura described them, appearing hale and healthy with no evidence of wounds or even bandages. As Ingelbert waved to him, Deglan noticed his arm was unencumbered by the plaster cast.

"I am not your enemy, Deglan Loamtoes," Fafnir said.

"Though long have you thought so. Please, meet with me on Skagen and I will answer all questions."

FIFTEEN

Flyn sat patiently while Deglan fussed over him. The gnome listened to his breathing, scrutinized his beak and felt along his body and limbs, kneading his stubby fingers deep into his feathers to feel the muscles and bone. Once, not long ago, Flyn would have made some jesting remark while Deglan poked and prodded at him, but he restrained himself. He knew from experience that Deglan was in no mood to be goaded. Besides, Flyn did not feel in the best of humor either. The herbalist finally stepped back, frowning, and rubbed a hand through his white hair and down his whiskered cheeks. Then, clearly unsatisfied, he stepped forward again and motioned for Flyn to lean down so he could pull down at the flesh under his eyes with his thumbs.

"Well," Deglan said, still peering at him, "your wattle will never be the same, otherwise . . ." the gnome removed his hands, "you are perfectly mended."

Flyn retrieved his sword and stood, allowing Inkstain to take his place on the low bench. Deglan did not spend near as long examining the chronicler.

"As if it were never broken," the gnome declared while rubbing at Inkstain's arm.

Flyn caught the man's eye over Deglan's head and gave voice to what they were both thinking.

"You sound disappointed."

Deglan cocked an eye at him over a shoulder. "Toad shit! I just don't like unfamiliar Magic doing my job for me. Now. What by Earth and Stone happened?"

Flyn walked a pace back and considered leaning on the wall of the cramped mariner's hut, then thought better of it. The crude little building looked ready to fall in at any moment. Flyn was amazed it stood up to the wind, which whistled constantly through the driftwood slats. He wished there were another bench. Despite Deglan's proclamation of his recovery, Flyn still felt weak in the legs, though he dared not admit it to the gnome, so he leaned forward on Coalspur's cross-guard instead.

"I remember little," Flyn admitted. "Tsura and Milosh found me. After that . . . just pain. When I awoke, Master Crane was beside me, as was Fafnir. The pain was gone and we were at sea."

"Crane and the Tsigani told me you were dying," Deglan groused. "Care to tell me how you got yourself into that condition?"

Flyn tried to look his friend in the eye when he replied, but ended up speaking to the floor. "No, Staunch. No, I do not."

"Master Crane, do you know?"

Flyn did not bother to look up to witness Inkstain's response. He had told him nothing. The chronicler must simply have shaken his head, for the next thing Flyn heard was an agitated expulsion of breath from Deglan.

"Fine. But what does the damn dwarf want with you two? Clearly, he is more than a bloody blacksmith!"

"He is a runecaster."

It was Ingelbert who had spoken. The man sat on the bench, his long face pale and drawn. He stared blankly at nothing for a moment, then looked up at Flyn and Deglan, his eyes quickly alternating between them.

"I saw him when he healed Flyn," the chronicler told them.

"And more clearly when he mended my arm. He, um, has stones adorned with runes. I recognized some of the, uh, some of the symbols. But I do not know what he wants with us."

Deglan looked dubious. "He has not spoken anything of his plans to either of you?"

"I was just coming around when you appeared," Flyn said.

He stole a glance at Inkstain, who had lapsed once more into a dull silence. The chronicler knew more than he was saying, Flyn was certain, but he left it alone. Crane did not look well. "I say we go hear what he has to say."

"You think you have a choice?" Deglan growled.

"We could just sail away," Inkstain mumbled, clearly disconcerted at the idea of meeting with Fafnir. He looked at Deglan, his eyes almost pleading. "You have a ship."

Flyn watched the gnome wrestle with the idea, his mouth wrinkling sourly. "Runecasting is old Magic, but damn potent in the right hands. The mastery of a single rune is lore hard-learned and Fafnir knows far more than that. He can obviously knit bone, close flesh. Probably purge infection and staunch bleeding, too. We have seen him turn arrows aside. And he may be capable of much more."

Deglan shook his head bitterly. "No, Master Crane. It blisters my kidneys to admit it, but it would be foolish to deny him. But! Agree to nothing. Make no bargains, swear no oaths. You do not want to find yourselves bound to this dwarf."

"As you are now bound to the Guild of Anglers?" Inkstain asked, a hint of regret in his voice.

"Never you mind that," Deglan barked.

"No," Flyn said, unwilling to be kept in the dark. "What does he mean? What did you do?"

"What I had to!" the gnome snapped at him. "They had a want, I had a need. We came to an arrangement."

Across the little room, Flyn saw Ingelbert's face fall even farther. "How long?" the chronicler asked.

"Fifty years," Deglan declared, his face challenging them to pass judgment.

Flyn let the tension ease for a moment. "That nasty little fellow outside. The one with the harpoon and terribly unfortunate face. He a part of the deal?"

"Hakeswaith?" the herbalist snorted. "He's the guild masters' cur. They say he is my guard dog, but he is really a sheepdog meant to herd me back to them when this is done. But the bastard thinks himself a wolf, and means to have my wooly lamb-arse for a meal."

"A twisted sack of crossed purposes," Inkstain proclaimed, almost to himself.

Deglan was chuckling, but Flyn refused to be amused. "I will deal with him."

"You will do nothing!" Deglan's black humor vanished. "I have managed my life for thousands of years without your interference, you preening gamecock! And I can damn well survive the meddling of a few fat fish merchants and one hideous whaler. While you, both of you, have attracted the attention of a damn dwarf wizard. Of the three of us, I would rather be Deglan Loamtoes than Ingelbert Crane or Sir Bantam Flyn!"

Flyn kept his elbows on the quillons of his sword and raised his hands in surrender. There was no reasoning with the gnome when he was in a temper. Still, his face, even scowling, was a welcome one to behold.

"Well then," Flyn said, directing his words to Inkstain and trying to give the man an encouraging look. "Shall we go and see what we can discover about Master Fafnir?"

"If only to get it over with," Deglan muttered.

Flyn kept his gaze fixed on Inkstain, who nodded reluctantly and finally stood.

The rickety door of the hut had barely to be pushed before the wind caught hold, flinging it open to clatter against the outside wall. Flyn waited for his friends to exit, then stepped out into the buffeting winds, squinting against the sand grit and sea spit.

Skagen was a remote stretch of land, all bleak, wet dunes and cold, wet winds. Whalers, smugglers and slavers all used it as a refuge when the Jutland Sea turned vicious with storms. A rough, makeshift community had sprung up on the peninsula to cater to the needs of the itinerant mariners. Stone cottages lay nestled in the sparse swaths of arable soil further inland, while a hive of ramshackle huts clung closer to the shoreline, poorly built and negligently maintained by generations of malingering sailors. Most of the wood used for construction was scavenged off the countless derelict vessels that had become beached on Skagen over the years.

Indeed, the largest building in the settlement was known simply as the Wreck and made primarily from the remnant of a great, overturned cog. The Wreck sat up on the highest dune, its broken hull now serving as a curious, curving roof, beneath which was housed Skagen's only tavern and meeting hall.

But that was not their destination. Fafnir had asked they meet him upon the shore when they were ready.

As Flyn exited the hut, two signs of movement caught his eye. The first was the odious man Deglan called Hakeswaith detaching himself from the wall of a neighboring hut. The other was Inkstain's owl swooping silently down and landing on the chronicler's shoulder. Flyn fancied he saw Inkstain flinch as the bird came to rest, but once it settled he appeared to take no further notice. Deglan completely ignored Hakeswaith, but Flyn did not miss the stare of hatred that the short man bore into the back of the gnome's head.

So. Both his companions had picked up unwelcome shadows. Flyn resolved to stay vigilant, but pushed both the whaler and the owl to the back of his mind. They were mysteries to be resolved later. Deglan was right. For now, Fafnir's designs for them were the most important matter.

They made their way down to the shore and walked through the sands away from the settlement until they reached a remote stretch of beach. Ahead, they could see Fafnir waiting, his hood pulled low over his face against the relentless gusts coming off the sea. None of the men from the longship were present, but a trio of other dwarfs stood nearby, one held between the other two.

Even from a distance Flyn could see this dwarf's hands were bound, his uncovered head bowed. The giant was there, too, standing removed from the dwarfs, watching Flyn and his group approach.

"Tell me that lofty lout's name again," Flyn inquired of his friends.

"Hafr," Deglan answered with scorn, "the Ever-Boastful."

"And why does he have a goat with him?"

No one had the answer to that.

Ingelbert drifted back a pace. "Be wary of him," he told Flyn, his voice so low that it was nearly swallowed by the roar of the waves. Flyn considered asking if Inkstain meant the giant or the goat, but the look on the chronicler's face withered the jest before it could be uttered. He nodded at the man and gave him a companionable clap on the shoulder not burdened by the sizable owl. He hoped the gesture was convincing. In truth, Flyn was not certain he could defeat the giant if this meeting went ill. Once, but no longer. The doubt rankled him, but he could not dispel it from his mind.

"Master Loamtoes," Fafnir called as they drew near. "Are you satisfied your friends have come to no harm at my hands?"

"Not yet anyway," Deglan conceded sourly. "Now what do you want with them?"

"First," Fafnir said evenly, gesturing to Hakeswaith. "Let us rid ourselves of those not welcome at this meeting."

Flyn watched as Deglan glanced back at the whaler with a calculating look, the barest hint of a grin cracking his face.

Hakeswaith stood where he was, frowning and obstinate, giving all present threatening looks, though he neglected to glare at the giant.

Deglan turned back to Fafnir. "He stays."

Flyn stifled a chuckle. The old mushroom hated Hakeswaith, but he vouched for the man simply to get one over on the dwarf.

"So be it," Fafnir said, unconcerned. He removed his hood.

Flyn was once again struck by how different the dwarf looked. Years ago, in Black Pool, Fafnir had been ruddy and vigorous, the red of his beard matching the healthy flush in his cheeks and bulbous nose. Now, his face was sunken and waxy, his hair a dingy black. Flyn had commented on the change to Crane when he first awoke on the longship, and the chronicler had informed him that Fafnir had not appeared so decrepit in Gipeswic.

His deathly appearance had become more pronounced during the voyage, deteriorating visibly with each passing hour. Were it not for this assurance, Flyn would have been hard-pressed to believe this was the same individual he had met in Airlann.

Fafnir spoke a word Flyn did not understand and the other three dwarfs stepped forward. The one in the center was dressed in rags and heavily chained, dragged forward by the pair flanking him.

These two were clad in shirts of darkened mail and stout steel helms. One bore a long-handled axe with a sweeping blade. All three possessed similar coloring to Fafnir, their beards coarse and black, contrasting sharply with the stark white of their flesh. The captive kept his shaggy head bowed, only looking up when Fafnir addressed him harshly in a strange, lilting language. There was malice in the bound dwarf's eyes, but also deeply rooted fear. The face of one condemned.

After a brief exchange Fafnir turned away from the captive.

"We dwarrow do not practice execution," he said gravely.

"Even for the vilest of criminals, the punishment of death is forbidden. Forbidden, not because we eschew bloodshed. And not because we are overly merciful."

With this, Fafnir signaled and one of the dwarf guards pulled a long, broad-bladed dagger from his belt and swiftly stabbed the captive, sinking the blade to the hilt. It was a sure, deft thrust to the heart, expertly done, and the doomed dwarf fell without a sound.

"Buggery and shit," Flyn heard Deglan hiss.

Fafnir looked down at the still form, watching as the blood ran free, rejected by the sodden sand. "What I have just done is a crime. Even for one such as this. He stole human women, murdered their husbands so he could keep them for bed slaves. When confronted by his kin to answer for this dishonor, he slew them. Two of his own brothers. But even this does not give me the right to take his life, for the death of a dwarf is not just a punishment for the individual, but a curse for our entire people."

"Damn you, Fafnir," Deglan cursed. "There is no need for this grisly display!"

"Not for you, Master Loamtoes," Fafnir returned. "But then you were not meant to be here. This I arranged for our young mortals here. It is important they understand."

Flyn was puzzled. He did not like the tone he heard in Deglan's voice, nor did he like the way the dwarf guards had stepped as far away from their executed captive as possible, yet retained their grip upon the heavy chains that were still shackled to the body.

"What is it, Staunch?" Flyn asked, readying himself to pull Coalspur free of its scabbard.

"S'bloody dwarrow dead," Deglan answered, taking a step back. "They do not stay dead. Bugger all Fafnir, take the bloody head off!"

"No," Fafnir said firmly. "They must see."

Flyn heard the clink of chain. Looking down he saw the shoulder of the corpse begin to twitch, then its slack fingers dug into the sand and the arm began to straighten as the dead dwarf began pushing itself off the ground. Flyn drew Coalspur, stepping between the rising thing and his friends. A low, moaning began to issue from the corpse's slack jaws, a protracted sound uninterrupted by breath. The lips moved, shaping the moan into words of the dwarrow tongue, their meaning lost on Flyn. It was a song, resonant and melodious, oddly beautiful despite its birth in a dead throat. The corpse was on its feet now. Its eyes were open and unblinking, looking exactly as they had moments ago when the dwarf yet lived, but now housing no emotion, no vital spark.

Behind him, Flyn heard the sound of feet running through wet sand, quickly receding. Hakeswaith must have fled, the craven.

The animated corpse turned, its head revolving slowly to fixate on Fafnir. It took a step towards him, arms reaching. It continued to sing, its voice never wavering. The guards hauled back on the chains, preventing the shambling figure from reaching the runecaster, but Flyn noticed their feet digging furrows in the sand and the taut expressions of exertion on their faces. Dwarfs were robust by nature, but it took both of the guards to hold their prisoner back.

"This is what we become," Fafnir said, his voice full of numb sorrow. "Vættir. What you would call a wight. Like the Fae, we dwarrow do not suffer death from age or illness, but when one of us falls to violence or mishap, this is our end. From the oldest among us down to our children. This is what became of this murderer's brothers. What he made them. He fled, of course, moments after his foul deed was done, but his brothers killed three more before they could all be destroyed.

"The vættir are stronger than living dwarfs and have only two desires. To go where they are called, and to end life whenever it crosses their ceaseless path. Fire will not touch them and their song can raise human dead. The only way to end them is to take off their heads."

Fafnir gave a nod and the dwarf with the axe tossed it to him. Catching it cleanly out of the air, Fafnir swung, severing the wight's head in one swift motion. The body fell heavily to the ground and moved no more. The guards dropped their chains with relief and one of them went to retrieve the head from the surf.

Flyn returned Coalspur to its scabbard, only taking his eyes off the fallen wight when Fafnir again began to address them.

"Too long have my people suffered this plague," he said solemnly. "Too long has this curse endured. And too long have I sought the three that can help me end it. You ask why I have need of you, Bantam Flyn and Ingelbert Crane? I need you to free the dwarrow from this doom."

"How?" Flyn asked.

Deglan jerked at his arm. "Dammit Flyn, shut your fool mouth!" The gnome stepped forward and thrust a finger at Fafnir.

"You wanted them to understand. Then tell them all of it, dwarf! Tell them why your kind are so afflicted."

"As you say," Fafnir nodded, turning away from the incensed gnome to look at Flyn and Inkstain. "History is an elusive thing. Even we immortals must make use of myth and legend to help us understand the great distances of the past which have moved beyond the reach of our knowledge. I can only relate to you what we dwarrow have come to believe, and I wager even the venerable Master Loamtoes has not the age to claim authority over the events of creation."

Flyn glanced down at Deglan after this remark, but the herbalist only fumed and held his tongue.

"Airlann is called the Source Isle of Magic," Fafnir continued. "But before it was risen from the waters, Magic had another home." The dwarf gestured out across the ocean, pointing to the north. "Middangeard. The world was new, untamed, raw, the very materials used to create it were unrefined. To guard and harness these primordial powers, Magic created eight beings, four mated pairs, and entrusted each pair with an Element. The two elves were granted Earth, at that time little more than unforgiving rock. To the dragons, Magic gave the molten beginnings of Fire."

Fafnir then gestured to Hafr, who stood picking his teeth, barely listening to the tale. "Frost was bestowed to the giants, not yet the softened brilliance that would become Water. The last Elementals were a pair of great birds, their true names lost to time, and they were given mastery of the maelstroms and gales, the savage forbears of Wind.

"Each Elemental pair gave birth to a race of mighty children and Magic slept, entrusting the world to the care of these beings. After untold centuries, the races quarreled. A war broke out between them and alliances were made. The elves and dragons melded their strength while the giants and the great birds united against them. The conflict put the very world in peril and needed to end, but neither side showed signs of relenting. Locked in a cycle of destruction, the end of all life drew near. And then a group of elves changed their allegiance, leaving their kin and dragon allies in order to join the giants and birds. This act shifted the balance and victory was at hand, the end of the calamitous war. But Magic awoke and, finding its creation in near ruin, was displeased. It ended the war between the Elementals and turned its ire upon them." Fafnir paused for a moment, his gaze growing distant and when he next spoke, bitterness had leaked into his voice. "But not all were punished. The dragons, and the elves who remained by their side, were spared. These Magic favored and allowed them to flee Middangeard, creating a new home for them. Airlann. Those left behind, the giants, the birds, and the brave elves who dared seek an end to the war, were stripped of their Elements and left to languish in a land laid to waste."

"The dwarrow," Inkstain said, his face full of discovery.

"You were once elves. The elves left behind."

"Yes," Fafnir said. "Our forms became stunted, the grace and beauty of the elves snatched away. The giants too, diminished.

However, not all of the Elementals allowed their powers to dwindle so easily. The mother of the great birds, fearing the loss of her immortality, drained the gift from her children. When that source was spent she used the last of her Magic and turned it on the dwarrow, placing upon us an enduring curse. My ancestors were weakened from their transformation, vulnerable, and could not stop the fell craft that descended on their bloodline. As they died, the vættir rose and marched to the call of the matron bird, tirelessly following her voice that drifted on the vestiges of the wind she once controlled. They seek her out, our dead, and when their steps bring them to her at last, she feeds upon them, devouring the last glimmer of their immortality to preserve her own. Once, eons ago, she had a true name, but now we dwarrow know her only as the Corpse Eater." Fafnir fixed Flyn with a hard stare. "She is the bane of my race. And the mother of yours."

"What?" Flyn said, unable to keep the incredulity from his voice.

"The coburn," Fafnir told him, "are the children of the great birds."

"Madness," Deglan said dismissively. "Madness wrapped in toad shit! The coburn were not even discovered until the Rebellion."

"So the elves say," Fafnir returned. "They kept them hidden, bringing them out of Middangeard and secreting them across the Tin Isles, using their most potent spells to conceal them. The evil rituals used by the Corpse Eater to steal the immortality of the coburn drove her mad and plummeted her children into barbarity. She remains little more than a beast, but over the slow crawl of many years, the coburn have overcome their savagery. Yet, only when the elves had need of the coburn did they reveal their existence to the world."

"The Rebellion," Inkstain said and looked over at Flyn, his mouth agape. "They established the Valiant Spur and marshaled the coburn against the Goblin Kings."

"They used them," Fafnir said with a sneer. "As is the way of the huldu."

"And this is all lies," Deglan snarled. "As is the way of dwarfs. Come, Flyn. There is no more need to listen to this."

Flyn gently shook his arm out of the gnome's pulling grip.

"Wait. I have never heard of any of this. Not as myth, tale or fable None of my brothers in the Order have made mention of it. How is that possible?"

"Because you are the first to hear it, Bantam Flyn," Fafnir replied. "The Corpse Eater stole the truth from the coburn when she cast you into brutishness and long did your race dwell in ignorance born from that betrayal. The elves chose to keep the secret, to what end I cannot say. Long did it take my people to rediscover your origins, as much was lost to us during our fall."

"Why reveal it now?" Flyn asked. "And why to me?"

Fafnir bowed his head for a moment and took a deep breath. When he looked up again, his face was suffused with hope.

He looked at Inkstain. "Master Crane, you know the dwarrow tongue. Please, translate for me."

Inkstain swallowed hard, casting a nervous look at Deglan.

When the gnome offered no objection, the chronicler nodded.

Fafnir walked back to the corpse of the prisoner. The guards had rid the body of its chains, but otherwise had done nothing to arrange its position. The head had been dumped unceremoniously nearby. Fafnir looked down at it for a moment and then began to speak slowly. Flyn understood none of the words, but the tone was one of great reverence and he noticed the dwarf guards bow their heads. As Fafnir spoke, Master Crane listened intently. The chronicler began to translate the runecaster's words, hesitantly at first, but he soon grew confident and his speech affected the same solemnity as the dwarf's.

"Woe to the dwarrow,
Our dead rest not,
In earth, in stone,
Nor under waves.
Neither flame, nor rot,
Our cold flesh touches,
Nor worm, nor crow,
Dine within our tombs.

"We are food for one,
Wind's ancient mother,
Called to her gullet,

We march on blackened feet.
All are risen,
All go forward,
In death enslaved,
A feast of corpses.

"Till the end of days,
She will glut upon us,
So that she may live,
Last upon the earth."

Fafnir turned away from the body and slowly approached.

He stopped before Flyn and raised his hand, gently placing it on the sheathed blade of Coalspur and once again spoke in dworgmál.

Inkstain echoed him in the tongue of the Tin Isles.

"To see her slain,
a blade must be wrought,
three must be gathered
And the eater sought."

Flyn met Fafnir's gaze and was surprised to see the dwarf's eyes well with tears, though he allowed none to fall. His voice faltered when next he spoke and though the language was strange, the sound of pain was unmistakable.

"Her bane to be forged,
Tempered and cooled,
Eight times in the hearts
Of beloved issue.
One you must find,
Among her lost children,
To wield this doom,
And see mother slain."

The dwarf then stepped away from Flyn and stood before Inkstain, continuing to speak. The chronicler grew troubled as he translated what was spoken directly to him.

"Of the two others,
A man there shall be,
Mortal and shunned,
Friend to folk Fae,
Though weak he seems,

Ever on his shoulder,
Winged and deathless,
A watcher will sit."

To Inkstain's obvious relief, Fafnir then stepped away and motioned up at Hafr. The giant attempted to feign apathy, but Flyn detected a hint of uncertainty in his face. He wondered how much of this the brute had heard before.

"A great champion,
To complete the three,
Guided by lust,
For glories new.
Though strong of limb,
A mile-tamer gone,
Deep in the horns,
All foes to the ground."

Fafnir lowered his arm and encompassed them all with a searching look.

"These hunters bound,
Together in purpose,
Shall seek with blind eyes,
The eater of corpses.
Upon frosty bough,
And rime-ridden root,
And there decided,
The fate of our race.

"Follow you this skein,
To seek such an end,
To set these links fast,
And make you this chain.
Heavy is the burden,
Long shall be the search,
Many paths unwoven,
Many lives undone."

With that, both dwarf and man ceased speaking, leaving only the sound of the wind and the shushing surf. Fafnir gave Inkstain a nod of gratitude. Flyn looked down and found Deglan deep in thought, his jaw bulging as he clenched his teeth, chewing upon some vexation.

"You are not just a wizard," the gnome said. "You're a bloody Chain Maker."

Fafnir said nothing, regarding the herbalist with a calm confidence.

"Care to explain, Staunch?" Flyn asked.

"Deluded dwarf prophets," Deglan answered sourly.

"Believe they can see the fate of individuals and manipulate them. Bring them together for whatever damn, dangerous purpose they are obsessed with seeing come to pass."

Flyn saw the two dwarf guards bristle at this and one of them made an aggressive step forward, but Fafnir halted him with a word. The affronted guard stepped back, his face still wroth.

"Master Loamtoes," Fafnir said with grim humor. "You perfectly display why I must travel in the guise of a steel peddler."

"So you are what he says," Flyn pressed.

"I see the potential in certain beings," the dwarf conceded.

"Those whose destinies may be intertwined with the Corpse Eater's destruction."

Flyn gave the dwarf a dubious grin. "May be?"

"I am not always correct," Fafnir admitted without sign of shame. "Many times the true nature of the augury has escaped me or I have misinterpreted the meaning of its words. There are few clues about the intended coburn, so I forged the sword and entrusted it to your Order in its earliest days."

Inkstain piped up. "The tapestry! Of the Battle of the Unsounded Horn. It *is* the same sword."

"Indeed," Fafnir affirmed. "There were many potent warriors among the first knights, but I had no way of knowing which would be the destined hand, so I left it in the keeping of the Valiant Spur, letting fate pass it from hand-to-hand over the centuries while I sought the other pieces."

"The mortal man and the great champion," Flyn said.

"Just so. But fate cannot be rushed and for a long time I wandered, keeping track of those with promise, but never able to bring them together. And then, several years ago, I found who I believed to be those prophesied. Both in Airlann."

"Faabar," Deglan muttered, casting a baleful eye at the giant. "That is why you gave him that sword. You can sense the weapons you have forged. You wanted him to come with you. The great champion."

Fafnir nodded.

"A mile-tamer gone," Deglan said derisively. "A mile-tamer is an old soldier's term for leg. It is a bloody play of words."

"What we in Middangeard call a kenning," Fafnir agreed.

The gnome threw a hand in the giant's direction, pointing at his peg. "This legless oaf fits your little omen. But Faabar's leg was not injured when you first met him."

"True," Fafnir replied. "But I saw the potential in him, nonetheless. And as you saw, he was indeed hurt. It was part of his fate. When I returned with the blade and heard of his wound, my certainty grew. And when the boy Padric arrived with the piskie, I saw the links at last begin to fasten."

"Piskie?" Flyn said, looking down at Deglan, but the gnome would not meet his eye. Flyn knew the name Padric. Padric the Black. The man he had almost killed at Castle Gaunt, presuming him to be Jerrod's heir before the truth of Pocket was revealed.

"You mean Rosheen?"

The dwarf smiled slightly. "Winged and deathless."

"The lad joined us on the hunt for the Unwound," Deglan said slowly. "You encouraged him to follow us, so you could get Faabar and him together."

"I did. But their fates, though intertwined, were not bound to the Corpse Eater. I brought the piskie to Black Pool where I sensed the coburn sword to now be, in hopes that the other two would find their way there. Little did I know that the fomori had been killed and Padric was sinking deeper into his true fate. However," the dwarf said, looking at Flyn, "I did get to set eyes on the new bearer of the sword and I knew the blade had finally found its chosen wielder."

Flyn looked at the weapon in his hands. It had been with him every day now for years, but suddenly it appeared to him a strange intruder.

"I found Hafr in Middangeard soon after," Fafnir continued. "And realized that 'deep in the horns' was not a reference to a fomori's age, but another kenning—"

"That he's a bloody drunk," Deglan cut in, looking at the giant with disgust. "This is madness! By your own admission you have been wrong before. How can you be so certain now?"

"When you seek the proper cure for an illness, Master Loamtoes," Fafnir replied, "are you not certain once you find it?"

Deglan stared hard at the Chain Maker for a moment, struggling for a retort. "I cannot listen to any more," he said at last.

He wheeled on Flyn and Crane, thrusting a finger up at their faces.

"You two should not believe a word of this! But just in case you are fools enough to, I hope you remember the last line of that convenient little prophecy."

The gnome turned away and stalked off down the beach, back towards Skagen. Flyn watched him go, feeling the fool. Try as he might, he could not recall the final words of the augury. He turned to Inkstain and the chronicler must have read the confusion on his face.

"Many lives undone," the man told him and ducked his head as he passed, following Deglan's tracks in the sand.

Flyn was left alone with the dwarrow and the giant. Fafnir must have been right about fate. Flyn could not force his feet to go after his friends.

SIXTEEN

There were no answers!

Ingelbert flung the tome off the table with a swipe of his arm, along with the low candle, empty cup and full plate. All spilled to the floor in a heap of graceless noise.

Immediately regretting his outburst, Ingelbert looked surreptitiously around, but in the raucous din of the Wreck, his loss of temper went unnoticed.

Sliding off the bench, he bent down and retrieved the book from the pile of flung food, dismayed to find grease on the pages and spattered wax from the upset candle. With a groan, he tried to undo the damage, but his efforts were feebly ineffectual. The stains were already set into the vellum. Not bothering with the rest of the discarded items, Ingelbert rose and set the tome carefully on the tabletop before flopping back down onto the bench. He stared at the sullied binding morosely. What was wrong with him? Never in his life would he have dared treat a book so. He once handled even the banal ledgers of the Valiant Spur with great care. Now he was dumping a centuries-old tome onto the floor of a tavern with the table scraps. And that, disturbingly, was the least of the changes he was manifesting.

What had happened in Gipeswic? To the clavigers, to the giant, to him? Horror and death and the release of fell powers. But how? Was it the book? If so, the pages offered him no clues. They lay splayed before him, unfathomable and inert. Since his abduction, Ingelbert had found no time to study the runes, but now that the truth of the dwarf's actions had been confessed he was determined to bury all the remaining riddles.

Deglan had been in no mood for more discourse after the revelations upon the beach and retired to one of the mariner's huts after seeking, and gaining, an assurance from Ingelbert that he was not fool enough to embark on the dwarf's deluded geis. Ingelbert did not fully share the bigoted gnome's skepticism, but he agreed readily. He had no intention of going anywhere save a quiet place to be alone. In the end, he found neither solitude nor silence.

The crude domiciles in Skagen were owned only by occupancy and the swell of men from Deglan's ship and Fafnir's crew had filled the available huts. Already, quarrels had broken out between the sailors over the lack of lodging. Ingelbert had been left with no other choice but the Wreck. For several hours, he drifted in the miasma of unwashed bodies, boiled fish, stale grog and fresh piss, trying to focus on his task. Before his time in Gipeswic, he would never have dared to enter a place such as this.

The overturned ship was awash in smoke and song, crammed to bursting with all manner of ruffians. Whalers drank with slavers, sellswords diced with wreckers and all caroused with the bevy of whores who had taken up permanent residence on Skagen. These women were also the local brewers, their bastard children selling spirits out of barrels while they sold their bodies.

As the sole purveyors of the two commodities that sailors hold most dear, the whores ruled Skagen from beneath the curved, clinker-built roof of the Wreck. They had slit more than a few throats to establish their dominance and preserved it with a ready willingness to slit more should they be challenged or abused. Fear of the whores' wrath kept the nightly peace in the Wreck. That, and the giantess they employed.

She sat at a table not far from Ingelbert, jesting and drinking with a group of rowdy patrons, her laugh by far the loudest. Her mirthful face was handsome beneath hair the color of embers, cut wildly short. Ingelbert had no reference in the reckoning of a giant's age, but to human standards she appeared just to the youthful side of middle-age. There was experience around her eyes and mouth, the confidence of womanhood still adorned with a spark of girlish mischief. Of all the boisterous distractions within the Wreck, she was the most difficult to ignore and Ingelbert had found his attention pulled away from his book by her laugh more than once over the last hour. He looked at her now, grateful she had not noticed his fit of anger and mistook it for a deeper aggression that needed to be quelled. Indeed, she was enjoying herself so immensely that he wondered how effective a peace-keeper she could actually be.

And then she stood.

When he refrained from slouching Ingelbert was near six and a half feet, but the giantess topped him by at least another two.

As she walked to refill her horn, he noted the rippling muscles in her thighs proudly exposed between the slits in her short, fur clout.

She had a woman's shape, but there was a firmness complementing every curve. Her bodice was made of cured hide, displaying a visibly strong back between broad, corded shoulders and a midriff etched with hard lines. She bore no weapons, not even a dagger, but her hands were wrapped in thongs of supple, well-used leather from the knuckles to the elbow.

"The Breaker don't service the guests."

Ingelbert tore his eyes away from the giantess and looked up to find a young whore looking down at him, her painted lips smiling.

"Um," he tried to return the smile. "I, uh, I am sorry. What, um, what did you say?"

"Ulfrun," the whore nodded at the giantess, who was now crossing back to her table, quaffing steadily from her frothing horn as she went. "Way you were staring, looked like you were of a mind to ask her for a thrust. Don't." The words had the sound of a friendly warning, but the whore's face was amused, almost conspiratorial, as if she and Ingelbert shared some private jape.

"Me though," she went on, flashing a knowing look. "I am not so unattainable."

Ingelbert gave what he hoped was a nervous laugh. He needed to decline, but not offend. In truth, he found everything about the woman repellent. Her lank, dirty hair, her pointed chin and red-rimmed eyes, the way her damp garments clung to her clammy skin. He had always been shy around women, but he suddenly found the instinct eclipsed by repugnance.

"Oh, um, I see," he said, hoping his feigned bashfulness was not immediately obvious. "Most kind, but, ah, I am afraid I am preoccupied this night."

The whore glanced down at the open tome for a moment and Ingelbert worried she was the ignorant sort who found knowledge a wondrous curiosity. He needed her to move on, not sit down and ask a torrent of wide-eyed questions.

"Aye, I see that," she laughed. "Long nose in them pages since you sat. One question?"

"Yes?" Ingelbert replied, convinced it would not be only one. The whore pointed above his head and laughed again.

"How do you keep *that* from shitting in your ale?"

Ingelbert followed the direction of the woman's finger, craning his neck up and around. Above him, perched on a protruding spar, was Gasten. The colorful patrons of the Wreck had barely glanced up from their revels when he entered with the owl on his shoulder. The bird had quickly flown up to the convenient perch and remained there, taking no interest in the clamor below.

The whore did not stay for an answer, sauntering off before Ingelbert had turned back around, but he found himself staring at the floor, considering her question. He tossed another look up at the owl. There were no signs of droppings, not on the spar, not on the floor. Inspecting his cloak, Ingelbert found none there either.

He knew he had never seen the owl eat, but proof of defecation had never occurred to him.

And there it was. An answer.

Ingelbert looked up at Gasten and knew for a certainty he had not been restored to true life. But how? He turned his eyes and his thoughts back to the green book. Huukayat. Owl. He had spoken the word and the bird had flown off of Edric's wrist and come directly to him. It was dead when he spoke the word again.

Could he have called it to him as before? Called it from death?

Ingelbert had just seen a corpse rise with his own eyes. The dwarf prisoner was stabbed through the heart, yet walked again before Fafnir made a permanent end.

Fafnir.

That the runecaster himself was responsible for everything crossed Ingelbert's mind. He could have revived Gasten and sent him to spy on Ingelbert. From his own mouth, the dwarf admitted to keeping track of those he believed held some value to his cause.

Ingelbert remembered how easily Hafr had found him that last, dreadful night in Gipeswic. Could Fafnir have been responsible for the clavigers' deaths as well? And what of the giant's sudden affliction of boils? Hafr had been ready to slay him and that certainly went against the dwarf's designs. Fafnir had rid the giant of his boils during the voyage, but could he not have also been the cause, to slow the brute's attack?

Ingelbert looked down at his hand, opening his fingers wide to gaze at his palm where he had caught the giant's falling blade.

There was pain now where there was none before. No wound was visible, but Ingelbert felt as if his hand had been sliced deeply with a dull knife. It was like his mind registered the injury, but his flesh refused to accept it. But even the pain was only a shadow of what he would have suffered if Hafr's sword had struck true. Had the blade been dull it still would have pulped his arm and killed him. By rights he should never have been able to stop such a powerful blow.

And why had he reached for sharp steel with a bare hand? Was Fafnir capable of such manipulation? He could turn arrows aside, but could he force a man to catch naked steel?

No answers.

There was nothing but a list of possibilities. The book. The owl. Fafnir. And the one common element that united them.

Ingelbert himself. Hafr had called him a wizard just before he struck. Was that the cause? Could Ingelbert be some kind of sorcerer? He thought back to his youth and found nothing in his flawless memory that would point to some dormant propensity for Magic. Surely Parlan Sloane would have sensed it and warned him.

The old man was more than a kindly savior of orphans. He possessed great wisdom and close friendships with the Fae. But he was now hundreds of leagues away. No, if Ingelbert wanted answers he had only one source.

Just then, as if summoned, Fafnir entered the Wreck. He was followed closely by Hafr and for the first time that evening the noise in the place perceptibly lessened. Ingelbert was surprised to see that Flyn was not with them. Fafnir scanned the crowded room and quickly settled on Ingelbert. The dwarf spoke a few words to Hafr and the giant made his way to the nearest tapped barrel.

Ingelbert quickly slipped the tome into his satchel as the runecaster made his way over. He sat across the table without waiting for an invitation.

"Shall we share a meal?" Fafnir asked pleasantly.

Ingelbert ignored this. "I have no, no intention of traveling with you."

"You had no intention of coming to Skagen," the dwarf replied with a smile. "And yet here we sit."

"Because you and that giant savage brought me here."

"I am a Chain Maker," Fafnir returned. "The proper links must be brought together before they can be made strong. Do you seek my pardon?"

Ingelbert shook his head. "I seek answers."

"Have I not given them?"

"What you chose to reveal," Ingelbert countered. "But there is more. I must know all."

"No man knows all, Master Crane."

"No man," Ingelbert agreed, watching Fafnir's face closely.

"But what of, of one dwarf?"

The runecaster laughed at that and Ingelbert detected genuine amusement. Still, Fafnir had a gift for deception and Ingelbert did not relax his scrutiny.

"What more can I tell you?" the dwarf asked with good humor. Ingelbert chose his first question carefully, needing some time to properly measure the wizard's responses. "Is the legend true? About Middangeard and the first Elementals?"

Fafnir considered this for a moment. His smile faded and he nodded shallowly as he thought. When he answered, the laughter was gone from his voice.

"Legends are born from a mating of distant truths and prideful lies. There are few written records remaining from those ancient times. Many were destroyed or taken by the huldu when they abandoned us for Airlann." A shadow of anger crept across the dwarf's brow and he leaned forward, his voice lowering. "That my people are murdered by their own dead is true. It is true that the cause of this curse is a foul beast from the depths of time. Is the Corpse Eater truly the mother of the coburn race? The augury proclaims it to be so and that is where I place my trust. I must believe! It is the last hope left to the dwarrow. A coburn is the only being that can slay her, this is all that matters in the end."

"And the other two?" Ingelbert pressed. "The weak man and the great champion? Do they matter so much?"

"Without them the destined coburn will fail," Fafnir proclaimed with certainty. "That I also believe. We dwarrow have a saying. 'One alone will fall. Two together can be divided. But three united cannot be cloven in twain.'"

"And if the three do not unite? If one refuses to accept his part in the augury?"

"If it is his true fate, then such a choice is impossible."

"And what of that fate?" Ingelbert asked. "Deglan believes that if we follow you, we will die."

Fafnir waved his words away with a broad hand. "The gnome is not part of this. His thinking matters not."

It was Ingelbert who leaned forward now. "It does to me! And if I am truly the man you seek, then it also matters to your precious portent. 'Friend to folk Fae,' remember?"

The Chain Maker smiled with appreciation. "I see that you do."

"That is why you had me translate the augury. You know I forget nothing."

"The least of your talents, too."

And there Ingelbert saw it. Another of the answers he sought, yet he had not asked the question. He did not need to, for it was revealed on the dwarf's face. Fafnir was not without guile, but at the mention of Ingelbert's talents his countenance became an open book, written in a language Ingelbert had no difficulty deciphering. Admiration nakedly displayed. Trepidation barely contained. Jealousy poorly hidden. Ingelbert had seen the exact expression countless times during his youth on the faces of his fellow orphans as he ceaselessly surpassed them in study. Parlan Sloan had also worn the same mask on occasion, though the envy was never present. Just pride for a gifted student and that hint of disquiet.

Fafnir had not worked a spell on him, nor bestowed him with any power. The dwarf believed he wielded Magic of his own volition. It was in his eyes. Images of the dying clavigers burst into Ingelbert's mind, sickening him. The burst flesh, the worms, the convulsions as one man bludgeoned his companion to death then did the same to himself. Ingelbert had caused all that. He had killed those men, and they had not died well. Ugly, nightmarish, prolonged death was dealt without lenity.

Ingelbert stared at his hands, once stained only with ink. He needed another explanation, another theory, another culprit. He felt his mouth opening and closing soundlessly, grasping vainly for words as his mind clutched desperately for another answer. It found none.

"Did you not raise the owl to ensnare me?" he asked Fafnir, abandoning all caution.

Fafnir's eyes darted up to where Gasten sat. It was a brief glance, almost reluctant. When the dwarf looked back, his words were slow, each carefully chosen.

"I cannot bring back the dead, Ingelbert Crane. Such power was denied my race when we were split from the huldu. Restoring benevolent life is the province of elf-kind and even among them, only the most puissant know the craft. Irial Ulvyeh and his line could accomplish it, but the huldu king has removed himself from the world and his daughter is long dead. This I am sure you know."

Again, the certainty of shared knowledge. The runecaster believed him a fellow wizard!

"In truth," Fafnir continued, "it was lore I feared lost. Until now."

Ingelbert's eyes had not left his hands, though he could no longer see them. He wept, with no concern for his company or surroundings. He wept without shame, feeling only bitter self-loathing and remorse for the men whose lives he ended.

Fafnir's voice was low, consoling, coming through the hot roar of his tears. "This talent is fresh."

"I thought it was you," Ingelbert admitted, his voice thick.

"No. I cannot foist power onto another. Your newfound Magic, whatever its source, is the reason your fate is tied to this quest."

"It is not me!" Ingelbert reached down and removed the tome from his satchel. He all but threw it at the dwarf, not wanting to touch it. The heavy book landed on the table before the runecaster, who regarded it with puzzlement. "You say you know not the source. There it is before you!"

Fafnir opened the cover with a flick of his thick fingers and frowned at the first page, then the second. He looked up at Ingelbert for a moment, his frown deepening, then returned his attention to the book, flipping to the middle and, a moment later, to the end. He exhaled heavily, fixing Ingelbert with a concerned stare.

"Master Crane, there is nothing here."

Ingelbert's stomach turned. "What?"

"It is old by human standards," Fafnir explained as Ingelbert reached forward to snatch the book back. "The runes are elvish, but it is merely a list. A quartermaster's log of supplies. It is nothing."

Ingelbert combed frantically through the book, turning pages with aggressive flicks of his wrist, eyes scanning feverishly over the symbols. Each was immediately decipherable. Numbers in front of words followed by brief notations. The runes no longer swam before his eyes, no longer stubbornly refusing to give up their meanings as they had for months. Foodstuffs. Pack animals.

Arms requisitions. There were even dates for each entry, though he was not familiar enough with the elven measure of time to discern them. It was as the dwarf said. Nothing. Some crumbling war record abandoned in the annals of the Valiant Spur, left over from their early days under elvish command.

"This, uh, this is not how it was!" Ingelbert fought against his own mind, feeling betrayed. "The writing, it, ah, moved. It moved! This is not how it was!"

"An old huldu spell," Fafnir told him gently. "Used to conceal the contents of the ledger from their enemies. In war, such things are great secrets. The enchantment, however, was unraveling. My contact with the book was enough to dispel what Magic remained."

The Wreck was alive with voices, all making merry in some fashion. Ingelbert sat with his head hung and his nose running, feeling crushed by the oppressive mirth.

"This cannot be me," he whispered at last.

Fafnir's large, calloused hand came into view, closing the book and pushing it out of sight. Then the hand retreated and only the dwarf's voice remained.

"Elf Magic does not wither with time. It was you who loosened the spell upon the book. That is a task few mortals can accomplish. Your sorcery is growing, maturing. It will progress quickly now that you are aware of its existence."

Ingelbert looked up at the dwarf, shaking his head. "No. I refuse this."

"You cannot!" Fafnir's voice turned hard. "The last mortal I recruited to my cause was as ignorant of my true nature as he was his own. As you were of yours. I sensed potential within him, as I did you when we met in the foundry. But your power Ingelbert Crane, your capacity for greatness, drowns what I saw in the other. Padric had venom in his veins, rage, a certain luck and a willingness to die. You. You are limned in the dust of broken kingdoms, emanating the echoes of falling towers. I felt joy surge from you as those men died, exultation, release. To kill one such as the Corpse Eater, we need one who shares her delight in depredation."

"That is not who I am!" Ingelbert protested. "That is not, not what I want to be."

"Which is the reason I do not hide it from you," Fafnir insisted. "I have erred many times in my search for those foretold in the augury. But in my mistakes I have learned that there is a similarity in those I am drawn to, a rough kindred. Had I not found him, Padric would have allowed his rage to overcome him. I saw in his future the jealous murder of a woman who cast him aside. And that is all he would have been, a killer. He would have ended his days dangling from a tree, nothing but a base cutthroat. But he turned from that path to follow me and though he was not the man prophesied, he found a better fate and helped save countless lives rather than selfishly taking one. I tell you, if you embrace your proper destiny you shall avoid a false one, one which will surely make you the despoiler you wish not to be. I need who you are, but I fear what you will become. You speak of refusing your part in this. Do so and you will be swallowed by the evil born of great might. Come with me! Help me banish a monster from this world and I swear to you, you will not become one yourself."

Deglan was nearly asleep when Flyn entered the mariner's hut. The sun was not yet down, but the weariness of the past days had caught up with him. Now that he knew his companions were alive and unharmed, Deglan succumbed eagerly to his exhaustion, reclining on the framework of rope some industrious sailor had constructed to better tumble whores and sleep off nights of excessive imbibing. Just as he drifted into welcome repose, the door creaked open and he jerked awake to see the young strut peering in at him.

"Hob's Teeth!" Deglan complained. "What?"

Unfazed by this asperity, Flyn ducked into the hut and shut the door. Leaning his large sword against the wall, the coburn slumped onto the bench opposite Deglan's mattress and stretched his legs out. In the closeness of the hut Deglan did not fail to see Flyn's muscles trembling.

"Rune Magic or no," he grumbled, sitting up, "you are not fully recovered."

"I am fine," Flyn whispered, leaning his head back and closing his eyes.

"Toad shit," Deglan said softly. It was a tone he rarely used, but one he learned while a Staunch of the Wart Shanks. Those war-torn years in the gnomish cavalry had taught him many things and one of the first was that warriors needed permission to admit weakness. "Tell me what happened, Flyn."

The coburn was so long in answering, Deglan thought he had fallen asleep. When Flyn spoke at last, he did not open his eyes, his words devoid of the laughter that usually dwelt at the edge of his voice.

"They instruct you endlessly, the Knights Sergeant. Drills with quarterstaff. Drills with spear. With mace and shield. Then the falchion and broadsword. And the glaive. You train in armor and without. In the mud, the rain. Drills, drills, drills. In my first year I mastered skills that most do not in thrice that time."

Deglan watched Flyn's face contort in an almost pained expression, as if the very memory of his martial tutelage taxed his already beleaguered body.

"What they do not teach," Flyn went on after a long breath, "what is never told, is what to do once you have your spurs. It is a proud tradition that every Knight Errant be allowed to seek his own purpose, free from interference even from the Grand Master.

The oaths of the Order must be upheld, its causes championed, but each knight must do so as he sees fit. I never understood what a burden that truly was. I once heaped scorn upon Sir Corc. I thought him a false knight, wasting his errantry with words, holding cowardly councils and hiding behind the countless letters he would write. Fool that I was. I know now that a questing life is only wasted if spent in pointless wandering, looking aimlessly for wrongs to right, which is all I could conceive of knighthood." Flyn sat forward and shook his head ruefully, finally opening his eyes. "I am not learned, Deglan. I have no gift for tongues nor knowledge of history. I lack the patience to seek an audience with an elusive potentate, as Corc did for years with the Lord of the Pile. I am not a skilled mariner like Blood Yolk, captaining a fleet to stand against the Raider Kings. I fight. That is what I know. All I know."

"Buggery and shit," Deglan swore. "You are looking for my damn blessing to go on this quest!"

"No," Flyn protested weakly.

"Yes you are! And you do not bloody have it."

"Deglan, I am not going."

Flyn said it blandly. There was nothing further, no laugh, no jest. Deglan found himself caught off guard, staring dumbly into the knight's resigned face. It was the last thing he expected from the hot-headed cock. The critical berating of Flyn's unfailing stupidity that Deglan had been prepared to deliver was useless.

"Does the dwarf know?" he managed, after a moment's slack-jawed puzzlement.

"Not yet," Flyn replied with a careless shrug.

"He will not take kindly to such a decision."

Flyn finally smiled, but there was no joy in his expression, only self-mockery. "He cannot kill me, Deglan. Not if he believes he needs me."

"We bloody know what he cannot do," Deglan argued. "It is what he can do that remains a mystery."

"You are getting what you wanted, Staunch," Flyn said coolly. "Do not grouse now about unknown dangers."

"What I want," Deglan countered, "is you and Crane still breathing."

Flyn gave a scoffing exhalation. "This is not about keeping us alive, Deglan. Not for you. This is about denying Fafnir whatever he wants."

Deglan felt his ears flush and he shot a hard stare at the coburn, fighting to keep his voice even.

"If you were not so recently hard-used, Bantam Flyn," he said, "I would rap my knuckles across your beak for those words."

The young knight's icy countenance held for a heartbeat then melted with genuine remorse. "Pardons, Master Loamtoes. It was unworthily said."

"Apologies are not necessary," Deglan said, waving him off.

"Explanations are."

Flyn nodded at this, thinking, clearly struggling. Deglan did not press further and waited, knowing the words would come.

"Did you know the Valiant Spur trains its squires for six years?" Flyn asked at last, seeking no answer. "After only two years I could best every one of my brother squires. I proved it at the tourney, and went on to defeat spurred knights. When Bronze Wattle yielded I was not even surprised. The most famed of the Knights Errant and he was just another defeated foe. I knew then I was the greatest warrior the Order had seen since Mulrooster. I was unbeatable." A flicker of pride played across Flyn's face, but quickly faded. "I went to Airlann and carried my arrogance with me, yearning to further test my prowess and resenting the knight who kept me chained. For months, I thought Corc a coward and openly impugned his honor time and again. It is a wonder we did not come to blows sooner, but as I said, Sir Corc is patient. When that patience finally shattered I learned the truth. I am not the most skilled fighter in the Valiant Spur. Neither was Bronze Wattle. No, it is a knight who did not enter the tourney at all. It is Sir Corc the Constant. He is the best of us. He is the one Fafnir truly needs."

"Bugger me," Deglan groaned. "You do believe that blasted augury."

"I believe the dwarrow need help," Flyn said defiantly.

"Then bloody help them! Do not shuffle this off on Corc!"

"He is who Fafnir wants, Deglan," Flyn's voice was beginning to rise. "They have known each other for years. Fafnir told me when he sensed the sword had moved

to Black Pool and he came with Rosheen, he suspected Corc had come into possession of the blade. The only reason he did not is because he did not compete in the
tourney."

"Clever bird," Deglan said with approval. "Likely he suspected the dwarf had
some hidden designs and did not play into his scheming hands."

"But if it is his fate . . ." Flyn urged, nearly pleading.

Deglan was out of patience. "Enough of this fate shit! Corc was not the one spirited away by a bloody wizard. His duty, his chosen duty, is to guard Pocket. And that
is far more potent than any conjured fate."

"I know," Flyn said, reaching into his belt pouch and retrieving a small object. He
held it forth and Deglan found it to be a wooden horse. "This is Pocket's. I found it
in his hiding place under the tower stairs. I intended to return it to him and I will. I
shall take up Corc's sworn duty and defend Pocket's secret and his life. Corc will be
free to return to the Order and resume his errantry."

Deglan stared at the toy horse in Flyn's outstretched hand and felt a wave of pity
settle in his gut. This was not the impetuous, insufferable gallant he once knew. This
was something broken. He looked up into the young coburn's face.

"When did you become a coward, Flyn?"

Had he been wrong, Deglan might have died in that mariner's hut and in some
way that would have been better. Being right though, he had to watch the last
desperate resolve of Bantam Flyn crumble, falling from his face as the horse fell
from his hand.

He slumped on the bench, staring blankly at the crude planking of the floor.
Deglan scowled at the sight. He was unwilling to allow the knight to descend further
into whatever self-piteous sinkhole was swallowing him whole.

"What happened to you?" he pressed without sympathy.

"Where is the strutting swordmaster? The insufferable bravado who leaps off
of towers to save falling chroniclers? Who fights skin-changers and Painted Men
without thought? Where is—?"

"HE WAS DEFEATED!"

Flyn erupted off the bench, shaking his clenched fist in Deglan's face. The coburn's
comb and torn wattle turned a deep crimson, his eyes blazing, streaming tears.

"Is that what you want to hear?" Flyn raged. "You sour, stunted little fuck!"

The words cut, but Deglan kept his face neutral. This was what he meant to draw
forth and now he needed to weather what he wrought. Flyn had grown threatening
still. His fist remained thrust in Deglan's face, but it no longer quivered. Like his
face, it was motionless.

"My father," Flyn intoned, "is a cruel, licentious savage. I tried to convince myself
that I did not hunger for his death, but it was a lie. His was the evil I most wanted
to purge from this world and I dreamed of the day I would slay him. I failed. He
defeated me. An ignorant, rutting, unwashed animal defeated *me*. Gallus was,
and because of my repeated failure, yet remains, the thing I most fear. When did I
become a coward? The day I did not help my brother kill him."

Deglan listened intently as the young knight unburdened himself, his fury cooling to shame and regret. Suddenly exhausted, Flyn let his fist fall and took an unsteady step backwards. Deglan thought he might tumble back down onto the bench, but the coburn kept his feet. He stared at nothing.

"I knew it too," Flyn whispered. "I knew I would fail. As I did before. You were not there, Deglan, not with us within the walls of Castle Gaunt. Earth and Stone be glad you were not! The Unwound were everywhere, waking and slaying. Men and goblins were dying all around us, Muckle was gravely wounded and suddenly we lost Pocket. By the time we reached him that husk was holding the damn crown over his head. I have never seen Corc move so fast. But I was faster." A terrible, haunted expression darkened Flyn's sightless gaze and Deglan keenly felt the walls of the bleak hut surrounding them both. "Whatever had possession of the husk, whatever held Pocket entranced, it laughed. A girlish laugh, full of loathing. It called the coburn up-jumped animals, and something . . . I do not know, like a pair of powerful hands reached into my core and—" Flyn clenched his hands into trembling fists and jerked them downwards in a snapping motion. "I became a wild and unreasoning thing. So did Corc. No oaths existed, no honor, just feral hatred and a need for blood. We fought like beasts. No weapons save what we coburn are born with. It was hideous, bloody combat. Again he emerged the victor, but this time my lesson was not in humility. It was in death. I have never forgotten the feeling of his spur impaling my throat."

Deglan felt his spine crawl and fought a shudder. He had not been there, that was true, but he knew what damage Jerrod's crown had wrought while in the clutches of the possessed husk, Slouch Hat. Curdle had told him everything in the days following the defeat of Torcan Swinehelm and his Unwound.

"Pocket restored our lives," Flyn continued, "but the memory remains. I greatly respect Sir Corc, and during our time on the island I came to love him, but between those bonds there is a blackness, one which we have never spoke of for Pocket's sake, lest we remind the poor boy."

The boy had not forgotten, Deglan knew. He and Moragh had nursed the little gurg through many difficult nights during his recovery. Pocket often awoke screaming, weeping and begging pardons for the misery he had been forced to unleash. The memory remained for all who survived the vengeance of the iron crown's keeper, but Deglan said nothing, knowing it would do Flyn no good to hear such things now.

"I am burdened by the brutishness of my race," Flyn said mournfully, "but I can draw no strength from it. Not like Gallus. Even Corc, so controlled and noble, can use that savagery to his advantage. Both bested me. Both my fathers. And now I am meant to slay the ancient mother of my race. She who is responsible for the very base nature of the coburn which I cannot overcome. If what Fafnir says is true, Gallus will be as nothing compared to this monster, this Corpse Eater. I cannot face her."

Deglan swallowed hard, trying to rid himself of the sour taste that flooded his tongue. "You must."

Flyn withered at the words, his face curdling with confused despair. "You would now push me towards the very quest you so sternly protested?"

Deglan did not answer right away. He motioned patiently for Flyn to sit and to his relief the knight obeyed after brief consideration. The coburn had difficulty meeting his eyes, shamed at his harsh words and rueful admissions.

"You have been running," Deglan began bluntly. "Never from a battle, but certainly from greater purpose. You squired only two years and then you were allowed to leave. Were I the Grand Master, I never would have allowed you to go with Corc to Airlann. You should have been made to stay and complete the remaining years of training set by tradition, best of the squires or not. You were faced with that possibility again when Lackcomb withheld your spurs. And you ran. There was a nice speech you made in that tower, about saving Crane's life and how you were not meant for knighthood. Corc believed it and . . . so did I. But you were running. Running away from more years as a squire, running away from the Order while running towards a vengeance that you knew would not wear well with those spurs. That vengeance has failed and you are called to something greater, so you seek a means to escape. You would accept exile and take up a mantle that is not yours. Whatever their origins, the coburn are not immortal and one day you may well have to take up Corc's duty, but that time is not yet present. You left the Roost so Corc would not have to, so he could remain by Pocket's side. Or so you claimed. Would you now abandon that choice, make yourself a liar, just so you can run once more?"

Deglan did not expect an answer, nor did he give Flyn time to voice one. "I do not trust Fafnir," he went on. "And neither should you. Yes, I did not want you to be caught up in his moonbrained plots. I deemed his quest a poison, one that would ruin you. But there is already something destructive running rampant within you, Bantam Flyn, and it must be purged before you are lost. I wanted you away from this business because I thought the quest to be an ailment. Now I see, it's the bloody cure."

"You could be wrong," Flyn whispered.

"Perhaps," Deglan said. "But between following your judgment or mine, which would you choose?"

By way of response, the young knight stood and reached for the greatsword leaning against the wall. His hand hesitated for just a moment, then firmly took up the weapon. Flyn turned to Deglan and nodded.

"Thank you, Staunch."

"Thank me if we come back alive."

Flyn barely blinked. "We, again? This time, I shall not attempt to dissuade you."

"Good," Deglan grumbled, stooping to retrieve Pocket's fallen toy. He held it up to Flyn and the knight took it from him with a thin smile. "You may have some wisdom yet. Now, let's go and tell that bearded bastard the happy news."

They made their way across the twilit dunes and climbed the sliding sands leading up to the Wreck. They spotted Ingelbert sitting with Fafnir. Deglan shouldered his way through the crowd towards them, Flyn striding easily behind. The chronicler looked immensely vexed and Deglan fixed him with a concerned stare once he reached the table.

"Master Crane?" he asked. "Is all well?"

It was Fafnir who answered. "We were just discussing our plans to set sail on the morrow."

Deglan scowled, but said nothing. He had resolved to cease battling against this current. Still, he was inwardly crestfallen that the chronicler had agreed to join the dwarf's quest. He wondered what Fafnir had said to convince the man to come. From the look on Inkstain's stricken face, it was nothing encouraging.

"Master Loamtoes and I will be joining you," Flyn told the wizard. Deglan watched relief flutter across Ingelbert's face at this news. Fafnir was less pleased, but he hid it well. It was a clever stroke for Flyn to announce Deglan's intentions of cooperation.

Fafnir was unlikely to deny his destined coburn.

"What, um, what about your bargain with the guild masters?" Ingelbert ventured.

"I will honor it," Deglan declared. "Once we are returned. The captain who brought me here is not a stupid man. He cannot take me back to Gipeswic by force. He is outnumbered by Fafnir's crew and will not risk a confrontation, especially not after what he saw our dwarf friend here do with the arrows. And if that is not enough deterrent, then a giant and a coburn knight make equally convincing arguments against courting a fight." Deglan fixed Fafnir with a challenging stare after he spoke, daring him to deny any support. In truth, Deglan knew he could easily be taken back to Gipeswic if the captain chose to press the matter and Fafnir did not lend aid. Flyn would step in surely, but in the coburn's current state he would not be enough against the wreckers. Thankfully, Fafnir voiced no opposition, merely nodding gravely before encompassing Flyn and Ingelbert with a grandiose gesture of his hands.

"You have my deepest gratitude," he said somberly. "And the gratitude of my people. This day has been long in the coming."

"Cause for celebration," Deglan said, his tone not matching his words. "We should drink to our success. Master Crane, would you be so kind as to fetch us a few tankards of the local brew?"

"Oh, um, certainly," the chronicler stammered, clambering out from behind the table.

Deglan cast a pointed look at Flyn, and the knight followed the gawky man through the throng. Once they were gone, Deglan slid opposite the dwarf. He was a little small for the human-sized table, but he did not let that bother him as he smiled at Fafnir.

"I take it there is not much welcome for me on your predestined path?" he asked with self-satisfaction.

"Not much," the runecaster agreed without rancor. "Indeed, there would be none at all, but Master Crane has opened my eyes to a few possibilities within the augury that make your presence tolerable."

"Lucky me," Deglan said lightly before allowing his voice to go quietly severe. "Heed this, dwarf. You may believe you have the aid of those young mortals, but you do not have their loyalty. I do. If you are playing us false, or if I catch one sniff of skulduggery, I will see to it they abandon your damn venture. Augury or no, your people can continue to kill each other as they rot."

Fafnir smiled darkly. "You really do hate we dwarrow."

"Do not take it to heart," Deglan shrugged. "I hate gruagach just as much and goblins more. And my own people too, most of the time."

"Such bigotry could be your undoing."

"Or yours."

"I do not fear you, herbalist."

Deglan could see that the dwarf meant it, so he smiled.

"Yes. I am just a lowly herbalist and not counted as one of the greatest among the gnomes. Not like you, who must be revered among your kind. A runecaster. A Chain Maker. A wielder of powerful Magic and a seer of shattering omens. Impressive. I have no such spellcraft. But be warned, wizard, if you risk matching wits with me, I swear by Earth and Stone you will find your better."

Flyn and Crane returned then, passing out horns of fragrant ale.

"It shan't make for a very good song," Flyn said with a deprecating chuckle. "What foretold quest begins in a tavern?"

Before anyone could respond, there came a great tumult from the depths of the Wreck. Cries of alarm and shouted curses accompanied the resounding crash of a wooden table flung with great force to splinter against the sloping wall. The press of bodies condensed as people scrambled to get away from the center of the disturbance. Many went directly for the door, fleeing the Wreck with a few cautious glances backward. Standing in the space made by the clearing crowd was Hafr, breathing heavily, his massive hand keeping a weeping woman pressed close against his leg. The giant was clearly angry, his gaze burning at the figure standing across from him, a fiery-haired giantess. She was certainly imposing, though Hafr was a head taller and far brawnier. Still, Deglan noticed the giantess did not lack for muscle, though she did lack any form of weapon.

"Unhand the girl," she ordered, her voice as powerful and captivating as her body.

Hafr barked laughter. "The whore is Hafr's for the night. She and as many others as it takes to satisfy him."

"She forsook your limp entreaties for love-play, Ever-Boastful," the giantess replied mildly. "Now unhand her."

"Hafr need make no entreaties when he has treasure to give," the brute returned. "The price is paid."

The giantess ran a leather-wrapped hand through her, messy, short cropped hair. "No amount of hoard-shine can bury her denial. She is not for you."

Hafr looked down at the trembling form of the whore he held fast and shook her, chuckling as she whimpered. Deglan noticed the giantess's fingers flex slightly at this provocation. All eyes remaining in the now-silent Wreck were fixed on the two towering figures. Deglan shot a glance at Fafnir, but the dwarf seemed unconcerned and made no move to intervene.

"Should you not muzzle your animal," Deglan suggested, but he received no reply.

"Perhaps we should, um, we should leave," Ingelbert said.

Deglan looked to Flyn, but the coburn seemed detached, staring pensively in the direction of the giantess's feet. A squeal of fright forced Deglan's attention back to the confrontation before him. Hafr had pushed the woman away roughly and retrieved his massive sword. Faabar's sword. Deglan felt his stomach sour.

"Come then," Hafr taunted the giantess. "If you would deny me sport, than you must provide my entertainment. Long have I wished to make battle with you, Ulfrun. Almost as long as I have wished to ravish you."

Ulfrun, the giantess, smirked. "Never will the sky-candle light a morn that sees me beneath you, Ever-Boastful." She nodded at the giant's sword. "Now put up that blood-worm lest I shatter your wolf's-joint."

Hafr's face grew grim at the threat and the onlooking crowd shrank further into itself. Deglan found himself wondering if he should not have taken Crane's suggestion and left the tavern.

A fight between these two could bring the Wreck down on their heads.

"You would challenge Hafr?" Hafr mocked. "You, Ulfrun Whore-Shield? You have won no glory, no renown. You know not your Doom Name. Unlike I." The giant spread his arms wide, just as Deglan had seen him do in the hallmote before the guild masters, though this time, holding aloft the dwarf-forged sword, the effect was much more intimidating. "I am Hafr! Champion of Utgard! I am called Ring-Breaker! Troll-killer! The Wyrm Wrangler! I know my Doom and seek it without fear. I am the Foretold! Dwarf-friend, the runecaster's Chosen! I am Hafr the Ever-Boastful!"

The giant charged, fast despite his false leg. The sword punished the air as he swung. Ulfrun sprang to meet him, her long legs bringing her swiftly under Hafr's arms, then bracing wide for the impact. The giantess crossed her wrists and caught Hafr's descending forearms, halting his stroke. Her right elbow struck hard into the giant's ribs while her left arm encircled his wrist. Hafr bellowed as bones crunched beneath the hammering heel of Ulfrun's hand. She placed a foot on Hafr's thigh and used it to vault herself high, wrapping the back of her knee around the giant's head. She twisted as she fell, allowing her weight to bring the brute down, locked between her calf and thigh. Hafr landed heavily on his back and Ulfrun released his head just in time to shatter his jaw with her fist. The giant lay senseless upon the ground in seconds.

The giantess rose and stared down at her fallen foe. As an afterthought, she brought her foot down on Hafr's wooden leg, snapping it in two.

"I am Ulfrun," she said. "The Breaker."

Deglan found he was staring slack-jawed, but that quickly turned into a hearty guffaw.

"Looks to me that you are down one great champion," he jabbed at Fafnir, laughing fully in the dwarf's face.

"I do not believe he is," Ingelbert said in hushed awe.

To Deglan's surprise the giantess approached their table.

Heedless of them, Ulfrun reached over and took Ingelbert's horn out of his hand, draining it in one long pull. Then she did the same with Flyn's. She handed the empty horns back with a grateful nod.

"Turgur's Balls, but that gives one a thirst," she said in way of explanation.

"Though strong of limb," Ingelbert recited. "A mile-tamer gone, deep in the horns," the chronicler looked to the prone form of Hafr, "All foes to the ground."

"Careful, thin man," Ulfrun told Ingelbert with good humor. "Honeyed word-play could lead to sticky love-play."

Deglan blinked hard then scowled at Crane. "A mile-tamer gone? She's not missing a leg."

Flyn laughed. "Yes she is."

Deglan shot him a quizzical look.

"You need more bawdy songs in your life, Staunch," the coburn told him, smiling.

"What?"

"He means I don't have a cock between my legs," Ulfrun said cheerily, then looked at Ingelbert and winked. "Leastways, not yet." The chronicler blushed fiercely and tried to stammer a reply, but what came out was incomprehensible. Flyn laughed merrily and the giantess joined him.

Deglan looked grudgingly over to Fafnir. "Well?"

The dwarf looked Ulfrun over for a moment. "It must be."

Upon hearing him speak, the giantess looked down at where the wizard sat, seeming to notice him for the first time. Her smile slackened only by a fraction.

"Turgur's Balls," she swore halfheartedly, then looked everyone over. "I've fallen in with a Chain Maker haven't I?"

"Yes," Fafnir replied simply.

The giantess breathed heavily, put out. "I best go tell the mistresses I will be gone for a span." She proceeded to leave.

Deglan was flummoxed. "Simple as that?"

Ulfrun turned around, barely halting. "Why? What did you lot do, get together in pairs and talk it through?"

SEVENTEEN

Middangeard.

For days it was nothing but a cold, uninviting coast viewed from the deck of Fafnir's longship. Flyn felt useless, staring at the distant skerries and occasional stands of dark trees as the men pulled at the oars, hauling the ship swiftly through the water, though the landscape drifted by at a crawl. Their crossing of the Jutland Sea had taken less than a day once the ship left the tide-pools of Skagen behind, but Fafnir changed their course when the first sea cliffs came into view, ordering the ship to skirt the rugged shoreline. They sailed endlessly, never out of sight of land, nor ever drawing nearer to it.

"Does he never mean to make port?" Flyn complained into the wind as yet another mist-laden fjord passed sluggishly across his impatient gaze.

"Not in Götland," Ulfrun replied without missing a stroke of her oars. "The Raider Kings upon that soil are many and strong. Gladly would they feed the eagles with this lot of sail-kissers. Nay, best we travel the whale's way for a while longer."

"You fear humans?" Flyn jibed, knowing Ulfrun would take no offense.

The giantess's easy smile played across her face, untouched by flush despite the harsh wind and her labor at the oars. "A wolf is smaller than you, is it not? And yet, you fear the pack."

"Be a fool not to," Flyn replied agreeably.

"Aye," Ulfrun snorted. "Be a fool not to."

Flyn smiled and nodded. He liked Ulfrun. Quick with a jest and slow to anger, she lacked the prickly pride of Hafr. Flyn wondered how much of that pride the lumbering braggart would have left, once he recovered from the injuries he sustained at Ulfrun's hands. Just her hands.

During the tedious hours on the ship, Flyn often replayed the giants' combat in his head. It had been obvious to him who would emerge the victor. It was written in Ulfrun's stance. The subtle, sure shifting of weight, the calculated bounce just before she sprang. Flyn had predicted the outcome, yet the feat still caused his memory to marvel. Hafr was still unconscious when they set sail and Inkstain had voiced concern that he would seek vengeance on the women of the Wreck once he awoke. Ulfrun merely shrugged.

"His marrow-sheaths will be a long time knitting," she said.

"And with that wooden mile-tamer shattered, he will be hard-pressed to catch the girls. Leastways, without that wound-wand in hand he is no danger."

"What?" Deglan had asked, his face crinkled in confusion.

Inkstain had to serve as translator for the first few days.

"Hafr's bones are, are broken. And his wooden leg. Plus, he no longer has a, a sword."

"That last part I knew," Deglan said with a satisfied smirk.

For reasons unknown, the giantess eschewed all weapons and had no interest in claiming Hafr's blade for her own. She was set to gift it to the whores when Deglan boldly pulled her aside, into a far corner of the Wreck. He talked for a long time and Ulfrun listened intently. Flyn could not hear his words, but stood by with Inkstain and Fafnir, watching. When the gnome was finished, the giantess thumped a hand on her knee and approached.

"The gnome spills a moving lip-stream," she said, her words directed at Fafnir. "Chain Maker, it is my wish the war-limb be returned to the worm-bed of this Faabar Brindleback. Mighty was he in life, and he should remain so in death."

"As you wish," was all the dwarf had said in reply.

From that moment on Ulfrun had the unwavering friendship of the most irascible Fae in the known world. Flyn had never seen Deglan take to anyone so swiftly. He doubted the old mushroom liked him half so well. Deglan had not wasted the gift.

He gave the sword over to the captain of the ship that brought him to Skagen with instructions to carry it back to Gipeswic. The blade was to be turned over to the guild masters as an assurance that Deglan would return to collect it and fulfill his bargain. The captain had agreed readily.

With one condition.

Flyn glanced towards the bow of the longship. Hakeswaith crouched just outside the canvas that served as Fafnir's cabin, clutching his harpoon and staring sourly at the sea.

"Reckon he still means to kill me?" Deglan asked from beneath his nest of furs. When Ulfrun had taken it upon herself to man the oars furthest to the rear, shooing the four sailors manning them off the benches, Flyn and his companions had taken up a place near her in the stern. Deglan had huddled down between the benches, out of the wind, and only emerged when nature forced his hand.

"He dooms himself if he tries," Flyn said. "Bloody foolish of the captain to send him along."

"He had no choice," Deglan's muffled voice replied.

"Hakeswaith is the guild masters' pet. If he did not stay, the captain risked the guild's wrath."

"We will watch him," Flyn declared.

"Oh, don't think I am not. Between him and this damn, chill wind, a gnome cannot get a wink."

Flyn looked down. "You look like an ugly bear cub."

Ulfrun laughed.

"Quiet you," Deglan told her playfully. "It gets any colder and I will be crawling into the nearest cave to hibernate."

The giantess took one hand off an oar long enough to slap the inside of her bare thigh. "Best wriggle in then, ugly cub. I need not wager, it *will* get colder."

"Bloody grand," Deglan grumbled.

Flyn looked back across the stretch of sea separating them from Middangeard, recalling his voyage from Albain to Airlann and how the climate had changed the closer they drew to the Source Isle. He and Pocket had laughed as the air grew chill and gawked at the fire-hued leaves crowning the trees of Black Pool's gardens.

Autumn held eternal sway in Airlann, brisk and bright, but across the choppy waves before him lay a land claimed by Winter. Even from a distance, Flyn could feel the bite of Middangeard through his feathers. He could endure the wind, the cold, and Ulfrun appeared to take no notice of either, but Flyn worried for Deglan, and for Inkstain most of all.

The chronicler stood but a few paces away. He too, had eyes for the shoreline, and a sunken, sick expression was fixed to his angular face. The wind tore at his shaggy, straw-colored head, and his long fingers clutched his cloak tight beneath his chin.

Though separated only by a low rowing bench, the man may well have been a hundred leagues away. Ingelbert must have felt Flyn's eyes upon him, for he turned and gave the slightest shake of his head.

"Götland," he said, nodding at the passing stretch of land.

"Gautland, as we say in the Tin Isles. Where they sow only cabbages."

Flyn frowned at this, hoping the thin man had not caught a fever. He glanced down at Deglan, but the herbalist did not seem concerned. From the depths of his furs, the gnome's eyes gave Flyn a reassuring look then cocked up to look at Inkstain.

"Thinking of your father?" he asked the morose chronicler.

"Ridiculous, I know," the man replied. "To wonder if he might still be alive, somewhere in that blasted countryside. Or perhaps out raiding? Making more, more bastards."

"If those are the choices," Deglan scoffed, "it is likely he is dead, Master Crane."

"Aye," Ulfrun agreed, between strokes. "And you might be grateful to him 'ere long. The blood of a fjordman can only serve you well here."

"And what else was inherited through that blood?"

Inkstain said these words so softly that Flyn was certain none of the others heard them. He maneuvered closer to the chronicler and leaned on the side of the long-ship. Flyn stood silently next to Crane for a long time, joining him in his silent study of the water.

"I regret that you are now entangled in this," Flyn said at last, keeping his voice low and directed out to sea. "It is my doing. And I am sorry for it."

There was no immediate reply. Flyn tarried until the silence became uncomfortable.

"I will leave you to your thoughts, then."

"You do not need to," Inkstain said, stopping his departure.

"My thoughts are constant, often unwelcome, companions. They can wait awhile."

Flyn settled his forearms back on the ship. After another long silence he cocked his head to look up at the brooding chronicler.

"You are still thinking, Master Crane," Flyn chided.

Inkstain shook his head and issued a small laugh into the ocean wind. "My head contains stubborn guests."

"The secret to avoiding undo thinking," Flyn said, "is rash action. I recommend challenging Ulfrun to elvish leg-wrestling."

A grin cracked Inkstain's long face and he half turned to look at the giantess. "Perhaps I should, I should start smaller."

"True," Flyn said, nodding with grave seriousness. "Flip Deglan into the sea a few times, bolster your confidence."

Inkstain quickly turned back to the water, his jaw clenched against an outburst of laughter.

"What are you two braying about up there?" Deglan's voice demanded from his cocoon of furs.

"Nothing, Staunch," Flyn responded quickly, keeping his voice perfectly even.

Next to him, Inkstain chewed on a few chuckles. He checked to make sure the gnome was no longer listening then leaned closer to Flyn.

"Perhaps a, a swearing contest would be more sporting."

Flyn recoiled with overwrought horror. "Do you want to die? I said rash action, not headlong destruction!"

"Indeed," the chronicler agreed with a sagely nod. "I have it. I will challenge Fafnir to a beard growing contest."

Flyn's laughter burst from his beak without any hope of repression. He felt every eye on the longship turn on him, but he did not care, for Inkstain joined him, expelling his own mirth. They stood together, shaking their heads at their own buffoonery.

"They are all impossible feats, I fear," Inkstain said, when he caught his breath. "I am made for study and poltroonery."

Flyn clicked his tongue at this. "I would not be so quick with that estimation. Here I now discover you are a pillager's son, the blood of the reaver hiding beneath the ink stains."

He said it jestingly, but must have misjudged the depth of Crane's momentary levity. The man's face fell somber once more.

"I have gone entire, entire years without thinking of it," he said. "But here, in his homeland, I imagine that will prove impossible."

Flyn squeezed the chronicler's shoulder. "I am sorry for bringing you here, Ingelbert Crane."

"You forced me to Gipeswic, Sir Flyn. Not here. I do not, do not require pardons from you."

Giving Crane a companionable pat, Flyn removed his hand.

"I understand. Coming here to find him. I know something of troubling sires."

Inkstain shook his head. "I did not come here to find him. That would be improbable and, and vain. But to see Middangeard, the place of his origins, his molding, that has an appeal. A chance to touch my own history."

Flyn ran a hand over his comb, fighting the words that were forming on his tongue. He was not normally one for wise counsel.

"Just do not try and change that history," he said at last.

"Believe me, it is folly."

"This entire venture is likely folly, Sir Flyn." Crane gestured across the water at the frigid shore. "Does that appear to be a clime where I will thrive? A land of raiders and the rule of the sword?"

"Well, let us see," Flyn said, lightening his tone. He directed Inkstain's attention towards the broad backs of the men rowing on the benches. "You are half fjordman. You share their height, their flaxen hair. They are well-built, while you . . . have the physique of a spear shaft."

Flyn met Inkstain's curdling look and smiled. He clapped the man heartily on the back and grew serious.

"You are no coward, Master Crane. You proved that with the gruagach in your study. The ink? That was deadly clever. You are the keenest individual I have ever known, mortal or immortal. Such a mind is a rare thing in a world full of strong sword-arms."

Inkstain pondered his words a moment, then gave Flyn a nod of gratitude.

The sound of Deglan's chuckling brought their attention back to the interior of the ship.

"Ulfrun?" the gnome asked between chortles. "Tell us again what you did with Hafr just before we took ship."

"I tied the beard of that nanny-goat to his testicles."

The heap of furs shook as the herbalist let loose, followed by the throaty laughter of the giantess. Flyn joined them in merriment and Inkstain cracked a smile.

"I will never tire of hearing that," Deglan announced when he caught his breath.

Flyn saw Hakeswaith look over, no doubt believing their laughter was directed at him. The whaler scowled for a moment, then went back to staring at the open water. It seemed they were not entirely rid of prickly pride, after all.

From the tent next to the man, Fafnir emerged and spoke to the ship's jarl, then thumped steadily down the center aisle of the ship. He passed Flyn and the others with nary a word, approaching the helmsman at the rear of the starboard side. The dwarf spoke a few words in the Middangearder tongue and the man at the rudder nodded once.

"Appears you shall get your wish, Sir Flyn," Ingelbert pronounced.

"Yes," Fafnir said, coming to stand among them. His face was ghastly pale. "We will put in today. Our time on the sea is at an end."

"Thank Earth and Stone," Deglan muttered.

The Chain Maker said no more, and strode back up the aisle towards the bow. As the dwarf left, Flyn noted the sway of his back had increased and his hair was now completely black, visibly thinning.

"He does not look well," Flyn said.

"Svartálfar always appear such in Middangeard," Ulfrun told him. "Corpse-white, black as night."

"Swart—?" Flyn could not get his tongue to form the word.

"Black elves," Inkstain said, coming to his rescue. "The dwarrow. The curse upon them must become stronger the closer they are to Middangeard."

"No," Deglan barked. "This is their natural appearance. What you have seen in Sasana and Airlann is a falsehood. Closer to the Source Isle, to Magic itself, dwarfs swell with power. That damn runecaster's red beard, hale countenance, sturdy frame, all a product of absorbed Magic. In Airlann, the dwarrow become as close to their elven kindred as remains possible. For thousands of years they were forbade from even setting foot on Airlann soil, lest they attempted to wrest control from the Seelie Court. In the end, the elves were looking in the wrong direction and it was man who overthrew them. Still, we Fae have always been very suspicious of a dwarf in our lands."

"You will soon know the feeling of such cold courtesy," Ulfrun said lightly. "For you, gnome cub, are about to set foot on their land."

Within the hour, the giantess's words came true. The men swiftly took the sail down, rowing the ship confidently between the skerries and into the mouth of a wide fjord. Cliff faces appareled with fog and snow rose sharply on either side of the inlet, standing in mute judgment of the ship as it slipped towards the shore. There was a sharpness to the air. The wind stilled, though something akin to a crackle played just at the edge of Flyn's hearing. The expanse of water was vast, the cliffs towering, and yet the clouds hung low in the sky, an oppressive ceiling of grey. The smell of the sea gave way to a hint of evergreens, the scent frozen in the air. Breath from Flyn's beak heralded itself in a vapor, joined by the fleeting phantoms of wet heat playing from the lips and nostrils of everyone on board.

Time slowed as the cold crept in, and the ship seemed to hold still. Flyn felt it was the cliffs that were indeed moving, pulled slowly away by the smothering march of clouds. The rocky slopes gave way to a haunting hinterland where ugly stalks of scrub grass reached pleadingly out of the snow. The channel began to narrow and a natural bay appeared before them.

"It seems we are expected," Flyn said, spying half a dozen figures standing upon the stony beach.

Deglan rose slowly, impeded by the furs that he refused to relinquish. The gnome struggled onto the bench to better see over the side of the ship.

"More dwarfs," he announced bitterly.

The beach held no buildings, no dock, but the sailors confidently steered the boat inland, throwing ropes to the waiting dwarrow so the vessel could be pulled close to the rocky shoals.

Fafnir emerged from his tent, now wearing mail and a stout sword.

Flyn felt the urge to don his own armor, then remembered his had been lost after Gallus defeated him. No doubt it now lay buried in the hole Wynchell had dug to be his grave. He had managed to acquire another harness for his sword, employing one of the sailors to fashion it from various leather trappings.

The fjordmen were vaulting the sides of the ship, landing competently in the shallows, the water reaching their knees. Flyn slung Coalspur's harness over his head and put a hand on Deglan's shoulder.

"Come, Staunch. I will help you to shore."

The gnome batted him away with a grimace. "I shall not be carried to land by a chivalrous gamecock!"

"Pardons," Flyn said, holding up his offending hand in a placating gesture.

"Ulfrun," Deglan said, turning away with a smile. "Would you be so kind?"

Flyn gave the back of the gnome's head a withering glare.

The giantess scooped Deglan up, furs and all, then jumped over the side. She barely got her feet wet.

"I have no such reservations, Sir Flyn," Inkstain said. "And would welcome some aid."

Glad to be of service, Flyn jumped into the water and turned to help the chronicler down. Inkstain handed his heavy satchel down first.

"Careful, please," he instructed. "I would rather this did not get wet."

Flyn gave him a reassuring nod, then reached up and took the satchel, holding it well above the water with one hand while using the other to aid Crane's descent. The man nodded gratefully once he was steadily standing in the shallows and together they sloshed to the shore. Once on land, Flyn returned the satchel to Inkstain's care, noticing the large green tome held within when the chronicler threw back the flap to inspect his possessions.

"Still carrying the records from the Roost?" he asked.

Inkstain looked up, a slightly embarrassed look on his long face. "Oh, um, yes I am, yes. Could not seem to, to part with them. They are pieces of history. It would grieve me if they were lost."

"I understand," Flyn told him.

Inkstain made his way up the beach and joined Deglan and Ulfrun under a stand of trees, the gnome stamping his feet against the cold. Flyn remained behind, waiting. When Hakeswaith disembarked, Flyn stepped into his path. The hideous whaler's eyes snapped up, full of anger and rimmed with alarm.

"No quarrel," Flyn told the man, though he did not bother with a friendly tone.

"What d'you want?" Hakeswaith demanded through his distorted jaw.

"For you to get back aboard ship," Flyn answered. "There is no need for you to go further. The sailors can take you wherever you will. Go back, Hakeswaith. This is your last chance to get free of this." The whaler's glare flickered with doubt for half a heartbeat, then his lips sneered around his broken teeth. "I go where the stunty goes." As the small man tried to step around him, Flyn grabbed his arm, pulling him close.

"Know this, worm! Deglan Loamtoes is under my protection."

Curiously, Hakeswaith did not bristle at his touch nor try to pull free. He laughed wetly in his throat, looking up with his malformed smile.

"You daft pigeon," he whispered. "Look around you. This is Middangeard. Protection or no, not a one of us is safe."

***

Ingelbert struggled not to shiver. His nose was beginning to run and he found himself sniffling more than breathing. He fought a rising panic. It was day, the wind was slight, it was not raining nor snowing. This was likely to be the best clime he experienced and already he was freezing. How would he endure nightfall?

"Here," he heard a voice from below him say. He looked down to see Deglan offering up one of his bear skins. "I am starting to sweat. And that is worse than shivering in these conditions, believe me."

Ingelbert took the skin with a shaking hand and wrapped it around his shoulders. His shivering ceased almost instantly, but then his teeth began to chatter. Ingelbert locked them together and made a grunt of appreciation at the gnome. Deglan Loamtoes, ever the observant caretaker.

A rustling of the branches over Ingelbert's head sent a dusting of snow down upon him. He ducked deeper into the fur, not bothering to look up. He knew it was Gasten. The owl had spent most of the voyage in flight and rarely in view. His presence made the sailors nervous and Ingelbert had been grateful for his long absences. Now that they were back on land it seemed the great bird had a mind to stay close once more.

Bantam Flyn joined them under the trees and together they watched the sailors unload provisions from the ship. Ingelbert hoped there were more bearskins contained within the bundles.

Four of the dwarrow who had met the ship loaded everything onto three sturdy sleds, while the remaining two hauled a large chest over to where Fafnir stood waiting with the ship's jarl. They set it down upon the rocks and immediately opened the lid. The chest was brimming with gold, silver and precious stones, wrought into torques, rings, crowns and bangles. Ingelbert saw the jarl smile as his eyes caressed the treasure. He extended a hand and clasped wrists with Fafnir, then motioned for two of his men to load the chest onto the longship. It did not appear the sailors would tarry long upon the shore now that they were paid. Indeed, Fafnir seemed to have no more use for them, for he quickly turned his back on the jarl and the ship, pulling one of the dwarfs aside, leading him to another stand of trees further inland.

Ingelbert focused on the distant branches, and another scattering of fallen snow signaled Gasten's departure. The owl flew swiftly and silently, reaching the copse well before the dwarrow, and perched upon a shadowy bough. As Fafnir and his comrade walked under the eaves of the wood, the sounds of their voices filled Ingelbert's head. They spoke dworgmál, the dwarrow tongue, and Ingelbert listened intently with Gasten's ears.

"How many more?" Fafnir demanded.

There was a pause. The other dwarf was hesitant. "Two."

Fafnir spat a word Ingelbert did not know, but it had the sound of a curse. "Why did you not send the valrôka to inform me?"

"I did, my lord, but the crows returned, saying there is an owl journeying with you, one that would not allow them to approach."

"It is the man Crane's creature," Fafnir said, sounding pensive. "He does not yet have full mastery of the bird, nor all his craft. What of the lower meadows?"

"They are safe, Chain Maker. Undiscovered."

There came another pause as Fafnir issued a sigh of relief.

"Then there is still time. Which two fell in my absence?"

"The tree of the Boar Helms and that within the Fatwood."

"Did the vættir escape?"

"The dead of the Boar Helms did not make it far before their kin cut them down. But—"

"The Fatwood tree was remote. Vulnerable. Aye, I know. Who has taken up the hunt?"

When the other dwarf answered, his voice was trembling.

"Hengest and Thorsa's band."

Fafnir cursed again, this time with much more vehemence.

"And likely the Roundhouse is with them. Those three together can bode only ill! We must move swiftly."

"There is more, Chain Maker."

"Tell me."

"At the barrow of the Fatwood. The tree was felled, but the valrôka claim the despoilers left one of their own behind."

"Alive?"

"No, Chain Maker."

"We must go there."

"What of the lower meadows?"

"Soon," Fafnir said, his tone losing patience. "Answers may prove more valuable than haste. The chosen slayers have been found, at last. Our people need not suffer much longer."

"We never lost faith you would find them, my lord."

Fafnir hummed a short laugh, tinged with sadness. "No, Skrauti, you did not. But there are many who did. Who, even now, will not believe. Come."

Ingelbert allowed his mind to drift away from Gasten's.

Fafnir had said his craft would grow swiftly, and the runecaster had not erred. Ingelbert had suspected a link with the bird the night he fetched Deglan to the Tsigani boat, and had used the tedious voyage from Skagen to further explore the possibility. He proceeded slowly at first, probing gingerly at the owl's mind as you would an aching tooth. He found no pain, no resistance. On the contrary, there was something welcoming in the sensation. Soon he was seeing through Gasten's eyes and hearing with his ears, though as yet, he could not accomplish both simultaneously. Several times he had been with the owl when it drove away flights of large, griping crows, but never suspected the black birds were attempting to reach Fafnir. Ingelbert could not have prevented it if he had known, however. He was not in full control of the animal, it was more that he was being allowed to share in something ancient and secret, and Ingelbert often felt as if Gasten was humoring him, as one would a child. It was unnerving, but with the trepidation came a certain longing.

Ingelbert had never feared to be a pupil, for at the end of all tutelage came an awakening of knowledge that could be possessed, stripped and molded, until it was his to wield upon command. History, languages, numbers, all these had begun as unintelligible mysteries, but at the end of the requisite schooling, Ingelbert could draw them forth with ease, to the forefront of his brain, if not always his tongue. This would be no different. Just as the truth of the green tome's contents had at last been laid bare, so too would this tangle of foundling Magic be forced into maturity and placed at his disposal.

Perhaps he should not have spied on Fafnir, but, Deglan's opinion to the contrary, Ingelbert was not blindly following the dwarven wizard. He knew there was much the runecaster had not revealed, this most recent conversation proved that, but it also proved that Fafnir believed in his cause, and thus, believed in the allies he had gathered. Whatever path this Chain Maker was about to lead them down, they were not being baited with mummery and invented prophecies. It was a small comfort.

They left the banks of the inlet within the hour. The six dwarrow who had met them split into pairs and pulled the pack sleds. They were each pale and black of hair, and outside of the one Fafnir had called Skrauti, Ingelbert did not readily learn their names.

They spoke only dworgmál, rarely giving voice except to each other.

They pulled the laden sleds tirelessly and without complaint, their competence with the labor clearly revealing a lifetime of such work.

Even when Deglan's short strides failed to keep the pace and the gnome was forced to join the baggage in one of the sleds, the porters showed no signs of frustration at the added weight.

"I was a Staunch of the Wart Shanks," Deglan proclaimed to balm his injured pride. "Always in the saddle. Never much of a foot-soldier. Still, even the most robust riding toad would not last long in this white waste."

Ingelbert did not doubt it. They traversed a wilderness mostly covered in snow, though naming it a waste was unworthy.

In truth, the land was quite beautiful.

Trees flourished around them, the dark green of their needles shining beneath cocoons of ice. The dense forests moated the open plains, the shadows beneath the verges an intrusive contrast to the white terrain. Above, the sky was the color of a sword blade.

Still, the inherent beauty of the country did little to blunt the toil of traversing its cold surface. Ingelbert's legs trembled after the first hour of trudging through the drifts, some reaching near his knees. His feet had been numb since wading to shore, and he feared what his toes would look like at day's end. If there ever was to be an end.

He found time difficult to judge. The sun was completely hidden behind the clouds, the light seeming to emit from the snow, not the sky. Whenever they were not sheltered by trees, Ingelbert was forced to squint against the glare coming off the blinding white ground. His face felt raw and burnt, and his lips began to chap, splitting painfully. With each breath, he felt as if his lungs grew smaller, atrophying with each infusion of frigid air.

Glancing up, he saw Bantam Flyn several strides ahead. The greatsword across his back must have become a hindrance, for the coburn now bore it across his shoulders, as if yoked to the weapon.

He stepped high, his talons punching through the cold crust.

Clearly, the going was not easy for the knight, but unlike Ingelbert, he showed no signs of flagging. Indeed, none of his companions appeared to know fatigue. Though the worst drifts neared their waists, the dwarrow took no notice of the snow, barreling through with a startling endurance. And Ulfrun may well have been strolling down a street of level cobbles. With Deglan in the sled and Gasten on the wing, Ingelbert felt abandoned, left to struggle on with only his own weakness for company.

A rock, hidden beneath the snow, caught Ingelbert's foot, tripping him up. The tumble was not painful, his fall broken by cold, giving powder. As he clambered to his feet, Ingelbert glanced back to see if he could gain any sense of their progress and it was then that he spotted Hakeswaith far behind. The whaler was doing his best to travel in the furrows left by the sleds, but the short man's legs were failing him. Using his harpoon as a walking staff, Hakeswaith made tortuous progress. Ingelbert had forgotten all about him.

"I told him to stay behind."

Ingelbert turned and found Flyn had also stopped to look back. The coburn's feathers were crusted with frost.

"It will do no good to wait on him," the knight went on.

"Compassion means nothing to a man such as that."

Taking a deep breath, Ingelbert turned and continued to march, suddenly grateful for his long legs. Ulfrun had been right.

His Middangearder blood was serving him well. Flyn waited for him to catch up before moving on. They traveled side by side for some time, neither speaking, saving their breath for the next high drift.

"I was lamenting my loss of armor," Flyn said at last, his laugh sounding more like a tired exhalation. "Now, I find its absence a blessing."

"It is a balm to know you, too, find this a tribulation," Ingelbert admitted.

"I am woefully mortal," Flyn chuckled, unhooking one arm from his sword long enough to dust some of the white flakes from his chest. "You know that better than most."

Ingelbert pondered this for a moment. "In truth, I do not, do not know you at all, Sir Flyn."

The coburn looked over at him, squinting against the wind.

The gusts caused what was left of his wattle to shake.

"You have the right of it, of course," Flyn said after a brief consideration. He faced forward again before continuing. "I have heard that old warriors see enemies everywhere. I am not yet old, and often behold friends where perhaps I should not."

"It was not my intent to imply that we, that we are enemies."

Flyn waved that off with good spirits. "No, no. Clearly, not enemies. But not yet trusted friends. I understand. However, we both serve the Valiant Spur. I have saved your life and you, in turn, saved mine. You discovered Pocket's secret and chose to help protect it, same as I. And we both have bloodthirsty barbarians for fathers. So, we may not be friends, Ingelbert Crane, but I think you would be hard-pressed to deny we are brothers."

The young knight had said all of this casually, his tone never wavering from the carefree way he so often used to express himself. And yet, Ingelbert felt the weight of the words. Flyn's whimsy contained an earnest fidelity, his admitted ease with forming kinships no longer a flippancy, but a well-wrought strength.

Ingelbert discovered he was grinning in a bemused, and possibly gormless, manner.

"Brothers?" he said.

Flyn shrugged beneath the weight of his sword. "Perhaps not. I was raised by gypsies. I see family everywhere, too."

They both released tired chuckles and spent a long time talking, no longer concerned with the travails of the march.

Ingelbert pressed Flyn further regarding his time with the Tsigani.

The knight spoke fondly of Milosh and his bear, and especially of the girl, Tsura. For his part, Ingelbert told of his time at the Dried Tear and of his mentor, Parlan Sloane. The crunch of snow beneath their feet mixed with their palaver of the past, and Ingelbert forgot about his numb toes.

During a lull in the conversation, Flyn paused for a moment and scanned the surrounding land.

"Wherever the wizard leads us, it is passing strange we have encountered no settlements."

"Upon my maps," Ingelbert breathed, "Middangeard is many times the size of Sasana, Kymbru and Albain put together. And I suspect Fafnir is purposefully, ah, avoiding others."

"You think he has enemies?"

"It is only logical," Ingelbert replied.

Flyn frowned, but did not appear overly troubled. "We have taken up his quest, which means we have also inherited his foes, and I do not relish being kept ignorant of those I may need to fight. Pardon me, Master Crane, while I go speak with our self-appointed guide."

Flyn quickened his pace and outdistanced Ingelbert with ease. Armor or no, the young knight's vitality was impressive. He soon caught up with Fafnir, and Ingelbert could see they began to converse, but could not make out the words. He was too tired to send Gasten over to listen in, and it would be a near impossible task with them on the move. For now, Ingelbert placed all his focus on his feet, one before the other, and hoped that soon his steps would lead him to warmth and respite.

Fafnir signaled a halt when the sky began to darken. They made camp within a cluster of pines, though the porters were careful to lay the fire under open sky, lest a sudden snowfall from the laden branches douse the flames. The dwarrow muttered to each other intermittently in their lilting language as they made preparations, and soon a stew was simmering in a pot over the fire.

Ingelbert lowered himself down on stiff legs next to the fire, reveling in its heat. It was some time before he was brave enough to remove his boots. He had only read about frostbite, but the descriptions had been clear. He found the affliction much easier to read about than to look upon, squeezing his eyes shut at the sight of his blue-black toes, and against the awful pain that made itself known the instant he beheld his stricken flesh.

"Buggery and spit," Deglan hissed as he waddled over to sit down. "I have something for that. Give me a moment to boil it up."

"No need," came a voice from behind them.

Ingelbert turned to find Fafnir approaching. The dwarf stepped around and knelt in front of him, drawing forth two small, irregular shaped stones from his pouch. Keeping the stones in the palm of one broad hand, Fafnir scooped up a handful of snow and clenched his fist tight. Ingelbert saw steam escape from between the wizard's fingers, and when he opened his fist only the stones lay within, fiery sigils now glowing fiercely upon them. Ingelbert had seen one of the runes when Fafnir had knit his broken arm. The other was unfamiliar, though it was certainly akin to those in the green elf tome. Ingelbert fought the urge to recoil as Fafnir reached for one of his agonizing feet, pressing the stones into the sole. The pain fled, replaced by a pleasant warmth, and within moments, Fafnir removed his hands. The frostbite had fled, leaving only pink, healthy skin behind.

"This is Help," Fafnir said, holding up one of the stones, then the other. "And this Protection. Tomorrow you shall not suffer so." He quickly treated the other foot, then stood, placing the runestones back into his pouch.

"My thanks," Ingelbert said, rubbing his mended toes.

The runecaster nodded, and without another word, walked away from the fire. Ingelbert spent several moments in sublime relief. He felt Deglan's eyes on him and looked over to see the gnome scowling at his feet.

"It doesn't stink," the herbalist complained. "Real healing should stink. Poultices. Salves. Ointments. Unguents. Teas. They smell, that's how you know they are working." The gnome became more agitated with every word and cast a baleful eye at the two dwarrow tending the stewpot. "Hoary bastards. Even their food has no aroma." He leaned forward to address the porters. "When. You. Cook. Food. It. Should. Smell."

The dwarrow looked at Deglan with a mixture of annoyance and confusion, then went back to their work.

"You can put something pungent on my feet, if it will keep you from grousing," Flyn said amiably as he sat down.

Deglan cast a critical eye at Flyn's talons. "Your damn chicken feet are just fine." He sounded disappointed.

"Fafnir says we are bound for a place called the Fatwood," Flyn said, ignoring the gnome's sour mood. "We will reach it tomorrow."

"And then?" Ingelbert asked.

Flyn shrugged. "That was all I could get out of him."

When the sun did finally set, their bellies were full and their bodies warm. The dwarrow stew had been almost as tasteless as it was odorless, containing mostly turnips, carrots and the fat of some animal, but it was hot and plentiful, serving well enough to stave off hunger and chill. There was mead also, which the dwarrow doled out from a sizable jug. Ulfrun did not seem satisfied with her ration, so Ingelbert offered her his horn. She accepted it with relish, easing herself down next to him.

"Be warned," she said with a wink. "It takes more than two horns of poet's draught to herd me into bed."

"No, um, no," Ingelbert tried to protest. "That is not, uh, not why I, um, not why I offered it to you."

The giantess smiled as she pressed the horn to her lips, delighted by his discomfort. After a deep pull, which must have nearly drained the vessel, she exhaled with great satisfaction, looking up through the branches into the night sky.

This close, it was impossible to deny she was the most impressive being Ingelbert had ever beheld, the savage menace of her race diffused over every part of her form. The size and strength of Hafr had been threatening, but with Ulfrun it was captivating.

Ingelbert was struck by how at ease she seemed, so comfortable out in the cold night, far from anything resembling safety or community. She had donned no additional garments since leaving Skagen, and as the bare skin exposed at her shoulders, stomach and legs seemed unaffected by the frost, so too did her demeanor seem invulnerable to despair. Untouchable.

Glancing about, Ingelbert saw that his friends were already slumbering, Deglan on one of the sleds, cocooned in furs, and Flyn on the other side of the fire. Fafnir had long retired into the small pavilion erected by Skrauti. Only Hakeswaith and two of the porters remained awake, the whaler having found enough common speech to enter into some dice game with the dwarfs at their own smaller fire on the far side of the camp.

"Ulfrun?" Ingelbert ventured. "What, um, what can you tell me of this place we are bound?"

"The Fatwood," Ulfrun replied, sucking at her teeth, "is an old forest. Much diminished now, it once covered a large stretch of these lands. This," she indicated the surrounding trees with a rolling finger, "was once a part of it. The svartálfar hid one of their barrows in the deepness of the forest, long ago." The giantess laughed darkly. "A hill housing hundreds of headless dead."

Ingelbert shuddered. "And what of the, uh, the lower meadows?"

Ulfrun cast a quizzical eye at him.

"It is, um, something I overheard the Chain Maker say," Ingelbert clarified.

"The lower meadows?" Ulfrun ran a hand through her knife-cut hair, then her confused expression slackened. "Ah! Your dworgmál is good, but not yet flawless. The Downward Fields is surely what you heard."

"The Downward Fields," Ingelbert repeated, nodding as he realized the error in his translation. "Yes, certainly that was it."

"It is a place sacred to the svartálfar," Ulfrun told him casually. "To my ken, none but their own kind has ever set foot there."

"I think Fafnir intends to take us."

"Perhaps," Ulfrun shrugged carelessly. "That one is known throughout Middangeard for wildness of thought."

"You think he is mad?"

Ulfrun found the question amusing, and fixed Ingelbert with a brilliant smile. "All who hold fast to belief are mad."

"Then why do you follow him?"

"For good or ill," the giantess replied, "conviction shapes the world. Protecting whores does not, though I loved them. I grew weary of sitting upon my rump." She winked at him again.

"Finely shaped as it is."

Ingelbert quickly grew uncomfortable with her bold gaze.

"I should, uh, I should seek repose," he told her.

"You," Ulfrun replied, cocking her head toward him, but returning her gaze to the sky, "should tell me a story."

"Um, a story?"

Ulfrun nodded grandly. "Singing would not be welcome among this slumbering lot. And . . . what do you call the svartálfar? Dwarrow? They are a dour bunch, besides. And methinks it is an ill thing to have honeyed drink without honeyed words. They call you Inkstain. The blood of books. And heavy do you encumber yourself with lore-traps. Surely you know a worthy lay to delight me this night."

"What, uh, what kind of story?"

"Great deeds of blood and battle delight me most," Ulfrun replied. "Noble sacrifice upon the fields of war. The din of spears breaking upon shields. Honor and glory and the passing of great chieftains." She flicked her large, laughing eyes at him. "And if you do not know such a tale, Inkstained Crane, then a debauched one will suffice. Filled with the lusts of strong men and the coaxed sighs of supple maidens."

Ingelbert swallowed hard.

"Um . . ."

EIGHTEEN

They reached the Fatwood before the following morning was old. If Fafnir had not announced their arrival, Flyn would have taken the place for just another woodland, albeit larger than any hitherto discovered.

"It's nothing but a grove of firs," Deglan griped from his sled.

"Bloody big grove, Staunch," Flyn said, staring across the white field separating them from the forest, taking in the march of the trees into the distant upcountry beyond.

The dwarrow porters dropped the guide ropes to the sleds when Fafnir called a halt, quickly retrieving broad-bladed spears from the baggage. They were nothing like the weapons Flyn had trained with as a squire. He doubted they were meant to be thrown, so heavy was their construction.

Skrauti directed his fellows to take up positions around the sleds, which they did with practiced efficiency. Fafnir approached his minion and they exchanged some quick words in the dwarf tongue, then he turned and addressed the group.

"I will venture in with the foretold three," Fafnir told them.

"The rest will remain here."

"Bugger that," Deglan proclaimed, hopping down from his sled. "I am going, too."

"Master Loamtoes," the runecaster said wearily, "this need not concern you."

Deglan tossed his hand around, pointing. "This beast my friends are supposed to kill? This Corpse Eater? She within that forest?"

"No," Fafnir said curtly.

Deglan seemed satisfied by that answer. "Well then, it concerns them no more than me. I'm going."

The Chain Maker remained resolute. "You will only slow us down."

"If I do, you can leave me behind," Deglan challenged.

Fafnir looked the gnome over, then turned away and began walking into the wood without another word wasted.

Flyn caught Deglan's eye. "Happy?"

"Not since the Age of Summer," the gnome replied bitterly, then turned to cast a sardonic grin at Hakeswaith. "Heel!"

The whaler spat between his teeth, but otherwise did not budge. "You either coming out of there with the rest, stunty, or you're not coming out at all. Either way, I've a mind to stay right here."

"Sit," Deglan told him and began waddling towards the forest.

The expanse of snowy field leading to the Fatwood's edge was barely a bowshot in length, but soon Fafnir's words came true and Flyn noticed Deglan was struggling. Ulfrun and Inkstain had no such difficulty, the long legs of the man and the even longer legs of the giantess bearing them steadily across the drifts. Flyn was certain they too were aware of the gnome's difficulty, but both knew better than to coddle him, so they continued on without slowing. Flyn adopted a careless pace to stay even with Deglan, hoping his little ruse would not earn him a berating. Thankfully, the herbalist allowed the gesture to go unchallenged and, slowly, the two of them reached the tree line.

A sudden wave of disquiet passed through Flyn's veins as soon as they crossed the forest's boundaries, a chill in his veins that was divorced from the wind. He had felt similar apprehension when he returned to Gallus's clutch, but that was born from within, pawing at him from his guts. This present sensation seemed to lick at him from the very air. Looking down, he detected a ripple of nervousness on the gnome's face as well.

"Nothing but a grove of firs?" Flyn asked.

"Shut up and draw that big damn sword," Deglan replied.

Flyn did as the gnome suggested, freeing Coalspur from its scabbard and slinging the harness back over his shoulder. The smoky metal of the blade defied the foreboding closeness of the trees, and Flyn was comforted by the weight of the weapon in his hands. Still, there remained a sinister hush to the wood, an unnatural stillness to the branches above, as if the trees cowered away from something lurking in their midst.

Ulfrun and Inkstain were already well into the wood by the time Flyn and Deglan caught up to them. The pair stood looking down at broad footprints in the snow, leading deeper into the heart of the forest. The only sign of Fafnir.

"Bastard really does want to leave me behind," Deglan snorted.

"If there is any peril ahead," Ulfrun said, "I believe the Chain Maker wishes to meet it first."

"Ahead?" the gnome exclaimed. "There is peril all around. Can't you feel it?"

Ulfrun nodded. "The Fatwood is old. Long has it hosted a throng of the dead against the very nature of a forest, which is life itself." There was no fear upon her face as she spoke, but Flyn noticed her usually relaxed demeanor was gone, replaced with a calm alertness.

"Well then let's bloody well get on, so we can get out," Deglan barked.

"I will lead," Flyn said, then looked up at the giantess.

"Ulfrun. Rear guard?"

"Aye."

Flyn followed Fafnir's tracks, the phantoms of the dwarf's steps leading directly through the snow-covered bracken without care for finding an easier route. Clearly, the wizard was driven by a single-minded purpose. Soon, the branches grew thick overhead and the snow underfoot sparse. The ground dipped downward in a long, meandering crease across the forest floor. Flyn dug his talons into the frost-hardened turf as he descended, reaching back to steady Deglan, who skidded along behind him. The gnome offered no protest, gripping Flyn's forearm with one hand, the other raised behind for balance. Flyn paused halfway down the slope to allow the herbalist a chance to rest, and to glance back uphill at Inkstain and Ulfrun. Neither were having much difficulty, so Flyn pressed on. They came to the bottom of the slope to find a near-frozen brook nestled in the gully. Here, Fafnir's tracks vanished entirely.

Flyn searched the banks and the facing of the opposite slope, but could find no evidence of the dwarf.

"I have him, Sir Flyn."

Flyn turned at Inkstain's voice and found the chronicler staring at nothing. He was perfectly still, paying no mind to the fact that he stood ankle-deep in the frigid waters of the brook. His eyes suddenly regained focus and he gestured down the length of the gully.

"That way."

"You are certain?" Flyn asked.

Inkstain nodded. "Gasten tracks him."

Deglan made a noise in his throat, scanning the branches above with disdain. "That damn bird is the only animal in this forest."

"Fafnir and we four are all that draws breath here, Master Loamtoes," Inkstain replied, his voice steady and distant.

The gnome cast a dubious frown the man's way, then turned his attention to Ulfrun. "That water looks to get deeper ahead. I don't fancy wading balls-deep down an icy stream. Do you mind?"

Ulfrun laughed, shaking her head as she bent to scoop Deglan up. "Saving your manhood by carrying you like a babe."

"Contrary to his bones," Flyn remarked, adding his own laughter.

Deglan tried to cast his own barb, but was cut short as Ulfrun hoisted him up to sit upon her shoulders, holding him steady with one arm gripped against his ankles. The gnome shifted dizzily for a second, then looked down at Ulfrun's ember-colored hair.

"You just be sure and watch for low-hanging branches," he warned her.

"Low-hanging?" Flyn mocked. "Staunch, you are now twice my height."

Deglan glowered down at him. "I can spit really far from here, Bantam Flyn."

Flyn let out one last chuckle, then proceeded to lead his little band down the gully. The water did indeed grow deeper, but they managed to find footing on the narrow banks and the thicker patches of ice. The slope to their left gradually receded, while the one they had descended grew steeper. Flyn took them up onto the left bank as soon as he was able, leading them away from the water at Ingelbert's direction.

The trees thinned, giving way to a vast, hilly clearing. A cold fog had settled within the cavity, idly caressing the uneven ground. Flyn could not see the far side of the clearing, nor much of anything beyond the reach of his sword.

Through the shifting fog, he could just make out a vast shape, a dense darkness in the ethereal white. Looking back, he caught Inkstain's eye and the man nodded grimly in assent. Flyn took a careful step forward, scrabbling up and over a rise of loose soil. He picked his way through furrows and shallow pits, getting fleeting glimpses of the terrain when the fog fled, only to rush back in and lay claim to the sight of the elusive ground. The mouldy aroma of stale earth grew potent and Flyn heard Deglan coughing somewhere behind him. Slowly, the shadowy bulk before him became more defined, and soon distinct shapes swam out of the fog. Great, broken branches and thick, exposed roots, and between them a trunk so large it rivaled the girth of a castle drum tower.

It was the remains of a tree. A huge, gnarled tree, felled and uprooted, impressive even in ruin. It lay upon a towering mound of grey, fetid earth, a bier of upturned soil foul to behold, for scattered in the dirt Flyn saw faces. Sightless eyes and mud-choked mouths, hair and beards caked with the muck of centuries. Heads.

They were all severed heads.

As Flyn drew closer, the mist gave way, as if it had wanted to shield him from this grisly sight, but now that he had come, heedless, it could no longer bear to remain. Flyn's talon sunk into something giving and he looked down to find a hand sticking up through the dirt, coal-black nails at the ends of pale, stiff fingers.

That one hand, once perceived, heralded the revelation of a thousand of its fellows. Everywhere there were limbs. Arms and legs half buried, the stalks of countless corpses liberated from the dirt. None of the bodies had heads.

Flyn paused upon a low rise, a rise compiled of death, and surveyed the horrible ground, the work of a mad ploughman, unearthing a crop of nightmare.

They were all dwarrow, the bodies. Male and female, many clearly, awfully, children. Despite the rank dirt, despite the obscuring fog, their faces were always visible, white flesh staring with empty sockets.

"No bones."

Flyn jerked and found Deglan standing beside him.

"These," the gnome gestured weakly at the bodies, "have been dead for uncountable years, but . . . the flesh remains."

He was right. There were no skulls, no protruding rib cages.

The dead flesh was aged, but preserved. Flyn felt sick. He had witnessed death in many ugly forms, even delivered it himself on occasion, but this was unlike anything from a battlefield. This was an obscene, purposeful display of something best left hidden. An untold number of lost lives, dismembered by those who loved them, who feared them. This was no memorial, no shrine to grief, it was the banished shame of a plagued people, unearthed to further their torment.

Flyn felt Deglan bump his leg purposefully and looked over to find the gnome pointing to the crest of the great mound. There, with head bowed before the remains of the great tree, stood Fafnir.

Flyn did not approach him, nor did any of the others. Only Inkstain's owl dared intrude, callously perching high on one of the fallen branches. At last, the runecaster turned to face them, looking down from the awful hill with eyes filled with tears.

"Is there no end to what my people must suffer?" Fafnir asked, his voice thick with sorrow. "Is it not enough that our dead rise to murder us? Must we also endure those we have ingloriously laid to rest be so despoiled?"

None gave voice to an answer.

"Now you shall learn why I have taken such steps to bring you here," the Chain Maker continued, his eyes slowly sweeping over each of them in turn.

Flyn resisted the urge to step back when the wizard's burning gaze rested upon him. "We dwarrow lived with the shadow of the Corpse Eater's curse for thousands of years before the augury came to me, and I have pursued it tirelessly since. Always searching, always hoping for those who would bring an end to the blight of the vættir, but I could never gather the chosen three. Those I believed to be the foretold slayers proved false, or died, or became entwined with greater fates. I had to learn patience through the bitterness of repeated failures. But I had faith in my people, in their resolve to outlast the curse. So long as the hearts of my kin remained steadfast, time was on my side, and this belief bolstered me through centuries of fruitless searching. And then, only a year ago, time began to run dry. The dooming of the dwarrow was proclaimed with the sound of falling trees.

"This," the dwarf said, gesturing mournfully at the fallen trunk and twisted limbs, "was once a Warden Ash. One of twelve trees planted by the huldu to keep our dead from rising."

"The elves gave them to you?" Deglan asked, his usual rancor gone.

"Yes," Fafnir replied with naked scorn. "But only after we came to their aid in the wars with the Goblin Kings. Our estranged kin finally deigned to help us, but their beneficence was not born from pity or charity. No, Master Loamtoes, the Wardens were not gifts. They were payment of the debt they owed."

Flyn was no scholar, but even he knew the elves owed the dwarrow much at the end of the Rebellion. Dwarven warriors turned the tide at the raid upon the Sullied Gorge and liberated the iron mines north of Black Pool, slaying the Toothless One in the process, one of Jerrod's most feared disciples. No doubt many of Inkstain's histories would credit the dwarrow with saving the Source Isle.

"Irial Elf-king himself came from Airlann at war's end," Fafnir continued. "Back to long-abandoned Middangeard where we knew only Winter, and sowed the seeds of the Wardens in the soil of our ancient burial grounds. Fire cannot consume dwarrow dead, so we were forced to behead our fallen, but with the blossoming of the elves' trees we were saved from such butchery. We began to lay our lost to rest with dignity among the roots of the Wardens, trusting in the Magic of the huldu to keep them in the Earth. The Warden Trees were as immortal as those who planted them and grew larger, stronger with each passing year. The Corpse Eater remained alive, but fewer were able to answer her call, fewer marched on black feet to her gullet, killing as they went. Some dared hope that we were at last delivered, that the Corpse Eater would be starved out and succumb to mortality.

"I warned against such folly, knowing she could only die at the hands of those I continued to search for, but few gave ear to my entreaties. The Warden Trees were protected by the most potent of huldu enchantments, repelling any who tried to harm them, destroying those who persisted. Mortal man came to fear them and shunned the places where they grew. My kin grew complacent, and reduced the guards upon the Trees. Fools that they were!

"I was away in the Tin Isles when word reached me that one of the Wardens had fallen, its garrison slain and then risen, along with the dead so long housed within the barrow beneath the Tree. Those responsible for this evil transgression could not be found and soon another Tree fell. And another, yet still the defilers remained a mystery. Nine have been left broken upon the ground with nary a sign of those who swung the axe. Until now!"

Fafnir cast an arm across the clearing, the gesture born of rage and triumph. "This was the tenth Tree to fall and it shall be the last! Skrauti tells me that the body of a man was found here, and wisely was it left unmolested until my arrival. Search it out. Search it out and we shall finally discover who so affronts the dwarrow!"

Gasten found the corpse within minutes, but Ingelbert said nothing. He was not sure why, save for a desire to look the dead man over before the dwarf arrived. Through the owl's eyes he saw him, hanging by the neck from a tree at the far edge of the clearing, too distant to be clearly seen from the mound and further concealed by the fog. Ingelbert made sure the others were busy in their own searches before following the owl's path. He picked his way across the corpse-strewn terrain, less repulsed by the profusion of bodies than was normal, and keenly aware of an overall detachment from the surrounding horror. He even kicked a head out of his path before he could stop himself, turning quickly to ensure Fafnir had not witnessed the disrespect before moving on.

Unlike the dwarrow dead, the hanged man was not immune to the effects of rot, though the lack of animals in the Fatwood had helped keep him more or less intact. The flesh was waxy, mottled with stains of black and purple. Wisps of pale hair clung to the scalp. He was not suspended from any great height, more trussed up for display. Ingelbert doubted he had strangled. His head was thrown back, the mouth still agape, though the lips had drawn back tightly with decay to reveal bad teeth. Likely he died from the shock and blood loss of the disembowelment he had suffered. As Ingelbert stepped around the spill of frost covered entrails, he saw the man's limbs had also been broken. A series of brutal tortures to produce a painful death, but performed quickly. An example.

"I see you found him."

Ingelbert did not startle. Gasten had warned him of Deglan's approach, sending a quick vision pulsing through his head.

It was the first time the owl had done that, but somehow it was not surprising.

"Yes," Ingelbert said, turning slowly. "I, um, am not much of a whistler. I don't suppose—?"

Deglan stuck two stubby fingers in his mouth and turned towards the clearing, blowing a piercing sound through the air. As they waited for the others, the gnome scrutinized the corpse.

"Poor bastard," he said simply.

Ulfrun was the next to arrive, followed by Flyn and Fafnir together. The dwarf wasted no time, striding up to the hanged man and producing one of the stones from his pouch. Ingelbert made sure he caught sight of the rune carved on its surface. Certainly not one he had seen before. The runecaster then snatched off one of the dead man's decrepit shoes and seized the tumid, black toes between his fingers. He squeezed until the rotting flesh burst, allowing the vile ichor that oozed forth to coat his thumb. This he rubbed over the runestone, staining the carved sigil which instantly began to smoke. Holding the stone close to his lips, Fafnir inhaled deeply, drawing the thick, putrid fumes into his mouth and nostrils.

Slowly, steadily, he exhaled and the smoke drifted up to the face of the hanged man where it entered his mouth as if he still drew breath.

Fafnir took a step closer to the swinging body and spoke to it in the tongue of the fjordmen. "What were you called in life?"

The corpse's head twitched on its stretched neck, the stiff jaw creaking. The black smoke drifted lazily out of the slack mouth, sliding over the grinning teeth. The voice choked out from behind a bloated tongue.

"Otkell."

Ingelbert heard Deglan curse behind him, muttering in distaste. Fafnir resumed his questioning. "Who felled this Warden Tree, Otkell?"

"Not I," the dead man groaned through his constricted throat. "Refused. Others . . . too craven."

"What others?" Fafnir demanded.

"Thralls," the corpse gagged the word out.

"You were commanded to destroy the tree?"

"I did not. Feared the curse. More than his sons."

Ingelbert saw Fafnir stiffen at this. Behind them, Flyn was asking for a translation, his voice edged with doubt. Ingelbert ignored him.

"Whose sons?" Fafnir hissed. "Who held you in thrall?"

The dead man's jaw clicked, the words boiling out of the smoke behind his frozen scream. "Crow Shoulders."

Ingelbert jumped back as Fafnir, with a howl of wordless fury, ripped his sword from its sheath at his side and sliced upward in one motion. The wide blade caught the hanged man in the ribs and cleaved the dead flesh in a vicious arc until it slashed directly through the rotting body, the keen steel emerging from the opposite collarbone. The lower half of the corpse fell to the turf, while the remaining arm, shoulders and head swung violently on the end of the noose. The smoke fled the dead man's mouth in a billowing rush, escaping through the branches above.

Fafnir stood transfixed, his blazing eyes upon the swinging remains. For a moment, Ingelbert thought the dwarf would again assault the carcass, but then he inhaled deeply, sheathing his sword.

"What by Earth and Stone was that all about?" Deglan demanded.

Ingelbert turned to face his companions, finding Flyn and Deglan in complete puzzlement. Ulfrun was grimly silent, though Ingelbert knew she understood the speech of Middangeard men.

She volunteered nothing, waiting on Fafnir.

"He gathered slaves," the dwarf said quietly. He spoke the tongue of the Tin Isles, but his words seemed meant only for himself. "Forced them to fell the Trees, knowing it would kill them. But they rose again. The song of the vættir calls mortal man to rise from death. That was why we found nothing!"

"Who?" Flyn pressed, stepping forward, forcing the dwarf to look at him. "Who is doing this?"

"Arngrim Crow Shoulders," Fafnir replied, still entranced by his own black thoughts.

"You know him?" Deglan asked.

The Chain Maker nodded. "A strong man and a great jarl. His enmity for the dwarrow runs deep."

Deglan's face grew sour. "What did you do to him?"

Fafnir was upon the gnome before anyone could react. He snatched Deglan by the throat, pulling him close and dragging him back out into the clearing, wrestling him around to face the field of exposed dead.

"What slight deserves this?" Fafnir screamed. "Tell me, elf's pet! Should we pay thus for the pride of mortals? TELL ME!"

Flyn was upon them now, struggling with Fafnir to release the gnome, who was now fighting to breathe. Try as he might, the coburn could not break the dwarf's hold.

Ingelbert stood watching. He should do something, he knew. Certainly interposing himself physically would be useless, but he felt he could stop the dwarf if he so desired. Turn the bones of his hands into wax or perhaps cause thorns to grow beneath his skin. The runecaster was so distracted with his petty anger, he would be unable to properly ward himself. Still, Ingelbert did nothing. He found he was intrigued by the shade Deglan's face was turning. The feeble scrabbling of his fingers across the dwarf's unrelenting grip. The gnome so often allowed his caustic tongue to wag without thought, it was a wonder no one had strangled him before now.

It was not until Ulfrun stepped in that Ingelbert realized he was viewing the struggle through Gasten's eyes. He recoiled from his cruel apathy, fleeing the owl's head and returning to his own shuddering body.

The giantess had shoved Bantam Flyn aside and crouched to place her formidable hands on the dwarf, though she exerted no force upon him.

"Chain Maker!" she said strongly. "Enough. This is unworthy of you. Let him go."

Fafnir ceased his throttling at Ulfrun's words, the rage falling from his face as his grip around Deglan's neck loosened.

The herbalist reeled away, coughing as he dragged air into his lungs.

Flyn helped steady him, casting an angry look at the runecaster.

"You—" the knight began, but Deglan grabbed his hand, cutting him off.

"No," the gnome said through a raw throat. "Let it be."

Flyn relented, though the wrath returned to his face each time he looked upon the dwarf.

"We should leave this place," Ulfrun insisted. "It serves no good to linger."

Ingelbert glanced up to the bough from which the remains of Otkell still swung. There, sitting upon the coils of rope which had hanged the poor man, was Gasten. The owl's imposing, orange eyes looked into Ingelbert's with palpable judgment, and he quickly turned away to join Flyn by Deglan's side.

Fafnir had already begun the trek across the barrow mound, once again leaving them behind.

"Are you well, Master Loamtoes?" Ingelbert asked.

Deglan rubbed his throat and tried to grin. "I once had a delivering mother clamp her thighs around my head. Her hold was tighter, believe me."

For the first time, Ingelbert beat Flyn and Ulfrun to laughter. It was forced, the child of fear and guilt, out of place in the surrounding reek, but Ingelbert did not care. He needed to dispel whatever merciless lethargy had seeped into his heart and guard against its return.

They left the Fatwood by the route they came, finding the sleds waiting for them, along with the porters and Hakeswaith.

"So you managed to survive, eh stunty?" the ugly whaler jeered at Deglan.

"Be comforted," the gnome said wearily, slumping down on one of the sleds. "It was a near thing."

Fafnir was already deep in conversation with Skrauti by the time they arrived. The Chain Maker was agitated and insistent, while Skrauti appeared to offer resistance, though his manner was placating. Ingelbert did not bother to listen in.

"Fafnir," he interrupted, keeping the anger from his voice, but allowing no timidity either. All turned to look at him. "No more dworgmál. Either speak so Flyn and Deglan can understand, or not at all."

The runecaster eyed him curiously for a moment, then gave a slight bow in his direction.

"As you say, Master Crane. I was simply telling my followers where we are next bound."

"This man who cuts down the Warden Trees," Flyn said, his tone insistent. "Who is he? What grievance does he bear the dwarrow?"

Fafnir took a deep breath and Ingelbert thought he saw the dwarf throw a quick, guilty glance in Deglan's direction. "I have sought those foretold in the augury a long time. And as I told you on Skagen, many were discovered that gave me hope. Arngrim Crow Shoulders is the descendant of one such man. I do not remember now if it was his sire or grandsire, the generations of man are too brief for me to recall. Crow Shoulders was but a babe, that I know. His forebear fit the augury."

"Mortal and shunned," Ingelbert recited, his perfect memory not allowing him to keep silent. "Friend to folk Fae. Though weak he seems, ever on his shoulder, winged and deathless, a watcher will sit."

"Just so," Fafnir said. "Tyrfing was his name, a tall man, but not overly strong for one born in Middangeard. His own people were wary of him, for he had a kinship with the valrôka, the talking crows who inhabit this land. These birds are far more canny than any animal, understanding the speech of man and dwarf. To the fjordmen, they are a dread omen and not to be trusted, but never was Tyrfing seen without at least one of the valrôka perched on his shoulder, whispering in his ear. This earned him the mantle Crow Shoulders and the scorn of his neighbors. I saw much potential within him. Though he had not the friendship of the Fae as the augury predicted, centuries of searching had taught me that not all things exist for a man in his present, so I waited to see if his future delivered a fellowship with any of the immortals from the Source Isle. Steel I have wrought calls to me and so I am able to easily find those who bear my blades. I gifted Tyrfing with a weapon of my own making and left him in the hands of fate, so that I could continue my search.

"It was many years before I returned to Middangeard and found he had died a pauper, the sword I gave him now in the hands of his heir. Arngrim was barely out of boyhood, but informed me of his sire's demise with a hatred long matured. Tyrfing had spent his final years as a braggart, pitifully proclaiming to all who would listen that he was the chosen man of a dwarf wizard and he would one day embark on a great geis and return with vast riches. Tyrfing descended into drunkenness and madness, waving his dwarf-forged sword around and talking to his birds. I never told Tyrfing of the quest, but the valrôka are cunning and must have sensed my purpose. I do not know why they tempted the man with stories of glory and power. Perhaps they were trying to goad him to greatness or maybe they simply toyed with him for their own amusement. His kinship with the birds already distanced him from his people, but his ravings turned him and his family into outcasts. Though his children were near starving, Tyrfing would not give up the sword, holding onto it jealously until it fell from his withered fingers on his deathbed.

"Arngrim took up the blade, vowing to use it to restore his kith. He killed the valrôka that continued to perch on Tyrfing's corpse and hunted the birds with a vengeance from that day forth. When I met the lad he already wore the makings of the cloak of feathers which caused him to retain his predecessor's name. He told me he would see me pay for the ruination of his kin, for the mother and sisters who went to their funeral pyres with empty bellies. As this youth spoke his blood oath, I saw the man he would become. Tyrfing Crow Shoulders had been a man worthy of derision, Arngrim Crow Shoulders would swiftly become one to fear. I should have slain him then."

"Why did you not?" Ingelbert asked, his curiosity sounding cold to his own ears.

"You wish me to say I spared him because he was still a stripling?" Fafnir replied with a small snort of self-deprecation.

"No. That was not the source of my mercy. It was the quest. Always the quest. I thought Arngrim would prove to be the man Tyrfing was not, the one to fulfill the augury. So I left him alive with the sword in his possession. Now, he pursues the revenge he swore would be his, and my people pay for my failures."

"The boy is now a man," Ulfrun said. "Time to bring him a thunderhead of war. Tutor him in the ways of vengeance."

Skrauti and the other dwarrow porters voiced assent, but Fafnir held up a hand, calming them. "Arngrim will know my displeasure for what he has done. The wrath of the dwarrow is terrible and we shall visit it upon him. First, there is a more pressing task before us."

"And that is?" Flyn asked bluntly.

Fafnir gestured to the north. "The vættir from the Fatwood barrow are on the march. They must not be permitted to reach the Corpse Eater. So many to feed upon will only make her stronger. They must be hunted down and destroyed."

"So many," Flyn repeated, frowning. "There are twelve of us. How many wights escaped the barrow?"

The Chain Maker met the knight's gaze squarely before answering. "At least a thousand."

Ingelbert felt the blood drain from his face. To the coburn's credit, Bantam Flyn did not so much as blink. Deglan was disturbingly silent.

It was Hakeswaith who finally spoke. "Impossible."

"Without help, yes," Fafnir agreed. "But there are some who already stalk the vættir. Some with whom we might ally."

"And be forever sullied by such an alliance!" Skrauti said with passion, but Fafnir silenced him with a look.

"Could we not get ahead of the wights," Flyn suggested. "Reach the Corpse Eater before they do and slay her?"

"The Corpse Eater dwells many leagues to the north, Bantam Flyn," Fafnir replied. "The vættir do not rest. They pause only to kill, and there will be little prey for them in this remote country. We cannot out-pace them. Even now, catching up will be difficult."

Deglan nodded in Skrauti's direction. "Your servant there seems put out. Who are these hunters he would rather not have as friends?"

Fafnir took a deep breath. "We dwarrow have our outcasts, the same as man. We refuse to name them, but I believe the giants call them—"

"Bone Chewers," Ulfrun finished for him, curling her lip.

"They are the most reviled of my people," Fafnir went on.

"Rightly viewed as dangerous madmen and guilty of irredeemable wrongs. A deranged cult, they are thankfully few, but none so skilled in dealing with the vættir. They pursue them relentlessly, almost as tireless as their prey, for which they ever hunger. For you see, like the Corpse Eater herself, these most twisted of my kindred have attained great power by consuming the flesh of our dead."

NINETEEN

Deglan came to love and loath the sleds. The first days in Middangeard, he tried to refrain from riding unless absolutely necessary, and for only long enough to regain some strength, a practice which quickly spiraled into a private torture. He would trudge through the increasingly impossible drifts, his legs screaming in protest as they quivered into uselessness, all the while yearning to be dragged along with the baggage. Then, inevitably, came the sinking moment when he had to call a halt, his pride ground to dust by the snow, save that last furious kernel which wailed as he clambered wearily aboard the nearest sled. The dwarrow porters never said anything, and Deglan tried to comfort himself with the delusion that they were secretly grateful for the momentary pauses.

Toadshit, of course. He was extra weight for the pair that was saddled with him. No matter. All he cared about was the sled. Each was a sanctuary and a cage, a means of deliverance and a source of shame.

Now, he always rode. It was simpler to endure the daily protracted feeling of weakness than repeatedly admit that the land had bested him. The dwarrow were not much taller than he, but the breadth of their bodies nearly equaled their height and they possessed a depth of seemingly limitless endurance. Deglan doubted even the heartiest gnome could manage the wilds of Middangeard. And it seemed all of Middangeard was wilderness.

He had lost track of the exact number of days since they left the longship, his memory not aided by the brevity of sunlight in this permanent winter. He guessed they were nearing a week with no sign of settlement. Deglan felt that was fortunate, for the quarry they tracked would destroy any living thing in its path. He was no loremaster on the subject of wights, but he knew they were dangerous in ones and twos. A thousand was a threat too terrible to measure.

Yet Fafnir was determined to catch them.

The path of the vættir was not difficult to follow. A broad swath of plowed snow led away from the northern edge of the Fatwood, a laceration upon the white so deep that the consistent flurries did little to mend it. Fafnir had them travel within the furrow, using the trail blazed by countless lifeless feet to give speed to their pursuit. Ulfrun would often scout ahead, her long, powerful legs transporting her miles away from the rest of the group. She always returned before nightfall, impressively, at a run.

One deep breath was all the giantess ever seemed to need to recover from such exertion before she would report to Fafnir.

The terrain ahead.

The best place to camp.

And no sign of the wights.

This unchanging report was the end to every tedious day of travel. Deglan's world shrank to the motion of the sled, the howling wind and the narrow view from beneath his hood, which was little more than the backs of two dwarrow laboring against a field of endless white. He tried to refrain from sleeping, to avoid further fueling the notion that he was a babe that needed caring for, but the boredom often lulled him into semi-consciousness.

At their nightly camps he made vain attempts to be of service, insisting on checking Ingelbert's feet, but ever since Fafnir worked his Magic the man suffered no more ill-effects from the cold. Hakeswaith too had received aid from the wizard's runestones, not that he would let Deglan tend him for any reason. The ugly sea-dog could be bleeding to death and never allow a Fae to touch him.

Just as well. Let the bastard die out of spite if it came to it. As for the rest of the company, they were a giant, a coburn and a bunch of dwarrow. None needed his assistance to remain hale.

Deglan hated admitting it, even inwardly, but there might have been some truth in Fafnir's claims that the coburn were conceived in Middangeard. Flyn had adapted quickly to the harsh climes, his feathers puffing out against the wind beneath his coat and cloak. Of course, the coburn were ever a hardy breed, and Flyn especially had more vigor than brains. The opposite could be said of Ingelbert Crane, but his gawky form hid a stunning endurance and he grew stronger by the day. It was not Deglan's imagination either. For too many centuries he had watched humans suffer infirmity not to perceive a definitive improvement in the normally tenuous chronicler. And Ingelbert's body was not the only thing that had steeled itself. Deglan had almost barked an approving laugh when Crane scolded Fafnir about speaking the dwarrow tongue, but his throat had been too sore. He was also less inclined to goad the dwarf.

The Chain Maker had almost killed him.

After the attack, Flyn would have quit this foolhardy quest if Deglan had asked him to. He loved the strutting rascal for that, though he would never tell him so. The end of their involvement in this blasted venture would have been welcome, but Deglan was not fool enough to further risk the runecaster's ire. Through the fog of strangulation, he had learned a frightening truth. Flyn could not overpower the dwarf. Deglan wondered if even Ulfrun could have in that moment. The giantess had spoken to Fafnir, but it was not her words that saved Deglan's life. No, Fafnir chose to let him go.

Through dimming eyes Deglan had seen it in the dwarf's face.

Mercy had been granted, not coerced.

Perhaps the wizard knew his chosen champions would disband if he squeezed the life from Deglan. Perhaps he had simply come to his senses, seen past his anger. It was not the first time Deglan's mouth had invoked the wrath of another. It was not even the first time his own words had put his life in danger. For unknown reasons, Fafnir decided to spare him, and somehow Deglan found that more disturbing than the memory of the dwarf's aggression. Would the wizard be so inclined to mercy if they tried to abandon his foretold quest? If his precious augury began to unravel around him? Could Crane or Flyn or even Ulfrun do anything to oppose him should it come to a confrontation? The pondering of each of these questions kept Deglan company during his lonely hours on the sleds. Each time he considered the answers he shuddered, knowing the sudden chill in his spine had nothing to do with the wind.

Deglan was lost in such dark musings when Ulfrun returned from yet another scouting foray. She was early and something was different, something in the set of her mouth.

Deglan was not the only one who noticed.

"The vættir?" Fafnir asked as the giantess came to halt.

"No," Ulfrun replied. "But something our Tin Islander companions need to see if they are to survive in Middangeard."

"And that is?" Deglan inquired, rousing himself from his stupor.

"Trolls," Ulfrun answered simply.

There was a momentary silence and Deglan took the opportunity to have a look at his fellow travelers. Skrauti and his porters looked to Fafnir with brave faces. Flyn merely slung his sword harness off his back with a practiced motion, and Ingelbert's expression was one of piqued interest. Hakeswaith's face had gone slack, the color drained from his wind-raw cheeks.

"Well then," Deglan said, grinning and hopping down from the sled. "Why tarry? Let us go have a closer look."

"How far ahead?" Fafnir asked Ulfrun.

"Not a league distant," the giantess told him. "And just off our path."

The wizard glanced up into the sky. "Night falls soon. I shall take my dwarrow and make camp. Show the foreigners what you will."

Ulfrun nodded to the Chain Maker, then quickly retrieved a sizable coil of rope from one of the sleds. She made a beckoning gesture and set off once more. Deglan hurried after her, not waiting to see if any of the others followed. He would need whatever lead he could get and was determined to keep up. Ulfrun kept a manageable pace and Deglan found the walk a welcome relief to his stiff limbs. Flyn and Crane quickly caught up to him, settling into a walk on either side. Deglan did not turn to see if Hakeswaith had been man enough to follow, but he soon caught the sound of the whaler's ragged breathing several paces behind.

The path of the vættir entered some rocky foothills interspersed with scrubby woodlands. Deglan almost cursed as Ulfrun began leading them uphill, but bit back the oath before giving it voice. It was not pride that stopped him. It was the hands of Bantam Flyn and Ingelbert Crane, gripping gently under his arms, aiding him up the rise.

"Thanks, lads," he said, allowing them to help him.

The steepness of the slope lessened before long and Deglan looked up to find Ulfrun waiting for them. She stood at the edge of the furrow left by the wights, staring across a small tract of flat land carpeted in snow. Deglan could see deep tracks cutting across the highland field, evidence of Ulfrun's previous passage.

"From here you must hold fast to your rudders of speech," the giantess whispered and, without waiting for an acknowledgment, set off once more.

Deglan cocked an eye at Flyn. "That means . . . keep quiet?"

"You are improving, Staunch," Flyn answered softly.

They went in single file after her, Ingelbert taking the lead.

Deglan stuck to the chronicler's heels, glad that Flyn was between his back and Hakeswaith's harpoon. The going was much easier, but the absence of the uphill exertion left him feeling very cold despite his hood and cloak of furs. Hob's Knuckles, he had a terrible urge to piss! There was no time, however, as Deglan had to run to keep up with Crane, who was likewise rushing to stay close to Ulfrun.

They entered a stand of trees stubbornly growing among a scrabble of boulders. Ulfrun turned sharply, and again struck uphill, quickly at first, then slowing to pick her way quietly across the rocks. Deglan grasped exposed roots with numb fingers to help drag himself over the terrain. He detected an absence behind him and turned to find Flyn had paused, quickly and deftly removing the steel spurs from his feet. The coburn affixed them to opposite sides of his belt, then swiftly caught up. Hakeswaith was less competent and tripped during the ascent, the barb of his harpoon scraping alarmingly against the rocks. Ulfrun stopped, her head snatching around to glare down the slope at the whaler. The man met her gaze boldly, his crooked jaw frozen into a defiant grimace.

They all remained perfectly still for a long time. Deglan could see by the lack of vapor that he was not the only one holding his breath. After what seemed an eternity, Ulfrun signaled for them to continue on.

They reached the top of the escarpment, where the trees once again laid claim to the ground, and Ulfrun turned to cut through the woods. If Deglan's sense of direction had not completely failed him, then he suspected they were now heading back to the path of the vættir, though much further up the slope than where they had left it. Ulfrun must have wanted to avoid traveling across open ground. Deglan allowed himself a self-satisfied grin when they emerged from the trees and his assumption proved true.

The furrow left by the wights was once again before them, narrowed significantly due to the encroaching crags at this height.

Surely a thousand wights would have been significantly slowed by the hemming of the rocks and cliffs. The dwarrow sleds would be hard-pressed to travel two abreast when they reached this spot on the morrow. Deglan found his soldier's mind waking, wishing they had caught up to the wights here, as the terrain made an excellent spot for an ambush against superior numbers. But Ulfrun gave him no more time to plan strategies than she did for him to piss, crossing the narrow track quickly, bending low as she ran. She made for the cliff face opposite the scrubby wood and they went right along after. Deglan sniggered into the wind at the thought of a mother goose leading her goslings back to water.

Ulfrun motioned for them to stay put and silently scaled the cliff. It was not overly steep, but probably ten times the big lass's height and slick with ice. She climbed confidently, but it took her a few moments to reach the top. Deglan used those moments to thump Ingelbert on the leg and direct the chronicler's attention up to Ulfrun's rather splendid backside. Crane took the bait, then quickly turned away to shoot him a disapproving look. The man was blushing and that caused Deglan's smile to widen.

Earth and Stone, he was enjoying this!

Perhaps it was the break from the monotony of the sled.

Or possibly just the distance from Fafnir and his underlings. More likely, it was the thrill of the hunt, a guilty surge of excitement when he was reminded of his service during the Rebellion. Those were terrible, death-filled days, but there were times when the danger had turned to delicious triumph and those memories settled fondly in the bones. He had helped ambush a group of Red Cap sappers on the slopes of Bwyneth Tor on ground much like this, though lacking the snow. The plan had gone perfectly and all seven of those goblin bastards lay dead with nary a hue. Deglan and every one of his comrades had come back from that maneuver alive. His mood sobered as he wondered if this night would prove equally fortunate.

When Ulfrun reached the top she lowered the rope down to them. One by one, they each ascended the cliff. Deglan knew Ulfrun could easily have hauled him up, but he was not about to dangle on the end of a rope like some gaping trout. He made the climb himself, and faster than either Crane or Hakeswaith. The burning in his shoulders and arms when he reached the top was a warm reminder that he still possessed some gumption, Middangeard be damned!

The sun was nearly down, but Deglan could see well enough thanks to his subterranean heritage, and he knew Flyn's eyes could detect variations in heat. Hakeswaith, however, would soon be limited by the brightness of the moon and stars, as would Crane. Then Deglan remembered the damn owl and quickly searched the sky and the surrounding cliffs. He failed to spot the bird, but knew he was likely around somewhere. Ingelbert's connection to that overgrown pigeon was yet another aspect of the chronicler that was mysteriously growing in potency. It was one of the reasons he had the man look at Ulfrun's rump, to keep him grounded, keep him human. As all Fae knew well, Magic had a nasty way of turning men to darkness.

The top of the cliff was little more than a ledge, winding around a pile of huge boulders. Ulfrun splayed one hand and made a slow pushing motion towards the ground. She then lay belly down and began to crawl around the boulders. Deglan was the first to follow her lead. As he burrowed through the trench of snow made by the giantess, he made note of the precipice to his left and could feel the drop deepening. He rounded the bend and found Ulfrun lying upon a broad shelf. She had turned to face the drop and Deglan crawled up next to her, slowly rotating until he too looked out over the pass. Below, he could see the foothills they had traversed not an hour ago, the path of the vættir an ugly black mark besmirching the snow.

Ingelbert crawled in next to him, followed by Flyn and finally Hakeswaith. They all lay in a row and, as soon as they were gathered, Ulfrun pointed to a spot in the pass directly below.

Deglan peered down and found a single dark shape shambling in the white.

The troll was big, and had they been on even footing would have over-topped Flyn by at least a head. Certainly not large enough to match Ulfrun in height, but its bulk was astounding. The creature slumped so greatly it appeared as if its head grew forth from its broad chest. Its protruding brow and strong jaw dominated its face, seeming to squeeze the beady eyes and flat nose between them. Long, twisted locks of dark, filthy hair were draped down its rounded back, dragging in the snow along with its knuckles. The arms were long and sinewy, thin-looking compared to the stout, bowed legs. Deglan could tell from the heavily swinging genitals it was a male, its naked flesh the color of old stones. The troll seemed to be wandering aimlessly, never still, though never going more than a few dozen lumbering paces before returning to where it began. Restless, even nervous.

Deglan lightly touched Ulfrun's arm and, when she looked over, he held up one finger. The giantess gave the barest shake of her head and held up two fingers, then pointed back down. Deglan returned his attention to the troll. At first, he thought it was an illusion, a trick of the fading light, but as he peered down he grew more certain of what he saw. Footprints appearing in the snow.

They drew towards the troll, who visibly relaxed as each new print came closer. Deglan noticed a faint distortion in the air above the troll's head and then, before his eyes, another creature appeared, seeming to wink into existence.

Where the male troll was slow and brutish, the female was lithe and graceful, her proportions those of a tall, well-formed human woman. She sat upon the male's swayed back, one long leg dangling over his shoulder, the other tucked beneath her. The posture radiated comfort, familiarity. She too was naked, her skin a few shades lighter than her mate's. The same torrent of matted hair grew from her head, but it was the color of blood. Even in the poor light Deglan's gnome eyes could detect the deep, vibrant color.

The female troll looked about for a moment, searching her surroundings, her comely face displaying all the keenness lacking in the male's. For one, heart-stopping instant, she looked up and met Deglan's eye. He froze, fearing to even blink. A low, agitated moan came from the throat of the male troll, but the female laid her hand gently upon his head as she turned away from the cliff, quieting him. Slowly, the troll began to walk away, down the slope, his broad back supporting the calming presence of the female. They were little more than a dwindling blotch on the snow when Ulfrun stood.

"It is safe now."

Deglan rose with the others, brushing the snow from his front. "Buggery and shit. I swear that thing looked at me."

"Aye," Ulfrun agreed. "The trollkona knew we were here. Thankfully, she also knew we sought no wound-tears."

"Are they so dangerous?" Flyn asked. "Only two?"

"Trolls are jealous creatures," Ulfrun replied. "The males are too territorial to allow them to congregate. Something you coburn share, is it not so?"

Deglan saw the shame settle into Flyn's shoulders as he nodded.

"So," Ulfrun went on, "two is all you will ever see together, so long as the troll-kona, the troll-wife, lives. It is enough. A troll pair which feels threatened is nigh impossible to kill. The males rival we giants in strength when they are angered. That battle-branch you carry would do little, Bantam Flyn, for so long as his mate is near, a troll's wounds knit themselves closed. But it is the trollkona which you must truly fear. She is a wife of charms, and the blood of spells is in her veins. She makes herself invisible and will use all her cunning and crafts so that her mate may make a raven's banquet out of their foes."

"Stinking, evil beasts," Hakeswaith muttered, spitting over the cliff.

"So the men of Middangeard believe," Ulfrun said. "They hunt them without mercy, the danger be damned. Few trolls there are now, though once they were many."

"I read they cannot survive without a mate," Ingelbert said.

Ulfrun gave the chronicler an approving look. "This is true of the trollkona. If her mate is slain, a female will quickly succumb to grief, dwindling away until she is no more. The males only become more fierce, should their wife be taken from them. Without her they must hide from the sky-candle, lest their shame be revealed in day's light and turn their flesh to stone. They retreat to a mountain-womb, living ever in enraged grief. Only then will male trolls be found together, living in a community of mourning and madness. Beware the caves of Middangeard, my friends."

Deglan looked out at the darkening landscape, nodding at the distance, though he could no longer see the trolls. "Those two are headed the way we came. Back towards Fafnir. Is it too much to hope they'll stumble upon our dwarrow friends and rend them limb from limb?"

Ulfrun threw a short laugh into the sky. "It shall be a day worthy of song if the Chain Maker is ever brought low by a pair of trolls, herb-cub. And trolls seek not to meet with any other. They are wanderers, ever in search of solitude and peace. Those two became trapped in the pass when the vættir came through, I ken. Now that the danger is gone, they travel on."

"If you are correct," Flyn said. "Then the wights are close."

"Another day and we will catch them," the giantess answered.

Deglan glanced up at her. "You did not tell the Chain Maker."

Ulfrun shrugged. "When I lay eyes upon them, he will know."

"Let us go," Hakeswaith growled. "I need food and a fire."

Deglan could hardly disagree, but as Flyn and the humans left the ledge he lingered with Ulfrun for a moment, staring out into the night.

"You stalled," Deglan said gently. "Had Fafnir known the wights were close, he would have commanded we press on. Likely run across the trolls. You feared they would be killed."

"Mayhaps I feared for us," Ulfrun replied without looking his way.

"Were that the truth you would not have brought us up here. You wanted to ensure they were spared."

Ulfrun took in a deep breath, blowing it out with great satisfaction into the frigid air. "Dwarves. Giants. Trolls. We are all of Middangeard. We are, all of us, children of Winter."

TWENTY

Flyn heard the vættir long before he laid eyes upon them.

Their song was borne on the wind, accompanying the flecks of snow that danced upon the air. A low, mournful sound impregnating the frozen hills with a haunting of life. It hummed in the earth, it carried on the breeze, and yet was banished from both, existing in exile, unwanted, unnatural and unceasing. The deep resonance of the dead.

When at last he saw the teeming chorus which gave voice to the song, Flyn's breath caught in his throat. Ulfrun had chosen their vantage well, leading them to the edge of a canyon through which the vættir marched, an incessantly moving mass of rotting raiment, black hair and white skin. Flyn stood with the giantess, Inkstain and Deglan, watching the distant wights traverse the valley.

He placed a hand above his eyes, shielding them from the glare of the sun reflecting off the snow.

"That is more than a thousand," Inkstain said, echoing Flyn's own thoughts.

"Six hundred more," Deglan announced.

Flyn removed his hand from his brow and looked down at the gnome. "You are certain?"

"Spent a couple centuries fighting goblin hordes," Deglan answered. "I got good at counting the enemy."

Flyn turned back to the valley. It was easy to forget that the old herbalist was a veteran of the bloodiest war in Airlann's history.

That was all it was to Flyn, history, and murky history at that.

Inkstain could no doubt conjure a clearer image of those days from all his reading, but Deglan remembered them from experience.

Flyn thought upon his own battles, especially Coalspur's tourney and the fight against the Unwound at Castle Gaunt. Those fleeting confrontations had taught him much. He tried to imagine centuries of war and the insight it would provide.

"How do you suggest we fight them?" Flyn asked.

Deglan considered the question, scratching at his chops.

"We can't. We don't have the numbers even for harrowing actions.

I do not know how much cunning these dead bastards have, but twelve against nearly two thousand leaves nothing but desperate tactics. I would say try and bait them over a cliff, or bury them in an avalanche, but it won't bloody kill them." The gnome cocked a glance to his right. "Of course, I am not leading this charge."

Flyn followed Deglan's gaze. Fafnir stood further down the canyon edge, alone. His hood was pulled low, his cloak fretting behind him at the whim of the wind. The runecaster studied the marching wights with a grim face.

"Give me a moment," Flyn told his companions.

He walked over and stood beside the dwarf.

"Beautiful, is it not?" Fafnir asked without removing his gaze from the wights. "The song."

Flyn hesitated before answering. "It is."

Fafnir chuckled. "You humor me, Bantam Flyn. You need not, truly. Hearken to the voices. From this distance the deep singing of the males dominates, but listen closely and upon the edges you can hear the high, clear voices of the women, and beyond that, the true, untutored singing of our lost children."

Flyn did as he was bid, cocking his head down towards the valley. At first, there was nothing, but gradually he heard it, a keen harmony floating among the roiling hum, here and there punctuated with sharp, sad notes, flung through the assonance.

Flyn found his eyes closing, to better concentrate, and without the disturbing sight of a herd of walking dead, he discovered the truth of the wizard's claim. The song was indeed pleasant to the ear.

When Flyn opened his eyes, Fafnir was facing him.

"The dirge of the dwarrow," the runecaster said. "Once sung to comfort the living as we laid our loved ones to rest. It is all that the vættir give voice. A song of mourning corrupted into a herald of doom. And yet, cruelly, it remains beautiful."

"How do you intend to silence so many?" Flyn asked.

"At my direction or not at all!" a voice from behind them shouted.

Flyn turned, quickly drawing his sword when he laid eyes on the strange group approaching them from the trees bordering the valley.

The dwarf in the lead was clad only in rough leggings under a kilt of animal hides. He was bare-chested despite the cold, displaying a sizable paunch, but his arms and shoulders bulged with hard muscle. The deathly pallor of the dwarrow was completely absent in this one, his skin healthily flushed and ruddy. His head was completely bald, but his beard fell past his waist, worked into three thick plaits and the color of a blazing bonfire. Indeed, he looked as Fafnir had when Flyn first met him in Black Pool, as the dwarrow do when in the Tin Isles, though far more savage. Shining bracelets adorned his wrists as well as the braids of his impressive beard. He held a long-handled war axe propped upon his shoulder, its curving blade broad and brutal. But it was not this dwarf's fearsome appearance which caused Flyn to draw Coalspur. It was the half-dozen massive creatures which loped around him. To Ulfrun they would have been wolves. Compared to the animals Flyn had seen, they were monsters. Each was as tall at the shoulder as the head of the half-naked dwarf.

Fafnir did not appear alarmed at their sudden presence. He had turned at the sound of the burly dwarf's voice and waited patiently as he and his huge companions drew near. It was no small wonder Flyn had not been warned of their approach, for dwarf and wolves alike moved with all the sound of candle smoke. With his back to the canyon, Flyn did not favor his chances if these bestial newcomers chose to attack. He glanced over at his companions and was relieved to find they too were approaching, Ulfrun in the lead.

Beyond them, Hakeswaith, Skrauti and the dwarrow porters remained motionless. Flyn did not expect the whaler to volunteer any aid, but was surprised that the dwarrow took no action. They had been unflinchingly servile to the Chain Maker until now.

Perhaps they knew their presence was not required.

The bald dwarf reached Flyn and Fafnir just ahead of their companions. He stopped and shrugged the axe from his shoulder, resting the blade in the snow and his hands upon the end of the haft, leaning upon the weapon. Beneath his heavy brow, his eyes were keen, and he fixed Fafnir with a look full of mirth and challenge. The wolves fanned out around him, their panting breath pushing past their long pink tongues as hot vapor. Ulfrun strode past the nearest without a care, leading Deglan and Inkstain. The gnome looked at the beasts with his typical chariness, but the chronicler's expression was unreadable.

"My friends," Fafnir said when they were all gathered.

"Allow me to present Kàlfr the Roundhouse." Though the words were courteous, Flyn did not fail to notice the iciness in Fafnir's tone. He spoke the language of the Tin Isles and the bald dwarf answered in kind, though his accent was thicker.

"Friends, Chain Maker?" Kàlfr laughed. "Never known you to possess such. Just puppets and servants. Those you have tricked into believing your greatness." The dwarf's mocking eyes left Fafnir, flicking around to take in Flyn and the others in turn. He laughed again. "Save the giant beauty, it looks to me like these here are babes to Middangeard. Pissing themselves at their first gander at storulvir."

The word was unfamiliar, but it was clear that Kàlfr referred to the monstrous wolves behind him. Their presence *was* unnerving. Flyn had seen a pack of barghests in Albain, but even those bloodthirsty hounds would be as pups to these storulvir. In the Tin Isles they were called vargulf, and the only one Flyn had laid eyes on was stuffed in the Campaign Hall of the Roost, a trophy made of the beast that Sir Pyle Strummer had slain after months of it preying upon the livestock of the Dal Riata. Sir Pyle had always said it was the most dangerous foe he had ever fought and thought himself fortunate to have survived the encounter. It must have been the runt of a litter, for Flyn did not recall it being so large as the six standing before him.

"Roundhouse," Fafnir said, his forced courtesy beginning to wither. "This is Sir Bantam Flyn of the Knights of the Valiant Spur. Ingelbert Crane, a scholar of the same order, and their boon companion Deglan Loamtoes. The giantess is Ulfrun, known as the Breaker."

Kàlfr was nakedly amused by the introductions, but his laughing eyes fixated on Inkstain, or rather on the owl upon his shoulder.

"Surrounding yourself with hedge-wizards now, Chain Maker?" the Roundhouse inquired with a smile. "Don't figure you have enough craft within you to bring the vulture-bitch down?"

"These are the Foretold," Fafnir replied, clearly nettled.

"And yes, there is power here, Roundhouse. It would be wise to remember that."

"Oh aye!" Kàlfr chuckled, casually cracking his knuckles.

"Attached myself to some, as it happens. You are not the only rune-twiddler here, Fafnir."

"Yes," Fafnir said dismissively. "I heard tell you traveled with Hengest Half-Rune. Tell me, have you found success in dealing with the risen of the Fatwood?"

"Slaying vættir takes time, Chain Maker, you know that. Or would if you stayed in Middangeard for longer than it takes to have a quick shit. But we've been whittling away at them, you can count on that. My storulvir brothers are well-fed." A sharp, meaningful smile split the bald dwarf's fiery beard. "Hungry for more, as always." Flyn saw a curl of disgust play at the corners of Fafnir's mouth.

"We would join the hunt," Ulfrun broke in. "See an end to these disturbed dwarrow."

Kàlfr's smile widened as he addressed the giantess. "Plenty of heads to sever. Hengest and Thorsa are with the rest of my brothers. They wait down in the valley, ahead of the vættir, preparing to carve off a few more chunks before nightfall. Follow me and I will take you to them. Then we will see if you can be of any use."

With that, Kàlfr the Roundhouse shouldered his axe and began walking away, his giant wolves padding after him.

"Come," Fafnir said and threw an arm into the air, signaling Skrauti at the sleds.

Flyn returned Coalspur to its sheath and shouldered the harness. As he started to move, he felt a hand snatch at his wrist.

"Half a moment," Deglan said, his grip tightening. His hand restrained Flyn, but his words were for Fafnir. "That bald bastard one of them dead-eaters you dwarrow are so ashamed of?"

"He is," Fafnir replied stiffly.

"And you bloody trust him?" Deglan demanded.

Fafnir shook his head. "Not at all. But Kàlfr lives to kill vættir and we will need him if we are to stop this throng from reaching the Corpse Eater. It is vital she not feed, lest she grow too powerful to slay. You are wise to be wary, Master Loamtoes. Especially of the storulvir. For all their appearance, they are not dumb beasts. They have their own speech and understand the tongues of Middangeard. It is possible Kàlfr has learned them in the language of the Tin Isles. Be mindful of what you utter, for their ears are keen." Without another word, the wizard trudged off, following the strange pack.

Flyn gently freed himself from Deglan's clutching fingers.

"Shall we?"

"Their ears are keen," Deglan scoffed. Fafnir was now a dozen strides away, but Flyn had no doubt he could hear the gnome. Deglan did not seem to care. In fact, he pitched his voice louder over the wind. "It's their damn teeth that worries me! And what about that shave-pate barbarian? Eating the dead and cavorting with horses wearing wolf-pelts. Hob's Teeth! It is not damn near natural."

"No," Ulfrun agreed, "it is not. The Bone Chewers embrace aberration. They consume the flesh of their dead to rid themselves of the weakness cast down upon the svartálfar when they split from their huldu kin. It is the only way a dwarf can dwell in Middangeard and possess the power they enjoy in your Tin Isles."

"They are a twice-cursed race," Inkstain said.

Flyn was startled by the chronicler's voice, though it barely broke a whisper. Inkstain rarely spoke of late and when he did, Flyn was not certain the man knew he was speaking aloud, so distracted was his tone. Indeed, he sounded as if he talked only to himself.

"First condemned by Magic for their betrayal," Inkstain continued, "and then by the Corpse Eater, so she might save herself from mortality. The Bone Chewers use one curse to dispel the other. Intriguing."

"And are thrice-cursed in the doing," Ulfrun said.

Inkstain roused himself at these words. "Thrice?"

"Aye," the giantess told him. "With time, wight flesh is all that will sate them. The meat of beasts, the fruit of trees, the crops of the earth, these no longer sustain. The hunt for the væettir becomes necessary for them to survive."

"And when pickings are slim?" Deglan asked. "When some vengeful, dwarrow-hating fjordman is not running around felling Warden Trees and freeing the dead? What then?"

Flyn did not wait for Ulfrun to respond. He knew the answer. "They murder their own, Staunch. They turn kinslayer."

"I bloody well knew that, you young, empty-headed rascal!" the gnome barked. "I am asking the question so the rest of you can hear the answer!"

Flyn forced a smile. "So that later, when all this turns ill, you can crow about how right you were?"

Deglan scowled up at him. "If I am as right as I think I am, there will not be anyone left to crow to."

"Think on it this way," Flyn said, laughing. "If you put as much energy into marching as you do in complaining, we would have reached the Corpse Eater by now." He clapped the gnome heartily on the shoulder and passed him by, quickening his stride to catch up with Fafnir. Deglan's voice called after him.

"I've no wish to speed you to your death, Bantam Flyn!"

Flyn did not stop, wishing to put some distance between himself and the old mushroom. He fought not to show it, but his patience with Deglan was thinning. His constant grousing, the barbs he cast at Fafnir and the other dwarrow, all of it was beginning to grate. It was an unworthy thought for a knight, but Flyn often felt they would have been better off if the gnome had stayed behind. He only slowed them down while on the march, but produced deep wells of energy when he wished to gainsay and cast aspersions. It was his way, Flyn knew, but it was beginning to take its toll. Deglan was deep in wisdom and experience, but he had a habit of forcing Flyn to think. Likely that was prudent, but in his heart, Flyn wanted to return to the comfort of courageous impulse.

He yearned to draw steel and charge into a battle without first gnawing at every outcome.

The defeat at Gallus's hands still weighed upon his mind.

Flyn could feel shame burrowed deep in his guts, holed up with fertile doubt. He feared the two would rut in the darkness of his placidity, and give birth to cowardice.

He needed to shake these skulking intruders loose, smoke them out of hiding with blood set to boil in battle, send them scurrying with the sound of ringing steel. His chance to do that lay ahead of him, with the wights and with the one who called them. The Corpse Eater.

For some time, Flyn walked alone, finding a pace between Fafnir ahead and the others behind. It was a welcome bit of solitude. His desire to be alone must have announced itself in his body, for none approached, though Ulfrun or even Crane could easily have closed the distance. Likely Deglan held them back, the perceptive old stoat.

Coalspur rode across his back, the tip of the scabbard dragging in the snow. Flyn hooked a thumb under the strap and hitched the harness down so the sword would ride higher. He often missed his squire's quarterstaff. A lighter, faster weapon, without the weight of steel, the weight of responsibility. The possession of Coalspur was a source of pride now turned into a constant burden.

Many times over the long, cold trek through Middangeard Flyn wished he wore a broadsword at his side as Sir Corc preferred. A falchion, a mace, anything quick to hand. But he had fought for Coalspur in the tourney, then argued for the privilege to bear the weapon when his victory became disputable.

It mattered little now. The sword was his. A large weapon meant for the scattering of superior numbers and for the taking of heads, qualities well-suited for a battle with the army of wights he witnessed in the valley. Soon, perhaps, he could wade into them, sword swinging, and deliver himself from the cares of his unwanted thoughts.

Kàlfr led them down into a wooded gorge, using a treacherous switchback littered with frost-crowned rocks. From a few turns up the steep trail, Flyn watched the dwarf and his wolves drift sure-footed down into the defile. Before descending himself, Flyn used his vantage to survey the landscape. The gorge opened off the valley proper, a sizable, slightly wooded outcropping. A good place to tuck away for an ambush. At the pace Kàlfr set, they were likely now in front of the risen dwarrow. Flyn suspected they were about to join up with the rest of Kàlfr's band and engage the wights. He found his steps quickening and soon reached the bottom of the slope.

The smell of wood-smoke reached Flyn's nostrils. Towards the center of the gorge a group of dwarrow and storulvir milled around a modest campfire. Kàlfr's wolves padded over to join at least a dozen others lounging near the flames, and Flyn spotted several more sitting among the rocks that formed the walls of the gorge, eyes and ears facing the entrance to the valley.

Sentries.

Kàlfr and Fafnir already stood among ten other dwarrow.

As Flyn drew closer he heard the guttural lilting of dworgmál being spoken between them. Fafnir conversed with a pair of dwarfs, one male and one female. The male wore no beard, but the hair atop his head was wild and dyed a bright blue. He was as slumped and pale as Fafnir, the skin beneath his eyes sunken and dark. A sleeveless coat of filthy skins draped to his ankles. His bare arms were crossed in front of him and he listened with a guarded expression to Fafnir's words.

The female dwarf turned her attention away from the Chain Maker as Flyn approached, staring at him boldly. Her hair was long and unbound, so blonde it was nearly white. Like the Roundhouse, she appeared infused with a palpable vitality, standing firm beneath furs and brigandine. Twin hand axes were thrust through her belt, well-used but sharp. As she eyed Flyn, he detected a feverishness in her gaze and a flush to her lips. So, another Bone Chewer.

The remaining dwarrow were as bent-backed and coarse-haired as Fafnir, though all had well-honed weapons close to hand.

Of armor there was little, the odd shield, here and there a hauberk, but everything spoke to a group girded for fast movement and long, grueling stretches living in the wilds.

Flyn did not interrupt and soon he was joined by the rest of his group. Only when they were all assembled did Fafnir turn and introduce them. The blue-haired dwarf was Hengest, also a runecaster. Flyn detected a hint of derision in Fafnir's voice when he acknowledged this, and a ripple of injured pride in Hengest's face added weight to the assumption that there was a difference between the two wizards' skill. Thorsa was the name given for the dwarf woman and Fafnir indicated she was Hengest's wife, but otherwise pointedly ignored her presence.

"Enough of this prattle!" Kàlfr the Roundhouse spat. "Best not get overly acquainted. Not all will survive this day and I do not bother learning the names of the slain."

The bald dwarf snatched up his axe and strode off towards the valley. The storulvir pack swiftly fell in behind him, and together they left the gorge. Only four of the giant beasts remained, the ones standing watch on the rocks above.

"The Roundhouse and his wolves will secret themselves in the valley," Hengest explained. "He shall strike from the rear once the vættir are contained within this gorge. Thorsa and I will take our warriors to the mouth of the valley and wait for the vættir to pass. We will bait the end of the throng and lead them back here, where you shall remain to bolster our trap."

"How many do you hope to bait?" Deglan demanded.

The blue-haired dwarf eyed the gnome for a moment before answering. "Half a thousand. Perhaps more."

Flyn started doing the calculation in his head, but Inkstain was quicker to the result. "Nearly twenty to one."

"Aye," Thorsa laughed, her bold eyes blazing. "Best to keep the odds easy for you maidens!"

Ulfrun returned the female dwarf's mirth. "I shan't hesitate to measure my cock against yours, she-dwarf."

Thorsa peered at the giantess with disdain before shifting her attention to Flyn. "Oh yes. The famed coburn so long sought by my misguided uncle, the Chain Maker. Tell me, rooster-man, have you the resolve to bear so weighty a mantle as an augury made flesh? Or will you break under the burden, as all the—"

"Silence, Thorsa!" Fafnir growled.

Hengest stepped forward to defend his wife, but he faltered when the Chain Maker turned his fury upon him.

"You do not yet have the craft to cast me down, Hengest Half-Rune!" Fafnir snarled. "Do not feign courage you do not possess for the sake of my sister's daughter, to whom you foolishly bound your troth."

Flyn saw the ten dwarrow under Hengest's command grow tense, their knuckles tightening around the hafts of their weapons, but he saw in their faces a reluctance to stand between the two runecasters. Thorsa had no such qualm and stepped full into Fafnir's face, quivering with fury.

"You speak of feigned courage, uncle?" she hissed. "You would not dare say such things to my love were the Roundhouse still near, runemaster or no."

"The Roundhouse?" Fafnir asked, a deep pity weighing upon his words. "He that is your true love, lost niece of mine? He with whom you place horns on your husband and consume the flesh of our dead kin! You are damned, Thorsa. It is no longer within my reach to bring you back from the pit within which you have flung yourself."

Flyn saw the Chain Maker's words cut, but Thorsa twisted the pain into a crazed smile. She leaned forward and whispered something in Fafnir's ear. Flyn could not hear what she said, but the pain passed from her face and settled in the countenance of the Chain Maker. Gloating with cruel satisfaction, Thorsa stepped back.

"We tarry too long," Hengest insisted, pulling at his wife's elbow. "Come. We must go before the vættir pass completely by."

"Of course," Thorsa said, almost merrily. "Remain here with your destined followers, uncle. We shall bring the catch to you."

Hengest and Thorsa gathered their dwarrow together and led them towards the neck of the gorge. Soon, they were lost from sight among the boughs of the evergreens and the haze of flitting snow. The four remaining storulvir came down from the rocks and followed after them.

Fafnir turned on his heel as soon as they were out of sight, looking to Skrauti and the other porters.

"Weapons," the Chain Maker commanded.

"My lord," Skrauti said, reluctance flooding his voice.

"Perhaps it would be wise to quit this place. Take the trail out and leave these swine to their fate."

"Agreed," Deglan threw in.

Fafnir shook his head morosely. "If only we could. But this must be done." He approached Skrauti slowly and placed a broad hand on his shoulder. "Weapons."

The loyal dwarf nodded, then humbly removed himself from his master's grip.

"Master Loamtoes, Master Crane," Fafnir said, as the dwarrow began retrieving their heavy spears from the baggage. "It would be best if you removed yourselves to the safety of the trail. Should this go ill, you would have a means of escape."

"Where the stunty goes, I go," Hakeswaith barked quickly.

Fafnir gave the diminutive whaler the barest of glances.

"Fear not, fisherman. I did not expect you would fight." The Chain Maker then turned to look at Flyn. "Though I would beg your sword-arm, Sir Flyn."

Flyn nodded. "You have it."

"And me, Chain Maker," Ulfrun said. "I will stand with you in this coming weather of weapons."

"My thanks, Breaker," Fafnir replied with a bow.

"I don't stand on a stool every time a mouse runs by," Deglan announced. "Hakeswaith can climb up on the hill if he wants, but I'll not stand next to him while his courage runs down his leg and turns the snow yellow around our feet."

Hakeswaith snarled and made to take a step towards the gnome.

"If you've no mind to fight, Hakeswaith," Flyn said, halting the man with a warning look, "it would be best not to test me."

The whaler's crooked jaw stretched back further over his hideous teeth. "Reckon I will enjoy watching all of you die." With that the man hustled off towards the rear of the gorge where the winding trail to safety waited.

"Whatever you intend, best do it with haste," Inkstain said.

"Hengest and his band have engaged the wights."

Flyn turned towards the chronicler and found him staring vacantly, the owl gone from his shoulder.

"Right," Flyn said. "No more time to argue, Staunch. Get to high ground."

"Bugger that," the gnome muttered, plucking a dwarrow hatchet from the sleds.

"Suit yourself," Flyn conceded, drawing Coalspur. "But stay close to me or Ulfrun."

"I pick you. Big lass is likely to step on me in all the excitement."

They fanned out across the width of the gorge, near the center. Flyn chose a spot relatively clear of trees, so his blade would not be hampered. Deglan stood behind him, safely removed from the reach of the greatsword. Ulfrun stood at Flyn's left, rolling her shoulders, flexing her fingers. Inkstain had decided not to join Hakeswaith and remained behind Deglan, his gaze still far away.

To Flyn's right and slightly ahead, Fafnir and his dwarrow took position. The porters all bore their hewing spears and broad, steel-rimmed shields. These they fixed close together as they stood shoulder to shoulder. Behind their small line, Fafnir drew his sword.

It was a stout weapon, wide in the blade with a heavy cross-guard.

The wizard also produced a runestone from his pouch and gripped it tightly in his fist.

From behind, Flyn heard Inkstain's voice.

"They are coming."

Gripping Coalspur in both hands, Flyn widened his stance.

He had not replaced his armor since losing it at Gallus's clutch. He felt suddenly thin, weak and exposed. Nothing for it now.

A figure darted out of the snowfall and Flyn raised his sword, but the shape proved to be one of the storulvir. The giant wolf sped towards them, its lean, savage muscles propelling it with preternatural grace. Three more came swiftly behind, followed closely by Thorsa, an axe clutched in each fist. Hengest and his dwarrow were at her heels. The blue-haired runecaster looked stricken. Flyn quickly counted the dwarrow. Nine remained, where twelve had ventured forth.

The storulvir darted between the trees without breaking stride, passing Fafnir and his men before flying past Flyn, kicking snow up all around him. They turned just beyond Inkstain, and came padding back to the center of the gorge. One came to stand near Flyn, between him and Ulfrun. Two others poised on the left of the giantess, while the last took a place to the right of Fafnir's formation. Flyn took all this in at a glance, noting that the ground to his immediate right between him and the Chain Maker remained uncovered. It was an ideal spot for the running dwarrow to form up, but only Hengest and Thorsa stopped to fill the gap. The rest fled past, and unlike the storulvir, did not turn around again.

Hengest collapsed to the snow, but his wife paid him no heed. She whirled around to face the direction she had just come, brandishing her axes.

"What happened?" Flyn called at the she-dwarf.

Thorsa must have found the question amusing, for she laughed. "We attracted too many! Nearly overwhelmed us before we could withdraw!"

Hengest struggled to his knees, his breathing labored.

"Tried to hold them. Runes . . . failed."

Flyn saw Fafnir throw a glance at his fellow wizard, but the older dwarf said nothing.

"Where was your bald friend with all his bloody wolves?"

Deglan asked.

"He will come," Thorsa exclaimed with relish. "He will come!" The song of the vættir began to fill the gorge, reverberating off the surrounding stones. At the far end of the defile, Flyn saw shapes moving, obscured by the flurries. The dirge of the dwarrow grew and the first wight emerged from the haze, slack mouth singing beneath a filthy, black beard. More came, until the mass of silhouettes pullulated into dozens of individuals squeezing through the neck of the gorge. The dirge of the dwarrow shook the snow from the branches of the trees, the choir of dead voices a punishing weight. Flyn could feel it in his ears, in his bones. He felt short of breath, as if the song was crushing the air out of his lungs. His knees began to buckle and Coalspur became a nearly unbearable weight in his hands. No longer was the music beautiful. It was despair made manifest.

To his left, Flyn saw Ulfrun struggling to stand. Behind, Deglan was unaffected and Inkstain too appeared immune. Flyn thought he saw a small smile at the corners of the man's lips. The storulvir howled in defiant protest, but the vættir could not be undone, their voices as inexorable as their steps. Coalspur fell heavily from Flyn's slack fingers as the music robbed him of strength. He wanted to run, but there was no will left to move his legs.

Through the din of despair, a lone voice began to rise. It was deep and true, somehow making itself heard above the tumult of the wights. Flyn's head began to clear and strength returned to his limbs. He looked over to see it was Fafnir who was singing, he and his defending dwarrow unbent in the maelstrom of the dirge.

The Chain Maker sung in dworgmál, the words lost to Flyn, but he felt an undeniable power rally his courage and he snatched Coalspur from the snow. The song of the vættir dwindled to his ear, eclipsed almost entirely by the slow, melodious voice of Fafnir. The storulvir ceased their howling and began showing the vættir their long fangs beneath snarling muzzles. Flyn hurried over and helped Hengest to his feet. Nearby, Thorsa's mad glee had been replaced with something akin to serenity, but she still made no move to help her husband. Hengest said something in the dwarrow tongue, his face full of disbelief.

Flyn shot him a questioning look.

"The Lay of the Sword-Dale," Hengest said. "By the Ancestors, he has learned the rune."

"The song?" Flyn pressed, full of strong desire. "What are the words of the song?"

Hengest peered at Fafnir, listening, and then he began to repeat the words.

"My brothers bold! My brothers, hold!
Honor now the oaths of old.
Stand ye firm, in war and woe.
Stand ye firm, against all foes.
This day of doom, this hour of spears,
Banish thought of flight and fear!

"For though we live, we yet may die,
To rise again, a singing wight.
I pledge my blade, I pledge my life,
To kinsmen brave in this fell strife.
Take steel in hand and steel your heart!
Together stand, or die apart!"

The vættir were nearly upon them, but Fafnir and his faithful stood fast, seven in the face of hundreds. They waited for the horde, stalwart in the face of living death. Flyn could not allow them to stand alone. Looking over, he caught Ulfrun's eye and saw she too had shaken off the effects of the dirge. The giantess winked.

Flyn smiled back at her and charged.

Coalspur was in his hands and the music of the Chain Maker in his ears. The wights were before him, his pumping legs bringing them closer. He flew past Fafnir's line, screaming the war-cry of the Valiant Spur. He could feel Ulfrun's pounding feet just behind him and saw the storulvir racing along on either side. He brandished his greatsword high and, as the vættir filled his vision, swung full into the mass of reaching, pale hands. His blade cleaved across arms and faces, slicing clean through the dead flesh.

The storulvir barreled into the wights, their jaws snapping.

They bit down on legs and arms, flinging the vættir aside with tosses of their large heads. Ulfrun leaped into the fray, scattering foes with sweeps of her powerful arms, picking up vættir and tossing them back into their fellows, preventing them from swarming her. Flyn continued to slash, severing heads where he could and limbs when he could not. Ridding them of a hand or arm did little to slow them. They did not cringe away from a cutting stroke, but came incessantly forward. Cutting off a leg felled them, but still they would crawl, blue-black fingers digging into the snow to drag themselves along. The wights felt no pain, they knew nothing of panic or fear. Fighting them was reduced to the killing stroke, the finishing blow. Nothing else mattered. Flyn allowed Ulfrun and the giant wolves to keep the vættir from grouping together, using their powerful forms to break up the masses. He quickly engaged the small, scattered groups and brought Coalspur down upon them. He became a butcher of filthy, half-clad corpses.

Flyn heard a yelp and looked to find one of the storulvir in distress. The giant wolf snapped and spun, looking for an opening to escape, but was pressed in from all sides by the mob of wights.

Flyn tried to reach the beast, to give aid, but too many wights stood in his path. He hacked at pale faces, tried to beat back the horde, but his progress was hopelessly impeded. The vættir overwhelmed the wolf, clambering upon it in droves, dragging it down until it was lost in a pile of grasping corpses. The size and strength of the vargulf was formidable, but beneath the press of bodies Flyn could hear the sickening sounds of the beast being torn limb from limb.

Casting about, Flyn caught sight of Ulfrun struggling against the horde. The giantess towered over the wights, but they clambered atop one another, using the bodies of their own fallen to reach her, trying to bring her down. Swinging Coalspur in reaping arcs, Flyn fought towards Ulfrun, but again he was faced with the folly of his attempt. There were too many wights. He could not hope to reach her.

A strident cry split the cold and Thorsa came cutting through the wights. Her axes whirled, dismembering the risen dead.

The she-dwarf charged headlong into the thick of the vættir, heedless of the peril. She made straight for Ulfrun, cutting down countless wights in a swath that led directly to the aid of the giantess. Thorsa's fury was terrible to behold, each sweep of her blades felling a half-dozen foes. Her warriors must have renewed their courage, for they followed her into the battle, though they could not match her speed nor her prowess. Hengest was with them, each fist clutching a runestone and limned with smoke.

Thorsa reached Ulfrun, giving the giantess a chance to win free.

Together, they were able to withdraw, using the path Thorsa had carved, kept open by her dwarrow.

Fafnir and his band had also joined the battle. They kept a close formation, keeping the wights at bay with their shields and using their spears to bring them down. Fafnir stayed behind the rough circle of protection formed by his retainers, his sword dispatching any wight that broke through. Two of the storulvir aided the Chain Maker, guarding his flanks. Flyn fought his way through to join up with Fafnir and together they were able to reach Ulfrun, Hengest and Thorsa.

The neck of the gorge was choked with fallen wights, but more were coming, streaming over the piles. Flyn watched them come. What strength of numbers he and his companions possessed were joined together. There was no time to plan, no time to rest his quivering arms. Flyn smiled to himself. This was how he preferred it.

He looked up at Ulfrun. "Once more?"

"Aye," the giantess breathed. "Once more."

They formed up around Fafnir and his dwarrow. Flyn and Ulfrun stood to the left of the shield wall, Thorsa and Hengest to the right with their six remaining warriors. The storulvir paced about, slavering, ready to dart in when and where they were most needed. The vættir pushed over the heaps of their brethren and began to enter the gorge. Onward they came, dozens, then scores.

Soon it would be hundreds.

Fafnir called the charge and Flyn did not hesitate. With Ulfrun beside him he went smashing through the vættir once again, swinging Coalspur with arms nearly spent. His first stroke sheared through the skull of a wight with no lower jaw, but that was the last detail Flyn was able to discern before he became lost in a morass of enemies. He swung, he slew, he beheaded, each fall of his blade bringing him closer to collapse. And no matter how many fell before him, more were always there. Flyn flailed uselessly, hopelessly against a rising tide of pitiless death. He did not know how the others fared. Only vaguely was he aware of Ulfrun, somewhere at the edge of his vision, striving to overcome, to survive. Flyn's strength was failing, he could feel it. His blade-strokes were slowing. Soon he would be forced to let the heavy sword fall and, like Ulfrun, battle on with nothing but his bare hands. He had his spurs, sheathed in steel of elven-make, but they would be of little use against the vættir.

The end was near and Flyn found he was content with the knowledge. He had fought once more and discovered no lack of courage. No cowardice dwelt within him. Gallus may have won their combat, but he had not defeated him, not utterly. He had done what was asked of him without fear, as was his vow, as was his duty. Perhaps his life had been unworthy of a knight, but his death would not be.

A child finally brought him down.

The murk of fatigue and death cleared for an instant, revealing a dwarrow girl nestled in the revolting drove of dead. She was so small, so fragile seeming, her burial smock covered in grime.

Flyn hesitated for just a moment, checking the downward stroke of his blade before it split her skull. Coalspur bit into the ground, the impact sending the sword tumbling from Flyn's numb grasp. He fell to his knees, his stamina at its end. The dwarrow child shuffled towards him, now near his eye level. She was a wight, like all the others. Corpse pale and black of hair. The flesh of her bare feet was mottled and purple. Her eyes were vacant and colorless, her small mouth agape, singing her soft, lonely notes of the greater, unconquerable dirge. She would be only one of many which would rend him apart, but Flyn resolved to keep his eyes fixed on her face alone.

He was still on his knees when the girl-child passed him by.

Another wight, this one a male adult, brushed by as he also passed.

Woozily, Flyn looked about. He was unarmed, on his knees, nigh helpless and surrounded by the vættir, yet none of them attacked.

He reached out and dragged Coalspur over to him, using the weapon to help him stand. On unsteady feet, Flyn surveyed the gorge. Ulfrun still stood, battling alongside one of the storulvir against scores of pressing wights. And there, across the waves of the risen stood Fafnir and Skrauti, fighting for their lives against several dozen. The vættir still hungered to end life, still strove to drag others down to join them in death, yet Flyn remained unassailed. He was left alone, ignored, adrift in a sea of walking corpses.

TWENTY-ONE

Ingelbert watched the battle turn ill through Gasten's eyes.

The owl's dizzying perspective revealed the neck of the gorge boiling over with wights. In the valley beyond, more were coming, pressing into the backs of their fellows, sensing life and striving to extinguish it with terrible, single-minded purpose.

Three of the storulvir had already been slain. The last fought fiercely next to the beleaguered Ulfrun. The giantess had put her back to the wall of the gorge, her fists caving in the skulls of every wight that came within reach, but the speed of her blows was flagging. The giant wolf next to her must have sensed the end, for it turned and scrambled up the rocks behind, turning to howl at Ulfrun, encouraging her to follow. The giantess beat back the vættir enough to turn and begin climbing. She joined the wolf among the boulders, out of the reach of the wights.

The vættir began to climb, using not only the rocks for purchase, but each other, crawling relentlessly over the backs of the mounding pile beneath. Ulfrun lifted a sizable boulder and sent it crashing down upon the teeming dead, breaking the growing pile into a cascade of snapping bones. The wights were undeterred and immediately began their ascent anew, the whole treading upon the broken. The giantess and the wolf had bought themselves some time, but the outcome would be the same. Death at the pale hands of the vættir was inevitable.

Gasten banked away, bringing Ingelbert to look down upon the main swelling of wights. Fafnir and his retainers fought back to back, completely surrounded. The Chain Maker's sword arm was tireless as he clove reaching arms and slack faces.

Even from such a soaring height, Ingelbert could smell the power emanating from the runecaster. Skrauti's shield was gone, but he fought valiantly, felling wights with great sweeps of his spear. The Magic unleashed by Fafnir's song was potent, for not one who stood with him had fallen. Nearby, yet separated by scores of the enemy, Thorsa, Hengest and a trio of their warriors still stood. The might of the Bone Chewer was undeniable, her axes taking a brutal toll on the vættir. Thorsa showed no signs of fatigue and strove with unnatural vigor to keep her dwarrow alive.

It would not be enough. Even now Thorsa cut the head off a wight who had been one of her hunters, fallen at the hands of the vættir only to rise as one of them.

From his vantage, Ingelbert saw the truth. Only one would leave this gorge alive.

Beneath Gasten's keen eyes, Bantam Flyn rose on unsteady feet. The young coburn looked around him, his beak agape, his large sword clutched weakly. Surrounding him was a tight circle of calm among fathoms of undulating horror. Strangely, the vættir left him be. Even when Flyn raised his greatsword wearily and struck the head off the nearest wight, the rest continued to pay him no mind. Dumbfounded, the knight began to push his way through the press, shouldering the vættir aside and making for Fafnir's position.

Ingelbert became aware of a sensation back in his own body. A form struggling against him.

Ah yes. Deglan.

Ingelbert returned to himself and found he still had the gnome clutched against his legs, holding him tightly beneath the jaw. It was cruel, but it would not do for the gnome to rush into the fray bravely, foolishly, and die. It would not do at all.

Deglan was spitting and cursing, his eyes rolled back to look up at Ingelbert balefully. The old stoat had not yet become so incensed as to strike at Ingelbert with the axe he still held. Even if he had, the steel would fail to wound. Ingelbert had hardened his flesh against weapons, consciously protecting himself with the same craft he had unknowingly wielded when Hafr tried to strike him down. He had also woven another ward, one that kept the sound of his heartbeat from reaching the vættir, prevented the heat from his skin and the smell of his blood from alerting them to the presence of life. Deglan too was within the boundaries of the ward, but if Ingelbert allowed him to break free, the gnome would be outside the protection in a single footstep. The wights would come for him then, and there would be nothing Ingelbert could do to save him.

The vættir were less than a stone's throw from where they stood, drawing closer with every moment as more of them flooded the gorge. Soon, the dwarrow would be overwhelmed, even Thorsa and Fafnir, then Ulfrun and the last great wolf, and finally, Ingelbert and Deglan. Though Magic protected them for the moment, Ingelbert could not move or the ward would be broken.

They were safe, but trapped, and likely the vættir would sense them despite the spell once the others were dead.

Ingelbert wondered how long Flyn would battle on after they had all fallen.

Would he continue to slay the væettir, one at a time, until he died from the effort? For a coburn, such a thing was possible. Ingelbert found the thought of such hopeless courage pitiful. Flyn should do the intelligent thing and save himself, as Hakeswaith had done. As Ingelbert should have done. He had been given the opportunity, but for reasons unknown even to himself he had stayed. The only notion he possessed for such a decision was a vague sense of yearning, of wanting to witness what took place here. Was it that Ingelbert desired to stand with his friends? Or did he simply want to see their deaths?

Through his own eyes, Ingelbert could just discern the shape of Bantam Flyn through the throng. He was now close to reaching Fafnir and his followers, the dwarrow standing atop a pile of dismembered wights. Of Thorsa and her band, there was no sign.

A great baying echoed through the neck of the gorge.

Ingelbert rejoined with Gasten on the wing and surveyed the ground below. The væettir in the valley lay scattered and motionless, destroyed by a sizable pack of storulvir that now charged into the defile, falling upon the wights in the gorge from the rear. Leading the pack was Kàlfr the Roundhouse, his massive axe sending heads flying with each great swing. The savage dwarf had left with only a score of the great wolves, but was now returned with near triple that number. The beasts tore through the wights, the head of the pack bowling through while those rearward savaged them with tooth and claw. Within moments, they had won through the neck and set upon the horde.

Ingelbert had thought Thorsa's fury was impressive, but the she-dwarf was nothing compared to the Roundhouse. The impact from his axe sent wights tumbling through the air, smashing bones, pulping skulls and separating limbs. His speed and ferocity outmatched even the storulvir. Swiftly, he cut his way through and, from somewhere within the mass of wights, he rescued Thorsa.

The she-dwarf carried the limp form of her husband slung over her shoulders. Together, the Bone Chewers made their way to Fafnir and Flyn. The storulvir fell in around them, tossing wights from their dripping jaws. Moving swiftly, the wolves opened up a path for the coburn and the dwarrow. Flyn led the dwarrow through while Kàlfr covered their escape.

They made for the slope where Ulfrun and the lone wolf stood besieged. Emboldened by the presence of the pack, the beast leaped down from the boulders, barreling into the climbing wights.

Ulfrun followed, reaching the bottom just as the pack began to shred the wights. The giantess joined Flyn and the dwarrow in the center of the screening wolves and they all began to flee towards the rear of the gorge.

Towards where Ingelbert and Deglan stood.

It was a strange sensation, staring down at himself from above, watching a charging pack of giant wolves speed towards his tiny body. Ingelbert could still feel Deglan struggling, his fear growing as the storulvir raced forward. At the last possible moment, Ingelbert returned to his own form, hauling Deglan off the ground as he turned to run. Snow exploded from all sides as the wolves darted around him. Ingelbert found himself in the center of the pack, running next to Flyn and Ulfrun, the giantess reaching down for Deglan. Ingelbert handed him up without breaking stride.

The back of the gorge loomed before them and there, nestled almost imperceptibly among the tumble of boulders, was the trailhead. The great wolves made directly for it, half a dozen of them running up the switchbacks to scout ahead. The others fanned out at the base of the rocks, turning to face the interior of the gorge. Ingelbert stopped with the others and looked back.

They had managed to distance themselves from the vættir, but the throng was continuing to pursue them.

"Go!" Kàlfr commanded, his bald head steaming in the cold. "I will hold them until you reach the top."

"I shall stand with you," Thorsa said, setting the still form of Hengest down upon the snow.

"And me," Flyn proclaimed.

"No!" the Roundhouse said roughly. "My brothers and me fight best alone. And you two will be needed if those horsemen wait for you at the top."

"Horsemen?" Fafnir demanded.

"No time to explain, Chain Maker," Kàlfr said. "Get you up that trail or stay here and be damned!"

Ingelbert did not wait to see what the others decided, but began hustling up the path. He felt suddenly cold, as if naked in the snow. No. It was a different feeling than that. It was as if something had left from his insides. He was now keenly aware of the danger nipping at his heels. He hurtled up the switchbacks, his teeth chattering. Shooting a look downward, he saw Ulfrun carrying Deglan a turn below. The gnome watched him, his crinkled face full of ire and suspicion. Behind the giantess came Flyn, followed closely by Fafnir and Skrauti. Two of the dwarrow porters now bore Hengest between them, laid upon one of their shields. Thorsa and a few wolves brought up the rear. Ingelbert could hear the sounds of Kàlfr and his beasts meeting the oncoming wights, but he did not venture a look. Instead, he returned his eyes to the trail ahead and kept running.

At the top, Ingelbert found no sign of Hakeswaith. The storulvir scouts had formed up protectively at the top of the trail, watching the flats between the nearby woodlands and the valley shoulder. As soon as the others reached the top, the wolves loped off, leading the group towards the trees. They did not enter the forest, however, but skirted its edge, setting a quick pace. It was not long before Thorsa called a halt.

"This is far enough," she announced. "The call of the Corpse Eater will pull the vættir off our scent. We will await the Roundhouse here."

"No," Fafnir said, his face haggard and drawn. "He could lead the throng directly to us."

Thorsa rounded on the Chain Maker. "He would never! None know the ways of the vættir better."

"That may be so," Ulfrun put in, "but this place is not defensible."

"Agreed," Flyn said. "We must continue on."

Fafnir took a single step towards Thorsa. "Stay here if you wish, niece. We are going. You may have lost a husband this day. Likely your lover is also slain. If you too would perish before nightfall, remain here. I care not."

Ingelbert saw the barest spark of anger flare in the she-dwarf's face, but it was quickly snuffed, replaced by a look of deep weariness. Was it the implication of Hengest's death? Or the possibility of Kàlfr's? Ingelbert was not schooled enough in the intricacies of love and passion to say. Whatever the cause, Thorsa seemed to come to the end of her previously unquenchable energy.

Fafnir passed her by and the others followed, including the storulvir. Ingelbert did not need to turn around to know that Thorsa chose to follow. Gasten flashed the image through his head.

With an audible snarl, Ingelbert pushed the owl out.

They slogged wearily through the snow for what remained of the day. Eventually, the woods to their right grew away from the valley. The storulvir continued to follow the tree line and the edge of the ravine was lost from sight.

The sun was low in the sky when the wolves halted in a craggy dell. They quickly sniffed the surrounding trees and the cluster of boulders, then bounded up among the rocks to rest.

"We camp here," Fafnir said, motioning for the porters to ease Hengest down at the base of an evergreen. The blue-haired runecaster looked awful. A blossom of black bruises ringed his neck.

The vættir had torn the storulvir to pieces, but it seemed they throttled their living kin so they could rise whole once dead. Fafnir immediately knelt beside Hengest, runestones already in hand.

Ingelbert could attest to the wizard's skill at healing, but likely Hengest was beyond saving. He did not even appear to be breathing.

Ingelbert glanced about the dell to see how the others fared.

Flyn looked as if he could barely stand, though he hovered close to Fafnir, clearly wishing to speak with the wizard, but unwilling to interrupt his tending of Hengest. Thorsa slumped to the snow as soon as she entered the dell, staring vacantly at the blade of the lone axe she still bore. Only Ulfrun seemed to have regained any strength since the battle. She set Deglan down and immediately began gathering wood for a fire. Skrauti and his dwarrow attempted to help her, but they moved sluggishly, clearly at the end of their strength.

Ingelbert sat himself upon a cold rock and tried to avoid catching Deglan's eye, waiting for the gnome to approach and demand an explanation for his rough treatment, but he never did. It was a small mercy. There would be no answer Ingelbert could give that would satisfy the herbalist. He had sought to save Deglan's life, but Ingelbert could not convince himself that feelings of mercy had guided his actions. He did it because he willed it, because in that moment he had found the gnome's need to uselessly sacrifice himself irritating. He simply reached out and placed

Deglan under domination. A Fae. A friend. And Ingelbert had mastered him as one would an unruly hound.

No one spoke for a long time. Ingelbert must have dozed, for next he knew, the fire was kindled and the moon risen. Hengest now lay before the flames, wrapped in Fafnir's own cloak. The Chain Maker sat beside him, one hand gently resting on the prone dwarf's chest, which was now rising and falling. Ingelbert marveled.

Was there no end to Fafnir's Magic? Deglan brooded close to the fire, sitting next to Flyn. Ulfrun stood just outside the ring of firelight, keeping a watch over the direction they had come. Thorsa had removed herself to the company of the storulvir, resting in the rocks which sheltered the dell. The sleds were gone, so there was no food, no furs. It would be a miserable, cold night.

It was Flyn who finally broke the silence.

"The wights did not attack me," the knight said, his voice low and taut. "I have been going over the battle in my mind. Every moment. They never tried for me. Why, Fafnir? Surely you know."

The question brought every eye to the dwarf.

"You are a coburn," Fafnir answered gravely. "A descendant of the Corpse Eater. Generations beyond reckoning separate you from her womb, but she can still feel you there, a child of her body. The vættir are nothing but food to her. She will not allow them to harm you."

"You knew this already," Deglan said. It was not a question.

Fafnir nodded slowly at the fire.

"Why did you not tell me?" Flyn asked.

"I have asked you to trust much, Bantam Flyn," the wizard replied. "Me. The augury. Unproven allies. Such trust has limits. Telling a warrior he can come to no harm at the hands of his enemy would sound as madness."

"And when I try to kill the Corpse Eater?" Flyn asked.

"What then?"

"It is against all that is natural to kill one's own child," Thorsa threw down from the rocks, her voice dripping with bitterness. "An unforgivable malediction."

Ingelbert saw Fafnir's eyes clinch shut at this, but otherwise did not acknowledge his kin had spoken. The Chain Maker looked back to Flyn.

"The Corpse Eater's struggle for survival is littered with atrocities. She will not hesitate to kill you to avoid her own destruction."

"You speak as if you know her well," Deglan said.

"Intimately," the wizard tolled. "We are wed in hatred. Just as a lover suffers over the absence of their beloved, be it from distance or death, such it is with me and the Corpse Eater. But it is not her absence which pains me, not distance nor death. It is her presence, her very life. In my heart I can feel her, her breathing, her pulsing blood. Her continued existence offends me. I yearn to rid her of that life, send her to the death she should have embraced in the unnamed ages of this world."

At that moment, the storulvir perked up, ears erect. They stood and dropped agilely down from the rocks, alert and sniffing.

"More wolves approach," Ulfrun reported. "It appears the Bone Chewer is with them."

Thorsa's face lit up and she came quickly down to stand with the storulvir, her breath heaving. Kàlfr and a dozen wolves entered the dell. The storulvir mingled quickly and Ingelbert was unable to tell the newcomers from those which led them to the camp. The Roundhouse carried a heavy burden slung over his shoulder, which he dumped unceremoniously to the ground. It was a headless corpse, one which wore a hauberk that Ingelbert recognized as belonging to one of Thorsa's own warriors.

Fafnir slowly removed his hand from Hengest and stood.

Thorsa had been about to embrace Kàlfr, but paused at the sight of the body.

"I did not withdraw until they all emerged from the throng," the Roundhouse explained, gesturing flippantly down at the remains before looking at Thorsa. "So you would know, none of yours walked as one of them."

Thorsa accepted this rough comfort with a grateful nod, but Ingelbert detected a hint of disquiet in her face.

"And the vættir?" Fafnir asked.

"Hundreds remain," Kàlfr answered. "They will go back on the march, but the rest of my brethren watch them. They will pick them off, a little at a time."

"Why were you so late to our aid?" Fafnir demanded.

Kàlfr tossed a hand at Thorsa. "This one was over eager.

Drew too many of the dead from the main group. I had to send a few of my wolves to gather a stronger pack. Figured you lot could hold until I had enough numbers to save your hides." The bald dwarf smiled widely. "You almost proved me wrong, Chain Maker."

Fafnir visibly bristled at the taunt, but managed to check his anger. "And what of these horsemen of which you spoke?"

Kàlfr stepped over the decapitated body and approached the fire. He did not even look at Fafnir as he spoke. "Saw them on the ridges as I was taking position. Both sides of the valley. Humans on horses, at least a score. They were tracking the vættir, same as us. Watching them. Thought they might lend a hand, but they vanished when Hengest and Thorsa engaged the walking meat."

Fafnir remained silent, but it was clear in his face he had an idea who these men might be. Ingelbert recalled the name given by the hanged man near the Fatwood barrow.

Arngrim Crow Shoulders.

He was the fjordman warlord said to be responsible for the destruction of the Warden Trees. Fafnir had been overcome with rage at the revelation. The same rage roiled at the edges of the Chain Maker's countenance now, but this time he kept control.

"No matter," Kàlfr went on, scraping melted snow from his pate with a calloused hand and flinging it into the fire. "We were victorious. The vættir in that gully will feed my storulvir for the next six months. So long as those fools guarding the last two Trees can keep them safe, there will be no cause to go on the hunt for a long time."

The Roundhouse took a deep breath, then stomped away from the fire. He bent and retrieved the body, flinging it back over one shoulder. "Come, Thorsa. It is time we had our reward. Bring Hengest. This flesh will revive him."

Thorsa looked at Kàlfr, then her eyes flitted to her unconscious husband and doubt filled her face. But there was something else struggling beneath. A lust. A craving. A hunger.

Ingelbert's stomach turned.

Fafnir stepped forward quickly and touched his niece for the first time, grabbing her arm firmly. "Do not do this, Thorsa."

"Thruni was young," Kàlfr said, slapping the rump of the corpse on his shoulder. "And powerful. A warrior, freshly killed. His gall will live in us for a fortnight and ensure Hengest lives."

The Roundhouse's tone was one of warning to Fafnir, but coaxing to Thorsa. She hesitated, uncertainty written in every muscle.

"Thorsa," Fafnir urged, his voice nearly pleading. "Hengest stood by you despite your transgressions, but he never partook in *this*. Do not dishonor him by making him a part of it unwillingly. I have done what I can for him, but he may yet die. Kàlfr's way will save him, but will Hengest forgive you?"

Thorsa's eyes welled with tears, but then her quavering lips hardened and she struck Fafnir across the face with the back of her hand, wrenching free of his grasp.

"You would speak to me of forgiveness!" she screamed.

"You! How dare you!"

Kàlfr placed his axe in front of his lover, gently easing her away. Thorsa allowed herself to be guided backward, but she continued to throw abuses at Fafnir.

"You claim the Corpse Eater's life hollows your heart, but her death will not make it whole, uncle! Too many times, with your own hand, have you cloven it in twain! You are as damned as I, Chain Maker! You may succeed in delivering our people, but that one act will never redeem you! Never!"

Kàlfr and Thorsa drifted away into the night, the storulvir departing with them. Fafnir slowly wiped the blood from his lip and went back to tend Hengest. Ulfrun resumed her watch and no one pressed the Chain Maker for answers, not even Deglan.

Ingelbert fell asleep to the sound of the campfire and the nearby howling of feasting wolves.

He was awakened in the middle of the night by an empty belly and full bladder. Rising on stiff legs, Ingelbert hobbled away from the comforting ring of pulsing light and relieved himself among the trees. As he returned, he saw that Fafnir had taken Ulfrun's place on watch. The dwarf's sword was sheathed at his side and a smoking pipe was clenched between his lips. Ingelbert approached him, making sure his steps were heard. The wizard turned and nodded at his presence.

"The night is long," Fafnir said somberly, briefly removing the pipe from his mouth.

"It is," Ingelbert agreed, rubbing his hands together.

Fafnir stared thoughtfully out into the darkness, blowing fragrant plumes of smoke.

"It was wise," the dwarf said after a time, "what you did today, Master Crane. Protecting yourself, and Master Loamtoes."

Ingelbert was only slightly taken aback. "You knew?"

Fafnir nodded. "I felt it."

"Deglan will never forgive me."

"Likely not," the runecaster agreed. "But you must accustom yourself to such feelings. It is one of the many prices demanded by Magic."

Ingelbert accepted this without comment. He had been without friends most of his life and would survive if his fellowship with Deglan was irreparably severed. Truly, he was more concerned about the price he was paying within himself. He was given to solitude, and always imagined he would end his days as a hermit, but the distance he felt from his companions, from his own emotions, from the world itself, all were growing. Desperately, he yearned to walk away, leave the others and travel alone. He fought the urge because he knew, once that first step was taken, there would be no coming back. He would have abandoned all loyalty, all responsibility, all compassion and offered himself totally to the gristmill of his own thoughts. The lives of others would become distant things, purposefully avoided, and when they did inevitably intrude, they would be nuisances best disposed of. Ingelbert saw all this clearly, a natural, logical progression beginning with the harsh way he handled Deglan and marching steadily along to cold, callous disregard for life. The images did not disturb him. Worse, the vengeful feelings that welled to the surface with the conjuring of these black thoughts were welcoming, familiar. Indeed, that incarnation of himself would wear with more ease than the man he was now, the man who suffered the company of others in a craven bid to retain any empathy.

"Hengest nearly paid the final price this day," Fafnir intoned. "His Magic twice failed him. The first by his own admission when they baited the vættir. He seemed befuddled, betrayed. The second failure I felt just before he fell." Fafnir closed his eyes for a moment, savoring the pipe smoke. "He was my apprentice, long ago. I housed him with my own family, tutored him in the lore of runes. My wife was fond of Hengest. Thorsa came to love him, but I warned him against her. I sensed the wildness in her. Many times I asked him not to follow her to unending shame. I begged him to set her aside and join me on the path to save our people, but he bound himself to her cursed choices and rebuked me. To him, I was the greater evil. So you see, Ingelbert Crane, I am no stranger to condemnation."

"What did you do?" Ingelbert ventured. "To deserve such scorn."

"He wished to wed one of my own daughters," the dwarf responded, his voice weighted with regret. "I denied him the chance." Fafnir became very still for a moment, frozen by some bitter memory. He issued a grunt that was half snarl, half sob and tossed the smoldering contents of his pipe into the wind. "Now, forgive me, but I must rest. Sir Flyn is to take my place. You too should seek repose."

Ingelbert could hardly disagree. He was weary to the bone.

As he turned to go back to camp, Fafnir placed a hand on his arm, halting him gently.

"One more matter," the dwarf said. "Hengest's failure today was not of his making. His runes were disrupted by another. It felt as if something leeched the power from him, used it to fuel a craft set against us. Did you feel it?"

Ingelbert shook his head. "No."

The runecaster eyed him for a moment, then released his grip.

Ingelbert left the dwarf alone. He had told the truth. No, when Hengest's Magic was stolen he had not felt it. He had done it.

Deglan had not yet slept. He kept his eyes closed, but remained awake, listening to Fafnir and Ingelbert converse. He was unable to catch every word, but his keen gnomish ears picked up enough to worry him. Or further worry him. He continued to feign slumber as Ingelbert returned to the fireside. Fafnir remained at watch a while longer, then roused Flyn to spell him as they had arranged. This was what Deglan had been waiting for.

True sleep began to tempt him as he waited for the dwarf to settle in, but Deglan fought it off, not wanting to miss his chance. When he was satisfied that the Chain Maker and the chronicler slept, Deglan opened his eyes and rose cautiously, using Ulfrun's heavy breathing to mask his footfalls. He moved so quietly that he accidentally startled Flyn when he came up beside him.

Thankfully, the coburn only jumped slightly and made no utterance of surprise.

"Buggery and spit, Staunch!" Flyn breathed, using Deglan's own parlance. "You should have been a cutpurse instead of an herbalist, you sneaking mushroom."

"Pardons," Deglan whispered. "I did not want to wake the others." Remembering that he had been able to hear Crane and Fafnir, Deglan took Flyn by the elbow and steered him further out into the field that approached the tree line.

"How fare you?" Deglan asked when they were well removed. "Any hurts I should look at?"

"None," Flyn replied, almost regretfully.

Deglan took a deep breath, girding himself for what he needed to say and the response it would undoubtedly receive.

"Flyn," he said quietly with a backward glance at the camp.

"We must leave."

"What?" the coburn asked.

"Stop it!" Deglan chastised him. "You are not that thick and you damn well heard me. We need to leave. You and I. Now. Get clear of this quest and out of Middangeard."

"We have come too far for that, Deglan."

"It is only too far when it is too late. And it is not too late. Not yet."

Flyn laughed, but Deglan heard the frustration hidden within. "Need I remind you, Master Loamtoes, that you were the one who said I needed to go on this journey?"

"Yes," Deglan returned. "Because I feared you had lost your damn resolve. Today proved you have not."

"Today proved nothing!" Flyn said, leaning down close. "I fought an enemy that did not fight back."

"Damn all coburn pride," Deglan growled. "You did not know that when you charged their lines, Bantam Flyn! Do not play the fool!"

"You seem intent on making me dance like one, Staunch. I was determined not to come here!"

"I have made many mistakes in my long life, Flyn. And I tell you the only ones I have ever regretted are those which I did not try and remedy. We can remedy this, this damn instant. Walk away from here with me."

"And leave Inkstain behind?"

Deglan could not help but groan at the mention of the chronicler. "He can damn well look after himself, mark me!"

"And you curse my pride?" Flyn scoffed. "Crane kept you from a battle that would have been your end and now you hate the man."

"That is not the way of it. The man is dangerous!"

"You have said the same about Fafnir."

"You think he is not?" Deglan asked, struggling to keep his voice low. "Crane is not the same bashful scribbler we knew at the Roost, and the only one whispering in his ear is that damn wizard! Think about what you're doing! Who you are following! This is a cursed land and has been for longer than even I can fathom. There is nothing that can be done. Believe me, I know when a life goes beyond the reach of all healing. Flyn, there is nothing here to save."

"There are the dwarrow," Flyn returned.

Deglan blinked hard, unable to believe the blind valor he heard in the coburn's voice. "The dwarrow? Outcasts? Exiles? They began their existence in betrayal. Magic stunted them so that they could easily be recognized for the deceivers that they are. Their dead do not rest, rising to kill the living."

"And once I slay the Corpse Eater that ends," Flyn proclaimed.

"Why?" Deglan demanded. "Because some cozening kidnapper told you so! Some charlatan who believes in auguries and talks to dead men and allies himself with cannibals! Fafnir will—"

"Dammit, Staunch, I do not hate him as you do!" Flyn hissed.

Deglan thrust a warning finger up at him. "That is not—"

"Yes it is!" Flyn exclaimed, riding right over his protestations. "You hate them and you want to see them continue to suffer. You cannot let it go, Deglan! Goblins. Dwarves. The wars. The past. Your own people! And now Crane. You hate them all because you cannot forget and refuse to forgive. You think the dwarrow deserve this fate and you want to abandon them to it. I cannot do that. I will not do that! It is my duty as a knight to try and set this right. And perhaps it is my penance as a coburn to undo the evil which has been wrought upon the dwarrow by the mother of my race."

It was Deglan's turn to laugh and he did it without a hint of mirth. "The Corpse Eater? Your ancestral matron? You truly believe that?"

"Yes. I do. After today, I have no more reason to doubt."

"So," Deglan said with derision, "she is your mother. And now you seek to slay her. Tell me, Flyn, how well did you account yourself when you sought a similar end for your father?"

Flyn was silent for a long time. When he did finally speak, his voice was flat and cold.

"You should leave, Deglan. You have no place here and I am at the end of my tolerance for you. You are as changeable as the wind and I am weary from listening to you bluster. You slow us down. You cause us to doubt. You are useless in battle and your skills as a healer are not needed. *You* are not needed. Go home. Go back to Airlann, or to whatever land you have not yet foresworn. In this errantry, you are nothing but a hindrance and I no longer want you by my side."

These words spoken, Flyn turned his back and walked away.

Deglan stood alone, rooted by grief. Anger tore at his head, pain pulsed in his heart, but neither won over to goad him to action.

The cold settled into his bones, yet still he did not move. He suffered with the knowledge that Flyn was right. He had forced the young strut to take up this madness. And he was useless. There was nothing he could do here. He fancied himself the voice of reason, but all were deaf to him now.

So lost was Deglan in thought that he did not hear the steps in the snow behind him until it was too late. He was grabbed roughly from behind, his spine wrenched backwards and the feel of cold metal pressed into his neck. Cold which began to burn. The touch of iron.

"Just you and me now, stunty," Hakeswaith's voice rasped into his ear.

Deglan grit his teeth against the rising pain of the harpoon.

"You going to kill me or help me get home? Make a damn choice."

The question gave the whaler pause. Deglan could not see him, but he felt his body tense, his breath hold. He was thinking.

Deglan used the moment to scan the distant tree line. Flyn was nowhere in sight. The cocky swain really had abandoned him.

Deglan's ears were beginning to fill with blood and he fought the bile rising in his throat. In another minute, it would not matter what Hakeswaith decided, Deglan would be dead, though he might go blind first.

"Difficult for either of us to make it out of Middangeard alone," Deglan wheezed. "What's it to be? Gipeswic? Or death?"

The harpoon came away and Deglan was shoved roughly forward. He spilled over onto the ground, retching and spitting, but the snow was a blissful relief against his blistered neck. Briefly, Deglan considered calling for help, but even without his iron-ravaged throat it would be useless. Hakeswaith would skewer him through the back if he tried to raise alarm. Rolling over slowly, Deglan found the whaler standing over him.

"Up," the man rasped.

Deglan did as he was told and Hakeswaith immediately grabbed him about the collar, hauling him away from the direction of the camp. The whaler walked backward, keeping an eye on the trees, watchful for any sign of someone coming to Deglan's aid.

"No need for such caution," Deglan told him. "I am as welcome back there as you are."

"Shut it!" Hakeswaith snarled.

Deglan's ear burst into pain as the man cuffed him solidly to punctuate his warning. Compared to the excruciation of iron, the blow was nothing.

"You bent-jawed fuck!" Deglan barked, undeterred. "Listen to me. You are getting your wish. We are going back to the Tin Isles. I will not fight you. Kicking me like a stray mongrel the entire way will only slow us down."

Hakeswaith halted, forcing Deglan to do the same.

"I'll not fall for your Fae chicanery," the whaler said, leaning in close.

"There are no tricks here, Hakeswaith," Deglan told him.

"And you have no choice but to trust me. Think on it. It is a long way to the coast and we do not know this country. You will have to sleep, and it's tiring work for one man to keep watch on a prisoner. Far easier to take me at my word and believe that I want away as much as you."

"Away?" Hakeswaith mocked. "Away from your friends? Expect I will believe that?"

Deglan leaned away from the man's foul breath. "My friends are blind fools. They are being led to slaughter and refuse to see it. Such is the stupidity of mortals. Fail to see sense when it's standing right in front of them. So tell me, Hakeswaith. Are you also that bloody daft?"

The whaler gave him a hard stare. Deglan could see every feature of his misshapen face, but doubted the man could make out much of his face in the darkness. It was a lucky thing, for Deglan was not sure his countenance would have given proof to his words.

Flyn was a fool, that was true enough, but was Deglan ready to leave him alone with this quest? It mattered little now. He was in Hakeswaith's power. There may come a chance to slip away, but how far would the rest of the group have traveled by the time such an opportunity came? Deglan would have no hope of catching them, even if he could track them. No, there was nothing for it.

Unless his friends discovered what had happened and came for him soon, Deglan was on his own.

"If I catch wind of one trick," Hakeswaith threatened.

"I die?" Deglan finished for him. "Well, that may be both our fates before long unless we find some supplies."

Hakeswaith said nothing, sullen and mistrustful. He was a seaman and useless in the frozen wilderness of Middangeard.

Deglan took a moment to think, quickly determining that their only hope was to backtrack to the abandoned sleds, which had been left behind in the gorge. He could only trust that bald dwarf barbarian had been correct and the wights had moved on, but it remained a risky venture. There were more dangers in Middangeard than the dwarrow dead. The storulvir, for one.

Deglan did not fancy an encounter with those monstrous wolves without the Roundhouse nearby, much as he found the dwarf loathsome. And then of course there were trolls. Deglan had to fight back a burst of bitter laughter. He was an herbalist in a land of perpetual freeze, accompanied by a cowardly fisherman.

Middangeard was going to make a meal of them both.

He need not have worried about the wights, the giant wolves or the trolls.

The horsemen found them first.

TWENTY-TWO

Despite the aching weariness in his body, Flyn found sleep elusive. He had reclined before the fire eagerly after Skrauti took his place on watch, nearly collapsing upon one of the pallets of fir branches prepared by the porters. Hugging Coalspur to his chest, Flyn allowed exhaustion to claim him, but guilt kept pulling his eyelids open. His temper had gotten the better of him. Deglan's jibe about Gallus had rankled Flyn deeply and he spat forth feelings that he swore never to give voice, feelings made all the more vitriolic by the mention of his defeat. By the Hallowed, would his father never cease to sour his judgment?

Fortunately, Deglan Loamtoes was the most obstinate being drawing breath and would never allow words spoken in anger to drive him off. Flyn would seek his pardon and the old stoat would grudgingly give it. This thought only comforted for a short time, however. Flyn's restlessness only increased as the stars arced across the sky and Deglan still had not returned to camp. The gnome was stubborn, but the cold of the night air could not long be endured.

Inwardly cursing his hot-headed nature and all cantankerous gnomes, Flyn rose. He walked to the edge of camp and paused next to Skrauti, standing vigilant with his spear.

"Any sign of Master Loamtoes?" Flyn asked the dwarf quietly. Skrauti gave only the barest shake of his head, clearly unconcerned. Deglan had done little to foster any fellowship with the dwarrow.

"I must go find him," Flyn said.

"Better to wait for sunrise," Skrauti suggested.

It was Flyn's turn to shake his head. "I cannot wait that long." He struck out into the field without wasting another moment. Fresh snow was beginning to fall, but it was just a light flurry. Flyn was easily able to follow the tracks he and Deglan had made when the gnome pulled him away to talk, leading to the patch they had trampled as they argued. Flyn was no tracker, but snow was a poor keeper of secrets. Someone had approached Deglan from behind and knocked him to the ground. There was no blood and the gnome had clearly risen, then left with his attacker.

Flyn broke into a run, keeping his feet in the tracks and his eyes on the path of footprints ahead. They had not gone far, Deglan and his captor, only moving to a stand of spruce a mile distant from the camp. Here, Flyn found the remnants of a meager, half-built fire. And a discarded harpoon. Flyn snatched it up.

Hakeswaith.

Flyn fumed, nearly crying out with impotent rage. They had distrusted the whaler for good reason, and maligned him, avoided him, ignored and neglected him. Flyn had all but forgotten him. He may as well have handed Deglan over to the man bound and gagged.

The fire had nearly burned out, but the moon was bright this night, illuminating the broad swath of horse tracks leading to, and then away from the trees.

Following the horses' path at a sprint, Flyn tried to determine the number of riders, but he had not the skill. The Roundhouse had said he saw mounted men on both ridges of the valley. Likely these were the same, but who were they? Flyn could not imagine Hakeswaith capable of winning allies to his aid unless the man possessed some riches he had kept hidden. And his harpoon had been left behind. Flyn still held the weapon in his fists as he ran, leaving Coalspur slung.

A smear of flickering orange appeared in the darkness ahead, just above the snow. Heat, radiating from the bodies of animal and man, surrounded by floating blobs of angry white.

Torches.

The sight drove Flyn on and he surged forward. He counted ten horses. No doubt the men upon them were armed.

Only fools would travel through Middangeard at night without something sharp close to hand. They kept a steady pace through the snow, but were not pushing their mounts, giving Flyn a chance to close the gap.

One of the riders must have been keeping an eye on their back trail, for Flyn was within a stone's throw of the group when two of them turned their mounts and charged. Flyn saw moonlight glint off mail, shield boss and spear tip. So, armed and armored, and bearing down upon him.

Flyn cocked his arm back, flung the harpoon, then immediately dove to the side. The pained screaming of a horse split the night as he rolled to his feet, slinging the harness off his shoulder and freeing Coalspur from its scabbard. A horse lay kicking in the snow not far from where he stood. The other was wheeling around for another charge. Flyn ran to meet it. The animal thundered toward him, snow bursting up from beneath its hooves. The rider's spear was lowered and trained, but Flyn did not break stride. He leapt at a full run, directly at the horse's head, issuing his war cry. The animal spooked, wanting to rear, but could not halt its own momentum. It turned just enough, and Flyn barreled into the rider, striking the man's shield with the full weight of his body, knocking him from the saddle. They spilled into the snow together, a tangle of weapons and limbs. Flyn felt the man beat at him with fist and shield, kicking at him as they both scrambled to rise. Flyn gained his feet first, but his foe was nearly as fast. He had retained his shield, but lost his spear, quickly filling his hand with a short-hafted axe from his belt. Flyn still held Coalspur.

The man was big and bearded, clad to the knee in mail. He had the look of a seasoned warrior. Flyn took one step forward and swung his greatsword in a massive cross-cut. The warrior had just enough time to get his shield up, but the dwarf-forged blade cleaved through the metal rim, shattering the wood beyond, then cut the man's arm off below the elbow before smashing into his side, shearing through mail and bone. A gurgle brought a gob of blood past the man's lips to splash into his beard before he dropped lifelessly to the ground.

Flyn looked about. The main body of riders was gone. With a frustrated jerk, Flyn pulled Coalspur free from the wreckage of the man's ribcage and immediately stalked over to the horse he had felled with the thrown harpoon. The animal lay still now, its limp body pinning the leg of its rider to the blood-darkened snow. The warrior struggled to free himself, gritting his teeth with effort and pain. His eyes widened as Flyn stood over him, then hardened with brave resolve.

"Where are your fellows taking the gnome?" Flyn demanded.

The warrior said nothing.

"Tell me and I will free you," Flyn said. "You have my word." The man began to mutter through lips taut with pain, but he spoke incomprehensibly in the tongue of the fjordmen. The words were unfathomable to Flyn, but the look on the man's face was unmistakable. Disdainful. Mocking. Resolute.

"It is against the codes of chivalry to slay a helpless foe," Flyn told the man, knowing his words would be but gibberish. "But I have not the time to free you. Luck to you this night."

To the warrior's credit, he did not fall to whimpering or begging as Flyn walked away.

The surviving horse had fled, leaving no chance of catching Deglan's captors. The snowfall had grown heavier. It was only a matter of time before the tracks were covered.

Lost.

Flyn needed speed and the ability to follow the horsemen once the trail was buried. He needed the storulvir.

Ingelbert awoke just before dawn, his mind astir. Cold and hungry. Such as it was every morn since he arrived in Middangeard.

But there was something else too. Another presence beneath his shivering flesh, the only contents of his grumbling gut.

Fear.

Even when warm and well-fed as a boy in the orphanage, Ingelbert often woke instilled with a creeping dread. So too in the Roost, later in life. It was a permanent, woefully familiar feeling that greeted him with each new day. Only with its renewed presence did Ingelbert realize that it had been absent since embarking on this frozen quest. He found the reunion unwelcome.

Though Ulfrun slept nearby, as well as Fafnir and his dwarrow, Ingelbert felt miserably alone, yet the thought of rousing one of his comrades was equally undesirable. He no longer wished to be here, in this hoary wasteland with these folk. He wished to be away, but the memory of the countless miles they had traveled over unfamiliar country nearly squeezed a sob from his throat. There was no escape lest he attempted to traverse the distance they had come alone. He could not do that, he would starve or succumb to the cold. Perhaps Ulfrun would take him? No, she would laugh in his face and know him for the pusillanimous weakling he was.

Ingelbert cast about with rising panic. He did not know what to do.

His eyes fell upon his satchel, lying upon the pallet. He had used it for a pillow, the scrolls and reams of parchment housed within cradling his head. Ingelbert grinned to himself in the bleakness of the morning. Dusty pages were ever a comfort. He had hauled the satchel over the entire journey and grown used to its weight, but had not the time nor inclination to study the contents since leaving Skagen.

Fighting down another wave of panic, Ingelbert picked up the satchel and placed it in his lap, gently pulling the flap back. The snow was still coming down, and though the trees offered some shelter, Ingelbert did not want to risk any of the loose pages. Only one bound book lay within the satchel. The great green tome. The elven war ledger. Reaching in, Ingelbert removed the book, then set it atop the satchel, raising his knees and making a lectern with his legs. He hunkered over the book, adjusting his cloak so that it fell protectively over the ancient, leather cover.

Reverently, Ingelbert opened the book, choosing a page towards the exact middle to better distribute the weight across his legs. The elvish runes warmly welcomed his eyes, no longer the ephemeral, shifting mystery they once were. Ironically, he had turned to a list of foodstuffs and he tortured himself reading accounts of field rations. The Pig Iron Rebellion had been a time of great hardship and the armies of the displaced Seelie Court had not eaten well, but even dried fruit and something described as "imperishable loaf" sounded a sumptuous feast to Ingelbert. He imagined the Fae resistance fighters, a thousand years ago, waking in rough camps such as this to face another day of battle and loss.

They were dubbed rebels by the Goblin Kings, but in truth, they were fighting to reclaim what was stolen from them. Their island, their lives. It gave Ingelbert a small amount of renewed mettle to know that many throughout history had found themselves opening their eyes to days frightful and foreign. Of course, Airlann had never known Winter, so no elven soldier ever awoke to a morning as cold as this. Still, Ingelbert was warmer now. The presence of the book had calmed his thoughts and his shivering had ceased.

Beneath his gaze the runes were a balm, nestled in a reassuring blanket of old pages.

As he continued to read, he noticed with dismay that one of the symbols was distorted. He had been so careful to keep the snow from falling upon the book, but a stray flake must have drifted past his cloak, settling on the page to melt and sully the ancient ink. Carefully, Ingelbert went to blot the offending spot with the cuff of his shirt, but when the wool touched the page, nothing changed. There was no moisture. Even now, the rune was continuing to change, the distortion spreading to the surrounding runes. Was the protection spell reasserting itself, returning the contents of the book to the cipher that foiled Ingelbert for so long?

No, the opposing page remained unchanged. The change was isolated, contained, a few runes coalescing into new shapes, but the language remained discernible. Ingelbert could still read what formed before his eyes, which widened as the runes settled.

Wake me.

Beneath these words, the existent letters again began to shift. The runes reformed, the same as before, but there was a slight difference in the movement. A strain. A struggle. Ingelbert could see and feel a great effort as the contents of the book reworked themselves.

Save me.

From the edge of camp came a rapid succession of soft thuds, snatching Ingelbert's attention away from the tome.

Clutching his cloak tight under his chin, Ingelbert rose slowly, peering in the direction of the sounds. They had ceased almost immediately.

Three. Ingelbert thought there had been three.

He waited, standing in a half crouch on his pine mattress, keeping his eyes fixed on the dell's borders as he returned the book to his satchel. In the gloom, he spied movement in the trees and let out a relieved breath when he recognized Skrauti coming back from watch. Ingelbert almost called to him to ask about the noise, but then, mindful of those still slumbering, decided against it.

Looping the satchel across his body, Ingelbert hobbled past the fire to meet the approaching dwarf.

He was only paces away when he saw the arrow buried in Skrauti's throat. Two more shafts were lodged in his chest. The dwarf shambled forward, eyes staring vacantly, his mouth slack, the dirge emerging as a choked mangle from his ruined windpipe.

Ingelbert almost cried out, but something punched hard into his shoulder. He heard that same strange thud and was knocked backward onto the earth, forcing the wind out of him in a nauseating rush. Looking over with watering eyes, Ingelbert saw an arrow shaft protruding from his right shoulder, just below the collar bone. Then the pain came. Ingelbert screamed, his cries cut short as another wave of agony forced his jaw to clench.

Skrauti's corpse was upon him now, grasping at him with horrifying strength, trying to seize his throat. A scything blade struck and the wight's head tumbled from its shoulders. Fafnir appeared and hauled Ingelbert to his feet.

"Move!" the Chain Maker yelled, pushing Ingelbert towards the deepness of the trees.

Arrows were raining down upon the camp, arcing over the trees, hissing as they fell. One of the dwarrow porters had been slain before he could rise, his body afoul with shafts. Next to Ingelbert, another fell with an arrow in his leg. Before the poor dwarf could rise, a second took him in the eye. Ingelbert tried to run, but the arrowhead tore into his shoulder as he moved, the pain causing his knees to buckle. A powerful hand grabbed him under his uninjured arm, helped steady him. It was Ulfrun. She too was bleeding and Ingelbert saw arrows sticking out of her upper arm and thigh. Together they made for the shelter of the forest.

Ingelbert leaned against a tree and turned back to the dell.

Near the center, Fafnir stood firm, head and eyes raised skyward, his sword gripped in one hand, a runestone in the other.

Arrows began to fly off course, deflected by the wizard's will.

Dozens of shafts spun away, but the lightening sky was awash with arrows. Another volley crested the tops of the trees, a swarm loosed from a hundred bows. Ingelbert's heart sank. Too many to ward. Fafnir watched them come and as they began their dreadful descent, the runecaster let forth a wrathful cry, flinging his arms to the side in a gesture of scorn. The tide of arrows parted down the middle, thrown aside with such celerity that they scattered into the upper branches of the trees.

The porter with the arrow through the eye began to rise as a wight. Fafnir quickly stepped forward and beheaded him with a clean stroke. The remaining three had retrieved their shields and held them aloft against the onslaught of falling missiles, two gathering around Fafnir, the other protecting the recumbent form of Hengest.

"Remain here," Ulfrun said.

The giantess sprinted back into the dell, making straight for Hengest. Fafnir took notice and focused his powers on the arrows falling near her. Ulfrun scooped Hengest off the ground and ran back for the safety of the trees, but another arrow caught her in the shoulder blade as she fled, causing her to grunt, but not to slow her steps. The dwarrow were not far behind. Ingelbert joined them as they fled, leaving the dell behind to dash between the trees. The exertion made him woozy, and he kept a hand pressed to his wound as he ran, trying to staunch the blood flow. The forest was not vast. Soon, a break in the trees appeared ahead, the bright white of a field bathed in snow and morning sun shining between the trunks. As they emerged from the tree line, Ingelbert came to a halt along with his companions.

The sun was not all that awaited them.

Warriors were arrayed in the field, draped in cloaks and mail, festooned with weapons. Helms adorned their heads and beards covered their faces, heavy with frost. Ingelbert calculated at least three score were gathered, waiting.

A trap.

A low growl issued from Fafnir's throat and he stepped forward, boldly approaching the assembled fjordmen.

"You are bonded to Arngrim Crow Shoulders?" the Chain Maker demanded harshly, stopping halfway between the tree line and the line of warriors.

One in the group answered. "Aye. He is our jarl."

Fafnir chuckled bitterly at this and Ingelbert was surprised to see him sheath his sword. "Likely he has offered up much treasure to the man who takes my head."

"To the man who slays Fafnir Rune-Wise," the same warrior confirmed, "his weight in hoard."

"Much treasure," Fafnir repeated. "Yet you bring sixty to do a deed that will be rewarded only to one. And twice as many men in the woods behind, coming up on us even now. Many men for the weight of but one to receive as payment. Mayhaps, Crow Shoulders warned many of you would die in this pursuit? A noble jarl, to speak so true."

"We do not fear death," the warrior proclaimed.

Ingelbert did not doubt it. This was Middangeard. The fjordmen left all their possessions to the firstborn son, leaving the younger issue to seek wealth by the sword. The Tin Isles had long been plagued by the raids of lesser sons seeking their fortune. So it had been for centuries, leaving the fjordmen inured to peril. The chance of one receiving a chest of rings and jewels was enough to inspire a hundred.

"You fear not death as an end," Fafnir said. "But what if it is not your end?" The wizard gestured back to the trees with a sweep of his arm. "Even now, one of my kindred lies dying. My own apprentice. Should he breathe his last while any of you lie slain, he will rise and call you from death with his song. Three of my loyal dwarrow yet live! Each of us that falls will become vættir and you, dead men, will not be deaf to our dirge. You too will rise. You fear not death, but to become draugr, is that a curse you dare court?"

Ingelbert watched a ripple of uncertainty pass through the warriors. Draugr was the name given to the walking dead of mortal man, a tragic offshoot of the vættir. They did not heed the Corpse Eater's call, but despised life as much as the dead dwarrow which spawned them.

The spokesman for Arngrim's men stepped forward, brandishing his axe. "Dwarrow do not rise if they have no head. We will just be sure to cut yours off before you die."

"Severing heads will be difficult with blades so dull," Fafnir said, raising a fist. A crumbling substance fell from the runecaster's clenched fist, staining the snow beneath a dingy orange. Ingelbert detected the distinct odor of rust upon the air. A rapid crepitation emitted from the warriors' weapons, causing several to let sword and axe fall from their hands in alarm as the blades were suddenly, violently, blunted. Fafnir opened his hand, allowing the wind to snatch the pile of powdery rust from his fingers, leaving only a glowing runestone behind.

"Now," the wizard intoned, drawing his sword once more. "Who will be the first to come try and take my head?"

The dwarrow porters rushed out to stand beside their lord, spears leveled. Ulfrun lay Hengest upon the ground, leaving him in Ingelbert's care with a nod, then strode out to join the dwarrow.

She bristled with arrows and bled as she walked, but her steps did not falter. Flexing her fingers, the giantess took position behind the dwarrow.

The fjordmen faltered, the loquacious one stepping back among his comrades.

"You!" Fafnir cried, singling the man out with a point of his sword. "Tell Arngrim Crow Shoulders that his pernicious deeds will not be forgotten. He dares to assault my people, raze our Warden Trees, to despoil our hallowed ground, to make war on me! I will remember! I will remember the pitiful, mewling mortal suckling that dared to so slight the dwarrow. And before his short life ends, I will exact the measure of these injuries upon him and his line." The wizard gestured dismissively with his outstretched blade. "Leave here and take you that message to your jarl. Or stand firm and I will merrily seed this frozen ground with your skulls."

Ingelbert swallowed hard, waiting for the men to make their choice. The tension drew on for what seemed an endless string of pounding heartbeats, then one of the fjordmen bent and snatched his fallen sword aggressively from the snow.

"Fucking dwarrow," he cursed, then cuffed the man next to him hard with an elbow, encouraging him to pick up his own dropped weapon. He did so, and then they all began to rearm themselves, their fury growing with each hand filled with iron.

So. It would be blood.

The fjordmen charged, screaming as they churned the snow.

Above the howling, Ingelbert heard a clatter as the dwarrow porters locked their shields. Ulfrun widened her stance, her sinewy legs bending to receive the charge. The giantess and the runecaster were formidable, but they were still outnumbered more than ten to one.

The fjordmen covered the distance and Ingelbert heard their weapons strike the dwarrow shields. The group enveloped Fafnir's band and soon all were lost from sight, save Ulfrun, who had turned to face the men attacking at the rear. With a vicious backhand she sent a man careening over his fellows, his feet leaving the ground. He fell hard to the snow and did not rise. The weapons of the warriors rose and fell about her and Ulfrun's face became a fixed grimace as the blows rained down, but Fafnir's spell was potent and the blunted blades drew no blood. Yet Ingelbert despaired. How long could Ulfrun hold out before she succumbed to the relentless bludgeoning?

A snapping sound came from behind Ingelbert. He froze, holding his breath. More sounds of movement came through the woods. Many footsteps, moving without concern for furtiveness.

The archers, come to join their fellows. Sinking to his knees beside the still form of Hengest, Ingelbert squeezed his eyes shut and waited for a final arrow in the back.

A low panting settled around him and Ingelbert opened his eyes to find himself surrounded by storulvir. The great wolves stared attentively at the battle in the field ahead.

"The Chain Maker's gone and found himself another fight."

Ingelbert turned towards the rough voice and found Kàlfr the Roundhouse standing behind him, the greataxe propped on his shoulder covered with gore. Thorsa stood next to her lover, her own blade bloody. Blood was also in her flaxen hair and splattered across her flushed face. The Bone Chewers each had a crazed look in their eyes, a suffusion of violent passions, barely contained.

Kàlfr's corded muscles were swollen with power, his bare torso steaming in the cold. An arrow was lodged in Thorsa's brigandine, just below the breast, but the she-dwarf took no notice of it. The maws of the surrounding wolves were stained a grisly pink.

Ingelbert surmised he had no more to fear from the archers who ambushed their camp.

He shot a glance back to the battle. Ulfrun still stood, swatting her foes aside with a purloined shield.

"Help them," Ingelbert pleaded, casting a look at the Bone Chewers.

"Not why we are here," Kàlfr said simply.

He and Thorsa approached, setting their weapons down and picking Hengest up off the ground. Together they draped him across the back of one of the storulvir, Thorsa keeping a steadying hand on her unconscious husband. She looked out across the field, her eyes blazing with intoxicated triumph.

"Come," she said. "Let us go."

Kàlfr grunted an assent and retrieved their weapons.

Ingelbert snatched at his arm. "You cannot leave them to die!"

The Roundhouse smiled through his fiery beard, relishing the moment. "Fafnir believes in a fated end. Let him discover if this is his."

The bald dwarf broke free of Ingelbert's grasp without effort and began to walk away, Thorsa and his wolves following.

Ingelbert clutched his wounded shoulder and, with a groan of pain, lurched to his feet.

Ulfrun still battled on. Men lay broken around her, but far fewer than those that still stood. With great effort, Ingelbert turned his back on her and went after the Bone Chewers.

"Please!" he called at Thorsa's back, struggling not to stumble as he hurried to catch up. "You must go back!"

"My uncle deserves no aid, mortal," the she-dwarf replied without turning or slowing. "You too should abandon him."

"What of Ulfrun?" Ingelbert pressed.

"The giantess is nothing to me."

His strength waning, Ingelbert had no more breath for further protestations. He continued to pursue the savage dwarrow, not knowing what else to do. He caught up with them when Kàlfr called a halt in the remains of the dell camp to retrieve the headless corpse of the porter Fafnir had cut down. The sight of the bald dwarf shamelessly loading the body onto the back of a wolf filled Ingelbert with disgust.

"Why do you do this?" he asked weakly from the edge of the dell. "Why do you debase yourself so?"

"Hold your tongue," Thorsa warned, her voice cold, her countenance afire.

Ingelbert looked at her and his disgust increased. "And you," he said, heedless. "You are the greatest mystery. Why come back for your husband when you flagrantly rut with another like a farm animal?"

The tree next to Ingelbert's head shuddered with a resounding crack and his face was stung with flying wood chips.

Thorsa's axe, flung from Kàlfr's hand, was buried deeply in the trunk.

"Enough," the Roundhouse said, his voice dangerously calm. "There is your answer, man child. Power. We do not quail from what we must do to regain the strength that was once ours. The Corpse Eater cursed us, but that same curse offered us an end to the affliction our huldu cousins bestowed when they fled to Airlann. Magic dubbed them faithful and lifted them on high, the true elves, while we were named the svartálfar, black elves, and left stunted, withered and frail. Kàlfr the Roundhouse will not be weak. But neither will I abandon Middangeard and walk the Tin Isles to bask in the Magic of the huldu as Fafnir does. No doubt you have seen him there, hale and strong, color in his flesh and fire in his beard. Such is as we dwarrow should be. But not skulking there in Airlann, standing proud here in Middangeard."

"You do not wish the Corpse Eater slain," Ingelbert realized aloud. "If she dies, the curse of the vættir ends and you are denied your wretched source of power. That is why you will not help Fafnir. You do not want his quest to succeed."

"His quest will not succeed," Kàlfr snorted with assurance, turning his back once more to leave the dell.

Ingelbert felt his mouth fill with sour spit. He stared at the back of the dwarf's bald scalp. This half-clad barbarian and his arrogance was offensive. So confident in his prowess, his crude strength, all gained from consuming the cold, dead flesh of his own kind. Thorsa too was crossing the dell, on Kàlfr's heels, the doting mate. They were animals. Worse, they were scavengers. Carrion.

Vile and proud.

The storulvir followed the dwarrow, padding along dutifully.

There were near thirty of them with the Roundhouse, all large and fearless, comfortable in this frozen wilderness. But for all their storied cunning, they too, like the dwarf they followed, were nothing but up-jumped animals. And animals needed to be mastered.

Ingelbert reached into the mind of one of the giant wolves.

The animal brain was a red miasma of heat and hunger, but there was something more, a light anchored in the fires of instinct. It was the effulgence of thought, the knowledge of loyalty. Within that light Ingelbert could see the exceptional intelligence of the storulvir that raised them out of the mere primal. They possessed language, understanding, free will, even compassion. All of these were housed and fed by a single, glorious flame.

Ingelbert snuffed it out.

The first wolf yelped, its steps made clumsy by the spasm that ran through its body as its affinity died. The rest of the pack halted at the sound, turning to face their stricken sister. Ingelbert took the rest of their minds in one swoop, stamping out their lights and reducing them to beasts. The storulvir began to growl, low rumblings coming from deep in their broad chests. Their fangs were bared, their hackles raised. The Bone Chewers paused, confusion spreading across their faces.

"Kàlfr? What is—?"

Three of the storulvir barreled into Thorsa, cutting off her words as they dragged her to the ground. The Roundhouse screamed at the wolves, trying to call them off, but they paid him no mind, their bodies shaking as they savaged the fallen she-dwarf. Thorsa's cries were shrill and terrified. Kàlfr raised his axe, preparing to strike, still yelling at the wolves to cease. Before he could bring the blade down, the pack attacked him.

The dwarf was fast, and dodged the first pouncing animal, his face a motley of confusion and rage. The next two wolves gave him no choice and Kàlfr brought his axe around in a vicious swipe, severing the head from the first and caving in the skull of the second in a single blow. Kàlfr cried out with anguish as the pair died. The others approached more carefully, spreading out to encircle the dwarf, their heads low. The three who brought Thorsa down left their prey to join the others, muzzles covered in fresh blood. Kàlfr pleaded with the wolves as they drew closer, but on the storulvir came, relentless. It was not for his own life that the dwarf begged.

It was for theirs.

The storulvir rushed in and Kàlfr's axe swung. The Bone Chewer was fast, fueled by vættir flesh, and his blade became a whirl of steel, scattering blood and the broken bodies of wolves.

And Kàlfr the Roundhouse sobbed as he butchered the pack.

When it was over, the dwarf fell to his knees in the center of the slaughter, his axe falling from his hands.

Ingelbert approached him slowly, ignoring the intense pain in his shoulder. Kàlfr held one of the dead wolves, embracing its large head as he wept.

"Power?" Ingelbert asked as he stood over the dwarf. "You have none, savage."

The Bone Chewer looked up at him, overcome with grief, though not yet broken. There was naked wrath in his streaming eyes.

"You have a choice," Ingelbert told him. "Live with what you have done, if you can. Or test me further with an attempt at vengeance. Choose the first and you may leave this dell, though I wonder, with so much of their blood upon you, will the storulvir ever again accept you? Choose the second, and it will be the end of you, Kàlfr the Roundhouse."

The dwarf's eyes flitted over to where Thorsa fell. Ingelbert followed his gaze. The she-dwarf had already risen, but the storulvir had mauled her so viciously, she could not stand. The wight which had been Thorsa crawled through the snow, one arm pulling while the other reached out for Kàlfr.

"Make your choice," Ingelbert said.

Kàlfr tore his eyes away from Thorsa and, gently laying the head of the great wolf on the ground, he rose. Picking up his axe, he fled the dell.

The wight continued to crawl towards Ingelbert, craning her neck upward to keep him within her empty sight. He watched her slow, pitiful progress for a while, fascinated and repulsed.

When she finally reached him, he allowed her to grip his ankle briefly, feeling the strength given to dwarrow in death in her curling fingers. With a disdainful kick, he released himself, walking over to retrieve the axe that Kàlfr had thrown into the tree. Ingelbert wrenched it free then strode back to Thorsa and, placing his foot on the back of her head, forced it down into the snow. He chopped down with the axe, severing the neck through with a single cut.

A crash of branches caused Ingelbert to look around.

Bantam Flyn came rushing into the dell, sword drawn. The knight was breathing heavily and the sight of the carnage in the ruined camp brought him to a halt. He stared wordlessly for a moment, taking in all the bodies, then looked at Ingelbert.

"Inkstain? What happened?"

"The storulvir turned on the Bone Chewers," Ingelbert told him.

"Why?"

"I know not," Ingelbert lied. "But there is no time for questions. Fafnir and Ulfrun need your aid. They fight the fjordmen." He pointed. "Go. Through the trees eastward and you shall find them. Hurry!"

The coburn nodded and ran off. Ingelbert hoped he would not be too late.

The agony in his shoulder was dreadful and he looked to see what could be done, surprised to find the arrow was not the only thing causing his pain. Gasten perched upon him, though Ingelbert had no recollection of him landing. The owl's head revolved lazily, looking across the horror of the dell. His talons were sunk deep into Ingelbert, piercing his flesh and drawing blood.

Flyn knelt in a pile of bodies.

He had hoped at least one of the fjordmen would yield, but the warriors of Middangeard fought to the death. His charge had taken them by surprise, shattering their ranks. Their mail was as silk beneath Coalspur's blade and many fell before they knew what attacked them. Flyn's entry into the battle had given Ulfrun a moment to rally. And a moment was all the giantess needed. She waded back into the fray, breaking limbs and smashing skulls, tossing broken men aside. Moving with a brutal grace, Ulfrun won through to stand at Flyn's side and together they came to Fafnir's aid. No longer surrounded, the Chain Maker and his dwarrow went on the offensive. Once again, Fafnir sang as he fought. The Lay of the Sword-Dale, that is what Hengest named it. This time, the dwarf was not present to translate, but Flyn remembered what the dworgmál words meant and he felt them provide strength to his sword. The remaining three porters were even more bolstered by the music and not one of them was laid low. Unlike Flyn, they gave the fjordmen no chance to surrender.

Breathing heavy, eyes fixed on the ugly pink slush surrounding the fallen, Flyn shook his head. These men might have given voice to where Deglan had been taken, but they all lay lifeless upon the ground. The crunch of snow signaled Fafnir's approach.

"I feared you lost," the Chain Maker said.

Flyn did not bother to look up when he answered.

"Hakeswaith took Deglan. I followed. But the fjordmen got to them before I did. They have been taken. I know not where."

"To Arngrim Crow Shoulders' fortress at Bólmr, no doubt," Fafnir replied.

Flyn stood and faced the wizard. "Then that is where we must go."

"We have not the numbers, Bantam Flyn," Fafnir said, then gestured to the warriors littering the snow. "These were just a portion of Crow Shoulders' strength. To attack him at his stronghold would be folly."

"You said you would do battle with this man when the wights were destroyed!" Flyn proclaimed.

"Now is not the time."

"I cannot simply leave Deglan behind!"

"You must."

The two words punched Flyn in the gut. It was not the bluntness which affected him, nor the placid expression on Fafnir's face when he uttered them. It was the truth that struck hard.

Flyn had wanted Deglan gone, even if only in a moment of anger. But fate had taken that moment and stretched it until his friend was now beyond his reach. He had feared it when the riders escaped him, a fear which solidified when he found the stor-ulvir slain, ridding him of any hope of tracking the horses. It mattered not that Fafnir knew whither they were bound, the dwarf was right, they could not hope to assault a position of strength. A part of Flyn wanted to throw curses in the Chain Maker's face, damn his caution and his quest. He could rescue Deglan alone or die in the attempt.

That was the old Flyn, the reckless Flyn, the very Flyn that Deglan had so often chastised him for being. The old mushroom would not respect him for throwing his life away in a vain display of pointless pride. Flyn had to remedy his mistake, not feed it with more foolhardy impulse. He had to trust that the old stoat could keep himself alive.

"I pledged you my aid," Flyn told Fafnir. "And you have it. But when this is done and the Corpse Eater lies dead, I ask you to return that aid and help me rescue Deglan Loamtoes."

Fafnir met his gaze firmly. "I swear it."

Fighting a sickening in his gut as he came to terms with his choice, Flyn slung Coalspur over his shoulder. "There is something you must see."

Without a backward glance, Flyn led Fafnir back to the dell.

Ulfrun must have followed, for he heard the giantess mutter a curse at the sight of the butchered storulvir. They picked their way through the carnage, towards the only living things remaining in the dell.

Hengest had regained consciousness, but awoke to a living nightmare. Weeping, he clutched Thorsa's severed head between his hands, his forehead pressed into hers. Inkstain stood precisely where Flyn had left him, staring vacantly at the grieving dwarf. The owl upon his shoulder swiveled its head to look at Flyn and the others as they approached.

Fafnir's face was unreadable, but he went straight to Hengest and gripped the beardless dwarf's shoulder, standing patiently until he composed himself. Setting the head of his wife gently on the snow, Hengest wiped his eyes and stood, then turned to face Fafnir.

"I offer gratitude for my life, Chain Maker," Hengest said, his voice still thick with tears. "I know it was your craft which delivered me from death."

Fafnir accepted this wordlessly, then glanced at Thorsa's ravaged corpse.

"Kàlfr the Roundhouse will pay for this," he said gravely.

"Vengeance is wasted on him," Hengest pronounced. "He chose to walk a cursed path. As did Thorsa. I was bound to her by marriage and stood with her as loyalty demanded. She entwined us with Kàlfr and I suffered it, but death has sundered our bond and I am free. A road of revenge would only fetter my life to the Roundhouse once more, and that I will not do."

"Then which road will you now take, Hengest Half-Rune?"

Fafnir asked.

"The one which leads to the end of the vættir, Chain Maker," Hengest answered, his voice hardening. "You once entreated me to walk it with you. If my past abjurations could be forgiven, I would join you now."

"Ever was your fate linked to this quest," Fafnir said. "I saw it centuries ago and ensured you became my apprentice. Gladly do I accept your return. Now, join your craft with mine and let us see to the hurts of our companions."

Flyn was uninjured and rested against a tree while the two runecasters turned their healing arts on Inkstain and Ulfrun. Both had suffered arrow wounds and the giantess was covered in a tapestry of weals from the battering she had endured at the hands of the fjordmen. Inkstain did not so much as wince when the arrow was removed from his shoulder and Flyn found himself watching the man with growing disquiet.

Deglan had warned him that Crane had become dangerous.

Certainly, he had changed, toughened, but in the harshness of Middangeard such qualities were needed to survive. Indeed, Flyn would have found it a wonder if Crane had remained unaffected by the travails they had all endured. Still, there was a coldness to the man not born from journeying through the hoary wastes, a distance that went beyond his usual propensity for solitude. Fafnir had claimed Crane was a burgeoning wizard, and even with Flyn's almost complete ignorance of Magic he could sense the sorcery surrounding the man. That bloody big owl was only the most obvious manifestation of Inkstain's power. Flyn felt it a small betrayal to be suspicious of one he counted as a member of the Order, but he was not certain the chronicler would lay claim to similar affection. Best to trust Deglan's word and count the man as dangerous, but Flyn would also trust his own instincts and continue to count him a friend as well. On a quest such as this, dangerous companions were an asset, especially when dangerous enemies abounded.

"Fafnir," Flyn said. "We need to reach a place of safety. Somewhere we can rest. Regroup."

The Chain Maker glanced up from tending Inkstain just long enough to signal he had heard, but did not answer until the chronicler's bleeding had ebbed.

"There is such a place," the wizard said at last. "Indeed, it has been our destination since we landed on the shores of Middangeard. A few more days' journey and we shall enter the Downward Fields."

Flyn noticed Hengest stiffen slightly, his attention briefly diverted from Ulfrun's wounds. The giantess too looked up sharply at Fafnir's words.

"Your people will suffer the presence of outsiders there, Chain Maker?" she asked.

When Fafnir answered, his voice, like his countenance, was tinged with darkness. "They will have no choice."

TWENTY-THREE

"So. People do live here," Deglan muttered to himself.

He lurched forward, his spine bending as the fjordman's fist struck his kidney.

The blow did not require much effort on the warrior's part, as Deglan was riding in front of the man, wedged uncomfortably between him and the pommel of the saddle. The punch was a welcome distraction from the ache of his crushed balls. Now he could look forward to pissing blood out of his already swollen genitals.

He said no more, but through watery eyes surveyed the tiny thorpe which the horsemen now approached. It was the first settlement Deglan had seen since arriving in Middangeard. The frozen land was sparsely populated, he knew, but Fafnir had taken special pains to avoid all contact with other folk, traversing only the deepest wilderness. The riders keeping Deglan company had no such designs. They had ridden through the cold night and now, not long after dawn, came upon a miserable cluster of buildings skulking in the snowy plains.

The thorpe consisted of maybe a dozen huts scattered around a long, low hall. In the early, weak light Deglan spotted several of the inhabitants from a distance, mostly women and children, but they quickly vanished into their mean houses as the column of horses drew closer. A few men watched them with wary eyes. Their willingness to remain in the open bespoke no courage.

They had the look of small game animals, fearful that running would only entice the predators. Like most Middangearders, the men of the thorpe were tall, fair of hair and beard, but they had the drawn, thin look of the slowly starving. One of the warriors barked something as he reined up, causing several of the men to scurry into their huts. They returned almost immediately with bread and sloshing horns, handing them up to the horsemen with deference.

Deglan heard the man behind him take a noisy pull from his filched horn, and felt liquid spill down his back as the lout dribbled. Deglan hissed involuntarily as the brew chilled his skin.

The smell of mead rose in the air and the warrior laughed at his discomfort, tossing the horn carelessly away before dismounting. A villager waited nearby, nervously offering a half loaf of dark bread.

The warrior snatched the bread with one hand and used the other to drag Deglan unceremoniously from the saddle. For once, he was grateful for the snow. He tumbled from the horse's back and would likely have broken a bone were it not for the drift that broke his fall.

The rough laughter of the other warriors echoed through the pale morning as they got down off their horses and began ungraciously seizing all that was offered by the groveling peasants. Struggling to stand, Deglan grimaced. He had often heard the fjordmen were as ruthless raiding their own people as they were the shores of the Tin Isles. Now he believed it. One loaf of bread was likely an entire day's food for any one of these poor families.

To his relief, his captors offered him nothing to eat. He did not wish to partake in this shameful pilfering of the destitute, but hungry as he was, he was not certain he could have resisted had they thrown him a crusty heel. Instead, his riding companion grabbed him by the collar and half shoved, half carried him into the long hall. It was dim and smoky within, the odors of animal and man oppressive, but Deglan closed his eyes with near ecstasy at the warmth of the room.

A few old men and women occupied the hall, their faces resigned to the unfortunate presence of their guests. Hakeswaith was kicked through the door, his ugly face bleeding from multiple small wounds. Together, they were herded into a corner of the hall and told with gestures to sit upon the floor. Deglan did as he was bid, reveling in the chance to be indoors, near a fire. He leaned back against the wall and stretched his legs out in front of him, wincing as the circulation returned, setting fire to his cramping muscles. Hakeswaith said nothing, probing gingerly at his split lip and welted forehead, results of their abduction.

Last night, the warriors had ridden boldly into their little camp, surrounding Deglan and the whaler in seconds. Deglan knew little of the fjordmen language and Hakeswaith had but a few words, none of which helped him when three of the warriors had come down off their mounts and beat him into submission. Not that Hakeswaith offered any resistance from the onset. Even had the man not been a coward to his marrow, there was little that could have been accomplished by fighting back, save die. Deglan had received a few kicks and cuffs as they herded him towards the horses, but otherwise had been unmolested until this most recent strike to the side. Ten men had taken them captive, but now there were only eight, two having ridden off after a few hurried words of alarm not long after the journey began. They never returned.

The remaining eight now filled the hall, shouting demands and slumping down on the long benches surrounding the central fire. Soon, more food and drink was brought to them. These ravenous curs were going to leave the thorpe with nothing. Deglan noticed that only the menfolk served the warriors, keeping their younger women out of sight. Clever, but with the amount of mead the warriors were quaffing they were likely to grow lusty regardless and then the rapes would begin.

After eight thousand years, human cruelty still sent Deglan's mind reeling into deep contemplations fueled by bitter anger and despair. None had gone hungry in the Age of Summer when the elves ruled from the Seelie Court. At least, none in Airlann. Here in Middangeard, where Irial Elf-King held no dominion even in those glorious days, the mortal children still died in droves, knowing little but Winter and famine. Wives and daughters were still ravished by hands slick with the blood of their husbands, their fathers. A hard life, a hard land, and it bred hard people.

Indeed, these men were such a brutal sort that Deglan was unsure why he and Hakeswaith were still alive. During the overnight journey he had listened closely to the few exchanges between the warriors and, even with his nearly complete ignorance of their language, he caught a handful of words which rang familiar.

Words which even now, as the men stuffed themselves, continued to float through the gibberish of their talk.

Svartálfar.

Jarl.

Arngrim.

So, Deglan found himself at the mercy of men pledged to a warlord who hated dwarrow. Surely these louts knew the difference between a dwarf and a gnome. Deglan did not much fancy the idea of dying, but having his head cut off because some oaf with a grudge mistook him for a dwarf was unconscionable. No, if they meant to kill him he would have died at the campfire, not taken for a jaunt on horseback. And since they weren't feeding him, their destination must be close. Perhaps. He could do little but guess.

Whatever was in store for him, he could take it. This was not the first time he had been taken prisoner. Bruised testicles, the occasional punch, and mead spilled down his back was nothing compared to the mines of the Goblin Kings.

He tried never to think on those torturous years, but sometimes, even centuries later, a deep sleep would betray him, offering no succor, only vivid dreams of chains. His unconscious mind would plummet back into a suffocating world of tunnels and whips, the cackling of goblins and the fear of cave-ins. Flyn declared Deglan's hatred tiresome, but he had earned whatever enmity he chose to hold in his heart, earned it during the sixty-odd years he had spent in the iron mines of King Sweyn the Third.

Somewhere north of Black Pool, Deglan and three thousand other slaves labored, forced to dig for ore destined for the foundries of the goblins. Iron was deadly to all Fae, including goblins, but the fanatical armies of Red Caps wielded the poisonous metal with glee to better slaughter the enemies of their human overlords.

Not wishing to waste the lives of his devoted servants in the mines, Sweyn valued his gnomish slaves. They were a subterranean people and did not succumb to madness while living underground the way humans so often did. The king's loyal goblins likewise thrived in the deepness of the Earth and were exceptionally efficient taskmasters, taking great pleasure in the domination of their cousins.

But while the goblins held the lash, it was the dwarrow who kept the workers imprisoned.

Mercenary dwarfs flocked to Airlann after the Usurpation, to gloat at the fall of the elves and glut upon the revitalizing effects of the Source Isle so long denied them by the Seelie Court. It was dwarrow blacksmiths who brought steel to the Tin Isles, forging the chains which hobbled Deglan and his fellow slaves. It was dwarrow sellswords who stood sentry in the mines, paid with the stolen treasures of the elves. So no, Flyn's valorous ideals did little to sway Deglan's long-held hatred. He had nurtured it over decades swinging a mattock into the blessed Earth, feeling the venom of the whip and the eroding agony of endless hunger.

Fortunately, a schism in the succession of the Goblin Kings eventually weakened Black Pool. The city was divided and the conflict between Hogulent the First and Only and the self-styled Goblin Queen quickly drained their coffers. The dwarrow, unpaid, abandoned their guardianship of the mines, leaving the goblins alone to manage an army of slaves. There was a reason the chroniclers later dubbed the Fae uprising the Pig Iron Rebellion.

The fight against tyranny had begun the moment Penda Blood Coin supplanted the elves, but the path to victory, the path which eventually led to the Restoration, it began in the mines.

It rankled Deglan that some histories credited the dwarrow with the liberation of the mines, when in truth, all they had done was leave their posts. During the war, Irial had let the lie persist, probably even spread the rumor himself, the crafty elven bastard, knowing the allowance of the little falsehood would allow the dwarrow to change their allegiance. They may never have come to the side of the Rebellion if they knew there to be ill will. Irial painted his dwarven cousins as heroes and thus, forced them to live up to the legend. Faabar used to tediously opine that the entire dwarrow race should not be condemned for the deeds of a few sellswords, but Deglan preferred to boil his grudges in a stew. It was more sensible to hate all dwarfs, all goblins, rather than try and figure who was worth trusting among the lot. One lapse in judgment could be lethal, he had learned that in the mines. He certainly was not about to begin looking for the fjordman with a heart of honey in this rabble of raiders.

While the warriors caroused, Deglan took advantage of the chance to rest and closed his eyes, unconcerned for whatever might happen next. The recollections of his past enslavement, normally an unpredictable haunting in his dreams, now served to steel him against his current plight. Deglan fell asleep knowing he could endure whatever these bearded bastards doled out.

He was roused with a kick. Through the door of the long hall, day was still strong. Several of the warriors were rolling themselves drowsily off the benches. So, this stop had been for rest, not rapine. A mercy for the denizens of the thorpe. This time.

Hakeswaith was already on his feet, his cuts clotted and beginning to scab over. The whaler kept his head bowed, so that the permanent snarl of his bent jaw would not be mistaken for defiance. They stumbled out into glaring white, the cold an invisible yet solid force. Deglan was hoisted up onto a different horse by a different rider. It seemed the pleasure of his company was best shared. Hakeswaith too was made to ride double, but he was placed behind his appointed guardian, a testament to how little the raiders feared the short fisherman. Putting heels to their mounts, the riders passed quickly through the village, leaving only a few steaming piles of horseshit behind for payment.

The riders took advantage of their rested steeds and set a quick pace. The horses were a shaggy, hearty breed, well suited for the grueling slog across the frozen plains. Soon, they came to what must have passed for a road in Middangeard. In truth, it was nothing but a well-traveled track, a natural rise in the terrain allied with the constant passage of man and beast to defy the snow.

Guiding their horses onto the track, the men again spurred them to greater speed. The track provided a decent vantage of the surrounding land and Deglan noticed broad patches of shining ice scattered among the fields. They were the faces of frozen ponds, growing larger and more numerous as the miles crunched beneath the horses' hooves.

Daylight was beginning to fade behind a shroud of steely clouds when the column reached the end of the track. It led directly to the edge of a vast frozen lake stretching across the horizon. The warriors did not hesitate and urged their mounts onto the ice.

Deglan had thought the drifts of the plains had seemed unchangeable and endless, but they were nothing compared to the expansive loneliness of the lake. Flat, stark, unwelcome cold in every direction. Water, sullen and primeval, imprisoned by the grip of Winter, as far as could be seen. The wind grew stronger, encouraged by the retreating sun, and Deglan found even the memory of warmth banished. Gritting his teeth, he could not help but grunt as the cold clamped down on his bones.

Just when he thought he would shatter from shivering, he caught sight of the opposite shore. As the column drew closer, Deglan soon realized he was wrong. It was an island, or would have been had the water not hardened, making it accessible by foot. It was a sizable swath of land, seeming to grow directly out of the encircling ice. A few holts clung to the edges, but the island had been heavily forested and the birthplace of the trees had become their graveyard. A great fortress made entirely of timber sat enthroned upon the island. Even from a distance, Deglan espied the impressive ring of earthworks supporting the upright beams of a high palisade. Behind the curve of the wall loomed a wooden tower house, its bulk gradually tapering with each level until it ended in a peaked roof.

The riders reached the island and the track once again appeared, leading towards a squat gatehouse built into the wall of the ring fort. At the foot of the earthworks lay a wide trench, circumnavigating the fort save for a narrow land bridge in front of the gate. At a hail from the riders the gates began to open, creaking as they were pulled wider. As Deglan's horse crossed the mound of earth bridging the trench, he glanced down and bit back a curse.

Dead men stood in the moat, gaunt and still, some little more than skeletons. Their bony fingers clutched rusted weapons and rotting shields. Dented helms sat upon their brows and ragged mail draped their loathsome forms. The trench was thick with them, all imprisoned by a layer of ice that encased their feet. One turned its head and watched Deglan pass, the empty sockets of its eyes staring at him with cold vehemence.

Draugr. The corpses of men called to rise by the song of the vættir.

So, the jarl of this fortress ensured his men continued to serve him even in death. His ability to marshal them here at his holdfast and ensnare them in the moat bespoke sorcery. Deglan's shivering intensified as the column passed through the darkness of the gatehouse and emerged behind the walls.

Within the fortress, the track became a proper road, cobbled with stones and covered in wood shavings. The tower house stood at the junction of the road Deglan traveled and another that ran perpendicular. The roads divided the sprawling circular interior into four equal sections, each containing four longhouses built to form a square. Warriors came and went from these longhouses, utilizing the open yards between to train and tend their horses. The sixteen longhouses could serve as barracks for over a thousand men, Deglan estimated, though it did not appear that many were currently occupying the fort. He saw women too, even a few children, each going about some chore.

The column made directly for the central tower, and Deglan craned his neck as they rode beneath its shadow. The fjordsmen were not skilled masons, but their woodcraft was truly impressive.

The tower's posts and lintels fit soundly together, the framework sturdy and level. Every surface was carved with elaborate decorations. The heads of dragons and ravens emerged from the ends of rafters at each corner of the steeply sloped roof.

Thralls emerged and took charge of the warriors' horses as they dismounted before the large double doors. Deglan was again pulled from the saddle, though this time care was taken that he did not fall. Hakeswaith was made to stand beside him and together they were led into the tower.

It was dim within, the air thick with heat and wood-smoke.

Almost the entirety of the first level was a single chamber, a grand hall with a high ceiling. Curved archways of carved wood surrounded the room and supported the floor above. Impressive hearths, pregnant with fierce fires, were set into the walls and adorned with mantles carved to depict the hunting of beasts.

Twelve men occupied the hall, some lounging on the benches, others sitting upon the trestles. They laughed and joked with each other, their voices deep and cruel. They were big and well-muscled, a few with shaved scalps, the rest with hair wild and long. All were bearded, clad in the skins of wolf and bear. Broad swords and long knives hung from their belts, while long-hafted axes stood propped against the walls or resting upon the tables. They smelled of murder.

"Berserkers," Hakeswaith whispered tremulously.

Deglan waited for their escorts to punish the whaler for speaking, but no blows fell. The warriors had adopted the same timid manner displayed by the peasants of the thorpe, the predators now acting the prey. No one spoke. Indeed, it seemed as if their guards were hoping not to be noticed. The berserkers grew silent as the warriors approached, though they did not bother to so much as look their direction. They continued to lounge about, but there was a subtle change to their posture, a menace in every small movement.

A yawn. A scratch. A shifting of weight. Each concealed a threat of sudden, unstoppable violence. Deglan felt that each moment he remained in this room, he tested the forbearance of these killers.

A door at the rear of the hall thudded open and another large man entered, this one made all the bulkier by a voluminous cloak woven entirely of black feathers.

Arngrim Crow Shoulders.

A dark beard, streaked heavily with grey, grew from his hard jaw. A sword was sheathed at his side and he kept a hand resting on the pommel as he approached, his sharp eyes taking in the room without moving. As Crow Shoulders strode past the berserkers, Deglan was struck by the strong resemblance between the jarl and the twelve men. He now noticed that two of the berserkers were identical twins, and all of them looked at Arngrim with that face of begrudging respect worn only by a man's sons.

A woman followed the warlord at a respectful distance, dressed in the simple smock of a thrall. She kept her head bowed as she progressed through the territory of the berserkers, and several of them shared leers and grins. So, not their mother. Her hair was a deep brown, long but tied up into a serviceable tangle. Deglan found the age of mortals difficult to judge, but the woman was still well within her child-bearing years.

Arngrim Crow Shoulders stopped in front of Deglan and Hakeswaith, exchanging a few words with the warriors who had captured them. Questions, followed by quick answers. Arngrim appeared displeased, but it was difficult to discern for sure through the jarl's frown, which was etched in stone. He dismissed the warriors and they left the hall with haste.

Crow Shoulders stared at his new captives for a long moment, but between the two of them, only Deglan held his gaze.

Hakeswaith had become fixated on the ground between his feet.

Cocking his eyes towards the woman at his side, Arngrim spoke.

The woman raised her head, but did not look directly at anyone.

"He demands your names," she said in the language of the Tin Isles. There was no trace of accent. Yet another daughter of the Tin Isles forcibly taken from her home and spirited across the seas to live enslaved in this cold pit.

Deglan addressed Arngrim directly. "I am Deglan Loamtoes, formerly a Staunch of the Wart Shanks pledged to Goban Blackmud, Gnome-King. Recently I took residence with the Knights of the Valiant Spur and was the herbalist for that Order. Currently, I am in service to the Guild of Anglers in Gipeswic, who would pay handsomely for my return. The man with me is Hakeswaith, also in service to the same masters and equally valued." The whaler did nothing to add weight to this claim.

He only stood by, quaking, eyes downcast.

Still, the gnome army, coburn knights and the rulers of a wealthy city were not trivial allies to name. With luck, this man was no ignorant fool and would see the wisdom in keeping Deglan alive.

The woman relayed his answer to her jarl, hopefully with some accuracy. When she finished, Arngrim growled another question.

"He says that you are in league with the dwarrow wizard, Fafnir Rune-Wise."

Deglan's answer was simple. "No."

Arngrim needed no translation and his scowl deepened.

"Brami," he said, and one of the berserkers approached.

The man smiled, showing a mouthful of bright teeth behind a flaxen beard. In a motion almost too fast to see, he hammered a fist into Hakeswaith's ribs. The whaler cried out and fell to his knees. Over the whimpers, Arngrim asked another question.

"Where are the Downward Fields?" the woman translated.

Deglan searched his memory, but came up with nothing. "I do not know."

Arngrim again gestured over his shoulder. "Reifnir."

Another of the jarl's sons stepped forward.

"Wait," Deglan told the woman. "I speak the truth. I would tell him if I knew."

Reifnir's foot took Hakeswaith under the chin, splattering the floor of the hall with bloody spittle and broken teeth.

"Stop!" Deglan exclaimed. "I know of no such place!"

"Where are the Downward Fields?"

"I do not know. I swear it."

"Hrani."

"Dammit! No!"

The third berserker was laughing, motioning for his brothers to cheer for him. Hakeswaith lay upon his back, mumbling for mercy through his shattered mouth. Hrani circled him wolfishly, deciding how to hurt the man. Deglan dropped down, shielding Hakeswaith and extended an imploring hand at the fjordman.

"Please. He will not survive much more."

Hrani looked to his father, his pitiless eyes dancing.

Arngrim considered, then spoke two words.

Deglan's vision exploded with color, Hrani's backhand blow tossing him to the ground. Sharp pain floating in a dull, aching pressure. His nose was broken. Deglan swallowed blood, waiting for the numbness to take hold and relieve the agony. He spat, shook his head to clear the swimming, sickening splotches from his eyeballs and sat up.

Crow Shoulders stared down at him and asked the same question. The woman looked pained, keeping her own gaze averted from the bloodshed.

"Where are the Downward Fields?"

Deglan probed his throbbing skull for a place, any place, within Middangeard. "The Ironwood," he ventured. "The Downward Fields are in the Ironwood."

"Hadding."

One of the twins stepped forward, his red hair heavy with filthy braids.

"Buggery and shit," Deglan swore and braced himself for the blow.

The twin hopped forward, raising a foot aimed for Deglan's face. At the last second, he brought it down hard, stomping Hakeswaith's knee. Deglan heard the crunch of bone even over the whaler's wailing.

"Dogs!" Deglan screamed at them. "We do not have the knowledge you seek!"

Hakeswaith continued to howl and Deglan wished the man would pass out, but even that small mercy was denied him.

"Where are the Downward Fields?"

Deglan had no answer, he could not even hazard another lie. He needed to keep the punishments focused on him. Eight sons remained, all eager for their chance to inflict pain. Hakeswaith would not survive one more assault. Arngrim gave him little time to think.

"Tind."

As the next berserker stepped towards him, Deglan began to chuckle. He had not the answer to save himself, and Crow Shoulders would not be fooled by desperate lies. That left only the truth. The truth was he did not know, but that would not satisfy this man. But life consisted of many truths.

Deglan continued to laugh, blood flowing from his nostrils.

The son called Tind stopped, a look of confusion on his face.

These berserkers knew what it was to laugh while dealing death, but it seemed they had never encountered one who would laugh in the face of it.

"You brainless swine," Deglan guffawed, rising to his feet.

"You do this all wrong."

The woman remained silent, unwilling to deliver his insult.

"Tell them!" Deglan snapped at her.

Jumping at his outburst, the woman quickly repeated his words in the tongue of Middangeard. Arngrim's face grew grim and Tind surged forward with an upraised fist, but was held back by his father's hand. Deglan did not waste the chance.

"Hakeswaith is a coward," he told the jarl, relieved to hear the woman's voice right behind his. "He would tell you all you wished to know if it would avoid the spilling of his own blood. He knows nothing. I know only that you wish vengeance on Fafnir the runecaster. You hate the dwarrow and him most of all, for what he did to your ancestor, Tyrfing." Deglan took a step forward. If the man was surprised at his knowledge, he gave no sign. Ignoring the blood flowing from his nose, Deglan held the warlord's stare, allowing him to see the truth in what he said next. "You need not beat me, Arngrim Crow Shoulders. Or this poor man here. If you want Fafnir dead, I will gladly help you kill him."

He said no more and the words of the woman ended a moment after his own. Crow Shoulders peered down at him, looking for him to falter, for evidence of the falsehood.

The jarl tilted his head back slightly, towards his sons.

"Hervard. Barri."

The named men came forward, moving for Deglan. He let out a breath, resigned to his end. He did not care that his own life was about to end, but was bitter with the knowledge that Hakeswaith too would die. Deglan hated the whaler, but the lifetime habits of a healer told him that not saving a life was a failure. With a final, defiant grin at Crow Shoulders, Deglan closed his eyes and waited for the fists of the berserkers to fall.

Powerful hands grabbed him under the arms, lifting him bodily off the floor. He felt himself being carried backward and only when he heard the doors of the hall kicked open did he open his eyes. The two berserkers hauled him between them, taking one of the roads towards the palisade. Just before the gatehouse they turned, striking off across the yard towards a low structure built into the earthworks under the wall. Wooden timbers framed a stout door guarded by four warriors. Seeing the berserkers coming, one of the men fumbled with a ring of heavy keys and unlocked the door, pushing it aside. The berserkers flung Deglan through the open portal and he landed hard in the dust. The door was slammed shut before he could rise and he heard the key secure the lock.

Wiping fresh blood from his nose, Deglan got gingerly to his feet. The only light came from the sun intruding beneath the door and sneaking through the narrow spaces between the slats, but it was enough for Deglan. The cold chamber was dug out of the embankment supporting the walls. Towards the back, Deglan could see the thick timbers of the palisade peeking through the dirt.

A latticework of timber framing kept the room from caving in and was tall enough for a man to stand upright.

The sudden clanking of a chain caused Deglan to stumble backwards as a shadow detached itself from the far wall, growing as it stood. The thing took a step forward, then another. A third step brought a metallic snap as the chain went taut, preventing the figure from coming further. The blaze of light from under the door fell upon a clawed foot, three toes ending in long talons.

It was a coburn, naked and fettered. He was so tall, he was forced to stoop in the confines of the chamber. His feathers were filthy, but beneath the dirt Deglan could see they were a drab grey, the colors of smoke and ash. Even his comb and wattle were near black.

"I know you," Deglan said, his voice still hushed with alarm.

The coburn bowed his head slightly and when he spoke, his voice was deep and gravelly.

"Sir Wyncott, the Dread Cockerel, at your service."

TWENTY-FOUR

Flyn looked up at the range of sullen mountains dominating the horizon. Crowned with snow and clouds, the tops of the peaks stood out sharply against the midday sky. He estimated the foothills were only a mile or so distant, waiting across a stretch of tundra.

Fafnir stood out in the white field alone, his head raised skyward.

The wizard kept a steady watch on the sun, which was now beginning to reach its zenith above the peaks. The last few days, Fafnir had taken to traveling well ahead of the group, sometimes with Hengest, but more often in complete solitude. Since the death of Skrauti, he spoke but little, even to the remaining porters. Flyn and the others followed his path, rarely seeing the runecaster until their nightly camps. Now, nearing noon, they had caught up to him keeping this strange vigilance. Flyn, Inkstain and Ulfrun had instinctively paused, deciding it best to wait for some signal to proceed.

"The Crone Fells," Ulfrun announced, nodding up at the mountains. "Beyond you will find few owners of speech and no hearth-ships of mortal men. It is a land of hunger and frost."

Flyn squinted at the march of peaks and chuckled. "How does that differ from the lands we have crossed?"

The giantess smiled. "More trolls."

"Grand," Flyn said with little enthusiasm.

"You have walked but the tamed side of Middangeard, sword cock. Once in the northlands, you shall see why it is a place even we giants rarely venture."

"How long will it take to cross the fells?" Inkstain queried.

Though his words regarded the mountains, Flyn did not fail to notice the man's stare, like that of the owl on his shoulder, was fixed on Fafnir.

Ulfrun shrugged. "That would depend on which passes we take. But I do not believe we are to cross those breath-stealers. I wager the Chain Maker means to take us beneath."

"The Downward Fields," Flyn declared.

"Aye," the giantess said. "Likely the wizard looks now for an entrance."

Flyn found it difficult to imagine a place Ulfrun had not dared set foot. "You have not ever been there?"

"No giant has. It is a jealously guarded secret of the svartálfar."

"Then why allow us admittance?" Inkstain wondered aloud.

"We are the Foretold," Ulfrun replied, certainty in her voice.

"You put a great deal of faith in Fafnir's prophecy," Inkstain said. The chronicler's voice was so numb, Flyn could not discern if he was complimenting or chastising the giantess. Either way, Ulfrun's face shone with amusement.

"I am giant-kin. It is rare that I encounter something greater than myself. When such things are before me, I easily recognize them, Inkstained Crane."

"I wonder what manner of welcome we will receive in this secret dwarrow haven?" Flyn mused.

"One fit for a returning king," came a voice from behind.

They all turned to find Hengest standing nearby. The beardless dwarf had spent the morning bringing up the rear with the porters. Flyn had not even heard him approach.

Despite his initial grief, the death of Thorsa seemed to be having a salutary effect on Hengest. His shoulders no longer stooped with guilt, his face was less creased with malingering shame. He was allowing the blue dye to fade from his unruly hair, an affectation Flyn suspected the dwarf had taken on to better match the vital appearance of his Bone Chewer wife and her lover.

Beneath the woad, Hengest's head was as black as any dwarf's.

"They can crown me if they desire," Flyn jibed, "but I think they would come to rue my rule."

"He refers to the Chain Maker," Ulfrun said, laughing.

Flyn looked to Hengest. "Fafnir is a king?"

Hengest shook his head as he came to stand beside them.

"His ancestors established the Downward Fields in ages past. Fafnir was to inherit from his father, but the burdens of leadership did not sit well atop the weight of prophecy. Fafnir bequeathed his right to his brother Reginn, who has reigned since before I drew breath. So no, Bantam Flyn, Fafnir Rune-Wise is many things, but a king he is not. Still, the Chain Maker will be received with honor."

"Even though many dwarrow believe him to be mad?"

Inkstain asked with a hint of challenge.

Hengest did not rise to the goad, but merely gave a resigned nod. "As you say."

Inkstain turned his attention back to Fafnir, clearly bored with the younger rune-caster. Flyn tried to catch Ulfrun's eye to see if she found the chronicler's growing arrogance disturbing, but the giantess seemed oblivious. Not for the first time, Flyn wished Deglan were still with them.

Turning to Hengest, Flyn saw a phantom of the old hauntings upon the dwarf's face.

"What ails you?" he asked.

Hengest took a deep breath, then shook himself out of his sudden malaise. "It is simply that I have not been here for a long time and never thought to return."

"This King Reginn," Ulfrun ventured. "He is your wife's sire?"

"You are more insightful than you appear, Breaker," Hengest replied without rancor. "Aye. Thorsa would have one day ruled the Downward Fields with me by her side, but . . . her fate lay down darker paths."

"So it is grave news you bring home this day," Flyn said, placing a hand on the dwarf's shoulder.

Hengest snorted. "Thorsa was dead to her lord father long ago. He will be glad the shame she brought upon his house has ended."

"What birthed her ire?" Ulfrun asked, her curiosity still courteous. "She bore such hatred for the Chain Maker. What did he do to make her turn Bone Chewer?"

"Forgive me, Breaker, but I cannot answer you. Fafnir was once my master and my uncle by marriage. He is no longer either, but he is still my kin. It is not for me to tell you his tale. But you shall know it soon enough. You three are the Foretold. I believe that now. Though as Master Crane says, I was long blind to the truth of the Chain Maker's purpose. As the augury's champions, no answer will be kept from you and no respect denied you, but all must come from its rightful source."

Fafnir was now approaching and Flyn waited with the rest until he stopped before them. The Chain Maker's face was dour as he addressed the group.

"It is time," he said curtly. "Only those with the will to relentlessly pursue the luster of gold may enter the Downward Fields. Keep your eyes fixed upon the face of the sun as you cross the field. Do not avert your gaze until you have reached the lee of the mountain. The porters shall go first to bring news of our arrival. Then you, Hengest. Ulfrun, you shall follow. Then Sir Flyn and Master Crane. I will be last to ensure you all find your way."

With that, Fafnir commanded the porters to proceed with a wave of his arm. The three dwarrow began hiking across the snow without hesitation, single file, each with his head turned skyward.

Flyn watched as they grew distant. They were still in sight when Hengest began to follow. Ulfrun waited for a nod from Fafnir before beginning her own trek. The height of the giantess allowed her to remain visible long after the dwarrow were obscured by distance. Flyn's eyes were keen and he had no doubt he would be able to see Ulfrun even once she reached the shadow of the mountains. He must have blinked, for he lost sight of her for an instant when she neared the end of the field and, try as he might, he could not descry her again.

"Go ahead, Sir Flyn," Fafnir's voice urged. "Remember, do not avert your gaze from the sun."

Flyn adjusted his sword harness, then looked up at the bright disc in the sky before setting off. It was more difficult than he imagined. Within moments, he was certain his feet were not cutting a straight path, though it seemed the others had found no such difficulty. He had to will himself not to look down and make sure he walked a direct course. Unsteady as his strides felt, the sun was still directly before him. Surely if he had strayed too far, his head would be turned to keep it in view. He trudged on, his world nothing but an increasingly bright nimbus eclipsing his vision. His eyes began to water and he squinted against the brilliance, needing desperately to blink, to turn away. He would be blinded if he kept this up much longer. Where was the mountain? He had come far enough, the damn blazing should have dropped behind the peaks by now.

Flyn became aware of a change in the air. Warmth, so long absent, fought for dominion against the chill that had taken up permanent residence beneath his feathers. The wind had ceased howling. Flyn's vision was still dancing with coruscations, but at the edges the sky had grown dark. Taking another step, he no longer felt snow beneath his talons. No, it was stone. He blinked hard, finding the normal blackness behind his squeezed lids now incarnadine. Quickly, the blotches of red began to fade and Flyn opened his eyes to find Ulfrun standing in front of him. The giantess, her mouth open in wonder, still looked upward. Upward, where there was no sky, no sun.

A cavernous hall of carved stone loomed above, stretching up, ahead and away. Massive damasked pillars supported a ceiling shining with gilded decoration. Etched runes and carved knot-work bordered the grim visages of dwarf-folk, all worked in intricate gold.

Renderings of dragons and storms, lightning and mountains, eagles and trees, they stood out against countless other images Flyn could not decipher. Stone braziers were carved directly into the supporting columns, the flames within infusing the gold with a molten light. Flyn could see no end to the hall ahead and turned to look behind. A solid wall of carved stone greeted him, unadorned save for an arch of runes carved directly into the surface. From beneath this arch, Fafnir emerged supporting Inkstain, man and dwarf passing through the very stones as if they were no more solid than air. Crane's face was haggard and drawn.

"Is he well?" Flyn asked, hurrying to help support the stumbling chronicler. As he placed Inkstain's arm over his shoulder, Flyn noticed the owl was nowhere to be seen.

"He will be fine," Fafnir grunted. "He faltered in the face of the sun. It can be a difficult passage for some. Where is Hengest?"

"He went ahead," Ulfrun answered. "Said he must needs speak with the guardian of these halls."

Fafnir did not look pleased with this news, but said nothing.

A group of armored dwarrow warriors was approaching, the clink of their mail echoing upon the stones. Relinquishing Inkstain entirely to Flyn, the Chain Maker went to meet them. The warriors struck the butts of their pole-axes on the flagstones and bowed low at the sight of the wizard, though they quickly rose as Fafnir began speaking to them in dworgmál. As the dwarrow conversed, Flyn looked to Inkstain.

The man was conscious, but just now beginning to take in his surroundings, his face as slack with marvel as Flyn's must have been a moment before.

Ulfrun came to stand at the chronicler's other side. "Are you well, book master?"

Crane gave them both a reassuring, if tremulous smile. "I, uh, yes. I believe I am, um, fine."

Flyn gave the man's narrow chest a companionable rub.

"How do you feel?"

"Warm," Inkstain proclaimed, sniffing deeply.

"I wager even you had nearly forgotten how that feels," Flyn jibed.

With a nod of gratitude, Inkstain removed himself from Flyn's support and stood under his power.

Fafnir returned from his discussion with the warriors. "My friends. Welcome to Hriedmar's Hall. Soon you shall have much-needed food and rest, but first, please follow me."

Without waiting for a response, Fafnir turned on his heel and began swiftly walking down the vast hall. Flyn gave his companions an encouraging look and they all set off after the Chain Maker. The ten dwarrow warriors fell into step around them, their faces impassive beneath heavy steel helms. As they walked the length of the great hall, Flyn continued to survey the place with awe.

Next to him, Inkstain was absolutely gawking.

Clearly they were beneath the mountains, in a cavern too magnificent to fathom, yet nowhere could rough stone be seen.

The floor was paved in a flawless parquetry of polished granite.

From the light of the braziers, Flyn could see himself reflected in the flagstones. An endless gallery of smooth columns rose to form stalwart arches which buttressed a ceiling of ribbed vaulting almost too high to be seen. And everywhere were the patterns of gold, flowing through the carefully crafted rock, pulsing with firelight, arteries of artistry. The time it would have taken to fashion this impressive hall made Flyn's mind roil. Even the imposing towers and keeps of the Roost seemed as cottages compared to this display of dwarrow stonework.

So enthralled was he by the architecture, Flyn nearly failed to notice the population of dwarrow traversing the massive space, individuals and small groups going about their lives. Miners and masons pushed carts loaded with ore, while farmers coaxed shaggy mules to pull wains full of root vegetables. A band of drovers swatted at a herd of muskox, expertly guiding the lumbering beasts through the resplendent hall. Seeing such rustic pursuits housed beneath such grandeur was strange, yet Flyn felt he witnessed the last vestiges of a lost age, an age before the world was host to the brevity of mortal life. The egregious barbarity of the coburn, the boorish scrabble of human existence, these were born from a practical haste, a need to survive before the ineluctable end of life.

Elves and dwarfs had no such concern. The perfection of goldsmithing and masonry was pursued in concert with agriculture and husbandry, without disparity. A painstakingly crafted statue was valued the same as a well-bred animal. With near limitless time, all were artisans.

Still, there was an obvious paucity to the inhabitants when compared to the size of the hall. Flyn saw dozens of dwarrow, but thousands would not have filled the area in which he now walked.

The glory of the construction was undimmed, yet the ancestors of the builders were not thriving beneath the roofs of their forebears.

Fafnir had often said his people were suffering under the weight of a curse, one that could not be endured much longer. Flyn now saw the truth of those words. This subterranean haven was built to be a lasting legacy of prosperity, yet the waning dwarrow that walked through its gullet seemed lost within the majesty, erstwhile inheritors now reduced to nomads within their own bastion.

After a long walk, Fafnir turned and began making for one of the many yawning portals set into the side walls of the great hall.

It was not until they were nearer the archway that Flyn noticed a stout stone bridge leading to it, spanning a frothing canal. As they marched over the bridge, Flyn looked down to see sturdy boats navigating the waterway, bearing crews of dwarrow anglers and various cargo. Once over the bridge, Fafnir's entourage passed under the archway, which was thrice the height of Ulfrun, and entered a passage much smaller than the hall, though no less adorned.

Various chambers entered onto the corridor from either side. Most were barracks and storerooms, though Flyn did spy at least one room that had the look of a bakery. Fafnir passed them all swiftly, heading directly for the opposite end of the corridor where another contingent of dwarrow warriors stood guard next to a set of double doors taller than Flyn. Solid steel and sparsely decorated, the doors appeared out of place within the intricate carvings of the wall. Fafnir did not slow his stride as he approached, motioning for the guards to admit him. They obeyed with ready haste and the doors were pushed wide. Fafnir walked straight through and Flyn followed without waiting for permission. Inkstain came through next and then Ulfrun, stooping a little to get past the threshold.

Fortunately the ceiling of the chamber beyond was high enough for her to stand upright.

The room was sizable, though modest compared to the scale they had seen. Great hearths stood blazing to left and right, each containing a spit being tended by a pair of she-dwarfs. From the smell of the meat, Flyn guessed it was boar, and his stomach announced its interest. Rugs of animal hide covered the floor and guards lined the walls. At the far wall stood a dais of stone overlooking the center of the room. Upon this dais an aged dwarf reclined on a chair made of shields. He was corpulent, yet not slovenly, his raiment of fine wool dyed blue-grey beneath a mantle of white fox fur. Draped across his legs was a great bearskin coverlet. His head was bald save for a circlet of gold upon his brow.

The black cascade of his beard fell past his sizable gut and heavy rings set with precious stones gleamed on several fingers. Hengest stood before this magnanimous dwarf, but stepped demurely aside as they all came into the room. At that same moment, a dwarven herald standing at the foot of the dais tossed his voice across the room.

"All hail Lord Reginn War-Loft, the Shieldborne, King of Hriedmar's Hall and Guardian of the Downward Fields!"

Fafnir went to one knee and Flyn followed suit, along with Inkstain and Ulfrun.

"Hail Chain Maker!" Lord Reginn bellowed, as they all rose.

He spoke the tongue of the Tin Isles, but his voice was laden with a heavy accent. "Hail, my brother." With a wave of his hand the fat dwarf beckoned for a servant, who quickly brought him a large drinking horn. This the king offered to Fafnir, leaning his bulk forward with great difficulty.

"Accept heat from my hearth and mead from my hand and be welcome here, for you are well returned home."

Fafnir approached the edge of the dais and took the horn, bowing his head respectfully. He took a deep drink, then gestured to where Flyn and his companions waited at the back of the room, motioning them forward. Flyn stepped forward as Fafnir introduced him by name. He now noticed that the king was crippled, the outline of his misshapen legs evident even beneath the heavy fur. Indeed, Reginn had all the look of a great warrior laid low by grievous injury, his muscle melted to suet. The chair of shields had two spears attached to the base, long and stout enough for the chair to be carried.

"You are all welcome here," the king tolled once the introductions were complete.

Drinking vessels were given to all and Flyn forced himself not to down his in one pull. Ulfrun had no such qualms and quickly asked for her horn to be refilled. Even Inkstain, normally so abstemious, seemed to relish the sweet warmth of the mead.

"So," Reginn said, his voice and face hardening now that all displays of hospitality were dispensed, "you have found your chosen three, brother."

Fafnir merely nodded.

Reginn's gaze rested on Flyn's face for a moment, then flicked up to Coalspur's pommel sticking up over his shoulder.

"The sword at last returns to the place of its forging, carried by the one who shall slay the Corpse Eater. Tell me, Sir, are you prepared to do this?"

Flyn gave a sturdy nod. "I am, my lord."

The king extended a finger and waved it from Ulfrun to Crane. "And these two? Has your poetry yet revealed their fate in this geis, my brother?"

"Their very presence here is enough," Fafnir declared.

"They have survived much, both before linking themselves to this quest and since. Middangeard would have claimed the lives of any but the Foretold."

Reginn's brow darkened. "As I hear it has claimed the life of one I once called daughter."

Fafnir shot Hengest a quick scowl before turning back to the king. "I would have preferred you heard such tidings from me."

"Why?" Reginn demanded. "Did you slay her? Or do you simply believe your right as Hengest's former master is greater than his as husband?"

"I grieve for Thorsa's end, brother. That is the start and the end of it."

Reginn waved off Fafnir's sympathy. "My only sorrow is that you did not bring me the head of Kàlfr the Roundhouse. But my troth-son tells me he has no want for vengeance. So be it. The choice is his."

Hengest produced a humble bow. "Thank you, my lord."

"Reginn," Fafnir said. "Have you had report from the Ironwood?"

The king quaffed deeply from his own horn before answering. "The giants still protect the Warden Tree entrusted to their care. No attempt has been made to despoil it. Whoever is behind the felling of the Wardens, they do not wish to risk the wrath of Turgur Summit King."

"That is wise," Ulfrun proclaimed.

"It is Arngrim Crow Shoulders, brother," Fafnir said. "It is he who strikes at us."

Flyn thought he saw the king suppress a smile. Reginn took another drink and when the horn left his lips there was a noticeable sparkle of mirth in his eyes.

"No warrior outlives all the enemies he makes in life, Chain Maker, be they mortal or immortal."

Fafnir weathered the jab well. "His vengeance has cost us much. Only two Warden Trees remain, but as you say, Crow Shoulders will not start a war with the giants and he will never find his way here. I need but a little time to allow my champions to rest and then we shall take our leave."

"I have watched over your family for centuries, Fafnir," the king said darkly. "A few days more will not undo my resolve."

"You have my gratitude. Now, with your leave, I will provide my champions with sustenance and rest."

"Go," the king allowed. "Seek your ease. Though I would have Sir Flyn tarry a moment. My armorers must take his measure if he is to be well-girded for battle. If you intend to stay only days, then no time must be wasted."

The reluctance in Fafnir's face made Flyn a bit uneasy.

Clearly, he did not want him to be alone with the king, but seemed to have no choice. After a moment's pause, the Chain Maker merely inclined his head and led the others from the room.

Immediately, a group of dwarrow approached Flyn and bade him remove his coat and harness. He complied and they set to work with lengths of knotted rope, measuring the length and girth of his limbs.

"You have my thanks, my lord," Flyn said as the armorers went about their task. "To equip me from your own forges is most generous."

"I will not send you to battle that bitch-beast in naught but feathers and a thread-bare coat," Reginn grumbled. Flyn smiled. The king's voice had fled, replaced with the bark of an old fighter. It was a tone Flyn had heard often from the raw throats of the Knights Sergeant.

"Have you faced her, my lord?" Flyn asked.

King Reginn shook his head with a small grimace. "No, though I made the attempt in my younger days before I wore a crown. Fafnir already pursued his own ends to see us free of the vættir, so I could do no less. My skill was not with runes or Magic, but in the wielding of arms. Alone I ventured north with spear and shield and axe, intent on becoming a great champion, the savior of my people, the slayer of the Corpse Eater."

Flyn heard the king's voice become momentarily plangent, the barest hint of a longing grin forming behind his beard.

"I never reached her. She dwells far to the north in the cradle of four great peaks. The mountains themselves are forever encircled by a tireless maelstrom, which we call the Mother's Gale. The winds nearly flayed the flesh from my bones, but I won through to shelter in the caverns beneath the mountains, hoping to find my way through the maze of tunnels and reach the vale between the peaks where she is said to live in a great tree beneath the eye of the whirlwind." The dwarf lord gestured half-heartedly at his covered legs. "But before I found the vale, this was done to me by a mourning troll, one of the crazed beasts without a mate. The caves at the borders of the Corpse Eater's abode are rife with them.

It crushed my spine, my pelvis, and my legs before my blade pierced his brain. For days, I crawled in darkness before my father's retainers finally found me. Only one healer in all of Middangeard could have helped . . . and he was away, chasing auguries. By the time my brother returned, my injuries were too far gone for his Magic to help." The king let out a bitter chuckle. "So you see, Sir Flyn, I was made to sit a throne."

"You are no less a warrior, Reginn War-Loft," Flyn declared.

"You flatter, coburn, but you do it well! If you return from this slaying, you shall have to tell me all of your battle with the Corpse Eater. Such a tale would do well for my powdered bones."

The armorers had finished their measuring and Flyn retrieved his sword harness from them with a nod of gratitude. He slung the weapon across his back and looked up to the king once more.

"Is there any more you can tell me of my foe, my lord?"

Reginn pondered a moment, then motioned for his guards.

"Not I. But maybe your own eyes."

Eight dwarrow, four to each side, lifted the king's chair.

They hoisted the thick spears onto their shoulders and descended the dais.

"Come," the king commanded as the throne passed Flyn.

He fell into step behind, along with half a dozen dwarrow guards.

Once out in the wider corridor Reginn called for him to walk alongside. They went once more into the intimidating vastness of Hriedmar's Hall.

"Ages ago, my ancestors founded this bastion," Lord Reginn intoned as they crossed the expansive width of the hall.

"Over the slow march of time, it has been used for many purposes. As a haven. As a vault. A prison. The fjordmen believe it to be a myth and the giants think none but our own kind are allowed admittance, but this is false. The huldu have been brought here on a few occasions, both as guests and captives. It was here that we dwarrow hosted Irial Elf-king when he returned to Middangeard following the defeat of the Goblin Kings. And there have been older, more puissant guests."

The king's bearers entered another corridor off the great hall, this one descending at a noticeable angle. There were no side-passages or junctions, no doors or chambers. This corridor was simply an avenue to greater depths. The king grew grimly silent and Flyn held his questions. The sloping passage went on for a great length, but the king's bearers never halted to rest nor slowed their pace, despite the immense burden of their substantial sovereign and his weighty throne. The wall sconces became less numerous and long stretches of deep shadow intruded upon the corridor between the pools of torchlight. Already weary, Flyn was not looking forward to the return journey uphill and did not envy the throne-bearers.

At last, the corridor leveled off and ran for a goodly stretch before terminating in a lofty chamber. Three sets of massive doors were housed within this chamber, one on each wall. Easily four times the size of a castle gate, these doors defied reason, their size made all the more incredible by the fact that each appeared to be a single slab of stone. No chisel had touched their faces, leaving them free of decoration. Flyn could not even see a means to open them.

Reginn commanded his throne be brought to the center doors, directly opposite the corridor. He craned his neck upwards, looking at the forbidding doors with a face full of eminence.

Reginn spoke a single word in dworgmál.

To Flyn's amazement, the doors began to swing inward.

Eerily, they made no sound as they moved. Only a brief, barely discernible sigh issued from the blackness beyond as ancient air fled captivity. The doors were still widening in a slow pilgrimage when one of the king's entourage handed Flyn a dancing torch.

"Enter, Sir Flyn," Lord Reginn said, his voice an intruder in the depths.

Grasping the torch, Flyn approached the tenebrous maw of the portal. His steps were carefully paced, not the reluctant plod of a craven nor the overzealous swagger of a buffoon. No, he enacted the pace of Sir Corc, the measured stride of a knight.

His torchlight glinted upon something above his head, an orange glow upon a curved shape. Then he saw another, lower down, and then a third far to the left of the first two. As his eyes quickly adjusted he saw dozens more. The curved shapes became large, metal links which quickly revealed great lengths of chain.

They came in from all directions, hanging in ponderous curves from high upon the walls, converging towards the center of the great chamber. Flyn walked on, torch leading. The edge of his feeble flicker of light timidly revealed a shape sprawled in the darkness.

Bones. Bones bound in chains.

As he drew closer, the form became more clear. It was an entire skeleton, though so large Flyn's torch could only shine upon sections at a time. Despite their size, the bones appeared brittle, calcified with untold age. The rib cage had mostly collapsed, crushed beneath the shoulder plates, large as wagons. Extending out from those were long thin bones, doubling back on themselves, the remains of massive wings. Flyn followed the length of the curved neck and found the heavy steel collar still surrounding one of the spinal bones. He worked his way through the web of chains until he reached the head. The hollow of the eye socket seemed to be both begging and accusing, the circumference of the cavity larger than a shield. It took Flyn a dozen steps to reach the hooked end of the beak. It was harder than the rest of the bones, still shining with a predatory luster. Had the jaws of this creature been open wide, Flyn could have walked down its throat without the need to stoop.

"The legends differ," said a familiar voice in the darkness.

Flyn turned, his torchlight falling upon Fafnir, standing alone.

"Some say that the first Hriedmar, for whom both the great hall and my father were named, lured the beast here with treachery and imprisoned him. Others tell that the monster came here of his own will, nearly mad with grief, and asked my ancestor to secure him lest he join his mate in bringing ruin to the world."

"The Corpse Eater," Flyn whispered.

"Yes," Fafnir said, nodding at the enormous remains. "This was once her consort. The Keeper of the Gales. The father of all coburn."

Flyn turned back to the bones, struggling to allow his mind to encompass what his eyes could not. "This is what you would have me fight?"

Fafnir did not answer.

"Would you have showed me this?" Flyn asked without turning. "If your brother had not brought me down here, would you have shown me this?"

There was silence for a time, then Fafnir's voice danced in the dark. "I know not, Sir Flyn."

There was laughter in the chamber and it took a moment for Flyn to realize it was his own. He turned to look upon the Chain Maker once more.

"You are right," he told the wizard. "Though next time you say those words, do not pause. You know not Sir Flyn. But that is no fault of yours, Chain Maker. I joined your company upon the heels of an ignoble defeat. The fight was unworthy of me, yet I courted it with a foolish passion. Following my burning heart nearly killed me and I discovered a fear of death where once there was none. Upon my recovery at your hands, I found all passion gone and guarded against its return. Were it not for Deglan's insistence I never would have joined this quest. I thought you needed a different coburn. And I was right." Flyn took a deep breath, aware that he was pacing, but unable to stop. His head kept swinging from Fafnir to the bones of the great bird and back again.

"You needed a warrior who fears not the end of his life, one who will laugh in the face of all despair. You needed the squire you met in Black Pool. The young strut who would have charged down the gullet of any beast with the knowledge that in victory or in defeat, he would win glory worthy of song! If you knew such a coburn, you never would have hesitated to show him a worthy foe."

Fafnir's face was troubled. "What are you saying?"

"That you, and the Corpse Eater, will soon become well acquainted with Bantam Flyn."

TWENTY-FIVE

Wake me.

Save me.

Ingelbert had slept indoors beneath thick furs next to a merry fire. He had eaten well, filling himself with rabbit and mushroom stew, boar ribs, and dark, dwarrow bread thick with butter. He was rested, sated and uninjured. Yet the words were still there, swimming before his eyes no matter which page of the elven ledger he studied.

Wake me. Save me.

He had spent his waking hours closeted in the chambers King Reginn had appointed him, near giddy with the blissful solitude. Only the occasional servant intruded to inquire of his needs. He accepted all offers of food, in the hopes that regular sustenance would dispel the entreating words upon the pages, but they were not the phantoms of a famished body or an overtaxed mind. They were real, incessant, and mutely desperate. After hours of study and contemplation, Ingelbert finally forced himself to perform an experiment he had been avoiding.

"Who are you?" he asked the book aloud, feeling foolish.

There was no answer. The same four words languished in the shifting ink.

Taking a deep breath, he tried again. "How do I wake you? Save you from what?"

Nothing.

Ingelbert set the book down on the bed, lying back among the pillows with a frustrated blow from his nostrils. He must have dozed, for when he awoke, his candles had burned down the length of several hours. In this underground realm, such candles were the only way to mark the passage of time, an elegantly simple innovation of dwarfcraft. Still, Ingelbert had lost all sense of night or day.

Rolling off his mattress, he went to the silver basin that rested on the trestle and tossed water on his face. Such an innocuous act, yet one that would have been unthinkable out in the frozen wilderness. Middangeard made a man forget what it was to be warm. An unobtrusive knock sounded from the door of the chamber.

"Enter," Ingelbert said in dworgmál.

A dwarf maid appeared, nodding respectfully. She crossed the room and quickly yet calmly fetched up the tray that contained what was left of the last meal.

"Will you be wanting anything else?" she inquired pleasantly.

"Um, could you tell me what the, uh, what the hour is? That is, on the surface?"

"The dusk of the evening," the maid answered readily.

"Ah," Ingelbert said with a show of understanding. In truth, he could not fathom how the she-dwarf knew that, but was too timid to ask. "Well, my, uh, my thanks."

The maid inclined her head and made for the door.

"Umm," Ingelbert stopped her. "Could I perhaps trouble you for ink and a, uh, quill?"

The maid nodded and left, closing the door silently behind her. She was not long in returning, bringing not only the requested items, but also a scroll of blank vellum. Ingelbert thanked her and she left him to his task.

The room contained a writing desk and chair suitable to his proportions, but he returned to his large mattress, coveting the feel of it after so many nights shivering on the ground. He was glad the maid had thought to bring the vellum, finding its presence comforting. No doubt he would find a purpose for it, but for now his quill was wed to a different mate. Taking the green tome in his lap, Ingelbert flipped through the pages until he found one mostly free of scrawled runes. It took a moment, but soon a section of the existing writing reformed.

Wake me. Save me.

Dipping his quill into the ink, Ingelbert raised it over the page. Finding a blank section, he lowered his hand, feeling his stomach sour as he sullied the ancient work with his own scribble.

Mimicking the simplicity of the pleas and the elvish script in which they were written, he wrote a single word.

How?

He stared at the four words of entreaty, his eyes occasionally darting over to look at the besmirching wet ink of his own contribution. Nothing changed. His simple question was long dry before Ingelbert found the will to try again. Wincing, he wrote again upon the page.

Wake. I, Ingelbert Crane, release you.

It amounted to nothing but more defacement. Frustrated by his fruitless efforts, Ingelbert pushed the tome off his lap, set the inkwell upon the open page and threw the quill into the pot.

What had he hoped to accomplish? Whatever sorcery affected the book, he was not likely to unravel it simply by random chance.

Fafnir had told him the text's original obfuscation was an old, enduring spell to keep the contents of the ledger secret. The runecaster claimed it was Ingelbert's inherent powers that slowly unmade the ward, ignorantly dispelling the Magic as he worked at translating the words. Ingelbert could not wish to be so lucky with this new manifestation. Likely, Fafnir could take one glance at the tome and present a solution, but Ingelbert had not seen him since settling into his quarters. Of course, that could have been because he had not left this room. Rest and privacy had become rare commodities and were not to be wasted. Sooner than Ingelbert would like, the Chain Maker would come to fetch him, and the journey would be taken up once more. Wind and snow and rough camps. Plenty of time to ask questions then. For now, Ingelbert was more than content to wait inside his chambers and keep well to himself.

Another resounding knock on the door caused his heart to sink. It was too soon for the servant to return and the raps upon the door were much more insistent. Cursing himself for conjuring this disturbance with thoughts of comfort, Ingelbert called for the knocker to enter. The door swung open and Ulfrun stepped into the room, stooping under the lintel. The rooms and corridors of the Downward Fields were constructed with ceilings easily able to accommodate humans and even giants, but many of the doorways were low. Ingelbert surmised this was a defensive feature of the architecture. A larger foe was far more vulnerable entering a room if he must partially crouch to do so.

Ulfrun stood up straight as soon as she was inside. The dwarrow had provided Ingelbert with fresh clothing, but it appeared they had no garments readily cut to fit a giantess. Ulfrun wore what might have been a heavy, floor-length robe for a dwarf, but it barely reached the top of her thighs. Ingelbert did his best to avoid looking at the sudden amount of well-muscled legs now standing before him.

"The scroll-bird loves his nest," Ulfrun pronounced, surveying the room with a grin. "Two days passed and you have not set foot out this burrow, Inkstained Crane."

"No need," Ingelbert replied.

Ulfrun seemed to chew on his response, nodding slowly.

"No need," she repeated vacantly.

"You have, um, you have rested?" Ingelbert asked, needing something to say. Really he wanted to know why she was here, but could not summon the nerve to voice so forward a question.

"Aye. But I grew weary of rest and have spent my hours treading Hriedmar's Hall. There is much to see here."

"I, uh, yes, I have no doubt."

Ulfrun squinted down at the tome upon the bed. "And what occupies your hours, loremaster?"

Slowly, so not to cause offense, Ingelbert reached out and retrieved the inkwell before closing the book. "Riddles."

Ulfrun made a face. "Songs would be better."

"Not with, uh, not with my voice," Ingelbert replied, laughing a little.

"Stories, then. I recall you spun me a most pleasing word-yarn at our first camp in Götland."

Ingelbert smiled, remembering. Ulfrun had requested some blood-filled epic or tawdry romance. Ingelbert knew of no such tales and lacked the imagination to invent one on the spot, so he had settled on what he did know. History.

He told Ulfrun about the lives of two dusk elves, Daigh Ulothdine and Easna Ulathdaigh. Both were born from a union of human and elf, but there their similarities ended. Daigh was a hunter, a warrior, as wild as he was fearless. Easna was patient and keen, a skilled ambassador as beautiful as she was insightful. Both joined the ranks of the Waywarders, the wandering agents of the Seelie Court. They found in their differences a rare power and together they became known as the Calming Storm, able to find a solution to any conflict. The pair proved to be invaluable to Irial Ulvyeh during the Rebellion and helped retake Airlann from the Goblin Kings. Though their partnership was forged in war, they came to know deep affection for one another. In the annals of elvish lore, the names of Daigh and Easna are lauded as lovers as equally as they are heroes.

During his youth at the orphanage, Ingelbert had often heard accounts of the two Waywarders at the knee of Parlan Sloane.

They were one of the old man's favorite subjects, and often his history lessons diverged into a tale of the Calming Storm. Ingelbert had recited some of their exploits to Ulfrun that first night, hoping they contained at least some of the elements that would please her.

He had chosen well, for the giantess had thanked him for the tale and gone to sleep smiling.

"It was not a story," he now confessed. "It was, uh, it was history."

Ulfrun shrugged, unsurprised. "The best word-streams spring from high up in the mountains of the past. I knew you for a learned mortal, Inkstained Crane, not a skald. Do you think we giants only find pleasure in pretty lies? That we value legends over the shaping events of time?" Her eyes grew hard. "Or is this simply what you think of those with milk-wells and a babe-canal?"

It took Ingelbert a moment to unravel Ulfrun's inference.

"Oh! No, n-not, uh, no. I do not . . . women are . . . I simply meant, uh, that I did not want you to think . . ."

Ingelbert felt himself drowning in stammers, but Ulfrun came to his rescue, her smile over his discomfort widening until she laughed merrily, her white teeth shining.

"Oh, but it is easy to pull your prick, Ingelbert Crane!" she proclaimed. "Come! Let us walk together and find some mischief."

Ingelbert held up a warding hand. "No. I, uh, I am in no mood for such things."

"Too much rest will make it all the more difficult when we return to the quest."

"Perhaps Sir Flyn would be a better choice of companion."

Ulfrun smirked. "I just came from the gamecock. He sleeps under a table, where his dreams will be well sweetened with the mead we shared. Now I desire other sport. Come, I will show you the Hall of Scrolls."

Ingelbert shook his head. "Please, no, I beg you. I really have no wish to leave."

Ulfrun sighed deeply. "Very well. You may stay here, but I will keep you company. We have a bed and the many hours of night to pass. Enough to keep idleness at bay."

"The Hall of Scrolls, you say?" Ingelbert said, standing quickly.

Ulfrun laughed and opened the door. For a moment, Ingelbert considered bringing the green tome, then decided he wished to be free of it, if only for an hour. Once in the corridor, Ulfrun motioned their direction, and Ingelbert was mildly surprised she led them away from Hriedmar's Hall. Though he had seen but little of them, Ingelbert knew the Downward Fields to be an expansive hive of corridors and chambers spread across several levels. Curving stairs and switchbacked ramps connected the upper floors to the lower depths. A system of canals wound through the entire subterranean community with sluice gates and ingenious locks employed to control the waterways. Despite its size and complexity, this kingdom beneath the earth was anchored by Hriedmar's Hall, which served as a sort of crossroads. Ulfrun must have been exploring for some time if she felt confident finding her way.

She led them to a ramp and descended two turns before taking a narrow corridor running next to a small canal. As they walked, Ingelbert and Ulfrun passed a pair of dwarrow obviously tasked with keeping the braziers in the area burning brightly.

Ingelbert wondered how many such teams were needed to ensure darkness never reclaimed the Downward Fields. Eventually, the canal entered a culvert and vanished, though the movement of water could still be heard behind the stone walls. Again Ulfrun took them down and the air began to grow humid. Inwardly, Ingelbert questioned the wisdom of keeping a depository of scrolls in a place given to such moisture, but he followed without comment. By the time Ulfrun finally stopped at an open archway set into the side of the corridor, Ingelbert's shirt was soaked through.

Peering through the arch, he saw a short stairway leading down into a murky room suffused with clouds of lazy steam. The vapors crawled up from the surface of at least a dozen, large circular pools. Benches lined the walls of the chamber and also sat intermittently along the central walkway. A handful of dwarrow relaxed in several of the pools with no separation between genders.

"What about the Hall of Scrolls?" Ingelbert asked, still staring dubiously into the bath chamber.

"Unlike you," Ulfrun replied with a wink, "I have no trouble inventing stories. If such a place exists, you are free to go find it, but here is where I intend to linger awhile."

With that, the giantess strode down the stairs and began making her way along the walkway towards the rear of the chamber.

Ingelbert almost turned around to begin the walk back to his chambers, but suddenly the thought of solitude was no longer so agreeable. The warmth of the bathhouse, the beauty of the carved stone tubs, the salubrious look of the waters, all were far more inviting. His mind made, Ingelbert began following the giantess.

By the time he caught up, Ulfrun had seated herself upon one of the benches along the rear wall of the chamber and was removing her boots. She glanced up as Ingelbert approached and smiled.

"That is the deepest bath," she told him, indicating the unoccupied pool nearest them to the left of the walkway. "The others are built for the svartálfar."

"Construction with the forethought of taller races," Ingelbert mused. "Fascinating for a dwarrow sanctuary, do you not agree?" Ulfrun hummed, clearly unconcerned, then stood and let her robe fall.

Ingelbert looked away quickly, but the brief glimpse of the unclad giantess set his heart to pounding. He heard splashing as she entered the water and kept his eyes lowered as he removed his own boots. After pulling his shirt over his head, he risked a glance at the pool. Ulfrun's back was turned, but the depth of the tub must have been built with humans in mind, or more likely, elves, for the water barely reached her lower back. Ingelbert found himself momentarily transfixed by the two dimples nestled within the muscles just above Ulfrun's backside. The cleft of her buttocks was just visible through the steamy water and Ingelbert had to force himself to look away. He removed his breeches quickly, thankfully able to complete the task and enter the tub before the giantess turned around.

The water embraced him, hotter than he expected. He allowed himself to sink, submerging his face. He felt the water working at his tangled hair and stayed down as long as his breath allowed. When he resurfaced, Ulfrun had turned to face him and settled down to recline in the tub, the water covering her from just beneath the collarbones. Her short hair was now soaked and slicked back, though somehow still appeared unruly. A somnolent look had crept into her face and she looked at him through half-closed eyes.

"Bless the svartálfar," she said with a contented sigh.

Ingelbert had to agree. The waters were miraculous.

"They must have found hot springs," he said. "Built the baths over them and harnessed the waters."

Ulfrun produced a languid smile. "Be silent and float."

It was good advice. For a long time they relaxed in silence.

Ingelbert kept expecting the water to grow cold, but it never did.

The heat kneaded his skin, caressed his muscles and blanketed his bones, chasing away the chill of Middangeard as no fire ever could.

At last, Ulfrun broke the silence. "You remember everything."

The giantess had not said it as a question, but Ingelbert felt obliged to answer. "Yes."

"Will you write of this quest, when it is done? Record our deeds in ink and trap them within a book?"

Ingelbert did not have a ready answer. It had never occurred to him to chronicle this journey that had abducted his life.

Perhaps a part of him knew it would be a worthless effort. What good would a written account of this quest do if there was no one left alive to deliver it?

"Why do you ask?" he queried, stalling.

"Memories are like a hot coal," the giantess answered, her words at ease. "They are passed quickly from one person to the next, but once they cool there is no more need to pass them on. The dead are remembered by those who feel the pain of their loss, sharing the stories to ease that pain. But soon, even for we immortals, there are none left who feel pain, for they too die, and so the stories cease to be shared. That is how the dead are forgotten. But a life written is never forgotten. I would have people read of me and, though they knew me not, still feel the pain of my end."

"You think this quest will kill you?"

"Possibly. But if it does not, something will, one day. The story you told me, of the álfar, the lovers, it did not contain their deaths, but they no longer live, do they?"

"No," Ingelbert answered, remembering when he asked Parlan Sloane the same question.

"I will remember them," Ulfrun stated with certainty. "And I feel pain that they no longer draw breath, because someone wrote of them. You should write of us, Ingelbert Crane."

"I could record what has transpired to this moment, but I doubt I will be witness to the end of this quest."

Ulfrun's eyes opened wider and she grinned. "Who is it now who believes his days draw to an end?"

"With reason," Ingelbert told her. "You and Flyn are great warriors, Fafnir is a potent wizard—"

"As are you."

"No," Ingelbert said, afraid to continue, but needing to say it aloud. "No, I am not. Fafnir is wrong about me. Without Gasten, I have no sorcery. I am sure of this."

Ulfrun frowned. "The night-gull did not follow you here. Why?"

Ingelbert paused, unsure how to answer, unsure how to explain. "We . . . struggled. Within. I do not know if he wished to keep me from this place or merely did not want to enter himself, but he fought my every step. I lost sight of the sun and became confused. I do not even know when Gasten departed, but he was gone when Fafnir found me."

"And he will return," Ulfrun assured him, "once you leave here. Birds do not wish to go where there is no sky."

"Ulfrun. I do not know if I want him to return. Without him I cannot survive in Middangeard, but with him, I . . ."

He lost all words. What was there to say? That the owl made him stronger and he relished it? That he had killed two men in Gipeswic and stopped a giant's blade with his bare hand? He had leached Magic from Hengest, held Deglan captive, compelled the storulvir to slaughter Thorsa. None of this he could have accomplished without Gasten and he feared what he was becoming, but he feared being helpless even more.

Suddenly, a torrent of hot water punched his face.

Spluttering, Ingelbert wiped the water from his eyes and found Ulfrun staring at him with an expression both sheepish and scolding.

"Pardons," she said. "But you looked about to weep. Giant men only shed tears for two things, the birth of their children and, if they be so unfortunate, the death of those children."

"I am no giant," Ingelbert complained.

"Which is why I offered pardon. Perhaps it is customary for mortal men to weep over some unspoken fear."

She was right, of course. Sulking and brooding resolved nothing.

"Without Gasten, I am going to die," he told her firmly.

"With him, I am going to cause others to die. Mayhaps it will be only our enemies, but it could be one of my companions. One of you. Or all of you. No matter which . . . I will enjoy it. Do you not see why that causes me to fear?"

Ulfrun's lips drew tight. "With the bird present, you are a changed man. We all see it. Deglan worried for you. The knight worries for you still."

Ingelbert swallowed. "And you?"

Something in Ulfrun's face changed. Her countenance hardened yet her eyes softened. She drew her legs back and gathered them under her, revealing a brief glimpse of her full breasts and firmly etched stomach before she lowered herself belly-down in the pool. She swam towards him, seeming to crawl through the water. Her shapely back and buttocks occasionally broke the surface, bright and wet.

"I have fought," she said quietly as she drew closer. "I have killed. I have delighted in victory, but the sight of wound-dew upon my hands has never given me joy. Battle is a skill, but should not be a passion. Songs, love-play, the laughter of children, these are life and these should be yearned for. These are what I yearn for."

She was very close to him now and knelt on the bottom of the pool, placing one hand upon the lip next to Ingelbert's head.

He felt her other hand fondle him beneath the water. Ingelbert jumped slightly, not from shock or revulsion, but from the exquisite sensation of her fingers upon his rigid flesh.

"You want me," she said, looking him in the eyes, clearly pleased with his body's response. "It is good and healthy to want a woman. It means you want life. Such desires should be pursued and celebrated. You remember everything, Ingelbert Crane, so remember this moment. Think on it often and allow it to fuel new desire. But, if one day the memory no longer arouses, if you find it no longer fires your blood, then you must ask yourself, what does? What does a man, or a woman, what do they want if not the wholesome pleasures of life? If, on that day, you find the answer is delight in slaughter, in ruin, in the mastery and pain of others, then you will have chosen death over life. But I do not believe that is your fate. So no, I do not worry for you."

Ulfrun moved forward until her body was pressed against his, then she shifted her hips slightly, breathing out through smiling lips. Ingelbert's eyes widened and his own breath caught pleasantly in his throat as an aching part of him was surrounded by a warmth more welcoming than the waters.

TWENTY-SIX

The Dread Cockerel raged.

The sounds of snapping chains and incomprehensible ravings filled the cell as the coburn struggled against his bonds.

Deglan crouched well out of reach, behind one of the support beams and away from the cell door.

"Sir Wyncott, calm yourself!" he urged from his place of safety. The Dread Cockerel did not heed him. He never did. Again he lunged for the door and again his chains rang stridently, defying his strength. The coburn's beak opened wide, issuing a string of hisses and agonized screeches. His talons scrabbled in the dirt as he tried to drag himself forward, but the steel links made a mockery of his efforts. The feathers beneath Wyncott's manacles had been rubbed thin long before Deglan was ever tossed into the cell, and blood ran freely from the raw flesh beneath the metal. The Dread Cockerel paid no more heed to his injuries than he did Deglan's voice. There was nothing to do but wait the frenzy out.

The first of these fits Deglan had witnessed awakened his healer's instinct and compelled him to approach the knight. He was rewarded with a cuff to the head from a wildly flung arm that nearly knocked him senseless. Since then, Deglan had learned to stay clear of the coburn when one of these rages was upon him.

What he had not learned was what caused them to possess the grim knight.

At first, he thought them a savage bid for freedom, some brave yet futile display of a coburn unwilling to be caged, but they were not simply born from anger over imprisonment. Deglan had talked almost relentlessly at Sir Wyncott about their current plight, discussing possible means of escape, yet none of these one-sided conversations had sparked any anger within the knight. Indeed, when he had control of his faculties, the Dread Cockerel seemed almost resigned to his captivity. Near as Deglan could tell, the fits were random and came without warning, even descending upon the coburn while he slept. Conscious or not, his eyes would suddenly become wide and vacant, imbued with a feverish luster. Then the babbling would begin, low grunts quickly escalating into bestial screams. Somewhere within the inane growling, the coburn was speaking, Deglan had no doubt, but he had only been able to make out one word, and that only because it was so oft repeated.

Prize.

Once the physical struggles began, however, all chance of deciphering speech became impossible. The Dread Cockerel would begin pacing, wringing his fettered hands, then throw himself at the door with abandon. The rattle of the chains and the plangent cries of the knight filled the cell, forcing Deglan to clap his hands over his ears until the fit subsided. When the inexorable strength of the chains finally defeated the coburn's labors, he always kept his feet for a time, moaning and pacing, slamming his manacles together. It was not until the exhausted knight at last slumped to the ground that Deglan dared come from behind the beam.

"You going to talk to me this time?" he asked when this latest fit subsided.

Sir Wyncott only shook his drooping head.

"I cannot help you if you refuse to tell me what ails you," Deglan pressed.

It was a well-used statement, grown feeble after days of fruitless utterance. The Dread Cockerel had a reputation for taciturnity, and being locked away beneath a wall had done little to loosen his tongue. All Deglan could gather was that the knight had come to Middangeard and been set upon by Crow Shoulders' men, specifically his twelve sons. The Dread Cockerel's face had become slack with haunted disbelief as he spoke of the berserkers.

"I never wounded one," the knight had said, his voice low with shame. "Not one. They are strong as ten men, each of them."

This was one of the longest strings of words Deglan had wrestled out of his cell mate. He sensed the pride of the coburn was fueling his words, forcing him to offer some explanation for his defeat and capture. The Knights of the Valiant Spur were formidable, and from his time at the Roost, Deglan had learned the Dread Cockerel was known as one of the most deadly. Certainly none other of the Knights Errant were spoken of with more fear.

From Sir Wyncott's tone it was clear he expected to be able to best a dozen men without difficulty, yet Arngrim's sons had disarmed him and clapped him in chains without a drop of their own blood spilled. Deglan had feared the berserkers when he saw them in Crow Shoulders' keep. He feared them more now.

Reaching forward, Deglan took one of the Dread Cockerel's wrists in his hands. The knight did not protest or pull away, nor did he even bother to raise his head. Deglan frowned at the chafed flesh beneath the manacles, knowing there was nothing he could do. He had been deprived of his herb satchel. Even if he still had it, his supplies would have been long depleted with as often as Sir Wyncott aggravated his wounds. Still, he had to look. It was his duty not just as a healer, but as the physician of the Valiant Spur. He and the Dread Cockerel were fellow captives, but they were also sworn to the same brotherhood. It was the only source of trust between them.

Sir Wyncott was an infamous blackguard among the knights, his drab appearance, laconic demeanor and dishonorable reputation making him all but an outcast. There were many, Sir Corc included, who believed his spurs should have been stripped from him. Well, they were now. The fjordmen had left the coburn with nothing, not even a stitch of clothing, but he seemed not to feel the cold. For truth, he seemed not to feel anything except the shame of defeat and the rage of his sudden fits. Not even curiosity intruded upon his torpor. Wyncott had not once asked Deglan how he too came to be a prisoner of Arngrim Crow Shoulders. For his part, Deglan volunteered nothing.

"What is the prize?" Deglan asked quietly, releasing the Dread Cockerel's wrist.

The coburn did not respond. Knowing it was pointless to press further, Deglan left him be, returning to the only tasks that kept him occupied; shivering and thinking.

Life in the cell was cold and cramped. Well, cold for Deglan and cramped for the Dread Cockerel. They were fed little, their meals consisting mostly of raw herring. Deglan had given his first few portions to the Dread Cockerel, but hunger eventually forced him to choke the nearly spoiled fish down. Other than keeping starvation at bay, the arrival of their rare provender provided an additional benefit in the form of Sigrun, the woman who acted as Arngrim's translator.

Long hours passed before the door of the cell opened.

Deglan stood, wincing as his frozen joints popped, and went to meet the thrall.

Sigrun always removed their mess buckets first, passing them to a pair of other slaves waiting outside with the guards.

Fresh buckets were brought in, along with the meager rations. As was her habit, Sigrun took a moment to inspect Deglan's face, cleaning the wounds made by the berserker's boot and scrutinizing the newer lump caused by Sir Wyncott. Under his guidance, she had managed to set his broken nose during her first visit, a procedure that had left Deglan in tears. Then, and every time since, the cell door was closed by the guards, leaving Sigrun alone with him and the Dread Cockerel. Deglan was no fool. He knew Crow Shoulders purposefully allowed the woman to linger by herself in order to gather information. Let the bastard think himself clever, so long as it provided Deglan a friendly face, even for only a few minutes. In his week of captivity, Deglan had learned little about Sigrun, save that she had been born in Kymbru, but lived most of her girlhood in Sasana. Even this information was hard-won, for she spoke little, adopting the silent, servile attitude so common in slaves.

"Hakeswaith?" Deglan inquired as Sigrun knelt in front of him. "Any word?"

The woman's deep brown eyes left his bruises only for a moment. "No. I have still not seen him." Try as she might to sound detached, Sigrun's voice contained an inherent compassion.

Deglan let out a deep sigh. For days he had been trying to gather some information on the whaler, but could not even discover if he were alive or dead. The beating Crow Shoulders' sons had given him was severe and it was not likely he survived. Still, Deglan wanted to know for a certainty.

Sigrun took a cold, damp rag to his cuts.

"They would heal faster if you brought me the herbs I asked for," Deglan told her lightly.

"I have not yet procured them," the woman replied.

Deglan gave an unconcerned grunt, hiding his disappointment. Days ago, he had asked for some specific supplies, claiming they would alleviate his and the Dread Cockerel's hurts.

This was true, but among the innocuous medicines, he had included a few herbs that could be useful in helping them escape.

Sleeping draughts and poisons were often better than a blade.

Naturally, he had not told Sigrun any of this when he innocently rattled off the requested components. Herbs were difficult to come by in the frozen lands of Middangeard, but nothing he required was unknown here. Either Crow Shoulders was simply disinclined to grant any request from his prisoners or someone in his holdfast knew herb-lore and warned the jarl of Deglan's ruse. He wondered if it was Sigrun herself. Like all thralls, the duty to her master was born from fear not loyalty, which would make it nearly impossible to win her as an ally. In Deglan's experience, it was easier to kindle the fires of betrayal in the human heart than it was to ignite selfless bravery.

"He still has not spoken?" Sigrun asked, her concerned gaze flicking to the Dread Cockerel.

"No," Deglan grumbled.

"His cries can be heard over half the fortress."

"The fits are getting worse. Without the medicine I need, I cannot help him."

Sigrun's jaw tightened. "I cannot get them for you."

Deglan nodded. "Why does Arngrim keep him alive? What does he want with a captive coburn?"

"He is a trophy," Sigrun replied softly. "Another display of Crow Shoulders' power. His sons would have him make a new cloak from the coburn's feathers."

Deglan glanced behind him to make sure Sir Wyncott had not heard. "Earth and Stone. Then it is only a matter of time before they kill him. And what does he intend to do with my hide? Make a nosebag for his horse?"

Sigrun made a face, chastising his dark humor. "I know not. But you claimed you would help kill the dwarf wizard. Did you lie?"

Deglan faked a wince at the rag's touch before answering, inwardly reminding himself to be cautious.

"Like your jarl, I hate Fafnir Rune-Wise. From Fafnir's own admission he caused great harm to Arngrim's family. Well, he is doing the bloody same with my friends! Give me an opportunity and I will plunge a knife into that meddling dwarf's heart."

Sigrun glanced towards the door of the cell, then looked back at Deglan and gave him a warning glare. "Such an oath will not help you. Would you have Crow Shoulders know you would deprive him of his vengeance? His must be the hand that slays the runecaster. None other."

Deglan shook his head at his own stupidity. "You are right. I am weary. I am simply trying to—"

"Survive," Sigrun cut in. "I know."

Deglan looked into the woman's face. It was a strong face, once comely but now lined with years. Not the years of age, but the years of enduring sorrow and hardship. Even her deep brown hair was showing streaks of grey, much too early for one so young. But her eyes remained vibrant, the harshness of servitude not yet corrupting her gaze. Deglan found friendship in those eyes, something housed within giving him permission to trust.

"I will help Arngrim," Deglan whispered. "If he agrees to spare my comrades, I will do whatever he asks of me."

Sigrun leaned close, worry and relief at war upon her brow.

"There is a dwarrow sanctuary—"

It was Deglan's turn to cut her off. "The Downward Fields, I know. I spoke the truth in the tower. I know not where they are."

"Then how can you hope to save yourself? Your friends?"

"I do not know!" Deglan barked.

Sigrun did not recoil from his outburst. A thrall was inured to far greater callousness than the yelled frustrations of a bitter, old gnome. She simply looked at him with deep sadness.

"Perhaps you do not need to help them," she said comfortingly. "The jarl sent men out to bring the runecaster here, but none returned save the riders who delivered you, and they lost two of their number in the doing. The dwarf has great Magic. That is what is whispered throughout the fortress when Arngrim and his sons are not present to hear. The warriors believe this Fafnir controls the birds and beasts, and has surrounded himself with invulnerable champions. The riders say one of them came after you the night you were taken. A swift fighter with a great blade."

Deglan could not keep the fondness from his face. He closed his eyes and breathed a tiny laugh. "Flyn, you witless swain."

A bellow erupted from the rear of the cell. The Dread Cockerel was on his feet, quivering with fury.

"PRETENDER!"

He charged, causing both Deglan and Sigrun to lose their balance as they scrambled closer to the door. The chains snapped taut, brutally arresting the coburn's headlong rush. The door to the cell was thrown open and the guards rushed in, spears leveled. Sir Wyncott strained against his bonds, still screaming.

"IMPOSTOR! PRETENDER! THIEF OF THE PRIZE!"

For one moment, Deglan thought the enraged coburn would rip the chains from the walls. In that instant, Deglan felt both triumph and terror. Triumph, for the Dread Cockerel would be free. Terror, because the coburn's gaze was fixed upon him. But the chains held and the guards quickly ushered Sigrun out before they too left the cell, slamming the door as they went, leaving Deglan alone with the incensed knight.

"THIEF! THE PRIZE IS MINE!"

Deglan swiftly skirted the Dread Cockerel and hunkered down behind the support beam, assaulted by the crashing of chains.

Soon, the coburn's cries degenerated into wordless, tortured noise.

At last, the noise abated, but Deglan waited longer than usual before coming out of hiding. He found the Dread Cockerel prone upon the floor, face down at the end of the chains' reach.

"Sir Wyncott," Deglan said, standing over him. "What is the prize?"

The Dread Cockerel stirred. Slowly, he roused himself and sat back against the wall.

"You are going to answer me, Sir," Deglan insisted. "What is the prize?"

Taking a deep breath, the Dread Cockerel spoke, his voice harsh and gravelly.

"It was taken from me," he said. "The prize of the tourney."

Deglan frowned, remembering a story Flyn had told him.

"Tourney? You mean Coalspur?"

The knight's eyes flicked up at him, brimming with suspicion. It was as if he took offense to any mention of the sword.

"I was undefeated," the Dread Cockerel said. "Hatch, Pitch Feather, Strummer,

Blood Yolk. They all fell. Stoward Thom, too. That upstart squire was the last. Flyn." The Dread Cockerel seemed to taste the name as he said it, finding it bitter. "But Tillory got in the way."

"You killed him," Deglan said, recalling the story.

The Dread Cockerel lurched to his feet. "The Grand Master was a fool to let him fight! The prize screeched in my head, blinded me with its fire! I was clumsy. Tillory fell to an unlucky stroke. He was newly returned from questing, tired. Refused a shield! He never should have been on that field. Lackcomb put him between me and the prize. The blood is on his hands. It should have been Flyn who faced me that day!"

"But it wasn't," Deglan said. "You slew a brother knight and disgraced yourself. The prize went to another. Coalspur was given to Flyn."

"Impostor!" the Dread Cockerel proclaimed through a raw throat. "The sword is mine. It called to me. It calls to me still!"

"Truly?" Deglan asked harshly. "Or are you merely mad? Driven to the brink of sanity by guilt and grief. You are the sullied knight of the Order, Sir Wyncott. You know that better than I."

These words seemed to take the strength out of the coburn's legs. He slumped heavily to the ground, his chains pooling around him.

"I thought as you," the knight said after a long silence, not looking up. "I thought lust for glory had overtaken reason. I begged forgiveness from the Grand Master and was allowed to return to errantry, to Outborders. The burning followed. The sword seared me across the leagues, punished me for every moment it was not in my grip. For months I endured, hoping that my next foe would slay me so I could be free from the anguish. Then one day, the pain was gone and stayed away for the meat of a year.

"But it returned. I could no longer deny the call of the prize. I sought it out, returning to the Roost to find it still within that popinjay's keeping. I would have challenged him in the Great Hall, but Corc the Constant interrupted. Then the gruagach attacked, set fire to the Roost. The young strut fled with the chronicler." The Dread Cockerel's eyes flicked up, boring into Deglan. "And you."

"You have followed us since Albain." It was not a question.

The Dread Cockerel nodded. "Those painted barbarians, the Pritani, delayed me in the mountains. You took ship at Caer Caled, but the prize told me where you were bound. I boarded the next ship to Gipeswic. The squire had gone. It mattered not. The prize again left a flaming trail in my mind. I found Flyn bleeding and broken, lying in the mud of the riverbank. The prize was there, stabbed into the muck above its unworthy bearer. It was within reach. I nearly touched it."

Deglan watched as lust filled the Dread Cockerel's face. He seemed lost in the memory, as if willing himself to return to that moment.

"But a bloody big bear stopped you!" Deglan barked, gratified to see his words snap the coburn out of his obsessive trance. "Flyn's gypsy family was looking for him, too. Pali found him just as you did and drove you off."

"That was no mere beast," Wyncott replied. "It nearly killed me."

"And you him," Deglan growled.

The knight showed no remorse, merely returned Deglan's hard stare and continued. "I was injured, but less grievously than the pretender. I thought I would soon claim the prize, but Flyn was spirited away, here, to Middangeard. I followed, but these humans found me before I found him. They deny me the prize, for now. But like the Pritani, like the bear, they will rue hindering my path."

"Sir Wyncott. Do you know what Coalspur is? The purpose of that sword?"

"It is the prize. It is my destiny."

It was not an answer, but the Dread Cockerel could not see it. There was such certainty in his voice, such conviction in his countenance. He was entirely possessed by a purpose he did not understand. Deglan's spine went cold and he backed away from the knight, returning sluggishly to his beam. He leaned against it, out of the coburn's sight and allowed his mind to swim in dark thoughts.

Deglan had never believed Fafnir's augury, that was no secret. Likely the others thought him simply a stubborn, cynical old stoat who refused to put stock in prophecy, but there was more to his doubt. There was always something missing from the dwarf's claim, something that had bothered Deglan from the beginning. He had lived for thousands of years and seen with his own eyes the ravages of great purpose upon mortals and immortals alike. Fate was not borne lightly, it always exacted a heavy toll. Lives were a tool to it, wielded and worked relentlessly until blunted by victory or broken by defeat. For all his hardships, Flyn never displayed the wounds caused by the manipulations of an unseen hand. He was headstrong and rash to a fault, but his choices were always his own.

The decision to leave the Roost, the defeat at the hands of his father, all were undeniably set into motion by the young strut.

Bantam Flyn, though a cocksure, flighty, insufferable knave, was ever the master of his own fate.

The Dread Cockerel was another matter. He was racked by unknown energies, tortured and tested without mercy. It would now be impossible to see Sir Wyncott's true nature, for it had long been enveloped in the crushing tides of omen. The sword sought its rightful wielder, called to him incessantly. How else could the Dread Cockerel have tracked Flyn across the known world? He mentioned a year of respite, when he was not harried by the absence of the blade. No doubt this coincided with Flyn's time on Pocket's island. Sir Corc had said the place was not chosen at random and contained more protection than simple secrecy and seclusion. The wards surrounding Pocket must have stifled Coalspur's call, granting the Dread Cockerel relief until Flyn departed the island.

Earth and Stone!

Sir Wyncott was not mad. He was the coburn foretold in the Chain Maker's augury.

With a snarl, Deglan punched his fist into the wooden beam. The bones of his hand throbbed in complaint and he skinned his knuckles, but Deglan ignored the pain. How could Fafnir, a Chain Maker, have failed to see this? Surely he must have sensed Flyn's nature was contrary to what the quest required. Fafnir admitted that this business with Arngrim felling the Warden Trees had forced his hand, made him desperate. He either knew or refused to recognize the truth. He had the wrong champion.

And what of Ulfrun and Crane? Was the wizard wrong about them too? No matter, the prophecy was not properly fulfilled.

Two of three chosen champions was not enough. Flyn was brave and skilled, but would that serve him on a path he was not intended to tread? If the Corpse Eater could only be killed by those foretold in the augury, then only one outcome awaited any who tried to slay her beyond the verge of that prophecy. Deglan always feared that Fafnir would get his companions killed, now he was sure of it.

He had told Sigrun he did not know how he could help his friends, but a plan was beginning to form in his mind. He worried at it throughout the night, avoiding any contact with the Dread Cockerel. Did he possess the resolve to go through with this scheme? More importantly, if he did, what was the source of that resolve, betrayal or selfless bravery?

By the time Sigrun returned, late the following day, Deglan had made up his mind.

"Tell Crow Shoulders, I beg to speak with him," he told the thrall as soon as she opened the door. "I know how to help him find the dwarf."

Sigrun hesitated a moment, reading his face. She nodded and left the cell without a word.

It was not long before she returned. She did not step inside the cell this time, but gestured for Deglan to emerge. Outside, it was snowing. The crisp air was a welcome change from the sour closeness of the cell. Four warriors awaited him, their looming forms draped in mail and woolen cloaks. The men surrounded Deglan and began herding him, not to the central tower, but along the interior of the curved wall. Sigrun followed a few paces behind.

Bólmr had four gates, housed at north, south, east and west.

The western gate was closest to Deglan's cell, but the men took him to the north gate, already thrown wide by the guards posted there. Following his escort, Deglan passed beneath the gatehouse and walked out onto the bridge of packed earth spanning the frozen moat. The men stopped in the middle of the bridge. And there, propped against the side of the bridge and leading down into the moat, a ladder waited.

Deglan glanced down at the loathsome ranks of draugr standing in the hoary trench, their feet encased in ice. They faced away from the castle, an uncountable number of mouldering sentries. As one, the heads of the dead men slowly revolved, looking up at the living occupants on the bridge. The warriors pushed Deglan roughly towards the ladder. He stumbled, but whirled around as soon as he regained his balance. Beyond the guards, Sigrun watched him forlornly. So, this was how they intended to dispose of him.

"Let me speak with your jarl," Deglan said desperately. "I can help him!"

The guards made impatient noises in their throats and stepped towards him.

"Climb down," Sigrun begged him. "Climb down before they throw you in."

Fixing the guards with a glare of contempt, Deglan backed up to the ladder and, grasping the ends of the poles, swung his foot down onto the first rung. The ladder was nearly five times his height and the rungs were spaced for a grown man's legs. It was a long and awkward climb down. Deglan took his time. He was in no hurry to die and kept pausing to look down at the waiting draugr.

The ice prevented them from walking, but each held a spear or a long-hafted axe in their skeletal hands. It would be easy enough for them to strike him dead as soon as he reached the bottom.

The dead men watched him descend, colorless eyeballs and empty sockets tracking his movement. He would be damned if some rotting, ensorcelled carcass was going to skewer him through the arse while he fumbled down a bloody ladder. When he was four rungs from the bottom, Deglan jumped, aiming for the wall of frozen dirt formed by the foundation of the earth-bridge, hoping to land outside the reach of the draugr. His feet hit the ice hard, then flew out from under him. Pain shot through his elbows and the back of his skull as they smacked the ice. Skidding briefly, he hit the wall and rolled to standing, putting his back against the dirt.

Before him stood a hideous forest of draugr, every head turned to the left, watching him. Then their chins raised, looking to the top of the bridge just as the ladder began to shake. Someone else was climbing down.

To Deglan's astonishment, Sigrun joined him in the moat.

The woman's last step down the ladder brought her well within reach of a draugr's axe, but the moving corpse only continued to watch her. Clutching her shawl tight under her chin with one hand, Sigrun extended the other to Deglan.

"Come," she said, her face pale and nervous. "They will not attack unless commanded."

"Comforting," Deglan grumbled and reluctantly took her hand.

Sigrun had to practically drag him the first few steps. They weaved their way through the dead men, going slowly to keep their balance on the ice. The cold air trapped in the moat was tinged with the reek of rust and rot. To their right, the wall of Bólmr loomed above, to their left, the lip of the trench and open sky. All around were the draugr. They were in various stages of decay, the skeletons far less unnerving than those still covered in bluish flesh and rime-crusted beards. They were equipped as an army, with helms and mail, weapons and shields. Deglan kept a wary eye, but it was impossible to watch in every direction. He could hear the creak of bone as the skulls swiveled to watch him pass and expected a pitted blade to kill him at any moment. After what seemed an eternity navigating this orchard of cadavers, Sigrun came to a halt.

Arngrim Crow Shoulders walked among the dead, his well-muscled form and feathered cloak making him appear huge among the wasted bodies of the draugr. The jarl turned as they approached, regarding Deglan with flinty eyes beneath a brooding brow. Beneath his cloak, the warlord wore mail and a sword hung at his hip. Deglan noted the weapon did not conform to the thick, one-handed blades forged by the fjordmen. This weapon had a wider, curved guard, longer grip and lighter pommel. Indeed, it looked very much like Flyn's sword, though smaller. A blade of dwarf-make.

Running a hand through his fierce beard, Crow Shoulders uttered a short sentence, then gestured at Sigrun with a broad hand.

"The jarl will now listen to your words," the woman translated.

"My lord," Deglan said, pacing his speech so that Sigrun could easily echo him in the tongue of Middangeard. "I cannot bring you to the Downward Fields. But I can bring you to Fafnir, wherever he may be. The wizard believes in a prophecy, and searches for the individuals foretold within its verses. He believed your sire, Tyrfing, to be one of those he sought." This time, the mention of Crow Shoulders' ancestor caused the jarl's face to grimace before Sigrun even translated Deglan's words. Quickly, he pressed on. "He was wrong. Fafnir's error brought ruin to your forebear. Now, he has seduced one within the order I serve with the same augury he used to cozen Tyrfing. Again, he has erred. My companion is not who he needs. But the augury is real, and the rightful champion is the coburn you have chained."

Deglan saw disdainful incredulity creep over Crow Shoulders' face as Sigrun repeated this.

"That is the cause of his rages," Deglan proclaimed. "Like the sword you inherited, Fafnir gave a blade to my friend, but he is not destined to wield it. Sir Wyncott, who you have imprisoned, is. He is compelled to possess the weapon, driven by fate. It is his sole purpose. If you release him, he will lead you to the sword. And to Fafnir."

Crow Shoulders had grown still. He was listening, thinking.

Time for the final gambit.

"The runecaster is powerful. And he has surrounded himself with powerful allies. If you confront them, they will fight and you will lose many men, mayhaps even your own life and the lives of your sons."

A bark of arrogant laughter followed this, but Deglan was undeterred.

"Fafnir is cunning and he will slip away in the chaos of battle. His chosen champions trust me, count me a friend. I can speak to them, show them the truth. Give me your oath that you will let them go free and I will see to it they abandon the wizard. I can leave him friendless and then no one shall stand between you and your vengeance."

His proposal made, Deglan set his jaw and looked firmly at the warlord. Crow Shoulders' face may well have been carved from stone. He considered a moment, then growled a short statement before striding past Deglan and Sigrun, making his way through the ranks of draugr, in the direction of the bridge. Sigrun's eyes went wide and she hesitated a moment before backing away.

"What did he say?" Deglan asked the thrall, trying to keep the desperation from his voice.

The woman turned without answering and quickly followed her master.

"Sigrun!" Deglan called after her. "What did he say?!"

"He wants to know if you speak the truth."

A spasm ran down Deglan's spine, one that had nothing to do with the cold. The voice came from behind him. It was thin and reedy. Familiar.

He turned and saw a gaunt form emerge from the ranks of dead. Tall as a man, it moved with a queer grace, silent and sure upon the ice. It was clad in clothes ill-suited for the cold. Simple boots and breeches, a thin tunic. Upon its head was a broad-brimmed covering Deglan knew well.

"Buggery and shit," he whispered. "Slouch Hat."

"Greetings, old friend," the husk said. He stopped in front of Deglan, his sack face twisted into a smile.

Deglan's mind reeled. The last time he had seen Slouch Hat was in Hog's Wallow, the home they shared for nearly a century.

The husk had fled the hamlet, believed to be the murderer of his master, Brogan. Soon after, Hog's Wallow was put to the torch by Red Caps, and Deglan's life had been thrown once more into the turmoil of growing war. Though he had not seen Slouch Hat again, he later learned they had become embroiled in the same desperate struggle against the Red Caps, a struggle which was supposed to have ended the husk's existence.

"You were dead," Deglan proclaimed.

"Why did you believe so?" Slouch Hat inquired, the black pits of his eyes narrowing. "Because I lay lifeless within Castle Gaunt? Abandoned along with the dormant remains of the Unwound? You did not see this for yourself, Deglan."

It was true. After the battle with Torcan Swinehelm's goblins and the awakened Forge Born, Deglan had been too busy with the wounded outside the citadel. By choice, he never set foot within the cursed walls of the Goblin Kings' stronghold.

Deglan shook his head, his jaw slack. "Rosheen said—"

Slouch Hat cut him off. "Ah, yes. Padric's piskie paramour. Well, I suppose I should grant her some accuracy. I was dead. Destroyed by the sorcery of the gurg child as I tried to remove Jerrod's crown from his head. I thought it only right, as it was my body that was used to place it on the poor boy's brow. It was killing him, and I felt remorse."

Slouch Hat shrugged his narrow shoulders and turned away.

He peered for a moment at one of the draugr. When he spoke again his voice was sorrowful.

"It was a cruel fate. That the boy should be half-Fae. The heir to the iron crown, poisoned by his birthright. I tried to save him, Deglan. But he had other designs."

Deglan kept his face passive. He had not been there, but knew the events well, having been told them by Flyn and Corc, Curdle and Rosheen. They had all been killed, or near to it, swatted down with dread powers turned upon them by Slouch Hat, who was possessed by the vengeful spirit of Jerrod's bed-slave. Pocket had saved them, keeping the crown upon his head so he could use its Magic to restore the lives of his friends at the cost of his own.

Or so Slouch Hat believed. Only a few knew the truth that Pocket had lived despite the grievous harm inflicted by the evil artifact.

"He restored you too, then," Deglan said. "Before he died."

Slouch Hat laughed. Even during happier times in Hog's Wallow, it was not a sound Deglan found pleasant.

"No," the husk said. "No, my salvation came from a different source. Though, admittedly, they shared a bloodline."

Reaching up with a hand made of bound twigs, Slouch Hat removed his name-sake. Beneath, upon the bare, rumpled dome of the husk's stuffed head, was a simple iron band.

Hissing between his teeth, Deglan took an involuntary step back. "Jerrod's crown."

"Yes," Slouch Hat said mournfully. "My fate appears bound to the lineage of vile men."

"You are damn well serving one now," Deglan groused.

The husk replaced his hat with slow deliberateness. "My kind was created to serve, Deglan. And only my first master was a good man, though even he was drawn to the study of the warlocks' origins. After his death I was passed down from one bucolic wretch to the next. Arngrim Crow Shoulders is no different from the rest, he just commands warriors instead of sheep."

"Crow Shoulders is not the mystery," Deglan spat back.

"He wants revenge, the same useless balm that humans and immortals have been applying to their pain since the birth of the world. It is you I do not understand!"

"My motivations are far more intricate. I would not waste time in an attempt to explain them."

"Toad shit!"

The curse caused Slouch Hat's face to crinkle with amusement. "I know you, Deglan Loamtoes. For all your many thousands of years, you are not a compli-cated being. Your judgment is as blunt as your speech. You are adept at healing and long-practiced in hating, but there is little more to you. That is why I know you are telling Crow Shoulders the truth. You will aid him, if you can save your compan-ions, and that will spare your life. Do not concern yourself with why I help the fjordman. Simply be glad I choose to help you."

"You want to help? Bloody help me escape! Earth and Stone, Slouch, we were friends once!"

"And that friendship is what prevents me from such schemes. Where would you go, Deglan? In the wastes of Middangeard escape is only another form of death. Better to stay a hostage and live. Have faith in your plan, keep true to your word. Convince your friends to leave the runecaster's side, so that you may return to the Tin Isles, to Airlann, where you belong."

"Then come with me! Leave this madness behind!"

"I cannot. I am needed here."

Deglan issued a disgusted groan. "Why? So you can command Crow Shoulders' corpses with that pederast's crown?"

Slouch Hat ignored this.

"Go home, Deglan," he said, nodding at the back of one of the draugr. "For some, it is already too late."

With that, the husk walked away and Deglan stared daggers at his thin form until he was lost from sight. After a deep breath, Deglan made his way slowly around to the front of the dead man Slouch Hat had indicated, a cold weight in his gut. The draugr's head turned to follow him, only resting when Deglan stopped to face it squarely. The thin, black hair was matted with frost, the jaw twisted into a permanent snarl.

"I am sorry," Deglan said softly.

Hakeswaith stared down at him, his eyes filled with more hatred in death than they ever held in life.

TWENTY-SEVEN

Flyn had dwelt only five days in the Downward Fields before his armor was ready. He was roused early by a knocking upon his door, followed by the appearance of one of the dwarrow smiths who had taken his measure in Reginn's throne room.

Suspecting this signaled the end of his respite, Flyn strapped the elven spurs to his feet and shouldered his sword before following the artisan out the door. A short journey brought them to a stifling forge where the other armorers waited, along with Hengest Half-Rune. The beardless dwarf's hair was fully washed of dye and shaved so short only a stain of black stubble covered his scalp. He had also abandoned his rude, sleeveless coat in favor of sturdy, somber-colored robes. A stout staff rode his fist, its top affixed with a heavy mace-like head fashioned out of steel in the likeness of a ram.

"Sir Flyn," Hengest said in greeting.

Flyn gave him a courteous nod, but was too captivated by the new coat of mail hung upon the arming stand to say anything.

No mortal smith could have completed a hauberk in so short a time, especially not one of such beauty. The thick rings were enameled white and woven so tightly together the metal looked almost like cloth. Shining spaulders added protection at the shoulders and a new belt encircled the waist, a dwarrow hand axe hanging from its frog. A pair of vambraces waited upon a nearby table.

"Remarkable," Flyn breathed, running a hand over the rings and nodding gratefully to the smiths. "Truly you are masters of your craft."

The dwarrow accepted the praise with humble bows, then quickly set about helping Flyn into the quilted gambeson before lowering the hauberk over his head. Though far from weightless, the mail was astonishingly light. Flyn had not worn armor since fighting Gallus. The feel of it was emboldening. He strapped the vambraces to his forearms and flexed his fingers. The smiths also provided him a new surcoat of heavy wool, dyed a cold grey. Lastly, Flyn slung Coalspur's harness across his back.

There was a brief exchange between Hengest and the smiths in dworgmál.

"They wish to know if any adjustments need to be made," Hengest translated.

Flyn took a moment and moved about the smithy, rolling his shoulders.

"None," he answered with a small laugh. "Though likely I am the only one surprised."

"Very well," Hengest said. "Then we are to meet the others."

With a final bow of gratitude to the armorers, Flyn followed the runecaster out of the smithy and they walked to Hriedmar's Hall, where Fafnir waited. Inkstain and Ulfrun were not far behind. They appeared much improved by the sojourn here, especially Crane, whose normally wan and worried face now wore a healthy flush. He was heavily dressed and laden with his book satchels, further evidence that their convalescence was at an end.

For his own part, Flyn was reinvigorated and eager to take up the quest once more. Warmth and wine were welcome comforts, but idleness was the thief of courage. It ushered in too much deep thinking, which only watered the blossoms of doubt. Flyn was glad he had learned some of Sir Corc's patience, however grudgingly, but now was not the time for such a virtue. Only a swift end to this quest would set Flyn on the road to retrieve Deglan and, after, the road home.

Of all assembled, Fafnir looked the least rested. Indeed, the Chain Maker appeared more haggard than ever. The black wires of his beard were wild beneath his alarmingly pale and haunted visage.

His garb was fresh, but his back drooped under his new cloak.

Only the wizard's eyes remained strong, his gaze steady as he looked over his chosen champions.

"My friends," Fafnir intoned. "I hope you have not found the hospitality of the dwarrow wanting. It is unworthy recompense for what you have already endured for my people. And yet I must beg more from you. The final measure of our journey is at hand. I tell you with certainty it will only grow more treacherous from here. No servants, guards or retainers shall accompany us. I will not risk any more of my people. Nor shall I offend your bravery with offers to abandon what we have begun. Know that if we succeed, you three will forever have the loyalty and gratitude of the dwarrow to call upon at your whim." The wizard gestured at a pile of baggage resting nearby. "Sleds will only hinder us in the upcountry, so we must each carry our own provisions. Come."

Without another word Fafnir grabbed one of the packs and began leading the group through the great hall. Slinging his own pack across his back, Flyn was suddenly grateful for the axe at his belt. The bag of provisions resting over his sword harness would make Coalspur slower to hand, for the entire harness had to be unslung in order to draw the massive blade. Fafnir was well ahead by the time Flyn got his kit properly situated. Hengest was a few steps behind his former master, while Ulfrun tarried some distance at the rear. Flyn found himself walking next to Inkstain.

"You seem hale," Flyn said, thumping the chronicler on his shoulder.

The man accepted the friendly cuff with a slight smile. "Yes. And you?"

"Plied with endless drink and well-fed," Flyn replied with a chuckle. "For so dour a people, the dwarrow are generous hosts."

"I see they have armed you well."

Flyn breathed a dramatic sigh. "Yes. I told them it would make a better tale if I fought the Corpse Eater wearing nothing but my feathers and a smile, but they insisted on the mail. I see you are still dragging half the Roost's library along. Surely King Reginn would keep the annals safe until we return."

"I cannot part with them," Inkstain answered simply.

Flyn found the man's response a little troubling and decided it was time to face Deglan's warnings.

"Well," he said, "I would rather see you wed to your books than that owl."

Inkstain expressed a hum and then was silent for a long moment. "Have you ever loved another, Bantam Flyn?"

The question caught Flyn off-guard and almost made him laugh. In truth, he did not immediately understand what the man was asking. Certainly, Flyn held deep affection for Deglan and, though he had known him only a short time, Inkstain as well. He loved Milosh as a father, Gulver and Tsura as siblings, bonds of fidelity that later extended to include Corc and Pocket. The love of his mother was now little more than an echo in his heart, one which, when thought upon, pulsed through his body as a pang of comfort and loss, gratitude and regret. So yes, he had loved and continued to love.

But something in Crane's voice hinted at a more visceral affection. It was this question that Flyn hesitated to answer. He had known lust as every coburn knows it, as a primal urge rife with red violence. In Gallus's clutch, it had nearly caused his destruction.

Mating for a coburn was not about love, as it could be for other races. It was about conquering and controlling. Denying another male access to the possession of a female was more important than the need to experience physical pleasure or the desire to father children.

Inkstain waited on his response, his expression a mix of embarrassment and pride.

For an answer, Flyn gave him a conspiratorial grin.

"Ingelbert Crane. You learned to sing."

The jest cracked the chronicler's timorous face into a self-conscious smile. "Yes. I, ah, I suppose so."

"What are you two clucking about?" Ulfrun called up to them, her voice playful.

"We," Flyn tossed over his shoulder, "were simply extolling the wonders of this underground sanctuary."

"You should visit the baths," the giantess replied quickly.

Flyn stifled a snort. Poor Inkstain was hopelessly outmatched, the fortunate fellow. Flyn gave the man a nudge with his elbow.

"You hear that? The giantess thinks we need to smell sweeter."

Inkstain ran a hand through his straw-colored hair and produced a nervous smile. "I, um, I have been to the baths."

To spare the man, Flyn hid his amusement by walking backwards so he could face the giantess.

"I am afraid you mistake tactics for uncleanliness, Breaker," he told her, putting just enough emphasis on the name for innuendo and making Ulfrun smile. "Where we are bound, I see an advantage in smelling like a troll."

"Do not insult trolls so, sword cock!"

"Pardons," Flyn bowed at her without breaking stride. "Let us simply call my lack of washing a blow struck in the war against vanity. I was far too comely as I was."

Turning back around, Flyn affected his swagger to give Ulfrun a display of his tail feathers and was rewarded with a bawdy whistle. Though he refrained from teasing Inkstain further, Flyn could not help but smile. Small wonder the habitually doleful chronicler was suddenly so transformed.

"I am happy for you, Master Crane, truly. But you have not answered me."

"But I have," Inkstain replied. "Though I admit a certain tendency towards tergiversation."

Flyn felt his brow wrinkle. "Did you just sneeze?"

The chronicler smiled, but his voice was sober. "Gasten will return. I am certain of it. I still do not understand his origins, but I know what he is. Power. Dominion. Protection. For me, these are seductive. But now I have a talisman against such forces."

"The charms of a giantess," Flyn said approvingly.

"Partly," Inkstain admitted. "More than that, it is knowledge. Knowledge that I am not irrevocably corrupted or, more importantly, that I am not so hopelessly dissimilar from others as I once believed."

Flyn started to respond, but was interrupted by Ulfrun stepping between him and Crane, laying her hands on their shoulders.

"If you two are composing ballads in my honor, I demand to hear them."

In good spirits, the three walked together, Flyn and Ulfrun jesting while Inkstain basked comfortably in their levity. But while Flyn's tongue produced puns, his mind swam with memory.

Inkstain's revelation had stirred the dregs of lost days to the surface.

Flyn had lain with a female. Once, many years ago, during his time with the Tsigani.

Milosh had docked at a human village which was home to a handful of escaped beldams. They were good workers come harvest time, so the villagers suffered their presence, but required they live on the outskirts of the community, lest some wandering male tried to claim them for his clutch. Human farmers were not about to fight a coburn on the hunt for fresh mates, no matter how helpful the females were. The beldams eked out a rough existence, though far better than the one they would have endured in some tyrant's birthing hut. Flyn still recalled the sudden, mysterious excitement which had come over him when Milosh arranged for him and Gulver to visit them. They went separately, of course, and Milosh set sail before the sun was up the following morning, lest Flyn or Gulver feel a desire to return and try to dominate the females. It was a dangerous chance the beldams had taken, and Milosh too. For the female coburn, the willingness to take that chance was born from desperation, but for Milosh it was simply a necessary risk. He believed if Flyn and Gulver were to join the Valiant Spur, they needed to know what it was they were forever renouncing.

The time Flyn had spent within the embrace of the female was a treasured memory, but one which he seldom recollected. It was too dangerous to dwell upon, the very thought enough to foment an unreasoning rage. He and Gulver had come to blows over the least thing for a fortnight after their respective couplings.

Once, Milosh was forced to call upon Pali to separate them. Many times since his night with the beldam, Flyn wished he had remained ignorant of such pleasures. More times, he wished she was again lying within reach.

Flyn's remembrance and his steps were soon brought to a halt.

Fafnir had led them to the western edge of Hriedmar's Hall and entered a wide, level corridor thick with dwarrow coming to and fro. Many pushed carts or drove wains pulled by mules and muskox. Among the loads Flyn saw bundles of oats, barley and rye, alongside baskets full of hazelnuts, plums and bilberries. Many wains were given over entirely to the transport of turnips and cabbages, piled high behind the driver. Though traffic moved in both directions, Flyn noticed most of the laden wagons came from ahead, their drivers making for Hriedmar's Hall.

"Now here is a tide of plenty," Ulfrun announced, frowning down into the passing wagons.

"Back to the surface we go," Flyn said, clapping Inkstain encouragingly on the back. "Back to the cold."

"I do not think so," the man replied. "Not yet."

It took some time to traverse the busy corridor, but it at last debouched into the first natural cavern Flyn had seen since coming underground. Unequivocally larger than Hriedmar's Hall, the cave spread out into the distance, the ceiling completely lost in towering darkness. Flyn stood stunned, but it was not the enormity of the place which caused him to marvel.

Where a moment before he had trod on flagstones, Flyn now found his talons striding over ground thick with strangely luminescent grass. Rolling plains sprawled out before him, dotted with thickets. Exchanging an awestruck look with Inkstain, Flyn and his companions followed Fafnir to the crest of a low hill. There was no sun, yet they could see far into the distance. An endless patchwork of cultivated fields lay next to rushing streams, little more than glittering ribbons in the distance. Somehow, the vegetation itself shone, imbued with a pale, inner fire. The light did not radiate, but was enough to reveal the individual blade or leaf which housed it. It was as if the land had leeched the stars and moon from the heavens, leaving a black void above an idyllic valley awash in purloined light.

The farmers and herdsmen emerging from the corridor behind struck out in different directions, taking the various tracks and paths that crisscrossed the landscape. As he watched them, Flyn began to notice other dwarrow working in the fields, sowing, reaping, harvesting, working the land and receiving its bounty.

"Well, now we know why the place is so named," Flyn said, leaning towards Inkstain. "Magic, I presume?"

The chronicler merely nodded, his eyes capturing the view.

"It is ancient Magic, Sir Flyn," Hengest told him. "A simple accomplishment for elf-kind, but we svartálfar have long been divested of such craft. Our ancestors, newly severed from the huldu, had the forethought to protect this resource. Now we can but preserve it, and protect it. It is the last such wonder in all of Middangeard. There will never be another of its ilk."

Ulfrun grunted. "Middangeard is Winter's thrall. Within our ever-frozen land, there are none who would not kill for this."

Flyn saw both Fafnir and Hengest struggle not to cast a distrusting look at the giantess. Only the younger runecaster succeeded.

"That is why we so jealously guard it," Fafnir told her, a shadow of threat in his voice.

Ulfrun took no umbrage at the Chain Maker's tone, nor was she cowed. She continued to stare boldly across the Downward Fields, surveying the land with an appreciative eye.

"Let us be on our way," Hengest suggested.

They set off across the fields, quickly embarking upon one of the trails. The cavern was colder than Hriedmar's Hall, yet nothing like the frigid land Flyn knew waited above. He wondered how long they could travel in this hidden tranquility before returning to the surface. His keen eyes could not see the cave's end, suggesting leagues. As they passed the borders of orchards and farms, Flyn had to keep reminding himself that he was underground, not simply walking at night. The illusion was easily banished by a glance skyward, where the shadows hid the stone ceiling, but did nothing to hide the feeling of its ancient weight hanging above. Flyn began to notice the tips of huge stalactites peeking through the inverted ocean of darkness. He shuddered and then did his best to avoid looking up.

After some hours, Fafnir took a narrower spur in the trail and began leading them away from the farmland. The fields quickly gave way to pitted heaths, and the track was often overgrown with thorny shrubs. The way gradually turned uphill and the trail disappeared entirely. Fafnir struck cross-country without pause and soon brought them to an expanse of cheerless downs. The grass lost its inherent luster and the view ahead diminished to the next hill.

"This reminds me of the lands just outside of Gipeswic," Inkstain muttered so that only Flyn and Ulfrun could hear him.

"These are barrows."

"A skull orchard," Ulfrun agreed. "The dead are beneath our feet."

Ahead, Flyn saw the curve of a low stone wall encircling a small rise, upon which stood a lone tree.

"Another Warden," Inkstain said.

Flyn frowned.

They had only seen the despoiled remnants of the Warden Tree in the Fatwood, but even felled, the prodigious size of the trunk had been apparent. The tree before them appeared to be no larger than a common elm. Still, Flyn thought the chronicler was right. The tree possessed an undeniable and unsettling presence, the branches motionless and menacing. And unlike all the other trees in the Downward Fields, this solitary sentinel was devoid of inner light. It stood grimly upon its pedestal of earth, mutely discouraging any approach.

Passing through an opening in the wall, the group walked to the base of the rise, where a carved stone lintel was set into the side of the slope. Beyond the lintel, stone steps led downward to a door, nearly lost in shadow.

Fafnir dropped his pack and produced a runestone from his pouch which immediately began to glow with pale, blue light.

Motioning for the group to follow, the wizard descended the stone stairs and uttered a word of command. The door swung open heavily, noiselessly, providing access to some sort of vault beneath the tree. Without a backward glance, Fafnir stepped beyond the door and was lost from sight. Flyn unburdened himself of his own bag and followed the dwarf down.

After a short passage, the stonework ceased and Flyn entered a roughly circular chamber with a dirt floor. The walls were bolstered with thick roots, as was the crude dome of the ceiling.

Deep, shadowy recesses lay between the gnarled and twisted tendrils. Fafnir stood in the center of the chamber before a small stone bench, his head bowed. The runestone was clutched in his folded hands, the light seeping between his thick fingers barely able to penetrate the deep darkness of the vault. Inkstain entered, followed by Ulfrun, hunched low in the confines of the chamber.

Hengest came last, the scant blue light revealing his face full of trepidation. The younger runecaster's gaze fell upon a spot on the wall to the right of the entrance and he made his way slowly over, then knelt down. Flyn heard him exhale sharply, his breath shuddering.

The room began to fill with whispers.

At first, Flyn thought it merely air whistling through the passage behind, but then, words began to creep at the edge of his hearing. Soft, sharp hisses. It began as one voice, but soon he heard another emerge, as if born from the first. There was a rhythm to their speaking, though he could not make out the meaning. He recognized the language as dworgmál when the third voice rose.

The rhythm began to break, intruded upon by a fourth voice. A fifth. Flyn looked at Inkstain and Ulfrun, and found their faces disturbed.

"What are they saying?" he demanded.

Inkstain shook his head slowly. "It is the augury."

And then Flyn could hear it too.

"We march on blackened feet."
 "Our dead rest not,"
 "a blade must be wrought"

Flyn knew none of the dwarrow tongue, yet he understood.

"One you must find,"
"Among her lost children," *"Upon frosty bough,"*
 "And rime-ridden root"

He lost count of the voices. They whispered over one another, rising and falling in a roiling din of hushed pronouncements.

"We are food for one," *"In death enslaved,"*
"Till the end of days," *"The fate of our race."*

The voices grew desperate, the whispers strident, and the fragments of prophecy sliced out of the tumult. Inkstain began to flinch and even Ulfrun seemed to quail beneath the onslaught of ghostly ravings. Fafnir was utterly motionless, but Flyn could see the wizard's eyes clenched shut as he too weathered the whispers.

"Heavy is the burden,"
 "She will glut upon us," *"A feast of corpses."*
"Her bane to be forged,
Tempered and cooled,
Eight times in the hearts
Of beloved issue."

A cry of anguish cut through the voices. It came from Fafnir. The wizard had fallen to his knees, his face a mask of misery, and the runestone fell from his hand. Free of the dwarf's clutches, the stone shone on, filling the chamber with light.

Flyn recoiled.

Eight wights hung from the walls of the chamber, suspended and imprisoned by the roots. It was they who spoke the augury, the words expelled from their yawning mouths. They leaned forward out of the shadows, pulled towards Fafnir by some invisible force, straining against their sinuous fetters. One, a female, was directly in front of Hengest and was reaching towards him with black-tipped fingers, trying to wrest free of the roots. Quickly, Flyn shrugged out of his harness and slid Coalspur free of its scabbard.

As soon as the blade caught the light, the heads of all eight wights snapped up to look at him, their colorless eyes full of condemnation.

> "*To see her slain,*
> *a blade must be wrought,*
> *three must be gathered*
> *And the eater sought.*"

The vættir now spoke in unison and Flyn realized that they were all she-dwarfs. Their hair was as white as their dead flesh, the dread energies now eddying through the chamber causing it to swirl in wisps around their stricken faces. The one to Flyn's immediate right was only a child, but she stared at him with the same malice as the rest.

> "*Heavy is the burden,*"

"Sir Flyn!" Fafnir called from the floor. "Do not strike! Sheath your blade!"

Keeping the naked steel in hand, Flyn hurried over to the Chain Maker and pulled him to his feet. Inkstain and Ulfrun rushed to their side.

> "*Long shall be the search,*"

"What goes on here?" Flyn demanded over the continued wails of the wights.

> "*Many paths unwoven,*"

With a shaking hand, Fafnir reached into his pouch, fumbling for his runestones. Two were in the dwarf's palm when his hand withdrew from the bag, but in a panic, he dropped them.

The runecaster bent to retrieve them, but the wights' voices overwhelmed him and he could not rise.

> "*Many lives undone.*"

"We must leave this place!" Inkstain shouted.

Flyn nodded his agreement and signaled for Ulfrun to help Fafnir. Before the giantess could move, Hengest stepped into the center of the room and snatched up the fallen runestones. Holding one in each hand, the dwarf shouted with great authority and smashed the stones together. A concussive force erupted from the broken stones and the eight wights slammed back into the wall.

Flyn saw the roots tighten their hold on the writhing she-dwarfs and slowly, one by one, their voices ceased. They hung limply and their milky eyes closed.

Silence again reigned within the vault.

"Turgur's balls," Ulfrun swore. "What are these hags?"

"They are the augurs," Hengest answered, dropping the shards of the runestones and going to Fafnir's aid. "They were his daughters."

Together, Flyn and Hengest propped Fafnir up against the small stone bench. The wizard looked grave. As Hengest tended to his former master, Flyn noticed an object resting beneath the bench.

It was a wide leather belt affixed with eight lengths of heavy chain.

Each chain was graven with runes and ended in a large manacle.

The sound of Fafnir's voice drew Flyn's attention away from the curious trapping.

"I was blessed," the wizard said, staring vacantly. "Eight lasses. Rare for we dwarrow. Eight beautiful heirs to the Downward Fields. I was to be the first King of Hriedmar's Hall learned in the mysteries of runes since Ivar Cinderteeth. We could have led the svartálfar to a new age. A glorious age." Fafnir closed his eyes for a moment. When they snapped open, the old steel had returned and the runecaster rose. Hengest bent to help, but Fafnir avoided his hand. He walked slowly over to one of the now dormant wights, the one just to the left of the vault's entrance, and regarded it for a long moment.

"Finna spoke the first verse of the prophecy while still a girl," the Chain Maker said, not taking his eyes from the corpse of his daughter. "Her sisters were not yet born. We thought it some child-rhyme, something invented, but with each utterance we saw Finna become more distant. Often she did not know what she had spoken." Fafnir walked down the wall to the second wight. "With Sefa it was the same, though new dooms fell from her young lips. The second verse."

The wizard stalked across the center of the chamber to approach the fifth body.

"By the time Vérún arrived, I was beginning to see the interwoven fates of others. In my heart I was overjoyed. To couple a runecaster's craft with a Chain Maker's sight, surely I would be the most powerful dwarf since our split with the huldu." Fafnir's teeth clenched and his next words were a wet growl. "Arrogance! Pride! Avarice! I was a fool. Three more children arrived and all were possessed with prophetic rantings. I came to understand their words, each part of a whole. My own daughters, the first eight links of the chain.

"For centuries I ignored the augury. Denied the doom preached by my own girls. I could see the skein, knew their words to be true, but did nothing. The augury continued to plague my daughters, each becoming more and more eclipsed by fits of foretelling. Finna and Sefa had been driven mad by the time I decided to act."

With a steady hand, Fafnir reached up through the roots and tenderly placed a hand on Vérún's bare, corpse-black foot.

Inkstain spoke, his voice hushed with dismay.

"You killed them."

A cold writhing settled in Flyn's gut and he looked around the chamber at the eight suspended corpses, coming to the terrible conclusion an instant behind the chronicler's quick mind. He stared at the blade in his hand, at Coalspur, renowned weapon of a celebrated Grand Master of the Valiant Spur, a sword he had revered, coveted, fought to win and found pride in possessing.

Opening his fingers, Flyn let it fall to the dirt.

"Winter's teeth, Chain Maker," Ulfrun hissed. "You did this?"

"I did," Fafnir replied, choking on the two words. "Belief in the augury requires acceptance of all its demands. To kill one as mighty as the Corpse Eater I had to forge a blade of dread purpose. Coalspur can never be dulled, can never be tarnished, its edge can shear through metal and stone. But for steel to contain such strength, it must be balanced with weakness. For all its potency, Coalspur can be unmade by one thing. The hearts-blood of the Corpse Eater. When the rune engraved upon the grip tastes that, the blade will shatter. To craft so fearsome a weapon required sacrifice. Sacrifice dictated by the augury. From my fourthborn's own lips I was told to kill my own children." Fafnir's voice broke and he threw his head back, unable to look at his champions, at the sword he had made, at the dead lining the walls. Then his jaw hardened and the dwarf leveled his gaze. One tear slid into his beard, the last drop of a grief Flyn could not fathom. When Fafnir spoke again, his voice was dull, resigned. His hand fell away from his daughter's foot.

"Eight times I tempered the blade and eight times I cooled the glowing steel by plunging it into the hearts of my sweet girls, quenching the heat with their blood. After Finna and Sefa, I vowed never to complete the sword. The price was too great. But Thrisa and Ingunn, having seen the descent of their sisters, pleaded with me to save them from their growing insanity. They begged to die. A century later, Vérún and Systa begged to live. I could not bear to give Gísla and Eilíf a choice."

Flyn looked at the last corpse, the one still in her girlhood.

Horror and sorrow would not allow him to gaze at her long. Fafnir continued to speak and though Flyn could clench his lids shut against the damning sight of the tomb, he could not shut out the wizard's confession.

"The sword complete, I renounced my claim to the throne and began to walk the Chain Maker's path, a path which will soon end, one way or another."

Bewildered and sickened, Flyn shook his head. "You had our pledge," he said to the floor. "We all three agreed to this quest. Why bring us here?"

"For you to kill the Corpse Eater, you must first find her," Fafnir answered. "She dwells in the reaches of the unforgiving north within the bosom of a great storm. The vættir can hear her call, distracted only by the need to kill. As you have seen, they ignore coburn, unable to harm the Corpse Eater's progeny. We must release my daughters. They will know a way through the Mother's Gale and through the tunnels of the mountains encircled by the wind. Flyn, you alone will accompany them to the beast."

Flyn glanced at the belt under the bench. "You intend to chain them to me."

"The vættir do not rest. Until they reach the Corpse Eater, their steps will not falter. Neither can yours."

"The journey could take days," Inkstain protested. "Weeks."

"Six days northward is the sea," Hengest said. "If one does not stop. Flyn will reach the Mother's Gale before he reaches the shore."

"And how are we to help him do battle if he is alone?" Ulfrun asked.

"We need only stay far enough removed to keep the vættir from turning on us," Fafnir replied. "And I can sense Coalspur's presence even if Flyn is lost from sight."

Flyn raised his head to find Inkstain walking a slow circuit of the chamber, peering intently at the roots. "To release the wights, this Warden would have to be felled."

Fafnir nodded. "That is the reason only my daughters are buried beneath its protection, why the dead of the Downward Fields are unceremoniously beheaded and interred in the surrounding barrows. Upon my brother's sufferance and that of his people I have squandered this tree, knowing it too would one day be sacrificed to the quest."

"The Wardens are protected by elven spells," Inkstain said.

"Any who harm them are cursed. We know that Crow Shoulders has sent countless men to their deaths in order to destroy the other trees. Surely, this one is no different."

"Only one of indomitable will and great strength can topple the Warden and live," Fafnir said. His eyes flicked to Ulfrun.

The giantess betrayed no emotion. She seemed neither daunted nor stirred by the task. For one so vehement as Ulfrun, this display of indifference bothered Flyn. Inkstain looked even more concerned.

"I told you all the journey would only become more perilous," Fafnir said. "For the Breaker, that peril is nigh. But I trust in the augury's words. 'All foes to the ground.' Ulfrun *will* bring the Warden down. Flyn, once she succeeds, you will need all the stamina of your coburn blood to survive the coming days. We leave only when you are ready."

These words spoken, the Chain Maker left the vault.

Flyn felt Ulfrun's hand upon his shoulder.

"I will do what I must," she told him. "This gallows-beam will fall. You must make your own choice."

Then she too departed. Issuing a vexed breath, Inkstain quickly followed her.

Flyn sat upon the bench and stared at Coalspur, resting in the dirt. The sight of it disgusted him. All weapons were forged to kill, but this one was made from murder. All for a belief. Flyn had forced himself to share in that belief so he could find purpose and lend his sword-arm to a cause. It was the duty of a Knight Errant to bring justice to the maligned. How many of his sworn brothers had embarked on quests with origins of this much evil? He had been worried idleness would stall his charge into glory. He never expected to learn he bore a butcher's blade.

Enough! He had regained his courage. He did not need this mad endeavor, his oath be damned. Let the sword lie here in this tomb among the innocents it slew. He would rescue Deglan without the Chain Maker's help and then he would be free of this blasted land. With a bitter exhalation, Flyn stood and went for the passage. Hengest's voice stopped him.

"This was Gísla."

The dwarf stood before one of the corpses, the same one he had knelt in front of when he entered the vault. He turned to look at Flyn, his face full of fond recollection.

"You should have seen her in life. Keen. Beautiful. Full of wit. She, Thorsa and I were of an age. And inseparable. I became Fafnir's apprentice just to be closer to her. I think she would have agreed to wed, but Fafnir refused me her hand. He knew, even then, what he was going to do. His choice destroyed his family. You know what became of Thorsa and it is unseemly to even speak of what befell Fafnir's wife. I have hated him for centuries, Sir Flyn. The curse of the vættir, the existence of the Corpse Eater, these had always been. I knew nothing else. To me they were ancient hardships, too vast to understand. I cared only for Gísla and myself.

"Now I know what Fafnir has known for a thousand years. The doom of the dwarrow will claim us all. It will be the end of my people, for none of us are greater than the curse. In the hopes of our salvation, Fafnir Rune-Wise did not just destroy his daughters, he destroyed himself. For the greater good of his entire race, he severed his happiness and his future. If this quest succeeds it will not be his name which is celebrated and hailed until the end of days as the savior of dwarf-kind. It will be yours."

Hengest leaned his staff against the wall and went to the center of the chamber, plucking Coalspur from the ground. He held it reverently.

"This is the blade which pierced the heart of my love," Hengest said. "She and her sisters died at the hands of their father a thousand years before you were born. You did not know them, you did not love them. Your grief is undeserved, Sir Flyn. And you cannot allow your soiled sense of righteousness to make their deaths meaningless."

The dwarf held the weapon out to Flyn and looked at him with flooded eyes.

"Please."

Ingelbert emerged from the vault to find King Reginn War-Loft waiting outside with a retinue of dwarrow warriors. The dwarf lord sat atop his throne which rested upon the doughty shoulders of its bearers. His warriors were arrayed in solid ranks behind him, beyond the low wall. Numbering two hundred, they were a bulwark of steel. Clad in plate armor, the warriors' black beards emerged past the lips of their helms. They were armed with broad shields and the stout hewing-spears favored by the dwarrow.

"An impressive company of field-reddeners," Ulfrun said, her voice coming from behind.

Turning about, Ingelbert found her sitting upon the slope of the Warden's hill, just above the lintel. He hiked up and sat down beside her, adjusting his book satchel to rest in his lap.

Together, they watched as Fafnir conversed with his brother in voices too low to hear.

"Why is the King here?" Ingelbert asked.

Ulfrun shrugged her corded shoulders. "Either to offer aid or hindrance."

"Perhaps his warriors will fell the Warden," Ingelbert said pointedly.

"I thought you too intelligent to try and talk me out of something," Ulfrun replied with a wry smile.

"I am," Ingelbert replied.

Ulfrun craned around to look up at the tree. "It matters not. The sword cock will never agree to aid the Chain Maker now."

"You think him so fickle?" Ingelbert asked bitterly. The question boiled out, unbidden. His sudden anger surprised him, but Ingelbert did not avert the hard stare he gave Ulfrun.

The giantess removed her attention from the tree and regarded him quizzically. "The wizard's deed offends you."

"Does it not offend you?"

"Aye," Ulfrun said, rubbing a hand aggressively over her short, wild hair. "Had I birthed children from my own body, no doubt I would have ripped the Chain Maker's head from his shoulders. Mother to one, mother to all, as we giants say. Luckily for Fafnir Rune-Wise, I have not endured the birthing bed, so my anger resides not in my womb, a most potent cauldron for wrath. I am no mother, but neither am I a maiden. The contents of this charnel house will not send me running. And neither will they deter you." Ingelbert said nothing, allowing his silence to give credence to Ulfrun's words.

"I do not think the coburn fickle," the giantess continued.

"I think him from another world. He is noble. Molded in honor. No doubt you know a better word for him, one we cannot conceive of in Middangeard."

"Gallant," Ingelbert said without hesitation.

Ulfrun smiled. Her face was not mocking. She seemed to savor the word, judging it worthy. "As you would describe him in song. You are capable of great lays, Inkstained Crane." She winked, making sure he understood her double-meaning. Ingelbert accepted the flirtation with a smile, his anger dispelled.

"I think you are mistaken," he said calmly. "I think Sir Flyn will surprise you."

"Why?"

"Because it is one of his gifts," Ingelbert replied.

Ulfrun hooked a thumb over her shoulder. "I must topple this forest-spar, if he chooses to proceed. Would not such a choice also vex you?"

"That is another of his gifts."

They looked at each other and shared a quiet laugh.

Ingelbert shook his head, exasperated and darkly amused.

"I will not try and stop you, Ulfrun. But I must understand why you so willingly embrace all that could end your life."

The question seemed to sadden the giantess. "We giants are immortal, but like the elves who became the dwarrow, we were cursed. The legends say that when Magic fled Middangeard, it took the Element of Ice from our keeping and softened it into Water to be guarded by a new race in Airlann. There the dragons and loyal elves were allowed to live, but the svartálfar and my own people were left here and punished. The giants diminished in both size and power, but Magic could only corrupt our immortality. We live eternal if not slain, but are cursed to seek a glorious end. When a giant becomes enamored with a destiny, we pursue it relentlessly. The earning and fulfillment of our Doom Name is a source of great pride."

"Even though it is a courtship of your own death?"

"Such is the nature of curses, lover."

Ingelbert valued knowledge above almost anything, but he feared to ask the question gnawing at his heart. "Has this quest revealed to you your Doom Name?"

"No," Ulfrun replied, disappointment etched into her voice.

But then her eyes brightened, gifting Ingelbert with her incomparable smile. "Which is why I know, one way or another, this tree shall not be my end." Reaching over, she squeezed his leg and then stood. "Come. Let us go and discover what the svartálfar discuss."

Taking Ulfrun's proffered hand, Ingelbert pulled himself to his feet and together they walked down the slope. Fafnir and Reginn's discourse appeared to be done, for the wizard watched them come, his back to the king.

Ingelbert and Ulfrun bowed respectfully to Lord Reginn.

"Well met, Breaker, Master Crane," the king said. "I come to bid you good fortune on your journey, but find that journey may be delayed."

"Much is asked of Sir Flyn, my lord," Ingelbert said. "He will do as he vowed."

Reginn nodded sagely. "I share your confidence. I do not bestow gifts to those I deem without grit. Which reminds me." The king reached under his robes and pulled a broad-bladed dagger from his belt. Flipping the weapon in his hand, he extended it down to Ingelbert handle-first. "My brother is not the only skilled smith in these halls."

Ingelbert took the dagger, finding the weight daunting.

"You forged this, my lord?"

"I am of little use wielding weapons, now," the crippled king answered. "So, I make them. It does not do for a man to venture into the north unarmed."

"Most gracious, my lord," Ingelbert said. "I thank you."

Reginn nodded, then swiveled to look at Ulfrun. "My brother tells me you are to fell the Warden."

"Aye, War-Loft," the giantess replied. Ingelbert looked down to hide a grin. Only Ulfrun could address a king as if he were a drinking companion.

Reginn thrust his arm out and motioned. From the ranks of his warriors came a dwarf bearing a great axe. The long haft was slightly curved and runes glinted upon the steel of the bearded blade.

"Perhaps," the king said. "This will help you cleave limbs of wood and bone."

The dwarf carrying the axe offered it to Ulfrun. The giantess gave the weapon the barest glance before addressing Reginn.

"I would not offend you, Shield-Borne," she said, "but when my foes fall by my hand, they fall by my hands."

Fafnir turned on the giantess, glowering. "You intend to challenge the Warden without the aid of a sharp edge?"

"Trust in the prophecy of your daughters, Chain Maker," Ulfrun said with a hint of vitriol.

Just then, movement at the vault's entrance caught Ingelbert's eye. Hengest ascended the stairs and approached. He bowed before the King, then faced Fafnir.

"Sir Flyn is ready," Hengest said.

Ingelbert could not resist giving Ulfrun a satisfied look. The giantess acknowledge his gloat with a wink.

"Ulfrun . . ." Fafnir began, but she was already making her way towards the hill.

Ingelbert watched her go, aroused and flummoxed by her sure strides. Behind, he could hear Fafnir addressing the King.

"Brother, best remove yourself."

"We will wait in the barrowlands," Reginn answered. "Should you need aid."

The sounds of clinking armor signaled the withdrawal of the dwarrow warriors, but Ingelbert did not remove his gaze from Ulfrun. She had reached the crest of the hill.

The Warden was nearly ten times her height and the giantess regarded it for a long moment before beginning a slow circuit of its trunk. Ulfrun's head was bowed as she walked, and Ingelbert realized that she was studying the root base. As she moved behind the tree, she was briefly lost from sight, but soon came around the other side. She paused then, one hand drifting up to rest upon the bark. Ingelbert winced, expecting some repercussions from the contact, but Ulfrun remained unharmed.

She ran her hand down the trunk and might have spoken, for Ingelbert thought he saw her lips move. Removing her hand, Ulfrun flexed her fingers, then, looking down at her feet, squatted.

She must have gripped two of the exposed roots, for the muscles in her arms grew taut, straining as she tried to straighten her legs.

Even from a distance Ingelbert could see the sinews writhing in Ulfrun's arms, her thighs rippling as she pushed upward. It seemed she labored for nothing. The tree stood tall and firm.

A low creaking began to be heard. The leaves of the Warden began to hiss as the branches shook. Ingelbert took a step forward, though everything about the tree was a warning not to approach. The air grew thin and cold, rife with fell energy.

Ingelbert could almost see it wafting off the Warden. He looked to Fafnir and

Hengest, finding the runecasters staring at Ulfrun's struggle with grim faces. A grunt of pain snapped his head back to the crest of the hill. Ulfrun's face was twisted in anguish. The exertion should have flushed the giantess's skin, but it was ghastly white. One of Ulfrun's hands suddenly jerked upward and she nearly spilled to the ground, but she ground her heels in and remained upright. A root had snapped, causing the upset in her balance. With a harsh snarl of celebration, Ulfrun seized another root and redoubled her assault. Incredibly, the tree began to lean.

But the struggle was not only physical. Ingelbert could sense the Magic as the tree protected itself, could smell the abjurations pouring into Ulfrun. Another root broke loose just as the giantess choked out a gob of blood. This time, she did fall.

Ingelbert tried to go to her, but was stopped by Fafnir's strong grip around his arm. He whirled on the Chain Maker, but found the dwarf pointing up the hill. Ulfrun coughed and spat crimson, but again got her feet under her. She spun and put her back to the trunk, hooking the roots with her hands and pushed again with the might in her legs. Ingelbert saw the roots begin to separate from the turf, tearing free of the hill. Ulfrun screamed and red rivulets spilled from her ears, standing out horribly against her blanched flesh.

The Warden was beginning to bend, but the giantess beneath would break first. Ingelbert could see it plainly, the inevitable failure. For every bit of ground the Warden surrendered, it took thrice as much from Ulfrun in vengeance. It could be moved, forced to release its charges, but not without a fight. A fight Ulfrun was losing.

"We must help her!" Ingelbert shouted.

"No," Fafnir said and the dwarf's grip on his arm tightened. "We dare not interfere with the augury."

Struggling feebly in the Chain Maker's clutches, Ingelbert let out a moan of despair. Ulfrun's heels were scrabbling in the dirt, exhaustion causing her to quiver. She began to slide away from the trunk, her body wracked with spasms. Dying, she fought on.

Ingelbert was nauseous, sick with rage. He yearned for Gasten. With the owl upon his shoulder, he could end this, cast off the pitiful runecaster's hand and leach away his power. Hengest's too. He would use the two stunted wizards like the blunt instruments they were and turn his fury upon the Warden. Even elf-craft would not oppose him. Their pathetic tree would wilt under the dread focus of his will. No amount of Magic could protect it from the blight of worms and rot he would conjure.

Within moments the great Warden Tree would be nothing but a decayed, etiolated log, the pride of elven Magic reduced to nothing but a breeding ground for mushrooms.

But he could not. Not without Gasten.

The Warden was now leaning heavily, but was far from falling. It clung to the hill, the gap Ulfrun had forced between tree and earth nothing but a maw, laughing at her defeat. The giantess crawled away from the tree, pink spittle drooling from her lips. Her head swung drunkenly as she rose on staggering legs and turned to face her opponent once more. With a gurgling cry of defiance, Ulfrun charged at the trunk, but there was no speed in her steps.

Her shoulder thumped ineffectually into the wood and she fell to her knees.

Screaming and cursing, Ingelbert thrashed against Fafnir's hold. He managed to break loose, but stumbled forward. Reaching out to break his fall, his hand came down upon something smooth.

Through tear-clouded eyes he saw the familiar pages of the elven ledger. The tome must have spilled from his satchel during his flailing and now lay open upon the grass.

Ingelbert saw his own fingers splayed upon the page, but they seemed distant, detached, floating serenely in his tears. He blinked to rid his eyes of the drops and they fell, becoming rain. He saw the back of his hand, the flesh suddenly soaked and within the brightness of reflection he perceived nine figures, shadowy and aloof. Eight stood opposed to one, drenched and occluded by the downpour. The single figure smiled and Ingelbert's sight was eclipsed by teeth running with rainwater. There was something familiar in that hungry grin, as if the owner of the bared teeth knew every crevasse of Ingelbert's hidden shame. The cruel smile faded and now only two figures stood in the midst of the storm, the smiler and a female. Between them, Ingelbert could see his own hand once more. He tried to remove it from the page, hoping to rid himself of the visions, but he was bound to the book. The female standing against the smiler turned her head and a pair of eyes appeared, lustrous and sorrowful. Ingelbert was reminded of Ulfrun's gaze, but as the eyes swallowed him, he saw they possessed none of her mirth. There was no dance of laughter, no spark of exuberance, only ancient wisdom and deep compassion beyond mortal boundaries.

The eyes spoke to him without voice, guided him without force. He felt his mind becalmed and he ceased trying to pull his hand away from the tome. Beneath, the written runes were moving, reforming, yet never settling. The eyes slowly closed and vanished.

Ingelbert inhaled sharply, realizing he had not been breathing. His hand was dry. There was no rain. Leaving the tome upon the ground, he stood and walked towards the hill. Nothing opposed him. His steps were light, his footfalls silent. The slope of the hill was as flat ground, so easy was the ascent.

Ulfrun was sprawled belly-down among the partially uprooted base of the tree, her face resting on one of the hard tendrils. Her eyes were open, glazed over and dim, but she still lived. Ingelbert could hear her breath coming in ragged shudders.

Kneeling beside her, he wiped the frothy blood from her chin. He smiled at her and, keeping one hand upon her cheek, he reached out and placed the other upon the tree.

The Warden instantly tried to repel him with a power primal and patient. He did not resist its attack, merely allowed it to wash past him. Keeping his eyes on

Ulfrun's, he comforted her without speaking and lulled the tree with his resting touch. The Warden was a sentinel of pure life, tasked with the keeping of death.

Below, in the vault, the tree's roots were intertwined with corpses, the imprisonment of their cold flesh its sole purpose. Ingelbert fed it the purity of life, forced it to forget the presence of the dead.

Slowly, the tree receded, relinquishing its long burden. As it succumbed, Ingelbert gathered all the life it had drained from Ulfrun and channeled it back to her. The vital force of the Warden was strong and Ingelbert was tempted to allow the giantess to have it, but he refrained. He gave Ulfrun only what was hers and allowed the Warden to leave the world with all it had brought.

Ingelbert could no longer feel the touch of bark on his hand. Ulfrun now lay fully upon the ground, the roots having fled.

Pushing herself to sitting, the giantess blinked, her eyes beginning to shine once more. The pallor fled rapidly from her face. She stared aghast at the empty hilltop.

"The Warden?" she exclaimed.

Ingelbert extended his hand and opened his fingers, showing her the single seed that lay resting on his palm.

The giantess was still laughing when Fafnir and Hengest trudged to the top of the hill.

Dirt rained down on Flyn as the roots withdrew through the ceiling. Fafnir's daughters fell to the ground, causing the chains around their necks to clatter. Hengest had helped Flyn put on the belt and affix the collars to the corpses before he left the vault.

Now, the eight chains ran from his waist to the prone wights, two directly out from his sides and the other six arrayed between in an arc. Flyn had slung Coalspur, but kept the dwarrow axe in hand. As the wights began to stir, he was glad for the precaution. The she-dwarfs rose in eerie unison and stared at him from behind their thin, white manes. Flyn bent his knees and flexed his grip on the haft of the axe, preparing to dispatch all eight if they rushed him.

The vættir opened their mouths and began to sing. It was the dirge of the dwarrow, the same song Flyn had heard from the horde of wights in the valley. In the confines of the tomb, the voices of Fafnir's daughters rang loudly, harmoniously. The music, given voice by the dead, was strangely beautiful.

To Flyn's immense relief, the wights turned and began walking towards the passage.

"Very well, my ladies," Flyn said. "Lead me to grandmother."

The chained wights traversed the passage with surprising ease, a mindless grace guiding their movements. Still, Flyn was certain travel was going to be difficult while tethered to eight corpses. The dead sisters fanned out after they ascended the stairs and began walking at a measured pace. Thankfully, they went right by Flyn's abandoned pack and he snatched it up without breaking stride.

A sharp whistle prompted him to turn his head. On the hill above, Inkstain,

Ulfrun and the dwarrow wizards watched him. The giantess raised a hand in farewell and Crane's voice carried across the distance.

"For the honor of the Valiant Spur, Sir Bantam Flyn!"

Flyn raised his own hand in parting.

A great clattering echoed across the barrowlands. On a distant hill, Flyn spied the chair of Lord Reginn, his host arrayed along the ridge. The warriors were striking their shields with their spears, sending forth a ringing salute of steel.

TWENTY-EIGHT

Deglan was encased in cruelty. The harsh winds of Middangeard buffeted his face, the savage laughter of the berserkers filled his ears, and in every direction his vision was choked with dead men. He was back in the wilds, in the cold, unforgiving embrace of this cursed land, eyes squinting against stinging flurries and the glare of the sun upon the snow.

Arngrim Crow Shoulders had called a halt to the march in an expanse of field hemmed by sparse holts. For days, Deglan had watched the vegetation grow steadily more scarce as he journeyed north with his captors. The trees here stood meekly, as if hoping to be ignored by the bleak tundra which held increasing dominion over the landscape. When the jarl commanded the column to stop, Deglan slid off the back of the horse he shared with Sigrun, allowing the woman to aid his dismount. She had led the animal towards the trees to be tethered and Deglan yearned to follow, to get out of the wind, but the sight of the deep drifts between him and the pitiful holt defeated the notion.

Gritting his teeth against chill and rage, Deglan glowered at Crow Shoulders' twelve sons as they tormented the Dread Cockerel.

Howling and hooting, the men kicked at the coburn as he whirled at the end of his chain, desperately trying to come to grips with his assailants, but the berserkers merely laughed and danced out of the way. One of them always held fast to the end of the chain collared to the Dread Cockerel's neck, and would jerk it taut should the knight get too close, pulling him to the ground. Deglan had never known a man who could outmatch a coburn in brute power, but every one of Crow Shoulders' bastards could manhandle their captive with frightening ease, their shaggy faces full of mirth as they made sport of his helplessness.

Deglan had watched this wretched scene repeat every time Crow Shoulders' army stopped and the Dread Cockerel's obsessed pursuit of Flyn's sword needed to be arrested. Fortunately for the knight, the rests were few, and mostly for the benefit of the horses.

After all, an army of corpses needs no respite.

Two thousand draugr had been released from Bólmr's moat on the day Crow

Shoulders gave the order to march. Save for his dozen offspring, the jarl brought no living men, leaving them behind to garrison his fortress. Deglan hated to admit it, but it was a wise plan. The Dread Cockerel, driven by fate, possessed a well of nearly inexhaustible endurance. Even the hardiest men would eventually be left behind, to say nothing of an army that needed to be fed. So, Crow Shoulders had assembled a force which needed no such provision; his twelve preternatural sons, two thousand walking corpses and a husk.

Deglan averted his gaze from the Dread Cockerel's plight and turned his scowl on Slouch Hat, who stood beneath the small stand of snow-laden evergreens. The husk was in deep conversation with Crow Shoulders, but the pair were too distant for Deglan to hear their words, especially over the wind. Standing beside the hulking jarl, Slouch Hat looked thin and frail, not needing so much as a cloak against the cold.

"Scheming, bloodless scarecrow," Deglan muttered to himself. He would have spit, but his face was swaddled in the depths of a woolen mantle, leaving only his eyes exposed.

The husk had always been too clever by half, and Deglan had no doubt that all of Arngrim's schemes had been birthed in his stuffed head. The felling of the Wardens, the use of the draugr, it all reeked of Slouch Hat's calculating mind. The husk's involvement explained much which had niggled at Deglan's brain. Despite his distrust for the dwarrow, they were a formidable race and he had been surprised that a mortal had dared risk their ire by despoiling the sacred resting places of their fallen. Even a feared warlord like Crow Shoulders courted his own destruction with such blatant aggression. But with a husk whispering in his ear, one which bore the crown and craft of the Goblin Kings, Arngrim must have been swollen with confidence. With Slouch Hat as councilor and ally, the jarl's revenge was within reach. Crow Shoulders wanted Fafnir's head, and by the look he now wore on his grizzled face, he believed he would soon have it.

The fool! He was being used. But for what?

"What do you want, Slouch Hat?" Deglan asked aloud. It had become a regular utterance, a question often asked of the wind since their march began. So far, the frigid gusts had not answered.

Another harsh bellowing of laughter brought Deglan's attention back to the berserkers. The Dread Cockerel was now face down in the churned snow, trying to rise, but the brothers had grown bored and were now dragging him around by the neck.

Hissing, Sir Wyncott managed to flip over on his back and gripped the collar with both hands to keep it from strangling him as he was pulled roughly across the ground.

It was said Middangeard bred hard men. Well, it had also packed ice around one already inflexible gnome. And he had had a bellyful of this barbarity.

"Enough!" Deglan growled, striding towards the guffawing pack of fjordmen. "I said enough, you pelt-wearing, bear-fucking sons of whores!"

He did not know if the men understood his words, but some insults are plain in any tongue. His sudden interference drew the brothers' attention and they ceased dragging the Dread Cockerel, fixing Deglan with predatory stares.

"Do you want to bloody kill him?" Deglan demanded, watching as the grins returned to the surrounding faces. The berserkers had found fresh prey. Predictable as hungry dogs.

One of them stepped forward and, grabbing Deglan by his thick wrapping of cloaks, raised him bodily off the ground in one fist. The man chuckled as he shook Deglan, spinning slowly in a circle to amuse his brothers with the display. The rough movement caused Deglan's hood to fall away from his head and the wind sliced into his suddenly exposed pate. When the man grew tired of shaking him, he pulled him close, forcing their eyes to meet. The berserker's beard split to show a wet, menacing smile. Then, the fjordman spoke in the tongue of the Tin Isles, heavily accented.

"We. Eat. You."

Deglan returned the smile. "And I will split your arsehole in half when you try to shit me out."

With that, he slammed his forehead into the man's nose.

His own eyes squeezed shut as pain and lights pulsed through his skull. When his vision cleared he found he was still dangling at the end of the berserker's arm. The lout was still smiling. He was not even bleeding. Opening his fingers, the berserker let Deglan tumble to the snow. Several of the other brothers loomed over him, their cruel faces twitching with the anticipation of violence.

Deglan felt someone grab him under the arms from behind and pull him to his feet. There was strength in those hands, but not the crude power of the berserkers. Craning his head around, he found Sigrun standing behind him. The thrall woman's face stared sternly at Crow Shoulders' sons and she exclaimed a string of words in the Middangearder tongue, tilting her head sharply to the side in a gesture of dispersal. The berserkers leered at Sigrun for a moment, before slowly backing away with overexaggerated deference, one of them even bowing. They allowed the Dread Cockerel to stand and escorted him over to the nearest tree, wrapping his chain around the thickest bough. They stood guard, but left the knight unmolested. For now.

Deglan shrugged roughly out of Sigrun's grasp and turned on her.

"Tell your master to control his damn litter," he said, thrusting a finger at the thrall. "Sir Wyncott will be of no use if those twelve animals kill him!"

Sigrun ignored Deglan's rancor and looked at him with weary, yet compassionate eyes.

"Are you alright?" she asked.

Deglan transformed his pointing finger into a dismissive wave. "Fine. It is I who should be asking that of you."

As one of the few beings on the march who actually needed rest, Sigrun was not looking well. As a thrall she was well accustomed to hardship, but five long days through the rough country with little food or sleep was visibly taxing the woman.

"You should be resting while there is time," Deglan told her.

"As should you," Sigrun returned.

"I am Fae," Deglan said, pulling his hood over his head once more. "I will succumb to this blasted clime long after you, my dear."

Sigrun's chin lifted slightly, her countenance hardening.

"Would you wager? I have survived much in my years of life, brief as they may seem to you."

Deglan allowed the strength of her stare to wither his own.

He was wrong to undermine her fortitude with his aspersions. A slave's life was beneath all things, save pity, and those who endured it did not deserve to have their resilience challenged or questioned.

Especially this slave, who had done him no wrong.

The day they left Bólmr, Deglan had become incensed when he learned that Crow Shoulders meant to bring Sigrun on this grueling journey. The jarl did not need her to translate, not with Slouch Hat nearby. Could the rutting goat not do without his bed servant for even one night? Deglan had learned the answer to that question during their first camp. He shared not only a horse with Sigrun, but a tent as well. It seemed guarding a gnome was woman's work. That is, until Crow Shoulders summoned Sigrun to his own tent, sending one of his sons to roust the poor woman from the feeble warmth of her pallet to attend him in the middle of the night. Deglan had soundly cursed the berserker, but had been forced to silence when the man began kicking snow through the tent flaps and atop his blankets. Once Sigrun was gone, Deglan was left alone and unguarded. After all, where could he go? Setting off alone across the hoary wastes was not an escape, it was a surety of death. The thrall had come back to the tent some time later, and Deglan could hear the exhaustion in her breathing as she lay down to catch what sleep she could with the remainder of the time allowed.

They had been given three such rests in five days, and each time Sigrun had her deserved repose interrupted by Arngrim's base needs. The latest rest proved just how base the jarl's needs were.

Upon Sigrun's return, Deglan heard her whimper slightly as she lay down. It was a tiny sound, quickly swallowed and silenced, but his healer's ears heard the pain and it had taken every bit of will Deglan still possessed not to rise and insist to attend to the thrall's hurts.

Had he his herb satchel, he would have, but with no supplies there was little he could do but shame the woman, so he feigned sleep and said nothing in the morning. Still, it rankled him deeply and he cast daggers at Crow Shoulders' feathered back during the following ride.

"Well?" Sigrun insisted, unsatisfied with his silence. "Would you wager?"

"No, I will not wager," Deglan said, keeping the bark from his voice. "I would see us both survive this. And Sir Wyncott, too."

"The coburn will outlive us all," Sigrun said, her eyes flicking over to where the Dread Cockerel was chained. "Theirs is a breed that values self-preservation."

Deglan snorted. "Well, so do gnomes."

"Truly?" Sigrun countered. "For I have seen a gnome openly challenge twelve known slayers, men who would surely have left him little but a pile of offal upon the snow."

Deglan raised his eyebrows and gave the woman a pointed look. "As a breed, gnomes value preservation. As individuals, I am bloody daft."

A small smile intruded upon Sigrun's wan face.

"My thanks for the rescue," Deglan added.

"Come," Sigrun said, extending a mitten-clad hand. "I have a fire prepared, and food."

Deglan followed her to a patch of ground the thrall had swept clear of snow. While it was tempting to build fires in the shelter of the trees, out of the wind, the rising heat often caused the snow to come dumping down from the branches. In Middangeard, an unexpectedly extinguished fire could prove fatal for those dependent on its warmth. Deglan had learned this the first time he griped about Sigrun's campfire placement and been soundly set straight by the thrall.

She now squatted before the fire and stirred the pot suspended above the flames. She ladled the steaming contents into a bowl and passed it to Deglan. He took it carefully, reveling in the warmth that seeped through his own mittens and into his fingers.

He sipped from the edge of the bowl, knowing that the frigid air would soon cool the soup. It was little more than broth, and Deglan drained it so quickly he could not have given testament to its taste. It mattered not, for it was the heat he savored. He nearly moaned with rapture when Sigrun offered him a second bowl.

"I wonder how long we shall stop?" he mused, keeping his eyes on the gorgeous flames.

"Crow Shoulders calls a halt only for food or sleep," Sigrun answered. "But never for both."

Deglan grunted his agreement and nursed the broth. The woman was right, of course. They would soon be on their way.

More hard riding on the backs of shaggy horses, the wind blistering any flesh it could touch. North. They moved ever north. A raven in flight would have discovered a queer sight if it happened to look down upon their company.

One coburn, afoot, clad in little more than rags leading twelve men draped in wolf pelts and the skins of bears. Each man was also afoot and bristling with weapons, loping like the predators whose fur they wore, keeping pace with the coburn through the drifts. A bowshot behind would be two horses and half a dozen pack ponies. Upon one horse, a large man wearing a cloak of black feathers, and on the other his female thrall, riding double with a gnome astride the saddle in front of her. And behind the riders, a hideous sight. A husk leading two thousand dead men across the snow, their shambling frames clad in rusting mail, their shambling steps leaving a dirty swath in the snow behind them.

This was how the army of Arngrim Crow Shoulders proceeded, every day and sometimes through the night. They had passed through lands ruled by other Raider Kings, men who would have called their karls to fight the encroaching warlord had he trespassed with a force of living men. But the sight of the draugr kept Crow Shoulders' fellow jarls behind the walls of their holdfasts and ringforts. No lord should expect his loyal retainers to fight the dead. There was no glory to be had, no wealth, only the horror of crashing spears with a foe who did not bleed, did not fear or flee.

None had challenged Arngrim and he had provoked none to action, leaving the thorpes they passed unharmed, taking not so much as a loaf of bread from the peasants. Today, however, Deglan had seen no sign of fort or hamlet and surmised that they had left the inhabited lands of Middangeard behind.

Crow Shoulders bellowed a return to the march before Deglan was through his second bowl of broth and he watched miserably as Sigrun dumped the remaining contents of the pot onto the fire. Slouch Hat strode close by on his way to rejoin the milling ranks of the draugr, but he did not spare so much as a glance at Deglan. He could feel the closeness of Jerrod's iron crown, hidden beneath the husk's hat, and a sickening ache settled in his head until the dread heirloom passed by.

Deglan spent the day's trek lost in dark thoughts. He settled into the uncomfortable trudging of the horse and his own brooding.

He could feel Sigrun at his back, the only thing warm and soft in all of Middangeard. Once, he felt drowsiness begin to overtake him and he lurched forward in the saddle. He would be damned if he would lean back against the woman and sleep, using her for his own comfort like the wretch that rode ahead of them.

Again, they rode into the night. Deglan's gnomish eyes saw well in the paltry light of moon and stars, but during their first night's march he had wondered aloud how Crow Shoulders and his sons were able to keep a proper path in the darkness. Sigrun had informed him that it was some spell of Slouch Hat's which bolstered their mortal vision. She too benefited from the sorcery.

That was when Deglan discovered the husk's mastery of the iron crown extended beyond commanding the draugr. It was an unsettling, though not unexpected, revelation.

The nights were long in Middangeard and seemed to lengthen the further north the army traveled. Arngrim called another halt hours before the sun was to rise, and commanded his sons to rest as soon as they erected his tent. The berserkers then built for themselves a massive bonfire and loitered around the popping flames. They always slept under the open sky, lolling beneath their bearskins and drinking sparingly from the store of mead carted by the pack ponies. They chained the Dread Cockerel nearby, but not so near that he benefited from the fire. Arngrim had barely seen fit to clothe the knight, giving him stinking rags, rife with holes. Amazingly, the coburn betrayed no discomfort and even appeared to sleep, as if the knowledge that he was once again on the path to claim Coalspur was enough to keep him warm.

Deglan helped Sigrun set up their own tent and they eagerly crawled inside. The woman was asleep as soon as she was prostrate and Deglan arranged the furs over her. He lay back and watched his breath expel in steamy torrents until he drifted off beneath his own coverings.

When the berserker's voice broke through his dreamless slumber, Deglan nearly screamed in fury. Sigrun was already sitting up, gathering herself to crawl from the meager shelter. In an impulse born from useless frustration, Deglan reached out and snatched her wrist without knowing what he was going to say.

Before his impotent entreaty could be made, however, Sigrun hissed in anguish and pulled her arm free. Even in the dark of the tent, Deglan could see her cradling the arm he had grabbed.

"I am sorry," he said, knowing he had not gripped her hard enough to cause harm. He recalled her nearly inaudible cry of pain from the previous camp. "Are you hurt? Let me look."

"No," Sigrun said, her voice soft and stern. "I must go."

Before he could do anything else, she fled the tent. Her steps and that of her escort crunched away through the snow.

Deglan sat fuming for a moment, then growled and scrambled out of the tent.

If he were foolish enough to confront Arngrim's twelve sons, then why not the man himself? He would demand that the jarl leave the woman be, at least for a night. At the worst, Crow Shoulders would strike his head from his body. Well, let it come.

Deglan had lived a damn long time and he would be buggered if he let the fear of death from a bunch of bloodthirsty Middangearders keep him from his calling.

The berserkers' fire was still blazing, but only one of the shaggy brutes was awake, his back turned. Deglan quickly sneaked around to the back of his own tent to block the man's view should he happen to turn. He could see the trail of footprints in the snow left by Sigrun and the other berserker. Oddly, they did not lead to Crow Shoulders' own tent, which lay only a little removed. No, the tracks led out away from the camp, across the drifts. The only thing which Deglan knew lay in that direction were the draugr. Was Arngrim surveying his army of corpses? Why would he wish Sigrun to join him out in the cold, among a horde of dead men left to mindlessly stand vigil through the night? Cursing into his mantle, Deglan set off, using the tracks already made to ease his slog through the deep snow.

The draugr made little noise, but two thousand of them packed together emitted an eerie assonance. Upon the wind, Deglan could hear the creaking of frozen tendons, the jingle of ragged mail, the plinking of snowflakes upon metal helms. It was more a palpable presence than a sound, the air impregnated with the existence of two thousand creatures which did not breathe.

They had been left within a small vale bordered by gently sloping ridges. Before Deglan began his trek down the easy grade, he paused, staring with distaste down at the assembled army standing lifeless in the moonlight. The wind tore the snow from the ridges, sending it sweeping down across the draugr, screening all but the nearest in an ephemeral curtain of swirling white.

Sigrun's tracks led down into the vale for a ways, but broke off before reaching its fullest depth. They climbed the ridge, leading to the last survivors of a grove of firs still clinging to life on the ridge, defying the frost. Deglan continued on, his lungs and legs burning by the time he fought his way to the top of the slope.

Voices caused him to duck and he crawled forward until he reached the trunk of the nearest fir. He waited, holding his breath, listening.

The voices came again, nearly swallowed by the whistle of the air through the trees.

Removing one of his mittens, Deglan dug through the snow at the base of the fir, wincing as the cold sliced into his fingers. Ice and snow were the domains of Water, but beneath the painfully cold powder was Earth. Deglan scrabbled bluntly at the frozen ground with his numb fingers. Magic may have renounced these lands eons ago, but it was still present, lingering within the Elements which it had created. Pushing his hand into the adamant dirt, Deglan implored aid from the Earth, as was the right of his race. He asked it to shield him, to bolster him. There was only a languorous response, the soil nearly lifeless. Deglan might have quickened the Element with his own blood, but he had no blade.

Still, he felt the cold in his body abate, calming his shivers, steadying his breath.

So bulwarked, he moved ahead cautiously, going slowly from tree to tree, keeping contact with the bark as much as he was able. The skeletal grove flirted with the edge of the ridge, but Deglan kept as far away from the slope as the trees allowed. The voices he heard grew nearer and he began to pick out the language of Middangeard. And then, through the trees, he spied four figures standing close to the edge. Arngrim Crow Shoulders was not among them. No, it was Sigrun and the berserker who had fetched her from the tent, conversing with Slouch Hat. Next to the husk stood a naked draugr, its armor and weapons lying in a heap upon the snow. The corpse had been a husky man in life and his pale flesh hung in folds around his middle.

Hunkering down behind a tree, Deglan peered around the trunk and watched as Slouch Hat said a few more words to the berserker before gesturing to the draugr. The fjordmen tore his sword free from its scabbard and lopped the head off the draugr with such speed and ferocity that Deglan startled. The heavy body fell to the ground, now truly lifeless. Sheathing his blade, the berserker bent and hoisted the corpse across his broad shoulders before turning his back and hiking back the way he had come, leaving Sigrun and Slouch Hat on the ridge. Deglan ducked behind his chosen tree as the man passed and felt his stomach turn.

So, Arngrim's sons had adopted the Bone Chewers' malediction. Like that animal Kàlfr the Roundhouse and his mate, Thorsa, the fjordmen were eating the flesh of the animated dead.

Small wonder they were so disturbingly powerful. And so increasingly crazed. Did Crow Shoulders know the madness he had condemned his sons to suffer? Even the dwarrow eventually succumbed to the corruption that came from such a vile source of power. From what Deglan had seen, these mortal dogs would not last another year before they were nothing but slavering beasts, incapable of speech or reason. Good. Let the bastards die with their brains afire and froth on their lips. It was a fitting end, but what orgy of bloodlust would they enact before then? Grimacing in the darkness, Deglan shook his head. Arngrim wanted revenge on Fafnir for the death of his sire, and had irrevocably cursed his own children to see that vengeance fulfilled.

When the man was fully lost from sight Slouch Hat turned to Sigrun.

"That should keep them sated," the husk said in the tongue of the Tin Isles. "By the time their craving returns, all this will be over." Sigrun was silent for a moment, clutching her shawl tight against the cold. "How much longer will we journey?"

"A few days more, I should think," Slouch Hat replied.

"Perhaps longer if the one the coburn chases loses his own way. Tomorrow we will reach the mountains and the way will become more difficult for you and the gnome."

"The Mother's Gale," Sigrun stated with no trepidation.

"Yes."

"What about the jarl?" Sigrun asked, a spark of challenge in her voice. "He is no longer young. Those winds could be his end."

Slouch Hat produced a thin, reedy laugh. "Crow Shoulders is driven by hatred. Though he partakes not of the draugr flesh, his hunger for the runecaster's death feeds his resilience. The mountains will not impede him. Once this dwarrow wizard is in sight he will be like a dog pulling at his chain and we will let him slip. He and his progeny can try to settle their pointless blood-debt with the dwarrow. Whatever the outcome, that feud is of no importance to us. No, it is you who will be in the most danger in the high passes. It will not be easy to endure the Gale, weak as you are."

Sigrun struck the husk. Had he been a man of flesh, the open handed blow would have split his lip. Slouch Hat's stuffed head snapped to the side at the impact.

"Never call me weak," Sigrun said, her voice low and measured.

Slouch Hat kept his face averted as he nodded. Slowly, his hand came up and reached inside his jerkin, drawing forth a dagger.

Deglan nearly rushed forward, but stopped when he saw Sigrun remove her mitten and push back the sleeve of her coat, holding the exposed flesh of her forearm out to the husk.

Slouch Hat took her wrist in his free hand and scrutinized something Deglan could not see. "It is healing less each time. I am sorry."

"Do it and let us have done," Sigrun told him, her voice muddled through clenched teeth.

With a swift sure jerk of the blade, Slouch Hat sliced into the woman's flesh. Sigrun choked as she tried to swallow a cry of pain. Blood poured from the wound, steaming in the air. Dropping the dagger, Slouch Hat pulled his tunic open and pressed the pumping gash to his straw-stuffed chest. Deglan watched as the blood soaked the husk's dry innards, the stalks absorbing the hot fluid. Sigrun's knees buckled and Slouch Hat guided her fall, kneeling with her to the snow, keeping her flowing arm pressed to him. The husk's hat was dislodged from his head and Deglan saw the iron crown beneath now glowing with an inner, eldritch fire.

Nausea gripped the back of Deglan's throat and a roar filled the space behind his eyes, forcing them closed. He could feel the iron, feel it feasting on the woman's blood, growing in potency. His head swimming, Deglan clutched the tree to keep from falling. Pushing himself fiercely off the trunk, he fled, stumbling in the cold drifts.

The tumescent power of the crown punched at the back of his skull as he ran. He had to get away, had to be far from here before the ritual was complete, before Slouch Hat sensed his presence.

Deglan collapsed so many times during his flight that his clothes were sodden with snow by the time he reached the tent. He kept his eyes away from the berserkers' bonfire and their terrible feast, no longer caring if they saw him. Diving into the tent, Deglan flung himself upon the furs, eyes, teeth and fists clenched painfully as he violently shivered. A moan escape from his clenched jaw and he battled against the cold and the dread and the poisonous effects of the iron crown.

Jerrod's crown.

When the last Goblin King fell to his death, the evil thing should have passed to his eldest son, the Gaunt Prince, but it never did, for he was slain at the Battle of Nine Crowns. Instead, the crown remained in the Tower of Vellaunus, until centuries later it was removed by a husk possessed with the specter of Jerrod's lover, slave and killer. Slouch Hat had become increasingly eclipsed by the young girl's vengeful spirit, until she used the husk's body to crown Jerrod's true heir at Castle Gaunt. Once in congress with the bloodline of the Goblin Kings, the crown's true power was made manifest. The fell energies Deglan had felt could only have come from the lineage of warlocks that marched nearly unbroken through the centuries from Penda Blood Coin to the Gaunt Prince, and from him to—

A shiver racked Deglan's entire body, wrenching his spine back and forth as he convulsed. He willed the spasm to subside, biting back cries of anguish, drawing on every vestige of his Fae blessings. At last, his torments subsided and he lay spent upon the disheveled furs, forcing himself to breath slow and deep. He must have succumbed to exhaustion, passing in and out of fitful sleep.

His body was cold and sore when he awoke, the thin haze of a frigid morning leaking into the tent. Sigrun lay asleep on the pallet beside him, her face hidden in the folds of her shawl.

When the cry came to break camp, she stirred and sat up, immediately setting to the task of rolling up the bedding.

"Sigrun," Deglan said. In truth, he had nothing in mind to say. He simply needed her to look at him.

She turned expectantly and when their eyes met, Deglan beheld a familiar gaze. It was all there in the eyes, the same hue, the same lonesome compassion, the same open, intelligent stare he had seen so many times in the homely face of a changeling boy.

Slouch Hat had always been too clever by half. Earth and Stone. He had found her.

TWENTY-NINE

"Don't go getting too far ahead, East!" Flyn scolded the back of the wight's head. "And you, Southwest, stop pushing your sister!"

Fafnir's daughters ignored his foolery and continued their immutable pace up the mountain trail. The wights walked, and sang, neither their steps nor voices ever faltering.

At first, the melodious dirge had been beautiful, even inspiring, but before the she-dwarfs even led Flyn out of the Downward Fields, he had grown weary of their constant wailing.

After the first day, he feared it was driving him mad. The only break he could force in the monotony of their voices was adding his own. Sometimes he produced bawdy harmonies to accompany the dworgmál melody. He would have felt ashamed had a dwarrow heard him, but once clear of their subterranean city, he lifted his voice lustily, finding comfort in the irreverence.

"The juggler dropped and the rooster crowed and that's how a cock got balls!"

Talking to the wights was another distraction. Fafnir had said their names, but Flyn could not recall them all, so he took to referring to the sisters as the eight points of the compass. Even this was absurd, for they did not encircle him, but were fanned out in front, guiding his steps at the ends of their chains. Still, it was eight names he could easily remember and provided some distinction to the nearly identical backs of the augurs' white heads.

Traveling while tethered to the sisters had been simple while traversing the byways of the Downward Fields. Flyn was easily able to settle into their pace, measuring his strides so that the chains refrained from dragging, but were not uncomfortably taut.

This ease had ended, however, when the wights led him through a narrow tunnel that gradually sloped upward. Still underground, it was impossible for Flyn to determine how long he hiked up that tunnel, but his legs were quivering and unsteady by the time it ended in a pile of loose boulders. Instinctively, he had slowed, preparing to stop and expected the wights to do the same, but they were undeterred by the obstacle. They continued forward and Flyn, caught off guard, was dragged until he stumbled and fell, face down.

He was down for only a moment, but the next he knew, the wind was screaming in his ears and his beak filled with snow. Getting his hands under him, he crawled until he could gain his feet. Pale sky and thin clouds were now above him, drifts of snow at his feet and Fafnir's daughters ahead, trudging inexorably forward. Flyn cast a look behind, finding a shoulder of snow-clad peak behind. He had left the dwarrow haven as unexpectedly as he had entered and was once again in the frigid wilderness. The land here was higher than when Flyn entered Hriedmar's Hall and he was never out of sight of one peak or another as the wights guided him across ridges between the mountains.

Since then, the journey had become torturous.

As Fafnir had warned, the wights never rested, never paused, neither obstacle nor indecision ever impeding their steps. It was as if they had perfect insight of the leagues ahead. They ascended ice-covered switchbacks without care and entered scrubby mountain forests Flyn would have judged impassable, but always emerged after effortlessly finding a suitable path. As the sun vanished behind the surrounding peaks and night swam into the vales, Flyn felt the first fibrous touch of worry enter his gut. As the wights pulled him through the darkness, the full weight of their single-minded nature fell upon him. Somewhere in the back of his mind, he had convinced himself that they would eventually stop.

He knew them to be dead, but his eyes, watching their limbs work for countless hours, were waiting for them to tire. But no matter what exertion he beheld, it was only an illusion. Their bodies did not know fatigue, and never would.

During that first night, Flyn lost all sense of direction. His coburn eyes were keen, but his ability to detect heat was wasted on his corpse guides. The moonlight was ever being hidden by clouds and the looming bodies of the mountains. In the shifting light, phantom images flew out of the shadows. Once, Flyn's heart surged to his throat as a deadly drop appeared under his next step, panic seizing him as he struggled not to plummet off the ridge. But the fall was unavoidable, for the wights would not allow him to adjust his path, pulling him towards the abyss. Crying out in desperation his foot came down on the black nothingness. He fell, but only because he expected to fall. The void was nothing but a group of dark boulders, seeming to be a yawning chasm against the snow. When his foot struck rock, the unexpected resistance upset his balance. Fafnir's daughters dragged him unceremoniously over the boulders until he regained his footing. Again and again, his trammeled sight betrayed him and the night was an interminable gauntlet of spills and false terrors.

When the sun rose, Flyn breathed a grateful sigh which crescendoed into a whooping cry of triumph.

"Well, my ladies," he said to the sisters, "my thanks for an unforgettable evening. Perhaps next time we could simply attend a peasant dance. A harvest festival? Maybe a wedding? Though I would have to warn any lads that fancy a jig with you lot. Your feet never stop. Especially you, North, you saucy wench."

To celebrate the end of the night, Flyn ate, slinging his pack of rations around while he walked and selecting a wedge of dense dwarrow cheese and a thick blood sausage. He forced himself to savor the meal, knowing his provisions were limited. The sound of his own chewing mercifully muffled the sisters' singing for a time.

Fortified by the food, Flyn took in his surroundings.

The night's travel had brought them further north and higher in elevation. Presently, the wights led him along a slowly spiraling trail, along the flank of a mountain. At first, Flyn could not imagine who would come into these remote heights often enough to leave such a path, but then his eyes fell upon his guides.

All vættir followed the Corpse Eater's call and many had been loosed of late. Flyn wondered how many dwarrow dead marched ahead of him. And how many behind?

Glancing over his shoulder, he was able to see far down the slope of the mountain and, just to his left, the deep of the valley below. It was then that he remembered his friends, supposedly following at a safe distance. Scanning the landscape below and behind, Flyn looked for signs of movement, but found nothing.

Likely they were just a short ways along the curve of his back-trail, hidden behind the mountain. Fafnir may have called a rest during the night, with intentions of making up the distance during the day.

Still, Flyn kept a regular vigil for signs of his companions, especially Ulfrun, whose long strides and incredible stamina allowed her to range far ahead of the rest.

The sisters continued their march and their dirge. With a smile, Flyn raised his voice in song.

"The juggler dropped and the rooster crowed and that's how a cock got balls!"

The sun was just beyond its apogee when Flyn and the wights reached the top of the peak. The thin air sliced through his coat and feathers, refusing to properly fill his lungs. The summit was a bleak, level stretch of rock, blasted bald by the roaring wind.

As they marched across, Flyn was afforded a grand vantage of the range. The mountains seemed to cover the earth, drifting slowly in a sea of clouds. Grey and blue ridges cut through the white, leading to impossibly high snowcapped promontories. Frozen lakes lay imprisoned in the deep vales. To every horizon the mountains reigned, towering in governance over an ancient land, carved from ice and formed by the brutal hands of time. But for all the majesty, Flyn's eyes were drawn to the furthest north, where a threatening mass of storm swirled, nearly solid with snow and frozen air.

It was a great maelstrom, its very size challenging Flyn's sanity. Barely perceptible behind the terrible funnel, in the eye of the storm, four peaks stood. The churning vortex that crowned the whirlwind hovered directly over the deepness formed between the mountains. Flyn was reminded of a castle, one of impossible proportions, its curtain wall constructed of deadly gales, blowing impregnably between the mountain towers.

Frightening as the storm appeared, Flyn saw desperation within its fury. The raging winds were the wildly swinging sword of a cornered warrior, the vicious snapping of an old, blind hound.

The Corpse Eater dwelt within the center of that storm, using the last vestiges of the Element which was stripped from her to keep the world at bay. Remembering King Reginn's tale, Flyn found further respect for the dwarrow lord. He had entered that storm alone and, more impressively, had crawled out of it again. It was a defeat, but one which Reginn had survived, though it had robbed him the use of his legs. Seeing the Mother's Gale with his own eyes, Flyn wondered if he could endure its onslaught. Each step brought him closer to finding out, but there was still a great distance to travel.

Hours later, Flyn found his trepidation growing as another night descended. The sisters had led him down from the mountain and then over another. They now marched along a saddle gap and Flyn saw a cluster of rime-covered trees nestled in the shadow of the next peak. It appeared they were heading directly for it, and Flyn quickly began unbuckling the girdle which fettered him to the wights. If he could help it, he was not going to spend another night crashing and tumbling along the trail. Once the belt was free from his waist, he held it before him in both hands. He chuckled to himself, knowing he resembled some strange farmer with the ghastliest team of plough horses. Unable to resist, he clicked his tongue at the sisters as they entered the frozen copse.

Eyes darting to the left and right, Flyn quickly searched for a tree of suitable girth. He saw one just ahead and ran forward, right up on the heels of the sisters, giving himself as much time as possible. Looping the belt around the trunk, he tried to get the buckles fastened, but his fingers were cold and clumsy. The slack he had gained in the chains began to recede as the wights pressed on. Flyn only had one of the straps threaded, but not buckled, and the belt began to pull away from the frost-slick bark. With a snarl of frustration, Flyn let the belt slip loose, but immediately began looking for another tree. They were almost through the copse when he found one, thinner than the last, but it was his only remaining chance. This time his hands were more nimble and he managed to affix the belt.

Fafnir's daughters were brought up short, but they continued to strain forward, the chains snapping. Flyn watched for a breathless moment, his eyes shifting from the wights to the belt.

The leather, like the chains, was dwarf-make and likely crafted by Fafnir himself. It showed no signs of stress, the steel rings which affixed the chains holding firm, not even stretching the leather.

Yet, the sisters feet scrambled forward, digging trenches in the snow. The tree began to bend and the belt slid up the trunk, catching on a branch. The frozen wood began to groan, the icicles adorning the branches creating a sharp music as they shuddered and broke. The tree was not going to hold.

Expelling a breath, Flyn sank to his knees, intent on capturing whatever rest he could, even if only for a few moments.

He watched forlornly as the belt bent the bough, ice and bark snapping under the stress. Flyn looked numbly around for a means to further secure the wights, but his weary brain could come up with nothing. After an agonizingly brief time, he rose and unbuckled the belt before the tree snapped in half. The wights continued on and he was left with no choice but to tether himself to them once more and follow.

The long hours of the night passed in currents of delirium.

He plodded along, lost in torpidity, his senses either plagued by unwanted sensation or usurped entirely by cold and darkness. Dead lasses sang in his ears, accompanied by the howling wind and the sound of his own ragged breathing. His feet became insensate. He felt as if he ended halfway down his legs, the pain chased by a hungering numbness that would eventually swallow him entirely.

Yet still his instincts were to live, and he reeled away from false assailants and imagined pitfalls, the only visions capable of breaking through his blindness.

Laughter stabbed through the sisters' dirge. Flyn was only dimly aware that it was his own. He mumbled inanely between laughs, feeble expressions of his wants.

"Must stop."

"Just need sleep."

"Only a moment."

His hand drifted down to the buckles at his middle, languidly caressing the metal. It would be a simple matter to unhook himself from the wights. Surely they could not get far while he slept. He would be able to follow their trail come the dawn.

"Lies."

"Lies!"

"LIAR!"

He laughed again, shattering the night with encroaching hysteria.

"Lazy. Lying. Lout!"

"Wailing. Wight. Women. White women!"

Opening his beak wide, Flyn allowed the mirth to pour out his throat. He gave in to the madness, surrendered to its release.

Quickening his pace, he began to run, throwing all caution aside.

Shoving past the middle two wights, he pulled ahead of his guides, the chains tight against his flanks as they grew taut behind him.

"Keep up my fair maidens! Onward! Come, South! That's the way, East! Northwest, no slacking! Forward!"

He could not go on much longer. But neither could he relinquish the quest to save himself. He had sworn an oath and if he was to fail in the execution of that oath, then best to do it on his feet, giving every last spark of vitality. He knew his mind was unraveling and that his body would soon follow. It was inevitable.

Nothing was unbreakable.

Inspiration burned through Flyn's crazed exhaustion. He stopped, barely able to keep his feet as the sisters overtook him once more, then passed him up. Snatching the hand axe from his belt, Flyn rushed forward on failing legs, approaching the rightmost sister.

"Forgive me, Fafnir."

Gathering the she-dwarf's hair in his free hand, Flyn pulled it up and away, exposing her neck. Careful not to strike the collar, Flyn swung the axe. In three strokes, the head was severed and the body dropped. Flyn went to the leftmost wight and repeated the grisly task. The two chains were now free and trailed behind, dragging narrow furrows in the snow. Flyn dropped the handaxe, then shrugged out of his pack and let it fall too, freeing his sword harness. He drew Coalspur.

The dwarrow steel caught the moonlight. Holding the great blade in one hand, Flyn pulled the two empty collars towards him by the chains, managing to gather them up and keep pace with the six remaining sisters. Dangling the collars from his wrist, he unclasped the belt. Allowing the heavy girdle to fall, Flyn held fast to the two steel collars, looping them over Coalspur's blade, letting them slide down until they rested upon the sword's cross-guard.

With a furious cry and the last of his strength, Flyn reversed his hands on the grip and slammed Coalspur point down. Four feet of dwarf-forged steel sank into the ground, pinning the collars to the earth.

The movement forced Flyn to his knees. Through bleary eyes he saw the steps of the sisters stall. They pulled, but the sword held fast. Collapsing to the snow, Flyn fell into oblivion.

Morning was old when he awoke. His mattress of snow was cold, but he lay a moment as his wits returned, basking in the bliss of stillness. As his eyes regained focus, they fixed upon Coalspur's hilt, the transfixed collars clinking against the quillons. At the end of the two tight chains the belt was suspended off the ground, pulled upward by the six wights still trying to follow a call only they could hear.

Flyn sat up, but did not immediately rise. Inwardly, he gloated. It had been a close thing, but he now had rest and a means of halting the sisters. Now all he needed was food. Flyn stood and walked back down the trail, finding his pack. He partook of more cheese and meat, also finding a skin within the provisions that proved to contain a strong wine, well-spiced with invigorating herbs. Sated and mildly warm, he dug around in the snow near his pack until he found the handaxe, returning it to his belt.

Shouldering the pack, Flyn continued backtracking.

The sight of the first corpse filled him with shame. He had only done what was necessary, but seeing the headless body sprawled pitifully in the snow, bare feet sticking from beneath the simple woolen dress, dispelled the loathing Flyn had developed for the she-dwarfs. He no longer looked upon a creature of living death, a cruel mockery of life. No, this was now the remains of a maiden, twice-slain, lying in the cold wilderness.

Flyn gently lifted her body and walked until he found her sister. He laid them side by side and retrieved their heads, arranging them with as much dignity as he could devise. These two had been North and Southwest, but Flyn did not utter those names aloud.

Their father would be along and use their true names to bid farewell. Flyn spent the rest of the morning resting, waiting to see if his companions would catch up. By noon there was still no sign of them. There was no use worrying. Three wizards and a giant made formidable company. The only course for Flyn was to carry on.

The noonday sun saw him belted once more to his guides.

It began to snow, the flurry increasing with each hour he traveled. By dusk, the fall was so thick Flyn often had a difficult time making out the sisters, only a dozen strides ahead. He had looped the two free chains across his torso and used them to again halt the wights for the night. Flyn tried to build a fire, but the snow and lack of dry fuel defeated his efforts. Hunkering down, he passed the night shivering into his puffed out feathers and taking tiny pulls off the wineskin, grateful to not be walking through the darkness. He managed some sleep and rose before the sun.

The snow had not abated and the trail the sisters followed was nearly covered. They strove on, oblivious to the growing drifts.

The snow clouds held sway in the sky and did not allow the sun to show its face. Only a thin gruel of light soaked through, barely enough to see through the storm. Flyn's world quickly shrank to the path the sisters cut through the snow. It was a realm of white and wind.

Soon, he could no longer hear the song of the wights over the screaming wind, its breath thick with frozen spittle. A great gust charged brutally from the side and knocked Flyn off his feet. He felt the pull of the chains as the wights walked on without a care.

Flyn tried to stand, but his feet could find no purchase, his talons scrabbling at nothing. His legs were dangling over the edge of a cliff! Flyn used his arms to try and haul himself away from the drop, but all he managed was to send armloads of snow cascading over the ridge. It was the wights who pulled him to safety, dragging him clear of the edge as they walked the precarious path without fear.

Once on his feet, Flyn squinted through the blizzard, using his hand to shield his eyes. He could just make out the path, the side of the mountain towering to the right and a sheer drop to the left. Snow-blind, he had not even realized it was there and his ignorance almost caused his end. He wanted to go more carefully, choose his steps, but the unshakable pace of the wights would not allow him the comfort of caution. Now that he knew of its presence, the chasm to his left seemed to call out to him, a great, hollow sucking of air as the wind raged through the abyss. Placing his right hand on the wall of the ridge gave him some sense of stability, but often the piles of rock and deep drifts kept him from reaching the stone.

The trail continued to ascend, further committing their journey to the high passes. Flyn hoped night would not fall while they still trod these narrow paths, trapping them at the edge of the perilous ravines.

Gaining the top of another peak, he was again knocked down as the wind barreled into him unchecked. Exposed atop the mountain, he was impacted by the full force of the gust. It felt as if he struggled through water, so difficult was it to move forward.

Even the sisters were slowed in the face of the blasts. Slowly, they made their away across the summit. Flyn could not tell where the snow beneath him ended and the sky began. The horizon was a motley of swirling white and grey.

A break in the wind eased the curtain of punishing flakes and Flyn's heart lodged in his throat. The wights were making directly for a sheer drop. Flyn could see the edge, a terrifying line of rock standing out starkly in front of nothing but dizzying sky. He dug his talons in, but they scraped feebly, unable to penetrate the thick snow. The sisters reached the edge and turned, briefly giving Flyn a glimpse of their faces before they lowered themselves over the edge and vanished.

Grabbing the chains in both hands, Flyn hauled on the links, trying drag the wights back. It was hopeless. Feet dragging, he was pulled to the brink. Flyn released the chains and spun, dropping to his belly. His knees went over the edge and he fought to find hand holds before the sisters pulled him to his death. One hand found a jut of frozen rock, his feet digging into creases in the stone. He tried to look down, to find his next purchase, but the blizzard blinded him. The chains at his waist tightened and he was pulled off the mountainside.

He plummeted through the laughing gales, terror choking his screams. He saw the edge of the cliff rushing away, then his vision was eclipsed by a horrible, rushing, white void. Falling, he felt the great height beneath him, his death waiting eagerly somewhere far below.

A hard jerk snapped at his waist, wrenching his spine. He seemed to float for a moment, then felt something slam painfully into him from above. One of the sisters. She tangled with him briefly as she fell, then plummeted past. Another followed, missing Flyn by a hairsbreadth. A jarring pain in his midriff signaled the abrupt end of their fall as the chains snapped. Spinning, Flyn slammed into the side of the cliff, knocking his scant breath sickeningly from his lungs. He dangled, and when the nausea evaporated, he was able to look about.

Above, four of the wights clung to the cliff face, the chains about their necks holding him aloft. Below, their fallen sisters hung from their own collars. Only one was moving. Flyn swung until he could grab at the rocks, finding a suitable grip and footing. He climbed down, trying to keep pace with the wights above. Their chains were in his face, constantly getting in the way, but he managed not to fall. One of the wights below also found purchase on the cliff, alleviating the weight that pulled down on him.

It was a long, arduous descent. The wights above had drawn even with Flyn by the time he spied the bottom of the gorge.

He focused on increasing his speed. If he allowed too much of a lead, they would force another fall. Thankfully, only the wight below completed the climb ahead. It continued on its way, but Flyn had been prepared. He jumped free of the cliff before he was pulled off, directing his fall towards a deep drift. There were boulders beneath the snow and he took a bit of a battering, but otherwise reached the end of the climb unhurt and alive.

The wights near him had also been tugged off the cliff, but picked themselves up and joined their sister, continuing their mindless pilgrimage. The other wight who had fallen never rose, her head twisted grotesquely beneath her collar. Flyn quickly drew Coalspur and severed her chain on the move, leaving her behind.

Fafnir's remaining five daughters led him through the ravine, their singing echoing off the walls. Sheltered from the wind and most of the snow, Flyn was able to recover his senses. The defile through which they walked began quite wide, but quickly narrowed, the frost-covered rocks giving way to pure ice. As the walls drew closer in, Flyn was left with only a sliver of sky above.

The snow barely drifted down, but the cold pressed in, emanating from the surrounding ice.

Soon, a toneless roar began to fill the ravine, reverberating from ahead. It grew in intensity, a nearly deafening, pressurized resonance. Looking skyward through the slit of the gorge, Flyn saw the wind slashing violently, churning and turbulent. Ice and snow were caught in the vicious eddies, granting the maelstrom substance.

Flyn frowned up at the bottom edge of the storm and was, for the first time, grateful for the guidance of Fafnir's daughters. They had led him beneath the Mother's Gale.

Ahead, the ravine terminated in the mouth of a cave, gaping out of the ice face. Flyn winced as he passed beneath the whirlwind, but was quickly within the shelter of the cave and soon, the din became nothing but a dull echo, humming through the ice.

The wights led him through a maze of frozen tunnels. At times he stumbled along in corridors black as pitch, while others seemed to glow, the ice imbued with sunlight, reflected and channeled into the depths of the caves. The tunnels twisted and turned, some ascending, while others sloped sharply downward.

More than once, Flyn lost his footing on the slick floor. Many of the passages were barely dwarf-height, forcing him to stoop and crawl. Others gave way to immense caverns, beams of light, infested with falling snow, spearing down from holes in the distant ceilings.

As they drew near the black mouth of one cave, Flyn's nostrils were filled with the stench of ordure. The stink poured forth, overpowering despite the cold. For the first time, Flyn felt the sisters change their pace, quickening their steps as they passed the reeking portal.

Sooner than he expected, the tunnel ahead ended in the radiance of snow and sun. The sisters led him out into the light.

They emerged into a large, roughly circular gorge. The feet of four great mountains formed the depression, their towering slopes completely surrounding the hollow and honeycombed with the mouths of caves. At the center of the vale stood a massive tree.

Flyn's beak stood agape as he craned his neck upward to try and absorb its inconceivable height.

The tree was completely devoid of leaves, its uppermost branches rivaling the surrounding peaks. The eye of the maelstrom was centered above the tree, leaving the entire vale free of the storm. As the wights began walking across the dale, Flyn leveled his gaze. Roots as large around as drum towers coiled up from the ice, supporting a trunk which the walls of the Roost could not have encompassed. The girth of the tree dominated the valley, leaving barely a bowshot between the root base and the slopes of the gorge.

Hoarfrost covered the wood, bloating the already huge branches.

Indeed, the entire tree was encased in murky rime, giving it a sickly, petrified appearance. Flyn detected movement all along the tree, which proved to be scores of vættir, walking along the roots, climbing the slopes formed by the ice, and scaling the boughs, each struggling higher.

At the top of the tree, the thick branches splayed up and out, and Flyn could see a pile of debris resting in the palm of the limbs.

A nest.

The vættir were making the long climb towards it and several fell while Flyn watched. Some were caught by shelves of ice growing from the trunk or nearby branches, but one plummeted to the valley floor to break upon the hoary roots. Flyn saw dwarf corpses half encased in ice at the base of the tree, some still moving, still trying to struggle out of their frozen prisons.

"Well, ladies," Flyn told the sisters, unbuckling the belt and letting it fall. "Off you go. As for me, I do not fancy another climb."

Doffing his pack, Flyn pulled Coalspur's harness over his head and dragged the blade free, tossing the harness and scabbard aside. Flexing his neck and shoulders, he gazed up at the distant nest, employing his coburn vision. He watched for a moment, scanning the cold heights, but could detect no heat. Could she have perished? Had she succumbed to time and now lay like her mate, a lonely, lost pile of bones? No, the gathering vættir proved she still lived. She was up there.

Filling his lungs with cold air and holding his sword aloft, Flyn crowed at the top of his voice, issuing the war cry of the Valiant Spur, a throttling screech of challenge. Thrice he crowed, each expulsion louder than the one before. His cries echoed through the dale. As they receded, Flyn waited and watched.

Movement caught his eye, above the nest in the highest branches. Heat began to appear across his vision, a muted blur the color of shifting flame. Flyn could see a shapeless bulk perched in the limbs, now beginning to emit a heat quickly turning an angry red. A pair of great wings unfurled, snapping outward, shedding a layer of snow and ice that hung briefly in the air before falling away from the extending feathers. A prodigious head snaked out from under one wing and Flyn saw it swivel to look down upon him.

The Corpse Eater opened her beak and answered his challenge with a shriek that shattered the ice around her.

THIRTY

"Your name is Beladore."

Deglan watched Sigrun closely as he said the words, but his statement did nothing to the woman. She did not even look up, merely continued to try and rub warmth into her hands through her mittens.

Crow Shoulders' army had stopped upon a wide plateau near the edge of the Mother's Gale. The winds this close to the maelstrom whipped into Deglan. The gusts kept him shivering, nearly kept him from breathing, but they would not keep him from learning the truth. He had waited long enough.

They were forced to abandon their mounts in the high passes and, though Sigrun remained close, helping Deglan struggle through the snow, the punishing gales shushed all attempts at speech. He yearned to question her, but that desire had been placed behind the need to survive the mountains.

When they reached the plateau, Slouch Hat was able to focus on quelling the winds and Deglan nearly collapsed with relief as the incessant pressure fled his body. Soon, the howling voice of the Gale receded. It was a queer sensation, looking at the solid twist of that seemingly living storm, its roar muted, its breath weakened.

Deglan became aware of his own breathing and the sharp sniffles of the woman beside him.

He took a quick look around. Slouch Hat was in council with Arngrim two dozen paces away. Half of the warlord's sons had left to scout ahead, loping off into the blowing snow outside the husk's protection. The other six were near the edge of the plateau, surrounding the Dread Cockerel, keeping him from marching headlong into the Mother's Gale. In that instant, Deglan feared for Flyn. Was he somewhere within those peaks? Or was his sword simply lying next to his wind-shredded corpse? No, if anyone could get through that storm, it was Bantam Flyn. But speculation and self-deluded comfort were a waste of time. Deglan had more pressing concerns.

He saw his chance and did not waste it on questions.

"Your name is Beladore," he repeated. "And you are no thrall. Leastways, no thrall of Arngrim's."

"Slouch Hat told me you might discover the truth," the woman said calmly, still intent upon her hands.

"He bloody well knew I would," Deglan growled. "Why do you serve him?"

The woman looked up and Deglan saw that there was no difference between Sigrun and Beladore. She had not changed because she had been discovered. She did not gloat or show dismay.

Indeed, Deglan could detect no difference in her bearing or countenance. Whatever name she used, this was the strong, haunted woman he had known while in his cell and throughout this blasted march.

"He is not easily denied," she replied.

Her answer caused Deglan to sneak another look at the husk.

During the slog through the passes, Slouch Hat had used the crown's Magic to blunt the force of the blizzard at times, but most of his craft was focused on navigating the draugr army through the passes. For all the husk's cunning, he could not successfully herd all two thousand. Many of the dead had been lost to ravines, their careless steps dropping them over the precipices.

Others simply trailed behind, the column stretched thin through the narrow paths. The reach of Slouch Hat's control must have had its limits, for the numbers of the army dwindled after each peak.

Even huddled in frigid despair, Deglan's old soldier's brain had kept track of the numbers, and he smiled into his mantle as more and more of the draugr were lost.

Now, barely half of the original two thousand remained.

Staring at the reaping winds between the four peaks ahead, Deglan thought the rest were doomed. He doubted even dead men could prevail against that maelstrom. Certainly he saw his own death within the towering cruelty of the gusting gyre.

"That is not the reason," Deglan said, turning back to Beladore. "Tell me the damn truth."

For a moment, he thought his brusqueness would cause her to refuse, but she took a decisive breath, holding it in for several heartbeats before answering.

"Who else can teach me about my bloodline?"

Deglan stilled. "You know."

"I am Jerrod's heir," she said, without pride or shame.

"Though in truth, I was told years ago, while in exile, by a crone I befriended." She gave a small, self-deprecating laugh. "But, in a place dubbed the Isle of Mad Women, it is unwise to believe any of what you hear."

"Until Slouch Hat rescued you."

The smile faded. "Until I escaped."

"The humans have long said there is no return from that isle."

"Well," Beladore's voice was a whisper, "there is no more isle, now."

The certainty in her hushed voice sent Deglan's hair standing. He opened his mouth to respond, but Beladore spoke before he could.

"You knew Ke—" she stopped abruptly, her face rippling with conflict. "You knew my husband."

Deglan scowled. She meant Kederic Winetongue, the human warlord who hated Fae and failed to see his most trusted warriors making deals with Red Caps, among other trespasses.

"I had the displeasure," he said through sour spit.

Beladore's head tilted slightly to the side. She seemed almost intrigued by his vehemence. "Could you possibly hate him more than I?" Her eyebrows rose slightly. "Slouch Hat is right about you, Master Loamtoes. Your capacity for grudges is bottomless."

"That hollow bastard is about to learn how right he is through personal experience."

The woman's face filled with sadness and pity. Pity, Deglan saw, that was directed at him. "I hope you will discover how wrong you are. But I wonder if even immortality could provide you enough years to change."

"And what of you?" Deglan spat back. "How many years will it take you to see your own folly? Why do you wish to embrace your ancestry? It is filled with nothing but evil, bloodshed, enslavement and madness. Why would you walk the path of sorcery when there are others to tread?"

"Like motherhood?"

The words lashed at Deglan from the woman's tongue. Her face was wroth for the first time. Deglan found himself cowed in the venom of that stare. Bugger. Did she know? He tried to speak, but produced nothing but a slack-jawed stammer.

"Do not search for sweet sympathies, Deglan Loamtoes," Beladore said, her voice quavering. "Believe me, there are no words that can heal my wound. Not even the most potent of elvish herbs in your ken could quell my pain for a single heartbeat. I know you were there. At the end, with my son."

Deglan needed to be very careful now. "I did not see it," he told her, truthfully.

"But I felt it!" Beladore's entire body shook with the exclamation, though her voice barely rose above a hiss. "His anguish and fear struck me down across leagues, his last moments filling me with excruciation, a pain only eclipsed by the great emptiness which followed. I thought I would die, hollowed out from the inside as I knew he was gone from this world. Nothing of him was left, nothing but an ache inside my womb that nearly devoured me, and a tiny, tearful whisper that I followed to Castle Gaunt.

"I knew something of my Magic by then. Unwittingly, I had unleashed it upon the isle in my grief, my power blooming as my son's was extinguished." She broke off for a moment, some terrible memory fluttering across her face. Deglan swallowed, wondering what fell deeds she had wrought upon that cursed island. Beladore shook herself, her eyes snapping up once more. "I carry his beginning within me. I needed to see the place that was his end. But all I found was the remains of a husk. I renewed his life with my sorcery, seeking only answers, seeking someone who could tell me what had happened to my little boy. What Slouch Hat could not tell me, the Forge Born with a name could, for I had discovered much more within that castle than I sought."

"The damn iron crown."

Beladore nodded. "My birthright. A dread relic too dangerous for me to yet master. The husk helped me use the power of the crown to command Coltrane to answer our questions. I know my son perished to save those who failed to save him. I know that he was brave and compassionate, loving those who allowed him to die. I know you accompanied his body, alongside the coburn knights who were his guardians." Beladore's face grew distant as she drifted in bitterness. When she spoke again, her teeth were clenched. "I even know the horrid name he was saddled with when he lived an orphan in their stronghold."

She could not say the name, and neither would Deglan.

"What did you call him?"

Beladore's grim visage was briefly broken by the barest of smiles. "Cadell."

Deglan kept his face placid. He wondered if Corc knew Pocket's true name. The knight had never said if he did. Deglan did not even know if there had been time for an exchange of words when this woman had placed her changeling babe into the knight's arms in order to save the child from Kederic Winetongue's wrath.

"What does Slouch Hat want in Middangeard?" Deglan asked, wanting to keep away from the subject of the gurg.

"That is for him to reveal," Beladore replied.

"Then at least tell me what happened to Coltrane."

"That I will. But you must tell me what became of my son's body." Deglan's mind raced. This woman was sinking rapidly into darkness. Within a span of years she could be the next Goblin Queen, if that is what Slouch Hat intended. Airlann would bleed if the Red Caps marshaled behind her. Telling Beladore that her son still lived could be all that was necessary to steer her from that fate.

Deglan could reunite them, let them live together in safety. Would she allow herself to be exiled to another island? Or would she take Pocket from his protected seclusion? More importantly, did Deglan risk telling her at all? She had already fallen prey to the husk's influence and, though his designs remained a mystery, he had the crown and the woman that was meant to wear it, at his service. The dwarrow and the men of Middangeard had already suffered. What could Slouch Hat accomplish if he attained both heirs to Jerrod's crown, mother and son? It was too dangerous for anyone to discover Pocket still lived. Yet, surely his grieving mother deserved to know. Once she did, it was possible she would renounce Slouch Hat and the crown, the joy overtaking all other emotion. And what of Pocket himself? Was it Deglan's right to rob the boy of the chance to know his mother's love?

Deglan weighed all of this in an instant. He made his choice and took a deep breath.

A shout of triumph rang across the plateau, ending Deglan's words before they began. The scouting berserkers had returned and ran to their father, savage joy in their yellow smiles.

They spoke excitedly, loudly.

"What are they saying?" Deglan asked.

"They have caught sight of the dwarf," Beladore replied dispassionately.

Slouch Hat broke away from the jarl and his brood, nimbly traversing the snow to approach Deglan and Beladore.

"Crow Shoulders goes to get retribution," the husk said without feeling. "Time for you to make good on your bargain, Deglan."

"I will talk to the wizard," Deglan proclaimed. "You just make sure Crow Shoulders keeps his word as well and leaves the rest be."

"You will have to rely on your own cunning for that," Slouch Hat said. "Sigrun and I will be proceeding into the Gale with the draugr."

"You said you would help me!"

The husk's face rumpled with weary curiosity. "Have I not? You are still alive. And I have no intention of harming your companions. I care nothing for them. Deglan, you made your proposal to Arngrim before you knew I was at his side. You should cease this belief that I am the cause of your predicament."

"This was my fool notion," Deglan agreed grudgingly, "but you could damn well be my salvation. You can command the dead, tame the wind. Tell me you cannot stain the snow pink with these louts with a thought."

"True," Slouch Hat conceded. "And should they choose to stand in my way, I will do just that, as I will with any who oppose me." Deglan could no longer look at the husk. His eyes went to Beladore and he briefly saw a curdled brew of feelings at war upon her face before her resolve hardened once more.

"I wish you luck, Master Loamtoes," she said earnestly. "I hope you soon find your way home."

There was an unspoken question behind her eyes.

"If you wish to visit Cadell," Deglan told her, "go to the Roost in Albain. There is a ridge on the eastern side of the promontory where the Valiant Spur cremates their own. That is your son's resting place. Fare you well."

Deglan turned away and saw Crow Shoulders had assembled his boys. They thumbed at their weapons and made jests to one another, basking in the promise of blood. It looked as if they intended to take Sir Wyncott with them.

As Deglan took a step to join them, he felt Slouch Hat's fingers claw into his shoulder.

"A parting gift, old friend," the husk's reedy voice said.

A dizzying wash of pain nearly spilled Deglan to the snow.

He kept his balance, but was bent double and watched as blood poured from his nose to adorn the white at his feet with crimson jewels.

"Buggery and shit," Deglan snarled, his voice thick with bile. "What did you do to me?"

He heard laughter and shouted jests issue from the berserkers. Their words waded heavily through his stuffy ears.

"By a giant's cock! Hrani, go and fetch that stunted fuck."

"Not I. It is said gnomes are grown from piles of dung. I will not sully my hands with his shit-skin."

"It would only make you smell sweeter, brother."

Roars of appreciative laughter erupted from the men and Deglan looked up, his head clearing.

Crow Shoulders gave an impatient wave of his arm. "Tell the gnome to come, hollow man!"

Deglan did not speak the fjordmen tongue, yet he understood every word. He glanced back at Slouch Hat.

"You are stubbornly blind to so much," the husk said.

"Best you are not deaf as well."

Deglan produced a rude gesture. "I would rather you had made me able to piss lightning." He turned his back on the husk and joined the Middangearders.

"So, which one of you she-bears has the smallest prick?" he asked, smiling.

One of the berserkers backhanded him. The blow was delivered lazily, yet it caused Deglan's teeth to slice the inside of his mouth and send him reeling. He righted himself quickly, looking at the man who struck him.

"So, you then," Deglan said, spitting blood at the man's feet.

"I shall call you Thumb Cock, until you give me your name."

Snarling, the man drew a seax and brandished the long knife in Deglan's face. "Name me such aloud again and it is not my name that will enter your ear!"

"Grand," Deglan said, ignoring the knife. "I was just trying to discern if you could now understand me as well. Clearly you do. Off we go."

"Enough!" Crow Shoulders barked. "Tind, carry the gnome. I will not be slowed."

The jarl set off and his sons fell in around him. Two of them held the Dread Cockerel's chain, pulling him along behind them, while another pair prodded him from behind with their axe hafts. Deglan was lifted roughly and placed on Thumb Cock's back.

The man's long hair smelled horribly, as did the skins he wore, but within moments the group stepped outside Slouch Hat's spell and the wind returned, ridding Deglan's nostrils of the stench. He gripped Tind's furs at the shoulder and clung to his waist with his legs, the man doing little to support him as he hurried through the drifts. To Deglan's relief, the berserkers did not go into the Mother's Gale, but skirted its edge. Soon, their steps turned away from the maelstrom and the ground sloped downward. The high country bordering the Gale was crisscrossed with crevasses and caves. It was astounding that Arngrim's sons had been able to track anything in this hoary waste, much less a wizard, but the six scouts soon led their father and brothers into an icy gulch.

The path down was little more than a trench, but it quickly widened as the ground leveled off. The berserkers went more cautiously now, fanning out with swords and axes in hand. Tind shook Deglan off his back without warning, causing him to fall rump first onto hard stones just beneath the snow. Standing with a wince, Deglan followed the men through the expanding gully. They were hemmed in by walls of loose stones mortared with ice, but the depth of the gully was only twice the height of the fjordmen and they did not seem overly concerned with ambush. Their steps were slow, but it was the patient pace of the hunter, not the fearful uncertainty of the wary. The walls soon receded into the snowbanks, emptying into a mountain pass that intersected the gully. An escarpment stood across from the mouth of the gully, a stone sentinel, guarding the crossroads of the pass.

At its base, Deglan could see a solitary figure.

He watched the berserkers cast smiles at their father, seeking his approval. Crow Shoulders gave them no such satisfaction. His focus was entirely upon the figure.

The warlord closed the distance, his cloak of feathers billowing in the wind. His sons followed in a pack, keeping both Deglan and the Dread Cockerel close.

"Hail, Arngrim Crow Shoulders!" the figure exclaimed.

The voice was not Fafnir's. It took Deglan a moment, but he recognized the figure as Hengest. His blue hair had been shaved off, but that beardless face was unmistakable. A heavy staff was in the dwarf's hand, a steel ram's head adorning the top. He stood calmly, as if waiting on the men, expecting their arrival.

The last time Deglan had seen Hengest, he was unconscious and near death. Surreptitiously, Deglan looked about for signs of the dwarf's companions; his savage wife and that bald braggart, Kàlfr the Roundhouse. Were Crow Shoulders and his sons about to be set upon by a pack of those bloody big wolves?

Deglan did not find that prospect entirely unwelcome, so long as he were not devoured along with the fjordmen.

Crow Shoulders stared at the dwarf for a moment, then turned swiftly and seized Deglan, dragging him forward. The warlord pointed at Hengest.

"Is this Fafnir Rune-Wise?" Arngrim demanded.

Deglan hesitated. Hob's knuckles, had the man spent his life pursuing a dwarf he had never laid eyes upon? Was this some test?

"There is no need to abuse the gnome," Hengest called out. "I am the runemaster's apprentice, come to see justice delivered to you, mortal. Justice for the atrocities committed against the dwarrow."

Crow Shoulders growled and shoved Deglan away. "You svartálfar will continue to suffer until I have the head of your master. Too long has he eluded me, and no underling he sends in his stead to shield his cowardice will prevent my vengeance."

Hengest smiled thinly. "The Chain Maker does not avoid facing you out of cowardice, Arngrim Crow Shoulders. You are simply beneath his notice."

"Chain Maker!" the jarl scoffed. "This was what he named himself to my father. A forger of destiny. Bah! A charlatan! He seduces men with lies and false promises, his witchcraft leaving them to rot in delusion. He is nothing but a deceitful soothsayer."

"No, mortal," Hengest replied, as if speaking to a child.

"His gift is true. But every link in his great chain must be tested to ensure it does not break. Your sire was simply made of inferior metal."

Arngrim chuckled grimly. "You speak true. He was a weak man. Speaking to birds was his only skill. Perhaps that is why your master gifted him with your precious dwarf steel." The warlord slowly drew his sword free of its scabbard. "To make him stronger. Well, I need no such steel to be strong, so I intend to return this sword to the wizard. Through his guts."

Hengest shook his head chidingly. "Fafnir has business within the Mother's Gale. Your search for vengeance ends here."

Arngrim tossed an amused look over each of his shoulders, encompassing his twelve sons. "You believe you have the power to oppose us, dwarf?"

The runecaster grinned. "No. Not me."

A shadow appeared above the dwarf, quickly passing over him as something large leaped from the escarpment at his back.

Ulfrun landed in the snow between Hengest and the berserkers, her knees bending to absorb the impact. The giantess straightened slowly, fists clenched. She was two heads taller than the fjordmen, and she swept them all with eyes glinting deadly purpose.

Deglan let out a sigh of relief. This was better than big wolves.

Arngrim sniffed, unimpressed.

"You think my sons have not slain your kind, giantess? They fear not immortals, for they are now more than men."

"Aye," Ulfrun replied. "I know what they are. Skin-wearers and Bone Chewers. Killers glutted on the dead flesh of the risen. They no longer fear the bite of the shield-snake or the piercing of war-reeds, believing their skin proof against weapons. Yes, Crow Shoulders, I know what they are. But you know not me.

"I am Ulfrun the Breaker. A daughter of Frost, the breath-stealer, the life-ender. I am called Whore-Shield, Boast-Ender, one of the Foretold. I am a fist of rage and hold quakes within my hands. You have incited a storm. The doom of your sons is my own and I face it without fear. I will put them in the ground and tear the roof from your hall. Look at me, Arngrim Crow Shoulders, and see the end of your murder."

The voice of the giantess was cold with confidence, hardened by certainty. Deglan saw doubt shadow the jarl's face. His sons, however, remained undaunted.

The berserkers began to converge, their feet pawing at the snow. Each man's breath grew increasingly guttural, pulsing out in white vapor. All eagerly approached the giantess, save one, who held fast to Sir Wyncott's chain, urging his brothers forward with fierce shouts.

Ulfrun did not wait for the men to surround her.

She charged forward, bent low, and swept a wave of snow at one of the berserkers. The man was taken off guard and before he recovered, Ulfrun barreled into him, her knee coming up hard under his chin. The berserker was lifted off his feet by the impact, flattening out in the air before landing hard. Ulfrun skidded to a halt and snatched the fallen man up, lifting him over her head and flinging him at two of his brothers. The trio went down in a tangle of sprawling limbs.

Deglan laughed, but his glee died in his throat as all three quickly rose again. He had sworn the one Ulfrun struck would have suffered a snapped neck. Blood poured from the man's mouth, staining his flaxen beard, and he spat broken teeth, but was otherwise hale. His weapons had fallen from his hands when Ulfrun hit him, but one of his brothers tossed him an axe. The berserkers eschewed the use of shields, preferring to wield a weapon in each hand, so there was no shortage of sharp edges now closing around the giantess.

Bellowing, the berserkers charged as one. Ulfrun ran to meet them. Just outside of the men's reach, she flung her legs to the side and dropped to the ground, twisting into a log roll. She knocked nearly half the berserkers off their feet, snatching one by the ankle as she sprang to her feet. With a vicious swipe of her arm she hammered the man's head into the side of the promontory, scattering his brains across the rocks.

Deglan heard a curse choke from Arngrim's throat and the man stared wide-eyed with horror as the limp form of his son slid to the ground. The other berserkers stood stunned, proof of their own vulnerability made brutally evident. Ulfrun did not squander the opening. She darted to the side, catching the man at the end of the line in the crook of her arm. She spun and wrenched, and Deglan heard neck bones grind to pulp.

Just then, Hengest, who had stood motionless, made a small gesture with his free hand. There was a sharp, metallic ring.

Deglan whirled to see the chain tethering the Dread Cockerel snapped in twain, sundered by an unseen force. The man guarding him was fixated on his brothers' battle with the giantess and took no notice. The coburn wasted no time, hooking his arm about the man's throat and throwing his weight backward. The knight fell to the ground, dragging the choking man atop him. Deglan saw the coburn's legs shoot up and around, then his feet hammered down, driving his natural spurs into the berserker's gut.

Arngrim spun, rushing to his fallen son's rescue. The warlord drew his sword back, readying to stab the Dread Cockerel, but the coburn kept the berserker between himself and the blade, denying Arngrim an opening to strike.

Snatching up the length of broken chain, Deglan swung it in an arc over his head, chopping down on Crow Shoulders' wrist.

The man grunted in pain, but kept hold of his sword. He whirled on Deglan, but as soon as the jarl's back was turned, the Dread Cockerel jumped to his feet, an axe now in his hand. Arngrim screamed as the coburn hamstrung him. He dropped heavily, the pumping wound in his leg steaming.

Deglan looked back to Ulfrun and found the giantess fully engaged with the remaining nine berserkers. She moved quickly, landing blows with fists and kicks, but her skin was now crisscrossed with red wounds.

"Help her!" Deglan cried, turning back to the Dread Cockerel.

The grim knight regarded him for a moment, eyes blazing, clearly struggling with the desire for vengeance against the berserkers and the insistent call of Coalspur.

The sword won.

Sir Wyncott turned his back on Deglan, on Ulfrun and her fight. The berserker he had gored still writhed upon the ground.

The coburn grabbed the stricken man by his hair and set off running, back towards the Gale, dragging the wretch behind, leaving a trail of vibrant red across the white.

"Buggery and shit," Deglan swore.

Ulfrun had managed to seize one of the berserkers, using him as a shield against the rest, but the fjordmen were now taken by frenzy and hacked without heed, butchering their brother to get to the giantess. Ulfrun flung the bloody carcass at her assailants, then kicked forward, stomping a man in the chest, knocking him away. A cry of pain escaped her lips as a berserker sword slashed her upper arm and another opened a gash in her thigh.

Deglan cast about and found Crow Shoulders struggling to stand on his lacerated leg. Deglan scanned the snow for the man's fallen sword and plucked it up. Its size made it unwieldy, but Deglan placed one hand around the grip and the other around the blade, trusting his heavily wrapped hands to provide protection from the keen steel. Trudging up behind Arngrim, Deglan straddled the man's back and wedged the blade up under his chin.

The warlord hissed and grew still.

"Call them off," Deglan demanded. "Call your curs off!"

Arngrim attempted to nod, but the blade bit into his flesh.

Deglan eased the pressure enough for the man to speak.

"Reifnir!" he shouted. "Hadding! Brami!"

It was no use. The berserkers were deaf to their father's voice, lost in the throes of bloodlust.

Six still stood against the giantess, but for each brother fallen, she bled from ten wounds. So covered was she in her own blood, Deglan did not know how she kept her feet. With a snarl, Deglan released Crow Shoulders, but kept hold of the sword. He hurried for the escarpment, where Hengest stood watching the battle placidly.

"Do something, damn you!" Deglan cried.

Hengest shook his head. "I cannot. The Breaker has declared her Doom Name. My interference would be a grievous slight."

"Then give slight, you hairless cretin! She will have her bloody life."

"And she would take mine for the favor. I am afraid there is nothing either of us can do."

Scowling, Deglan turned back to watch the fight that was quickly coming to an end.

Ulfrun had felled two more, but the last four sons waded in, two to the front and two to the flanks. Deglan recognized Tind among them, closing in from the right. The giantess bolted left, catching the berserker's swinging axe with her forearm, snapping the long haft. She slammed her fist into his face, staggering him, but was unable to deliver a killing blow, her momentum halted by pain as another man shoved his sword through her leg. Ulfrun spun, leading with a reaping swing of her arm, but the berserkers sprang away. The motion caused the giantess great pain and she lost her footing on her injured leg, falling to her good knee.

The man she punched quickly recovered, his nose pouring blood, but with his axe broken, he was left with nothing but a seax.

The sword was still in Ulfrun's thigh, stabbed completely through, and the brother who left it there accepted an axe from his twin, leaving each man now with only one weapon. Their frenzies had faded, replaced by a killing calculation far more deadly. Deglan grimaced. Ulfrun may have stood a chance if the bastards had remained berserk. Now they were thinking, watching.

So was Deglan.

Bloody Nose was on the left flank with his long knife. He would need to get damn close to harm the giantess. Axes were held by the twins in the center, while Tind, at the right flank, grasped the last sword.

"Well that is just poetic," Deglan muttered and made his move.

The berserkers charged together, going for the kill. Tind never saw Deglan coming. Using both hands to lift Arngrim's sword, he swung low. Deglan was no warrior, but he was skilled at amputations. The dwarf steel sheared through bone with frightening ease, taking Tind's foot off at the ankle. The man tried to take another step on an appendage that was no longer there and fell face first into the snow.

The twins swung their axes, but Ulfrun flung her torso backwards, flattening her back nearly to the ground. The berserkers' hews passed harmlessly over the giantess and she sprang back up, snatching the twins' heads in her hands and slamming them together, shattering their skulls. The last man came on, his dirk poised in a downward strike aimed for Ulfrun's eye. Catching his arm, the giantess rolled and before Deglan could blink she had the man pinned beneath her, his head caught behind her knee. Her jaw set firmly, Ulfrun gave a quick jerk of her hips and the muffled sound of a broken neck preceded the pinned man's final twitch.

Through a face horribly streaked with blood, Ulfrun glared at Deglan. She rose slowly, keeping her transfixed leg stiff.

"You," she said, her voice hoarse with pain and exertion.

"You deprived me of my Doom."

"Oh, come off it!" Deglan groused. "This way you still get to drink, fuck and sing! Besides, you said you were meant to kill them all." He waved a hand at Tind, whimpering on the ground.

"Well, this one still lives. So, you are bloody welcome!"

"I do not kill helpless, footless men."

Deglan could not help himself. He started laughing. "By his own admission, he does not have much of a cock either."

A smile cracked Ulfrun's face. "Mayhaps killing him would be a mercy then."

The giantess too began to laugh, throwing her head back.

Deglan's eyes squinted closed as he gave himself over to grim humor. A sudden, dull, squelching noise caused him to jump slightly, interrupting his laughter. Opening his eyes, Deglan found Hengest dragging his ram-headed staff out of the ruins of Tind's skull. Shards of sticky bones fell from the steel-wrought horns.

Deglan gave the dwarf a disgusted look.

"A poor deed," Hengest admitted. "But necessary. This feud must end here."

The runecaster's head turned. Deglan followed his gaze.

Arngrim Crow Shoulders had crawled to the carnage. He struggled to each of his sons, one by one, placing a hand on their still, broken forms. He was weeping.

At last, he came to Tind and cradled his gory head.

"End me," the warlord pleaded, tears mixing with his son's blood.

"As you wish," Hengest said. "But it shall not be my hand. Your father had a gift, Arngrim. He was friend to the valrôka."

Deglan heard a caw from behind and turned. What he saw caused him to curse and take a step back.

The escarpment was suddenly choked with scores of large crows. Their heads were cocked downward, staring at Arngrim with unsettling keen eyes. Deglan had not even heard them alight, but there they perched, nearly covering the stones, a mass of croaking, restless black.

"We runecasters also know the language of the valrôka," Hengest continued. "They were pleased to hear that the man who has hunted them ceaselessly, worn their feathers upon his back with disdainful pride, would be brought low."

Crow Shoulders looked up at the escarpment, his black beard full of frost and frozen tears. He stared at the birds dully for a moment, then bowed his head back to his dead son.

"Come," Hengest said, motioning to Deglan and Ulfrun.

They all moved off, the giantess limping.

Deglan flinched as the sound of fluttering wings filled the air behind him. Angry caws arose in a chorus, accompanied by the high shrieks of a man being torn apart by sharp beaks.

At last, distance and the howling wind swallowed the terrible noise.

Deglan stopped and thrust a finger up at Ulfrun. "Sit."

The giantess nearly collapsed as she tried to lower herself to the ground. With a deepening frown, Deglan inspected the sword through her leg. "This will need to come out."

Ulfrun nodded once, her jaw clenching. Deglan instinctively reached for an herb satchel that was not there. He turned to Hengest. "Have you the craft to stop bleeding?"

The runecaster paled slightly, his face growing dubious, but he set his jaw and removed a runestone from his bag. "I will do what I can, but we should get her to Fafnir."

"Where is Flyn?" Deglan demanded, probing the skewered flesh around the blade.

"Within the peaks beyond the Gale," Hengest answered.

"Alone?"

"Yes."

"We were on his trail," Ulfrun put in, "but were forced to divert when we caught sight of Arngrim's forces."

With a practiced yank, Deglan pulled the blade free. A sharp intake of breath was the only sound the giantess made in response to the pain. Deglan stepped back and allowed Hengest to go to work with his Magic. The blood flow ebbed slightly, but only the wound made by the blade's exit at the back of Ulfrun's leg fully closed. After a time, Hengest stepped back.

"That is all I can do," he said, his expression contrite.

"Much improved, Half-Rune," Ulfrun said, standing slowly.

"My thanks."

The giantess still bled from a dozen deep cuts and she seemed unsteady on her feet. Deglan stifled a growl in his throat.

There was nothing for it. Without his medicines, he was powerless to help her.

"We need to get to Fafnir," he said.

"He goes to confront the husk sorcerer," Hengest told him.

"His name is Slouch Hat," Deglan said. "And he has an army of dead men."

"We saw," Ulfrun said, her voice shuddering as she put weight on her leg.

"Does the Chain Maker have a way of fighting nearly a thousand draugr?" Deglan snapped.

Hengest seemed to find the question amusing. "He has Ingelbert Crane."

THIRTY-ONE

Fafnir gave the signal to move as soon as Arngrim and his men left the plateau. Deglan and the captive coburn went with them.

"The fjordmen have taken the bait," the Chain Maker said.

Ingelbert was relieved to see that none of the draugr went with them. Hengest and Ulfrun had a difficult enough task.

Inwardly, Ingelbert had doubted the efficacy of this plan, but it appeared all was now proceeding as Fafnir predicted. With the jarl and his warriors drawn away, there was a chance to deal with the greater threat. Ingelbert followed the dwarf away from the ridge that had been their vantage, losing sight of the plateau as they hurried down the slope.

"Make haste, Master Crane," Fafnir insisted needlessly.

Ingelbert allowed the slope to speed his descent, sliding more than stepping, keeping a hand on the steep grade behind to help steady and steer. The dwarrow wizard, despite his shorter stature, still outpaced him.

The Chain Maker had burned with a fierce energy since finding two of his daughters beheaded on Flyn's trail. Their final demise, as well as their respectful arrangement, was clearly the work of the young knight. Fafnir had stared at their decapitated forms for a moment, then stooped to brush the fresh snowfall from their faces.

"Finna. Eilíf. Go you to deserved rest, my loves."

The bodies were those of Fafnir's eldest daughter and his youngest. Eilíf still had the appearance of a girl. Ingelbert had looked away then, feeling he intruded on the dwarf's grief. His eyes met Ulfrun's and they shared a silent commiseration. What torture to bid farewell twice. Nearby, Hengest regarded the bodies with an odd mixture of sorrow and relief.

After a time, Fafnir stood, keeping his back turned as he spoke.

"It is strange that I should grieve for those that were already dead," the Chain Maker said. "I know this. I ended their lives long ago, but the guilt of my deed never leaves me. The prophecy, however, demanded I find some peace or I would not have been able to continue, and so I resigned myself to my daughters' end centuries ago. Until I encountered you."

Fafnir turned and looked directly at Ingelbert. His eyes burned with anger, but his voice was full of a strange, morose wonder. Ignoring Hengest and Ulfrun completely, Fafnir continued.

"Your first display of sorcery was returning an owl to life. Such power is unfathomable, especially in mortal man. And only days ago, I beheld your banishment of the Warden Tree, commanding an elven spell to relinquish its purpose. Unknowingly, you had done this before, with the elven ledger, but to come so far, so quickly, surpassed even the vast gift I saw within you." Fafnir took a step forward. "There is huldu Magic within you, Master Crane! Since Skagen, a hope has been growing within me, though I resisted its kindling. I dared believe your place in the augury was my own redemption. That you were meant to restore my daughters to life, give them back what I had stolen. It was folly to have such a hope, but I could not resist. I admit, that hope still burns, but now, for Finna and Eilíf, it matters not. My fragile wish for them is forever beyond reach. And so I grieve anew."

Ingelbert had no words. He could barely meet the dwarf's eye. What could he say? Fafnir's hope *was* folly. The elven Magic came from the green book, Ingelbert was certain of that now. It channeled power through him, used him as a vessel, just as Gasten had done. And the owl had not returned, despite Ingelbert's certainty that he would. It was just as well, for Gasten's influence was prurient and corrupting. His presence was ever a herald of woe.

Fafnir would find no resurrection for his lost children while Ingelbert was within that dread bird's sway. They were contrary forces, the book and the owl, and yet they came from the same source. It was as if Ingelbert sat before a blazing fire. The book was the warmth on his skin. Gasten was his flesh burning within the flames. Nurture and destruction. Comfort and calamity. Ingelbert had somehow found himself poised between the disparate dominions of two entities far greater than he. But Fafnir had given his life over entirely to the currents of greater powers, he was a creature of belief. How could he be made to understand?

"I am not mad," Fafnir said, seeing Ingelbert's hesitance.

His steady gaze faltered, and he flicked looks at the others. "Fate will determine how this ends for us all. But there is a difference between what the Chain Maker knows and what the father wants."

Fafnir stalked off then, without another look at the forms of his daughters.

Mere hours later, Ulfrun had spotted the draugr. They marched through a lower pass, the horde easily visible even through the eddying snow.

"This stinks of a warlock," Fafnir muttered, frowning down at the column of dead men. He shot looks at Ingelbert and Hengest.

"Can you sense it?"

Hengest nodded readily, his eyes not leaving the army below. Ingelbert gave no response. Other than a natural sense of foreboding at the sight of the draugr, he felt nothing. Reaching a hand into his satchel, he touched the elven tome. Nothing.

Though his wizardry would not manifest, nothing prevented Ingelbert from conjuring his knowledge of the past.

Warlock was the name given to the human sorcerers who would later become the Goblin Kings. It meant oathbreaker. Long before they ruled Airlann, that was all those wicked men were, traitors and deceivers. The elves were their patient teachers, never suspecting they tutored their own usurpers. At least, not until it was too late.

Perhaps, if we had dealt with them as more than unruly pupils, we may have prevented the Usurpation.

Ingelbert froze. *We?*

Slowly, he moved his hand off the tome and out of the satchel. The thought had not been intrusive. On the contrary, it had come naturally. For a moment, history had become memory. Pangs of centuries-old regret still lingered in his heart. He could not sense the warlock, but for a single, connected moment, he had known him.

"Yes," Ingelbert said, confirming Fafnir's appraisal. "The sorcery of the Goblin Kings is at work here."

Fafnir squinted down at the column. Slowly, his arm came up and he pointed. "There."

Ingelbert followed the dwarf's finger to a thin figure at the head of the column. Unlike the throng behind, it bore no weapons or armor. Indeed, so unencumbered was the figure, that it appeared to walk atop the snow, gliding strangely over the drifts, barely needing to bend into the blustery wind.

"There is a smaller group," Ulfrun informed them. "Not a mile ahead of this army. I think it is Crow Shoulders. I believe he has Deglan Loamtoes prisoner."

Fafnir turned away from the pass below. "Show me."

And so they had spent the day following, watching and planning. Fafnir was eager to vent his furor, but all thoughts of retribution against Arngrim Crow Shoulders seemed to have fled.

He only had a mind for the warlock. Ulfrun, too, was overtaken with an obsession for their foes, though her brooding stares were directed down at Arngrim's dozen raiders.

"What is it?" Ingelbert had asked her, coming to stand by her side. The giantess had barely been able to relax her vigilance while she spoke with him.

"The hanged man in the Fatwood," Ulfrun replied. "He spoke of Crow Shoulders' sons. Those twelve below are they. I must bring battle to them."

Ingelbert was disquieted by the finality in her voice, but said nothing. Ulfrun would not suffer his worries.

"I wish you were accompanying me," she said after a time.

Breaking her gaze away from the men below, she turned and smiled at him. "To record the battle, praise my prowess and fury within one of your books."

Ingelbert returned the smile. "You shall be beautiful and terrible to behold."

"Aye," Ulfrun breathed. "Luck to you, Inkstained Crane."

"And you."

Not long after, she had left with Hengest. Within an hour, Crow Shoulders pursued. Now, it was time.

Ingelbert reached the relative flatness of the plateau a few steps behind Fafnir. The dwarf already had his sword in hand, a runestone clutched in the other fist. The massive whirlwind of the Mother's Gale dominated the sky, raging between the peaks. The plateau was an anvil, unceasingly smote by hammers of wind, kicking up frozen sparks. Squinting against the blizzard, Ingelbert pawed at the hilt of his dagger, but left it sheathed when he saw the assembled draugr, a dense smudge in the swirling white. What good would a dagger, even one of dwarf-make, do against hundreds of dead men?

As they drew closer, the draugr regarded them with cold, impassive stares. Ingelbert wondered if it was Fafnir's Magic keeping them from attacking, or simply that the sorcerer controlling the army had not yet noticed their approach. His question was answered when the draugr suddenly parted, opening a lane between their ranks and causing Fafnir to pause. That momentary reluctance told Ingelbert that this was not of the runecaster's doing. So, they were expected. The Chain Maker strode boldly through, leaving Ingelbert no choice but to follow. The dead did not try to deter them, but merely turned their heads and bodies to mark their passing. As they emerged from the ranks, the wind abated, as if they had crossed an unseen threshold into a bubble of calm.

A few dozen paces away, closer to the Gale, stood a pair of figures. The warlock was tall and unnervingly thin, wearing a broad-brimmed hat. Next to him stood a shorter figure, well-bundled against the cold, but Ingelbert could still see a woman's shape beneath her layers of clothing.

"So, this is what tries to thwart prophecy?" Fafnir snarled, still moving forward. "A straw-stuffed man!"

Ingelbert saw that it was true. The warlock was a husk, his face a sack with hollow pits for eyes. Ingelbert had only ever seen one other. When he was boy, a troupe of minstrels tarried for a time near the orphanage, and their harpist had been a husk of unequivocal skill. The scarecrow now before him was far more sinister than that musician of childhood.

"I am called Slouch Hat," the warlock said with a dip of his chin. "We have met before, Fafnir Rune-Wise, though I am sure you do not recall. You wore the guise of a steel-peddler and came to the village of Hog's Wallow, whose elder I served."

Fafnir took another step towards the husk. "It was believed you slew the man."

Slouch Hat shook his head. "Of that I was guiltless. I have never taken a life."

"No," Fafnir said, his voice dropping low and deadly. "You only throw a pebble and watch the avalanche. My people have suffered and died because of you, hollow man. Crow Shoulders despoiled our barrows at your advice. That much is now plain."

"The vættir are dead, dwarf," Slouch Hat declared briskly.

"I have no care for your offended sense of honor."

"Our dead slay our living!" Fafnir roared. "They are a threat to all life!"

"Only until they have been devoured," Slouch Hat returned without emotion.

It was Ingelbert's turn to surge forward, offended by the husk's twisted logic. "And what of those who stand here?" he demanded, throwing an arm wide at the surrounding draugr. "They are walking corpses where once they were breathing men. Cursed now to living death because they were forced to take axe to the Warden Trees."

The husk's abyssal stare regarded Ingelbert from beneath the brim of his hat. "Who are you?"

The question was unexpected. "I, uh, I am, Ing-Ingelbert Crane."

"And what is your purpose, Ingelbert Crane?"

Recovering his composure, Ingelbert met the husk's calculating gaze. "I am the chronicler to the Knights of the Valiant Spur." Slouch Hat turned slightly towards the woman at his left.

"Indeed?"

"He is far more than that," Fafnir proclaimed.

Slouch Hat ignored the dwarf. "The life of a thrall is over the moment they enter bondage, Ingelbert Crane. The fjordmen have a terrible custom of slaying a jarl's servants upon his death. There is no freedom from thralldom, save the end of life. Arngrim Crow Shoulders condemned his slaves to die in the felling of the Wardens. I merely told him the trees must be toppled."

"To draw me out?" Fafnir demanded. "It was a clever lie. It may not have worked."

"True. But it furthered my aim."

Fafnir's glower deepened. "And what is that?"

"To feed the Corpse Eater," Slouch Hat replied.

Fafnir's patience snapped and he nearly charged the husk.

"Why?" Ingelbert asked quickly, his question stalling the dwarf's anger.

"In the hopes that she will shed her savagery," Slouch Hat said, his tone suggesting the answer was obvious. "That she will regain some of her intellect and majesty. At the very least, to elevate her from the dumb beast she has become."

Ingelbert's mind worked quickly. He was beginning to find this husk intriguing. "You seek an ally."

"That would be useful," Slouch Hat conceded. "But I will settle for a witness. A voice to tell me the tale of the last of the first Elementals. An account from a being who saw the beginnings of the world and the end of Magic's favor in these lands. A witness to events that must not repeat."

Ingelbert's intrigue turned to awe. "You want to prevent Airlann from succumbing to an Age of Winter."

The folds of Slouch Hat's face twisted into a disquieting smile. "For a start. I only tell you this in hopes that you will understand my goal as greater than your foretold quest. Abandon your intent to slay the Mother of Gales. I have no wish to harm you." Fafnir chuckled darkly. "It is not our quest to abandon. The foretold slayer of the Corpse Eater is already within her lair."

"Poor, deluded prophet," Slouch Hat scolded. "You have the wrong champion."

Ingelbert saw a wrinkle of doubt appear at the corner of Fafnir's eye.

"My allies hold the true slayer in chains," the husk continued. "I am sorry, Chain Maker. You have failed. Leave here with your companions and your life. If I can save the poor fool you convinced to march to his death, I will."

Waves of heat began to distort the frigid air around Fafnir's fist. Without taking his eyes off Slouch Hat, the dwarf slid the smoldering runestone across the edge of his sword. Steel and stone scraped with a sharp sibilance and the blade burst into flame.

Fafnir pointed the burning sword at Slouch Hat. "You claim there is no blood on your hands. I say, there will be none on mine when I scatter your dry carcass into the Gale."

"The Magic of a runecaster," Slouch Hat scoffed, addressing the woman at his side, his voice instructional. "Such feeble artifice."

The husk extended an arm, thin fingers splayed. The flames licking up from Fafnir's sword died as quickly as they ignited.

Slouch Hat closed his fingers, seeming to snatch at the air. The blade shattered with such force that Fafnir was thrown to the ground. Ingelbert flung his arms up to protect himself from the flying steel. He was unharmed, but the dwarf was bleeding from scores of small wounds caused by the fragments of his sundered sword. Fafnir's eyes blazed with pain and fury. He stood, a bestial noise rumbling in his throat.

"Do not," Slouch Hat warned.

Fafnir reached into his pouch, drawing forth a pair of stones. He gripped one in each hand, his jaw set with concentration.

The ground began to rumble, layers of snow parting as a fissure opened at the runecaster's feet. Ingelbert flung himself backward as hulking shards of ice erupted from the crack, spearing upwards in frightening succession as the fissure snaked towards Slouch Hat.

The husk watched the ice charge him, his only motion to calmly push the woman away from his side. The shards came within a hands-breadth of the warlock before violently reversing course, surging back across the trench which birthed them, back to towards their conjurer. Ingelbert shouted a wordless warning at Fafnir, but the dwarf did not budge. Arms flung back, the runecaster leaned forward, bellowing defiantly as he tried to halt his own spell. The ice slammed into him, unchecked, shattering with the impact. Fafnir was flung into the air and landed among the draugr.

"Enough!" Ingelbert yelled at the husk.

"He dooms himself with his stubbornness," Slouch Hat replied.

Heedless of the dead men, Ingelbert ran to the fallen dwarf.

He still lived, but his breath was ragged, his eyes unfocused.

"Destroy him," Fafnir wheezed.

Ingelbert shook his head uselessly. "I cannot."

The Chain Maker groaned, struggling to rise. Ingelbert heard the husk's voice drift through the press of draugr.

"Yield, Fafnir Rune-Wise. I cannot allow you to delay me further. Yield, or I must leave you to the dead."

Ingelbert looked desperately around. The draugr were slowly coming closer, rusted weapons clutched in desiccated fists.

He could no longer see Slouch Hat through the bodies. Fafnir kept trying to stand, but his legs would not support him. His breath sounded wet and labored.

With shaking hands, Ingelbert threw open the flap of his satchel and removed the heavy ledger. Propping the spine on his forearm, he allowed the book to fall open, placing his free hand on the pages. He closed his eyes, trying to rid his mind of the approaching corpses. He thought of the eyes he had seen in the Downward Fields. Those gorgeous, lustrous eyes that seemed to hold the wisdom of ages imprisoned. He willed them to appear, but only succeeded in summoning them to his imagination.

Opening his eyes, Ingelbert stared at the pages, searching for aid. The runes remained fixed to the page, an innocuous accounting of provisions.

The draugr closed in and panic seized him. He snatched his knife from its sheath and sliced the meat of his palm, slapping the wound onto the pages.

"Wake!" he screamed.

His blood stained the vellum, barely flowing in the cruel cold.

"Wake! Please!"

A shadow fell over Ingelbert and he looked up to find Slouch Hat standing over him. The draugr had ceased moving. The husk reached down and plucked the tome from Ingelbert's unresisting grasp.

"What," the husk mused, "do you have here?"

He flipped idly through the pages, his sack face creasing with interest. After a time he peered over the splayed tome.

"Tell me, chronicler. Do you know what these pages contain?"

Ingelbert lifted his chin pridefully. He was no wizard. He was nothing that could stand up to this warlock. But he always had knowledge and, in this quest, had discovered a mote of courage.

This husk would see both before the end.

"It is an elven ledger," Ingelbert replied with the sureness of expertise, "dating from the Battle of Nine Crowns. Once, it was protected by a spell of occlusion, but I unraveled it, so that the contents could be read. You hold an accounting of the stores of armaments and provender quartered by the grand army of Irial Ulvyeh and his allies during the final days of the Pig Iron Rebellion. That book is the property of the Order of the Valiant Spur and in my safekeeping." He held his injured hand up. "You will return it to me."

Slouch Hat made no move to comply, his eyes returning to the book. "My first master was a scholar. The man was obsessed with the history of the Rebellion, especially the Battle of Nine Crowns. Two armies marshaled that day, one of Red Caps, the other of allied Fae, but they did not meet. No, instead it became a duel of royalty. The sovereigns present on that battlefield met to treat, but the talks descended into violence. Do you know the names of those august peers who fought that day, Master Crane?"

Ingelbert stared up at the husk, trying to read his intent. His question sounded earnest, not mocking or scornful. Still, Ingelbert could not discern why he asked it. That sack face betrayed nothing, but so long as they conversed, Ingelbert remained alive. He could hear Fafnir still fighting to breathe, lying upon the snow. Perhaps he would recover given enough time. If Ingelbert could provide that time, the rune-caster might find a way to defeat this warlock.

"Jerrod the Second had been murdered in Black Pool," Ingelbert replied, his voice measured and steady. "Thrown from the Tower of Vellaunus. The Gaunt Prince was left to lead the Red Caps alone, and it was he who met with the other eight lords. Princess Aillila Ulvyeh represented the elves. Allied with her was the gnome king, Goban Blackmud, Vindwor Secret Keeper, high-king of the dwarrow, a human lord known as Tattered Iefan, the self-styled Coburn King, the queen of the sylphs—"

"You are a learned man," Slouch Hat cut him off, his eyes never leaving the book, "and far too intelligent not to have guessed at the true nature of this book. I am certain you know it is more than a tally of arrows and radishes. Forgive me, but it is too dangerous to leave in your keeping." The husk snapped the ponderous book shut with one, reedy hand. "It shall remain with me. You would be unwise to remain here. I am only taking a small contingent of the draugr into the Gale. The rest will soon be beyond my control. I hope you can drag the dwarf to safety before they are free of restraint."

Slouch Hat turned away and the draugr parted to let him pass. Ingelbert sprang to his feet, rushing at the husk's exposed back. A draugr bashed him with a rotting shield before he went two strides. He fell back to the snow, his head ringing. Blood filled his mouth and his vision swam with sickly radiant blotches. By the time his sight cleared, the draugr had reformed themselves into a barricade. Slouch Hat was gone, along with the tome.

Ingelbert grit his sore teeth in fury. That book was his charge. The husk was nothing but a thief! A pilferer of relics! He was no better than some fjordman raider, plundering what he did not deserve. He thought himself clever, wielding stolen sorcery, but Ingelbert knew him for what he was, a pretender to power. He would show this ragged scarecrow what came of such arrogance.

He would teach him the price demanded by delusions of ill-gotten Magic.

The sound of buffeting wings was welcomed by his ears.

He looked skyward to see a black shape swooping towards him.

The aches in his mouth vanished, replaced by sharp pains in his shoulder, which he ignored, and a familiar weight. He did not even bother to glance at

Gasten as he rose to his feet, allowing the owl to feed off his wrath. Vengeful humors coursed through his blood, stemming from the talons that punctured his flesh and befouling him to the core. Ingelbert did nothing to curb their corruption.

Within, he envisioned his fluids turning black. Stained. He embraced the change and banished the chronicler. Ingelbert Crane was of no use here. He much preferred that disparaging sobriquet created by the stinking coburn. Ingelbert had thought it foisted upon him, not realizing the advantage in such titles.

Under Inkstain's gaze, the surrounding draugr began to bloat, their cadaverous forms rapidly putrefying despite the cold.

They swelled, as if under the heat of an oppressive summer sun.

Their degraded mail split against the pressure of bursting flesh. The nearest draugr began to collapse, spilling chill-stiffened entrails upon the snow. He walked through the opening, stepping on the grisly piles.

"Slouch Hat!" he sang out.

He laughed as the husk, mere steps from entering the Mother's Gale, whirled around. The woman next to him also turned, her eyes widening as she beheld the crumbling draugr.

"You are like some favored farm animal," Inkstain chuckled. "Named for your most prominent feature! Did you truly think, *Slouch Hat*, that you could take what is mine?"

"Very well," the husk said regretfully, and waved his hand sharply.

A torrent of unseen sorcery tried to tear Inkstain in half. He weathered the pain, laughing through his clenched jaw. Gasten beat his wings in complaint. The Magic faded and Inkstain took another step.

The husk's face creased with uncertainty. "Fafnir was right. You are far more than you appear. Perhaps this is safe with you. Take the book and go."

Slouch Hat extended his arm, offering the tome back.

"That?" Inkstain sneered. "The tally of arrows and radishes? That is nothing. I want what is mine. What you hide beneath your peasant's hat. It should have come to me. And I will not allow you to place it on the head of some laundress with diluted blood."

"How could he know?" the woman hissed, gripping Slouch Hat's arm.

"You are so fond of history lessons, husk," Inkstain wheedled. "Tell me, do you know the names of the august peers who survived the Battle of Nine Crowns?"

"There was only one," Slouch Hat replied, his words slow with uncertainty. "Goban Blackmud, the gnome king."

"It seems," Inkstain said, stepping nearly within arm's reach, "that is no longer true."

Slouch Hat's eyes fell upon Gasten. "You!"

"Give me my crown, straw man."

"No!"

The husk dropped the tome and threw his arms protectively around the woman.

The snow burst upwards as Slouch Hat's feet left the ground. He launched himself backward into the air, holding the woman close, cradling her head as their flight took them into the Mother's Gale. Caught in the currents of the whirlwind, they rose higher, spiraling deeper into the storm.

Inkstain watched them dwindle as they rose, pulled towards the towering eye, where they were lost from sight.

He snorted, impressed with the husk's mastery of the crown's powers. Eschewing the pull of the Earth was difficult. This body was not yet up to the task, but that did not mean Inkstain could not follow.

He turned briefly, amused curiosity bringing his gaze to Fafnir. The dwarf still lived, sprawled upon the snow. Inkstain had destroyed only a few dozen of the draugr, and the remainder, free from the husk's influence, were stalking towards the runecaster.

Inkstain grimaced. Dwarrow were loathsome creatures, reduced to scribbling Magic upon rocks and trinkets. This one would besmirch the world no longer. As soon as the dead men reached him, he would be butchered. Inkstain turned his back on Fafnir and, stepping over the green tome, entered the Gale.

He strode through the fury of the maelstrom, making his way assuredly for the slopes of the nearest peak. The winds may well have been the breath of a babe, for all they hindered him. He was shielded in sorcery. The nearly solid barrier of blowing snow blinded him, but he neither stumbled nor halted. He could smell the wickedness that dwelt within the vale of the mountains. It guided him, seduced him. Soon, he came to a cave and left the screaming vastness of the storm behind, entering a dark gullet of stone and ice twisting deep into the mountain. He walked on.

The maze of caves did not confuse him, guided as he was by the alluring beckon of death. The most direct route to the vale brought him through a large, foul-smelling cavern. The air was heavy with musk and excrement and decaying meat. Wrinkling his nose in distaste he began to traverse the expansive chamber.

Movement caught his eye along the cave walls. Great, lumbering shapes with sloping shoulders and protruding brows moved away from him, spooked by his presence. Inkstain stopped in the center of the cavern and smiled.

Mourning trolls.

There were eight of the brutes, every one a male. The giantess had warned Ingelbert of their kind. These dull, crazed creatures had lost their mates and congregated in the depths of mountains to share their madness and hide from the face of the sun. Though barely taller than Inkstain, they were nearly as broad as they were tall. Any one of them could pulp a man's skull with one, knuckle-dragging hand. The thews of their arms were capable of crushing a grown bear. Yet they cowered, peering at him with frightened eyes from behind their filthy, lank hair. Even their dim, tormented brains could sense the danger he posed, their savage instincts warning them not to challenge his trespass into their lair.

He toyed with the notion of bending the trolls to his will, but quickly dismissed the thought. Day still reigned outside. If he compelled the beasts into the sun of the vale, they would become stone. Amusing, but a waste.

Inkstain left the cave, left the trolls cringing in the darkness.

He needed no minions. He needed only this body and the Magic that now made it mighty. That presumptuous husk thought to palaver with the Mother of Gales. Inkstain would immolate him and retake the crown, use it to make the Corpse Eater his slave. As for the woman who accompanied the husk, she would become his consort. The scarecrow had been leeching her blood to fuel his craft, but there were other ways, older ways, to wrench power from her body. A husk was ill-equipped for such methods, but surely the body of Ingelbert Crane could be made to take her, willingly or unwillingly, and plant the surest means of true resurrection.

No longer would he be imprisoned in books or languish in the corpses of birds. No longer would he suffer the feeble forms of scribbling annalists. Through the womb of his own distant progeny would he return. He would claim all that was his by rights. The crown. The goblins. The Source Isle. All of this he would place under his rule and more. The world would remember his name and shudder at its utterance.

He would once again be the Gaunt Prince.

THIRTY-TWO

The Corpse Eater swooped down upon the vale.

Flyn watched as she left the heights of the massive tree almost leisurely, allowing herself to fall for half the distance before throwing back her wings to slow her descent. He heard her feathers snap the air and held his ground, gazing up at the beast he was meant to slay. From her high perch, the beast had appeared large.

As she drew nearer the earth, her true size came into daunting focus.

Each of her feet could easily have clutched a bull, the curving talons as long as Coalspur's blade. Just before the great bird touched ground, her wingspan swallowed the sky. Flyn flung up a warding arm against the onslaught of snow kicked up by the sudden burst of air and heard the ice crackle as the Corpse Eater found purchase on the frozen turf. As the upset snow began to settle, Flyn swallowed hard.

The Mother of Gales towered over him, keeping her wings unfurled in a threatening posture. Her head lowered at the end of a long neck, drooping from the hunch between the massive bird's protruding shoulders. Flyn doubted even Coalspur could sever that neck in one blow, for the appendage was thicker than a battering ram. Both the beast's head and neck were bald, covered only in wrinkled, flaccid flesh, the unhealthy hue of decaying meat. A desiccated wattle hung from beneath her cruelly hooked beak, but otherwise she resembled a monstrous, deformed vulture. The plumage of her wings was impressive, but elsewhere her feathers grew sparsely. Patches of filthy, bone-colored down grew at her chest, the hunch of her back, and between her legs, but everywhere else the pale skin was left exposed, hanging slack over the bones.

For all her size, the Corpse Eater's body was wasted and sickly.

Even in the frigid air, Flyn could smell the sour reek of her feathers, the odor of malingering disease.

Opening her massive beak, the Corpse Eater hissed at him, a long grey tongue emerging to drip a foul ichor upon the snow.

The stench of the grave wafted from her maw, the opening as large as a castle door. Flyn steadied himself against the noxious vapors, but did not take a single step backward. He held Coalspur before him, knees bent, ready to move. At the end of her sinuous neck, the Corpse Eater's head began to sway, the motion reptilian. Her unblinking eyes took turns watching him and her wings slowly drew close to her body as she settled. She took a step to the side, leveling her head with Flyn, keeping just out of his reach. He prepared for the strike that was sure to follow, hoping he was quick enough to dart out of the way before that terrible beak could snap him in twain.

But the beast did not lunge.

She merely watched him, displaying more in those black eyes than the vigilance of an animal. There was interest, even fascination.

Flyn used the time, quickly assessing a means of attack. A drawn-out battle with this immense creature would only end in his defeat. If he seized the initiative, he might dive beneath her head and roll beneath her breast. A quick thrust would see this monster done, if he struck true. Fafnir had said that Coalspur would shatter once it pierced the monster's heart. No doubt it would take the entire length of the massive blade to reach that vital organ. Flyn was wary to make a move before he knew his foe's speed. To rush in could be his death. So too would be his end if he delayed overlong.

Flyn tensed, readying his charge.

A sibilant echo drifted into his ears. The sound was unbalancing and Flyn fought a sudden wave of dizziness. He shook his head violently, trying to rid himself of the sound and keep his focus on the Corpse Eater. She had not moved, simply continued to watch him, her head moving rhythmically. Flyn waited until he could again hear only the wind, but no sooner had the strange echo faded, then it returned. He reeled, now aware that the undulating whisper was in his head. Words drifted out of the nauseating din.

Why. Come. Offspring.

Flyn struggled with the new sensation, trying to keep his other senses dominant while this voice intruded directly into his mind. *Why. Seek. Me.*

The Corpse Eater regarded him with predatory curiosity, her eyes articulating the questions where her tongue did not.

Questions.

Flyn hoped that meant she could only speak to his mind, not read his thoughts as well. If his foe knew his every intent, this battle would be brutal and brief. Flyn hesitated. He had not expected a conversation. Fafnir had said that the Corpse Eater was nothing now but a crazed beast. The Chain Maker, it appeared, was mistaken. The hissing in his head grew insistent.

Why. Come?

"Earnestly?" Flyn replied, finding his voice. "I wanted to know why, if we coburn are truly your creation, I cannot fly? All these fetching feathers, but no wings! Seems a shame, that."

The Corpse Eater seemed to consider his question, her dulled brain working at his speech. At last, she formed a response.

Magic. Demanded. Lesser children.

Flyn stifled a chuckle. The old girl may not have been mindless, but she clearly did not comprehend levity.

"That is how I have oft viewed myself," Flyn sighed with a careless shrug. "A lesser child. Alas. Oh well, no harm done. I quite like having arms. Hands are good, too. They hold swords."

From beyond the Corpse Eater, movement caught Flyn's eye. All across the vale, the vættir were approaching, abandoning the tree to march towards the creature which silently beckoned them. Fafnir's daughters had only just reached the roots when the Corpse Eater landed. They now turned, retracing their steps. The Corpse Eater paid them no notice, keeping her gaze fixed on Flyn.

The voice returned to his head, less disorienting now that he expected its presence.

Your ever-life. Gone. Offspring. I cannot return it.

"Is that what you think I seek?" Flyn mused. "Immortality would be wasted on me. I make a habit of putting my life in constant peril." He slowly swept his gaze over the immensity of the creature before him. "Obviously."

Then. What?

Flyn tightened his grip on Coalspur. "An end to life-eternal, Mother of Gales. Yours."

The Corpse Eater hissed again, her beak hanging open as her words flooded Flyn's mind, dripping with venom.

The stink of black elf. Upon you. Encased in their metal.

"Yes," Flyn admitted, undaunted. "I aid the dwarrow against you. You have wrought enough despair upon them, Corpse Eater. It must end."

The Corpse Eater's head jerked backward. She drew herself up, flexing her wings in agitation.

It ends. With the last black elf!

The bird's breast was now far above, but so was her head and that vicious beak.

Flyn saw his opening and sprang, taking three charging steps before flinging his feet out in front, dropping to slide upon the ice. He heard a screech of alarm from the Corpse Eater and saw the shadows of her pinion feathers appear violently upon the snow as she spread her wings. Flyn directed his slide straight between the bird's legs. Coalspur was too large to swing from his prone position, so Flyn braced the blade against his vambrace, hoping his momentum would cause the blade to slash into the Corpse Eater's leg, hobbling her.

The sword sliced nothing but empty air.

Shooting a look above, Flyn saw the Corpse Eater had hopped upward, using her wings to give her lift, but she did not go far. She twisted her long neck, craning around and down to strike.

The ice erupted just behind Flyn's head as the huge beak pierced the ground where he had been a moment before. Flyn's slide was slowing. She would not miss a second time. Digging his talons into the ice, Flyn gained his feet and spun, leading with Coalspur in a great, sweeping cut. The blade came around just in time, connecting with the Corpse Eater's onrushing head, her mouth agape. The sword struck her upon the bulbous front curve of her upper beak, the sharp steel rebounding off with a strident ring. Flyn felt the force of the blow reverberate down his arms. The Corpse Eater recoiled, her head jerked backward by her agile neck.

Flyn felt his guts drop in despair. Coalspur could cut through rock, steel and the iron flesh of the Forge Born, but had failed to even crack the osseous beak of the Corpse Eater. Shaking off his consternation, he got moving. There was nothing to do but fight on and hope the monster's flesh proved less resilient.

The Corpse Eater recovered quickly from the blow, giving Flyn only a few moments to close in. He was nearly within reach, preparing to thrust for the bird's guts when she flung herself backwards, flapping her great wings to push away from his blade.

Flyn was nearly bowled over by the beating of air and feathers. No sooner had the bird danced away, she changed directions, seeming to suspend in the air for a heartbeat before rushing headlong directly for him. The beak spread wide, sharp-edged and wicked, hungry to spill his blood. Flyn did not risk another strike, but dove forward, trying to get under the path of the dreadful swoop. He avoided the beak and rolled to his feet, ready to strike at the exposed belly passing over. The Corpse Eater's feet slammed into him before his blade met flesh. Flyn hit the ground hard, pummeled between the ice and the creature's curved toes. He felt the Corpse Eater's claws open, attempting to snatch him up. Her rear talon scraped across his shoulder, but the dwarf-mail spared his flesh a rending. Fortunately, the monster's flight carried her past before she found a hold.

Battered, Flyn stumbled to his feet. The Corpse Eater was now across the vale, close to the great tree, but she began to turn, tipping one wing earthward to come back around for another pass.

Gripping Coalspur in both hands, Flyn readied himself. He was tired, in body and mind. He no longer had the stomach to scurry beneath this beast. One mighty swing, straight down between her eyes, at the last moment. That was all he could think to do. She might survive it, but he would never know.

"Move aside."

Flyn whirled at the voice, finding Inkstain standing behind him. The chronicler's face was fixed on the Corpse Eater, as was that of the owl upon his shoulder. Something in Inkstain's face, feverish and wild, made Flyn do as commanded. He hurried over to stand at the man's side and turned back to the rapidly approaching bird.

Inkstain raised one hand, palm up, his fingers curled.

The Corpse Eater let out a horrible squawk, twitching in mid-flight. Her sudden convulsions caused her wings to draw inward and she lost her loft, careening off her chosen course.

"By the Hallowed," Flyn swore. "What are you doing?"

"Causing her pain," Inkstain said simply, his lips drawn into a thin smile.

The Corpse Eater's spasming form ripped a furrow in the ice as she hit the ground, veering away from where Flyn and Crane stood. As her stricken bulk skidded and plowed through the crust, she collided with Fafnir's fettered daughters. Flyn winced as the five wights were bowled over, quickly lost from sight beneath the crushing weight of the grounded bird.

The Corpse Eater came to a halt a bowshot to their left, surrounded in a haze of upset snow and ice crystals. Flyn wasted no time, breaking into a run to reach the creature while she was vulnerable. He had not made it ten strides when her head rose from the trench of hoary earth. Flyn stopped, knowing he would not close the distance before she took flight once more. Inkstain drew up beside him.

"So," the chronicler said. "The old quim has some fight left in her."

Flyn frowned at the man's uncharacteristic crassness. "I see Gasten has returned."

"Yes," Inkstain said, snorting through his nose. "It seems I am surrounded by stinking fowl."

Flyn ignored the barb and pointed at the Corpse Eater, now on her feet. "Well, old mother hen will offend your nose the worst."

"Oh, I do not think so."

Inkstain began strolling towards her. Flyn nearly reached out to stop him, but stayed his hand. It was unwise to hinder Crane when he was in this humor. Deglan had dubbed him dangerous and, of course, the old stoat was right. The stuttering scribbler had just brought down a beast whose power was wrought in the heat of creation.

And she did not look pleased.

The Corpse Eater stepped out of the rift, her vengeful eyes and hissing beak directed at the sauntering chronicler. She did not take flight, her movements betraying a lingering daze over whatever affliction Inkstain had unleashed. As her taloned feet emerged from the trench, Flyn saw one was entangled by the chains of the augurs.

The wights were still attached to them, their shifts filthy and torn, their limbs twisted and broken. At least two still moved, and Flyn could just make out their song over the sound of scraping chains.

Heedless of her impediment, the Corpse Eater screeched and thundered toward Inkstain, who raised a hand once more. The beast stumbled and weaved, but did not abandon her charge. Flyn saw her eyes squeeze shut against some phantom agony and she dipped her head, as if fighting against a current, but still she came on, bearing down on the chronicler.

"Crane!" Flyn called out, seeing the inevitable. "Move!"

The chronicler ignored him, not budging from the onrushing monster's path. The Corpse Eater's head swung across from the end of its neck, swatting Inkstain with the brutal curve of her beak. Just before the horrendous blow connected, Flyn thought he heard the man laughing. Inkstain was lifted fully off his feet, catapulted an awesome distance in the span of a heartbeat. He landed hard, not a knife-cast from where Flyn stood. Somehow, the owl upon Crane's shoulder had clung to him, only detaching and taking flight an instant before his human perch struck the ground.

Flyn fought the instinct to rush to his fallen companion's side, instead keeping his attention on the Corpse Eater. The giant bird continued forward on her own momentum for a few seconds, then slowed, turning to face her assailants. She seemed cautious, taking sidling steps as she watched, her gaze flicking from Flyn to Crane, waiting to see if he rose.

He did not.

Flyn now stood between the Corpse Eater and her tree. He could feel the vættir approaching from the distant trunk behind, could hear their dirge drawing closer. Was that what the beast was waiting on, for the wights to come and tear them apart? The vættir did not attack coburn, but had their master lifted the ban, giving them leave to kill her progeny? Certainly, Crane would not be spared. Flyn took a step towards the man, keeping his sword and eyes trained on the Corpse Eater. She made no move to stop him.

Indeed, she was no longer looking at him. Her attention had shifted skyward. Continuing to creep towards Inkstain, Flyn shot a quick look up and over his shoulder, trying to follow the beast's gaze.

Near as he could discern, she was looking at her own nest, high in the cradle of the boughs. The distance was too great for Flyn to see any detail. While turned, he took a moment to check the progress of the wights. There were too many to quickly count, and would soon be upon them. Even if they continued to ignore him, he would be stuck fending them off until Crane regained his senses, if the man still lived.

He was only a stride or two away from his companion when the Corpse Eater began to flex her wings. Her eyes were still raptly affixed on the nest. She moved cautiously, as if reluctant to take flight, and Flyn was not certain whether it was the attack from Inkstain that fueled her uncertainty, or what she saw in her nest.

Either way, she was moments from taking off, leaving Flyn and Crane to deal with her walking food.

If they remained, they were doomed.

Flyn darted for Inkstain, reversing his grip on Coalspur so that he held the sword point-down in one hand. The long blade dragged along the ground as he knelt, scooping Inkstain's slack form in the crook of his sword arm. For all his height, the gangly man weighed little and Flyn managed to drape him face down over his forearm. Hearing the slap of wings, Flyn whirled to see the Corpse Eater push away from the ground, intent upon her destination.

Awkwardly hauling man and sword, Flyn rushed to get directly beneath the giant bird's path, keeping his eyes on the tangle of chains still wrapped around her foot. As the immense shadow passed overhead, Flyn leaped upward, reaching with his free hand.

Feeling metal slap his palm, he gripped hard and cried out in pain as he was wrenched off the ground. The shoulder bearing Crane's weight burned, threatening to tear loose. He had to fight the need to let the man go and allow him to fall towards the rapidly retreating ground. Through eyes tearing in the rushing air, Flyn looked up.

He had grabbed hold of a loop of slack chain, one strand in the knot-work that entwined the Corpse Eater's claw. Fafnir's daughters dangled around Flyn, hung by their collars at the ends of chains now taut with the speed of the ascent. Three of the five still moved, their mouths open in a song stolen by the surrounding roar.

They reached for him with fractured arms, eyes blazing with the need to kill. Flyn felt Crane stir in his arm, then begin to thrash, panicking at his predicament.

"I have you!" Flyn screamed, his own voice sounding weak in the turbulent air. "Do not struggle! We will fall!"

It was no use. Inkstain continued to writhe, weakening Flyn's hold.

"Crane! Stop!"

The man could not hear him. He tore free and slipped through Flyn's embrace.

The sudden emptiness in his arm was horrifying and Flyn cried out in dismay. Kicking out, he snatched desperately with his feet and felt his talons catch something yielding. A sudden weight jerked at Flyn from below, causing his grip to slip further down the chain. Grunting with effort, Flyn looked downward.

He had Crane. The chronicler's heavy cloak and the strap of the man's satchel were caught in his toe claws. The poor man was staring up at him, eyes wide and entreating. He was yelling something, pleading, but Flyn could not make out the words. He would need to let Coalspur go, if he had any hope of reaching down to pull his friend up to the chain. Then, beneath Crane, Flyn saw branches, layers of them stretching below, crisscrossed with formations of ice. The Corpse Eater's flight leveled out and she began to descend, towards a solid jumble of frosty debris. Flyn released Crane and waited a heartbeat before he let go of the chain.

He dropped, landing upon the unforgiving surface of the nest. The wind was knocked from his lungs and he rolled to his back, sickened. Coughing and nearly retching, he stood, using Coalspur to help himself rise.

A frigid miasma hung over the vile eyrie, limiting Flyn's vision. He found no immediate sign of Crane or the Corpse Eater.

Haphazard logs, encrusted with ice and frozen droppings, spread out beneath his feet. He guessed the nest covered an expanse larger than a castle yard, but only the nearest edge was visible, not two dozen paces from where he landed. Flyn saw huge, up-sweeping branches rising from beyond the precipice, the curved fingers of the bole which supported the nest. He was certain he had dropped Inkstain safely, but scrambled his way over to the edge to be sure.

Leaning precariously over, Flyn peered down.

The bottom of the vale was barely perceptible, nothing but frighteningly distant patches of white peeking through cracks in the spider web of massive boughs. Anyone falling from the nest would likely never reach the bottom, their body breaking on countless branches and spurs of ice before coming to rest, shattered and pulped, somewhere in the vertiginous heights. Flyn saw nothing to indicate Crane had plunged to his death, though he did spy the movement of a few wights, slowly making the climb. Many of the branches were wider than ramparts, creating rime-covered avenues for the vættir to travel. At points the limbs grew so far outward they nearly touched the walls of the surrounding cliffs, and Flyn could just make out the black openings of caves high in the crags.

Small processions of vættir trickled from the cave mouths, traversing the branches as bridges, bypassing much of the slow climb from the vale. That would be Flyn and Crane's egress from this dread tree, if they came down alive.

Stepping back from the edge, Flyn turned towards the interior of the nest and began making his way towards its center.

Out of the stinking mist loomed large, bloated pods. At first Flyn thought them to be eggs, and a cold foreboding seized his spine, but then he came upon one which had split open. A grisly cascade of denuded bones and skulls was disgorged from the fibrous fissure, the pile spilled among the existing detritus of the nest. The pods were not eggs. They were regurgitated pellets the size of boulders, all that remained of the vættir once the Corpse Eater had supped upon their living carcasses.

Flyn began to hear the dirge of the dwarrow and made for the sound. Through the mist, the bulk of the Corpse Eater took shape, her back turned. Taking shelter behind the loathsome pellets where he could, Flyn made his way closer. What remained of Fafnir's daughters was still attached to the great bird's foot, the living corpses feebly crawling about atop her talons. A handful of other vættir milled about in the bird's shadow, waiting to be eaten.

Flyn could hear another voice, this one not singing, but speaking.

The space between the Corpse Eater and him was devoid of cover, forcing him to creep closer with only the putrid vapors for concealment.

A pair of figures stood before the Mother of Gales. She watched them with the same attentive brutishness she displayed during her brief discourse with Flyn.

"Do you believe the elven patron still lives?" asked the taller of the figures in a voice strained and reedy.

If the Corpse Eater answered, Flyn did not hear. Likely, she spoke directly to the mind of the questioner.

"Thousands of years you have spent on vengeance, and the dwarrow are far from extinct. Turn your hatred upon that which originally cast you out, on Magic itself."

Flyn could see the speaker more clearly now. His steps halted as recognition dawned.

It was the husk from Castle Gaunt, the one who slew him and all his companions with dark sorceries before Pocket restored their lives. He had spoken with a different voice that day, the voice of a phantom girl who held him enslaved, yet it was the same husk with the same shapeless hat, Flyn was certain. The woman next to him was a stranger, however, so Flyn was bewildered when she suddenly looked directly at him.

"Join us, Bantam Flyn," she said.

All eyes turned towards him, the empty pits of the husk and the turbid wells of the Corpse Eater. The great bird opened her beak silently, but made no aggressive motion. Warily, Flyn stepped so that both the strange pair and the Corpse Eater were directly in front of him, husk and woman to his right, the creature to his left.

"My lady," Flyn addressed the woman, "you have me at a disadvantage. You address me with familiarity, but I am unacquainted with your name."

A wry, tired smile crept upon the woman's face. "You speak gallantly and well, Sir Flyn. So unlike your mentor." Flyn's face must have betrayed some surprise, for the woman's smile faded and she dipped her chin. "Yes, I know Sir Corc the Constant. I know the names of both coburn who failed to protect my son."

Flyn managed to mask his shock this time. He bowed deeply, allowing himself the risk of relaxing his vigil upon the Corpse Eater and the husk sorcerer.

"I misspoke," Flyn said when he straightened. "I am well acquainted with your name, Lady Beladore. I offer you deepest regrets, in the name of the Valiant Spur, for the loss of your son. Pocket was one of us, and was dear to me. I counted him a friend and a brother. I carry the guilt and the grief of his death with me, always." He saw his words absorbed by the woman, her face softening with sorrow and hardening with bitterness. The lie came easily to Flyn's tongue, borne upon deep currents of truth. "But you should know, lady, it was the hands of the husk which now stands beside you that slew your child."

"As I have already revealed to her, coburn," the husk said without emotion.

"He was powerless to stop himself," Beladore said, her voice struggling to remain steady.

"As were we to stop him," Flyn replied with courtesy.

"Only such fell craft could have prevented us from saving Pocket."

Beladore flinched. "You make excuses?"

"I offer the truth. Pocket was the only one with the power to prevent his end. But he chose to save us, his companions, whom he loved as family. I wish he had made a different choice."

"As do I," Beladore replied, her voice nearly a whisper.

"Now," Flyn requested, "if you and your scarecrow would kindly step aside, I must dispatch this creature." He turned his attention back to the Corpse Eater and raised his sword. The great bird bunched her furled wings and coiled her neck, hissing once more.

An incredulous laugh scraped from the husk's mouth.

"That simple? You have no curiosity of our purpose here?"

"None," Flyn replied, keeping his eyes on the Corpse Eater. "Remember, I have met you once before, husk. That encounter ended with my death, yours, and that of the little boy who saved me at the cost of his own life. I do not know what you told the lady to make that tragedy palatable, but I have no wish to hear it. For you see, I do not, will not forgive you. You killed me once, and you may do so again. As before, there is nothing I can do to prevent it. But I know my purpose here and I will see it through." He shot a quick look at Beladore. "Forgive me, lady. You know my name, but not my nature. Fighting is what I do. Red Caps and skin-changers, Unwound and wights. I have battled them all and am rather skilled at it, but I am also an impetuous rascal. I bolster this failing by surrounding myself with deeper thinkers, but none of them are here at the moment, so I must ask you again. Remove yourself to safety." Beladore did not move, but the husk did, stepping forward.

"Allow me to be your deeper-thinker," he said.

Flyn shook his head. "Not likely."

"This is not a battle you need fight," the husk insisted, throwing an arm up at the Corpse Eater. "You are not the one meant to face her, as you have been led to believe. But the deceitfulness of the dwarrow goes far beyond their fallacy in interpreting prophecies. Did they claim she cursed them, corrupted their immortality in order to retain her own? Lies! I have heard it directly from her. She did not create the blight of the vættir to extend her days, but to punish the dwarrow for robbing her children of eternal life."

Flyn tried not to heed the husk's words, but the calm surety of that thin voice penetrated all attempts to ignore him.

An unwanted question came to Flyn's tongue. "The dwarrow? They took the immortality of the coburn?"

The black elves. Took from you. Not I!

Flyn looked up at the Corpse Eater, her calamitous stare challenging him to doubt.

"I am sure you know the legend," the husk asserted, "of the forebears of Middangeard's Elementals. One of them stands before you. It is no myth. She and her mate created your race. So too did the giants, the elves and the dragons have such mighty parentage. But not the dwarrow, for they were once elves, stunted and forsaken by Magic. Their progenitors, the mother and father of elf-kind, went to Airlann with their favored kin, as did the dragons. The giants and the coburn were left here, abandoned, but they had their mighty forebears to guide them. The dwarrow had nothing. Nothing but what they could steal."

Flyn's mind raced, the voice of the Corpse Eater accompanying his scattered thoughts.

Deceivers! My mate. Imprisoned. Mother giant. Father giant.

Imprisoned. Leeched to death.

A chill entered Flyn's blood at the mention of the Corpse Eater's mate.

He had seen the remains, the great, shackled skeleton housed deep within

Hriedmar's Hall. It had been kept behind a set of massive gates, one of three. Fafnir had said that the great bird's incarceration was a mystery, but admitted that it might have been the result of a trap set by a dwarrow lord of bygone days. Did the other gates conceal the mouldering bones of the first giants, entombed by the dwarrow? Could the immortality of dwarf-kind truly be invested by such skulduggery?

"No!" Flyn snarled. "Fafnir has no wish to capture the Corpse Eater. He wants her dead to end the threat of the vættir."

"Of course," the husk agreed. "The lore of stealing life-eternal has long since slipped beyond the ken of dwarfs. But the deed has been done, to you and your kind in the ancient past. Your matron wanted to destroy the dwarrow for that ignominious act, and now you would slay her for it at the behest of those who deprived you of your birthright."

A humorless laugh played across the nest. Flyn turned, equally relieved and troubled to see Inkstain appear out of the putrid haze. Relieved to see his companion alive, troubled to see the owl returned to him.

"You are a fine one to speak of stolen birthrights, hollow man," Inkstain declared with dark amusement. "Did you truly believe I could not follow you up here?"

"Ingelbert," Flyn said. "You know this husk? Does he speak true?"

"That is not who you think it is, Sir Flyn," the husk put in quickly.

Inkstain came to stand beside Flyn, his dancing, lucid eyes taking in all present. They eventually rolled around to settle on Beladore and stilled, deadening. Flyn saw the woman blanch under that stare, though she remained firmly rooted in place and countenance.

"Who can say what is true?" the chronicler said, his voice adopting an odd, sing-song inflection. "Immortals lie, as willingly and readily as those of us with limits to our years. You coburn are mortal, that is true. Whether by the craft of those hideous dwarrow or this delicious carrion-creature matters not at all. History is an old whore, only interesting if you delight in hearing of all the depraved things she used to do. I much prefer the debasements of today."

Flyn was loathe to admit it, but the husk was right, this was not Ingelbert Crane. But the chronicler had known the dangers, better than any of them, and admitted to the struggles he faced under the owl's influence. He had confided his fears to Flyn, as well as his means of combating this corruption.

"Remember Ulfrun, Master Crane," Flyn told him.

The man laughed low in his throat, his eyes never leaving Beladore. "Ah yes, the giantess. Those were some exceedingly wet ablutions we shared. But that frolic is now behind me, in the tiresome past. I am now focused on the conquests to come."

"Dammit, Ingelbert, enough! Find control!"

"Strike him down, Sir Flyn!" the husk exclaimed.

Inkstain chuckled, his lascivious gaze finally leaving Beladore. "This one?" he asked, pointing derisively at Flyn. "He dare not. Far too noble, far too chivalrous is our flocculent cock here. He lacks the viciousness of his race. By the Hallowed, he is practically a castrate." The chronicler turned to face Flyn, his face aglow with mockery. "And that is where the husk speaks most truthfully. You are not the foretold coburn. And not because that half-wit runecaster was wrong about his paltry prophecy, but because you are entirely too sparing. You hear one measly possibility that the Mother of Gales is not the malevolence you wanted her to be and it causes you to doubt, to think of mercy! You are worse than a craven, Bantam Flyn, you are a poet, trapped in the body of a killer." Inkstain's smile widened. "As it happens, I am caught in the opposite dilemma." He waved two fingers over his shoulder in a lazy, dismissive gesture.

Beladore vomited blood.

It came without warning, the woman suddenly choking on a torrent of crimson. The husk rushed to her side, catching her as she collapsed.

"Crane, no!" Flyn cried, readying his sword to strike.

"Thwart me and she dies!" Inkstain proclaimed, his warning sweeping Flyn and the husk. The man smiled as Flyn lowered his blade. "You see? A slave to compassion. But I would not drop your guard too far, gamecock. You will soon need that ludicrous sword."

The chronicler slowly began walking towards the Corpse Eater. The great bird grew skittish at his approach, but did not attack or flee, seemingly rooted in place by the man's mere presence.

"I am going to give you a gift, Bantam Flyn," the leering swain who was once Ingelbert called over his shoulder. "I am going to give you the monster you desired."

Inkstain was now directly beneath the Corpse Eater's head, nearly standing between her feet. She made no move to oppose him, nor did the gathered wights. Turning to face Flyn, the chronicler smiled.

"She is nearly as old as time itself, yet her hold on reason is wonderfully tenuous. Imagine what would become of her if that hold was completely severed. Oh, do not fret. You need not imagine. I will show you."

The Corpse Eater screamed, throwing back her head to trumpet a deplorable agony to the sky. Inkstain stepped away as she shivered violently, molting feathers and digging into the logs with her talons. Her head leveled, snaking forth from her neck, and when she opened her eyes, they bored into Flyn. There was nothing left in those pitiless orbs but brute savagery. Pure, hungering madness.

With a screech for blood, the Corpse Eater launched herself directly at Flyn, her wings unfurling. The open beak came at him with terrible speed and Flyn tried to jump aside, but he was struck by the monster's shoulder. Feeling ribs crack, Flyn folded at the middle, pinned to the bird's wing bone by the speed and force of her movement. He felt the pounding footsteps of the beast jostle him and then they ceased, replaced with a punishing press of wind upon his back. The wing on which he clung flapped and he was dislodged, tossed up momentarily, only to have the wing slam into him once more. He tumbled across the Corpse Eater's back, screaming in terror as he saw, beyond her tail feathers, the top of the great tree receding below, surrounded by the stone embrace of the mountains.

Desperately, he grabbed hold of the tuft of feathers between the pumping wings and clung one-handed. Crosscutting gusts of wind nearly threw him off, but he pressed himself to the Corpse Eater, face-down, the solid stink of her separating him from the cold void. Some unseen force began to lift him, starting at his feet. He looked down and between his dangling talons saw a great eye, the white world with the vale for an iris, the denseness of the tree its pupil. The Corpse Eater was climbing quickly, her ascent nearly vertical. Flyn could feel the downy feathers between his fingers slipping as his own weight pulled at the plumes. He twisted, facing the horrifying emptiness of clouds, and kicked the steel of his spurs into the Corpse Eater's back. Her screeching protest could be heard over the tumult of beating wind.

Flyn's stomach charged to his throat as the climb turned into a dive. All his senses became useless, his world nothing but a shrieking haze of fear. Any instant, he expected to find himself free of his foe, she having killed him while he yet breathed, existing in impotence until the ground received him. Yet, somehow, he held on.

Survival, however, was no victory. It would be fleeting for all his fortune and effort. He would tire long before this beast, she who was mother of Wind. Eventually, he would join the clouds.

Knowing it was impossible, Flyn fancied he could hear the beating of the Corpse Eater's heart, just beneath his shoulder. He would never be closer.

Focusing on the unsettling motions of the bird's flight, Flyn held on, waiting. When, at last, he could feel his back resting level upon her, he ripped his spurs free and rolled, knowing he had only a moment. He gained his feet, and as the unseen hand of the wind punched him, he plunged Coalspur down. The blade sunk through feather and flesh, and Flyn's precarious perch lurched beneath him as a screech pierced his ears. He clung to the sword, using it to defy the wind's might and tried to push the blade deeper.

The sky and earth switched places, revolving with frightening speed.

Flyn floated in emptiness.

Coalspur was still in his hand, half the blade darkly stained.

The mind-shattering chaos of the flight was gone, replaced by a near serene weightlessness, the roaring air no longer threatening, but embracing. Flyn's sight was keen once more, his plight displayed before him with detached clarity. It did not feel as if he were plummeting to the earth, and the crushing dread of such a death was absent. The powerlessness provided a freedom from all care.

Below, he could see the vale just off to his left. Just as Flyn thought it would never grow any closer, it began to swell, taking up more of his vision with each speeding moment. He judged he would come down among the bordering peaks, somewhere in the heights above the vale.

As the end drew near, Flyn found his acceptance dwindling, quickly replaced by stark terror. His panic mounted as a stretch of stark white rushed to end his life. It was a ridge, snow-blanketed and flat, nestled among the craggy shoulders of the mountain.

Flyn's eyes darted around, streaming tears from the punishing updraft. He nearly laughed at his own desperation. What did he search for? And then he did laugh at what he saw.

It began as a smudge, a blackness on the white. Quickly, it became a hole, a vertical shaft, sunk into the ridge. It was a sizable, roughly circular crevasse. The earth, it appeared, desired to devour him. Flyn would not disappoint and began adjusting his fall, aiming for the icy gullet. Swimming in the air, he directed his feet at the yawning hole and gripped Coalspur two-handed over his head, point-down. Screaming with triumph and terror, Flyn entered the throat of the mountain.

The shadowy wall of the pit was before him, the bottom an unknown distance below, eager to jelly his bones. With all his might, Flyn thrust Coalspur into the rocks. The steel bit through, gouging into the stone, the speed of Flyn's fall forcing the blade to carve deep. He held firm to the grip, riding the sword as it sliced a furrow down the wall of the pit. The joints in his arms screamed in burning protest, promising to snap, but he held firm until finally, the blade slowed and his plummet came to a halt.

With an expulsion of breath, Flyn grabbed hold of the rock face with his feet, taking some of the weight off his wrists and shoulders. He hung there, trembling for what seemed an eternity.

At last, he opened his eyes and surveyed the shaft. Down, an impenetrable pool of shadow, the dark and distant gut of the mountain. Above, a circle of sunlight, now no larger than a plate.

"Up it is," Flyn said aloud, his voice croaking.

He hung one-armed from his sword for a moment, reaching down with his free hand to unbuckle one of the elven spurs. Wielding it as a spike, Flyn began climbing, keeping Coalspur in the trench it had carved and sliding the blade up, twisting it just enough to bite before pulling up and stabbing with the spur. Thus, aided by the steel of dwarfs and elves, Flyn made his slow, steady pilgrimage towards the light.

The trench made by Coalspur ended some distance before the mouth of the shaft. Keeping the spur buried deep in the rock, Flyn pulled the sword free and resumed his climb, one-handed.

After many muscle-trembling rests, he reached the lip.

Flyn hooked his sword arm over the edge of the pit, hauling himself up until his forearms rested on the ice. He clung to the edge of the hole for a moment, his eyes closed, his wattle resting on the cold stones between his arms, breathing deeply.

When he opened his eyes at last, his heart sank.

The Corpse Eater waited upon the ridge, unslain. She was less than a stone's throw from the pit, staring at him with eyes eager for retribution. One wing protruded oddly from her body and her black blood smirched the snow at her feet.

Flyn chuckled darkly. He did not have enough strength left to haul himself out of the shaft, much less do battle with this beast, however injured. She began to stalk towards him, her lower beak nearly dragging the ground.

"Be warned, Mother," Flyn said, grinning weakly. "I shall likely stick in your craw."

Her breath was upon his face when an object came whirling through the air. It thudded into the side of the Corpse Eater's neck and she stumbled, hissing. Flyn saw a long-hafted axe buried in the bird's flesh. He looked to the right, the direction from which the weapon had come, and found a coburn standing in the shallow of the ridge. The mail and furs of a fjordman covered his drab, grey feathers, a long dirk in his hand. Only one coburn was that tall and grim. The Dread Cockerel.

Flyn nearly burst into hysterics as revelation flooded his exhausted mind.

The husk had said he was not the proper champion, not the foretold slayer. Here stood the proper knight, the one with the viciousness needed to bring this beast down, the one who would have won the tourney and received Coalspur as prize if not for unhappy chance. This quest was never Flyn's fate. It was housed within the determined stare of the Dread Cockerel.

"Sir Wyncott!" Flyn yelled and, flinging his arm out, sent Coalspur spinning across the ice. The motion upset Flyn's purchase and his feet began to scrabble on the slick stones. He clung with the last of his strength, making sure his cast had been true.

The Dread Cockerel stopped the sliding blade with his foot and, hooking his talons beneath the blade, kicked the weapon into his hand.

"Cocky strut," Flyn whispered with a smile, before allowing himself to fall.

THIRTY-THREE

"Will he live?" Deglan demanded as soon as Ulfrun set him down. Hengest looked up from the prone form of Fafnir and nodded, quickly reaching into his pouch for his runestones. Deglan tried to watch him work, but his gaze kept returning to the mouth of the cave that now sheltered them, and the howling maelstrom without. Ulfrun stood just under the threshold, watching for signs of pursuing draugr.

It had been a near thing, pulling Fafnir out of that mass of murderous dead, but Ulfrun and Hengest had managed it, while Deglan watched from near the edge of the Gale. With the giantess hobbled and the Chain Maker barely coherent, their only chance of escape had been to enter the clutches of the storm. Were it not for Ulfrun, Deglan would have been lost in those punishing winds, beaten down and buried by snow. When she scooped him up, she had handed him something square and heavy, and only now was he able to look at what he held in his arms.

Ingelbert's book. The bloody big, ugly tome, covered in green leather. The thing was practically as large as Deglan's torso.

He thumped over to Ulfrun, wincing as he drew nearer the storm, its voice shrieking through the cave.

"It was the only sign of him," the giantess said as soon as he drew near. Her vigil of the storm never wavered, but Deglan saw through her brave face. Clearly, Crane and the giantess had grown closer since Deglan's capture. The signs were etched in her brow, the corners of her eyes and the set of her jaw, which bulged irregularly as she grit her teeth. Knowing she would accept coddling about as well as he would, Deglan said nothing.

Behind them, Fafnir began to gasp. Together, Ulfrun and Deglan came away from the cave mouth and approached the dwarrow. Hengest was helping the Chain Maker sit up, just enough to prop him against the rough stone wall. The older dwarf looked ghastly.

"Crow Shoulders?" Fafnir asked, his voice fringed with coughs.

"Dead," Ulfrun told him. "He and his brood."

"Where is Crane?" Deglan asked, giving voice to the question Ulfrun would not.

Fafnir lost focus for a moment, drifting on a sudden wave of fear. "Taken," he said at last.

Hengest put a steadying hand on the Chain Maker. "By the warlock?"

"By his son."

Deglan frowned with confusion. "Slouch Hat is a bloody husk. He has . . . no . . . sons."

A frozen stone dropped into Deglan's gut. Slouch Hat wore the iron crown. The crown of Jerrod the Second. That twisted tyrant had many children, but only one who could invoke the look of drowning dismay that Fafnir now wore.

"The Gaunt Prince," Deglan hissed, feeling his mind unraveling at the prospect. "How is that possible?" But his frayed thoughts quickly wove themselves into an image of an owl.

"Gasten."

Fafnir nodded weakly.

Dropping the tome, Deglan flung himself at the stricken runecaster, grabbing fistfuls of his cloak and shaking him.

"You encouraged him! Convinced that poor boy he was a sorcerer! You pushed him towards it!"

Through his rage, Deglan could feel Hengest trying to pull him off. Ulfrun made no move to interfere.

"You did this!" Deglan cried.

"I felt only his power," Fafnir protested. "I knew not its source."

"You did not want to know!" Deglan growled, shoving the dwarf further against the cave wall. "You saw only a tool for your precious quest. A confused young man, easily swayed and you have damned him!"

The wizard did not struggle under Deglan's abuse, merely looked him in the face, morose and defeated. "I swear, I did not know."

Shaking his head with scorn, Deglan released the dwarf and stepped back. His mouth was sour. When he spoke again, his own voice sounded tired and tedious.

"Crane is the Gaunt Prince's puppet. And Flyn," he flung the name down at Fafnir, "is not the proper champion."

The Chain Maker's face clenched with inner turmoil. "I know."

"Now?" Deglan pressed. "Or always?"

Fafnir struggled to swallow. "Does it matter?"

"No." It was Ulfrun who answered.

"No," Deglan echoed, scowling. "None of it matters. None of it will matter. You have done nothing, Chain Maker, but fashion the deaths of all foolish enough to follow you. You have erred at every turn of this quest."

Fafnir regarded him with a spark of defiance. "Save one."

"And what is that?" Deglan spat.

"I allowed you to come."

The dwarf's gall kindled fresh rage in Deglan. He would dare make a mockery now? But before Deglan launched into another tirade, he saw the stone-faced earnestness in the wizard's face.

"You are right, Master Loamtoes," Fafnir said, struggling to rise. Hengest bent to help him. "You were right on Skagen, when we spoke in the Wreck. You had the loyalty of Crane and Sir Flyn. The loyalty of fellowship. That is a gift I would never earn. After all, one does not earn the loyalty of a wielded implement, one simply takes it in hand and forces it to purpose. As you say, they were tools to be used. Nay, they were weapons. And I loosed them upon the Corpse Eater, for she needs to die. Ulfrun and I will continue on that path, but you, Master Loamtoes, you must do what fate demands of you. Save your friends."

Deglan snorted. "They are lost, dwarf! I lived beneath the Earth for enough centuries to know that these caves are expansive. I could wander for days!"

The lids of Fafnir's eyes slowly drooped and the dwarf lifted his chin, concentrating. "The sword Coalspur quickly approaches the vale. That is where the Breaker and I must go." The Chain Maker's eyes opened and he looked to Hengest. "What of Sir Flyn?" The beardless dwarf came out of his own momentary reflection and answered readily. "Above us, and deeper in the mountain."

Fafnir nodded once. "Then they are parted. Go. Take Master Loamtoes to Flyn."

Without pause, Hengest tightened his grip on his ram-headed staff and began walking deeper into the cave. Deglan caught his arm, stopping him.

"How do you know where Flyn is?"

"I aided in the forging of his mail," Hengest replied.

"Come."

Together, the four traveled through the frigid cavern, but soon came to a junction of tunnels. Fafnir nodded assuredly at one spur, the most level. "This is our road."

"And this ours," Hengest said, pointing to a larger, upward sloping branch.

"Luck to you," Ulfrun said, nodding at Hengest, at Deglan.

"Come with us," Deglan urged the giantess.

Ulfrun shook her head with little vigor. "I must go where the augury commands. I must chase my Doom."

"Toad shit! Flyn and Crane need you."

"No, you ugly bear cub," Ulfrun replied with a small smile.

"The gamecock needs *you*. As for Inkstained, he needs that word-prison." She lifted her chin towards the tome in Deglan's arms.

"We share affection, it is true, but memories of lust and bed-play will not aid him now. Aye, they may do harm, if the songs of this Gaunt Prince are true."

"She is right," Hengest said from over Deglan's shoulder.

"Go," Ulfrun said with encouragement. "Help. Heal. I have a battle-hunger, and the mother of Wind awaits."

The giantess turned and followed Fafnir down their chosen tunnel. Deglan watched her for a moment, then went with Hengest into deeper darkness.

Flyn snapped awake with the feeling that he still fell. A cold, stone surface was pressed into his face, his chest, his belly, pulsing pain wherever it touched him. As consciousness returned, a leaden ache settled into Flyn's skull and he tasted blood, could smell it through a thick foulness in the air. Spitting and blowing, he expelled the coppery fluid from his beak and nostrils, only to have more flood warmly back into the cavities. The pain barking through his right shoulder was nearly audible, the agonizing sensation accompanying the ringing in his addled head. He could feel something gripped in his hand, a cold weight at the end of the pain, and had a vague recollection of plunging the elven spur into the side of the shaft before the world vanished.

Opening his eyes, the world returned, red and roiling.

Grotesque blotches, limned in orange and crimson, swam before him, emerging from perfect blackness. Flyn heard grunts and low bestial groans rumbling from a chorus of surrounding throats.

Crying out against the pain, he scrambled quickly to his feet, holding the spur out at the end of an arm quaking with injury. Flyn spun in place, finding the shambling red blobs encircling him, closing in. He began to discern the suggestion of bandy legs and long, corded arms extending from broad, cruel shoulders.

Flyn recalled seeing such a shape before. A male troll. Save for his mate, that one had been alone and revealed under the light of a winter moon. Now, near ten of the creatures ringed him, seen only by the heat of their reeking flesh.

Instinctively, Flyn reached for the axe at his belt, but found the ring empty, the weapon falling free at some unknown time during his aerial grapple with the Corpse Eater. Unmated trolls were said to be crazed, deadly and monstrous, overcome with savagery at the loss of their females.

Flyn chuckled in the darkness. So like his own kind, these trolls, except coburn became unreasoning at the presence of their females, a lust for flesh descending into lust for blood, an inbred barbarity which some believed Flyn lacked. Gallus had called him a cockless coward, a castrate in a metal shirt. Inkstain had cast similar aspersions up in the nest, likening Flyn's valor to weakness.

Viciousness, he claimed, was the essence of all coburn. Certainly, the Dread Cockerel was vicious. A more merciless knight there has never been, according to Corc. And now Sir Wyncott fought somewhere above, with Coalspur in hand and the weight of prophecy upon his head, while Flyn skulked in the darkness, weaponless and surrounded by snuffling beasts.

He still wore his metal shirt. The armor would provide little protection against the pressing trolls, however. They had not yet charged, but Flyn could hear them becoming more incensed at his presence, their stentorian expulsions of breath growing with aggression.

Flyn felt his own blood boiling. To be torn asunder by these low fiends was not a worthy end for a knight. A dung-filled crevasse was no fit grave. This was a place of darkness and discarded bones, the den of pitiful, pitiless animals. That was what should die in such a place, an animal. He could give them that, allow himself to become lost in the blood red haze. It was not absent in him, for all the insults. Twice had he unleashed the savage side and fought at its urging. Once at Castle Gaunt, when compelled by sorcery and again against his father. Both times, he should have died.

Flyn felt his breath quickening with mounting fury. Not again. It was not his way, not his strength, but that was no weakness. Only an animal would die in this pit, so he would not become one and thus, he would live and emerge, a knight with a purpose. No longer to slay the Corpse Eater, that task had been willingly passed, but to free Ingelbert Crane from whatever malevolence caused his evil comportment. These beasts would not stand between Sir Bantam Flyn and the salvation of a member of his order.

Reaching down, he unbuckled his other spur. He now held both in his hands, points down, his fists rolling slightly in front of him as he pivoted.

Nine. Nine trolls.

Flyn smiled. "Perchance this is worthy of a knight, after all."

He stilled, ceasing to turn in place, and focused on one of the beasts. It lumbered toward him, flanked by its fellows. Another two strides and Flyn would be within reach of those terrible, thick-fingered hands. He spun, turning completely around to charge the troll that was behind him a moment before. The surrounding brutes bellowed with aggravation at his sudden movement.

Ignoring the others, Flyn flung himself at his chosen opponent.

The troll responded with a clumsy, surprised swipe of its arm. Flyn jumped, avoiding the blow and, landing briefly atop the beast's low-scything forearm, he vaulted over the troll. Twisting as he began to fall, Flyn stabbed downward with the spurs in his hands, plunging them deep into the creases where neck met shoulder. Hot blood spurted and Flyn planted his feet into the stricken troll's back, pushing away as he yanked his weapons free.

Howling, the wounded troll stumbled forward, his legs buckling beneath him. He spilled onto the cave floor, his tumbling bulk interrupting the charge of three of his brethren. Two more came at Flyn from the sides.

From a crouch, he flung his legs back over his head and rolled, avoiding the cauldron-sized fist from the faster of the two, causing the blow to strike the slower troll instead. The meaty thump of hard knuckles on thick skull resounded in the cave as the hapless creature fell senseless.

"Bad luck, large one," Flyn gloated.

He darted to the left, flanking the troll who had just inadvertently brained his companion. As he sped by, Flyn hammered one of his spurs dagger-like up into the beast's exposed armpit. The elven steel punctured the tough skin with ease, releasing a torrent of blood as Flyn withdrew the point on the run.

The six uninjured trolls were now converging on him, but Flyn cut a wide path around, skirting the cave wall. He dragged the spur in his left hand along the rock as he went, hoping to detect a tunnel opening into the cavern, some means of escape, but the sound of scraping steel was uninterrupted. Not wanting to lose his momentum and the advantage of speed, Flyn shot back towards the center of the cave, charging directly at the trolls. The six had gathered into a group, their dull minds prodding them to congregate against danger.

Wasting no time, Flyn charged into the circle of monsters, dropping to slide beneath the bowed legs of one troll, ripping the unfortunate brute's swinging genitals with a vicious swipe. Skidding clear of the squealing wretch, Flyn gained his feet and came up directly in front of another foe. It grabbed for him, but he dodged within its reach and punched his spurs into its soft midsection in a rapid series of brutal blows.

"Shall we dance?" Flyn laughed.

He left the blades embedded in the troll's flesh upon the last strikes and used them to heave the beast around just as his fellows attempted to lend aid. The impaled troll hollered as he was beaten savagely from behind, the fists of his brethren pummeling him in an attempt to reach Flyn. His living shield began to topple, and Flyn spun away, taking the dripping spurs with him. In their fury, the trolls were unaware that their quarry had escaped and continued to bludgeon their fallen comrade.

Flyn made a quick count. Four of the brutes were mercilessly beating the now limp troll into the floor, while the one Flyn had gelded was writhing weakly upon the ground. Two more lay unmoving a short distance away. Flyn hesitated.

"I thought there were nine of you?"

A primal roar erupted at Flyn's back and, before he could act, great crushing arms seized him. The breath was forced from his lungs in an agonizing rush as his ribs began to bend inward. His right arm was pinned at his side, while his left flailed from above his assailant's enclosing arms. Flyn stabbed backward, trying to strike the troll's face with his free spur. The beast began to shake him violently, upsetting his attacks. In his shuddering vision, Flyn saw the other trolls had discovered his predicament and abandoned their rage-murdered kin. In another moment, they would be upon him and help their brother tear him to pieces.

Releasing his grip on the steel spur, Flyn reached backward and grabbed a fistful of his attacker's filthy hair. Pulling with all his might, he forced the brute's head downward, moving his own head aside so that the troll's chin now dug into his shoulder. With savage instinct, the troll opened his growling mouth and bit down. Flyn grunted against the painful pressure, but his mail saved his flesh a gnashing. He continued to pull down on the troll's head as he bent in the middle, straining against the hold, lifting his feet until they were struck out directly before him. The four uninjured trolls reached for his talons, eager to rend his limbs.

Crying out with desperate exertion, Flyn jerked his legs up and felt the arms around his midriff slacken. Hauling on the troll's head for leverage, Flyn flipped up and landed astride the brute's shoulders, immediately slamming the natural spurs on his heels into the unwilling mount's chest.

Finding his fortunes suddenly reversed, the offended troll bellowed with pain and frustration, flailing his long arms in an attempt to smite Flyn from his perch. His right hand still lodged in the monster's locks, Flyn jerked the troll's head, causing his arms to wildly slap at the other brutes. They recoiled, but their stricken brother lumbered forward, as if he could flee the pain clinging to his body. Digging his spurs in, Flyn held fast, riding the crazed troll as he barreled into his cave-mates, thrashing them with agony-fueled blows.

As soon as his roaring steed burst free of the press, Flyn drove the remaining elf spur into the troll's throat before jumping free. Gargling his own blood, the brute careened into the cavern wall and fell in a heap upon the ground where he noisily expired.

Flyn stood, facing the remaining trolls, and let forth a war cry that rattled off the stone.

"Come, oafs!" he challenged, his voice mixing with the echoes of his screech. "Come, animals!"

He took an aggressive step forward and the trolls shuffled backwards. Flyn could feel his feathers standing away from his flesh, every quill puffed out contentiously, the skin beneath itching for further combat.

Five of the trolls were down. Three of the fallen were unmoving, the other two crippled and moaning where they lay. The remaining four were unharmed, yet they flinched away from Flyn, cowed and timid.

"Run and live, beasts," Flyn said, striding forward.

The trolls hurried away from him, their size making a mockery of swift, fearful movement.

Just then, light burst into the cavern. It came from Flyn's left, radiant and livid. The roiling red shapes of the trolls were dispelled, replaced with the reeling forms of the creatures revealed in full brightness. Throwing up grey-skinned arms to hide their eyes, the beasts dipped their shaggy heads, lowing in pain and fright.

Blinking against the nimbus, Flyn watched the trolls flee, even the injured, loping heavily into the safety of the dark tunnels dotting the cavern walls.

The source of the effulgence dimmed, hard shafts of light receding until only a warm glow bathed the cave. Hengest stood in the mouth of a tunnel, the light emanating from his raised fist.

Behind the dwarf, stood Deglan Loamtoes.

"You chased away my playmates," Flyn jested, his laughter coming out strained and raw.

Deglan crossed the cavern, something large hugged against his chest. As he drew closer, Flyn recognized Ingelbert's ledger.

"Hello, Staunch. Decided to give up medicine for chronicling?" Flyn watched the gnome bite back and swallow a reprimand. "I know. I am a preening, foolhardy, reckless popinjay."

"You are," Deglan agreed. "But, Earth and Stone, it is good to see you!"

"And you, you mouldy old mushroom."

Hengest walked over, his runestone still illuminating the cavern and the bodies of the trolls.

"They played rather rough," Flyn said.

The hairless runecaster squinted at the fallen creatures. "We should go. There may be more."

"Agreed," Flyn exclaimed, quickly finding his lost spur and buckling the pair on to his feet. "Neither of you appear to have a sword I could beg."

"Fresh out," Deglan said, and then his tone became grave.

"Flyn, Crane has been consumed by the influence of that damned owl."

Flyn put a hand on Deglan's shoulder. "I know."

Quickly scanning the cavern, he set off towards one of the tunnels.

"Dammit, you impatient wastrel!" Deglan complained, hurrying to catch up. "It's the Gaunt Prince!"

Flyn breathed a hum and quickened his pace, entering the tunnel.

"Hob's teeth, you unschooled strut, do you know who that is?"

"Some long-dead son of a Goblin King," Flyn said, intent on the tunnel floor and keeping alert for branching passages. "The heir to the iron crown. You forget, Staunch, I was sent to kill one of those before, by you, a certain saucy piskie, and a bunch of other strange sorts. And that Goblin King turned out to be nothing but an unlucky farm boy. Well, Ingelbert Crane is just an overly clever chronicler. We are going to remind him of that."

"You know where he is?" Hengest asked from the rear of their little column.

"Within the vale," Flyn called over his shoulder. "In the Corpse Eater's nest."

"And you know the way?" Deglan asked, his voice dubious.

"Up," Flyn answered. "We need to keep going up. The vale is littered with caves. It is how the vættir reach the tree. If you hear their singing, we should head towards it."

"Comforting," Deglan grumbled.

"Sir Flyn," Hengest said. "The Magic living in Master Crane is most potent. The spirit of this Gaunt Prince nearly killed Fafnir Rune-Wise, and that is not something to scoff at."

Flyn paused, turning around to face his companions. "I know. He broke the

Corpse Eater's mind on a whim. She would have killed me if the Dread Cockerel had not intervened. He fights her now, if he yet lives."

"The Chain Maker and Ulfrun the Breaker have gone to aid him in her destruction," Hengest told him.

"Good," Flyn said, though inwardly he wondered how well Wyncott would take to allies. "As for whoever holds Crane enthralled, I know not his full intentions, but he is up there with that husk from Castle Gaunt and . . . a woman."

"Beladore," Deglan intoned.

"You saw her too?"

"I did."

Flyn looked into the gnome's frowning face and they shared a look which bespoke of shared secrets, shared vows. They each asked and answered the same question without speaking, and were each relieved to find all secrets, all vows, intact.

"Who is she?" Hengest asked, clearly noticing their silent commiseration.

"The last surviving heir to the crown of the Goblin Kings," Deglan replied evenly.

"Inkst—" Flyn started, then caught himself, "rather, this Goblin Prince, wants her for something, though he is not afraid to harm her. She is in grave danger."

"We all are," Deglan said, peering up at the tunnel ceiling as if he could see through stone.

Flyn took a deep breath. "I need to stop him. Hengest, can you protect me from his sorcery?"

The runecaster thought deeply for a moment. "There are stones I have which will ward you, but they will not guard for long. You may have mere seconds."

Flyn nodded his understanding. He turned to set off up the tunnel, but a thought made him pause once more. Looking over Deglan's head, he locked eyes with Hengest.

"There is one other thing I would have you do."

Through the owl's keen eyes, Inkstain watched the Corpse Eater and smiled. She had made short work of Flyn and was now engaged with the other coburn on the nearby slopes just inside the Gale.

"The dark one is doing quite well," Inkstain said. "Far better than the fop. He wields that sword as if he were born to it, which, of course, he was."

The grey-feathered coburn did not have Flyn's alacrity, yet moved with the undeniable persistence of the tides, wading in to slash dauntlessly at the Mother of Gales. The great bird stuck to the ground, hindered by the one injury Flyn had managed to deliver.

Inkstain's smile broadened at the sight of the battle and the feeling of the chronicler struggling to reassert his own will. With the owl away, the mewling man had found a foothold and was feebly trying to reemerge. It was a treat to sense him squirming about, clinging to the small belief that he would regain control.

Tired of witnessing the Corpse Eater snap and hiss, Inkstain returned to his own vision to bask in a different spectacle.

The woman convulsed upon the ground, her jaw clenched so tightly she could not even scream out the agony that wracked her body. Slouch Hat knelt over her, his thin-fingered hands fighting to restrain her thrashing.

"Women are so very difficult to hurt," Inkstain mused.

"The nature of childbirth naturally inures them to pain. Indeed, they welcome it. As lusty girls they yearn for their first tearing penetration, hating and craving their own desires. And then they endure the birthing bed, wishing against all reason to return to that nightmare of sweat and blood again and again until they are old, dried-up crones, nursing the memory of the pains they savored in youth." The woman managed a squeal through clenched teeth, a sharp, high sound of torment. "So, you must slather them with the most excruciating energies just to get their attention."

Inkstain could feel the husk trying to break his spell, thumping crudely and ineffectually at the edges.

"You see, straw slave, there is more to sorcery than simply stealing a crown of power. You must know where to strike and how. For all your cunning, you must use every ounce of the craft you have stolen simply to keep that slattern alive." Inkstain clicked his tongue, reveling in the husk's helplessness and the bending spine of the woman flopping upon the squalid floor of the nest.

"Let her die, Slouch Hat. Then you can turn the crown on me. You may emerge the master of such a contest. Truly, I do not know how much the body of this skinny annalist can suffer. It might be you are the victor."

The husk did not respond, redoubling his efforts to calm the woman's affliction. Inkstain paced around them.

"You were right not to crown her. I concede she is my descendant, but no human has worn that circlet for a thousand years. It would have destroyed her. Mortal blood has such a fickle memory, so easily diluted by time." Inkstain knelt down beside the woman, opposite the husk. "But you, hollow man, you have no blood. Nothing for sorcery to pollute. You are a perfect vessel. Which, I suppose, is the reason father's little cunny used you to leave the Tower of Vellaunus. And so, here we all are."

The woman whimpered as Inkstain traced a finger between her tightly closed eyes and down the bridge of her nose. Her flesh was damp with sweat, despite the cold. Inkstain brought his finger to his tongue, tasting her salt.

"I can see why you strive to save her," he told the husk.

"But it leaves you vulnerable. I could set you afire at my leisure, or summon a flock of ravens to pick you apart, one stalk at a time. Mayhaps I will force the woman to wear your hat while I rape her."

Inkstain stood suddenly. "Half a moment! The cockfight has once again become interesting!"

Returning to the owl, he saw the Corpse Eater had at last returned to flight, the grim coburn clutched in her claws. He struggled most valiantly, still battling with the big sword, but had not landed a telling blow by the time the Corpse Eater reached the vale. Inkstain was able to leave the owl and watch with his human eyes as the great bird shot over the tree, quickly entering a dive towards the vale. She tried to release the coburn, drop him to his death, but he clung to the chains still tangled about her talons as Flyn had done before. Quickly, they dipped beyond the heights of the nest and Inkstain once more used the owl as his vantage.

The grey coburn waited until they were near the ground, then let go of the chain, rolling to break his fall. The Corpse Eater swooped level with the ground, quickly leaving her foe behind. The Mother of Gales was fleeing.

Inkstain wrinkled his mouth in disappointment. Perhaps he had not broken her mind enough, if she could resort to such tactics.

He started to turn away, but movement caught the owl's eye.

Ulfrun emerged from a cave mouth directly in front of the Corpse Eater and near level with her flight. As the great bird sped through the air, flapping her wings to pull up and leave the vale, the giantess leaped out. She caught the bird's neck, gripping it in a bear-hug with her arms and legs. Using her powerful muscles to exert tremendous torsion, Ulfrun wrenched the Corpse Eater's neck around, forcing her flight into a headlong twist. The giantess still held fast as the bird slammed into the ridge. A small avalanche accompanied the tumbling monster to the floor of the vale.

Inkstain grinned. "I can see why you tumbled the giantess, chronicler. Most impressive."

Dazed, but alive, the Corpse Eater struggled to rise against the press of snow and ice. Of the giantess there was no sign. The grey coburn came rushing across the vale, towards the grounded beast, cutting down every wight in his path. Inkstain felt a surge of power enter the vale and directed the owl to look at another cave, this one opening at the ground. Here, the runemaster strode forth, though visibly still frail from the chastising he had received from Slouch Hat. The vale was now teeming with wights and they began to shuffle towards the dwarf, a tide of corpses.

Inkstain smiled. "Fafnir truly is tenacious. Could it be his augury will be fulfilled?"

Uncaring, he shrugged and turned back to Slouch Hat.

"Have you not broken that little curse? If you do not hurry she will be quite insane. You deserve to be so humbled, husk. To be reminded of your proper station. That is why I do not burn you now. I will not stoop to taking what is mine by force from a servant who should offer me my crown on bended knee!" Leaning down, Inkstain pushed his face beside the husk's and whispered at him. "You will know your place and then this woman will be bent to hers."

"Buggery and shit," Deglan cursed, scowling at the twisted, rime-covered branch before him. "You do not expect me to cross that?"

"I am afraid so," Flyn replied.

After hurrying on cramping legs through the caverns, keeping up with the strut's blistering pace, Deglan had finally gained some relief when the tunnel they traversed leveled out. His comfort, however, was short-lived, for they had only gone a few hundred paces before they saw a glaring portal of white sunlight ahead. Reaching the exit, Deglan had gawked at the massive trunk before him.

They were high up the ridge, the underside of the horrid nest they sought visible above. The cave mouth was joined to the tree by one thick, serpentine branch that had pushed its way into the rock face with the slow, irresistible growth of countless years.

Though wide as a wagon track, the limb's curved surface was encrusted with frost and a covering of snow, no doubt hiding all manner of knots and knobs ready to trip a foot and send an unsuspecting gnome plummeting to his death.

"Bugger that," Deglan declared, stepping back from the edge of the tunnel. He watched as Flyn clambered down the eroding stone and dropped to the branch, his taloned feet clutching the slick bark.

"Come on, Staunch," the coburn urged, holding a hand up.

Clutching the tome tight to his body with one arm, Deglan took Flyn's hand and lowered himself down, sliding painfully on his backside until his feet touched the branch. He had to move forward to make room for Hengest, so he grabbed the back of Flyn's belt and eased his feet forward. Once the dwarf gained the bough, Flyn led them slowly across.

Deglan fought the urge to look down and when he failed at that, he fought the urge to piss himself. He could hear the spike on the butt of Hengest's staff striking the crust behind him, the dwarf jabbing the steel deep to steady himself. Flyn had his talons to keep his footing and Deglan had Flyn, unwilling to relinquish his hold on the coburn's belt. Thankfully, Flyn never asked him to.

After a ponderous eternity of shuffling his feet, Deglan reached the hoary wall that was the tree's trunk. The branch widened where it joined the tree, and the three of them were able to stand in a cluster while Flyn surveyed the best possible ascent.

Deglan watched with a growing sense of unease as the coburn's eyes followed the path of a narrower, up-sweeping branch just above where they stood, which thrust out over the vale for a dreadful distance before curving to cradle the edge of the nest.

"No," Deglan groused softly as he saw Flyn decide on their course.

"It is the only way," the knight said, reaching out for the tome. Deglan handed it over and Flyn tucked it between his ragged surcoat and his mail. Squatting, Flyn motioned at his back. "Up you come, Staunch."

"Why me?" Deglan asked, then pointed at Hengest. "Take him first. I will wait here and see if you make it."

"I will manage on my own," the dwarf said.

Deglan flicked a squinted eye at the runecaster's heavy staff.

"You going to climb one-handed?"

"No," Hengest replied and reached into his pouch to produce a runestone. Muttering something in the dwarrow tongue, he placed the stone in the socket of the staff's wrought ram's head.

When the dwarf released the staff, it remained suspended in the air at his side.

"Clever," Deglan admitted. "I don't suppose you have another of those stones to shove up my arse."

Still crouched, Flyn laughed. "Come on, you."

Groaning, Deglan clambered onto the coburn's back. As soon as Flyn stood, Deglan shut his eyes.

"Bugger. Shit. Bugger. Shit. Bugger. Shit."

He felt his own weight sway as Flyn made his way out onto the smaller branch, certain that he was going to cause the coburn to become unbalanced and drag them both down. Slowly, Deglan felt his head pitch forward as Flyn leaned down to grab the bole, proceeding on his hands and feet. The coburn went alarmingly fast in this manner and soon Deglan felt himself raised back to nearly upright. A sudden jostle signaled Flyn's initial bound as he began to climb the nearly vertical branch. Deglan opened his eyes, only once, immediately regretting the impulse. He hung out over the brink, beyond the other branches, nothing below but laughing wind and the blurry white of the vale, mind-numbingly distant. Beyond and above Flyn's head, Deglan saw the edge of the nest, the ends of dozens of sundered, jumbled logs drawing closer.

Deglan lay face down on one of those logs when Flyn deposited him at the top, breathing in grateful, shuddering breaths.

The coburn went back to the edge and leaned an arm down to help haul Hengest up the last stretch. The dwarf's staff rose up beside him and he took it in hand once more. Deglan got to his feet as Flyn handed the tome back.

"You think this will help him?" the knight asked.

Deglan could only raise his eyebrows, but Hengest was more certain.

"That book is rampant with huldu Magic," the runecaster pronounced. "I think it may be what kept Master Crane from succumbing for so long and what prevented Fafnir from sensing the warlock's presence."

"A blessing and a curse," Deglan said.

"Yes," Hengest agreed. "But, if anything has the power to deliver Master Crane, it is within those pages. Here." The dwarf handed Flyn his staff. "This will make a good mace, and the craft used to forge it may deter some of the Gaunt Prince's sorcery."

Hengest then proceeded to tuck various stones in the coburn's surcoat, beneath his vambraces and in the pouch on his belt.

"My thanks," Flyn told him, once the dwarf was finished.

"Thank him if we survive," Deglan said, receiving a clap on the shoulder from the knight.

Flyn then took the lead, swiftly traversing the fog-laden nest. Deglan glanced back at Hengest when they passed the first pellet bursting with dwarrow bones, but if the dwarf was unnerved he showed no sign. Walking through the unhealthy vapors, they soon came to the center of the nest.

Slouch Hat knelt on the ground next to Beladore, who twitched weakly as she lay, blood and vomit leaking from the corners of her palsied lips. Deglan tried to run to her aid, but Flyn shot out a restraining arm. Following the coburn's stare,

Deglan saw what should have been a familiar figure appearing out of the haze. The tousled mop of coarse, flaxen hair, the thin limbs and narrow shoulders, the large, long-fingered hands, all features which defined Ingelbert Crane, yet it was not he. The splayed stance, the arrogant set of the head, the proud, confident bearing, none of it belonged to the chronicler.

Deglan had never laid eyes on the Gaunt Prince in life, but looking now upon the visage that once belonged to Crane, he had no doubt who was behind that ravenous smile. The voice which greeted them was painfully familiar, but everything in its inflection, its mocking cadence, was an affront to the gentle, hesitant tones of the man they knew.

"Still alive, Bantam Flyn? Living things have grown more stubborn while I slept."

"Ingelbert!" Flyn exclaimed. "Hear me. Fight him."

The Gaunt Prince threw back his head and laughed throatily at the sky. "Do you expect such an entreaty to be of any use? Your simpering annalist cannot heed you! He has gone somewhere shrunken and cold, believe me. He no longer has thought or voice, and yet you think you can bid him return with naught but brave words!"

Laughter filled the air once more and Deglan nearly choked on bitter rage. Clutching the tome, he scanned his surroundings quickly, looking for the owl, which was forebodingly absent. At his side, Flyn joined the Gaunt Prince in laughter.

"You have the right," the knight said, the mirth leaving his voice as quickly as it had come. "Forget the words."

Flyn charged, swinging Hengest's staff one-handed in a swift upward backhand. Still laughing, the Gaunt Prince leaned away from the blow, proceeding to step nimbly and also avoid Flyn's return strike. It was disturbing to see Crane's gawky physique move with such speed and grace, comfortable in the deadly dance of combat. Flyn pressed the attack, but Deglan could see he was holding back, not willing to use his full prowess against what he still perceived as Ingelbert Crane. His clemency quickly cost him.

Dodging a downswing, the Gaunt Prince lunged forward and Deglan heard Flyn grunt in pain. Springing back just as quickly, the man smiled, a dripping dagger in his hand. Blood flowed freely from Flyn's side, staining his surcoat. The Gaunt Prince had punched the blade through the mail as if it were not there. Deglan's trained eye saw that the wound was not mortal. Flyn was being toyed with, used to increase the warlock's pleasure.

"I can smell the wards on you, coburn," the Gaunt Prince needled. "All the little dwarrow trinkets." He laughed again, rolling his mocking eyes at Hengest. "You are more pathetic than your master. Scribbling runes! I wonder, have you left any protection for yourself?"

Hengest's hands suddenly shot to his head as a scream erupted from his lips. Blood leaked from his eyes. Deglan went to the dwarf's side, catching his fall. He pawed ineffectually at the suffering runecaster, unable to do anything to curb his pain.

The Gaunt Prince returned his attention to Flyn, watching him calmly as the knight tried to quell the blood flowing from beneath his ribs. "I need no sorcery for you. A thousand years ago I was the most feared fighter living. Of your kind alone, I have slain scores. It will be a sweet delight to kill again with my own hands." He smiled, thinly. "Or rather, your friend's."

Deglan saw Flyn's face contort with hatred and he surged forward. He held nothing back now, swinging the heavy staff in lightning arcs, forcing the Gaunt Prince to give ground. Yet even on the defensive, the man was smiling, savoring the sport. Deglan glowered as he watched them duel, uncertain Flyn could prevail and unable to help him, unable to help anyone.

His attention was dragged back to Hengest. The dwarf clutched at him with clumsy fingers. Looking down, Deglan saw Hengest's other hand struggling to reach into his pouch. Quickly, Deglan released the clasp and stuck his own hand in, finding a single stone.

"Clever bastard," he whispered. "You did keep one."

Hengest took the runestone from him, his eyes closing tightly at its touch. The blood streaming from his eyes began to ebb.

"The husk," the dwarf wheezed, pushing Deglan feebly.

"Go." Nodding, Deglan rose. Taking the tome with him, he scurried over to Slouch Hat and dropped to his knees on the other side of Beladore. She was barely breathing, her eyes half closed and rolled to white. The husk's sack face was creased with concentration, his hands pressed into Beladore's chest and abdomen. Just when Deglan thought the woman would succumb, she lurched upward, her back bending as a tortured wail escaped from behind her locked jaws.

"Earth and Stone, Slouch, do something!"

"I cannot," the husk hissed. "I cannot break through."

Deglan snatched a glance at Flyn and the Gaunt Prince, battling a few dozen strides away. The coburn was tiring, but the man remained full of sinister vitality.

"We need you," Deglan said, turning back to Slouch Hat.

"We need that cursed crown to stop him."

"Quiet!" Slouch Hat hissed. "If I leave her side she will die. She must not. She is the key to everything."

Deglan pulled his lips back in a silent, helpless snarl, looking around desperately. Flyn fought on, but it was clear he was flagging. Soon, the Gaunt Prince would tire of the contest and end him. A few paces away, Hengest still lay on his back, clutching his stone, alive, but barely. At Deglan's knees, Beladore continued to choke on her own screams and fluids. He could not help, he could not heal! A woman lay in agony, afflicted and suffering, and there was nothing he could do for her. Nothing, except . . .

"Let her die."

The husk ignored his words, continuing his unseen struggle with the forces which racked Beladore's body.

"Slouch Hat!" Deglan cried. "Let her die!"

"No!"

"It is the only way. Do you not see? You said it yourself, she is the key to everything. Look at her, she hangs on the brink of death, but does not die. The Gaunt Prince needs her too! He is only doing this to keep you distracted. He is not as powerful as he claims. It is a damn bluff, Slouch! Let her go!"

The black pits of the husk's eyes left Beladore, and bored into Deglan. Then, slowly, his hands came away. Beladore shuddered and retched, violently convulsing, her limbs pounding the logs beneath her. Quickly, she descended into small, pitiful twitches and her breathing grew shallow.

Flyn grunted as the Gaunt Prince's dagger sliced into his forearm. He had never known a foe to move so swiftly. Bleeding from a half-dozen wounds, Flyn had not so much as touched the man.

"Do you grow weary, coburn?" the warlock gloated. "Shall I make an end?"

"For one who called me a poet," Flyn returned, "you delight in your own voice."

The Gaunt Price smiled and Flyn saw the anticipation of the killing stroke. He would not be able to prevent it, the man was too fast. Then, the smile withered and the man's eyes widened, leaving Flyn to glare at a point over his shoulder.

"You impudent husk!" the Gaunt Prince exclaimed.

Flyn sprang, using the opening, but before his strike could land, the Gaunt Prince snarled and outstretched his arm. Flyn's forward rush was instantly arrested as he was catapulted away, borne aloft by a wave of fell energy. His entire body felt afire from within and he screamed, feeling the runestones beneath his armor shatter. He hit the rough surface of the nest and tumbled over himself, the staff flying from his hand. The smell of his own singed feathers filled his nostrils.

Rising onto his elbows, Flyn turned his head to see the husk standing away from Beladore and Deglan, facing the Gaunt Prince. Both had their arms flung wide, leaning toward one another as the air between them crackled. Flyn knew nothing of Magic, but he knew a battle when he saw one. Slouch Hat now fought the Gaunt Prince as fervently as Flyn had moments before, though the blows could not be seen.

All sound seemed to have been sucked from the world, and then the Gaunt Prince screamed, snatching at his skull with one hand. "Return to your prison, warlock!" Slouch Hat cried out.

Falling to his knees, the Gaunt Prince flung his free hand out in a furious motion, sending a wave of pale fire scything towards the husk. It caught Slouch Hat clean in the midriff, slicing him in half and continuing directly at Deglan. Flyn screamed, but had no time to even gain his feet before the wave struck the gnome, exploding with a blinding flash as it impacted. A blackened, smoldering lump was flung into the air, vanishing in the fog.

Flyn shot to his feet and whirled to face the Gaunt Prince.

Ingelbert Crane stared back at him.

The chronicler was on his knees, slack-jawed and bewildered. A shadowy motion above the man caught Flyn's eye.

It was Gasten, swooping down, claws opening.

Flyn sprinted forward, covering the distance swiftly and leaped, snatching the owl out of the air before its talons could sink into Crane.

Flyn used his fall to force the owl to the ground. Its wings buffeted his face, its beak and claws tearing at his eyes and the soft flesh of his comb. Through the physical pain, Flyn could feel a greater agony, one which lanced him to the core. His mind was flooded with tormented visions. Burning cities and orgies of bloodshed, battlefields strewn with hacked corpses. A man stood among the dead, tall and terrible, naked to the waist. Crimson droplets of the slain shone upon his pale, sinewy torso and shaved pate. He beckoned for Flyn to approach as a heavy rain began to fall, rinsing the gore from the man and causing his flesh to glisten.

The figure smiled and the rainfall ran down his teeth, pooling in his lower lip before dripping from his angular chin. Promises of power were ensconced in that smile, promises of dominance in combat and ever-lasting life.

Flyn refused them all.

Surging through the boiling in his brain, he cried out in defiance, returning to himself just as the owl escaped his grasp. He dove for it again, but the creature flapped beyond his reach and was gone. Breathing heavily, Flyn picked himself up and looked around. Hengest and Beladore still lay upon the ground, but the vapors geysering from their lips showed they yet lived. Slouch Hat was sprawled near the woman, in two halves. The upper half still moved. Flyn stared as the husk raised his head and rolled to what was left of his stomach, using his arms to drag himself towards Beladore. Movement in the mist beyond caused Flyn to start.

Deglan appeared with the charred remnants of the tome in his arms. Flyn nearly fell to his knees as he breathed a sigh of relief.

"Where is Crane?" the gnome asked, hobbling forward.

Flyn cast about, but found no sign of him.

"That way," Hengest croaked, raising enough to point.

With Deglan at his heels, Flyn hurried off in the direction the dwarf indicated.

They found Ingelbert looking out across the swirling sky, standing at the end of a narrow bough which struck out well past the edge of the nest. Flyn was troubled at the chronicler's precarious position, but relieved to see that Gasten was not with him. He and Deglan walked to the border of the nest.

"Look," Ingelbert said, his voice once again recognizable.

"The Gale is abating."

Flyn focused beyond the man and saw he was right. The maelstrom was weakening.

"Earth and Stone," Deglan breathed.

"They have done it," Flyn said, shaking his head in wonder.

"The Corpse Eater is dead."

Ingelbert turned around slowly. He regarded Flyn and Deglan for a moment, all the usual hesitancy returned to his face.

The slackening winds tugged at his clothes and hair.

"I, uh, I am glad to see you both alive."

Deglan snorted, lifting the burned book, "Thank your bloody ledger. Makes a damn fine shield."

Flyn chuckled and Ingelbert smiled, but it did not spread beyond his mouth.

"He was in there all along," the chronicler said. "The Gaunt Prince. I did not mean to, I did not mean to release him." The man's voice broke and his chin fell, his narrow shoulders slumping beneath his frayed cloak. "He escaped to the owl's corpse and then, then to me."

"He is gone now, Crane," Flyn said gently, stepping forward. Ingelbert recoiled, moving closer to the end of the branch.

Flyn froze and shot a concerned look at Deglan. The perch was hardly wide enough for both the man's feet.

"Master Crane," the gnome warned. "Be careful."

Ingelbert stilled and looked at them, his mouth twisted with contrition. "He is not gone. He is, uh, a contagion, Deglan. You understand? A part of him lingers."

"I understand, lad," Deglan replied, a note of apprehension in his soothing words.

Ingelbert gave a small, embarrassed laugh and looked distantly at the ground. "Swear an oath, Bantam Flyn. Swear an oath for me."

Flyn nodded. "Name it."

Ingelbert's eyes came up and met his. "Do not try and save me."

"Ingelbert . . ."

"I want your word, sir, that you will not try and save me," the chronicler said firmly. He made a sheepish gesture to the cloudy expanse behind him. "This is not the tower in the Roost. No stairs to catch us. But I know your bravery, Flyn, and I know you would try. Please. Swear you will not."

Flyn could not keep from looking at Ingelbert's rocking ankles. He suddenly recalled the man's pleading face as they hung from the Corpse Eater's claws. He had begged something, something Flyn could not hear.

"Do I have your oath?" the man pressed.

"Ingelbert," Flyn tried to keep his voice steady, "I would not let you fall before and I will not now. There must be another way."

"There is not. Your oath."

"Dammit, man!" Deglan exclaimed. "Step to us!"

The chronicler's eyes welled, but his voice was calm. "He will return. The Gaunt Prince will return."

"And you will resist him!" Flyn insisted. "You have before."

Ingelbert gestured at the book. "I, I had aid. Aid you must also seek if you want to defeat him. Wake her. Save her. Call her from the dark. She is the only one who can oppose him."

"Who?" Flyn asked.

"Give me your oath and I will tell you."

The chronicler's face was implacable, waiting on an answer.

Clenching his fist, Flyn looked down at Deglan. The gnome gave the barest shake of his head.

Flyn groaned with frustration. He paced fretfully, unable to step forward for fear he would goad Ingelbert off the bough. "No! You will not ransom your own life with riddles."

"It is not a riddle, Bantam Flyn. It is history."

"Which I know nothing of and you do, so step towards me and we will stand against what comes together!"

Flyn felt himself beginning to panic, his unease growing alongside Ingelbert's unnerving calm.

"You see friends everywhere, Bantam Flyn. But tell me truthfully, what do you see when you look at me now?"

Unbidden, an image of Ingelbert's smile, twisted by the Gaunt Prince's madness, swam in Flyn's mind. He pushed it away, steeled himself against the thought as he looked into the chronicler's long, sad, familiar face.

"I still see a friend," he proclaimed. "A friend and a sworn member of the Valiant Spur. You remain my brother, Ingelbert Crane. Remember that and do not do this!"

"I shall remember," the man said, his voice hushed with regret. "I am grateful that I will remain your friend. Your family. But I can no longer be your ally. Alive, I remain a path for the Gaunt Prince to return."

"Crane!" Flyn shouted as Ingelbert took another half step backward.

Ingelbert held up a calming hand. "I cannot defeat him, Flyn. That is for you to do. The world needs selfless bravery such as yours." For an instant, the chronicler's gaze shifted to Deglan.

"And level heads, to do what courageous hearts cannot."

"Master Crane," the gnome said, his voice grimly weighted.

"Do not force me—"

"I cannot defeat him," the chronicler repeated, looking at Flyn once more. "I can only deprive him."

Ingelbert's face filled with fondness and he stepped back.

"NO!"

Flyn darted forward, but was tripped up as Deglan jumped into his path, grabbing his legs. Hitting the logs of the nest, Flyn craned his head up to look at the bough.

It was empty.

There was nothing but cold, remorseless sky. Frozen with disbelief, Flyn stared at that terrible void for a long time.

A shaking at his legs pulled him out of his stupor. Deglan still clung to him, his body rocking with sobs. Sitting up, Flyn gathered the gnome in his arms and hugged him tightly.

"What did you do, Staunch?" he whispered.

"My part," Deglan replied, his voice thick with tears. "I needed to save you. Both of you."

THIRTY-FOUR

Flyn was eager to be down from the nest, but the going was slow. Hengest and Beladore were still weak, and she insisted on carrying Slouch Hat herself. The lower half of the husk's body had been reduced to little more than ash, and he now clung to Beladore's back, his body ending at the waist. Once they gained the caves, they moved cautiously, watchful for trolls.

"This is where we must part," Slouch Hat said at a seemingly unremarkable junction. "Do not allow my physical plight to give you confidence. It would not be wise to attempt to stop us."

"And you would be wise to flee Middangeard with all haste," Hengest returned with cold menace. "The dwarrow will forever hunt you for your part in this."

"There is no longer cause to stay," Beladore said. Flyn thought the woman looked years older, the shadow of the Gaunt Prince's torments lurking in the lines of her face.

"And what did you hope to achieve?" Deglan growled.

"Not achieve, Master Loamtoes," Slouch Hat replied.

"Prevent. Middangeard is a glimpse of Airlann's future. The Age of Autumn will end and when it does, this same dead cold will encase the Source Isle. The elves have had their chance, and twice the world has suffered under their stewardship. It is only a matter of time before they abandon Airlann as they did Middangeard. The Seelie Court is silent, Red Caps are on the rise, your own people in Toad Holm are corrupted. It is time for the Fae to relinquish control and allow the world to be governed by forces other than Magic." Flyn saw Deglan struggle with the husk's words, his jaw chewing bitterly upon a retort that never came.

"But the Mother of Gales has been vanquished," Slouch Hat continued, "and, with her, our need to remain."

"I heard you speaking with her," Flyn said. "What did you hope to discover?"

"Perhaps one day, Sir, I can tell you," the husk said. "One day, when our goals align."

"Not bloody likely," Deglan grumbled.

"You freed Ingelbert," Flyn told the husk. "At the end, you severed the Gaunt Prince's hold over him. For that, I thank you."

Slouch Hat gave the barest nod. "Let us go, Beladore."

"My lady," Flyn said as the woman turned to go, causing her to pause. "The protection of the Valiant Spur was once promised to your son. We failed in that duty." A flicker of old pain settled with the new upon the woman's face. "But, I believe that protection extends to you. If you would trust our Order, just once more, we would welcome the chance to make amends and, perhaps one day, assuage your grief."

Beladore's countenance hardened. "You think you can replace what I have lost with chivalry and hospitable words?"

Flyn struggled in the wrath of the mother's stare, struggled not to look at Deglan, struggled not to say the four words this poor woman needed to hear.

"I am merely trying to offer you another choice," he said at last.

"I have made my choice, knight," Beladore replied.

Flyn bowed to her. "As you will. I would but beg one thing more. I told you I carried the grief of your son's loss with me. I spoke true." Reaching into his belt pouch he pulled forth Pocket's little wooden horse. "This belonged to your little boy. He held it and played with it during his time at the Roost. Please, accept it."

Beladore's eyes widened as he placed the toy into her hand.

She stared at it for a long time, holding it as one would an injured bird. When she looked up again, there was a resentful gratitude on her face. Flyn bowed again, saving her from voicing any thanks.

When he straightened, she was already disappearing into the shadows of the tunnel, the mutilated husk upon her back.

Flyn allowed Hengest to lead their own path, proceeding in silence for some time until they emerged from the caves.

Outside, dusk was descending quickly, but there was more than enough light to marvel at the vale. Hundreds of wights lay strewn about, spreading from the cliff-sides to the roots of the great tree. No longer walking, no longer singing, they were as they were meant to be, lifeless at last.

They found Fafnir lying among a heavy pile of dead, his eyes closed. His hands were clutched into blackened fists, still smoking from the power of the runestones lodged within. Flyn could see no visible wounds upon the wizard, yet he looked as lifeless as the corpses which cradled him. He had stood against an army of his risen kin and prevailed, but whatever crafts he had wielded against his foes appeared to have leached all vitality from his body.

Flyn stood by while Hengest knelt at Fafnir's side. Deglan too, squatted beside the dwarf, his fingers reaching instinctively for a pulse. The Chain Maker's eyes fluttered open at his touch. The gnome removed his hand while Hengest began rummaging in Fafnir's rune pouch.

"You will find only one stone," Fafnir managed, his words thick and labored.

Hengest removed his hand from the bag and marveled at what he held in his palm.

"The Lay of the Sword Dale. My lord, why? With this, you would not have fallen."

"And exhausted the power of the rune," Fafnir managed, "sundered the stone. Take it. Learn the rune. One day, you will sing behind your shield so that your allies shall stand firm. The Lay will serve you well on the path now before you."

"What path, my lord?" Hengest asked.

Fafnir's eyes drifted over to Deglan and tarried for a heartbeat before rising to settle on Flyn. When he spoke again, his breath was spare and ragged.

"To aid those who have aided us so faithfully," the rune master answered. "Master Loamtoes, Sir Flyn, you have my thanks."

Deglan remained silent, but Flyn shook his head, finding he had no stomach for gratitude. "Others are deserving, my lord. Not I. I am not the one you needed."

Fafnir's eyes closed, and for a moment the pain fled his face. "You are wrong. The chain is now complete. You were the stoutest link. Had you broken, this destiny would have lay snapped, unfulfilled. Because of your bravery, the doom of the dwarrow is over."

"The vættir are no more," Hengest declared softly, placing a hand on Fafnir's shoulder. "You can rest."

Fafnir's eyes opened once more and agony flooded over his brief serenity.

"Then," the wizard pushed the word passed his swollen tongue, "I will not rise?"

"No, Chain Maker," Hengest assured his former master.

"You will not rise. Rest. Go to your daughters."

Fafnir smiled weakly, drew in a shuddering breath and stilled.

Flyn and Deglan withdrew and waited silently while Hengest said some words over Fafnir in dworgmál. Looking towards the western edge of the vale, Flyn saw the distant lump of the Corpse Eater's fallen form. He ran a weary hand over his comb, unable to fathom why he still lived when so many other powerful beings breathed no more. Once Hengest's respects were concluded, they made their way towards the monster's carcass.

She lay not far from the base of the cliffs, the ground around her littered with fallen rock and ice, and the decapitated remains of at least a dozen vættir. The Mother of Gales was twisted grotesquely in death, her beak agape, her tongue lolling upon the snow. Her large eyes were open, devoid of madness and life. Flyn felt they stared at him accusingly.

"Earth and Stone," Deglan said, scowling distastefully at the beast, then jumped back as one of her wings twitched.

"Buggery and shit, she lives!"

Flyn tensed, then laughed as the pinion feathers were thrust aside, revealing the limping form of the Dread Cockerel. The grim knight paused when he saw them, standing a moment beneath the wing of the creature he had slain. After a moment, he stepped forward, releasing the curtain of feathers to fall back behind him.

As he approached, Flyn noticed his right hand was drawn up close to his chest, bloody and mangled.

"Well fought, Sir Wyncott," Flyn said, nodding his head with respect.

"My thanks, Sir Flyn," the Dread Cockerel replied in his gravelly voice. "Especially for the use of your blade."

Flyn gave the drab coburn an incredulous look. "Mine?"

The Dread Cockerel issued what might have been a laugh.

Whatever the sound, it was not pleasant.

"The property of no one now," he said, motioning at the Corpse Eater with his uninjured hand. "The blade lies shattered in her heart, though a few slivers I still carry." He held up the ruin of his sword hand.

Flyn found he could not look at the Dread Cockerel's wound, could not face the price he might have paid himself.

"And what of Ulfrun?" Deglan asked.

The Dread Cockerel looked about, frowning. "I know not."

They found her kneeling between two of the tree's massive roots, cradling Ingelbert's head in her lap. Ulfrun looked up as they gathered around. She did not weep, her sorrow dammed up behind her strong face.

"Who will write of him?" the giantess asked, her voice brittle. "He was to record our deeds, but . . . who will write of him?"

Flyn had thought no one who fell from that tree would reach the bottom. He had been wrong. Yet, Ingelbert was oddly whole, filthy from the fall, but not bloody or broken. Only his sightlessly staring eyes and blue-tinged flesh gave evidence of death.

Hope igniting in his heart, Flyn turned on Hengest. "Save him." The dwarf looked at him with confusion.

"Save him," Flyn repeated, stepping towards the runecaster.

"Surely you can do something?"

"Sir Flyn—" Hengest began, his face full of pity.

"Look," Flyn pressed, hearing the pleading in his own voice and pointing at Ingelbert. "His wounds are not great! Restore him. Do something!"

Hengest remained silent. Looking about desperately, Flyn saw Deglan.

"Staunch," he said, rushing over to the gnome. "You can heal him. I know you can! Please."

Deglan shook his head, his face begging with Flyn to stop.

"He is gone, lad."

"But he looks hale. It should be possible!"

Hengest's voice drifted through his mounting despair, saying things Flyn did not want to hear. "The Magic in his veins was strong, Sir Flyn. Even at the end. Do not let his appearance deceive you. He is beyond help."

Flyn paced, tearing at his comb, unable to accept it. He himself had died and been restored, along with others. Pocket had done it, using the power of the iron crown.

"Slouch Hat!" Flyn exclaimed, casting desperate looks at his companions. "I will find him, bring him back and—"

"BANTAM FLYN!" Deglan roared. "This is what Crane wanted!"

Flyn snapped, screeching at the sky, every feather standing away from his body. Looking up, he saw Gasten sitting upon a low branch of the great tree, staring contemptuously down at him.

"YOU!" Flyn screamed, pointing violently at the owl. "You! I will end you for this! Do you hear? Do you see? Look upon me, Gaunt Prince, and behold your slayer! I swear on the life you have taken, I will turn all-purpose to your destruction!"

Gasten unfurled his wings and took flight across the vale.

Flyn flung his words at the retreating bird. "This I vow!"

Deglan stared critically at the Dread Cockerel's injured hand and took a deep breath.

"Sorry to say, but I doubt you will ever wield a sword again."

The grim coburn stared at his crippled appendage for a moment, then dismissed it as he turned his eyes on his other hand, raising it up before him.

"Yes," the knight intoned. "I will."

Finding he had no argument, Deglan continued the bandaging as best he could.

Not wanting to tarry in the death-covered vale, the group had left through the caves, taking Crane's body with them. Hengest had insisted Fafnir remain where he fell, claiming the Chain Maker would desire nothing else.

Using the tunnels, they were able to avoid the plateau where the draugr still milled and made a rude camp in a pitiful, frozen stand of firs well away from the yawning caverns and their troll inhabitants. The night had been long and cold, yet Deglan slept soundly, rising with the sun to do what good he could with no supplies.

As he tied the last strip of scrounged linen about the Dread Cockerel's wrist, Flyn approached with Ulfrun beside him. Hengest remained deeper in the copse, conversing with several of those bloody big crows that had torn Arngrim to pieces.

"Sir Wyncott," Flyn said, "can you escort Master Loamtoes safely back to the Tin Isles?"

The Dread Cockerel nodded once.

Deglan peered at Flyn. "You truly are staying?"

"I am."

Deglan shot a look at Ulfrun. "You going to watch out for him?"

The giantess smiled. "I am."

"What of you?" Flyn asked. "Where will you go?"

"The Roost," Deglan replied readily. "The Guild Masters of Gipeswic be damned. My scruples can weather a broken promise to those fat fishermen."

Flyn hesitated a moment, but finally found his tongue. "Do you think the Roost is truly where Ingelbert would have wanted to be?"

Deglan forced himself not to look at the shrouded form lying among the trees. "For truth, I do not know. If you have a better place in mind, I would hear it."

Flyn ran a hand over his comb while he thought. "He mentioned the orphanage of his youth with some fondness, and a man there named Parlan Sloan. Perhaps that would be best."

Deglan nodded, remembering Crane mentioning both the place and the man. "Then Sir Wyncott and I will go to Sasana first, lay him to rest there."

Flyn turned and gazed at the body, forcing Deglan to do the same. It would be a long journey, but the cold of Middangeard would keep Crane preserved until herbs could be found suitable to the task.

They relaxed their morose vigil when Hengest joined them, the runecaster glancing up to watch the crows quickly receding into the sky.

"The valróka bear word to Hriedmar's Hall," the dwarf informed them. "Lord Reginn will send an escort for you, Master Loamtoes. Keep a southerly course and the birds will report your movements. You will have supplies and a company of dwarrow warriors within a few days. They will see you safely until you take ship. If you feel you need them in the Tin Isles, you need but say the word and they will follow."

Deglan nodded his appreciation, trying not to seem too pleased with the prospect of leaving this hoary waste behind.

"And what of you two?" he asked, wagging a finger between Flyn and Ulfrun.

"We follow Beladore with all haste," Flyn answered. "The Gaunt Prince will stay near her, so that is our road. Hengest has agreed to join us."

"How will you track her?" the Dread Cockerel inquired.

"Through the rune Sir Flyn had me inscribe and conceal on an item he gave her," Hengest replied.

Deglan frowned. "You do not think Slouch Hat will sense it?"

"Most likely," the dwarf admitted. "But he would need to destroy the item to dispel the rune."

"Something Beladore will never allow," Deglan said, looking approvingly at Flyn.

"That is my hope," the coburn said. "If she does, then I am wrong about her. About everything."

"We should make haste," Hengest urged.

Flyn nodded his agreement, then looked up at Ulfrun.

"What say you, Breaker? Fancy a chase?"

"Aye," the giantess said, grinning hungrily.

Flyn laughed. "I feel naked going on errantry without a sword."

"Well, there is a bloody sharp one lying near Crow Shoulders' bird-scattered bones," Deglan told him.

Hengest grunted in approval. "The sword of Tyrfing. Fafnir forged that blade. It would serve you well, Sir Flyn."

"I remember the spot," Ulfrun announced. "Come."

"I will be with you in a moment," Flyn told them. "Your pardon, Sir Wyncott, I need a word with Deglan."

The Dread Cockerel strode off with the dwarf and giantess, leaving Deglan and Flyn alone.

"You must tell Sir Corc everything, Staunch," Flyn whispered.

"I intend to," Deglan assured him. "The question remains, what do you intend to tell Beladore? Would you risk revealing that Pocket still lives?"

"Not while she is surrounded by warlocks and evil counselors, no. But if I can rid her of those influences . . ." Flyn paused for a moment, weighing his thoughts. "Then yes, Staunch, I will tell her. She deserves to know. We may fail. I may fail. Slouch Hat is not to be trifled with and the threat of the Gaunt Prince is far worse. He could very well return to Airlann. Ingelbert said he could be stopped, but only by some woman. Do you know what he meant?"

Deglan blew hard through his nostrils. "Crane said it was history. So, not a woman. An elf.

"At the Battle of Nine Crowns only Goban Blackmud survived, the king of my people at that time. He always said that he would not have lived were it not for

Aillila Ulvyeh, daughter of the Elf-king, that she defeated the Gaunt Prince at the cost of her own life. It appears now they did not die. Perhaps Aillila trapped the Gaunt Prince, banished him somewhere and she went as well. Hob's teeth, I do not know, I am no damn mystic! But I think the elf princess is who helped Crane, who he believed could help us."

"Then she too must be freed, as the Gaunt Prince was freed," Flyn ventured.

Deglan shrugged. "All I can do is bring what is left of the ledger back to Airlann and try to make contact with the Seelie Court. But Slouch Hat was not wrong, Flyn. The Source Isle is no longer strong. There may be little we can do."

"Save try."

Deglan smiled at the young knight. "Save try."

Flyn clapped a hand down on his shoulder. "Thank you, Staunch."

"I am not going to bloody kiss you good-bye."

"No," Flyn laughed. "I thought not."

Deglan shooed him off. "Get you gone, you puffed-up rascal."

Bantam Flyn smiled broadly and began to depart, walking backwards. "Farewell, you mouldy old mushroom."

Deglan watched the young knight join his new companions and, with a parting nod to the Dread Cockerel, led them out of the copse. The trio struck off together across the white land, coburn, dwarf, and giantess, the fallen children of Middangeard.

Deglan chuckled to himself. Flyn was right. He did look naked without a sword.

EPILOGUE

Wynchell's clubbed foot ached from walking under the weight of the armor. Using the long haft of the pole-hammer as a walking stick, he trudged through the underbrush, each step taking him farther from the clutch than he had ever been. He kept casting furtive looks over his shoulder, fearing he would discover Gallus pursuing him. Hating his lingering fear, Wynchell pressed on.

The shaft of the hammer was not exactly straight. Wynchell had fashioned it himself, working during the precious hours of night when he was left forgotten in his little hut. It had taken him near a month to find the tree Sir Flyn had described, and he had almost given up hope of its existence when, one morning in the hazy glow before the dawn, he spied the carving in an elm. Two spurs, carved into the bark. The resting place of Sir Haward the Lambent, a knight slain by Gallus and buried by a young Flyn.

Wynchell's chores prevented him from digging immediately and he spent the entire toilsome day thinking of the tree, his mind distracted. Had Gallus been in good health he would surely have noticed and beat Wynchell bloody for his daydreaming, but the tyrant no longer left his hall, trying to recover from the wounds Sir Flyn had given him.

Finally, night came. Wynchell had spent a lifetime yearning for the embrace of darkness and the seclusion of his hut, struggling through each day's labors just to escape to the solace provided by the fleeing sun when Gallus took to the pleasures of his mates and neglected his crippled slave. Wynchell would flop down on his pallet and partake of what meager food he had before slumber claimed him. Sleep was his only pleasure, a blissful absence of all things save dreams. The clutch, Gallus, the beldams and brood huts, they all vanished behind his exhausted lids.

But not that night.

Quivering with anticipation, Wynchell had gathered tools and set off for the tree, renouncing his bed for more work. Only this was not Gallus's forced drudgery. He dug for his freedom.

Under the moon, he battled the dirt with his spade until finally, neck-deep in a pit, he found what Flyn had covered all those years ago. The bones of Sir Haward gave Wynchell a moment's pause, but he reminded himself that the foul deed had already been done.

Gallus had condemned the knight to this rude grave, not he. He was unearthing the pride of the Valiant Spur, bringing it back into the light. Removing the mail, the spurs and the steel hammer-like head of the weapon Flyn had called a raven's beak, Wynchell returned the bones to the soil. He took his treasures back to his hut and spent the night not in sleep, but in awed study of the artifacts.

Over the coming weeks, Wynchell set to the task of cleaning and repairing the mail, polishing the spurs and scouring the hammer of rust. Sleep became as unwelcome a distraction as his daily chores. Sir Hayward's hauberk was riddled with holes and grown ragged at the edges, the corroded links falling free in places.

Wynchell had played with the idea of digging up Flyn's mail, but that supposed grave was still fresh in Gallus's mind. If he found it disturbed, then all would be lost. Wynchell could not take the risk.

For nights on end he wore the armor, growing accustomed to its weight and restrictions. He drilled himself in the use of the raven's beak, swinging the weapon inexpertly at the air, not daring to strike a tree lest the new pole snap or the noise awake Gallus.

And then, one day, there was nothing else he could think to do, no more preparations to make. Doubt filled his thoughts, causing him to stall. For days he waited, going about his work during the day and sleeping once more at night, his armaments hidden in his hut.

Fear of death plagued him, but so too did the fear of staying. He found himself taking little rebellious chances, leaving tasks undone, courting Gallus's ire, but it never came.

Unable to endure his own reluctance any more, Wynchell donned the hauberk and took the raven's beak in hand, thumping through the stretch of forest separating his hut from the clutch.

The morning was dreary, the leaves pattering under a spitting rain.

Wynchell's heart beat painfully in his steel-clad chest as he approached the filthy curtain covering the door of the hall. Cursing all doubt, he stepped through, leading with his hammer.

The stink of the place was gagging. Many of the mates and beldams were within, fleeing to the walls as he entered. Wynchell looked up at the raised platform which housed Gallus's chair of lashed bones, expecting to find the tyrant glowering down at him, radiating murder.

The chair was empty.

Half a dozen pullets occupied the platform, squatting behind the chair where Gallus's pile of sleeping furs lay. The females cast glances down at Wynchell, their faces full of a nervous curiosity. Approaching carefully, he mounted the stairs of the platform, keeping his hammer poised before him in both hands. He had never in his life set foot upon the platform. As his head drew even with the floor he saw the pullets clustered around the furs.

They drew back when he reached the top and Wynchell froze.

The thing upon the bed was bald and reeking. What feathers remained clung to the mottled flesh in greasy patches. A festering poultice covered the flaccid belly, saturated with gangrenous fluids.

"Gallus," Wynchell called at the emaciated wretch upon the furs. The once-mighty tyrant gurgled and gagged, trying to look towards the sound of his name, but his eyes were burned blind by fever. Staring in morbid fascination, Wynchell tried to recall the last time he had seen the old bird. So obsessed was he with his plotting and preparation, he had not fully realized his tormentor's absence.

He knew Gallus was recovering from the battle with Flyn, accepting it would only be a matter of time before he was once again hunting and rutting with the same vigor as always. In Wynchell's mind, Gallus was simply reclined in his hall, being nursed by his mates and taking his ease. Only it was not so.

Gallus was not recovering. He was dying. The gut wound from Sir Flyn's blade had never healed and slowly ate the tyrant from within.

Glancing about, Wynchell saw the females looking at him, some with fear, some with menace. One approached with a bronze skinning knife in hand.

"This day was near," she told Wynchell, gesturing down at Gallus with the blade. "Old as he is, it was coming soon, fight or no. We could not have that young strut claim us. Be years upon years afore he died, and us under his talons through all of them."

"Will you try and claim us?" another of the pullets asked boldly, standing to brandish a hide-scraper. "Suffer the same as the pretty one, if you do."

Wynchell looked back at Gallus, his head shaking slowly.

"No," he said at last. "No, I am leaving."

Turning away, Wynchell descended the stairs. A young beldam, lacking the grit of her elders, timidly grabbed at him.

"What shall we do?" she asked, her voice hushed and fearful.

"Stop waiting for him to die," Wynchell replied, pointing with his beak to the platform above. "Cut his throat. Take the clutch. Rule yourselves."

With that he left the fetid hall.

Now, the river was before him. Wynchell followed it for days, keeping a course roughly northward, wondering how long it would take to reach Albain. Could he even find the Roost? He hunted and fished when he could, eating better than he had under Gallus's niggardly ways. He slept beside campfires under the stars, and soon, the desire to look over his shoulder fled. No one would be pursuing him. Gallus was dead, and so was Wynchell's old life.

On the fourth day, a boat appeared from behind a bend in the river at Wynchell's back. He stood upon the bank and watched it approach. Ignorant of the world and not knowing what else to do, he raised a hand in greeting, expecting the vessel to sail by, but he received two surprises. The second was that the boat pulled close to shore and dropped anchor, the smiling man aboard offering him passage. The first was the large animal sitting in the bow.

Wynchell loosed a puzzled breath. "A bear on a boat."

ACKNOWLEDGMENTS

Expressing gratitude to individuals has only one pitfall: the inevitable neglect of at least one person who rightly deserves mention, but fails to get it due to the weary and numb brain of an author at the end of the long journey to publication. For those worthies who do not see their names here, forgive me.

Respectful mention to the late, great Pete Postlethwaite, whose genius acting inspired a certain foul whaler.

To those in my extended family who read *The Exiled Heir* unsolicited and reached out with kind words.

As always, oodles of gratitude to Cameron McClure.

To Betsy Mitchell and all the folks working behind the scenes at Open Road Media, I appreciate you.

Heartfelt appreciation to my test-readers; Matt Gale, James MacMurray, Chelsea Voulgares, Brad Starnes, and Rob Strickland. Their honest and keen critiques forced me to rethink, rewrite and (hopefully) improve this tale.

An extra hat-tip must go out to Rob, my dear friend, whose creation of Hafr at the gaming table not only inspired the character in this book, but ultimately led to the inception of Ulfrun, for which I am very grateful.

Of course, to Mom. Thanks for patiently reading the work in progress, chapter by chapter. Thank you for accepting me and these yarns of mine, and for loving us unconditionally, flaws and all.

Unfathomable love to Wyatt, my little boy, for saving my life on the day he was born and many days since.

ABOUT THE AUTHOR

Jonathan French is the author of the Autumn's Fall Saga and *The Grey Bastards*. His debut novel, *The Exiled Heir*, was nominated for Best First Novel at the Georgia Author of the Year Awards in 2012. His second book, *The Errantry of Bantam Flyn,* was a top ten contender on the Kindle Norse/Viking Fantasy bestseller list. French has also served as consultant on the cultural impact of the Dungeons & Dragons franchise. He currently resides in Atlanta with his wife, son, and two cats.

THE AUTUMN'S FALL SAGA

FROM OPEN ROAD MEDIA

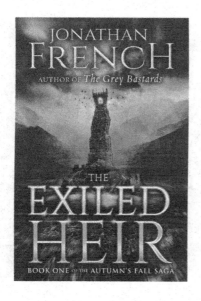
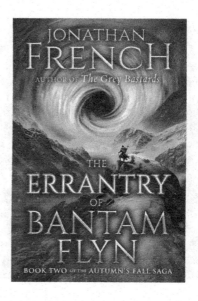

INTEGRATED MEDIA